HEROD

THE MAN WHO HAD TO BE KING

by Yehuda Shulewitz

PENINA PRESS

Herod
The Man who Had to Be King

Published by Penina Press
Text Copyright © 2012 Yehuda Shulewitz

Cover Design: Shanie Cooper
Editorial and Production Director: Daniella Barak
Editors: Batsheva Pomerantz and Malka Hillel-Shulewitz

Soft Cover ISBN: 978-1-936068-26-5

First edition. Printed in Israel

Distributed by:
Urim Publications
POB 52287
Jerusalem 91521, Israel
Tel: 02.679.7633
Fax: 02.679.7634
urim_pub@netvision.net.il

Lambda Publishers, Inc.
527 Empire Blvd.
Brooklyn, NY 11225, USA
Tel: 718.972.5449
Fax: 718.972.6307
mh@ejudaica.com

www.UrimPublications.com

DEDICATION

In memory of our son
Jonathan Asher
who fell while serving
in the Golani Brigade of the IDF

ᘓ

Contents

Contents

Preface

For and About the Author

I am not sure when this novel first took root in the mind of Yehuda Leib Shulewitz, my late husband, who left us during Passover 2007.

Perhaps it was when he came to Israel in 1947. Then a young, demobilized soldier who served with the US Army in Europe during World War II, he opted to take the opportunity under the GI Bill of Rights to realize a dream: to study Jewish History in Jerusalem, particularly the Second Temple period. So he left his home in Peoria, Illinois and made his way by ship to the Promised Land.

After touring the country and staying for a while on the religious kibbutz, Yavne, he began his studies at the Hebrew University on Mount Scopus. (Later, he wrote a touching article about that brief, impressionable period). It was brief because Jerusalem came under siege. A number of the Americans went back to the US. Yehuda remained in the blockaded city until he decided that he was of little use to the country getting weaker due to the bombardment and lack of food. So he took a chance and made his way by foot over the hills, somehow avoiding Arab villages and brigands, until he finally arrived in Tel-Aviv. Only on the very last leg of the journey did he get a lift in what he described as "an old jalopy." Recovered from the effort, he immediately enlisted in MACHAL – Hebrew acronym for *mitnadvei chutz l'aretz* – Volunteers from Overseas. He was sent to join the nascent Israel army in the Galilee where – coincidentally? – his book begins.

Spirits were high, though supplies of nearly everything were low. Nevertheless, here too they were victorious, despite the invasion of five well-equipped Arab armies.

After the War of Independence, Yehuda returned to his beloved Jerusalem where the Hebrew University was reorganizing having lost its campus on Mount Scopus. Combining his studies at Terra Sancta, (rented for the duration – which lasted until after the Six Day War) with work at the Jewish National Fund. The articles he wrote then make pleasant reading and gave vent to his love of the Land of Israel and the challenge of renewed Jewish statehood.

9

Yehuda, of blessed memory, wrote a lot. Bulging files of articles, radio scripts that were broadcast (sometimes in several languages) and two full-length plays testify to his exceptional literary ability and the scope of his interests: polemics on Judaism and papers on its leading historic characters such as Sa'adia Gaon, and a dissertation on Judaism and the early church.

As an archeology buff, he wrote and published articles, particularly on the digs in and around Jerusalem while keeping abreast of the progress in Herodian, where he dreamed up some sections of his book which was the one subject that could distract him from his love of European and American drama.

On quite a different level, he was very interested in economics having earned a degree in the subject from the University of Illinois. Yehuda highly valued the 27 years he worked at the Bank of Israel as Editor of English Economic Publications. Believing that they were an ambassador for Israel abroad, he took pride in maintaining their high level of language and style.

It was only after Yehuda finally received an advanced degree in Jewish History from the Hebrew University that he embarked on this historical novel about which he had already filled several small notebooks. Still working full-time, he spent whatever was left at the Hebrew University Libraries in Givat Ram and on Mount Scopus. His research was done in the days preceding Internet when all information had to be gleaned from books. And that was fine! The library and its surrounding books were second home to Yehuda. He oft consulted with his professors at the university, especially the late Shmuel Safrai, whom he greatly admired.

Yehuda was once asked by this writer why he went into such detail rather than take more of the "poet's license" that was surely his prerogative when writing a novel, even a historic one. He was adamant on that score: As a historian himself, all facts available had to be woven into the story. Where there were gaps or dry facts made a minimum of "dressing up" necessary, then imagination could come into play. This is obvious when perusing the card index of facts he set up – a veritable Who's Who of this fascinating, if tragic period about a hundred years before the Temple was destroyed and before mighty Rome became a subject for history books.

Yehuda was an observant Jew with a deep love and understanding of Judaism; an intellectual whose vast knowledge was only equaled by his too modest and unpretentious nature.

He almost completed this volume before he died. It has been a privilege for me to add the finishing touches and make it available to you, the reader. I think you will enjoy the way Yehuda made "his" period come to life.

Malka Hillel-Shulewitz
Jerusalem
Sivan 5771
July 2011

Chapter One

Herod, the Young Governor of Galilee

The Proud Commander

The day dawned overcast and a stiff breeze blew up, rattling the shutter that shielded the bedroom window from the morning light. The clatter grew louder, prompting Damos to quietly enter the room in order to secure the shutter. He had received orders not to waken the governor at the usual hour, and was afraid the noise would disturb his sleep. He did not relish a tongue-lashing this morning. He was not bothered by his master's invective when he sensed that it was not meant to be taken seriously; in fact, when the young governor of Galilee called into question the legitimacy of Damos's birth or hurled other epithets at him in a rather odd dialect of the Greek vernacular sprinkled with Aramaic, Damos found it hard to keep a straight face and not reveal his amusement. But he did not feel the least amused when the governor was in a bad temper and proceeded to taunt him. Then Herod's swarthy cheeks would crease deeply, his eyes take on a hard, metallic glint, his lips tighten; then he was not ruggedly handsome, but stern, harsh, imperious, his voice high-pitched and menacing.

Damos tiptoed across the room, casting an anxious glance at the recumbent figure. He did not know that his precautions were being observed through the half-opened eyes of his master. The rattling of the shutter had put an end to Herod's sleep, brief as it was, but he decided to allow himself the luxury of a little extra rest. When he had awoken his head was fuzzy from the night's revelry, but as he began to relive the evening a glow of warmth suffused his whole being, clearing away the cobwebs in his mind. Last night's celebration did not differ much from the others tendered in his honor during the past month, but he heartily enjoyed them all – the feasting, the entertainment, the comely female admirers. Above all, he was pleased by the warm praise he had received from Sextus Caesar, governor of Syria and kinsman of the great Caesar in Rome.

He was glad that he had made his headquarters in a predominantly Greek town not far from the Syrian border. His father had advised a Jewish town or village, but young Herod knew that, despite the high rank to which Julius Caesar had elevated him, Antipater was inclined to be rather cautious in his dealings with the Jews and tried to avoid offending their religious and national sensitivities. He, Herod, was less concerned whether he ruffled their feelings. *Their* feelings? But wasn't he too a Jew, or at least partly so? His father's father had accepted the Jewish faith after their northern neighbors had subdued Idumea and given the inhabitants the choice of either converting or being expelled from their land. No, no one had asked Herod whether he wanted to be a Jew, and no one could make him regard himself as one. But why think of that now? Why let that sour his wine, disturb his delicious recollections?

For a whole month now the neighboring Syrian Greeks had let Herod know how grateful they were to him for freeing them from the menace of Hezekiah and his band of ruffians. Brigands, that's what they were, even if the Galileans insisted they were patriots waging a guerrilla war against the hostile heathens. The campaign against them had not been easy. They would attack and then slink away to some secluded cave where they remained in hiding until the next raid. But Herod had relished the challenge they posed. His father knew what he was doing when he appointed him governor of Galilee. This was rugged country, both physically and with respect to the Jewish inhabitants. Relations between Jews and Gentiles – Greeks and Hellenized Syrians – were unfriendly on the whole. On top of this, the smoldering embers of the civil strife between the followers of the two rivals for the Judean throne, the Hasmonean brothers Hyrcanus and Aristobulus, which had rent the country two decades earlier, still flared up from time to time. But Herod welcomed this turbulent situation, as it had given his father and himself their golden opportunity. Antipater was now the power behind the throne and he, Herod, was governor of Galilee no less, the bold, vigorous hand that was needed at this crucial hour. He was showing the Galileans and, more important, his Roman overlords his mettle. He had lured Hezekiah out of his lair with a brilliant stratagem and captured him and all the surviving members of his band. He had personally led his men into the fray and cut down two of the bandits with his own sword. A pity he couldn't have engaged Hezekiah in personal combat: that would have made his victory sweeter yet. As it was, Hezekiah had been taken alive. When Herod ordered his execution, Hezekiah did not bat an eyelid. Herod had wanted him to cringe and plead for his life, but he breathed defiance and spat in his face. Well, he'll spit no more.

After Damos left the room, Herod peered through the chink in the shutter and saw that the morning mist was beginning to disperse before the first rays of the sun. He yawned and stretched himself; soon afterward he dressed and ate a light breakfast.

Headquarters was a short distance from the handsomely furnished villa that served as Herod's residence. This was an arrangement he preferred, as it offered him greater privacy and enabled him to indulge his taste for beautiful objects: Grecian urns and vases, polychrome bowls, crystal glassware, a colonnaded courtyard flanked with statuary. Antipater disapproved of the statuary in view of the Jewish abhorrence of any violation of the Second Commandment. But Herod was not going to let that interfere with his love of beauty, whatever its form. *A peculiar religion it was that had been foisted on him*, Herod mused as he made his way to headquarters.

The inhabitants of the town had grown accustomed to the sight of the young broad-shouldered governor striding to his headquarters, usually alone but occasionally accompanied by an aide. He enjoyed the brisk walk in the early morning air. It invigorated him, and his spirits responded to the beauty of the scenery: the neat homes flanking the cobblestone streets, the scented jasmine and honeysuckle, the stately cedars, the mountains marching away into the dim horizon, their peaks now garbed in an iridescent mantle of variegated soft hues. The blood pulsed in his veins, and his jet-black eyes sparkled above high cheekbones, long aquiline nose, and thick lips framed by a black mustache and short pointed beard. He exuded an air of self-assurance and determination.

His entry into the single-story stone headquarters building set the staff into a flurry, and an air of bustle immediately replaced the early morning somnolence. He nodded to his subordinates and cast a sidelong glance at the couriers sitting on a bench awaiting their turn to submit their dispatches. One of them rose and approached the governor, saluting him smartly.

"I have an urgent message for you, sir. It's from..."

"There are channels," Herod cut him short. "Report to the adjutant."

"But, sir, it's extremely important. It's..."

"The adjutant," came the curt, imperious reply.

Herod turned on his heels and entered his office, a large room containing a long table, a number of chairs, two cabinets, and a camp bed; a fairly large window looked out on a well-tended garden in full bloom. He signaled to his staff officers to follow.

"I say, Aratus," he smiled at his second-in-command as the latter drew up a chair, "you're a bit green around the gills this morning. The celebrating is getting you down, I take it."

Aratus's temples throbbed, but he managed a weak grin.

"Never mind," said Herod, seating himself; "we deserve it. Besides, we're going to have our hands full with other matters soon enough."

Herod enjoyed the daily meetings with his staff officers. All of them were young and in the full vigor of manhood. As governor he was responsible for the administration of Galilee, military and civil, and he displayed equal zeal in attending to the latter. But the most urgent problem was suppressing the rebellious elements, a by no means easy task in this hostile territory. To ferret out and seize the ringleaders required both strong-arm and more subtle methods.

Herod was pleased to learn from Phillipos, a short, brawny Antiochene, that the troops were nearly up to full strength, with the number of sick and wounded smaller than expected. "And their morale?" asked Herod.

Phillipos hesitated before replying: "On the whole quite good, sir."

"What do you mean, on the whole?" said Herod, fixing the officer with a piercing look.

"Well, as you know, the Cilicians haven't been paid yet. They're getting restless, and some have been heard to say they'd like to waylay a few rich Jews."

Herod's expression immediately darkened, his eyes narrowed, and his jaws set hard. "There'll be no waylaying or looting by the troops," he snapped in his most authoritative voice. "There are enough problems without having the rich merchants on my back. Some of them are friendly to our cause and have been quite cooperative. Tell the men that if anyone dares to disobey my order, he can say goodbye to his head. I want that made absolutely clear." He paused before adding: "You can also tell them that they'll get their pay soon."

Herod turned to Arthenates for an intelligence report. He did not have an enviable assignment, and both knew it, but he enjoyed Herod's complete confidence. They were friends from childhood, and the governor valued his loyalty and shrewdness. Like Herod, he was of noble Idumean descent, a native of Marissa who had lived many years in Jerusalem and hence knew the people intimately; he was also familiar with the politics of the court, especially the jockeying for position and the lingering bitterness engendered by the struggle for the throne by the two Hasmonean brothers. But this knowledge did not stand him in good stead in Galilee. He found the inhabitants tight-lipped and sullen on the whole. They were vociferous enough in their complaints about taxes and other grievances, but his attempts to discover their political views and allegiance, to uncover dissension and its fomenters, were more often than not frustrated. He did know that the Galileans intensely disliked the "Idumeans" – Antipater and his two eldest sons, especially Herod – who were the power behind the throne occupied by the well-meaning but weak Hyrcanus. It required all his subtlety and cunning, and not infrequently harsh methods, to pry a modicum of information out of the Galileans.

He felt Herod's eyes boring into him. His brow furrowed, giving a somewhat odd aspect to his broad face framed by a clipped black beard. "As you know, there has been much less trouble the last couple of weeks," he said, "but we suspect that new centers of resistance are springing up."

"Suspect?" Herod bent forward, his eyebrows arching sharply. "You're not sure?"

"Our sources of information are not certain. They say there is growing disquiet – a lot of murmuring about the death of Hezekiah and his men."

"What did the Galileans expect?" Herod shot back in a scathing tone. "Did they want me to crown those brigands with laurel wreaths and give them a place of honor at my table?"

Arthenates was slow in responding; he spoke in measured accents: "They claim you didn't have the right to execute them."

Herod banged his fist on the table and leaped to his feet. "I didn't have the right?" he flared savagely. "Bandits! Murderers! Perhaps I should have let them capture us? Do you know what our fate would have been?" He drew a finger across his throat. "That's what it would have been!"

The officers were taken aback by the vehemence of Herod's outburst. They stared at him curiously as he started to pace back and forth, his hands clasped behind his back. It was almost a week since he had received Antipater's letter informing him that feeling was running high in the capital over the execution of Hezekiah and his men. The leading families were becoming more and more resentful over the growing power of Antipater and his sons, and were trying to stir up Hyrcanus against them. They claimed Herod had violated the law in putting the men to death; only the Sanhedrin, the supreme legislative and judicial body, had the right to try capital cases. The mothers of the deceased had come to Jerusalem and every day gone to the Temple to wail and clamor to have Herod stand trial for his crime. Antipater, of course, defended Herod's actions, but there were powerful enemies in the court.

At first Herod had been upset by the news. He knew his family did not lack for enemies, especially among the aristocratic ruling class, who were jealous of the high position Antipater and his sons had attained and were apprehensive about their own positions. But he was not one to shrink from a challenge. He believed in himself; he felt instinctively that he was destined for great things. He did not expect his path to be smooth or particularly peaceful; he would encounter resistance and have to overcome many obstacles, but overcome them he would.

Herod stared out the window. In the nearby field a company was being put through its paces, a sight that cheered him. These were *his* soldiers. At the age of only 25 he was commander of these fine seasoned troops; he was governor of

Galilee. His star was in the ascendant. Then why did Arthenates's report disturb him so much?

"So the Jews claim I didn't have the right to execute those bandits, do they?" he said turning to face his staff officers. "And you, Cleon, what do you say to that?"

Cleon was surprised at the question. He was a military man through and through and failed to see where any problem existed. "To me it's as clear as day. Hezekiah was an enemy who carried out raids. He knew the risks involved. If he won, the others suffered; if he lost, he had to pay the price."

This was the opinion of all the men except one. Like Arthenates, Dalleas had lived much of his life in Jerusalem and knew about the strife between the two Hasmonean brothers over the royal crown. But unlike the others, he also knew about the rivalry within the walls of the Sanhedrin between the two constituent parties, the Sadducees and the Pharisees. He knew very little about the religious differences between them, but he did know that the Sadducees hailed from the aristocratic circles – the upper priestly class, the big landowners, the wealthy merchants – while the Pharisees, led by the sages, came from the poorer strata and were considered to be more pious in their religious practices yet more liberal in their interpretation of the Law. Relations between them had been quite acrimonious in the past, and while they were now much less so, their debates could still generate considerable heat. But on one point they saw eye to eye – the inviolability of the rights and powers of the Sanhedrin. Dalleas had warned Herod about its likely reaction when he ordered the execution of Hezekiah and his men, but the governor was in no mood to listen.

Dalleas glanced up to find Herod's gaze fastened on him. "And you, Dalleas, I take it you don't agree with the others?"

"I once expressed my views on the subject," replied Dalleas dryly. "I hope my fears prove unfounded."

Herod drew himself up full height; his lips twisted into a scornful grimace. "The Sanhedrin is nothing but a bunch of old fools!" he snapped contemptuously. "Do they think I owe my appointment to them? I am not answerable to these men. It was my father and hence Caesar himself who appointed me to restore order in Galilee. It is to Rome that I am responsible and not Jerusalem!"

There was a knock on the door, but it was drowned out by Herod's words: "This is not a matter for debating," he went on fiercely; "it's a question of..."

The door opened and the adjutant stepped inside, wearing an apologetic look.

"Don't interrupt!" Herod shouted at the hapless intruder.

"I'm sorry, sir," the adjutant retorted quietly, "but I think you should know that the courier who wanted to hand you a dispatch when you came in is from the king."

"The king?"

"Yes, sir. He says he has a message for you and was ordered to deliver it to you personally."

Herod paused before replying coldly: "Very well, admit him."

The courier entered, a thin, slightly built man in his thirties. He saluted the governor and handed him a scroll enclosed in a leather case. Herod broke the seal and extracted a letter. As he read it his face underwent a transformation, first paling and then reddening. He angrily rolled up the letter and looked the courier full in the face, his eyes blazing with defiance.

Hyrcanus, king and high priest, had summoned Herod, governor of Galilee, to appear before the Sanhedrin to stand trial for the death of Hezekiah and his men.

Herod is Summoned to Stand Trial

The Temple was crowded with so many worshippers that Hyrcanus thought it more reminiscent of a pilgrim festival than the New Moon. It was his wont to officiate on the New Moon and the Sabbath in addition to the holy days, including of course the Day of Atonement, when the service had to be performed entirely by the high priest. Perhaps it was his imagination, but he sensed a certain tension in the air. As he gazed upon sea of faces, he wondered what had attracted so many people, especially women.

In his early days as high priest such a multitude would have made him nervous, but he had long since overcome his fear of not measuring up to the demands of this most exalted office. A great deal of water passed under the bridge since that day more than two decades ago when he had first officiated in the Temple, but he still clearly remembered his apprehension that he might disappoint the assembled and especially his mother, the revered Queen Alexandra Salome, who was not confident that he would acquit himself as befitted a Hasmonean. Now it was second nature for him to perform his sacred office. He loved the pomp and ceremony of the ritual; in fact, he felt more at ease, a greater sense of adequacy and fulfillment, in the Temple than anywhere else, more so than in the privy council for instance.

The service, which had begun at daybreak, was now well advanced. Hyrcanus himself had made the morning offering of the unblemished lamb, after which the priests had gathered in the Chamber of Hewn Stone to recite, together with the people who had begun to arrive, the Ten Commandments, the *Shema* (prayer of commitment to One God), and other prayers. Now it was time for the incense-offering, one of the most impressive of the day's rites.

A hush fell over the large throng of worshippers, who had crowded as close to the sanctuary as was permissible. Hyrcanus, accompanied by the prefect and two other priests, strode with measured steps to the sanctuary, where stood the golden incense altar, along with the shewbread table and golden candelabrum. He waited for the prefect to intone, "Lord High Priest, pray burn the incense," whereupon he and the other two attendants prostrated themselves and withdrew, leaving Hyrcanus alone in the sanctuary. He heaped the contents of the incense ladle, which he carried in his left hand, on the coals. A thick cloud of smoke rose upward to the ceiling, spread out and then descended, filling the sanctuary with fragrant odor. Hyrcanus inhaled deeply and pleasurably, after which he prostrated himself and withdrew to wait for the other priests to file into the sanctuary and prostrate themselves. When the last one had departed, he raised his hands to bless the assembled. His voice was not very strong, but he pronounced the benediction in majestic accents, and when he uttered the divine name the worshippers prostrated themselves and fell on their faces. The scene never failed to stir him; to him it was the high point of the ritual.

The service of the morning daily offering concluded with the wine libation upon the sacrificial altar, which was preceded by the sounding of silver trumpets by two of the priests and the waving of a flag by the prefect as a signal for the choir to begin singing the prescribed hymn to the accompaniment of musical instruments. This being the New Moon, there followed the additional sacrifices designated for the day.

After the service Hyrcanus retired to his chamber to change his garments. Although it was a warm day, the interior of the Temple was quite chilly. He went over to the charcoal brazier to warm his hands and in particular his feet, which like everyone else he was forbidden to shod while in the Temple courts.

"The service went very well today, sire," the attendant in charge of the high priest's wardrobe commented after Hyrcanus had warmed himself.

"Thank you," replied Hyrcanus with a feeling of keen satisfaction. "There was an unusually large number of worshippers today. I wonder why."

"I don't know, sire," said the attendant, helping Hyrcanus to take off his outer vestments, after which he withdrew to let the high priest complete his disrobing in privacy.

The feeling of anticlimax which he frequently experienced after officiating began to creep over Hyrcanus: The luster died out of his dark brown eyes and his features sagged perceptibly. As he made his way toward the exit, the thought of the urgent problems awaiting him in his capacity as ethnarch weighed heavily on him. He failed to notice a tall, dignified figure overtaking him.

Hyrcanus's face lit up when he beheld Nehunya, one of the leading members of the Babylonian Jewish community. He was a successful man in every respect, and this was apparent in his demeanor and speech. Not yet fifty, he was reputed to be quite wealthy, the owner of a flourishing trade in wine and spices and possessor of extensive estates. He was also learned, having spent several years of his youth in the homeland studying at the feet of the sages of the day. In addition, he was an accomplished diplomat, whose services were frequently employed by the exilarch, the official lay head of the Jewish community in Babylonia. Hyrcanus could not help feeling a tinge of envy whenever he was in Nehunya's presence, for while in position and honor the high priest was second to none, Hyrcanus's path, unlike Nehunya's, had been a thorny one that left him scarred.

"The Lord has dealt graciously with you," observed Hyrcanus. "You look remarkably well."

"Thank you. I do my best to cooperate with Him," said Nehunya with a grin.

"You have denied us your presence and sagacious advice for too long a time. Nearly two years, if I'm not mistaken."

"A little longer, I must confess," replied Nehunya. His beard, trimmed square in the Babylonian fashion, was still black. His deep-set eyes, also dark, were intelligent and lively, and this, together with his high cheekbones, straight nose, strong white teeth, and tanned visage, gave him a striking, urbane appearance.

"My business interests and public activities are a relentless taskmaster," Nehunya went on. "You can't imagine how intense my longing to see the Holy City again can become. To visit the Temple is not only a mitzvah [commandment or good deed], it's an inspiration – especially when the high priest himself officiates."

Hyrcanus acknowledged the compliment with a diffident smile. He could not escape the suspicion that there was more to his friend's visit than he cared to disclose. "You will of course be my guest," he said cordially. "Unless you have other plans, that is."

"I shall be delighted and honored," replied Nehunya, nodding politely.

The two men started to make their way to the bridge used by the nobles to reach the Hasmonean palace and their mansions in the Upper City. Their progress was slow, for at every step Hyrcanus stopped to acknowledge the greetings of worshippers.

When they neared the gate leading to the bridge, they came upon a startling sight – a score or so of women dressed in black and wailing loudly. Nehunya stared at them with a puzzled expression. He glanced at Hyrcanus and saw that his countenance had clouded; the high priest swallowed hard and hunched his shoulders; he seemed to have visibly aged.

"What is the meaning of this?" asked Nehunya.

"We'll soon find out," was the resigned reply.

As Hyrcanus approached the women, the wailing grew louder and more importunate. Nehunya tried to make out their mournful cries but could distinguish only one word; it was on everyone's lips: "Herod." It was uttered in unmistakable derision and hatred, accompanied by the waving of clenched fists. Nehunya immediately grasped the import of the scene: The women were beseeching Hyrcanus to avenge the death of their sons, who had perished with Hezekiah at Herod's hands. One of them tried to take hold of Hyrcanus's robe, but the guard stationed at the gate intervened and started to push the crowd back. When a space had been cleared, Hyrcanus signaled to him to desist. Seeing that the high priest wanted to address them, the women gradually fell silent.

"My dear women," Hyrcanus said in a consoling, fatherly voice, "I can understand your anguish and fully sympathize with you. To lose a son is to lose the apple of one's eye; there can be no greater blow to a mother's heart..."

"Then make Herod stand trial," came a shrill demand, which was echoed by the other women.

Hyrcanus raised his hand for silence. In a subdued voice he continued: "Will Herod's trial bring your dear sons back to life? If it would, I would not hesitate one moment. But alas, it cannot do so. We mortals cannot quicken the dead. We can only pray that their souls will rest in peace until the great day comes when the Almighty will restore them to everlasting life along with all the other worthy people who have perished from off this earth."

"What about justice?" one of the women called out. "There must be justice in the land! Murder must not go unpunished!"

The cry for justice rent the air. Nehunya saw beads of sweat glistening on Hyrcanus's forehead and a pallor spreading over his face. Should he intervene and try to help the high priest? He was inclined to do so, but thought better of it. Silently he watched Hyrcanus reasoning with the women. But they were adamant in demanding that Herod be brought to trial. Nehunya had to admire Hyrcanus's patience, his willingness to endure what must have been an agonizing experience, one that he could have terminated by simply ordering the guard to disperse the crowd. At the same time, Nehunya could not help sympathizing with the women. He heaved a sigh of relief when Hyrcanus finally convinced them that their plea would not go unheeded and they started to drift away.

Hyrcanus remained glued to the spot, his shoulders bent and an abstracted look in his eyes; he was shaken and emotionally spent. "Now you have the answer to your question," he said in a dull voice. "You know the meaning of the demonstration, and I know why there were so many people in the Temple today." He drew himself up. "Come, let us continue on our way."

Hyrcanus wore a frozen expression as they passed through the gate and started to cross the bridge spanning the Tyropoeon Valley; it was clear to Nehunya that he was brooding.

"Yours is not an enviable position," he commiserated. "To be high priest, yes, but to be king, that's a different matter."

"Not king," Hyrcanus corrected him, "ethnarch. That's the title the Romans conferred on me," he added with a frown.

"It makes no difference to us what the exact title is," said Nehunya with a deprecatory gesture. But he knew that Hyrcanus's statement was fraught with considerable significance. Whether he was ethnarch or king, the fact remained that he was beholden to the Romans for his appointment as "political head of the nation" and even worse, the high priesthood. For Judea was no longer an independent but a subject state. Nehunya realized the dilemma facing Hyrcanus: As high priest he presided over the Sanhedrin, the supreme legislative body of the Jewish nation and the highest tribunal, which alone could try capital cases like the one in question. But as king – or ethnarch – he was answerable to Rome. There was the rub, for the largest and most powerful Jewish community outside the homeland was that in Babylonia, now part of the Parthian empire, the arch-enemy of Rome.

"How do your ministers and counselors feel about the business with Herod?" asked Nehunya reflectively.

"They and the nobles have been urging me to summon Herod to trial," Hyrcanus replied in a low, flat voice. "They claim that Antipater and Herod are getting too powerful, and unless they are put in their place we'll pay dearly for it. Malichus is particularly vehement in his opposition."

"I see," said Nehunya, pursing his lips.

Hyrcanus fixed Nehunya with a grave expression. "Let me ask you as a trusted friend and a representative of the Babylonian community: How do our people there feel about the situation?"

Nehunya had anticipated this question, yet he was uncertain how to reply. If he were perfectly candid, he would hurt Hyrcanus's feelings. How could he tell him how distressed the Jews of Babylonia were at the turn of events in the Holy Land? The loss of Jewish independence had pained them grievously. They believed it could have been prevented or at least mitigated.

"As for myself," he said, choosing his words carefully, "I can appreciate your predicament. It isn't only Antipater and his sons you have to contend with, but Rome, whose backing they enjoy. But the Romans also need you. If they want peace and quiet in the land, and I'm sure they do, they must ensure that your authority is not undermined. If they are made to understand how much Antipater and his sons are resented, then hopefully they may try to allay the people's suspicions. Frankly, I too take a dim view of our Idumean friends. I agree with your ministers and counselors that Antipater and Herod are too ambitious, and unless they are put in their place, you and all of us will pay dearly for it later on."

"Then you think Herod should be made to stand trial?" asked Hyrcanus. Upon receiving a positive reply, his brow furrowed deeply. Had he expected Nehunya to advise differently? There was a sinking feeling in the pit of his stomach. He lowered his gaze on the scene below. The Tyropoeon Valley stretching southward, the section called the Lower City, was teeming with people going about their daily business. A cacophony of sound could be heard in the distance: the hawking of wares displayed in front of numerous workshops and stalls, the pounding of hammers, the braying of asses, cackling of hens, and bleating of sheep and goats. How different from the atmosphere of the Temple, he mused. Men were permitted to work on the New Moon, but he always found the contrast between the Temple Mount and the Valley very jarring.

At least the scene was a peaceful one. Time had helped to mitigate the agony caused by the bitter fighting fifteen years earlier, when the Romans had besieged the Temple and after overcoming the defenders, slaughtered the priests who had carried on with the sacrifices until they were struck down, their blood mingling with that of the animals, and massacred thousands of inhabitants. The guilt and depression that had tormented Hyrcanus at the time eased with the years, but would never be completely eradicated. It still caused him occasional nightmares: In his sleep he could see the Roman siege engines battering the walls of the Temple, where his brother's followers had fled for a last-ditch stand. Hyrcanus had felt like a helpless spectator, a puppet manipulated by others, with no volition of his own. He had been torn by conflicting emotions, and to this day he was not certain if he had acted wisely or justly. True, Antipater had convinced him that Aristobulus would not be content with wresting the high priesthood and throne from him, but was plotting to do away with him completely. Antipater had urged him to flee Jerusalem and seek outside help in order to regain the two crowns he had legitimately worn. *And with what consequences,* he brooded morosely. The Temple had been invested, thousands of his people slain, and Aristobulus was dead, as was his son Alexander, who was not only Hyrcanus's nephew but also his son-in-law.

Relations between Hyrcanus and Aristobulus had never been very brotherly. They differed greatly in character, but Hyrcanus could not accept this as sufficient reason for the intense rivalry his younger brother harbored against him. Even as a youngster Aristobulus had assumed an air of superiority, which he asserted at every opportunity. He bitterly resented the fact that as the firstborn Hyrcanus had been appointed high priest by their mother upon her assumption of royal power and that he was also heir to the throne. Hyrcanus had been deeply hurt and humiliated when after her death Aristobulus had deprived him of both crowns. But for all that, Aristobulus was his own flesh and blood. Now he was no more; his restless, driving energy, his elated, animated manner were a thing of the past, a mere memory. His whitened bones lay in the royal sepulcher at Modi'in, the village where a century earlier their forebear Mattityahu had raised the banner of revolt against the despotic Syrian ruler Antiochus Epiphanes, a struggle that had led to the restoration of an independent Jewish state. Had the wheel turned full circle? Hyrcanus sometimes wondered gloomily.

"If I do as you and the others urge me and summon Herod to stand trial," Hyrcanus said to Nehunya in a subdued voice, "there is a grave risk of antagonizing Rome."

"Not if the matter is handled properly. You must display firmness without arousing Rome's anger."

Hyrcanus threw Nehunya a puzzled look. "I'm afraid I've only mystified you," Nehunya chuckled. "It's a common fault with those who dabble in diplomacy. Let me explain myself. Rome respects law, and it's not part of its policy to interfere with the religious practices of other people. It must be made clear that Herod is guilty of violating Jewish religious law, and hence the matter falls under the jurisdiction of the Sanhedrin."

"But will Rome see it in that light? I doubt it."

"You have to make certain that it does. What's the alternative? If Antipater and his sons are allowed to gain further power, the consequences could be very dire – for you personally and for the entire nation. I'm not referring only to the loss of whatever sovereignty is left of your political leadership. The fact that the Idumeans were forced to convert has made them Jews in name only – superficial Jews. There are numerous Greek cities in the land, and this, together with the presence of Rome, makes the pagan-Hellenistic influence a real threat to our way of life. That we dare not ignore. We paid a dear price for that in the past. We cannot afford a repetition; it would be disastrous."

These words were uttered in a calm, deliberate tone as if they had to do with some trivial matter. But to Hyrcanus their import was clear: This was a call for action – action that was liable, despite Nehunya's assurance, to anger Rome. No, the matter was not so simple as Nehunya and the others thought. A false step could prove fatal. Once before he had let himself be talked into pursuing a rash course; he had no intention of repeating the mistake.

* * *

It was Hyrcanus's custom to invite a few guests to dine in the palace after the New Moon service. Most of them were close friends or his advisers, but they also included people from different walks of life. Some of whom, while highly honored at the rare privilege, felt awkward at first in the presence of such distinguished company, but Hyrcanus went out of his way to put them at their ease. He tried to keep the conversation pleasant, but almost invariably it would drift to current affairs and frequently became quite heated. He had a feeling that this might happen today, but with Nehunya present he hoped the guests would prefer to hear how their brethren were faring in the Parthian empire.

Nehunya was in fact the center of attention. He had many friends in Judea, and was happy to meet some of them again after what was for him a comparatively long absence. He was particularly delighted to find Shemaiah among the guests. They had been fellow disciples of the eminent sage Shimon ben Shetah, and both had gone on to achieve renown – Shemaiah as the leading sage of the day, and Nehunya as one of the most prominent members of the Babylonian Jewish community and a confidant of the exilarch.

Nehunya was especially desirous to meet Malichus, currently Hyrcanus's favorite counselor, who was urging him to dissociate himself from Antipater and his sons. What intrigued Nehunya was whether this represented a basic change in policy orientation. Hyrcanus was not noted for bold action; if Malichus had supplanted Antipater in Hyrcanus's favor, this would constitute a drastic departure from his pro-Roman stance. What is more, Malichus was a military man, who twenty years ago had fought against the Romans, not the type of person one would normally expect Hyrcanus to prefer.

Nehunya, who prided himself on being a good judge of character, was even more puzzled after being introduced to Malichus. He had the bearing of a commander who was used to having his orders obeyed implicitly. He had a squat, powerful frame, and when he turned sideways one could see the muscles quivering under his tunic. His ruddy face was framed by a thick reddish beard sprinkled with gray. A low brow sat over steely black eyes, a short, broad nose, and full lips. His voice was deep and authoritative, and when conversing with a small group he would make a conscious effort to modulate it.

After allowing his guests time to exchange a few words with one another, Hyrcanus led them into the dining hall, where they took their places around a long oak table. The smallest dining hall in the palace, it had an intimate atmosphere for the thirty or so persons present. The fading sunlight cast a soft glow on the fluted columns and marble walls adorned with mosaic frescoes featuring clusters of fruit, as well as on the table, which was set with gilded dishes and silver wine goblets.

Menservants brought in baskets of warm bread and platters of roasted lamb garnished with olives and various vegetables, and filled the goblets. Nehunya was hungrier than he thought, and he had to exercise self-restraint to keep from overindulging. He mused, with a grin, how different this dinner was from those he heard about in the Parthian court: Here there was no music or singing or dancing girls, just talk. But the talk was pleasant, and he was glad to see Hyrcanus relaxed with no trace of the tension evident earlier in the day. When the dessert was being served, Hyrcanus rose to his feet and after rapping for silence, addressed the guests:

"We are honored to have with us today a dear friend from Babylonia. His visit is totally unexpected and thus all the more welcome. Apart from the exilarch, no one has been more active on behalf of our brethren in what is undoubtedly the largest and most influential Diaspora community. I am sure that you are all as eager as I am to take advantage of this opportunity to learn from a first-hand, authoritative source what is happening in the Parthian Empire in general and Babylonia in particular. It is with great pleasure that I call on Nehunya ben Abba to enlighten us."

Nehunya had anticipated an invitation to say a few words and had jotted down some notes on a small piece of papyrus. But before he began, Malichus was on his feet. "If the high priest and ethnarch will permit me," he said in his powerful voice, "I would like to make a suggestion. Instead of hearing about what is happening in Parthia or Babylonia, I think it would be more profitable to hear what a leader of Babylonian Jewry has to say about what is happening *here,* right here in the homeland, in Jerusalem in fact. Today we witnessed an extraordinary event – yes, I saw Nehunya there: Women were crying for justice, demanding that Herod stand trial for murdering their sons along with gallant Hezekiah. It was a moving sight, one that won't be easily forgotten. Let us hear what our honorable friend has to say on *this* subject, which has given us no peace of mind."

Malichus's suggestion evoked a positive response from the guests, much to Hyrcanus's annoyance. The encounter with the women had unnerved him, and he yearned for a respite. All week long he and his advisers had discussed the question of Herod. Malichus had become increasingly exasperated at what he called Hyrcanus's procrastination and demanded that he do what he was morally obliged to do. *He was evidently determined to force the issue even if it spoiled the festive atmosphere*, Hyrcanus thought glumly. He threw Nehunya a questioning look. When his guest nodded his acquiescence, Hyrcanus reluctantly acceded to Malichus's request.

Nehunya slowly rose to his feet, searching for an opening to his talk in place of the one he had intended to use. He exuded an air of distinction, and when he began to speak his listeners were no less impressed by his eloquent Aramaic. After some introductory remarks he said that, with all due respect to Malichus, he didn't think it was fitting for him to advise the high priest and his distinguished ministers and counselors how to deal with Herod. This did not mean, however, that he and his fellow Jews in Babylonia were not concerned about the matter; they were concerned about everything that happened in the homeland.

"As I see it," he continued, "there are two aspects to the question of Herod: the political and the *halachic*. I will confine myself to the first of these, the political aspect.

"The issue cannot be divorced from developments in the surrounding world. And who better than you who are sitting around this table know that the question of Herod is inextricably bound up with the Roman presence in Judea. We in Babylonia understand and sympathize with Judea's plight. We know that

25

when a storm is raging a tree must bend with it, otherwise it will break in two. But if the tree bends too low and too long, it will be permanently deformed."

Nehunya stressed that there was a limit to how low Judea should bend. "But, you may argue, Julius Caesar has been very benevolent to us. Has he not shown great respect for our religious sensitivities? Has he not lightened Judea's tax burden, especially during the sabbatical year, and conferred other privileges? Yes, this is all very true; he has done all this. But there is only one Caesar. Have you forgotten how Pompey laid siege to the Temple and slaughtered thousands of our people? Have you forgotten how only a few years later Crassus plundered the Temple, stripping it of all its gold and other treasures? And what for? To help finance his conquest of Parthia, a campaign which fortunately failed miserably and cost Crassus his life. Caesar is mortal; who knows what will happen after he goes the way of all flesh?

"What has all this to do with Herod, you are probably wondering. Those who demand that he stand trial are motivated not only by the desire to see justice done, but underlying this is concern over the growing influence of Antipater and his sons and their pro-Roman policy. And therein lies the danger. For Rome and Parthia, the two mightiest empires today, are contesting for hegemony over this part of the world. Parthia has vivid memories of Crassus's invasion of its territory. What is more, Parthia suspects that Caesar is contemplating or perhaps even planning a new invasion. Now, if Judea openly sides with Rome, this could conceivably have unpleasant consequences for the Jews in Judea and also harm the good relations we in Babylonia enjoy with the Parthian monarch. And so..."

"Are we to understand, then, that you are in favor of trying Herod?" Malichus broke in somewhat impatiently.

Nehunya was a little nettled by the interruption, but quickly regained his composure. "As I have already mentioned," he continued, turning first to Malichus and then to the others, "I do not feel that it is right for me to advise you what to do. This must be your decision. My intention is merely to describe the political considerations involved, as I see them, in order to help you reach a decision. Judged from the purely political aspect, there is a danger either way, of offending Rome on the one hand and Parthia on the other. That must be absolutely clear to you. But there is another aspect to take into account, the religious or *halachic* aspect.

"Yes, I witnessed the women pleading for justice, and I was moved by it. Who better than we Jews know the meaning of justice? For as the psalmist has declared: 'Justice and judgment are the foundation of the Lord's throne.' If you decide to summon Herod to stand trial, it should be primarily on religious grounds. As I explained to the high priest, the Romans respect other peoples' religion, and if it is shown that this is essentially a moral, religious issue, there is less likelihood of antagonizing Rome. They must be made to understand that in executing Hezekiah and his men without a trial, Herod violated our sacred law, and so the matter falls under the jurisdiction of the Sanhedrin. But this brings us to the *halachic* aspect of the issue, and this is not one that I am competent to discuss. I know that I have not fully answered your question, but I hope that I have at least made one aspect of the problem a little clearer."

Hyrcanus thanked Nehunya for his incisive analysis, but before he finished, Malichus rose to make another suggestion. Hyrcanus protested that this was a festive dinner and not a meeting of the privy council. Malichus replied that the presence of two outstanding authorities offered a unique opportunity to hear a fresh view of this vexing problem. They had just heard an explanation of the political considerations involved, and who better than the eminent sage Shemaiah could analyze the *halachic* considerations? It would be a great pity not to take advantage of the opportunity. Hyrcanus reflected a moment before asking Shemaiah if he agreed to the suggestion.

Shemaiah was about the same age as the high priest and had witnessed all the tribulations that befell him. He had been distressed by the conflict between the two Hasmonean brothers and the internecine strife that had convulsed the country. He was also distressed by the sweep of the Roman tide through the Eastern Mediterranean region, which had engulfed the state of Judea. He sought some explanation of this phenomenon. Was it punishment for Israel's sins? Was Rome the Almighty's rod wherewith to chastise His people for their backsliding? But what backsliding? He did not perceive that the people were more lacking today than were their fathers. On the contrary, there was a growing thirst and respect for learning. The Pharisaic teachers found the people eager to be taught and to obey God's will; they welcomed and responded to the sages' efforts to interpret Scriptures with a view to applying its eternal truths to changing conditions, to imbue all life with holiness.

Shemaiah was not one who kept aloof from the political scene, who secluded himself within the four ells of the Law. The opposite was true: He took an active interest in affairs of state, and his counsel was frequently solicited. He was fully aware of the unpopularity of Hyrcanus's pro-Roman leanings and especially the growing influence of Antipater and his sons, but he nevertheless had a warm spot in his heart for Hyrcanus, who was essentially a kind, well-intentioned man. Like his mother, Queen Alexandra Salome, he was favorably disposed to the Pharisees, and thanks largely to this, relations with the Sadducees were more harmonious than during his father's reign. Not that the two parties would ever see eye to eye on numerous fundamental beliefs and practices. The Sadducees, drawn from the wealthy priestly, merchant, and aristocratic classes, were more worldly, and they rejected the doctrine that the Oral Law was just as valid as the Written Law – a stance which the Pharisaic sages clearly saw was bound to have an inhibiting effect on Israel's divinely ordained way of life, for changing conditions necessitated *halachic* solutions. But despite the differences between the two parties, they were united in their stand toward Antipater and his sons.

Shemaiah rose somewhat laboriously from his seat. He was of medium height and broad-boned, but his long blue flowing robe with its four dangling fringes made him seem taller than he actually was. There was something noble in the set of his features, which lent him an air of quiet, unassuming authority that commanded the respect of all who came within his orbit. He had lively dark eyes under bushy brows, a smooth forehead, a thick shock of black hair turning gray around the temples, and a neatly trimmed beard.

"It is with a sense of great responsibility that I respond to the request to explain the *halachic* aspect of this question, which has stirred our people as perhaps no other one has done in recent years," Shemaiah began in a low voice. Everyone leaned forward to better catch his words, and some even cupped their ears; but as he went on, his voice rang clearer and stronger, heightening the impact of his words.

"As a teacher of our sacred Law, I am obliged to speak on all issues and problems that affect our lives, both as individuals and as a nation. Thus it is only natural that like everyone else I too have certain thoughts on the matter concerned.

"It was with great interest that I listened to the previous speaker lucidly and convincingly explain that aspect of the problem he felt was within his competence. I was not surprised, therefore, to be called upon to comment on the *halachic* aspect. I will describe very briefly the underlying *halachic* considerations without, however, expressing an opinion as to the guilt or innocence of the person concerned. For as a member of the Sanhedrin, I would be one of the elders before whom Herod would be tried, if it comes to that. It would be a capital case, with a man's life at stake. As a judge, I must be free of any prejudice; I must be scrupulously fair and objective, for it is written in our Holy Scriptures: 'Take heed what you do, for you judge not for man, but for the Lord, who is with you in judgment.'"

Shemaiah paused for breath. There was not a sound in the hall; all eyes were focused on the speaker as he continued:

"*Halachically* speaking, what is the problem? Put simply, it is this: Has Herod committed a transgression for which he must be tried by the Sanhedrin? There are two possibilities. One, did Hezekiah and his men rebel against the king? If so, then the king, or his agent, in this case Herod, had the right to execute them. For it is written in the book of Joshua that 'whosoever rebels against the king's commandment and hearkens not to his words he shall be put to death.' But, and this is the second possibility, if Hezekiah and his men did not rebel against the king, if their actions were directed solely against a foreign power, then Herod had no right under our sacred Law to put them to death without a trial. Only a duly constituted court composed of qualified judges – the Sanhedrin – could decide their fate. In this case, in flouting the authority of our judicial system, a dangerous blow has been dealt to one of our most cherished sovereign institutions, a blow which could have very grave, far-reaching implications."

Shemaiah turned to face Hyrcanus with a grave expression. "You, High Priest, must answer that question. Search your heart and ask yourself, did Hezekiah rebel against you or did he rebel against Rome?" Shemaiah took his seat amid complete silence. Hyrcanus compressed his lips and heaved a sigh.

Antipater's Advice to His Son Herod

It was a dark, gloomy day. Heavy black clouds scurried across the sky, and the trees swayed wildly, whipped by a northwesterly wind. The smell of rain was in the air. Ordinarily Herod did not mind such weather; he found it both challenging and invigorating. But today his mood was as black and threatening as the weather, something his slave Damos and his subordinates were plainly aware of. He knew they were trying to steer clear of him. "I'd better pull myself together," he told himself. His father was due to arrive today, and it wouldn't do to be seen like this.

Herod stared out the window. Why was Antipater coming to his headquarters of all places? It was about a three-day journey from Jerusalem; they could have arranged to meet at some point midway. The sealed letter delivered by courier was in his father's own handwriting; evidently he did not want his secretary to know its contents. It was couched in an urgent but reassuring tone; nevertheless Herod's blood had boiled when he read it. His headache was now excruciating; when he closed his eyes he saw blinding flashes of light. He picked up an earthenware jug and let cool water trickle over his face. This helped to ease the pain and soothe his taut nerves a bit. He decided to summon his adjutant, but immediately changed his mind. Although it was not yet noon, he was tired from lack of sleep. He went over to the camp bed and stretched himself out full length; within a few minutes he was snoring lightly.

Herod was awakened by his adjutant, who informed him of the approach of a carriage accompanied by an armed escort. The nap had refreshed him and his headache was gone. He splashed water on his face, combed his hair, and straightened his military tunic. When the party drew up before the headquarters building, he went out to greet his father.

After embracing his son, Antipater stepped back to scrutinize him. His smile turned into a frown. "Your face is drawn and there's too much shadow under your eyes," he observed in a slightly high-pitched voice. "That's not the way I expected to find the governor of Galilee."

Antipater was lean, like Herod, but shorter. Despite the long journey, he was immaculately dressed and groomed: His cloak, made of heavy rich-looking stuff, was clasped by a bejeweled girdle; his beard and mustache were neatly trimmed, oiled, and scented. He looked every inch the shrewd man of affairs; he had keen black eyes that quickly detected the weakness in others, a rather large nose, and thick lips. There was, of course, a strong physical resemblance between the two men, but a marked difference in disposition: Both were strong-willed, but whereas Herod was imperious, impulsive, and quick-tempered, Antipater kept a tight rein on his thoughts and emotions, never losing his composure.

After introducing his father to his staff and ordering Damos to bring refreshments, Herod ushered Antipater into his office. No sooner had the latter seated himself than Herod started pacing the room, nervously fingering his sheathed dagger.

"What does that old goat take me for?" he flung at his father. "Does he think we're playing games in Galilee? Can't he see..."

"Hold on, son," Antipater broke in with a chiding gesture. "Have you forgotten your elementary manners? You're not at all curious about the welfare of your family – your mother, your brothers, your sister, not to mention your wife and son?"

Herod stopped in his tracks. "I'm sorry, you're right. This business has so enraged me that I forget myself." He drew up a chair opposite his father and asked solicitously, "And how are they all? How's Mother? Is she feeling better?"

"May the almighty ones be praised!" replied Antipater with outstretched arms and eyes rolling upward so that the divine powers could better perceive his sincere gratitude. He had been exposed all his life to the monotheistic faith, but with characteristic caution he invariably used the plural when addressing or referring to the Deity, just in case there was more than one roaming the heavens. "She's feeling a little better; hasn't had an attack in weeks."

Herod was relieved at the news. His mother's health had been a cause of considerable concern. Born into a noble Nabatean family, she had in recent years suffered frequent bouts of some mysterious malady that would leave her depressed and subject to hallucinations. The physicians had prescribed various cures, but with limited success. She had also tried the remedies recommended by the native priest of the Idumean god Cos, and in desperation Antipater had even turned to other practitioners of the art of healing. While the various medicaments, incantations, and charms had a palliative effect, they failed to cure her.

"And Salome?" asked Herod warily.

Antipater looked down at his long folded hands, then picked an apple from the bowl in front of him and sank his teeth into it. "Delicious!" he pronounced, smacking his lips. "Are they grown locally?"

"How is Salome getting along with Doris?" asked Herod a little sharply.

Antipater took another bite before replying in a casual tone: "About as well as can be expected."

"Hmm," Herod muttered. He knew what that meant. His sister was headstrong, jealous, and according to some an inveterate intriguer, but he refused to place any credence in that, putting it down to sheer spite. He had hoped that his sister and his wife would hit it off, if only for the sake of family peace and considering that they came from similar backgrounds, Doris being the daughter of a prosperous Idumean trader. Well, maybe in time, Herod thought hopefully. He inquired about his three brothers, especially Phasael.

"Phasael is doing quite nicely," Antipater said with more enthusiasm. "To be governor of Jerusalem requires a great deal of discretion and tact. He's learning fast."

Herod shot his father a quizzical look. Was there a note of disapprobation in his remark? Observing his son's nettled expression, Antipater hastened to add: "Phasael is suitable for Jerusalem, but he wouldn't do for Galilee. This is rough country, its inhabitants are tough and rebellious, hot-heated supporters of Hyrcanus's opponents. That's why I chose you for this province."

Antipater often marveled at the difference between his two eldest sons. He saw some of his own traits in both, but they possessed others which he could only assume were inherited from his wife's side of the family. Phasael was calm, cautious, and conciliatory, but fell short of his younger brother in astuteness, resourcefulness, and ambition – traits which Herod possessed in abundance. But one side of Herod's character puzzled him – a highly suspicious nature and a tendency to react intemperately and even violently when angered. Antipater never forgot how as a youngster Herod had once caught a young Bedouin making off with a lamb from the family estate at Marissa, and with savage fury had thrashed him to within an inch of his life. Antipater had admonished him that, while theft must be punished, it must be within reasonable limits. When he learned that Herod had dispatched Hezekiah, he was not very surprised. But he was perturbed, a feeling exacerbated by subsequent developments.

Herod rose from his chair and, hands on hips, strode over to the window. "You admit that this is tough country and that's why you appointed me to govern it," he declared somewhat heatedly, gazing at the stormy scene outside. "Then why all the fuss and commotion? Who am I governing it for? For that fool Hyrcanus? It was you who appointed me, and with Caesar's approval. Haven't you drummed it into our heads that Rome is master of the world, and whoever is master of Rome is our master, whom we must serve faithfully?" Herod swung around and faced his father with a challenging expression. "That's exactly what I'm doing," he said in clipped, precise accents.

Antipater had to concede the validity of Herod's statement. It was true that he had preached to his sons the need to faithfully serve and to make themselves indispensable to whoever ruled Rome. This had proved to be a most felicitous guiding principle, for it had brought him high position, influence, and wealth. Of course, this might not have come about were it not for the rivalry between the Hasmonean brothers. How wise of him to have seen in Hyrcanus his great opportunity; with strong-willed, martial Aristobulus he would not have had a ghost of a chance. It had been easy to convince Pompey that Rome's interests would best be served by Hyrcanus, with Antipater pulling the strings of course. But what a time he had with Hyrcanus! He had no stomach for a fight. To prod him into action was a Herculean task, requiring all his cunning and persistence. Sometimes he wished Hyrcanus possessed a little of Aristobulus's spunk. That was why he was astonished at Hyrcanus's sudden manifestation of boldness now. Not only astonished, but worried, for if it was not nipped in the bud, everything he had achieved so far would be in jeopardy. This was a very precarious and delicate situation, He would have to proceed carefully and with the utmost adroitness, not only with respect to Hyrcanus, but also with his own son, whose eyes were now boring into him.

"Do you think you were really serving Rome's interests when you executed Hezekiah?" asked Antipater in a bland, matter-of-fact voice.

Herod stared at his father with an incredulous expression. "How can you have any doubts about that? Hezekiah was a bandit chieftain who terrorized non-Jewish villages on both sides of the border and even dealt roughly with his own countrymen who were friendly to the Romans. And didn't Sextus Caesar himself commend me for capturing him?"

"For capturing him, yes, but not necessarily for executing him."

"What was I supposed to do – treat him like royalty, with lavish banquets and spectacular entertainment?"

Antipater ignored the biting sarcasm. "No, not that either. But you have evidently forgotten one of the cardinal principles of Roman imperial policy. I thought I had made it clear to you, but it seems I was mistaken."

"I don't know what you're referring to."

"Then allow me to refresh your memory. But first, please sit down; my neck is beginning to hurt from looking up at you. Thank you. Now, as you are perfectly aware, the Roman Empire is a huge, sprawling one, embracing many different states and peoples. For Rome they are a source of wealth and power. But empires must be handled with care if they are to endure. This means that the subject people, who are anyway resentful at their loss of independence, must not be mistreated, otherwise they will rebel at the first opportunity. So it is to Rome's interest to interfere as little as possible in the internal life of the subject peoples or client states. In the case of Judea this refers primarily to its religion: its observance and no less significant, its institutions, of which the Sanhedrin is the most important, apart from the Temple itself. Now do you understand?"

Herod shook his head. "Not entirely."

"What is it you don't understand?"

"For the life of me I don't see where I trampled on anyone's religious sensitivities. Maybe their national pride, but nothing more than that. You say the Romans don't interfere in the internal affairs of the subject peoples. I admit I haven't had as much experience with the Romans as you have, but one thing I'll swear to: No Roman commander, let alone Sextus Caesar, would have acted any differently than I did. He would have disposed of that gang of brigands without the slightest compunction or mercy. What's more, those brigands knew the risk they were taking and what their fate would be if they were captured. It's absurd to think otherwise."

"What you say may be true," Antipater conceded: "A Roman commander would very likely have acted just as you did. But that's why *you* are governor of Galilee, and not a Roman."

Antipater rose and strode over to one of the cabinets in the room and picked up a statuette gracing its top. He examined it closely. "A beautiful piece of work," he commented with unfeigned admiration. "A goddess and one of her maidens, I believe. The man who fashioned this must have devoted many hours of loving labor to it. An exquisite thing to behold." He returned the statuette to its place, then turned to Herod. "You prize that statuette, don't you?"

Herod regarded his father with puzzled eyes. "I do, but what has all this to do with what we are discussing?"

"If a Jew – a real Jew, that is, not one like us – saw the statuette, do you know what his reaction would be? He'd say that, apart from the fact that the female figures are – er, rather scantily clad, it's a violation of the Ten Commandments. His religious upbringing wouldn't let him appreciate the statuette as you do. And the same applies to the execution of Hezekiah. He'd say that man is created in the image of God, and to take human life is to commit one of the worst sins. Only the Sanhedrin is empowered to sentence a man to death, and that only after a proper trial. In executing Hezekiah you infringed its authority. You have united all Jews against yourself and me too. It's a real hornets' nest you've stirred up, and I'm afraid we might get stung."

"What do you suggest, then?" Herod reflected a moment, and in that short interval his countenance underwent a transformation: His eyes narrowed to two tiny slits, the veins stood out on his neck, his lips became a thin line, his voice was biting. "Are you suggesting that I appear before that body of hair-splitting old men, to put my fate in their hands? No! I say, a thousand times no! They want my blood, they do. But they won't have it!" he thundered, his whole body trembling with rage. "*They* are going to judge *me*? Not on your life! I'll fight before I abase myself before those weasel-faced old goats. Let them dare try to judge me. I'll show them who they're dealing with!"

All the while Herod was pacing the room like a caged tiger, gesticulating vehemently, pounding his fist first into the palm of his left hand and then on the desk, his face contorted with wrath. Antipater sat through this performance with a placid expression, not saying a word until the torrent of invective showed signs of subsiding.

"Now that you've gotten that off your chest, perhaps you will be kind enough to listen to me," he said calmly. "But do sit down, your prancing is making me dizzy. That's better. Now what was it I wanted to say? Oh yes. That you are upset and angry is understandable. It's hard for you to keep your cool at the best of times, and this is certainly not the best of times. But if you want to make your mark with the Romans, you will have to keep your emotions under better control, and above all, think and act logically."

"I think what I've said and done is logical enough, even if I may be a little excited right now."

"You may think so, but as an impartial judge I beg to differ. Take one small example: The members of the Sanhedrin, who are men of learning and some distinction, you call weasel-faced old goats. Now, I know what goats look like and I've seen weasels in my lifetime, but I have yet to see a goat with a face like a weasel's."

This remark, accompanied by a grin, produced the desired effect. Herod's lips twisted into a thin, wry smile.

"But seriously," Antipater continued, "you must learn not to act or make decisions rashly, especially when they can have grave repercussions. And believe me, what you have done is bristling with potential grave repercussions. If you arouse the people to the point of rebellion, Rome is going to have second thoughts about you, and by implication me too, since I appointed you governor of Galilee. I have managed to establish a good rapport with the Romans over the years, and I don't want it ruined by any impetuous behavior on your part. Have I made myself clear?"

For a long moment Herod reflected on his father's words. "Then I'm to throw myself at the mercy of the Sanhedrin, to appear before it in black like a common criminal? Is that what you want?"

"No, not by any means. You will not appear before the Sanhedrin in black like a common criminal. You will appear before it as befits Antipater's son: not craven or downcast, but wearing your military dress, with your head held high. Nor will you be defenseless: You will be accompanied by a small bodyguard – just large enough to impress upon the worthy judges that not only are you serving Judea, but Judea has a – er, patron to consider."

Herod stared at his father incredulously. "I don't understand. You just now admonished me for acting rashly, warning me not to antagonize the people."

"That's true. I warned you against antagonizing them, but I didn't say not to *overawe* them. You see, my son, we now find ourselves in a rather desperate

– no, that's too strong a word; let's say, awkward position. Until now Hyrcanus saw the wisdom – nay, the necessity – of cooperating with the Romans, without whose favor he would not be the high priest and ethnarch. But for some strange reason he has decided to throw caution to the wind. Instead of continuing to accept my advice, which has served him so well until now, he prefers to lend his ear to our dear friend Malichus, whose views on where Judea's true interests lie differ from our own. The high priest and ethnarch evidently doesn't realize what a perilous course he has chosen. I regard it as my sacred duty to make him see the error of his ways, to convince him of the need to re-ingratiate himself with his – er, patron. And that is why, without flouting the Law, it is unfortunately necessary to overawe the guardians of the Law. Have I made myself clear?"

Herod mulled over this explanation. His mind was not entirely at ease. "And what if the Sanhedrin is not overawed? It's my neck that is at stake, you know."

"Don't worry, son," Antipater replied with a sly grin; "your neck will be safe and sound. Sextus Caesar knows that you are more useful to him with your neck intact. He may have to be reminded, though. Perhaps you wonder why I made this rather long journey instead of asking you to meet me somewhere closer to Jerusalem. I can assure you it's not because I enjoy having my intestines bouncing up and down for three days. Damascus is not very far from here, and that's the seat of Sextus Caesar's administration. I have an irresistible urge to renew my acquaintance with that delightful city – the scene of my fateful meeting with Pompey fifteen years ago."

Hyrcanus Warned by Sextus Caesar

One of Hyrcanus's favourite rooms in the royal palace was the study. After a long, tiring day devoted to Temple affairs and other official duties, he liked to retire to this small, cozy room in the western wing. It commanded a panoramic view of the Upper City, with its stately mansions, the city walls, and the surrounding hills, over which the setting sun cast an iridescent mantle that evoked a sense of wonder and serenity.

His father, Alexander Yannai, had made little use of the room, for even when he was not campaigning with his army, he had little time or inclination for such sedentary pursuits as books. Hyrcanus, on the other hand, had at an early age discovered the pleasure they offered and spent many happy hours here. He sorely missed the study during the three years he was deprived of the high priesthood and royal crown, and upon returning to the palace one of the first things he did was to refurbish the room. He installed cedar paneling, added cabinets for the books he had collected in the meantime, and covered the floor with a new peacock-blue rug. On the thick-veined knotted desk, over which hung a two-wick bronze oil lamp, he kept a tray of reed quills and styluses, an inkstand, and a wax tablet for jotting down notes. He sat on a high-backed chair, and four other chairs were ranged along the wall for visitors, usually sages with whom he studied or carried on a learned discussion.

Clad in informal attire, Hyrcanus was immersed in a piece of wisdom literature, Ben Sira's *Ecclesiasticus*. He enjoyed rereading the moral maxims and sage advice written over a century earlier by this widely traveled Jerusalem scholar and man of the world. From time to time he would glance out the window and watch the sun sinking behind the hills and the first stars making their appearance. His reading was interrupted by the pitter-patter of children's feet dashing down the corridor. From the peals of laughter he knew who his visitors would be, and he smiled in anticipation. The door burst open to admit a five-year-old boy and his sister, two years his senior. The youngsters threw their arms around Hyrcanus's neck and gave him a loud kiss.

"And did you, Jonathan Aristobulus and Mariamne, get permission to enter my study and disturb me?" Hyrcanus said, screwing up his face in mock severity.

"Indeed I did not," was the boy's gleeful reply. "When I want to see Grandpa nobody is going to stop me." And with that declaration he jumped onto Hyrcanus's lap to receive a warm kiss in return.

Hyrcanus drew Mariamne to him and gave her an affectionate hug and stroked her long black tresses. To him these youngsters were two little suns that radiated warmth and light, that never failed to dispel the darkest clouds in his sky. "Children's children are the crown of old men" – how apt that proverb was. He would love them just as much if they were plain-looking, but it was obvious that Mariamne was going to blossom into a very beautiful young woman and her brother into a handsome young man. "May the Lord bless them and keep them," he silently prayed.

This was one intrusion on his study that Hyrcanus did not begrudge. He asked them how they had spent the day and listened attentively to their enthusiastic recounting of their adventures. During their brief visit the dish of sweetmeats on the desk dwindled rapidly, much to his amusement; he knew they were devouring all they could before their mother came looking for them. They had no sooner consumed the last tidbit than she appeared with a handmaid to shepherd them to her apartment.

With their departure the study seemed oppressively quiet. Hyrcanus shook his head, thinking how wonderful it was to have these two lively youngsters around him. He could not help regretting that he had no male issue. In this respect he envied his late brother, who had fathered two sons and three daughters. Thrice Hyrcanus's wife had miscarried. More than once it was suggested to him that he consider taking another wife who might prove more fruitful and give him a male heir, but he would not hear of it. Elisheva had loyally stood by him through all his travails, and he had no intention of rewarding her in such an ill manner. He knew how grieved she was that she had not given him more children. He would comfort her by reminding her of Elkanah's encouraging words to Hannah – who subsequently gave birth to the judge and prophet Samuel – that she was better than ten sons. But he was grateful that he had a daughter at least. Alexandra was the epitome of filial devotion, and he valued her clear-sighted opinions even when they differed from his own. Her present unhappy state troubled his conscience, for he had encouraged her to marry her cousin Alexander. The match had been proposed in the hope of healing the breach between Hyrcanus and his brother, but things had not turned out that way. Aristobulus and his two sons continued to rebel against the Romans and made further attempts to wrest the throne from Hyrcanus. They paid dearly for their rebelliousness: Aristobulus was poisoned in Rome by Pompey's followers, and Alexander was executed on Pompey's orders by the proconsul of Syria.

Hyrcanus resumed his reading of Ben Sira, but found it hard to concentrate. His thoughts kept wandering to his young visitors and, despite his attempt to put it out of his mind, the forthcoming session of the Sanhedrin. When Alexandra reappeared within the hour, he welcomed the diversion.

"I take it the children are asleep?" he said.

"Aristobulus is, Mariamne is getting ready for bed," she replied, drawing up a chair opposite her father. She noticed the empty dish on the desk. "I assume that it wasn't you who ate up all the sweetmeats," she remarked with a look of amused resignation.

"I plead innocent," replied Hyrcanus with a grin.

Alexandra knew how much he valued the time spent in his study. It was therefore obvious to him that she must have some compelling reason to speak to him. He never begrudged her the opportunity to discuss her problems or simply to have a chat – not before her marriage and certainly not now when she no longer had a husband in whom to confide. She had a strong character, like her grandmother Queen Alexandra Salome, but without the excessive pride of her late husband and her father-in-law, which he had found so irritating. He rolled up the scroll and put it aside.

"Ben Sira can wait for another day. What's on your mind, daughter? Is it the children?"

"No, I just feel like talking to you, that's all. Ever since this business with Herod came up we haven't had much chance for a little chat. I can see how much it has affected you."

Hyrcanus's eyebrows arched sharply. "Is it that obvious?"

"To an outsider probably not, but I'm not an outsider."

Alexandra was wearing a plain light-blue tunic without any ornaments or jewelry. This, however, did not detract from her regal appearance. She had a noble, finely molded countenance, with long dark eyes, a finely chiseled nose, and a determined mouth; her thick black hair was drawn into a tight knot at the back of the head. Her voice was full and rich, pleasing to the ear.

She was acutely aware that his subjects had an ambivalent attitude toward her father. They respected him as high priest but less so as king – or ethnarch, as the Romans designated him – even though he sincerely believed that he was acting in their best interests. Whenever she had explained this to her late husband, he would ridicule her, saying it was mere humbug intended to salve his conscience for letting himself become a tool of Antipater, who was a mere puppet of Rome. It was he, Alexander, and his father who were concerned for the honor and self-respect of their fellow Jews. Their many arguments on this subject had cast a shadow over their marriage. She loved her father but had to admit there was more than a grain of truth in Alexander's contention. And what was the outcome of all this? To what a sorry pass had matters come, she ruefully mused: Her husband and her father-in-law put to death, and she a widow still in her thirties. There were times when she envied the lot of the plain housewife and would willingly have changed places with any of them, to be able to enjoy her home, her husband, her children, in peace and tranquillity, to busy herself with the daily chores and concerns of the household, untroubled by matters of high politics, not to be privy to plans to take up arms against the Romans and wait in trepidation for news of the outcome of the battle and the safety of her husband, her father-in-law, and other kin. But then a voice inside her would remind her that she was a Hasmonean, a member of the ruling house that had performed valiant deeds and elevated the honor and prestige of the nation, whose name was enshrined in the annals of her people. This would uplift her spirits and enable her to carry her head high. She often wondered why her father seemed to lack this sense of family pride. Now that he had apparently adopted a bolder stance, she thought it a propitious time to broach the question as delicately as she could.

"No, I don't think it is wrong to take pride in our Hasmonean blood, not at all," he said. "Our family has done much that is a credit to our people. But you must not overlook the fact that not all our deeds have been worthy ones, not all have been acclaimed by the people. Your great-grandfather John Hyrcanus, for instance, did not deal kindly with the Pharisees toward the end of his life; your grandfather Alexander Yannai dealt still more harshly with them, and to our great shame put many of them to death and forced others to flee or to go into hiding, not to mention the death of many of our people in foreign and civil wars. Some of his subjects were proud of his conquests and rejoiced to see Hellenistic cities like Gaza, Ptolemais, and Gadara, to mention a few, become part of the realm, but many more were made unhappy by his ceaseless warfare with its toll of Jewish lives, his heavy taxation, and the growing Hellenistic character of the court. And this after our ancestor Mattityahu and his five sons had fought to free the country from the pagan-Hellenistic yoke.

"I don't claim to be entirely blameless myself," Hyrcanus confessed. "The good Lord knows that I have tried to serve Him and our people faithfully, but my conscience is troubled. Am I to blame for what happened to your husband and his father? I have asked myself that question countless times; it has cost me many a sleepless night. My brother was very much like our father Yannai, and I feared for our people if he held the reins of power."

Hyrcanus paused briefly. He had been speaking in a quiet, unemotional tone, as though relieved to unburden himself. Alexandra waited for him to continue. "But did this give me the right to do what I did? I'm not sure, I'm not at all sure. When the day comes that I have to render an accounting to the Almighty, perhaps then I will know."

"On the day of final reckoning we are all wise," said Alexandra with a serious expression. "If only we knew with certainty what is right and good we could spare ourselves a lot of trouble and grief."

"Quite true. This applies to all us mortals, and even more so to one who is head of a nation. Being the head of a nation is not all honor and glory, as most people seem to believe. I have advisers, no lack of them. One counsels one course, another a different course. But they don't have to bear the consequences of their advice if it should not turn out to be as good as they think. But I do. The final decision and responsibility rest with me, and I've agonized over many a decision in the past, and the present too. When I see that to some innocent people they bring suffering, I too suffer. Those who criticize me, and I know their number is not small, can't appreciate what I have to endure."

The occasions when Alexandra had so intimate a talk with her father were rare indeed; in fact, she could not recall when he had ever bared to her his inmost thoughts and feelings as he was doing now. Yet she regretted having broached a subject that led to a brooding introspection. He deserved his hour of contentment, free of all concerns and anxieties.

"I don't think many will criticize the big decision you've made this time," she said in the hope of lightening his mood. "Everyone seems relieved by it."

Hyrcanus, however, showed no sign of being buoyed up. For a long moment he remained silent, staring vacantly out the window. When at last he spoke, his voice was flat, toneless. "I only hope it was a wise decision."

Alexandra regarded her father with some perplexity. "Do you still have doubts on that score? I thought the matter was settled in your mind."

"I thought so too. But something is troubling me."

"Antipater?"

Hyrcanus was struck by her keen perception. "What makes you say that?"

"Your daughter doesn't have blinkers on her eyes. I've noticed how unconcerned and light-hearted he seems to be. A man in his situation should feel differently."

"Yes, he should," agreed Hyrcanus with a frown. "He's made himself pretty scarce the past few days, and as for the trial, he hasn't even mentioned it. It's not natural; it makes me uneasy."

"There's no need to be. As long as you're convinced that you've done the right thing, there's nothing to worry about. And now I must go back to the children."

After Alexandra left, Hyrcanus picked up the scroll and tried to resume his reading, but found it hopeless. A knock on the door startled him out of his musing. He recognized the knock as that of the chamberlain and bade him enter.

"I'm sorry to disturb you, sire, but a courier has arrived with a message for you – from Sextus Caesar."

"Sextus Caesar!" Hyrcanus uttered with an expression of surprise mingled with apprehension.

"That's correct, sire. Shall I admit him?"

For a moment Hyrcanus was flustered. Why would the governor of Syria be writing to him? "Yes, yes of course, admit him."

Upon entering the room the courier saluted Hyrcanus in the Roman manner and extracted a sealed letter from his girdle. Hyrcanus took the letter and motioned to the courier to be seated, but he said the message was quite clear and required no reply.

"You have traveled a long distance," Hyrcanus said in a tolerable Latin. "Let me offer you some refreshments before you proceed on your way."

"Thank you, but I was ordered not to tarry." With this crisp reply, he saluted, made an about-face, and departed.

Hyrcanus stared at the letter, hesitating to open it, for he sensed that it was not calculated to please him. With a resigned look he broke the seal and unrolled the papyrus. As he read it, he turned pale and distraught. The message was blunt and left no room for doubt. In his mind's eye he could see the haughty face of the Roman governor as he dictated the letter in an imperious voice:

> Sextus Caesar, Governor of Syria, to Hyrcanus, son of Alexander Yannai, the high priest and ethnarch of the Jews, greeting. It has come to my attention that Herod, son of Antipater, whom I confirmed as governor of Galilee, has been summoned to appear before the Sanhedrin in Jerusalem to answer charges of having executed one Hezekiah and certain members of his band of brigands. You are hereby informed that Herod was acting in full knowledge of and in conformity with

my instructions to maintain peace and order in the province of Galilee. It greatly displeases me that one who has rendered a signal service to Rome should be summoned to stand trial for faithfully fulfilling his office. As high priest and ethnarch of the Jewish nation, you will be expected to see that no harm befalls him nor any reproach cast on his good name. I shall personally hold you responsible for any contravention of my express wishes in this matter.

Drama in the Sanhedrin

Jerusalem seethed with excitement on the day of the trial. Already at dawn, when the Temple priests were summoned to their stations and ordinarily a somnolent air still lay over the city, the inhabitants began to stir. It would be some time yet before the trial got underway, not until the morning sacrifice, but the Jerusalemites could not contain themselves. It was hard to believe that Herod, the despised Idumean, was going to answer for his crime. The venue was the Chamber of Hewn Stone, situated on the southern side of the Temple court. It was large enough to admit only a comparatively few spectators, but this did not deter the denizens, who were determined to get as close as possible to the scene, to watch the arrival of the main personages involved and to follow the proceedings even by word of mouth.

Long before the smoke of the morning sacrifice could be seen curling upward from the Court of the Priests, the narrow streets and lanes of the Lower City began to fill up, and soon a mass of humanity was converging on the site of the trial. The air buzzed with animated chatter, and there was little doubt from the tenor of the people's remarks where their sympathies lay. When the first group of elders made their appearance, a wave of excitement swept through the throng of spectators. They jostled one another and craned their heads to catch a glimpse of the judges. It was only with some difficulty that a path was cleared for the sages and priests who comprised the supreme judicial and legislative body of the Jewish nation. They wore a serious expression, as was usual when they had to deal with a capital case, and they conversed in low voices. Their robes, mostly in gray and brown hues, flowed in loose folds almost to the ground. From each hem dangled the ritual fringes; a phylactery gleaned on each forehead, and the black thong of the second phylactery was twined about the fingers of the left hand.

While awaiting the arrival of the high priest Hyrcanus, the elders stood around chatting with one another, but once the trial got underway they would take their places on three semicircular tiers of benches. Only the most privileged spectators were allowed into the chamber, where space was at a premium today.

All members of the privy council were present, as was, of course, the defendant's family. Much to everyone's surprise, Antipater had a confident, cheerful mien, and he nodded affably to friends and adversaries alike.

When Hyrcanus entered the chamber, the elders rose to their feet and remained standing until he took his seat on the stone dais facing them. A quick look told him that the full complement of 71 members was present for what all knew would be a historic trial. At a signal of his hand the elders took their seats and waited for the defendant to be ushered in so that the proceedings could begin. Hyrcanus turned to issue instructions to the two scribes seated at separate tables below him, the one on the right assigned to take down the arguments in favor of acquittal, and the one on the left, those in favor of conviction.

The scribes had to ask Hyrcanus to repeat his instructions, for he had spoken in a low, indistinct voice. From the drawn look on his face, and especially the shadow under his eyes, it was obvious that he had not slept well, a fact they put down to sheer excitement at presiding over such an extremely important trial. They could not know that Hyrcanus had had a very fitful night: He had tossed and turned on his bed for a long time before falling asleep, and then his sleep was disturbed by a dream that left him shaky. He was standing on a hillock overlooking the road to Jerusalem and watching Roman legions marching six abreast on the city, led by Pompey and his staff. On they came, cohort after cohort, their armor and weapons glinting in the sunlight, their faces hard and steely, seasoned troops with many a campaign under their belts, who expected and would show no mercy. Then the siege engines rolled by – catapults and battering rams that were frightening to behold. Their rumbling was punctuated by the staccato tramp of studded military boots, an endless stream that flowed closer and closer to the Holy City. At the sound of a trumpet blast the troops charged ahead and began scaling the northern wall under a barrage of stone missiles and arrows that sent screaming defenders plummeting to their death. The Romans poured through the breaches in the wall into the narrow lanes and alleys, cutting down young and old like a field of grain before the reaper's scythe. Then they rushed to the Temple and struck down the priests offering the afternoon sacrifice. Hyrcanus shouted to the soldiers to desist, but no one heeded him. He wanted to stop them with his own hands but was rooted to the spot, paralyzed. He called out again, but with the same result. At this point he woke up, bathed in a cold sweat, his heart pounding fiercely. It took him a few minutes to regain his bearings, after which he got out of bed and poured himself a drink of water from a pitcher. Opening the shutter to his bedroom window, he saw that the city was quiet and asleep, the Temple, homes, and massive walls clearly outlined in the bright moonlight. Everything looked peaceful, and Hyrcanus, greatly relieved, uttered a prayer of thanks. He got back into bed, but it was a long time before he fell asleep again.

His head was still fuzzy when he repeated his instructions to the two scribes. He then ambled over to discuss some technical points with Shemaiah and Avtalyon, the two leading members of the Sanhedrin, with whom he enjoyed a warm relationship, admiring their erudition, humility, and piety, their broad, humane outlook. Shemaiah expressed his concern about the huge crowd milling about outside. He knew they expected the Sanhedrin to find Herod guilty and to exact the maximum punishment.

"It's not surprising that they believe Herod to be guilty," he confided to Hyrcanus. "But they must realize that in a capital case we are bidden to bend over backward to find the least scrap of evidence in favor of the defendant, for we are dealing with a man's life, and life is sacred. I know people will say, 'What about Hezekiah and his men? Didn't Herod snuff out their lives? And isn't he likely to put more men to death if he is allowed to go free?' Nevertheless, we are duty-bound to give him a fair trial. Nor can we inflict capital punishment for a crime that might be committed in the future. To do so may be expedient politics, but it would be a travesty of justice; it would open the door to proscriptions. That may be the Roman way, but it is not our way, the divine way. No, as great a menace as Herod may be, we have to give him a fair trial."

Hyrcanus was about to comment on Shemaiah's observation when a strange noise made him and all the assembled prick up their ears. In the distance could be heard what sounded like the clatter of approaching horses. But how could it possibly be? After a few minutes the crowd began to cry out, and their angry shouts penetrated the chamber. Hyrcanus, who had meanwhile resumed his seat, ordered an usher to see what was happening. He hurried to the entrance, and opening the door was dumbstruck by the sight that greeted his eyes. It *was* a troop of horsemen – dismounted foreign soldiers armed with swords and spears. They forced their way through the entrance, and from their ranks stepped forth Herod, bold and dashing, dressed in purple, his hair and beard curled and oiled. A gasp of horror swept the chamber. It was strictly forbidden for anyone to enter this hall of justice, or even to approach the Temple Mount, with arms, let alone foreign troops with swords and spears. The elders stared aghast as Herod strode to the middle of the semicircular rows of benches, before the seat of the presiding judge.

"You have summoned me to appear before the Sanhedrin," he announced in a loud, defiant voice. "I have come."

Folding his arms across his chest, he cast a scornful glance at the elders. They could not believe their eyes. In capital cases the accused would present himself in a humble, meek manner, his hair disheveled, his garments black. But what astounded them even more was Herod's audacity in entering the chamber with an armed bodyguard. Their weapons glinted menacingly; from their fierce looks there was no doubt in anyone's mind that at a single word of command they would strike down all the members of the Sanhedrin. The entire assembly was petrified. The elders looked at one another in wonder and fear; no one dare to speak up.

Hyrcanus's heart missed a beat when he beheld Herod announcing his presence. Never in his wildest dreams could he imagine such a thing happening. He must collect his thoughts. He was the high priest, the president of the Sanhedrin; it was up to him to do something. But what? He desperately wracked his brain, but to no avail.

Like the others, Shemaiah was taken aback by this incredulous turn of events, but he quickly regained his composure. He saw very clearly the implications of Herod's brazen act. He had not come as the defendant in a capital case; he had come to intimidate the highest tribunal of the Jews. This affront to the dignity of the Sanhedrin made Shemaiah's cheeks burn. He knew, however, that it was not Herod alone who was intimidating the Sanhedrin; he would not dare to defy it in such a manner were it not for his Roman overlords. Shemaiah hesitated, but only for a moment, for the words of the holy Bible rang in his ears: "God standeth in the congregation of God: In the midst of judges doth He judge." He waited for Hyrcanus to say something, but when the latter remained silent, Shemaiah realized that he was paralyzed with fear and irresolution. Shemaiah rose to his feet and addressed Hyrcanus: "With your kind permission, High Priest, I would like to say a few words to the Sanhedrin." Hyrcanus readily assented. Shemaiah waited until he had everyone's attention. He glanced at the soldiers' weapons, but was no longer afraid. He turned to his colleagues.

"High Priest and honored colleagues," he began in a strong, clear voice, "what we are witnessing today is unprecedented in the history of this august body. Before us stands a man who is charged with a capital crime," Shemaiah went on, pointing at Herod. "A man who admittedly holds a high position, who wields great influence and power, but nevertheless one who has been summoned to stand trial for a most serious crime. We are accustomed to seeing the defendant in such cases dressed and comporting himself in a humble manner, his hair untrimmed, his garments black. We are not accustomed to seeing him dressed in purple, his hair neatly combed and oiled, his demeanor proud and, yes, even arrogant; and what is even more astonishing, surrounded by soldiers who presumably are ready to kill us if we should condemn him. Where the accused found the audacity to conduct himself in this manner we know only too well. But this Sanhedrin is Israel's supreme tribunal. It is to us that the people of Israel look for wisdom and justice.

"It is written: 'Ye judge not for man but for the Lord, and it is He who is with you in judgment.' If the Lord is in our midst, are we to be craven, are we to be cowed by the impertinence of this man or any other man? We must not shirk our responsibility; if we are derelict in our duty, who can foretell what the end will be? Heaven forbid, but I fear it will be a dire fate, for the nation and for us personally."

Shemaiah paused for breath. He perceived that the look of alarm had vanished from the elders' faces, to be replaced by a determined expression. "The man before us is no ordinary man," he resumed, pointing at Herod. "He is a man of considerable talent, the governor of Galilee no less – an exalted position." At this remark Herod felt a flush of pleasure; in spite of himself, he was fascinated by the sage's words and had to admire his courage. Shemaiah faced his colleagues again. "But we are commanded by our great teacher Moses, 'Ye shall not respect persons in judgment.' High or low, they must answer for a crime imputed to them. They must be given a fair trial before a competent court. It is up to us to see that the accused is so tried. Pay no heed to the armed soldiers who have accompanied the accused into this hall of justice. Do not let fear or hatred pervert your vision, do not harbor any prejudice in your hearts, but judge justly. For as the prophet has said, 'I the Lord am exalted by justice.' May the Lord be exalted and may He guide us in our deliberations."

Shemaiah remained standing a few seconds, and then he slowly turned and bowed to Hyrcanus before sitting down. The atmosphere in the chamber was transformed. The elders, visibly moved by their colleague's plea, buzzed with excited whispers. Hyrcanus rapped for silence, and the noise gradually died down.

"After hearing the eloquent words of our distinguished colleague," he said in a voice that betrayed no agitation, "we shall proceed with the trial. But first, I must ask the defendant to order the removal of his bodyguard. We cannot sit in judgment in an atmosphere of intimidation."

Everyone turned to see how Herod would react to this request. His visage darkened; he felt a surge of hot anger at this impudent demand, and for a second he contemplated drastic action. But Antipater rose to his feet and, catching Herod's eye, motioned to him to comply. Herod swallowed hard and whispered some instructions to the commander of the troops.

"Very well," Herod said to Hyrcanus in a harsh, menacing tone, "my bodyguard will leave the hall. But they won't be far away."

The soldiers started to file out of the chamber, their features hard and ominous. The elders heaved a sigh of relief, even though they knew the bodyguard would be within calling distance. When the last of the soldiers disappeared through the door, Hyrcanus requested Herod to take the defendant's seat. Herod bristled at this request and was about to refuse point-blank; he was restrained by a desperate sign from his father. But how could he humiliate himself in such a manner? He respected his father's judgment and acumen, and to him filial loyalty and obedience was an inviolable obligation. Nevertheless, he wished he had followed his own instinct in this matter and not let his father talk him into appearing before the Sanhedrin. The situation was highly disconcerting, not at all to his liking. He debated with himself whether to continue with this farce, which he could end in a trice. When Hyrcanus repeated his request, this time a little more insistently, Herod's blood boiled. He felt an irresistible urge to crush these contemptible pedants; and he knew he could do so as easily and with as little compunction as he would crush an obnoxious insect.

Antipater, reading his son's thoughts, realized the situation was extremely precarious. He knew what Herod was capable of doing in an ugly mood. He was ignoring his father's advice, the reasons why he must go through with the business, distasteful as it may be. One false move, one rash act, and all that Antipater had built up, all his hopes and plans, would be ruined. He started to wend his way toward the dais. Herod, already highly incensed, did not relish his father's intervention. Swallowing his pride, his eyes flashing defiance, he took the seat reserved for the defendant. The trial began.

Never before had he been subjected to such a degrading experience, and he vowed that one day he would have his vengeance. To be sure, the proceedings started mildly enough. Hyrcanus called on Avtalyon to explain the basic issue in question which, he was sure, all the members were acquainted with. Speaking dispassionately, Avtalyon briefly reviewed the salient facts: Herod's appointment as governor of Galilee, the raids carried out by Hezekiah, the final skirmish with Herod's troops, and the execution of Hezekiah and his men at Herod's command.

"As our honored colleague Shemaiah lucidly explained at a recent meeting in the royal palace," Avtalyon continued, "the question before us boils down to the motive behind Hezekiah's acts. Was he rebelling against Hyrcanus or against Roman rule? If against Hyrcanus, then the latter had the royal prerogative to condemn him and to empower his agent – in this case presumably Herod – to execute him. Thus Herod would not be guilty of a criminal act. But if it is proved that Hezekiah was rebelling against the Romans, then Herod had no legal right to execute him. According to halacha, he would be guilty of committing a capital crime, and consequently he would have to be tried by a competent court. This is the question we have to address ourselves to."

Hyrcanus thanked Avtalyon and declared that in accordance with prescribed procedure he would first recognize those who wanted to argue for acquittal of the defendant. Not unexpectedly, their number was not large. The most prominent was Saul ben Eliezer, a longtime opponent of the Hasmonean house, whom he regarded as usurpers of the royal crown. The crux of his argument was that, even if Hezekiah had rebelled against Hyrcanus, the latter had no prerogative to condemn him, since the right to wear the royal crown belonged exclusively to the Davidic line, as was the case in First Temple times and which could be deduced from numerous scriptural passages.

Another elder argued that Herod could be regarded as an agent of Hyrcanus, for even if the latter had not appointed him governor of Galilee, he had tacitly agreed to his appointment. Therefore, assuming that Hezekiah had rebelled against the Romans, Hyrcanus, as the principal, had to bear responsibility, at least indirectly, for the crime. Two elders questioned Hezekiah's motives, believing that he and his men were inspired equally as much, if not predominantly, by the desire for plunder, and hence they should be regarded more as violators of the law than patriotic freedom fighters.

These were the only ones to speak in Herod's defense. As opposed to them, speaker after speaker refuted their arguments, citing *halachot* (Oral Law), precedents, and relevant scriptural passages. The testimony of the witnesses was also overwhelmingly against Herod.

The number of elders who expressed their opinion or indicated a desire to do so was large, as was the number of witnesses. The sun had long passed its zenith, and the shadows playing on the walls of the chamber were growing longer. It was obvious that the trial would not be concluded that day. The Sanhedrin could sit only until the afternoon sacrifice, and if a verdict of acquittal was not reached by then, the trial would have to be adjourned until the following day in order to give the elders time to reflect and perhaps find some new arguments or evidence in favor of the accused.

Fatigue began to overcome Hyrcanus, and he waited impatiently for the moment when he could close the session. But if he was suffering from weariness, Herod was enduring what everyone realized was a very trying experience. His visage betrayed his feelings: His lips were compressed tight, his eyes smoldering with wrath. Several times, when the speaker referred to him disparagingly, he angrily leaped to his feet. Perhaps it was just as well that the elders did not know how fierce was his hatred of them, that he had sworn to settle scores with them one day.

The sudden blaring of trumpets and the clash of cymbals rent the air; the Levite choir burst into song, signifying that the afternoon sacrifice was being offered. With a sigh of relief, Hyrcanus adjourned the court. The elders and spectators rose from their places and began to leave the chamber, the spectators chatting animatedly, the elders in subdued tones. The huge crowd outside the chamber parted to let the elders through. They had managed to get a fairly good picture of what was happening inside. As the day wore on their apprehension over Herod's bodyguard had waned, and by late afternoon they had virtually forgotten its presence. They were reminded of it afresh when Herod emerged from the chamber and joined his troops.

Hyrcanus was exhausted. A poor night's sleep, the day's dramatic events, and the lengthy proceedings had drained him physically and mentally. He mechanically acknowledged the good wishes of the spectators and stopped to exchange a few words with some of the elders. He was relieved when at last he got into his litter, which he had ordered even though it was a comparatively short walk to the palace. Many thoughts crowded upon him, but he brushed them aside. He wanted simply to relax from the fatigue and strain of the day. He failed to hear the approach of another litter that was overtaking him, and he became aware of it only when it passed him. Hyrcanus watched impassively as the litter came to a halt, but the wan look on his face vanished when he saw who stepped out – Antipater, looking as fresh and energetic as in the morning.

Hyrcanus was in no mood for this encounter, which instinct told him was not coincidental. For more years than he cared to remember he and Antipater had worked hand in glove, and he knew that if not for him he would very likely not be where he was today. The bond between them had been forged of iron and, as much as he hated to admit it, even in blood. Yet he had found it necessary, if not to completely sever the bond, at least to loosen it. When he had been finally persuaded to try Herod, one of things he feared was Antipater's reaction.

He was intimately familiar with his driving ambition, his shrewdness, and his uncanny ability to turn events and men to his own advantage. More than once Hyrcanus had thought their cause was doomed, yet Antipater had managed to emerge unscathed, more firmly entrenched and powerful than ever. When he had informed Antipater of his decision to summon Herod to stand trial, he expected a violent protest. Much to his surprise, Antipater did not reveal the slightest sign of consternation. For a moment or two he stood rigid, scrutinizing Hyrcanus with a frozen smile. Hyrcanus wondered what thoughts were racing through his mind. Antipater nodded respectfully, and in a calm voice said, "If you permit me to say so, I believe that in bowing to public pressure you are making a grave mistake, and one day you will come to realize that." That was all. Since then the two had seen very little of each other, and it was clear to all that there was an almost total rupture between them.

Suspicious and uneasy, Hyrcanus watched Antipater advance toward him. But there was nothing in the latter's features or demeanor to betray any sign of coolness or ill-feeling; on the contrary, he appeared to be in a good humor, "I congratulate you on the excellent way in which you presided over the trial today," he said in a friendly tone.

Hyrcanus, more mystified than ever, remained silent. Much to his surprise, Antipater's mood seemed to undergo an abrupt change; he regarded Hyrcanus with a grave expression. "From the drift of the proceedings it doesn't look too good, does it?"

Hyrcanus hesitated before responding. He did not want to hurt Antipater's feelings, but at the same time he was wary of possible pitfalls. "As the presiding judge, it would be inappropriate for me to voice an opinion on this point," was his cautious reply. And then, relenting a little, he added in the hope of injecting a warmer note: "As you know, in cases like this, when it appears that majority opinion is against the defendant, the trial is adjourned to the following day in order to let the elders see if they can find any new evidence or any extenuating circumstances that would warrant a change of mind."

"Ah, yes, quite so," remarked Antipater in a lighter vein. "A most admirable system, one that probably has no equal anywhere. You are indeed fortunate to be presiding over such an eminent court, and the court is indeed fortunate to have such an eminent person at its head. But then, I have always known you to be a just man. And a prudent man – one who always puts the good of his people above all else. Happy be it when the two go hand in hand – justice and prudence." Antipater paused briefly before adding in a voice pregnant with meaning: "But alas, it is not always so, is it?"

Hyrcanus stared at Antipater, wondering what lay behind his words. "I must not detain you any longer," Antipater said. "Peace be unto you." After a polite bow he returned to his litter, but before getting in he turned and called out: "By the way, I shall be at home this evening. Should anyone wish to communicate with me, he'll find me in."

Hyrcanus watched Antipater's slaves lift up the litter and move on. Fatigue weighed heavily on him, and he found it hard to think clearly. Antipater's enigmatic words puzzled him, but one thing was certain: there was some cryptic meaning, perhaps even an oblique warning, in this seemingly innocuous encounter. However, he decided to banish it from his mind for the time being. It was only after he had eaten a warm meal and rested awhile that he found himself reviewing the day's events. It was hard to believe that so many things had happened in the course of a single day. First, there was the consternation caused by Herod's singular appearance and his effrontery in entering the Chamber of Hewn Stone with a bodyguard of armed foreign soldiers, some of whom might have been Romans. Romans? Of course! How could he have forgotten – the letter from Sextus Caesar? Hyrcanus sat bolt upright, his senses fully alert. What was it the governor of Syria had written? "It greatly displeases me that one who has rendered a signal service to Rome should be summoned to stand trial for fulfilling his office. I shall personally hold you responsible for any contravention of my express wishes in this matter."

So that was Antipater's veiled message! In bland, seemingly innocent phrases he was reminding Hyrcanus of Sextus Caesar's warning. The clever fox! "Justice and prudence," Antipater had said; "happy be it when the two go hand in hand, but alas, it is not always so." And what was that oblique compliment he had paid him? "A man who always puts the good of his people above all else." That sly Antipater; he knew exactly where he was most vulnerable. Hyrcanus had once confided to him the trauma he experienced at Pompey's investment of the Holy City: the massacre of the priests in the Temple while they were carrying on with the sacrifices in the face of imminent death, the slaughter of innocent civilians. Antipater had replied that this was the inevitable price that had to be paid in the circumstances. Without it Hyrcanus would never had been appointed high priest and ethnarch; presumably someone else would have been appointed to these offices, with the consequence that there would very likely have been even greater devastation and loss of life over the years. And who knows? Judea might even have fallen completely under the Roman yoke, with no vestige of freedom or sovereignty.

And now what price would have to be paid? What could Sextus Caesar exact from Hyrcanus and his people? Scenes from last night's dream flashed before him: the advancing legions, the siege engines, the slaying of men, women, and children. Would Sextus Caesar dare go to such lengths? Could Hyrcanus risk incurring his wrath and thereby precipitate a possible catastrophe?

Hyrcanus groaned and wondered if it was all worth the anguish he had to endure. True, he liked being high priest; he loved the pomp and ceremony of the Temple service, the respect accorded the holder of this sacred and most exalted office of the Jewish nation. But there was the other side of the coin: the weighty responsibility that this office – and that of ethnarch – imposed on him, the difficult and fateful decisions that had to be made. Like the present one. Human lives were at stake. In one scale was Herod; in the other, who knows how many innocent lives? Hyrcanus began to pace the room, his mind in a turmoil. "O Lord," he pleaded, "help me to do what is right."

He desperately longed to consult with someone. But who? His ministers and advisers were all dead set against Antipater and Herod and their Roman masters. They would hardly counsel prudence but forceful action, heedless of the consequences. Shemaiah perhaps? He feared no man; he was sustained by an abiding faith in the Almighty. But twenty years ago Hyrcanus had seen priests slain while performing their sacred duties in God's own house. When Hyrcanus beheld the swords and spears in the Sanhedrin and the hard, merciless visages of the soldiers, he knew they were capable of mowing down all the elders in the chamber like stalks of ripe wheat, and with no more regret. "No, Shemaiah, my dear friend, it is not as simple as you think," he murmured in a grim voice. "You don't know the Romans as intimately as I do, and perhaps it is just as well that you don't. If I were to be responsible for your death or that of the other elders, I could not go on serving the Lord; my life would no longer be worth living."

Hyrcanus continued to debate with himself, weighing the pros and cons, but deep down inside he knew he had no choice. Finally, with a heavy heart he sat down at his desk and picked up a quill and sheet of papyrus. It was a short message he had to write, just a few sentences advising Herod to secretly flee the city that very night. But how to frame it so that the proper connotation would be put on it, sounding neither timorous nor self-abasing, was no simple matter. It was only on the third attempt that he felt he hit the right note. He rolled up the letter, poured some wax on it, and sealed it with his signet ring.

After summoning his most trusted courier, he instructed him to immediately deliver the letter to Antipater himself and to no one else, impressing upon him the need for the utmost secrecy and caution. With a resigned expression, Hyrcanus watched the courier leave the room. He knew that the dispatch of the letter was fraught with grave implications, yet curiously he felt a sense of detachment, as though not he but someone else was taking this desperate step. The reaction was bound to set in later, and he feared it would fill him with foreboding.

Chapter Two

Herod Escapes, Appointed Governor of Coele-Syria

Alexandra Visits Exiled Antigonus in Chalcis

It was good to get away from Jerusalem for a while. For all her love of the city, Alexandra had felt the need for a change of scenery. She had always been an avid traveler, but since the death of her husband she was often depressed and could not muster any enthusiasm for travel, or even for keeping up with her usual social obligations. Her father, understanding her frame of mind, did not press her on this, but tried in his quiet, unobtrusive way to keep her spirits up until time would hopefully work its cure.

When not long after Herod's aborted trial, an invitation for a visit arrived from Antigonus, her brother-in-law and cousin, she was at first inclined to turn it down. She had not seen him since he was granted asylum by the prince of Chalcis after the traumatic events two years earlier, and would have liked to see him again but hesitated because of the strained relations between him and her father. Hyrcanus, however, had urged her to accept the invitation, assuring her that his skin was thick enough to withstand any barbs Antigonus might hurl.

The long highland journey to Chalcis was a pleasant one, and Mariamne and Aristobulus bubbled with excitement at the sights. It was early autumn and free of the oppressive, enervating khamsins (hot, dry desert wind), so they enjoyed comfortable weather. Aristobulus, having heard adventurous tales involving hostelries, had his heart set on spending the nights in such lodging places, and was dismayed to learn that his mother had arranged to be put up with friends wherever possible. To placate him, Alexandra promised to stop off at inns for daytime breaks. They were, of course, the center of attraction, and the guests and local inhabitants crowded around to greet them. Ever since she had gone into mourning she had little contact with people outside the court, and the enthusiastic expressions of loyalty to the Hasmonean house rekindled a spark in her breast. By the time she arrived at Antigonus's villa, she was feeling more like her old self.

This was her first visit to Chalcis, capital of the principality of Iturea. Lying at the foot of Mount Lebanon, some 25 miles from Berytus, it was a delightful place. From the spacious, well-tended grounds of his villa on the outskirts of the town, Antigonus pointed out the magnificent prospect. Chalcis was girdled with thickly-wooded hills honeycombed with caves – "excellent hideaways for brigands," he chuckled. Clearly visible to the naked eye, Mount Hermon towered aloft, crowned with a gleaming white snowcap. Peering down a narrow valley that stretched in a northwesterly direction, Alexandra could glimpse the blue waters of the Mediterranean. The villa lay atop a knoll carpeted with a lush-green lawn and bright flower beds bordered with neatly trimmed hedge rows and interspersed with cypress and pine trees.

Aristobulus and Mariamne, having been taken in tow by Antigonus's young daughter, were scampering over the grounds and poking into all the nooks and crannies. They did not realize, nor would they have cared in the least, that they were being observed by their elders, who were seated on a stone bench and sipping cool drinks and were particularly amused by Aristobulus's intense interest in the kidney-shaped pond upon whose lily-strewn water glided a number of swans and various other fowl. This intrigued him so much that his whole body quivered with excitement, and he called to his two companions to come over and join him.

"He's a cute little darling," remarked Antigonus's wife, Roxane. "We grownups are inclined to take life's simple joys too much for granted."

"When we grow up we find that life's joys are simply too little granted us," retorted Antigonus with a faintly cynical smile.

Although accustomed to Antigonus's somewhat sardonic wit, Alexandra was not sure whether it was an innate trait or more an affectation, a sort of defense mechanism against the rough winds that had buffeted him. He had some annoying traits, but she was nevertheless quite fond of him. He had the handsome features of the Hasmoneans and cut an imposing figure. Tall, well-proportioned, with broad shoulders and sturdy limbs, he gave the impression of being able to render a good account of himself in any contest of arms. His hair and beard were a thick black and trimmed short, a long thin nose sat above finely molded and mobile lips, his dark-brown eyes were keen and piercing, and when he was not serious, they had a mocking glint. Even when he was being deliberately provoking, Alexandra found him interesting. She could never be sure what turn his mood would take, and she was always braced for his verbal skirmishing. *It was fortunate*, she mused, *that his wife was unassuming and patient.*

"I must admit you're right, my dear," Antigonus said in response to Roxane's comment about Aristobulus, "he is a cute boy. And his sister is going to be a raving beauty. Fortunately, their souls are still unscarred, and may they always be so." Turning to Alexandra, he lowered his voice: "We have all been through a great deal of late, haven't we, cousin? It's time we put the past behind us and look forward to the future – a better and happy future. I propose we drink a toast to that," he added, getting up to refill the glasses.

Alexandra lowered her eyes; it was not going to be easy to forget the past. And knowing Antigonus, she could not help wondering what sort of a future he was looking forward to. But his optimism was contagious; she picked up her glass to join in the toast.

It was a long time since she felt so relaxed. She loved Jerusalem, with all its bustle, the throngs of pilgrims who converged on the Temple from all parts of the country and the various lands of the Diaspora, the stimulating conversation in the palace of statesmen and diplomats, the edifying discourses and instruction of the sages, the knowledge that here was the hub of the world, at least the Jewish world, where one felt the divine presence most intimately. But she also loved the charm of places like Antigonus's residence, whose pastoral peace and beauty were balm to her soul.

"You have a lovely place here," she complimented her host. "Your taste is written all over it."

"Thank you, cousin, but I'm afraid I can't take all the credit for that."

"You have made some big changes, dear," Roxane reminded her husband.

"Yes, that's true; I have made some changes to suit my own taste, but basically we have to thank our bandit chieftain."

Alexandra was not sure how to take this reference to the man who had befriended Antigonus. She had heard stories about the propensity of the Itureans to brigandage, but did not know how much credence to put in them; and even if true, it would not make this people much different from other neighbors of Judea.

"Bandit or not," she remarked with a grin, "it's fortunate that Ptolemy was kind enough to give you asylum. We were so relieved when we heard the news."

Antigonus put his glass down on the small table set before them. "We?" he said, lifting his eyebrows. "Excuse my impertinence, but may I ask who else besides you was made happy by the news?"

Alexandra sensed that she had inadvertently trodden on slippery ground. "All of us, of course," she replied a little hastily.

Antigonus made a wry face. "I can hardly imagine that you would be referring to your two lovely children. Nor can I believe that your father was overjoyed to learn that I am residing in this handsome villa so deucedly close to the borders of his realm."

Alexandra, familiar with Antigonus's tendency to blow innocent remarks out of all proportion, sought to disperse the clouds that had suddenly gathered; but she feared that no matter what she might say, he would put the wrong construction on it.

"You misjudge my father, Matti," she protested conciliatorily, using the diminutive of Antigonus's Hebrew name. "You may not believe it, but in spite of everything that has happened, he bears you no ill will. There is nothing he would like more than to patch up relations with you, to let bygones be bygones."

"To forgive and forget, you mean?" Antigonus retorted somewhat tartly. "That's very noble of him, but don't you think it's a little late for that? A lot of water has flowed under the bridge. And a lot of blood too, including that of my father and brother."

"I know," Alexandra commiserated. "Your father was my uncle, and your brother my husband. That's all the more reason why it's so important to end the feud, to put the past behind us and look forward to a better and happy future. Didn't we just drink a toast to that?"

Antigonus rose to his feet and ambled over to the sundial mounted on a granite pedestal a few steps away. Leaning against it, he gazed vacantly at the distant scenery, reflecting on her words. The silence was broken only by the twittering of birds darting among the trees and the buzzing of bees. When he turned to reply, there was an uncustomary opaque look in his eyes. And when he spoke, it was without any trace of bitterness or sarcasm.

"The problem is not essentially a personal one, of Antigonus versus Hyrcanus; it's a national issue. I have reservations about my uncle, I won't deny it – strong reservations. But in reality we were not opposed so much to him as against the Romans. We were fighting against the subjugation of our people after a century of independence – independence won under the leadership of our forebears."

"And you think we have completely lost our independence, even when the Sanhedrin can meet without hindrance and the Romans acknowledge my father as high priest and ethnarch?"

Antigonus stared at Alexandra with an incredulous expression. "Alexandra, really! You amaze me. How long has your father been ethnarch? Not even a year yet – appointed by Caesar, who, even though I may have a grievance against him, is far above the usual breed of Roman despots."

Alexandra knew that the grievance Antigonus harbored against Julius Caesar was a festering sore. When he had bested Pompey in the struggle for mastery of Rome and forced him to flee the country, Caesar had released Antigonus's father from his imprisonment in Rome with the intention of sending him back to Judea with two legions at his disposal in order to win support against the Pompeians. The plan, however, had miscarried, for some Pompeians poisoned Aristobulus while he was still in Rome, and his elder son, Alexander, was beheaded in Antioch upon Pompey's orders. Antigonus had recently reminded Caesar of the distressful denouement of the enterprise and pleaded to be appointed high priest, considering that his father and brother had given their lives in Caesar's cause, while Hyrcanus and Antipater were not Caesar's true friends, for they had previously been closely associated with Pompey. Caesar, however, had not been swayed by this argument; he was more impressed by the aid Antipater and Hyrcanus had extended him when he was battling a strong enemy force in Egypt. He realized that Antipater could be relied upon to subordinate the interests of Judea to those of the Roman Empire, a factor that outweighed any moral obligation he might have owed Antigonus. Antigonus had smarted at what he regarded as a gross breach of faith, but he was too experienced in the devious ways of statecraft to be surprised. He also knew that the title of ethnarch was devoid of any real political power, which was vested less in Hyrcanus's than in Antipater's hands.

"And if your father does possess the title of ethnarch," continued Antigonus in a more strident tone as the recollection of Caesar's ingratitude rankled him anew, "he can thank that oily Idumean serpent of his. If it weren't for that sycophant..."

"Matti!" his wife called out sharply, "don't be an insufferable boor. Once you get on that subject you work yourself into a rage and will end up annoying our guest. Why don't you drop it?"

Antigonus glared at his wife; his lips twitched as he struggled to restrain himself. "Roxane, dear," Alexandra hastened to calm the brewing storm, "I'm quite used to my cousin's fulminations. I assure you that I won't hold it against him if he wants to vilify that 'oily Idumean serpent,' as he calls him. In fact, I find his description of Antipater a very apt one."

"If you think the description fits, then why don't you try to talk a little sense into your father?" Antigonus shot back. "Tell him to get rid of that leech before he completely enslaves the nation to the Romans."

"Wiser people than I have counseled him to do that," Alexandra replied unruffled. "But you – and they too – forget that Antipater was appointed *epitropos* (guardian) of Judea not by my father, but by Caesar himself. One cannot ignore that small detail."

Antigonus poured himself another drink. He asked the women if they would also like one, and upon receiving a positive reply, he refilled their glasses. "I must say," he resumed after taking a few sips, "when I heard that your father had summoned Herod to stand trial, I couldn't believe it. It was the first time I've seen him show any spunk. Just think! Hyrcanus dared to defy Antipater and by implication even the great Caesar himself. Incredible!"

"It was a step he took only after long, careful consideration. There were many factors to be weighed, and there were great risks involved. I can vouch for that."

"There are risks involved in everything we do A leader is expected to face and, yes, even to take risks. A pity, though, that after putting on a brave show for once, your father got cold feet in the end."

The latter observation, uttered in a scornful voice, stung Alexandra. "Cold feet!" she exclaimed with some indignation.

"Yes, what then? When it seemed certain that Herod was going to be convicted the next day, he fled the city. How do you explain that?"

Alexandra was disconcerted. She did not know what exactly had happened that night, but there were some who claimed that her father had a hand in Herod's disappearance. The rumor pained her greatly. When she had queried him about it, he was deliberately vague, neither denying nor confirming it. She could only conclude that if he had been a party to Herod's hasty departure from Jerusalem, something drastic must have happened to make him take such a desperate step.

"I see words fail you," Antigonus taunted her. "I'm not surprised. Well, there's going to be the devil of a price to pay, I'm afraid. You may not know it, but Herod fled to Damascus to Sextus Caesar, cousin of the great Gaius Julius, and got himself appointed governor of Coele-Syria, no less. That makes him a neighbor of mine – a most undesirable neighbor, I can assure you."

At this point Roxane excused herself to see to dinner, first admonishing her husband to keep his cool. The children were out of sight, but their animated chatter was clearly audible. A breeze had blown up and Alexandra began to feel chilly. Antigonus asked if she would like to go indoors, but she expressed a preference to remain. He offered to bring her a shawl and a hot drink.

Alexandra tried to relax until his return. She thought she would close her eyes awhile, but the late-afternoon sun caressing the surrounding hills, transforming their mantle of autumnal foliage into a dazzling mosaic of color, was overwhelming. "How wonderful it would be," she mused, "to be able to enjoy the beauty of nature without any worries or problems." She sighed softly, knowing that this was but a fleeting moment of repose, a brief interlude in a life crowded with tumultuous events and personal concerns. She envied Antigonus for living, even if only temporarily, amid such delightful rustic scenery, but immediately reproved herself. Her cousin had gone through a great deal and suffered much. True, he was ambitious and did not lack for pride. While to some this was regrettable, to others it enhanced his natural gift of leadership. It was no wonder, she reflected, that like his father and brother he had time and again inspired thousands to flock to his standard. Almost always he had taken the field against foreign forces superior to his own, especially in training and discipline, with the result that he invariably suffered defeat. This, however, failed to daunt his resolve or that of his followers, who were always ready to rally around him again. He had been wounded more than once and twice taken captive to Rome.

If he was enjoying some respite now, who was she to envy him? But could one as restive and dynamic as he lead a quiet, tranquil life for long? She doubted it.

When he returned she asked him how he was enjoying life amid such enchanting surroundings.

"You mean my life of enforced leisure? You may be surprised, but it has its advantages. For one thing, I have plenty of time to think."

Alexandra frowned. "When you have a lot of time to think, I'm worried."

"Oh, my dear, how can you have such gloomy ideas? Surely you don't take such a dim view of your cousin?"

"I'm very fond of my cousin, even if I don't always appreciate the wisdom of his deeds. They have not always produced happy results, not for his followers, his people, or even for himself. I'm not sure he realizes that. That's why I'm worried."

Antigonus gave a short laugh. "Alexandra, you're being melodramatic! You will twist my words and impute to me the most sinister of motives." And then in a serious vein, he added: "Do you honestly think I have forgotten all that I have gone through the past few years? Would you like me to bare my chest and show you the scars of my wounds? My memento of the battle at Machaerus is a real beauty. And I assure you that I can think of more pleasant ways of seeing Rome than as a captive of war."

"You were taken to Rome as a captive not once but twice," Alexandra reminded him in a gently admonishing voice.

"Yes, twice; your memory doesn't deceive you."

Alexandra looked her cousin full in the face. Her eyes were deadly serious, even a little frightened, like a doe's eyes. "I'm afraid there won't be a third time, Matti. Don't try it again, I beg of you – for your own sake."

Antigonus stared at Alexandra for a long moment and then lowered his gaze. When he looked up, the grin had vanished from his face, to be replaced by a look of cool reserve. "What makes you suspect that I'm thinking in that direction?" he asked guardedly.

"I know you too well. I know what's happened in the past, and I know the stuff you're made of. You've got the Hasmonean pride in your blood, and it won't let you rest content."

Antigonus reflected on this remark. "Yes, I admit that I have the Hasmonean pride in my blood. And frankly, I'm glad of it. I'm proud of what our family has done for the nation. We restored its independence and for a hundred years gave it leadership. We took over the helm of a nation puny in size and power and made it much bigger and stronger, a nation respected and even feared by our neighbors. We pushed out the borders closer to where they were before the Exile; we built a sound economy, with a flourishing seaborne commerce and a thriving home trade."

Antigonus paused a moment, and then continued in a grave tone: "It grieves me to see what's become of all this – all our wonderful achievements squandered. It grieves me all the more because a certain member of our family has tarnished the glorious name of the Hasmonean house; he has even lent his hand to the deprivation of our freedom, and the way things are going, who knows what greater adversities may be in store for us?"

These words cut Alexandra to the quick; a pallor spread over her face. "You have a very harsh opinion of my father," she uttered almost inaudibly.

"I'm sorry that I have to hurt your feelings," Antigonus said, relenting a little. "Believe me, I'd much rather be able to laud your father, to say that I respect and honor him for his valiant deeds, his strong, inspiring leadership; but how can I?"

Alexandra drew herself up, her eyes beginning to smolder. "No, you can't, Matti, because you don't understand that a Hasmonean can be anything but a gallant warrior. You can't appreciate that sometimes it may be necessary to be flexible in order to preserve the gains we won and still possess."

"To preserve our gains!" Antigonus snorted. "What your father is doing, or rather, has already done, at the prodding of that scheming Idumean viper is to bend the necks of our people under an alien yoke. And this after we Hasmoneans had fought and shed our precious blood to liberate the Temple, the people, the land from the pagan conqueror."

Alexandra realized that she had touched her cousin on a very sore spot. She did not relish pursuing the subject further, as it was liable to lead to bitter recriminations. Yet she felt duty-bound to defend her father's honor, or at least to try and explain his actions. Above all, she was worried that Antigonus might be planning to raise the banner of revolt again despite the outcome of his previous attempts.

"I know you can't condone what my father has done. But you aren't even willing to try and understand him. You claim we are under the Roman yoke. In a way I suppose you're right; we're not as free and independent as we were before the Romans came on the scene. But neither are we an enslaved nation. Caesar is no mad tyrant like Antiochus, and Rome is not Antiochus's Syria. Rome is a mighty empire on the march. Bigger and more powerful nations than we have had to bow before it. We have to reconcile ourselves to that fact, unpleasant as it may be."

"I see Antipater has poisoned your thinking too," Antigonus reproached Alexandra scathingly. "He has always twisted your father around his little finger, but I thought you were made of sterner stuff."

"You're mistaken if you think Antipater has influenced me. I hold little brief for him. I know him for what he is, and deeply regret that he wormed his way into my father's confidence. But even if he is a self-seeking opportunist, that doesn't alter the basic fact that he may have a realistic grasp of the situation facing Judea."

"That remains to be seen. Rome is not the only power in this part of world, nor is it at all certain, in spite of what you, your father, and that Idumean serpent think, that it is the mightiest power. Crassus discovered that the Roman legions were not invincible. All the gold he plundered from our Temple didn't help him to defeat the Parthians six years ago. He paid dearly for his folly: The bulk of his army perished and the Roman eagles were taken to Parthia, where they remain to this day – to the great disgrace of mighty Rome."

At these words an uneasy feeling swept over Alexandra. Was Antigonus thinking of allying himself with the Parthians? It suddenly occurred to her that this would seem a logical course to him. The Romans and Parthians were sworn enemies, rivals for domination of this part of the world. Moreover, there was a large, influential Jewish community in the Parthian Empire; they had reason to distrust the Romans, and a valiant prince of the Hasmonean house would strike a responsive cord in their hearts.

"Matti, are you in league with the Parthians?" she asked bluntly.

Antigonus was taken aback by this question and did not reply immediately. "No, I'm not in league with the Parthians," he said at last in a matter-of-fact voice.

"But you're thinking of doing so, aren't you?"

Antigonus turned his back on Alexandra and gazed abstractedly at the distant snow-covered crest of Mount Hermon, his arms folded across his chest. His eyes narrowed and a determined look transformed his features; he looked every inch the Hasmonean warrior-statesman who fired the imagination and enthusiasm of his people.

"I have not found the Romans particularly appreciative of our branch of the Hasmonean house," he declared in a frosty voice, facing Alexandra. "Even Caesar, who has ample reason to be grateful for our services, has failed to show any appreciation. In statecraft, as in private life, it is useful to have friends; nay, it is an absolute necessity."

* * *

The visit with Antigonus did Alexandra a world of good. For a fortnight she was able to relax and to enjoy the sites of Iturea. Antigonus and Roxane went out of their way to make her stay, and that of her two children, a pleasant one. Apart from the first day, they did not discuss politics, preferring small talk or innocuous subjects. Her hosts gave several dinners in her honor, and Ptolemy, the prince of Chalcis, also gave a lavish reception.

Alexandra found the prince a colorful person. Squat and swarthy, he favored highly aromatic perfumes and oils and bright-hued robes made of silk and other fine stuff. His fingers were adorned with gold and silver rings set with precious stones, and on formal occasions an ornate jeweled pendant dangled from the lobe of his right ear. He had a roguish look, and his eyes twinkled impishly when he regaled his guests with what were undoubtedly embellished tales of adventures he had experienced in his fifty-odd years. Alexandra began to suspect that Antigonus's description of him as a bandit chieftain might not be so wide of the mark after all. He was fond of horses, and arranged two races during the visit, to the great delight of the youngsters, to whom he took quite a fancy.

On the return journey to Jerusalem, Mariamne and Aristobulus gleefully discussed this jovial man who had lavished his attention and gifts upon them. Their excited chatter kept Alexandra in good humor, but as they neared Jerusalem a disquieting note crept into her thoughts. She would have loved to continue enjoying the relaxed, carefree mood of her visit, but the memory of her talk with Antigonus on the first day returned to disturb her peace of mind. Knowing how scathing he could be on the subject of her father, she realized that subsequently he had made a conscientious effort to avoid hurting her. But from the few remarks he did make, and even from what he left unsaid, it was clear that his feelings toward her father were as harsh as ever.

Was her father as ineffectual as Antigonus claimed? She had to acknowledge that Antipater and his two eldest sons had risen to positions of power. But was her father to blame for that, or did he have to bow to the inescapable fact that Judea was caught up in the Roman tide and that to keep it safely afloat required dexterous steering, involving, unfortunately, some swallowing of national pride? Antigonus, she knew, would ridicule such rationalization.

As for Antipater, that was a different matter. Maybe Antigonus's description of him as an "oily Idumean serpent" was too astringent, but there was more than a grain of truth in it. She had to admit that he was very crafty; even when defeat stared him in the face, he invariably managed to turn the tables. One example, of which her father regretted in retrospect, had to do with the audience of the two Hasmonean brothers with Pompey some 20 years earlier. The rival claimants to the Judean throne had presented their gifts to the Roman, flushed with his recent victory over the pirates who had preyed on Roman shipping off the coast of Cilicia. Antipater, astutely assessing Pompey's mood, had prevailed on Hyrcanus to voice his suspicion that Aristobulus might have had a hand in the acts of piracy, a charge calculated to put him in Pompey's bad graces without the Roman even bothering to check its veracity.

A more recent example was that alluded to by Antigonus on the first day of the visit. When he had appealed to Caesar for the high priesthood in place of Hyrcanus on the grounds that his father and brother had suffered death in Caesar's cause, Antipater had cunningly pulled the rug from under his feet and emerged with enhanced power and honor.

It was obvious to Alexandra that Herod was cut from the same cloth as his father. Nevertheless, there was a glaring difference between them: Herod too was ambitious and crafty, but he was more arrogant and had a cruel streak that was absent in Antipater. Antigonus in one scale, Antipater and Herod in the other – her father was not having an easy time of it, and who knows if the going would not get rougher yet? If only there was some way she could help him, but what could she do other than give him the love and support of a devoted daughter?

The day was drawing to a close when Jerusalem's skyline hovered into view. Alexandra's spirits never failed to be uplifted at the sight. The city, dominated by the Temple, sat like a crown on the crest of one of the spurs of the Judean Mountains. On two sides the ground descended abruptly to the verdant Kidron Valley, curving below the eastern declivity, where it separated the Temple Mount from the Mount of Olives, to the southern slope of the City of David, where it fanned out to converge with the second valley, the infamous Ben Hinnom. Beyond the Mount of Olives the terrain and vegetation presented a stark contrast: a bleak, tawny, corrugated desert stretched as far as the eye could see, framed by the distant Mountains of Moab, which in the glowing rays of the sunset displayed all their purple splendor.

Mariamne and Aristobulus shook off their drowsiness as they approached the city. The cottages and homesteads were more numerous, and the road, twisting, turning, ever-rising, was more heavily traveled. A stiff breeze had blown up, dispelling the midday heat. Alexandra opened a chest sitting on the floor of the carriage and extracted shawls for herself and Mariamne and a light cloak for Aristobulus. After draping herself and the children in these garments, she leaned back in her seat. The youngsters, however, were too excited to sit; they stuck their heads out the window to better observe the view and to wave at passing vehicles and wayfarers.

The road dipped suddenly, obscuring the city from view, but a few minutes later it reappeared. The Temple Mount loomed closer and closer. A thin, barely visible thread of smoke coiled upward from the Court of the Priests and wafted serpentine-like in the breeze – evidence of the wood that had been heaped on the big altar to keep the fire smoldering throughout the night. The precincts and walls of the Temple were shrouded in a checkered mantle, as light and shadow contended with each other. At this time of the day, the Temple had a deserted look, soon to be blanketed by the gloom of night. But this did not detract from the overwhelming majesty of this citadel of the spirit, which exercised an irresistible lure over Jerusalemites and pilgrims alike.

When Alexandra's carriage entered the palace square, she was surprised to see a fairly large number of litters and even some carriages parked there. There were also more guards than usual. Recognizing the royal carriage, the officer of the guard strode over and saluted.

"Why are there so many people here?" Alexandra inquired. "Is something special going on?"

"It would seem so," replied the officer. "All the king's ministers and other advisers are in conference with him."

"Has anything happened during my absence?" she asked a little nervously.

"I can't say for sure. There are rumors, but I can't vouch for them. All I can tell you is that I was ordered to double the guard."

When Alexandra and the children entered the palace, she found a number of sentries posted in the long corridor. As she passed the room where the meeting was taking place, one of the participants emerged. Peering through the opened door, she recognized the ministers of the realm, the commander of the army, some of her father's other advisers, and, oddly, the sages Shemaiah and Avtalyon. Catching her father's eye, she waved a greeting. The grave expression on his face softened a little when he beheld his daughter and grandchildren. He nodded to her, gesturing that he would come to them when the meeting was finished.

It was not until Alexandra had unpacked with the help of a handmaid and she and the children had eaten a light meal that Hyrcanus appeared. Mariamne and Aristobulus threw their arms around his neck and hugged him tightly. Alexandra noticed that the tense look he wore when he entered the apartment evaporated in the warm embrace of his grandchildren. When he asked them about the trip, he was treated to an animated account of their experiences. Alexandra knew that he had weighty matters on his mind, but he did not seem to be in any hurry to dismiss his grandchildren. With a sigh, he finally released them to the handmaid, who led them to their bed chambers.

"How good it is to be young and carefree," remarked Hyrcanus wistfully. "And you look fine too. I'm glad to see the trip did you good."

"We all enjoyed ourselves immensely – more than I expected," replied Alexandra. "It was good to be away from all the problems and worries. But unfortunately one has to come back and face reality." Gazing steadily at her father, she asked in a low, urgent voice: "What is it now, Father? What has happened while we were away?"

Hyrcanus hesitated briefly before replying in a deliberately casual tone: "We have received reports that Herod is marching on Jerusalem."

Alexandra gasped; her face turned ash white. "So! Antigonus was right, after all. He said there was going to be the devil of a price to pay."

Seeing how agitated she had become, Hyrcanus hastened to reassure her. "I'm sorry this had to happen to spoil your homecoming. But there's no need to worry."

Alexandra regarded her father with a baffled expression. *How could he be so calm?* she wondered. "How serious is the threat? How far has he advanced?" she asked in a voice full of trepidation.

"It seems he's crossed the border, which means he's probably three or four days' march from here. But we're taking adequate countermeasures. With the Lord's help, we'll overcome this threat."

"But the Romans!" she exclaimed. "Herod wouldn't have dared do such a thing without their help or connivance."

"He undoubtedly has the consent and possibly the backing of Sextus Caesar. But we very much doubt that his cousin Julius will regard this with a favorable eye. In fact, we suspect that he knows little or nothing about the matter. We're dispatching an urgent message to him."

"What good will that do if Herod is already on the march?" she asked hastily. "It will take days, maybe weeks, for the message to reach him."

"Quite true," replied Hyrcanus, strangely unperturbed. "But we have good reason to believe that the very knowledge that such a message has been sent will have the desired effect."

Herod Attempts to March on Jerusalem

Antipater's residence was not the largest or most palatial in the Upper City of Jerusalem, but it possessed a character of its own. Originally built by his father after being raised to high office by Alexander Yannai, it had been enlarged with the growth of Antipater's family. The style was predominantly Hellenistic: The living quarters and other rooms were arranged around a court, and colonnades, loggias, and porticoes relieved the solid, heavy lines of the building, lending a note of graceful elegance.

Antipater took special pride in the banqueting hall. Since the list of personages who enjoyed his hospitality had become increasingly long and impressive, including the rulers of the neighboring principalities and even high-ranking Roman officials, he had lavished considerable attention and expense on it. One of the walls was adorned with a limestone frieze, another with a panel of spirals and carved woodwork, while the third was covered with tapestries. The fourth wall was faced with polished stones varying in shape and color, including black basalt, flesh-red granite, and green and black-veined malachite. In winter brightly colored rugs covered the floor, but during the rest of the year its geometrically patterned mosaic delighted the eye. In this room Antipater kept his favorite mementos and bric-a-brac. Some of the artifacts stood in wall niches, while others were displayed in two large ebony cabinets inlaid with ivory and amber. In the corners of the room stood glazed painted amphorae, and flanking the door opening onto the court were two massive urns.

Some of the ideas for the design of the room, notably the stone-faced wall, originated with Herod, who had to convince his father that the overall impression was not at all garish. At the present moment, however, Herod had no eye for the beauty of the banqueting hall, and least of all for that of the more modest room where the family dined when there were no guests. The evening meal over, the small three-legged tables had been stacked in a corner, except for Antipater's. He was enjoying a second helping of dessert, and wore a faint and inscrutable smile as he ruminated on his encounter with Hyrcanus when returning from the trial a couple of hours earlier. Herod, who had doffed the purple robe in which he confronted the Sanhedrin, had a dark, surly look. He was still seething at the humiliating treatment he had received at its hands. He had no appetite and had pecked at his food only at the urging of his mother.

Cypros, the daughter of a wealthy Nabatean nobleman, was rather plain in appearance and bearing, an impression heightened by the bouts of depression to which she was subject in recent years. She was proud of the high position to which her husband and two eldest sons had risen, but at the same time was more than a little bewildered by it and did not feel at ease in her role.

Not so Herod's sister Salome. Antipater, whose enjoyment of his dessert was disturbed by his daughter's malicious remarks about Herod's tormentors, which were uttered in a high, grating voice, cast a sidelong glance at her. It puzzled him how the comparatively meek and mild Cypros and someone as suave and polished as himself had begotten a daughter with traits he had to admit were not the most endearing. Not everyone could be comely or winsome, but there was a hardness about her that clearly showed in her features. The corners of her mouth were more often than not drawn down in an expression almost scornful. Her black eyes, under a heavy shadow of khol, had a cold, calculating look which warned others not to rub her the wrong way. Her expensive garments and jewelry showed her slim figure to advantage, but the effect was spoiled by her forbidding countenance and manner. That she was haughty Antipater put down to the fact that he was one of the most powerful men in the land, if not the most powerful. But he would have been happier if she were not such an inveterate schemer. He too did not scruple to intrigue, but he was a statesman. Salome, however, seemed to have a mania for intrigue, deriving an intense satisfaction from trapping her victims. Like a spider, she would carefully spin her web and patiently wait for her victim to get hopelessly entangled and struggle to extricate himself. In her younger days Antipater had taken her to task about this a number of times, but seeing how little effect it had, he resigned himself in despair. He only hoped she would not cause too much trouble with Herod's wife Doris.

Not that Doris was the proverbial woman of valor. When Antipater had arranged the marriage of his son to the daughter of an affluent Idumean merchant of his acquaintance, he had his eyes on the material advantages which it promised. He had of course made inquiries about her personal qualities, and was assured that she would be a suitable match. But knowing Herod's predilection for comely maidens, he hesitated, even though this was not necessarily a decisive factor – one could enjoy the best of both worlds. Doris had a rather scrawny figure – too bony for the masculine taste, Antipater thought. She had a small, pouting mouth, a short, broad nose, and pale green eyes. All this he was aware of before arranging the match. What he discovered only afterward was that she also had a bristly nature, and was quite ready and able to pay Salome back in kind for her spiteful gossip and uncivil behavior. She had borne Herod a son, whom he dutifully named after his father. The elder Antipater had hoped that this would make Herod a little more attentive to his wife, but he continued to neglect her, making her all the more vexatious. Antipater was pleased to see that she got on quite well with Phasael at least. This was not surprising, though, for while he fell short of his younger brother in ambition and astuteness, he was a genial sort who managed to stay on good terms even with those in the opposite camp.

The atmosphere in the dining room was charged with tension. Apart from Antipater and Phasael, everyone seemed to be on edge and extremely irritable. Herod was railing against the Sanhedrin, against Hyrcanus, against the Jews in general. Cypros and Phasael tried to calm him, but to no avail. Doris, a frequent victim of Herod's black moods, sat morosely, hardly speaking to anyone. When the family's pet saluki nuzzled up to Herod, he pushed it away with his foot; the dog slunk away with a whimper and hurt look.

Antipater was seemingly oblivious to all the commotion. When a slave entered and informed him that a messenger had arrived from the royal palace, he broke into a broad grin and ordered the slave to show him in. The others fell silent, and with an inquisitive expression watched the messenger hand over a sealed letter. Antipater exchanged a few words with him and gave him a generous tip. After the messenger left, he broke the seal and began to read the letter, obviously pleased with its contents. The others waited impatiently to learn what tidings had come from the palace.

"Well, now this puts a different complexion on things," Antipater announced cheerfully. "This should interest you, son," he said, handing the letter to Herod. "Hyrcanus has some excellent advice to offer."

Herod hurriedly read the letter. His visage, however, remained frozen, his fists tightly clenched. "Excellent advice!" he growled. "To run away like a scared dog from that pack of sanctimonious old men? That's not the way I intend to end the matter."

"When you've had time to reflect a little more calmly, you'll realize that in the present circumstances this is the wisest course," Antipater patiently counseled. "So let's forget your injured pride and not waste any time."

Antipater took a few steps toward the window, his hands clasped behind his back. "The question is, where to go? Obviously it will have to be outside the borders of Judea. As it happens, I've already given a little thought to the matter. I think the best solution, in fact the ideal one, would be to call upon our good friend Sextus Caesar. He was extremely pleased with your handling of Galilee and is not unaware of your appearance before the Sanhedrin. I'm confident that he will not only grant you asylum, but will find useful employment for your talents."

This struck everyone as an excellent idea. Herod too had to admit that it possessed considerable merit, although in his present sullen mood he leaned to more direct, belligerent action. At first he argued for such a course, but was finally convinced of its futility. When at last he acquiesced, the atmosphere in the room was transformed.

"Time is precious," declared Antipater peremptorily. "I suggest we all lend a hand to speed Herod on his way."

Soon everything was ready, including one of Antipater's sturdiest carriages and fastest horses. The family took leave of Herod indoors in order not to attract attention. Cypros tearfully kissed her son goodbye and, clasping an image of Koze, prayed that the god protect him and prosper his way. Antipater waited for the others to bid Herod farewell, and then clapped him on the shoulder.

"Remember, son, Sextus is a servant of the Empire, and likes to feel that his efforts are appreciated." He handed Herod two exquisitely wrought golden goblets wrapped in satin. "Give this gift to Sextus in my name, together with my felicitations." He reached under his robe and extracted a leather pouch. "This pouch I'm giving to you. It contains precious gems. Don't be niggardly in expressing your gratitude to whatever important officials you may have dealings with. You'll find that it will smooth your path remarkably." With this piece of advice, Antipater embraced his son and sent him on his way.

* * *

In his more candid moments, Sextus Caesar admitted to himself that if he were not the cousin of the great Gaius Julius, conqueror of Gaul and half of Britain, Imperator and Dictator of Rome, he would not be comfortably ensconced in a handsomely carved chair behind a large lemonwood desk in the spacious three-storied building on the broad main street of Damascus that was the headquarters of the governor of the Roman province of Syria. But was that not the way of the Fates? Of course, one had to cooperate with them: How did one advance if not by taking bold risks or being well connected? And by Hercules, he could honestly lay claim to both. He had attached himself to his cousin's fortunes, and together they had risked life and limb to push out the borders of the Roman empire, suppress rebellious tribes, put down patrician traitors of the people, and gotten rid of that pompous ass Pompey. Yes, he deserved to hold the governorship of this province, and he intended to make the most of the opportunity. He was not a superb general like Julius – such genius was rare enough

–but he would show the scoffers that when it came to governing he did not take a back seat to his illustrious cousin.

When he peered into the mirror – which was frequent enough – he liked what he saw. His hair was still black and fairly thick – unlike his cousin's, which had become quite sparse of late, much to his chagrin. His features were clean-chiseled, his brow lofty above keen, dark eyes, an eagle nose, and a determined chin. Not very tall, he had an agile frame, a body hardened by military and athletic discipline. He set great store by appearances, and was a fastidious dresser.

As was his wont, he had eaten a frugal breakfast and, despite the oppressive khamsin, was in excellent spirits when Herod was admitted to his presence.

"Well, my good man," he said jovially after thanking Herod for his father's gift, "and how was the trial? How did it feel to be queried by your doctors of law? I must say, you look a bit off-color. Surely it couldn't have been as bad as all that, or is it this khamsin that's got you down? As for myself, you can give me a moderate or even cool climate any day. Now take Gaul, that's where you find pleasant weather. Not like that blasted island of the Britons, where the damp seeps through your garments and chills you to the bone no matter how many layers you put on. Try sleeping in that kind of weather while on the march. But enough of the weather. Tell me about the trial. We Romans have a passion for legal proceedings, and especially trials. And what lawyers we have – the best in the world. Awful exaggerators – they can stretch the truth quite a bit – but magnificent orators! They sweep you off your feet, especially our Cicero. You can't beat a good trial for entertainment. Now let's hear about yours. How can your distinguished sages interpret the suppression of brigands as a contravention of law? I'm intrigued."

Herod proceeded to describe the trial, omitting any mention of his manner of dress and his armed escort. It was plain to Sextus that he had not found the experience a pleasant one. Herod's jaws quivered and the muscles of his neck tightened as he struggled to check the blind rage that welled up in him.

"And so your doctors of law were ready to condemn you, eh?" remarked Sextus, shaking his head incredulously. "By Hercules, it still baffles me. When I have time, I must make a study of the Jewish system of jurisprudence." Sextus scrutinized Herod with a sly expression. "And what happened in the end? I see you're here – a free bird, so to speak."

Herod told about Hyrcanus's message. It was clear to Sextus that Antipater had not mentioned to his son the stern letter the ethnarch had received from the governor of Syria. "Very interesting!" he exclaimed upon learning how effective his communication had proved. "It seems our friend Hyrcanus is not so foolhardy, after all." His voice took on a confidential ring. "I can tell you that I've been more than a little concerned about him of late. I was beginning to wonder if he knew where his true interests lay. I'm glad to see that he's come to his senses."

Sextus regarded Herod steadily for a moment. "Now that the trial is behind you, let's talk about something else – your future. But first, we'll have some refreshments."

Sextus ordered a slave to bring wine and sweetmeats. Within a few minutes he returned with a tray laden with cakes, a flagon of wine, a pitcher of water, and two silver goblets. He mixed the wine in a glass bowl and started to fill the goblets.

"Callias, this is a fitting occasion to initiate the gift of my good friend Antipater," Sextus interrupted him, pointing to the golden goblets on his desk. The slave returned the silver goblets to the tray and proceeded to fill the golden ones, after which he withdrew. Sextus fingered his goblet with an appreciative eye. "Beautiful workmanship! Please tell your father that I shall treasure his gift." He sipped his drink slowly, savoring the aroma of the prized Falernian wine, all the while chatting about the merits of the various national drinks he had sampled. When an assistant announced the arrival of other petitioners, Sextus replied that he had important business to discuss with Herod. Knowing how busy the governor was, Herod wondered why he was engaging in small talk instead of getting down to the main purpose of his visit, and he was becoming increasingly disquieted. Sextus's last remark put his mind at ease.

During the time that he governed Galilee, Herod had conceived a liking for Sextus despite their markedly different characters. He appreciated his understanding of the mentality of the native population and his firm but wise governance. And now he had just declared that he had important business to discuss, which Herod hopefully understood to mean that he would find "useful employment for his talents," to use Antipater's expression. Yes, his father was right – as usual, Herod had to admit. He had a remarkable knack for sizing up situations and those who held the reins of power, to determine the most effective course of action. There was a great deal he could learn from his father, who was second to none in the art of diplomacy. Herod waited expectantly for Sextus's proposal, taking pains not to appear too eager.

After his fill of refreshments, Sextus wiped his lips and fingers on a napkin and pushed the dish and empty goblet aside. When he had heard of Herod's arrival the day before, he gave some thought to the question of how to use this young man who had proved his resourcefulness and loyalty to the Roman cause. The organization of the Syrian administration was not entirely satisfactory. Sextus was finding the task more complicated than expected, and he was in need of loyal, competent lieutenants. He suspected that some officials he had inherited were secretly Pompeian supporters. They needed close watching, and here Herod could be useful. Yes, he would fit very well into his administrative machinery.

Sextus pushed back his chair and crossed his legs. "Now let's see what post we can offer you. There's a district north of Damascus that's proving a bit troublesome and needs a strong hand. But I think an older, experienced administrator is called for there. And there's that unruly district on the eastern border, where my governor wants an assistant. In Coele-Syria I have a governor I trust as much as I would a slave let loose in a harem. It would be advisable to replace him, but that's a very important district; it's probably too tall an order for you, I dare say. And then there's Samaria, which was once part of your country." Sextus stroked his chin. "Hmm, now that's an idea. The Jews there may not be delighted to have you as governor, especially after the business of Hezekiah and the trial, but there's no love lost between the Jews and the Samaritans. Also, there are some Greek cities there. Yes, that's probably the best place to assign you. What do you say to that, my man?"

When Sextus mentioned Coele-Syria, Herod's heart had leaped up. He knew how strategic this district was, and to be appointed its governor would be a real test of his ability. He relished the challenge. Moreover, it would give him command of a sizable armed force, just what he needed to take revenge on his enemies in Jerusalem. But how to persuade Sextus? He chose his words carefully.

"I'm deeply flattered that you consider me worthy of such an important post as Samaria. There's nothing I desire more than to prove I'm deserving of your trust. I know I could competently govern Samaria, but if I may be so bold, sir, I'd like to say that I feel sufficiently confident of my ability to govern Coele-Syria in your best interests."

If Sextus had not been aware of Herod's burning ambition, he would have been surprised at this suggestion. How old was he – 25 or 26? And think of it, he wants to govern Coele-Syria of all places! Geographically Samaria was actually part of his own country. But this business of the trial may have left him with a bad scar. Yes, that's probably it. But Coele-Syria? Was he up to such an important post? He was still quite green. On the other hand, he's undoubtedly got what it takes, and sooner or later he's bound to rise to the top.

"Coele-Syria is a very important district," said Sextus, measuring Herod with a keen eye. "It has considerable strategic value: It's a sensitive area for our defenses. It's also a rich source of income for Rome. I'm sure you could look to its defenses quite capably. But, and I want to emphasize this, even though we have reduced taxes substantially, it has provided Rome with no little revenue. To keep it that way and retain the goodwill of the inhabitants requires a combination of firmness, tact, and political savvy."

Herod, keeping his gaze level, replied in a confident voice. "I fully appreciate that, sir. I can assure you that if I'm appointed governor, Sextus Caesar – and Rome – will have no reason to regret it. You will find that the district will be ably administered by one totally loyal to the governor of Syria. Nor will Rome, or the governor of Syria, be the poorer for it; on the contrary, I can assure you that you will enjoy an even larger revenue."

Sextus's lips twisted into a broad smile. He liked this reply; he liked this young man whose fidelity and ability he did not doubt in the least. Still, he needed someone to govern Samaria and preferred a non-Roman.

"I'll tell you what, my good man, we'll kill two birds with one stone. You're young and energetic; I'll let you govern Coele-Syria and Samaria too. If we find that it's too tall an order, we'll decide what to do. But in the meantime I want you to have a go at both districts, one north and one south of Galilee. That way you can keep a close eye on Galilee too – a rather troublesome region, as we have both discovered," Sextus added with a grin.

When Herod had entered the headquarters of the governor of Syria, he was dispirited, the future uncertain, even bleak. When he emerged he was elated. Just as when he had assumed command of Galilee, so now too he felt instinctively that his guardian spirit was favoring him. The conviction that he was destined for big things had been blunted by the trial, but now it was stronger than ever. The blood pulsed in his veins; he was ready to tackle the most challenging of tasks.

He set about his duties in his typically energetic manner. He decided to appoint a trusted lieutenant to act as his deputy in Samaria and to devote most of his time to Coele-Syria. He found that the administrative machinery there was swollen and flabby, which surprised him, as he had always associated Roman rule with the utmost efficiency. In discussing the situation with his chief assistant, he learned that the Greek and Roman officials were quite able on the whole, but many of the indigenous employees seemed to think that fawning servility and wholesale flattery were an adequate substitute for industriousness and competence. The first thing Herod did upon assuming office was to start streamlining the bureaucracy, weeding out the incompetents and making it clear to the others what was expected of them.

The officials in the higher echelons also began to feel the weight of Herod's authority. Not a few resented this, regarding themselves as superior to this upstart foreign puppy. Those who were unable to conceal their feelings found themselves confronted with an ultimatum: to come off their high horse or be recommended to the governor of Syria for transfer to another post or even dismissal. These measures, while they did not enhance Herod's popularity with the staff, produced a more efficient apparatus. He saw to it that brigandage was suppressed, the collection of taxes reformed, with a larger share of the revenue transmitted to Sextus Caesar, and services improved. Nor did Herod neglect the establishment of an efficient spy system. As in Galilee, he regarded this as an indispensable instrument for governing the district and for ensuring his personal safety.

Once he was confident that the administrative machinery was functioning properly, Herod wasted no time in preparing for a march on Jerusalem. His father had written him that the Sanhedrin was outraged to learn that he had fled Jerusalem and was insisting that he be summoned to reappear before it, even though he was governor of Coele-Syria and hence safely out of its reach. Antipater was of the opinion that Hyrcanus would have no choice but to bow to its pressure and at least formally order Herod to return to Jerusalem, but that the summons could safely be ignored. Herod, however, hoped that Hyrcanus would yield to its demand and had resolved to answer any such summons in his own way, for he was determined to avenge his humiliation by the Sanhedrin. He realized that there might be a problem with Sextus, but he was confident that he could convince him that Rome's interests were at stake and that such an action was for its own good.

It was not long before a courier arrived from Jerusalem. When Herod was informed of this, his face lit up. The courier, a rugged young man who looked none the worse for his long journey, saluted Herod. "I have been instructed to deliver this to you personally, sir," he announced, handing Herod a sealed letter.

Herod broke the seal and hastily read the letter. It was a summons to re-appear before the Sanhedrin. If he had not been expecting it, he would have exploded with rage; instead, he was filled with intense satisfaction.

"I have been ordered to inquire if you wish to send your reply back with me," the courier said.

Herod stared at him for a moment. "Yes, I do," he said in a frosty tone. "You can inform the Sanhedrin that I acknowledge receipt of its summons and have every intention to reappear before it – in my own good time and in my own way."

The armed force at Herod's disposal was composed mostly of Greek-Syrians. To beef it up, he decided to recruit Samaritans, who, he knew, would eager-ly join in a march on Jerusalem. They had never forgotten the conquest of their territory eighty years earlier by John Hyrcanus, grandfather of the present high priest and ethnarch, nor had they forgiven the razing of their temple on Mount Gerizin. In deciding to recruit Samaritans, Herod was running some risk, for it was essential to keep his ultimate objective a secret as long as possible, both from the authorities in Jerusalem and even from Sextus himself. He therefore told the Samaritans that the force was intended for policing the borders against brigands and to suppress anti-Roman elements.

Herod appointed Roman officers to whip the force into shape. When the time came, he of course would lead the troops, but his administrative duties were too pressing to allow him to personally take a hand in their training. Be-sides, because of the need for secrecy he deemed it wiser not to do so. But as often as he could, he watched the men being put through their paces. His heart swelled with pride, for this was not a small force like the one he had in Galilee, but a much larger, professionally trained army. These were his men, his troops, and with them he was going to show his enemies what sort of a person they were dealing with.

Herod now had to decide how to win Sextus's backing for his march on Jerusalem. What if he hesitated or even refused outright, or decided to refer the matter to his cousin Julius, as would be the natural thing to do? Herod would have to be at his most cunning. He would have to convince Sextus that as governor of Syria he had to suppress this brazen threat to Roman sway over Judea, and that immediate punitive action was imperative. To bolster his argument and to prompt him to act without referring the matter to Rome, Herod decided to produce "indisputable evidence" that the authorities in Jerusalem were secretly negotiating with the followers of the late Pompey, who were causing Julius no end of trouble in Rome and especially in North Africa. Knowing that the Pompeians threw the fear of death into Sextus, Herod was counting on his forgetting or disregarding the Jews' favorable attitude toward Julius, and was confident that his stratagem would turn the trick. To manufacture the proof did not present any great difficulty. He possessed letters and other communications that Hyrcanus, Malichus, and other ministers had written to Antipater, and he would merely have to instruct his expert forger what to write. This, he was sure, would convince Sextus of the need to act at once. He was right.

* * *

When Antipater learned about Herod's defiant reply to the courier, he was both puzzled and perturbed.

"It baffles me," he said to Phasael, drumming his fingers on the table. "I don't like the tenor of his reply, especially as I had advised him to ignore the summons. I have a strong suspicion that he's playing the fox with us. What do you think?"

Phasael inwardly agreed with his father, but love of his brother inclined him to circumspection. "I really don't know what to think. His reply does make one wonder, but I'm sure he's smart enough not to do anything rash."

Instead of reassuring Antipater, this statement only made him more apprehensive, for he knew that in the heat of anger or frustration Herod was capable of acting irrationally. He decided to send a message to his son that very day asking him to elucidate. When Herod received his father's communication and a request to send his reply back with the courier, he made a wry face. Certain that his father would take a dim view of his proposed move, he framed an evasive answer. He now had to act fast, not only because he knew that his father's suspicions would not be allayed, but on the contrary would probably deepen, and also because it was imperative to finish the business before word reached Rome. He had already mapped out his strategy, and as soon as he got the go-ahead from Sextus, he set his plan into motion. It was clear that both speed and stealth were essential for success. If he marched his force of some 3,000 men en masse from Coele-Syria, the news would soon get to Jerusalem, allowing the authorities sufficient time to take countermeasures. He therefore decided to infiltrate his men into Samaria, dispatching small detachments via different routes and with the entire movement staggered over a period of about two weeks. This way he hoped to avoid arousing suspicion until his entire force was assembled in Samaria, the springboard for the march on Jerusalem. Since not even small bodies of troops could move through Galilee without being detected, he ordered the unit commanders to hug the coast as much as possible, thereby skirting Galilee and avoiding most of the Jewish towns and villages. For the time being he decided to let only his most trusted lieutenants be privy to his ultimate objective.

Despite these elaborate precautions, Jewish scouts detected the crossing of the border on the very first day and informed their officer. When other units were observed the next day, the officer dispatched an urgent message to Malichus, stating that the detachments were moving down the coast, with their final destination and objective as yet unknown. Malichus was puzzled by the movement of relatively small units, but being extremely suspicious of Herod, he alerted the commander of the army and informed Hyrcanus and the other ministers of the situation. On the third and fourth days similar reports reached Jerusalem, and it was now clear that the troops were heading toward Samaria.

"Our information indicates that a fairly large force is being assembled in Samaria," Malichus told Hyrcanus. "In view of all the evidence and the prevailing circumstances, there can be no doubt that it constitutes a distinct threat."

Hyrcanus's face was pale and drawn. Ever since he had been apprised of the situation, he was a prey to growing anxiety. It was with considerable misgiving that he had agreed to summon Herod to reappear before the Sanhedrin. He had warned the elders of the possible consequences, but they had insisted that the honor and dignity of the Sanhedrin overrode all other considerations. In his heart he knew they were right, but he shuddered to think how Herod and especially his Roman masters might react. What he had feared was now a palpable reality.

"There is no doubt that Herod is up to some mischief," Malichus continued, seeing that Hyrcanus was sunk in gloomy thought. "I suggest that a council of state be urgently convened to discuss the situation and decide what action to take."

Hyrcanus looked up, a glimmer of hope appearing in his eyes. "Yes, by all means," he said in a lighter vein; "an excellent suggestion."

The ministers of the realm, the commander of the army, and the two leading members of the Sanhedrin, Shemaiah and Avtalyon, were requested to meet in the royal palace on the following day after the afternoon sacrifice. They found that access to the palace had been sealed off to the public, and it was heavily guarded. Mounting the wide staircase leading from the broad square to the entrance of the palace, they nodded to the officer of the guard, who checked each of the arrivals to make certain he was among those whose name appeared on his list. In the entrance hall they were greeted by Hyrcanus who, although he wore a serious expression, welcomed them warmly and bade them enter the conference chamber. When the last of the ministers arrived, Hyrcanus took his seat behind a long oak table and called the meeting to order.

"Gentlemen," he began in a steady voice that did not betray any nervousness, "you have been summoned to a conference of the greatest import. The reason, I believe, is known to all of you. A new peril has arisen to threaten the realm. It is our task to ascertain the nature of this peril and decide what steps to take to ensure the safety of the realm. Since the situation has both military and political implications, I shall call upon our honored colleague Malichus to brief us on the latest developments and to give his assessment."

Malichus, holding a wooden-backed waxed tablet on which he had jotted some notes, rose to his feet. Although wearing civilian garb, his whole bearing was that of a military man. He carried himself erect and exuded an air of resoluteness and authority. He briefly studied his notes, then put the tablet down on the table and began to explain the situation.

"Why is Herod doing this?" he asked in his strong voice, addressing the question that was uppermost in everyone's mind. "What are his possible motives and objectives? This, I regret to say, is still largely a matter of guesswork; we have not yet discovered the reason for this move. But the most likely assumption is that it has to do with the summons to reappear before the Sanhedrin, that Herod aims to revenge himself on the Sanhedrin and possibly also those most strongly opposed to the growing influence of Antipater and his sons. Another possibility, which may seem less plausible but cannot be ruled out, is that he actually intends to seize power. While the troops and equipment at his disposal are, to my mind, inadequate for a siege, he may be planning to overwhelm the city's defenses by surprise and eliminate all hostile elements."

Following his review of the military aspect, Malichus went on to discuss the political implications. He expressed surprise that Herod had been allowed to embark on this adventure, which ran counter to the policy displayed toward Judea by Julius Caesar. Malichus wondered if the latter had actually sanctioned, or was even aware of, Herod's move. After touching on several other points, Malichus concluded with the observation that, while the military situation could be adequately dealt with without having to reconvene the council of state, it must devote serious thought to the political aspect and decide what course of action should be taken, not only by the army, but more importantly, on the diplomatic level.

After Malichus sat down, Hyrcanus called on the other members to voice their opinion. To a man they viewed the situation with grave concern, regarding it as a threat to the safety of the Holy City and the very existence of the state of Judea. Various conjectures were made as to the possible reasons why Sextus Caesar sanctioned such an action, but for lack of definite information they were groping in the dark.

Meanwhile the sun had gone down and night began to close in. When a servant entered the chamber to light the lamps, Hyrcanus recessed the meeting in order to let the men repair to the dining hall for a light meal and to relax a little before resuming the discussion. Also, various courses of action had been proposed, and he wanted to give the men a chance to discuss them among themselves.

Refreshed by the warm food and drink, the conferees were soon able to sum up their discussion and to decide on the practical steps to take. The first and most pressing were, of course, the military countermeasures. Malichus's proposal for the defense of the city was approved with a few minor changes, and other action was agreed upon. As for the politico-diplomatic aspect, the consensus was that it hardly seemed likely that Julius Caesar would have consented to such an adventure, and that it was probably undertaken without his knowledge or at least without a proper acquaintance with the situation. It was therefore decided to dispatch an urgent message to him, apprising him of the facts and requesting his intervention. Even though the message would very likely arrive too late to forestall Herod's designs, it would at least let Caesar know who was responsible for the trouble.

Hyrcanus was about to close the meeting when one of the members asked whether they were pledged to secrecy. Assuming that they were, it was hardly conceivable that the convening of the council of state could be kept secret, for the sight of the ministers making their way through the Upper City to the royal palace must certainly have excited curiosity, especially of the most important person who had not been invited – Antipater. Hyrcanus asked Malichus for his opinion.

"The point raised by our honorable colleague is a very important one, and he did well to call our attention to it," Malichus said in deep, measured accents. "I agree that it is not reasonable to think that our meeting can be kept secret. The fact that we shall immediately begin to take military countermeasures can hardly be concealed from the public. On the contrary, the people will have to be informed of the danger facing them and be prepared to join in the defense of the city. But as regards the other measures decided upon, especially the dispatch of a message to Caesar, not one word of this should reach the ears of outsiders, least of all Antipater."

Malichus's words were greeted with nods of approval. Hyrcanus assumed that his advice would be accepted, but as a matter of formality asked whether anyone wished to add anything or even to express a different view. To his surprise, Shemaiah rose to his feet.

"On the face of it, Malichus's counsel would seem to be most prudent, especially as regards Antipater," he began in his customary low voice, which would gradually gather volume. "From our discussion there seems to be considerable doubt whether Julius Caesar has sanctioned Herod's adventure, or if he is even aware of it. And as for Herod, we know that it was his father who persuaded him to appear before the Sanhedrin, and we saw how perturbed he became when Herod, aroused to the point of fierce anger, seemed about to commit some rash act. May we not have reason, then, to think that Antipater is not in accord with his son's action? In recent years Antipater has shown a tendency to gain his ends by political stratagem rather than armed conflict, especially when the prospects of success seem rather slim, as in the present case. And when we wonder at a move that seems to be inconsistent with, and even contrary to, Julius Caesar's benevolent policy, I feel safe in assuming that Antipater too may not be privy to this adventure, or at least does not acquiesce in it. Should we not, therefore, prefer a solution that avoids the shedding of blood, the loss of human life? I propose that we let Antipater learn about the message we intend to send to Caesar. Antipater will fully realize its importance, and hopefully will dissuade Herod from proceeding further. Our message to Caesar will then serve a dual purpose."

No one could dispute the wisdom of Shemaiah's advice, not even Malichus, who acknowledged that the sage's proposal was by far the better one. It was left to Malichus to devise the best way of letting Antipater get wind of the message to Caesar.

* * *

Before Herod's troops began to cross the border, camps had been laid out at three different sites in the vicinity of Samaria, capital of the province bearing that name. Herod reached his headquarters several days after the first of the units had set out, and took over command of the force. He ordered his workmen to immediately start building siege engines, and in less than two weeks the army was ready to move. He had not told the troops why they were being moved to Samaria or what their real objective was. This he would do only when they set out for Jerusalem. He knew that the city's walls were very sturdy, and so he intended to rely on speed and surprise to force an entry into the city. Knowing that Hyrcanus was haunted by fear of a hostile Roman force, he was confident that when the high priest and ethnarch woke up to find a Roman-equipped army inside or battering at the gates, he would soon capitulate.

Herod ordered his men to strike camp and to assemble on a broad field outside Samaria. While the units were streaming in from different directions after daybreak, he conferred in his tent with his staff officers, describing Jerusalem's approaches and defenses and explaining his plan. When the last of the troops arrived, he dismissed the officers and told his orderly to help him with his cuirass and greaves, after which he buckled on a short broad sword and donned his helmet. The armor was too constrictive for his liking, but since they would be moving through hostile territory, he deemed it advisable to be properly protected. He emerged from his tent to find the staff officers waiting for him on their steeds. He flashed them a big grin. They were pleased to see their commander in high spirits, for usually when occupied with official duties he was serious and inclined to wear a stern expression. Herod mounted his white Arabian stallion and led his suite to a small mound in the center of the field. His eye roamed over the regiments drawn up on three sides of a large square: the light- and heavy-armed infantry, the spearmen, the archers and slingers, the cavalry, the siege engines. His heart swelled with pride at the sight, and he assumed a keen, aggressive look. Suddenly a fanfare of trumpets rent the air. The soldiers stiffened to attention as the commander and his staff left the mound and began a round of inspection. This took the better part of an hour, and Herod was palpably pleased.

"This should strike terror into the hearts of the enemy," he remarked to his staff officers with a toss of his head upon returning to the mound. They lined their steeds in a row, with Herod's in the middle. The sun, rising fast in a clear sky, lit up the tops of the surrounding hills and the silvery leaves of the olive groves dotting the slopes. The swords, spears, and helmets glinted menacingly in the light. Another flourish of trumpets resounded over the field. Herod eased his stallion forward a few paces in order to address the men. He spoke in a loud, clear voice, first in a fairly fluent Greek and then in a stiff Latin. He began by explaining that various reasons had made it advisable for him not to reveal their true objective, but now they were to know: Jerusalem!

This announcement had an electrifying effect. The soldiers had wondered why they were sent to Samaria via a circuitous route, but it had not occurred to them that their objective might be Jerusalem. A cheer rose from the ranks, at first rather feeble, then growing in volume as more voices joined the chorus, until it swelled across the countryside. After a few minutes Herod raised his hand to restore silence.

The authorities in Jerusalem, he went on to explain, were responsible for the unrest along the Syrian border – the raids against peaceful villages, the loss of innocent lives. They encouraged the brigands who waylaid caravans bringing wares to the markets, depriving the inhabitants of both essentials and precious articles while enriching themselves. It was imperative to end this intolerable state of affairs and mete out justice to those who were to blame. The objective was not to destroy Jerusalem and wipe out its inhabitants, but to force their way into the city and seize the principal villains. No mercy was to be shown to anyone who offered the slightest resistance. He knew his men would acquit themselves well, and assured them that they would be amply rewarded for their valor. In conclusion, he stated that the gods had willed this campaign and the omens were favorable. He raised his right hand in the Roman salute. A thunderous cheer burst forth from over 3,000 throats.

After another fanfare of trumpets, the army started to move. Herod's heart was light and every nerve and fiber of his being awake, tingling with exhilaration. The thought that he might not return from the campaign safe and sound never occurred to him. Fear for one's life and limb was for others; for him life was full of glittering promise: Greatness and glory awaited him.

The army advanced at a fairly rapid pace along the main road which dipped and curved across the rugged terrain in the direction of Jerusalem. Herod reckoned that it would take three to four days to reach their objective. The first night they encamped in the vicinity of Shechem (known about 100 years later as Nablus), on the second, near Aphaerema. It was here, when the sun had already sunk behind the hills, that Herod received unexpected visitors – his father and brother. He stared in disbelief when they entered his tent. The lamp flickered fitfully in the breeze that blew through the opened flap, throwing moving shadows on the sides of the tent and giving a yellowish hue to Antipater's and Phasael's visages.

"Well, son, have you no words of greeting for your father and brother?" asked Antipater in a gently chiding tone.

Herod was dumbstruck; he stood rigid as though riveted to the spot. This was the last thing he expected – or wanted.

"I take it our visit was not expected, nor does it seem to please you," Antipater went on with a bland smile. "Since you have evidently forgotten your manners and lost your tongue in the bargain – only temporarily, let's hope – I shall take the liberty of inviting myself and your brother to sit down." He thereupon seated himself on one of the camp-chairs and motioned to Phasael to follow his example.

Herod, his thoughts thrown into disarray, blurted out in low, staccato voice: "Why have you come? What is it you want? How in the name of all the gods did you know I was here?"

Antipater flung up his arms. "Whoa there, son! You're firing questions faster than a Pisidian archer can shoot. Let's take your questions one at a time. Why have I come here? To see my second-born, of course. Isn't that a perfectly natural thing for a father to do? What is it I want? Well, I think that's just a slightly different version of your first question, to which I have just replied. And the third question – what was it again? Oh yes, how did I know you were here? Well, let's just say that your brother and I happened to be on our way to – er,

Sepphoris – yes, that's it, when we stumbled, quite by chance of course, on this little encampment, and after due inquiry we learned, much to our pleasant surprise, that the commander of this small party of armed men is none other than my own son."

Herod gave his father a piercing, exasperated look. His head was in a turmoil, his face overcast.

"This small group of men encamped here," Antipater continued, seeing that Herod was not in a very sociable mood, "it's not a hunting party by any chance is it? Because if it is, I pity any poor game that may be roaming these parts. They don't stand a ghost of a chance – not with all these swords and javelins and bowmen you have. And if my eyes don't deceive me, there are even a few catapults and battering rams too. Oh, if there are any wild boar in the neighborhood," Antipater went on, shaking his head and clucking his tongue, "I wouldn't give them any odds at all against those monsters. I must hand it to you, you're well prepared for any eventualities. Don't you agree with me, Phasael?" said Antipater, glancing at his eldest son. "It warms the cockles of my heart to see how thorough Herod is in his preparations. Even helmets and cuirasses – to protect your tender skins against the bites of vicious mosquitoes and other insects, no doubt. Very original and quite effective, I'm sure. I must commend you on that."

Antipater paused a moment and fingered his beard. Herod was becoming increasingly taciturn and darker under the relentless, sonorous flow of his father's derision. "Well, well," exclaimed Antipater, slowly rising to his feet, "you seem to be about as talkative as a tortoise. Apart from three short questions – two really – you haven't spoken a word. But tell me, am I correct in assuming that the game you're hunting may not be around here but possibly further afield – say, Jerusalem?"

Although Antipater continued to wear an affable smile, his eyes bored into Herod, making him feel like a raw youngster. Beads of sweat glistened on his brow, his cheeks twitched. He opened his mouth to say something, but the words froze on his lips. He turned his back on his father.

"Your silence is answer enough," Antipater declared in clipped accents, abruptly dropping his bland manner. "You can thank your lucky stars that I found out, quite by chance, about your adventure – your reckless, asinine, imbecilic adventure!" These last words were spat out in a sharp, stern voice.

Herod, stung to the quick, swung around to face his father. "Reckless, asinine, imbecilic, you say!" he spluttered, his features twisting into a pained grimace.

"Yes, that's exactly what I said," retorted Antipater, his look hard and reproachful. "Before I ask if you've thought about the possible consequences of your little escapade, let me ask, what in the name of all the gods who may be troubling themselves with us poor mortals, made you commit such a folly? Well, why don't you answer? Was it because you're still nursing a grudge against the Sanhedrin and want to wreak vengeance on it?"

Herod felt a surge of cold hatred for the members of the Sanhedrin. When he spoke, the words came out with savage intensity: "Yes, I have a grudge against the Sanhedrin, against those who subjected me to the most odious humiliation, who sought to make me abase myself in the dust, to grovel at their feet. And that includes the man who issued the summons for me to suffer this unforgivable indignity."

"That man happens to be the one who let you escape Jerusalem scot-free, who in many ways has been your benefactor, and mine too," remarked Phasael, who until now had been a silent witness to the exchange between his father and his brother.

"You can also add," interjected Antipater in a slightly softer vein, "that if it were not for him, it is very unlikely that we would have risen to positions of power – none of us, including you, Herod. I think you should bear that in mind and take a little more generous view of the man."

"How can you advise that after what he's done? He's practically severed all ties with you."

"Only temporarily," Antipater calmly conceded. "It's true that at the moment our relationship has cooled a bit, but the Fates are a bit fickle at times; eventually they straighten themselves out."

"And if we have risen to power," Herod continued to challenge his father, "it's not because of any benevolence on his part, but because of our determination, our iron will, our own wits."

"Quite likely," replied Antipater He fixed his son with a severe look; his voice took on a harsher tone. "But what you're planning to do now will ruin everything we've achieved so far. Even if you can't find a little charity in your heart for Hyrcanus, what exactly do you expect to gain by this crackbrained jaunt of yours? Surely your thirst for revenge can't make you totally blind to the possible consequences."

Herod's jaws quivered and his eyes narrowed, flashing defiance. "There is one thought uppermost in my mind: to show that Herod is not a man to be trifled with, to be put in the dock like a common criminal. I was the governor of Galilee; I am now governor of Coele-Syria and Samaria. It is *I* who should put *them* in the dock: Hyrcanus and his whole pack of graybeards. And one day I'll do just that, and more!"

Antipater shook his head slowly. He clapped Herod on the shoulder. "Son," he said commiseratingly, you're all worked up. Your pride has been hurt and I can understand and sympathize with you. But one thing I've always tried to impress on you and Phasael: Never let your emotions get the better of your head. You have to weigh the possible consequences of every act. You haven't done that in this case. I don't know what exactly you intend to do once you get to the walls of Jerusalem, but one thing I can assure you: You'll arouse the inhabitants to the point of poisonous hatred, as if they don't dislike us enough already. They'll fight like lions. Every house will be turned into a fortress. You don't stand a chance. You don't even have the slightest chance of breaking into the city, do you realize that?"

Herod slipped away from his father's clasp. His eyes were troubled and uneasy. "What makes you so sure of that?"

"Because your moves have been known in Jerusalem from the very first day you crossed the border," Phasael said. "Steps have been taken to strengthen the defenses, and they are more than adequate. I can vouch for that."

Herod's face fell. He stared in consternation, first at his brother and then at his father. "Is that correct?" he asked his father in a barely audible voice.

"Yes, it is," replied Antipater, slowly nodding his head and folding his arms on his chest. "If you think you're just going to stroll through the gates or knock down the walls with a few catapults and battering rams, I'm afraid you're badly mistaken. Since I myself was responsible for rebuilding a good part of the walls, I can tell you they're more than a match for your siege engines. You'll have a bloody battle on your hands, and take it from me, you'll be defeated. And with that defeat we can say goodbye to all our achievements and hopes for the future. And even if by some miracle you should be victorious, you'll still be the loser."

Herod's brow furrowed deeply. "What do you mean?"

Antipater started to pace the tent, flapping his arms vigorously. "Excuse me, son, but I'm getting a little cramped and chilly. I can't seem to take these chilly evenings as easily as in my younger days." After a few minutes he felt better and began to elucidate calmly and patiently.

"In planning this little expedition of yours, did it ever occur to you that we are beholden to the master of Rome? It was Julius Caesar who appointed me *epitropos* of Judea, and it was he who appointed Hyrcanus ethnarch and high priest. Did you take his likely reaction into account?" Antipater paused briefly before continuing. "There's something else I'm very curious about. Julius's cousin Sextus must surely know about this business. How did you manage to get his backing? And how did you explain this to your troops? This has puzzled me ever since I got wind of your move."

This question disconcerted Herod; he paused to arrange his thoughts. He explained what he had told the troops and how he had convinced Sextus that this action was in Rome's interest, for his spies had proof that the authorities in Jerusalem were in secret communication with Pompeian supporters. He did not mention how this "proof" was procured.

In spite of his vexation, Antipater was inwardly amused at the lengths Herod had gone to in order to obtain Sextus's approval which, in view of the

Roman's earlier warning to Hyrcanus, would very likely have been forthcoming without an elaborate fabrication. He decided to let his son remain in the dark about Sextus's message to Hyrcanus.

"I'm astonished!" he exclaimed in feigned surprise. "I would never believe that Sextus would sanction this adventure on such flimsy grounds. He's going to find himself in hot water with his cousin."

"Why?" asked Herod uneasily.

"How did you and Sextus expect to keep this secret from Julius? When he finds out he's going to be furious."

"We had to act fast. There was no time to inform him first and await his approval. He was to be notified afterward."

Antipater snorted at this lame explanation. "For your information, a courier is on his way to Julius with a message from Jerusalem giving full and accurate particulars about this lamentable business."

At this piece of news Herod stiffened perceptibly; there was a sinking feeling in the pit of his stomach. It was clear that the enterprise which he had prepared with the most meticulous care was doomed. An overwhelming sense of frustration and despondency swept over him.

"All my plans thwarted, all my hopes dashed to the ground," he murmured. "It was I who set this machinery into motion – I, the commander of this force. How can I stop it when we've come so far? What sort of a commander will the troops take me for? One with milk in his veins. I'll be the laughingstock of my men."

Antipater clasped his son by the shoulder. His look was reproving yet compassionate. "My son, a wise man prepares for all eventualities. On the way here I gave a little thought to this question too. I hit on a possible solution, but since I wasn't aware of all the details, I wasn't sure what exactly to suggest. Now that I know what you've told your troops, the solution is simple. You explained to them that this was to be a punitive expedition, intended primarily to end the brigandage, the raids against the Syrian border villages, which, by the way, have been relatively quiet since the destruction of Hezekiah's band. All you have to do now is to tell them that the authorities in Jerusalem have become aware of your formidable force and are duly impressed. So much so that they have dispatched an embassy to seek terms with you and to eliminate the unfortunate cause of this misunderstanding. Your objective has therefore been achieved."

Herod swallowed hard and turned his back on his father. "A wretched ending to all our preparations," he muttered wearily, "a poor test of our valor. The men were promised an ample reward. How will I hold my head up in their presence?"

"Double their pay, triple it, even. That should satisfy their valor – and let them keep their heads intact at the same time."

Herod moved away from his father, mulling over this suggestion. He knew he had no choice, even though the denouement would leave a bitter taste in his mouth. After awhile he turned around to face his father with a resigned yet determined look.

"Out of filial respect and in view of the circumstances you have described, I have no choice but to accept your advice. But one thing I swear: The next time I march on Jerusalem there will be no turning back. Either Jerusalem falls or I fall."

Sextus Caesar Murdered, Cruel Cassius Commands

When Antipater told Cypros that Cassius was passing through Judea in order to deal with Julius Caesar's followers in Egypt and had summoned him to a meeting in one of the coastal towns, her eyes dilated with fear. Too many terrible things had been happening of late. First was the murder of Sextus Caesar a little over a year ago by a Pompeian sympathizer. This had upset Antipater, but he reconciled himself to this "distressful but not uncommon deed." And then came the assassination of Julius Caesar. That someone as powerful as the dictator of Rome should be struck down in the Senate House of all places had shaken Antipater to the core. For several days he had secluded himself in his home. This was so uncharacteristic of him that Cypros had been extremely worried. And now she was worried again. Who knew what Cassius wanted of her husband? There was something forbidding about this Roman; this she had perceived nine years earlier when, as proconsul of Syria, he had been a guest in their home. When she confided her fear about the meeting to Antipater, he shrugged it off.

Could it be that he had already recovered from the trauma of Caesar's death? And had he forgotten the incident of the oak tree? This still gave her the shivers. A bolt of lightning had struck the oak tree on their estate at Marissa, splitting it in half so that it had to be uprooted. Antipater had attached no importance to the matter, but Cypros took it as an ill omen. If only it were possible to go to the shrine of Koze and ask the priest what it portended. But this was Jerusalem; there was no such shrine in this city or anywhere else in the country, not even in Idumea since that wicked John Hyrcanus had banned the worship of Koze. There was only one way to find solace: She possessed an icon of Koze and would invoke it to watch over her husband and protect him from the dangers that seemed to lurk on every side.

On his way to Cassius, Antipater leaned back in his carriage seat and closed his eyes. But he was not relaxing; he was trying to fathom why the Roman had summoned him. Granted he had been on excellent terms with Caesar and had come to his aid when he was hard pressed in Egypt, for which service he owed the high position to which he had been elevated. But he doubted that Cassius would hold this against him. Like Caesar before him and Pompey too, Cassius needed loyal allies, and in Antipater he could repose his complete trust. Moreover, he would certainly put an end to Hyrcanus's capricious favoring of Malichus and his influence. It would not be difficult to make Cassius appreciate the wisdom of this. But there was something unpredictable about the man. This Antipater had discovered when Cassius took control in Syria after the ignominious defeat of the Roman legions by the Parthians nearly a decade ago. There was a harsh, unsympathetic streak in him that was disconcerting.

Antipater experienced a feeling of revulsion when admitted to Cassius's presence. It turned his stomach to greet the man who had been the prime mover in the conspiracy against Caesar, whose hand may even have been the first to plunge a dagger into his body.

"I congratulate you on your notable success," said Antipater with a perfunctory bow and summoning up the trace of a smile.

Cassius dryly acknowledged Antipater's greeting and motioned to him to be seated. Apart from a desk and several chairs, the room was bare of furnishings, only slightly less sparse than a headquarters tent.

"You have kept yourself in excellent shape," said Cassius stiffly and with a tinge of envy.

"Thank you, sir. I am pleased to see that the gods have also been kind to you." Antipater twisted his lips into what he hoped was a genial smile. In reality, he was taken aback at how much Cassius had aged since their last meeting. He was leaner than ever and so pale that Antipater wondered if he were ill. He had a typically Roman nose and thin lips; his cold gray eyes were narrow and hard, his cheeks taut and scarred, giving his features a somewhat sinister aspect.

"You no doubt want to know why I have summoned you," said Cassius brusquely without further ado.

"I assume it is because you want to make use of my good services," replied Antipater guardedly.

Cassius measured Antipater with a stony look and spoke in clipped, almost harsh accents: "I see we understand each other perfectly. At the moment the situation is uncertain both in this region and in Rome itself. It's impossible to know how things will turn out, but there's no doubt that we're going to have our hands full with Antony and that young Octavian. My army must be brought up to full strength and prepared for any eventualities. That, as you can well appreciate, is an expensive business."

Cassius paused to let the import of this statement sink in. The question of tribute was one of the possibilities Antipater had considered. Knowing Cassius's record on this score, he dreaded to speculate about the sum he might have in mind.

"You can count on Judea contributing its fair share," he replied, keeping his gaze and voice even.

"Good! It may interest you to know that I have requested other cities and kingdoms to contribute too. From Judea I want 700 talents."

Upon hearing this sum, Antipater's heart missed a beat. He had expected a large, even exorbitant, tribute, but nothing like this. For a moment he was nonplused; the smile disappeared from his face and his brow furrowed deeply.

"Permit me to point out, sir," he said, trying to conceal any hint of dismay, "it will not be easy to raise such a sum. Judea is a small country and has had to pay heavy tribute over the years until –" He was about to say, "until Julius Caesar had eased the burden," but checked himself. Cassius, however, read Antipater's mind. He compressed his lips and gave Antipater a piercing look. "I did not say or think it would be easy, but it will be done," he pronounced in an imperious tone that brooked no contradiction. "I trust I have made myself perfectly clear."

He rose to indicate that the meeting was over. Antipater, however, remained seated, pondering how to broach a very delicate point: How to inform Cassius that he and Hyrcanus were no longer enjoying cordial relations, that Malichus had in fact supplanted Antipater in Hyrcanus's favor. Should he apprise Cassius of the situation and thereby foil Malichus's plans? His instinct warned him that the Roman would interpret this as a sign of weakness, lowering Antipater in his estimation. He must try another tack.

"In the interest of our common cause, permit me to point out the existence of – er, what I would call a rather anomalous situation in Judea."

Cassius stared at Antipater coldly. He had many matters to attend to and was anxious to get on with them. But he relented and, without changing his expression, sat down. "And what is that?" he asked gruffly.

"Caesar – the late Caesar, that is – had not clearly delineated the authority and powers that were to be exercised by the ethnarch and high priest Hyrcanus and those that were to be exercised by myself, your humble servant. If you have deemed me worthy to be in charge of collecting this – er, contribution to your laudable cause, it would be most inadvisable if it were to cause unnecessary friction with the ethnarch. It would..."

"And so?" Cassius broke in impatiently. "What is it you want from me?"

"It would prevent any unpleasant misunderstanding and make my task much easier if you were to inform the ethnarch that it is your express desire that I be assigned sole responsibility for collecting the tribute."

Cassius, wishing to end the meeting and seeing no harm in this request, quickly agreed. "I shall instruct the ethnarch accordingly," he said with a gesture of dismissal.

* * *

"In what kind of a mood did you find Cassius?" asked Herod when he and Phasael met with their father in the family mansion.

"He was his usual jovial self," replied Antipater, making a wry face and thinking that he would prefer to encounter a serpent than confer with that dour and dangerous man.

"And the tribute, how much is he demanding?" inquired Phasael.

"A mere 700 talents."

Herod and Phasael stared at each other in astonishment. "Impossible!" exclaimed Phasael. "Judea can't raise anything close to that amount."

"Neither could Rhodes raise the tribute imposed on it, which happened to be twice as large," Antipater reminded him. "When the citizens of the island failed to show any great enthusiasm in responding to this trifling request, Cassius stormed the port, ordered the people to hand over their wealth, and those who refused – well, he very considerately permitted them to join their ancestors. It seems our venerable Roman friend is not overly sensitive in such matters."

"Either way we lose," remarked Phasael dismally. "If we exact that sum we'll bitterly antagonize the Jews, who anyway don't love us. And if we don't produce it – well, I wouldn't like to be near Cassius when he learns of our failure."

"We don't have much choice, do we? Between the two evils it's obvious which is worse. So, somehow or other, we'll just have to scrape up 700 talents for our august, charitable Roman. Phasael, you'll be responsible for collecting 500 talents from the Jerusalem area, and Herod, you'll raise 100 talents in Galilee."

Phasael's paled. "How can I possibly raise an extortionate sum like that?" he muttered.

"Take an example from your brother. He's acquired a lot of experience, both in this country and in Coele-Syria."

"But I'm not like Herod. I can't use his strong-arm methods."

"I'm afraid you have no choice," said Antipater dryly.

Unlike his brother, Herod was by no means dismayed at the prospect of raising his share of the tribute. On the contrary, he welcomed the challenge and was confident of his ability to succeed, which he knew would not go unnoticed by Cassius.

"I take it, then, that I'm free to use whatever means I consider necessary?"

"As long as there is no violence," Antipater cautioned him. "I absolutely forbid any bloodshed. I don't want a repetition of the Hezekiah affair. Is that clear?"

"Yes, perfectly. Just a little twisting of the arm, but not the neck," commented Herod with a grin.

"I want both of you to emphasize to the people that we have been ordered to do this by Cassius. It's not something we ourselves would have chosen or preferred."

"There's one small detail that puzzles me," said Herod.

"What's that?"

"If Phasael is to raise 500 talents and I'm to raise 100, that adds up to only 600 talents."

"That's correct."

"Where are the other 100 talents to come from?"

Antipater leaned back in his chair, a crafty smile playing on his lips. "The other 100 talents will come from the Emmaus region. And for that task I can think of no one more eminently suited than my very able colleague and dear friend Malichus."

An incredulous look crossed Herod's and Phasael's faces. Knowing their father, they assumed that there must be a good reason for this decision, which to them seemed not only incongruous but fraught with danger.

"I'm afraid I don't understand your choice," remarked Phasael, shaking his head. "Especially considering that Malichus has been our most vocal and hostile rival, our bitter foe. You can't expect him to try and exact tribute for the Romans. It would go against his grain; why, it's downright preposterous!"

"Why do you think it's preposterous?" asked Antipater in a calm voice. "Either he raises the money or he doesn't. If he succeeds, then we shall have done our duty by our magnanimous Roman friend. Of course, it's quite likely that in the process of doing so Malichus will discover that his fellow citizens are not overjoyed at the idea of contributing to the Roman war chest – a fact which would undoubtedly dim his luster in their eyes. And if he doesn't come through with 100 talents, there's Cassius's reaction to take into account. Cassius's temper, I need not remind you, is not exactly the sweetest we have had the good fortune to encounter."

"What difference does it make to Cassius which of us raises his quota or not?" Herod wanted to know. "In fact, how will he even know who you have assigned the quotas to?"

"Ah, that's what's bothering you, is it? I shall of course inform Cassius upon whom I have conferred the honor of sharing this rare privilege. I have the utmost confidence that you two will raise your quotas, thereby warming the cockles even of his heart. Now, should Malichus for some reason or other let Cassius down, I shudder to think what might be the consequences."

Concern among the Peaceful Farmers of Emmaus

The sun was only a little beyond its zenith and Zechariah's body was already beginning to ache. He leaned on the handle of his plow, breathing heavily, and wiped the sweat from his furrowed brow on the sleeve of his heavily stained dun-colored tunic. Measuring with his eye the piece of land he had hoped to finish today, he realized he would not make it.

"If I'm not going to get this much done," he said with a resigned expression, "then let it be a little less."

He unhitched his ox and led it to a grove of pine, where he took shelter from the hot sun. He picked up a jug of water and tilted it, taking a long draught and letting a few drops trickle over his rough weather-beaten face.

Could it be that the years were beginning to tell on me? he wondered pensively. In the old days, he thought nothing of working from dawn to dusk, except when there was a khamsin; then his lungs and nostrils would be caked with dust, his mouth parched no matter how much water he drank, his body soon fatigued. But ordinary summer heat? He would laugh at those who complained about it. He felt at his best, of course, in cool, bracing weather, but he could not order the weather to suit his taste; one had to take the bad with the good, for they both came from the Almighty.

Sometimes when he had quenched his thirst, a thought would cross his mind: How could the good Lord and His faithful servant Moses have been vexed with the Israelites when they were trekking across the burning wilderness and bemoaning the lack of water? But he would immediately rebuke himself, for it was not for him, a God-fearing son of the covenant, to question the ways of the Almighty. Nor was it for him to ask why He gave abundant rain in some years and withheld it in others. Last year the rains had been less than adequate, and this past winter they were even more scanty. When the blight of drought had threatened to descend upon the land, a fast was proclaimed and special prayers recited beseeching the Lord for rain. But He did not seem to be in any hurry to answer the prayers, although Zechariah did not doubt that He would do so in His own good time. Until then it would not be easy, he thought with a sigh.

Emmaus was blessed with a number of springs, which normally provided enough water for the inhabitants' household needs and for irrigating the areas under vegetables and sometimes even the vineyards during the rainless summer months. But this year's drought drastically reduced the flow of spring water, so that it had to be largely restricted to use in the home. Zechariah was not too worried about the olive groves which covered the terraced hillsides, for without any connection with the rainfall, the olive crop had a unique cycle of its own, a bumper yield generally being followed by a poor one. The vineyards and grain fields, however, were a different matter, especially the former, for grapes were one of the main earning crops of the Emmaus region. The drought would sharply reduce the income of the Emmaus farmers.

Despite his lean build, Zechariah was still strong of limb. His keen, friendly eyes peered out from under thick brows and over a long, thin nose. His short, round beard was sprinkled with gray. When he thought about it – which he tried not to do too often – he found it hard to believe that he had already reached his fiftieth year – a full jubilee, he wistfully remarked to his wife Hannah. But the Lord be praised, most of the time he felt as fit as when he was in his prime. Not today though. Now, if Avner were here to help him, he could have gotten much more done, but he had sent his son with a cart of hay to the neighboring village. Well, if the Lord so willed it, then let it be.

Resting against a large, smooth rock, Zechariah let his eyes roam over his farmstead. Years ago it had been much bigger, but he had given parcels to each of his three eldest sons upon their marriage so they could support their families which, may the evil eye have no power over them, were multiplying rapidly. "What will we do when the day comes for Avner to take a wife?" Hannah had asked him not so long ago, for it was doubtful if his present holdings could support two families. They would have been if he had not been forced to sell some of his land to meet the heavy taxes levied over the years by the rapacious Romans, may their bones be crushed! There would have been enough land for all four of his sons and still leave him with ample sustenance.

"A pity that Caesar was assassinated," he had lamented to his wife. "He was different from the other Romans, and if he were still alive, things would be much better."

"You wait and see," his neighbor Saul had warned him when news reached Emmaus of Caesar's assumption of power a little over three years ago. "He'll be as bad as that Pompey, who robbed us of our freedom and sucked our blood."

Zechariah had no reason to question this dire prediction. But much to everyone's surprise, Caesar had turned out to be a benevolent ruler, who respected the Jewish people and their ways and lightened their tax burden, even remitting the annual tribute in the sabbatical year, when the people were bidden to let the land lie fallow. But now that Caesar was dead, who could tell what the future held in store for Judea? When Saul, who seemed to know before everyone else in Emmaus what was happening, told him that Cassius Longinus had arrived in Syria to take control there, Zechariah groaned, for all knew what a vulture he was.

These were very uncertain times, and Zechariah had already experienced enough strife and unrest. Whenever he prayed in the Emmaus synagogue, and especially when he went up to Jerusalem to offer a sacrifice, he would utter a special prayer for peace. But as with the rain, the Almighty did not always see fit to bestow this blessing on His people. And no wonder – there had been too much backsliding, too much discord and strife. In his younger days he had witnessed the two sons of Alexander Yannai contesting the royal and priestly crowns, in the process of which much innocent Jewish blood had been shed. And this after Yannai's forebears had freed the land from the cruel Syrian king Antiochus, who had forbidden the Jews on pain of death to keep the Lord's commandments, including the observance of the Sabbath and the circumcision of new-born sons, and who had desecrated the holy Temple and converted it into a shrine to Zeus, sacrificing swine on the altar and forcing the people to worship idols instead of the one and only God, besides committing other abominations. And after all this, after the yoke of the cruel oppressor had been cast off, how could Yannai's two sons take up arms against each other and by their own hands cause the land to run with the blood of their fellow Jews? Was it any wonder that the Almighty had despaired of His people and, as the prophet had predicted, sent his rod – the Romans – to chastise them? To such a pass had things come.

Zechariah heaved a deep sigh. He wished Avner a happy youth free of the tribulations he had endured. But he knew that his youngest son was restless; there was fire in his veins, and he was not willing to sit back quietly and let events take their course. He felt strongly about the Romans and was chafing at the bit.

Zechariah yawned. He tried to fight off the lassitude creeping over him, to keep his eyes from shutting, because he knew that if he didn't, even for only a moment, he would doze off. If only the heat would let up; there was much work to be done, he muttered, his head drooping on his chest. At this rate he would not get the field plowed, he thought hazily, his whole body relaxing against his will. After what seemed a few short minutes he heard a buzzing near his ears. "I wish that bee would stop pestering me," he mumbled. He raised his hand to chase it away, but instead of a bee he encountered a human hand. He looked up, startled.

"Avner! How did you sneak up on me so quietly?" he asked, yawning widely. "I didn't hear you coming."

"Of course not, Abba [Father]," replied Avner blithely. "When one's sound asleep he usually doesn't hear very well. I was even humming a new ditty I picked up last week, but only Kalba the ox appreciated it."

Zechariah wondered how long he had been asleep. It could not have been very long judging from the position of the sun. But it was just as well he had dozed off, he thought; it would refresh him and enable him to get on with his work. He slowly rose to his feet and stretched himself.

"How do you manage to stay so fresh and peppy, son?" he asked, rubbing his eyes. "Surely you're not immune to the heat."

"I'm not, but when there's good news who cares about the heat?"

Zechariah's aching tiredness had lifted, and things were looking brighter now; the problem of the drought and of Avner's parcel of land did not seem so oppressive as before. Avner always made him feel better; he was a cheerful lad, who did not seem to be bothered by any troubles or worries. That is, except when discussing politics, or what he called "the situation." On this he had very strong views, and spoke with contempt and indignation against those "miserable puppets of Rome who were ruining the country."

Avner was by no means a son of Zechariah's old age, but he was the youngest of his seven children. Not yet 17, he already surpassed his brothers in height and physical strength. He had black hair, a smooth, slanting forehead, and an ardent face with dark-brown eyes.

"What did Gad offer in exchange for the hay?" inquired Zechariah.

"He said he wants to discuss it with you. He's the one who told me the news."

"What news?"

"The news I mentioned a minute ago. Two things really. First of all, Barzilai is coming to spend a few days in Emmaus – with his family."

Zechariah frowned. "I don't see what's so important about that. And I think you'd be well advised to take a similar view."

Avner, expecting such a reaction, was not the least daunted.

"And by his family I take it you mean Rachel?" Zechariah went on.

"Of course! Who then? What interest do I have in his married sons and daughters?"

"I've told you more than once that you shouldn't be taking too much interest in Rachel," Zechariah gently reproved his son. "You're just wasting your time and making Barzilai angry besides. Not that I care two figs if he's angry, but I hate to see you building up your hopes when nothing can come of it. When the time comes, you should think about a girl of your own class."

"But Abba," protested Avner with a shrug of his shoulders, "I don't hold Rachel's class against her."

"Maybe you don't hold Rachel's class against her," Zechariah retorted with some exasperation, "but her father holds your class against you. And it's he who helps the Lord determine who her spouse will be. He's made it quite plain that it's not Avner, son of Zechariah, a tiller of the soil who lives by the sweat of his brow and is a Pharisee to boot."

Avner knew that his father was a kindly man who took to heart the biblical injunction not to hold a grudge. But the friction between him and Barzilai was due to more than personal reasons. What particularly annoyed Zechariah was that while both came from the same background – in fact, both had been born in Emmaus to families of farmers – Barzilai now identified himself with the Sadducees, the party composed largely of wealthy aristocratic and priestly families.

"What does Barzilai know about Sadducean beliefs?" remarked Zechariah with more than a trace of sarcasm. "In fact, what does he even know about Pharisaic beliefs? May the Lord forgive me, but his knowledge of Torah is pathetic. If he's struck it rich by buying up the produce of other farmers and selling it and his own crops at fancy prices, that was his good fortune, and who am I to envy him for that? But when the Almighty saw fit to deny us rain, and our crops were blighted so that we didn't have enough to provide for our families and pay the extortionate taxes imposed by those Roman vultures, it wasn't right of him to exploit our misery."

Avner failed to see what wrong Barzilai had committed.

"What wrong!" Zechariah snorted. "To help impoverish his fellow townsmen, that's not wrong? When they didn't have a spare *pruta* (coin) to tide them over those lean years, he could have lent them money and waited until they were able to repay it, instead of buying up their land at ridiculously low prices. Sure, he's a big landowner now, and not a few of his Emmaus neighbors and friends – or former friends – are no longer independent but tenant-farmers, paying him for the use of what was their own land."

Barzilai was accustomed to return to his Emmaus residence at least once or twice during the year. Not to collect the rents due him – for this he had an agent – but because he liked a change of scenery and also because he still had a nostalgia for the place where he was born and lived much of his life. "He just wants to lord it over us and show off how rich he's become," Zechariah's neighbor Saul insisted. But Zechariah knew that he had no need for that. He had tasted luxury and power in Jerusalem, and while he no longer possessed the authority he once enjoyed, he was as wealthy as ever. Several years ago he had purchased a mansion in Jerusalem's Upper City, and it was now his permanent home. Besides his holdings in the Emmaus region, he owned land elsewhere in Judea – some of it a reward for commanding one of Aristobulus's army units during the three years the latter sat on the throne. Antipater had several times urged Hyrcanus to confiscate these estates, but he would not hear of it.

Avner did not have to be reminded by his father that Barzilai did not approve of his continued friendly relations with Rachel. She herself had told him this on their previous visit to Emmaus. Before setting out, Barzilai had given Rachel to understand that she was no longer a child and had to behave accordingly.

"But Abba, Avner and I grew up together. What harm is there in seeing him again? It's unfair of you," she had protested.

"It's not unfair," he had admonished her. "You have to realize that you're now a young maiden of marriageable age – a rich, desirable maiden. I arranged good marriages for your two older sisters, and they're very grateful to me for that. I intend for you to marry equally well."

"But Abba, I'm not going to marry Avner. I just want to see him and talk to him, that's all. It will be boring for me otherwise."

Barzilai had regarded her with a severe, authoritative expression. "If it's going to be boring, then you had better stay in Jerusalem with your sisters."

Rachel was on the verge of tears. She knew it was pointless to oppose her father's will. The visit had not been an enjoyable one for her, but she had managed to see Avner briefly. When she told him about her father's admonition, he stared at her in silence for a long moment. "Do you really want to see me, Rachel?" he asked with an uncharacteristic serious look.

"What a question!" she replied without hesitation. "Of course I do. We're old friends, aren't we?"

"Yes, but when you think about it, your father is right. You're no longer a child, and neither am I."

"Oh, you silly thing! Of course we're not children. But what has that got to do with it? We're still good friends, aren't we?"

Avner gave Rachel a searching look. She was slender and tall for her age, her face rather thin, her dark-brown eyes sparkling, as they usually were, for she smiled often, a wide, pert smile. Her nose was also thin and slightly turned up. Was she beautiful? Avner had never considered the question before, nor did it particularly matter, for until then he had regarded her simply as a pleasant companion with a lively sense of humor and somewhat saucy manner. But after that visit he found that she was increasingly encroaching on his thoughts. During the daytime he was too busy with his work on the farm to think of anything else, but often at night he would see her in his mind's eye as she was the day she told him that she was now of marriageable age. "And if she does get married, what does that matter to me?" he asked himself. "Of course she's going to get married some day, and so am I, God willing." But the more he thought about it, the more restless he felt. When he heard that she was coming to Emmaus, he was determined to see her, whether her father liked it or not.

"And the second item of news you heard?" said Zechariah, cocking his eye. "I hope it was a little more significant."

"A courier arrived from Jerusalem this morning with a message for the town elders."

"From Jerusalem?" exclaimed Zechariah, his eyebrows rising sharply. "Why wasn't I told about this? I'm one of the elders."

"I understand that the courier gave the message to Eliezer, who was supposed to notify all the other elders."

"Do you know who the message is from and what it says?"

"Malichus will be coming to Emmaus tomorrow. He wants to meet all the elders in the synagogue."

Zechariah could not contain his surprise. Until quite recently Malichus had been Hyrcanus's chief counselor, having supplanted Antipater. But after Cassius's arrival on the scene, the cart had been turned around again, and Antipater regained his preeminent position, at least in his dealings with the Romans.

What could Malichus possibly want of the inhabitants of Emmaus? Zechariah wondered. His intuition told him that this visit spelled trouble of some sort. Ever since Caesar's death he had been apprehensive, for it was hardly likely that those who had conspired to assassinate him would treat Judea as leniently as Caesar had done. When Zechariah recalled Cassius's previous presence in Judea, especially how he had fallen upon the town of Tarichaea in Galilee and enslaved its menfolk, he spat in disgust.

"I'm going to be at the meeting tomorrow," Avner said in a casual tone.

Zechariah stared at his son with a curious expression. "I thought you said Malichus wanted to talk to the town elders?"

"That's right. But no one said others couldn't come too."

Zechariah grinned. His son was quick-witted, he had to admit. But Avner's decision struck him as quite brazen, and he feared Malichus would not tolerate such audacity. Avner, however, was adamant.

"On one condition, son," Zechariah grudgingly gave in; "that you don't provoke any argument with Malichus or annoy him in any way. Don't forget, he's the king's confidant and deserves proper respect, not to mention the possible consequences of any brash remarks or behavior on your part."

Zechariah had good reason to warn Avner, for he was outspoken in his hatred of the Romans and their stooges, Antipater and his two eldest sons, and also spoke disparagingly of Hyrcanus. He was a fiery patriot, and this caused Zechariah no little anxiety. They had many arguments on the subject. Avner could not understand how his father reconciled himself to the presence of the Romans or the nominal rule of someone like Hyrcanus, who had let Antipater lead him by the nose while Judea became more and more a mere vassal of Rome.

Zechariah had explained time and again that he had little love for the Romans, but Judea didn't have much choice. He did not admit to Avner that he was disillusioned with the more recent Hasmoneans, who had frittered away the fruits of the glorious victory won only a century ago. He was about Avner's age when he had been impressed into Alexander Yannai's army to fight his campaigns of aggrandizement. He had been a sorry witness to the civil strife between Yannai's two sons, when Jew had taken up arms against Jew, with the result that the country had fallen almost completely under the heel of the Romans. Not that tiny Judea could have stemmed the onrush of the Roman tide, but it might at least have retained a greater degree of sovereignty, some shred of independence. No, he didn't like the Romans any more than Avner, but when a strong wind blows up, it is the tree that can bend with it that survives. And with the Almighty's help Judea would survive; nay, it would outlive the heathen Romans, for the Lord would not forsake His people.

Avner was not the only one whose curiosity got the better of him. News of Malichus's impending visit spread like wildfire, and the synagogue was packed on the morrow. There was not a single male adult who did not down his tools to hear the tidings from Jerusalem.

Malichus arrived shortly before noon accompanied by an armed escort. They were greeted at the entrance to the town by a delegation of the leading elders, who escorted them to the synagogue. When he entered the hall, Malichus was surprised to find it thronged.

"I thought I made it clear that I wanted to speak to the town elders," he declared gruffly, jerking his head. Since his purpose in coming to Emmaus was of a delicate and not particularly pleasant nature, he had no desire to address a large audience, who were sure to react sharply to the message he had to convey. At first he was angry at what seemed a deliberate disregard of his request, and was inclined to order the hall cleared of all except the elders; but after consulting one of his men he relented.

The din in the hall died down when Malichus rose to speak. Zechariah, sitting in the front row with his fellow elders, noticed that he seemed ill at ease and eyed the audience with some suspicion. And no wonder, for Malichus explained to them, in a voice heavy with scorn, about the tribute laid upon the land. A gasp rose from the assembled when they heard the sum – 700 talents; when they learned what quota had been set for the Emmaus region, they stared at one another in dismay. For a second or two there was a deathly silence, then a chorus of angry protests burst forth.

"Quiet!" Malichus shouted in his powerful voice above the tumult. "I didn't ask to have the whole town gather here. If you're going to bray like a pack of asses, I'll send you all out."

Malichus's threatening visage and imperious warning had their effect; the hubbub died down.

"Now that you're here," he continued in a calmer tone, "if anyone wants to ask a question or make a comment, you may do so, but only in an orderly manner and after getting permission."

Everyone present seemed eager to take advantage of this opportunity, but Malichus gave priority to the elders. One after another they hammered home the same point: Emmaus and the neighboring towns and villages could not possibly pay such a heavy tribute – an unheard-of sum which was extortion on a grand scale. They related how last year's drought had played havoc with their crops, and this year's rains were also scanty. Malichus listened patiently to their complaint, and decided to reply to it before calling on the others.

"I'm just as dismayed as you are at the sum Cassius is demanding. That it's extortion on a grand scale I fully agree. I also know that you have suffered from drought the past two years. Don't think for a moment that I enjoy bringing you this message. You well know what love I have for the Romans; I would love to see them out of this land. But let's not fool ourselves, Cassius is no Caesar. He is cruel and ruthless. You had a taste of him eight or nine years ago. You remember what he did to one of the towns in Galilee: He made slaves of the menfolk. That's his method. I know you haven't been earning much lately. But what can we do? You'll have to dip into your nest-eggs, whatever you've manage to save over the years."

"Save, did you say?" scornfully remarked one of the elders. "How much do you think we've been able to save? First there was Pompey, who sucked our blood. Then there was Gabinius and then Crassus and then Cassius, and now again Cassius. Do we not have to provide for our old age? Do we not have children to marry off? Are we to tell them not to marry because of Cassius?"

This protest was echoed by the entire audience. Malichus's countenance clouded over, for he had to acknowledge the justness of their grievance.

"My friends," he said with a conscious effort to soften his voice, "I know your are speaking from your hearts. Your suffering is my suffering. But the Romans don't give a damn about that. Whatever you have you'll have to give up some of it. Either we raise our quota or face – well, I don't have to tell you what Cassius is capable of doing."

At this point Avner rose to his feet and signaled his desire to speak. Zechariah, observing the look of burning indignation on his face, was nervous. He silently prayed that his son would not antagonize Malichus. Avner received permission to speak.

"You have come to ask us for tribute," he began in clear, loud accents. "If you were to ask for extra taxes or an extra offering in the name of our high priest and king for the benefit of our country and our people, we would make the sacrifice, no matter how hard it might be. But you do not come to raise money for the good of our people or our land; you come to raise tribute for the hated Romans, who have degraded us, who have put our necks under a foreign pagan yoke. You are a loyal patriot, sir, a lover of freedom – you have amply proved that. How is it, then, that you are now doing the bidding of the foreign conqueror? How can you expect us to make this sacrifice on behalf of the loathsome Romans?"

At these bold words Zechariah groaned. To a man, the assembled felt as Avner did, but no one dared voice such thoughts, which were liable to goad Malichus to fury. With bated breath they riveted their gaze on him. They saw him stiffen and his expression darken. No one could guess how much Avner's words disconcerted him. He regarded Avner with a curious expression; he had to admire this young man, who had the pluck to speak out plainly on what was an extremely sore point, one that had caused him too great anguish. For he knew that he had been cunningly maneuvered to the edge of a precipice; one false step and he would go hurtling to his doom. Antipater had succeeded in ingratiating himself with that malevolent Cassius and regaining his position of power. He had Malichus just where he wanted him, and was gloating over his crafty stratagem. Malichus's gorge rose; how he hated that sly, fawning Idumean! If only he could pay him back in his own coin, but he knew that for his own safety he had to tread with extreme caution.

Malichus would have liked to reply to Avner's question with some quotation or parable, but he couldn't think of anything suitable. He let his gaze sweep over the crowd, and then focused on Avner, regarding him steadily.

"Look here, young man," he said brusquely, "that's a delicate question you asked me. I see that you have as much love as I do for the foreign conqueror in our midst. For that more power to you! Would that all our people felt as you do. Now, let me say this," he continued, glancing at the wall of faces in front of him, "I'm a military man, you know that. When we're threatened by an enemy, we have to decide on our strategy. If we think we're equal to the task, we deploy to blunt the enemy's advance and then counterattack in order to crush him. If our forces are too small or too weak, then we might put up only token resistance and skillfully withdraw in order to conserve our strength for another day when we can attack with a reasonable chance of success. That's the way we have to look at this business of the tribute. Don't think that I am any keener than you on collecting it for the benefit of the Romans. But I can only repeat, I have no choice and neither do you. Like soldiers, we must face up to this unpleasant business and make the necessary sacrifice. Regard it as a strategic retreat, if you like. I can tell you this: Cassius is not in an envious position. He's far from secure; he has enemies at home – Mark Antony for one, and they say young Octavian too. So we can hope that this plague will not last long. But in the meantime we mustn't give Cassius any excuse to inflict his brand of justice on us. It will be cheaper to pay this cursed tribute. So let's all contribute our share and let the Romans be damned."

Publius Quintus and Cassius Discuss the Situation

Publius Quintus woke up feeling out of sorts. He had a rough time the day before and had slept fitfully. Lydia, his comely Syrian mistress, had done her best to soothe him, but did not succeed. When the first chink of light stole in through the shutters, he crawled out of bed, taking care not to wake Lydia, who was breathing evenly and a look of complete serenity on her face. He envied her peace of mind.

Even though Publius hardly made any noise, Lydia woke up. Through half-closed eyes she watched him dash cold water on his face and don his military garb. He had a well-proportioned, muscular physique and ruggedly handsome features. A surge of passion welled up in her. Quietly she slipped out of bed and, tiptoeing to the other side of the room, threw her arms around him. He had a strong urge to take her in his arms. Nevertheless he tore himself from her embrace.

Lydia had given herself to many men, but to Publius she gave her heart as well. She had a lithe, long-limbed body, which would probably thicken with the years, but since she was not yet in her thirties, this did not trouble her in the least. Her oval face was framed by jet black hair, which now hung loosely below her shoulders and flowed almost to her waist; later it would be gathered up in a chignon at the back of her head. She had almond-shaped eyes, a finely chiseled nose, and a small, voluptuous mouth.

"What is troubling my handsome Roman god?" she asked.

Publius had made it a rule not to discuss political or military matters with his mistresses, even to be discreet in what he revealed to his wife. He knew that with rare exceptions women were incapable of keeping secrets or confidential information to themselves, and woe betide him who thought otherwise. But he could see no harm in telling Lydia something about yesterday's stormy meeting in Cassius's headquarters, especially as he was still rankling from the tongue-lashing he had received. He warned Cassius that if it were not for the fact that they had been comrades since youth and had gone through thick and thin to-gether, he would retire to his family estate and let Cassius find himself another lieutenant. Contrary to what was commonly believed, Gaius Cassius Longinus could be amiable enough with close friends; if not, Publius would long ago have left him. With others, however, he could be bitingly sarcastic and given to violent outbursts of temper. He did not cultivate the love of his officers or men, and dealt harshly with the slightest breaches of discipline or signs of slackness. It was only because he was an able general that he could induce his troops to give a good account of themselves. It was he who, as quaestor to Crassus, had extri-cated the remnants of the Roman army after its crushing defeat by the Parthians nine years earlier. The survivors knew that if not for him they too would have perished in the inhospitable wastes of that huge, sprawling land, and would not today be enjoying their families or attending gladiatorial contests or chariot races, or preparing to take the field again under his banner.

"But if you're his second-in-command and lifelong friend, why did he treat you so disrespectfully?" Lydia wanted to know.

Publius, seating himself on the bed, explained that Cassius had been in a vile mood for two main reasons. In the morning he had received information that Mark Antony and Octavian, Caesar's nephew and adopted son and heir, were about to patch up their differences, which spelled trouble for Cassius, the prime instigator of Caesar's assassination. Cassius would have to prepare for an inevitable showdown with his two rivals, and he was none too confident of the outcome, especially as a bad omen had greatly upset him.

Lydia, who possessed a wide assortment of amulets and other charms to ward off evil spirits, was intrigued by this information and wanted to know what had disturbed him.

"It happened shortly after we came to Syria," said Publius, scratching his head. "We were encamped with our army when a storm suddenly blew up. We ordered the men to take shelter from the pelting rain, and while they were scurrying to their tents, some wild swine rushed into the camp and overturned everything in their way. Cassius asked the augers for the meaning of this incident, but they claimed they weren't sure what it portended. Cassius knew they were lying, and it was only when he threatened them with dire punishment that they said one could possibly infer from this his immediate rise to power and his subsequent overthrow. Well, if Cassius has been rather pale of late, you should have seen his face then: It was as white as snow."

A worried expression crossed Lydia's countenance. "I don't like that at all, not that I give a hoot about your Cassius. I'm sure I wouldn't like him from what you've told me about him, but you're his second-in-command. If anything should happen to you..."

"Now, now, my pet, don't worry your pretty head about that," Publius reassured her, touched by her concern. "First of all, if Cassius continues to forget that we're old comrades, he'll have to look for another second-in-command. And secondly, even though you might not like him, he's an excellent general and has a large army at his disposal. Only he could have saved what was left of our forces after the Parthian campaign. If not for him, none of us would probably be alive today."

"Don't say that, darling," Lydia beseeched him. She took Publius's hand and pressed it to her lips. "The gods were kind to Cassius – too kind. He didn't deserve to live. You did, but not him."

"Why do you say that?"

"Because you just told me that he was the one most responsible for Caesar's murder. That was a wicked crime. What made him do it?"

"If I try to answer that I'll be here all morning," declared Publius, hoping that Lydia would not press the matter. But she was not to be put off so easily. "Then make it brief," she insisted.

Publius gave Lydia an odd look. She had never evinced any great interest in political affairs, and he doubted if she had a bent for things intellectual. In this respect she differed from many of the upper-class Roman women who had taken to stuffing their heads with book learning, and with it acquiring a taste for independence – too heady a taste in his opinion. He wondered why Lydia was so curious about Caesar's death; after all, he was not the first prominent person to suffer a violent end, nor would he be the last. In fact, it seemed that not very many of Rome's leading political figures were dying peacefully in bed in recent years. When he thought about it, he had the feeling that the fabric of Roman society was irreparably rent. In his early years he would smile at those who bemoaned the loss of the old Roman virtues, the growing corruption of politics and morals; he put it down to the usual lament about the good old days. But by the time Caesar had become dictator of Rome, the people were fed up with the degeneration of government – the buying of votes, the intimidation of juries, the murdering of political rivals to such an extent that the Tiber seemed to be always full of corpses and the rostra decorated with the nailed heads of senators and other nobles who had belonged to the party displaced from power. And this after a century of slave revolts and class war provoked by the growing concentration in the hands of a comparatively small number of aristocratic families of the immense wealth pouring in from the conquered provinces. Many had come to the conclusion that the republic was in effect dead and dictatorship inevitable. That is why Caesar was able to be voted dictator for life. This, in essence, is what Publius tried to convey to Lydia in a simple, brief manner.

"And did Caesar disappoint the people? Was he good for Rome?"

"Whether he was good for Rome depends on which side of the fence you're sitting on. What's good for some may not be good for others."

Lydia burst into laughter. "Publius, dear, you're a soldier. Why don't you answer like a soldier and not like a fence-sitter?"

Publius was nettled by this remark, whose relevance escaped him. "All right," he said a little huffily. "Did Caesar disappoint the people – the common folks, that is? No, not at all. Besides distributing corn to the needy – which others had done before him – he distributed land to the poorer citizens. He started a big building program to provide jobs for the unemployed. He reduced debts and excessive interest rates. And as for government, he tolerated no incompetence or waste, and severely punished those who tried to buy or bribe votes or were guilty of other politically corrupt practices. He reduced provincial taxes, sometimes by as much as a third, and, I must admit, on the whole he appointed efficient governors and other officials."

Lydia was impressed by this catalog of virtues. "If he did so much good for Rome, why did they murder him?"

Publius hesitated before replying; he shrugged his shoulders. "Well, as I said before – a statement which for some strange reason greatly amused you – it depends on which side of the fence you're sitting on. And, if I may repeat myself without the risk of provoking some derisive comment on your part, what's good for some may not always be good for others. The nobles and patricians naturally resented the curtailment of their privileges, even if only to a relatively slight degree. But you have to hand it to Caesar, he treated them gallantly. He canceled all sentences of banishment and even pardoned all returning aristocrats. Take Cassius and Brutus, for example – the ones who led the conspiracy against him.

101

Even though they had been opposed to Caesar, and in fact could be regarded as his enemies, he forgave them and appointed them to responsible positions. And he did the same to others who had opposed him. But they didn't hold him in gratitude for this; they were always plotting against his life."

Lydia shook her head in disbelief. "I can't understand them, especially your Cassius. They must be either very foolish or very wicked."

"They thought Caesar wanted to become king, and the Romans hate kings as much as they love money."

He was relieved to see that this answer seemed to satisfy Lydia. He was therefore spared the need to go into the details of Caesar's growing power and the excessive honors showered on him, to the point where some had thought it was only a matter of time until he became king or emperor. And who could tell what that might have led to? For a bad monarch would be no better – in fact, he would probably be much worse – than a chaotic republic. Publius himself thought Caesar was unwise to have accepted all the honors and privileges, which had outraged not a few honest citizens. If he accepted the honor of always wearing a laurel wreath, Publius could understand that; after all, Caesar was known to have been greatly troubled by his baldness and could be forgiven this concession to vanity. But as for the celebration of his birthday by public sacrifice, the Senate's naming him father of his country and having this title stamped on the coinage, and many other such honors – that was carrying things a little too far. Some claimed that Caesar's enemies had encouraged the heaping of all these honors on him in order to make him odious in the eyes of the people. Publius had not dared to query Cassius about this allegation, but it would have been in keeping with the latter's character. He was not sure whether Cassius's hatred of Caesar was motivated so much by concern over his growing power as by a peculiar quirk in his own nature – an intense envy of and bitterness toward those in high places, men who had achieved success and public acclaim.

"And that's why Cassius barked at you yesterday – because of Antony and Octavian?" Lydia interrupted Publius's musing.

"What?" he muttered abstractedly.

Publius was growing impatient; he had no particular desire to confront Cassius today, but it was getting late. "Look here, pet, I can't spend the whole morning chatting with you. If I show up late, it will cause eyebrows to rise, not to mention Cassius's ire."

"So what? Let him wait; he has it coming to him."

"All right, but I must be brief." He got up from the bed and started to pace the room as he continued with his account. "It was shortly after Cassius got the report about a possible reconciliation between Antony and Octavian that he received Malichus."

"Who's he? You've never mentioned him before."

"No? Maybe I didn't. He's a confidant of Hyrcanus, the ethnarch of Judea, and now his chief minister. It seems there's bad blood between him and Antipater, whom I've mentioned to you more than once. When Cassius told Antipater he was imposing a tribute of 700 talents on Judea, Antipater evidently divided responsibility for its collection among his two sons and Malichus, who, it seems, has no great love for us Romans. Last week Antipater handed over 600 talents to Cassius, explaining that this had been raised by his two sons, while Malichus had failed to raise his quota of 100 talents. Well, you should have seen Cassius's face when he heard that. He actually got some color in his cheeks. He also had some ungracious things to say about Malichus, but I'll spare your delicate ears the details. He praised Antipater and his two sons and said that he wanted Malichus to report to him at once. Yesterday he came."

Before continuing, Publius went over to a small table next to the window and picked up a goblet. Lydia hurried over to pour him some wine from the mixing bowl.

"Thank you, pet." He took a long draught and smacked his lips. "Ah, that's better. That should put a little pep into these creaky bones of mine."

"And your tongue too, I hope," said Lydia, eager to hear the rest of the story. "Now tell me about Malichus and Cassius."

"It was quite a scene, as good as anything I've seen on the stage. Cassius even outdid our famous actor Roscious. He stormed and raged at Malichus, who, I must hand it to him, bore it all stoically. When he thought Cassius had finished, he started to explain why he hadn't raised his precious 100 talents, but Cassius cut him short. He exploded again, and his face turned purple – and that's saying something, considering that its normal color is more like white-wash. Eventually Malichus managed to get a few words in edgewise. He said the people of the Emmaus region were unable to pay the sum demanded because they had been very heavily taxed during the past 20 years, with the exception of the three years Caesar was in power. Well, that sent Cassius's blood boiling still more, and he foamed with rage. Malichus should have known better than to mention Caesar, but after the dressing-down he had received, you can't blame him for not thinking of all the niceties. Cassius threatened that if he wanted to keep his head, he had better produce the 100 talents, and pretty damn quick."

"What has all that got to do with you?"

Publius sipped some more wine before replying. "When Cassius is foaming at the mouth, woe betide anyone who may be in his presence. After dismissing Malichus, he asked me what punishment I'd suggest. I told him that Malichus was hardly likely to forget Cassius's warning, and advised giving him a little more time, because the reasons he gave seemed plausible enough to me. Cassius, to put it mildly, took a dim view of my advice. 'If Antipater and his sons can raise their much larger quota, then Malichus can certainly raise his,' he growled.

I said that Antipater's sons probably had no qualms about using unpleasant methods to collect their quotas, since they feel less sympathy toward the people than Malichus does. Needless to say, this did not convince Cassius one bit. And now, my pet, I must be off, or I'll be the butt of his anger today."

Publius bent down and kissed Lydia as he departed.

* * *

Cassius took special pains not to antagonize his lieutenant, for he knew that Publius's threat to walk out on him was not an idle one. With no end of trouble in sight, he needed the loyalty of all his men and especially his friends. It was not easy for him to keep a tight rein on his temper, because every time he thought of what mischief Antony and Octavian were probably brewing for him, his gorge rose. "How stupid of me to let Brutus talk me into leaving that arrogant, lecherous Antony alive," he fulminated, pacing his Spartanlike headquarters.

Publius, sensing that Cassius was about to work himself into a frenzy, muttered some innocuous reply.

"That was a bad blunder on my part," Cassius went on irritably. "I shouldn't have paid any heed to Brutus's pious insistence that we act with strict justice and spare Antony. Justice!" he snorted. "What a joke! What Roman knows what justice means today? The sight of the severed heads of senators and pompous nobles nailed to the rostra must have been too much for Brutus's squeamish stomach. And who would have dreamed that this puny, sniveling puppy Gaius Octavian would try to avenge the death of his swell-headed uncle and to take over the reins of power?"

Publius knew that once Cassius got on the subject of Caesar he was in for a tedious tirade. He kicked a campstool out from under the table and seated himself with a resigned look, as the flow of invective continued.

"Even now my stomach turns sour when I think of how that insolent, dandified charlatan would strut around with his laurel wreath, his wide-fringed sleeves, and his high red shoes. And an ordinary chair wasn't good enough for him in the Senate House. Oh no, he had to park his exalted buttocks on a golden throne. And as if that wasn't enough, he had to deface Rome with all those statues of himself. He even had the gall to let one be marched alongside those of the gods at the games in the Circus, and another erected in the Temple of Quirinis with the inscription 'To the Invincible God,' and another one set up alongside those of the ancient Roman kings on the Capitol. Imagine that! It wasn't enough for that libertine to make his presence felt in every high-born lady's bed, he had to make his odious presence felt in all Rome. Every time I passed one of those stone monstrosities, I wanted to puke."

Publius, who was only too familiar with Cassius's denunciations, knew that he had about exhausted the list of major sins, but had gotten himself so worked up he would probably start cataloging the innumerable less glaring ones. Wearied to death of the subject, Publius racked his brains for an escape, but a perverse desire impelled him instead to pour oil on the flame.

"From the way the plebes carried on at Antony's funeral oration," he drawled, "I'd say that not everyone was repelled by Caesar's high red shoes or fringed sleeves or even his statues."

Cassius, who had been pacing the room furiously as he hurled his vitriolic strictures on the late dictator, stopped dead in his tracks. He glared at Publius with a savage expression. Publius observed, with a look of sly satisfaction, how his jaws quivered with rage, and was sure he was aching to lash out at him but wouldn't dare. Cassius, remembering his resolve not to antagonize his lieutenant, gnashed his teeth.

"The plebes!" he snarled. "What do the mobs of Rome really know about their beloved benefactor? Would they have wanted a king to order them about and force them to bow and scrape before him? They too would have been glad to be rid of that lump of arrogant insolence, if not for that dunderhead Brutus."

"Brutus?" queried Publius with a quizzical look.

"Yes, Brutus. When Antony got hold of Caesar's will and insisted that he be allowed to read it in public, I was the only one who opposed it, but that soft-headed Brutus had to override me. What a blunder! And now both of us may pay dearly for it. When the scurvy mob learned that Caesar had left his garden to the people and bequeathed 300 sesterces to every citizen of Rome, they took leave of their senses. Is it any wonder that so many turned up at the Forum for Caesar's last rites?"

"You have to admit they were quite moved by Antony's eulogy," said Publius daringly.

"Moved? Any ham actor can move the rabble."

"I personally thought he was quite good. And that climax was superb drama!"

Cassius glared at Publius. He had, regretfully, to concede the point. In the first part of his oration Antony had been restrained, and Cassius and his accomplices breathed a sigh of relief. But as Antony went on, he grew more and more impassioned, and after working himself up to a fiery pitch, he picked up Caesar's robe, stiff with blood, and unfolded it for all to see, pointing out each of the 23 gashes where the daggers had pierced through. At this the mob went berserk; their wails and frenzied cries still rang in Cassius's ears. On the spot they made a pyre from all the wood they could lay their hands on, and as the flames began to consume Caesar's body, his veteran troops threw their weapons on the fire, actors their costumes, musicians their instruments, and women their precious ornaments. Some began to shout, "Kill the murderers!" At this, Cassius and his colleagues looked at one another in consternation. They hastily dispersed to their homes, and some even fled Rome. This probably saved their skins, for some hotheads had seized firebrands and ran to the homes of the conspirators in order to set them ablaze with all their occupants. But thanks to their formidable bodyguards, the conspirators managed to escape the mob's vengeance.

"And all because of that debauched, villainous Antony," Cassius spluttered, his eyes blazing. "We'll settle his hash good and proper and that of the prissy juvenile too."

With that remark Publius realized that Cassius had finally wound down on the subject of Caesar and was ready to get on with the business at hand. Now the subdued and able general, Cassius took his seat behind the table, which was covered with maps, rolled parchment, and waxed tablets. For the next hour or so the two discussed plans for the forthcoming campaign. When they finished, Publius rose and prepared to take his leave.

"Not so fast!" Cassius called out. "There's another piece of business we have to deal with. We've got to decide what to do with that Jew – what the devil is his name again?" asked Cassius with a vicious scowl.

"Malichus," Publius reminded him with a grimace. Truth to tell, Publius wasn't sure whether Malichus was a native-born Jew or one of the Idumeans who had been forced to convert. But it was obvious from the way Cassius spat out the word "Jew" that he entertained no great love for this people. It was curious, thought Publius, how the Romans reacted so differently to the Jews, whom they found strange, so unlike other peoples, who inhabited the empire. The Romans either thoroughly detested them, or were intrigued by their national customs and especially their belief in an omnipotent and omniscient God, who they claimed was lord of the entire universe, including Rome.

"When I warned that worm Malichus yesterday," Cassius went on testily, his lean head craning forward, "I meant every single word. If he doesn't cough up 100 talents, and pretty damn quick, I'll have his head. I've relieved much better men of their heads. In fact, I've a good mind to do it even if he does produce the money. When I think how he had the nerve, the insolence, to answer me back, my blood boils. He..."

"I understand he's Hyrcanus's principal adviser," Publius interjected. "You can't blame him for trying to honorably defend the interests of his fellow citizens. When he pointed out that Judea had been milked by Roman officials until Caesar came upon the scene, you have to admit he was speaking the truth. Caesar did treat the Jews much more leniently than his predecessors."

Publius realized he was treading on dangerous ground with this observation, but he could not resist the temptation to give Cassius another jab. It was common knowledge that the Jews had so highly regarded Caesar that they mourned him for several days after his assassination. Cassius scowled at Publius and his lips twitched, but he stifled his rising ire. Publius grinned with satisfaction.

"The fact that this scoundrel is Hyrcanus's principal adviser cuts no ice with me," Cassius retorted gruffly. "In fact, I've even a good mind to replace Hyrcanus as ethnarch. He was too close to Caesar and he's become too uppity of late. This young son of Antipater – what's his name again?"

"Herod."

"He's got the makings of a good client king. I'm toying with the idea of having him appointed in Hyrcanus's place."

"He too is Jewish."

"A half-Jew, if that, I've been told; but more a Roman by inclination. A much more dependable sort, one who knows how to get things done. Not gutless like Hyrcanus or a knave like Malichus."

"You've already got plenty on your plate. Why look for more trouble? I understand that the Jews detest Herod; they'd bitterly resent such a change."

"The Jews! The Jews!" Cassius spat out savagely. "Are they your only concern? A small, pestilential, obnoxious race! They're a boil on my buttocks. A plague on them all! If they don't know by now that Rome is master of the world and that our word is law, we'll have to teach them. I'll give that slimy worm Malichus ten days to raise his 100 talents. No, one week at the most. And if he doesn't come through, the towns he's responsible for – how many are there?"

Publius referred to one of the tablets. "Four: Gafna, Emmaus, Lydda, and Thama," he read out wearily.

"The inhabitants of those four towns will find out what it means to disobey Cassius Longinus. All able-bodied males will be sold into slavery."

Publius stared blankly at the tablet. Without looking up, he could feel Cassius's harsh, vindictive gaze boring into him. "It will take Roman spears to enforce that order," he uttered in a low, flat voice.

"I know that," Cassius affirmed stiffly. "And to command those spears I need an officer of exemplary competence and unimpeachable loyalty to Rome." Cassius's thin lips twisted into a crooked smile. "I can think of no one more suitable for that assignment than Publius Quintus." Cassius paused briefly to let the significance of this announcement sink in and to savor Publius's discomfiture. "I'm confident that as a loyal servant of Rome you will see to it that my order is faithfully carried out."

Malichus Meets His End in Tyre

Hyrcanus did not look forward to the journey to Laodicea. It was only with great reluctance and out of a sense of duty that he, like the other client-kings in the region, was proceeding to this city, which lay on the Mediterranean coast some 50 miles south of Antioch, in order to bring a gift to Cassius and to congratulate him on his victory over Dolabella. He had hoped that Dolabella and not the malicious Cassius would gain the upper hand. Dolabella had proved to be a friend, both when Caesar was alive and after his assassination. As Caesar's appointed governor of Syria, he had responded favorably to Hyrcanus's request to exempt the Jews of Asia Minor from military service so that they need not violate the Sabbath or eat forbidden foods, and to enable them to observe their other religious customs. After Caesar's death Dolabella had helped persuade the Roman Senate to confirm Caesar's favorable decrees concerning the Jews.

If Hyrcanus did not view the impending meeting with pleasure, he knew that Malichus had even less reason to do so. He had, in fact, tried to beg off. Hyrcanus could understand his attitude, for since the sudden death of Antipater while dining in the royal palace with Malichus and several other guests, Herod and Phasael suspected poisoning and were convinced that Malichus had been the perpetrator. Malichus was aware of their suspicion, which he assumed had been conveyed to Cassius, and even though they pretended to be friendly toward him, he knew that this masked their hostility. Moreover, he had good reason to detest and to be wary of Cassius. Because he had not raised his share of the tribute that had been imposed on Judea, Cassius had vented his wrath by selling into slavery all the able-bodied male inhabitants of the four towns in the region Antipater had assigned him. If Hyrcanus had not given 100 talents of his own money to cover Malichus's quota, the latter would undoubtedly have met a dire fate.

Shortly after dawn of a fine autumn day Hyrcanus and Malichus set out from the palace in the royal coach, accompanied by an armed escort. It was chilly at this early hour, and Hyrcanus was glad to be wearing a woolen cloak. The pale saffron rays of the rising sun were playing on the Temple walls, and tiny figures could be discerned moving about in the precincts – the priests going about their duties. Gazing at the Tyropoeon Valley and Lower City, Hyrcanus could see only a few people stirring in the shadows of the small houses huddled on the slopes of the quarter; soon, however, it would come alive and resound with the shouts of human voices and the braying of asses. Generally when leaving Jerusalem, Hyrcanus felt a sense of anticipation, a welcome respite from the burden of his office. Today, however, he was uneasy and would have welcomed an opportunity to put off the trip.

"You did not sleep well, sire?" asked Malichus in his deep, rumbling voice.

"Probably as well as you did," replied Hyrcanus with a wan smile, observing the shadows under Malichus's eyes and his somber appearance. Neither spoke any more until they reached the city gate. As he watched the walls of

Jerusalem dwindling behind them, Malichus felt an unaccustomed oppression of spirit. *This will never do*, he told himself. *I must pull myself together*. To dispel his gloomy thoughts, he began to relate anecdotes about his army life. This helped and soon he was engaged in a lively discussion on various personal and political matters. On the second day, Malichus was in a reasonably good humor as they made their way through Galilee, but when they approached the Syrian border on the following day he lapsed into long silences. This was so unlike him that Hyrcanus scrutinized him with a puzzled look. Hyrcanus himself was not in a very communicative mood, and he made an effort to shut out all thoughts of what might lie ahead or what happened in the past few weeks. But he was unable to put out of his mind the fateful dinner in the palace. Antipater had been in good spirits, and no wonder: When Cassius had assumed the governorship of Syria after Caesar's death, he saw to it that Antipater was restored to his former position. Hyrcanus had to acknowledge that Antipater behaved decently enough, ignoring, or pretending to ignore, Hyrcanus's deliberate attempt to distance himself from him. Antipater had even displayed a polite attitude toward Malichus, who he knew bore him malice. They had been dining around the long oak table, and in his usual suave manner Antipater had been recounting an amusing encounter he had that morning with a foreign dignitary when the servants brought in the soup course under the careful eye of the butler. While they were eating the soup, Hyrcanus saw with horror how Antipater suddenly turned pale; he half-rose to his feet, his face contorted with pain. He clutched his stomach or his heart – Hyrcanus was not sure which – and then collapsed. In the ensuing confusion Hyrcanus had the presence of mind to summon the royal physician, but by the time he arrived Antipater was dead.

Hyrcanus was profoundly shaken by this distressful event, and the recollection of it left him in a cold sweat. Although he and Antipater had grown apart of late, this could not erase all the years of close association and even friendship. They had shared many vicissitudes and triumphs. Hyrcanus was fully aware that the overwhelming majority of the people and all his followers had viewed Antipater's growing power with dismay and aversion, but he had known this useful Idumean at first hand and admired his considerable talents. He had been ambitious – of that no one had any illusions – but he had tempered it with personal charm and unerring political acumen, as witnessed by the safe course he had steered in the face of the various changes of ruler in Rome. Not many could pull off such a feat. Nor had he failed to display a respectful attitude toward Hyrcanus. He would miss the old fox in spite of everything. Ecclesiastes probably had a point in asserting that the memory of the dead is forgotten, but Hyrcanus would never forget his longtime counselor and minister.

While Hyrcanus was musing in this vein, Malichus was deeply troubled in mind. A soldier nearly all his life, he had faced danger – and death – times without number, but had accepted this as the inevitable lot of a man of his profession. Today, however, he was full of disquiet and foreboding. He did not know whether to blame it solely on the impending meeting with Cassius, to which, thankfully, he would not be accompanying Hyrcanus. He hated the very idea of being near this man, who had humiliated him as no one else had ever done and, even more galling, had forced him to send his son to Tyre as a hostage in order to discourage any possible sedition on his part. He would rejoice to see this arrogant Roman get his just deserts. And who knows? Perhaps that day was not too far off. For Malichus had information that Mark Antony and Octavian had composed their differences and, together with Lepidus, were about to form a triumvirate. This undoubtedly presaged a showdown with Cassius and Brutus, the leaders of the conspiracy against Caesar.

The plebeians had been shocked at Caesar's assassination and hated his murderers. However, battles were decided not by the masses but by trained, disciplined legions. Nevertheless, Malichus believed that Cassius's days were numbered. "What I wouldn't give to see it come to pass," he said to himself. In the meantime the thought of being in the same city with him filled him with repugnance. Only the knowledge that at Tyre he would be able to see his son gave him some relief. He was longing to see him. His career as a soldier had frequently kept him away from home for long spells, and his son had grown into adolescence and then manhood much too fast, thought Malichus nostalgically.

As the coach made its way along the coastal road, Hyrcanus idly gazed at the azure waters of the Mediterranean, their surface ruffled by whitecaps rolling in toward the shore and lapping the tawny sands. He was feeling pleasantly drowsy and shut his mind to all cares and worries. But not so Malichus. Amidst his grim musing, the idea occurred to him to spirit his son out of Tyre and return to Judea. As he mulled this over, his heart grew lighter. He would have to invent a plausible excuse for his sudden decision not to proceed with Hyrcanus to Laodicea. And once it was known that he had helped his son to escape, it would bring Cassius's wrath down upon his head, and he would be a marked man. But Cassius, he was sure, would soon have his hands full with Antony and Octavian. It was a dangerous step he was contemplating and might end disastrously. Should he take the risk? He was weighing the pros and cons when Tyre came into view. Malichus was familiar with the city, having visited it several times, but it was many years since Hyrcanus had last set foot in it. He did not have a soft spot in his heart for the city. During the Maccabean wars, it had joined Sidon and Ptolemais in attacking the Jews of Galilee, and even in relatively recent times the Jewish community there had suffered many indignities. Moreover, some of the male inhabitants of the four towns in the Emmaus region whom Cassius had enslaved were sold in the slave market of Tyre.

As they approached the city, they saw a fairly large number of ships heading into or out of the harbor. There were slow-moving freighters, most of them riding low in the water, as well as fishing smacks and men-of-war: menacing-looking triremes and fast, sleek galleys with sails bellowing in the breeze. Piled on the wharves were bales of goods, and swarming about them were merchants, porters, and stevedores. Much of the outgoing freight consisted of glass, silk, and the purple dye for which Tyre was famous. Beyond the wharves narrow streets and alleyways teemed with sailors, workmen, shoppers, and others, who were milling about or picking their way past carriages, litters, and drays pulled by oxen, mules, or stout horses. The bazaars and stalls were crowded with customers, and the taverns and heavily scented, rouged women offering their personal services did not lack for patronage. The driver of the royal coach experienced considerable difficulty in making his way through the heavy traffic.

"Wouldn't it be advisable to skirt the port area, sire?" the officer of the royal escort asked Hyrcanus.

Hyrcanus, who had been enjoying the sights and did not entertain any thought of danger, threw Malichus a questioning look.

"The Jewish quarter lies a little beyond the port area," Malichus told the officer. "We will be lodging with the archon of the Jewish community. Clear a way for us and keep your eyes open."

With the escort opening a path, the carriage was able to proceed more rapidly, and soon they reached a broad thoroughfare. It too was heavily traveled but much less congested. Approaching them they saw what appeared to be an important personage mounted on a white steed and flanked by two bodyguards. To their surprise, it turned out to be Herod. When he reached the coach, he peered through the window and, observing who the passengers were, grinned broadly.

"This is a pleasant surprise," he exclaimed, dismounting and handing the reins to one of his men. "You honor Tyre with your presence," he said to Hyrcanus when the coach had come to a halt. He nodded perfunctorily to Malichus, who regarded him with a cold, suspicious expression.

"Since it is well past noon, I presume you intend to spend the night here," said Herod.

"We are on our way to Cassius," replied Hyrcanus laconically.

"Then you still have a long journey ahead of you. Please do me the honor and be my guests for the night."

"That's kind of you," said Hyrcanus a little dryly, "but we will be the guests of the archon of the Jewish community."

"Far be it from me to trespass on the archon's hospitality. But you must let me show you some of the sights tomorrow. There are many interesting things to see in Tyre."

"We won't have any time for that," interposed Malichus frostily. "As you have said, we still have a long way to go."

"Heaven forbid that I should delay you," replied Herod with a conscious effort to maintain a friendly mien. "But if you were to spend only an hour or two, it would be very much to your profit, and you could still reach Laodicea in good time."

Hyrcanus, who was not looking forward to paying his respects to Cassius and was eager for some diversion, welcomed the suggestion. "I think we can manage it, Malichus," he declared.

That evening, after dining in the archon's residence, Malichus excused himself in order to visit his son. The archon offered to send a servant with a torch to accompany him, but Malichus said he knew the city and could find his way. It took about an hour to reach the home of the former Roman magistrate Rufus Galba, where his soon was being held hostage. Rufus, a middle-aged man with an amiable yet authoritative manner, welcomed Malichus and summoned the latter's son. He ordered a slave to bring a platter of fruit, and after exchanging pleasantries with Malichus let the two withdraw to the son's room where they could speak in private. Malichus walked over to the door and bolted it quietly.

"Why did you do that?" asked the young man, perturbed by his father's precaution and drawn look.

Malichus studied his son intently. How much he resembles me, he thought. Just growing into manhood, he had the same sturdy build, ruddy complexion, and reddish hair. Not normally given to sentiment, Malichus could not suppress a feeling of pride mingled with apprehension. He dearly loved his son, and if anything should happen to him, he would know no peace of mind. In an undertone he related what had been happening lately: the sudden death of Antipater; Herod's suspicion of poisoning, for which he secretly accused Malichus while pretending to be friendly to him; the impending visit to Cassius; and the encounter with Herod today, which to all appearances was of a fortuitous nature but which he believed otherwise.

"I've been uneasy ever since leaving Jerusalem," Malichus confided. "It may sound foolish, but I sense danger in the air. Herod's honeyed words only made it worse. I'm returning to Jerusalem tomorrow and I'm taking you with me."

The boy stared at his father with an alarmed expression. "If you do that, you'll be in even greater danger. Cassius will take drastic action against you."

"If he has the time and mind for it. He's going to have his hands full with Antony and Octavian, who are preparing to take the field against him and Brutus. I'm counting on that to distract him."

"What about Hyrcanus? How can you desert him like that?"

"Nothing will happen to Hyrcanus. I'm the one who is under a cloud of suspicion."

"It's a risky business, Abba," the boy said, unable to hide his anxiety. "You're endangering your life. Don't do it – not even for my sake."

Malichus was deeply touched by his son's solicitude. He put an arm around his shoulder. "I'm doing this for my sake as well as yours. If they're scheming to do me harm, I'm afraid they'll do the same to you. Now, not one more word of protest." Keeping his voice as low as possible, he continued: "Here's my plan. Listen carefully. In the morning I have to accompany Hyrcanus on a sightseeing tour of the city, which he let Herod talk him into against my better judgment. At noon or thereabouts, I'll come here and we'll tell Rufus that we're going out for a short walk before my departure. I'm sure we can allay any suspicion he might have, especially if you don't take anything with you. Is that clear?"

The boy nodded mutely. When Malichus took his leave, after embracing him warmly, his eyes filled with tears. He uttered a silent prayer for his father's safety.

Next morning, after a good night's sleep and a hearty breakfast, Hyrcanus was in a more cheerful mood. While waiting for Malichus, he chatted with his host about local Jewish affairs. He was especially interested to know how many of the men who had been sold into slavery on Cassius's orders were in Tyre and how they were faring. The archon gave him what information he had.

"Malichus thinks Cassius and Brutus are heading for a showdown with Antony and Octavian," said Hyrcanus. "He's confident that Antony and Octavian will gain the upper hand. If they do, I'll appeal to them to release our people, and considering the close ties they had with Caesar, I'm hopeful they will respond favorably."

At this point Malichus appeared, looking stouter than usual. Hyrcanus stared at him curiously, wondering if his eyes were deceiving him. It did not occur to him that Malichus was wearing a breastplate under his robe. After Herod's arrival was announced, Hyrcanus and Malichus bade the archon farewell, saying they should be back around noon.

As they emerged from the archon's residence, Herod greeted them cordially. Hyrcanus responded with a faint smile, Malichus with marked coolness. Herod pointed out their respective litters and bade them be seated.

Malichus glanced at the litter-bearers and saw that they were unarmed; Herod's escort consisted of two mounted guardsmen. "The royal escort," Malichus reminded Hyrcanus hoarsely, "I want them to accompany us."

"When you are the guests of the governor of Coele-Syria what need have you of the royal escort?" asked Herod calmly. "You can rest assured that my escort is more than adequate."

Hyrcanus and Malichus exchanged glances. "I think we can rely on Herod's protection," said Hyrcanus.

Malichus was seized with doubt – a gray, nagging doubt which heightened his morbid suspicion. He demurred in a grating voice, and it was only with great reluctance that he accepted Hyrcanus's decision. As he stepped into the litter, he fingered the hilt of his sword to make sure it could be quickly unsheathed.

Herod, avoiding the crowded bazaars and main thoroughfares, guided them through the various quarters of Tyre, pointing out the ruins of the ancient city, the palatial homes of the upper-class citizens, and the magnificent public buildings and gardens. The last sight he chose to visit was the harbor. At his suggestion the party stepped out of the litters and continued on foot across the sand toward the ancient mole. As they were nearing it, two men appeared on horseback. They were wearing plain tunics and striped headcovers; from a distance they gave the impression of being Jews or native Syrians, but as they drew closer, Malichus guessed they were Romans. All his senses were alert as he watched them dismount and approach. He instinctively glanced at their weapons: Besides the customary dagger, they each had a long thin sword. If they were Romans – and Malichus was almost certain they were – he wondered why they did not carry the short broadsword used by the Roman army. The two men saluted Herod.

"I beg your pardon for disturbing you, sir," one of them said, "but I have a message to deliver."

"Is it so important that you have to disturb us here?" asked Herod irritably.

"We were ordered to deliver it at once."

"Well, let's have it then."

"It's not for you, sir, but for –" The man glanced at the name written on the rolled scroll. "It's for Malichus."

At the mention of his name, Malichus's eyes narrowed and his mind raced furiously. Who could be sending him a message? Who even knew he was here of all places? "I'm Malichus," he said in a suspicious tone, his hand instinctively reaching for the hilt of his sword.

The courier took a step toward Malichus and handed him a sealed scroll. Malichus glanced at the seal but did not recognize it. At that moment, when his eyes were averted, the two men whipped out daggers and lunged at him. They aimed blows at his breast, but to their astonishment failed to pierce the concealed armor.

At this sight, Hyrcanus shrank back horror-stricken, his voice paralyzed with fear.

Malichus had been momentarily dazed by the dagger blows, but quickly recovered his senses. In a trice he unsheathed his sword.

"What is the meaning of this?" Herod thundered at the two assailants. "By whose orders dare you..."

The two men paid no heed to Herod. They advanced on Malichus from opposite directions, aiming at the lower part of his body. Realizing that he had been lured into a trap, Malichus was determined to make his adversaries pay a dear price. He wielded his sword deftly and pierced their guard with powerful thrusts. But he himself received deep cuts. The blood poured from his wounds, and he began to lose consciousness. Before collapsing he had the grim satisfaction of seeing one of the attackers writhing on the ground, bleeding profusely.

The two men had fallen on Malichus so swiftly that Herod's escort was taken by surprise – or so it seemed to Hyrcanus. By the time they intervened, Malichus was already engaging his foes and had been mortally wounded. Herod ordered one of his men to shield Hyrcanus, but this proved unnecessary, as the surviving assailant was clearly incapable of doing any more harm.

"Disarm him!" Herod shouted.

The second bodyguard seized the sword which hung limply in the wounded man's hand and pinned his arms in a tight vice.

"What is the meaning of this?" Herod barked. "Who are you? Who sent you here? Don't you know this man was my guest?"

The wounded man was breathing heavily, with blood streaming down his face and body. "Cassius," he muttered.

Upon hearing Cassius's name, Hyrcanus's face turned ashen. He glanced at Herod, who seemed to freeze for a moment.

"Cassius?" remarked Herod with an incredulous expression.

"Yes, sir."

Herod fixed the man with a piercing look. "Perhaps you will be good enough to explain yourself."

"Only if you release me."

Herod signaled to his bodyguard to free him. "Now talk!" he commanded.

The disarmed man wiped the blood from his wound on the sleeve of his tunic. His face was convulsed with pain; he spoke in a low, strained voice.

"Cassius had received secret information that Malichus was planning to stir up a revolt in Judea. And so he ordered his execution."

This statement startled Hyrcanus. He knew nothing about any such plot. Could Malichus have planned something like this without his knowledge? It seemed implausible. He did not know what to think. His heart was as heavy as lead. With slow, faltering steps he walked over to Malichus, his eyes wet with tears. Malichus's beard was matted with blood. Hyrcanus stared at him for several minutes; he sighed deeply, a profound, pained sigh.

"This human clay," he uttered in a barely audible voice, "how fragile it is."

Herod approached the prone figure and, bending down on one knee, felt Malichus's pulse. There was no beat. He rose to his feet, his face a somber mask. Turning to Hyrcanus, he said commiseratively: "He was a brave man. I won't pretend we were friends, but I salute his courage." He ordered his men to carry the body to the litter and to treat it with the utmost respect.

As the party made its mournful way over the sand, Herod glanced sideways at the dead man. A grin of keen satisfaction creased his face: He had avenged his father's death at the hands of this despicable creature. When informed of Antipater's sudden death while dining at Hyrcanus's palace, he had been so grief-stricken that he thought he was going out of his mind. After learning the circumstances, he did not have a shadow of doubt that his father had been poisoned by Malichus. He had not been taken in by the condolences of that two-faced, perfidious blackguard. Two years ago, even a year ago, Herod would have immediately sought revenge, but the business with Hezekiah and his father's advice not to act rashly had stayed his hand. More than once he had an overwhelming desire to finish off Malichus, to run him through on the spot. But Phasael had urged him to abide his time and pretend to believe Malichus's protestation of innocence until they could employ a subtle stratagem that would not stir up the population against them. He had suggested informing Cassius of their suspicion. Herod had immediately written him, adding that he had secret information that Malichus was scheming to foment an uprising against the Romans. Cassius's reply had been prompt and forthright: Malichus must be put to death, but not at Laodicea. He did not want his triumphal celebration marred by an execution, as it would undoubtedly upset the client-kings. Not that it would hurt to bring home to them that it was inadvisable to try Rome's patience. Herod had been puzzling how and when to do away with his enemy when he learned that one of ex-magistrate Rufus's slaves had overheard Malichus planning to spirit his son out of Tyre and return to Jerusalem. That settled the matter: Malichus would have to be eliminated without delay.

After Laodicea, Herod had good reason to feel pleased and even lighthearted, for the first time since his father's death. When he had informed Cassius of Malichus's end, the Roman was delighted.

"Excellent!" he exclaimed. "You're to be commended for getting rid of that insolent piece of vermin. A pity that it cost me one of my tribunes and another one got cut up a bit, but it was a small price to pay."

Herod was particularly gratified with his own performance. He had played his role so skillfully as to allay any suspicion on Hyrcanus's part; in fact, he had succeeded in making the latter believe that he had actually protected him against an attack on his life by the two "assailants." Ordinarily Herod would not have cared a whit about Hyrcanus's reaction; his conspiring with Malichus against his father was reason enough to arouse his fierce anger. But Herod was now playing for big stakes, and it was necessary to ingratiate himself with Hyrcanus. For at Laodicea, Cassius had not only reappointed Herod governor of Coele-Syria and given him command of a body of infantry and cavalry as well as a modest fleet, but even more important, he had intimated that he would one day make a fine king of Judea. Herod was not sure what he meant by "one day," and he deemed it unwise to press Cassius on the point; but the very fact that the Roman had mentioned this supreme honor had filled him with unbounded elation. His father had been content to pull strings behind the curtain; that was the most he and his sons could hope for, he had contended. But Herod had different ideas: He had his heart set on reaching the top rung of the ladder, and he was determined not to let the opportunity slip by. There were some problems that had to be dealt with – quite knotty ones, to be sure – but nothing that could not be resolved with clever thinking and the right tactics.

First of all, there was Hyrcanus himself. Besides being high priest, he was king of Judea – or, to be more precise, in Roman parlance, "ethnarch." But he was getting on in years, and one does not live forever. Besides, if Hyrcanus continued to act in defiance of Rome's interests, as he had done at Malichus's urging, Herod had no doubt that he would find himself stripped of his powers and replaced by someone more reliable. True, Rome preferred wherever possible to have a member of the ruling house on the throne, especially if he commanded the loyalty of his subjects – a policy calculated to ensure the least opposition to Rome's grand design. But one could not expect to tweak the Roman eagle's beak and get off scot-free.

There was another consideration Herod had to reckon with. Whatever one thought of Hyrcanus's backbone and his capacity to rule, he possessed one incomparable advantage: He was a Hasmonean. To the people of Judea – or at least the overwhelming majority – the very name of this house still stirred their imagination and loyalty. The Hasmoneans were the legitimate ruling house. Herod did not have to be reminded by Phasael that to the Jews Antipater and his sons were mere Idumeans, "half-Jews," puppets of Rome, unloved commoners. Yes, there were difficulties he could not lightly dismiss or afford to ignore. It would tax his ingenuity to overcome them, but overcome them he would. The goal he had dared to dream about – the goal his father had argued was beyond their grasp – was now less remote. He must not let it elude him. He would have to avoid overplaying his hand; he must proceed prudently and let the pieces fall into place until he emerged triumphant.

Chapter Three
Cassius Exits, Antony Enters, Antigonus Encouraged

An Unwelcome Surprise
at the Royal Palace in Jericho

Malichus's murder plunged Hyrcanus into a deep despondency and left a void in his life. He felt adrift, a rudderless ship in a storm-tossed sea. He brooded on the meaning of life, and his thoughts were somber. Like Job, he wondered why life is given to the bitter in soul. He recalled the apothegm in the *Wisdom of Solomon* which he had always considered unduly pessimistic: "Our life shall pass away as the trace of a cloud and shall be dispersed as a mist that is driven away with the beam of the sun." The author of this work, concerned with the problem of why the wicked appear to prosper and the righteous to suffer, taught that the punishment of the righteous serves to test or educate him; his reward will be granted in the world to come, where he will be vouchsafed eternal life and happiness. Although Hyrcanus subscribed on the whole to Pharisaic views, he found it hard to believe that this world is merely a corridor to the next. But now, in his present mood, this particular passage ran like a refrain through his thoughts.

Hyrcanus's wife and daughter were worried about him. But they were hopeful that with the advent of the High Holidays followed by the week-long celebration of the Sukkot harvest festival, when the Temple would be thronged with pilgrims from all parts of the country and the Diaspora and the city assumed a joyful air, Hyrcanus would snap out of his depression. His spirits did in fact rise as he officiated in the Temple and received dignitaries from Babylonia, Rome, Alexandria, and other Jewish communities abroad. But after the holiday season he again sank into a state of depression.

"Why don't we go to Jericho now?" Alexandra suggested. "It will do all of us good to get away for a while."

Like many high-ranking priestly and other aristocratic families, it was Hyrcanus's custom to spend some time each winter in Jericho, where the sunny sky and balmy air made it an ideal place to escape the severe Jerusalem weather during this period. Even as Alexandra spoke, a freezing rain pelted the windows of the palace and turned the streets into raging streams; the sky was a solid mass of dull gray, unrelieved by a single patch of blue, and the drafts penetrating the spacious rooms of the palace chilled Hyrcanus in spite of his heavy garments and numerous braziers. The icy hand of winter held Jerusalem in its merciless grip, and the very thought of escaping it by a relatively short journey appealed to Hyrcanus. But in another fortnight it would be Chanukah, the Festival of Lights, which commemorates the victorious struggle for national-religious freedom under the leadership of his ancestors. He would not dream of absenting himself from Jerusalem at this time.

"That's an excellent suggestion," he said to his daughter, "but I must be here for Chanukah. After Chanukah we'll go."

In the second week of the month of Tevet the family set out for Jericho. Hyrcanus was glum and withdrawn as they passed through the main gate of the city and ascended the Mount of Olives, which overlooked the Temple and the city, spread out like a sprawling mosaic below. He glanced at the spot where the large bronze altar stood, and observed the smoke curling fitfully upward in the late morning breeze, drifting this way and that – very much like himself, he reflected drearily.

For the first hour or so the countryside was covered with a verdant mantle, thanks to the abundant rainfall. But the further they traveled along the twisting, descending road, the warmer the air became and the sparser the vegetation until the desert took over. Hyrcanus began to feel drowsy; soon his head was lolling on his breast and he started to snore lightly. From time to time his catnap was interrupted by the animated chatter of Mariamne and Aristobulus, who commented excitedly on every passing landmark and the flocks of goats and sheep grazing nearby. The day was drawing to a close when the fortresses of Taurus and Dok hovered into view, and below them the city of Jericho, a veritable emerald in a tawny setting.

When the carriage drew up at the Hasmonean palace, the sun was sinking low on the horizon.

"Look at that gorgeous scenery!" exclaimed Mariamne as the sunset touched the distant Mountains of Moab with velvet and deep purple hues and transformed the Dead Sea into a wine-dark mirror. Hyrcanus never tired of the twilight view of the Jericho panorama, and as he drank it in, his spirits rose, leaving him more cheerful than he had felt in weeks.

The arrival of the royal family created a stir in the city, and the palace immediately became the center of its social and intellectual life. Hyrcanus preferred to spend the early part of the day by himself or in the bosom of his family. He would rise early, and in the cool morning air would ramble about the surrounding countryside or stroll through the palace grounds, where graveled paths wound past flower beds, arbors, fountains, and lily-strewn ponds. After a mid-morning snack he generally relaxed in a comfortable chair on the terrace, where he would study awhile or watch the youngsters enjoying themselves in the royal swimming pool. Swimming pools were a rarity in the country, and Hyrcanus doubted if there were any equal to this one. It was fed by an aqueduct that conveyed abundant water from various springs in the vicinity and Wadi Kelt, and also supplied the Hasmonean palace and neighboring villas with water for drinking and other household uses, as well as for the numerous ritual baths, flower gardens, and palm groves.

When he thought about it, Hyrcanus found the idea of a swimming pool rather incongruous for a person of his station – a deeply religious man who was high priest of the Jewish nation. However, it was not he who had built it, but his father Alexander Yannai, who had acquired some Hellenistic tendencies. Hyrcanus had once discussed the matter with the sage Shemaiah, who said that while in principle he opposed any embracing of Hellenistic ways, since the pool was already in existence he saw no reason why it could not be used by the royal family in the privacy of the palace grounds. To Hyrcanus's grandchildren at least, this was a welcome decision, and the pool became one of the highlights of their annual winter stay in Jericho.

One afternoon, while lounging on the terrace with his wife and daughter, Hyrcanus idly watched Mariamne frolicking in the pool with some of her girlfriends.

"My granddaughter has become quite a beauty," he remarked to Alexandra with a feeling of pride mingled with pensiveness. "She's no longer a young child, to be petted and caressed by a doting grandfather. It won't be long before we have to start considering a suitable match for her."

When Alexandra did not respond, Hyrcanus thought she had not been listening. He was about to repeat his remark when she spoke in a subdued voice: "I hope that whoever her destined spouse is, the Lord will bless her with a peaceful, happy life."

These words brought an anguished look to Hyrcanus's face. The Almighty had not seen fit to bless him with male issue, and his only daughter had endured more than a fair share of suffering. He knew that marriages were arranged for a variety of reasons, with the romantic element playing only a minor part, if even that, especially among royalty and the aristocracy. But he also knew that the marriage partnership usually ripened into a relationship of mutual respect and true love, particularly when the union was blessed with a growing number of offspring. So it had been with Hyrcanus, even though he had only one child. His wife, chosen by Queen Alexandra Salome, had proved to be a loyal, devoted helpmate, a pillar of strength in his most difficult hours. He could have rejected his mother's choice, but he had obediently accepted it and was forever grateful to her.

After this conversation Hyrcanus did not return to the subject of Mariamne. In the warm, sunny climate of Jericho he devoted himself to study and relaxation, in addition to friendly chats with neighbors and guests, shunning as much as he could all thought or discussion of national affairs. He was thoroughly enjoying this respite from his daily concerns. It was therefore with no little annoyance that one day he saw what appeared to be a foreign trooper galloping up the road toward the palace. He sensed that this spelled trouble of some sort and resented the intrusion on his privacy. To his surprise, the rider turned out to be a courier bringing a message from Herod, which stated that he desired to pay his respects and would be pleased to know when it would be convenient to do so. At first Hyrcanus was inclined to reply that he would receive him upon his return to Jerusalem, but realizing that Herod would take umbrage at this, he grudgingly suggested the following Wednesday.

After the courier's departure, Hyrcanus puzzled over the possible reason for this request. He had not seen Herod since Malichus's murder, and as he reread the message, he recalled the distressful events of that day.

"Whatever he wants to see you for, you can be sure he's conniving at something, and it's not to our benefit," Alexandra commented tartly.

Hyrcanus expected his daughter to react negatively, for she had a deep distrust of Herod. When he had related to her what happened on the beach at Tyre and expressed his pleasant surprise at Herod's protective attitude toward him, even shielding him against any possible attack on his body, Alexandra had been highly skeptical. "It's not like Herod," she said contemptuously. "He wouldn't be considerate of you unless he had some ulterior motive. I can't believe that he didn't know Cassius had ordered Malichus's murder."

Herod arrived with his escort around noon of the appointed day. When he stepped out of his carriage, it was obvious that he was in good spirits.

"You are very fortunate to be vacationing in this delightful place," he said after exchanging greetings with Hyrcanus. "It's no wonder you look so fit. After the beastly weather up north, this is paradise."

Herod, who had a strong sense of aesthetics, admired the well-tended grounds, varicolored garden beds, scented shrubs, and climbers gracing the white walls surrounding the palace. "Beautiful!" he exclaimed with a sweeping gesture of his hands. "There are lovely spots in my province, but few that can compare with this. Whoever designed the palace and grounds was a real master."

Hyrcanus, his reserve thawing a bit, led Herod and his escort into the palace and instructed the chamberlain to conduct them to their apartment so they could rest up from the journey and change their garments.

When Herod emerged, he was attired in a splendid robe and his hair and beard were oiled and perfumed; he was the picture of robust health and spirits, radiating an air of courtly self-esteem. He proceeded to distribute gifts to his hosts. Alexandra acknowledged an admirable gold broach in a coolly polite manner, while Mariamne waxed more enthusiastic over a silver filigree bracelet inlaid with onyx stones. Herod was pleased at her response, and his eyes lingered on her longer than what seemed proper to Alexandra.

"I can't tell you how happy I am to see you looking so well," Herod remarked to Hyrcanus after the others withdrew. "When Phasael wrote me that you were in a deeply troubled mood after the – er, unfortunate incident at Tyre, I was greatly concerned. I don't like to reawaken unpleasant memories, but I must confess I had strong pangs of conscience. I felt that to no small degree I was to blame for what happened."

Hyrcanus winced at the recollection of that terrible day. "There is no reason for you to feel guilty," he said in a flat voice. "What happened was not your fault."

"Nevertheless, it was at my suggestion that we were walking along the beach when the horrible encounter took place."

"I doubt that it would have mattered much. If Cassius was bent on dispatching Malichus, he wouldn't have hesitated to do so regardless of the place."

"No, he probably wouldn't have. But since you were my guests – under my wing, so to speak – I was responsible for your safety."

"You did what you could to protect me," said Hyrcanus dryly.

"It was my elementary duty." Herod leaned forward in his chair and rested his hands on his knees. "In protecting you I was doing what my late father would have expected me to do. You and he had long worked together for the good of the country. One can't find many examples of such a praiseworthy relationship between those responsible for guiding the destiny of their nation. I sincerely hope that relations between our two families will continue to be marked by close harmony. It would benefit all concerned – us personally and, above all, the people of Judea."

Hyrcanus's eyebrows lifted sharply and he gave Herod a searching glance. *Does he really think I'm so gullible as to believe he's concerned for my welfare and that of the people of Judea?* he wondered. *Can the past be glossed over as if it had never existed?*

"Do not think me audacious," Herod went on, seeing that Hyrcanus did not respond to his last statement, "but I would like to suggest that if we joined hands, your house and ours, we could raise Judea to new heights. Together we could ensure its safety, its prosperity. It would become one of the most beautiful countries, with splendid cities and ports, magnificent buildings, attractive gardens and colonnades. Judea would become the envy of all the nations."

Hyrcanus perceived that Herod was being swept up in the fervor of his vision; his eyes sparkled with vivid intensity, the words flowed faster and faster. Hyrcanus had never seen him like this before, and he was both puzzled and amazed.

"You paint a glorious picture, but I must admit I don't know what you're driving at," said Hyrcanus in measured tones. "Your words would seem to imply that I am not concerned for Judea's welfare, or at least not sufficiently so."

"Heaven forbid!" Herod shot back. "If you have gained such an impression, then please accept my humble apologies. You have performed, and are continuing to perform, a noble service to the nation. And the people are rightly grateful to you for that. What I'm trying to say is that by joining hands we could do even more; we could achieve unparalleled prosperity, and above all, we could make Judea safe from foreign adversaries."

Hyrcanus knitted his brow and gave Herod a swift, questioning look. "And how do you suggest we join hands? The same way your late father and I did?"

Herod kept his gaze level; his voice took on a graver, more resonant timbre. "I propose that we cement relations between our two houses – between the great and noble house of the Hasmoneans and the house of Antipater, who for three generations now have faithfully served the Jewish nation, beginning with my grandfather Antipas and your father Alexander Yannai. And how better to cement such relations than an alliance of the most enduring kind possible – an alliance based on marriage."

Hyrcanus gaped at Herod. Was he actually proposing marriage? Such an idea was too incredulous for words. His ears must be playing tricks on him.

"I see my proposal has taken you by surprise," remarked Herod with a confident grin. "I thought it might, and I confess that I understand your reaction."

"And whose hand, may I ask, are you asking for?" inquired Hyrcanus in a wary tone. "Alexandra's?"

Herod crossed his legs before replying. "Alexandra possesses sterling qualities, and the most noble of men would deem himself fortunate to win her hand. But it is your granddaughter I have in mind."

"Mariamne!" Hyrcanus felt the blood draining from his face. "She's only a child."

"I hardly think she can be called a child. She is growing into maidenhood and is already of marriageable age. It's true she is young, but the betrothal could take place now and the nuptials at some later date, whenever you deem appropriate."

When Hyrcanus had discussed the subject of Mariamne with Alexandra a few days earlier, he had given a little thought about who might be a suitable match. He had mentally run through the list of aristocratic priestly families who had eligible sons. And now here was Herod with his startling proposal. The idea was so incongruous that it made his head swim.

"I would like to point out that such a union would be in the best interests of your house and the Jewish nation alike," Herod went on. "I need not remind you of the delicate situation in which Judea finds itself. Rome is the dominant world power, and in all due modesty I can claim to enjoy excellent relations with those standing at its helm. An alliance of our two houses would ensure Rome's continued friendly policy toward Judea, with all its attendant benefits."

Hyrcanus regarded Herod thoughtfully. "I'm aware of the fact that Rome is the leading power today," he said slowly. "But looking at the situation from a distance, so to speak, the picture does not seem to be as clear as you make out. Rome has been wracked by civil strife for years. Leaders have come and gone. Even now thunderclouds are gathering on the horizon. Cassius and Brutus are being challenged by Antony and Octavian, and a showdown seems inevitable. Does this indicate strength and stability? Is it on this that you would have me pin Judea's fortunes?"

Herod's brow furrowed. He could not gainsay Hyrcanus's estimate of the situation. This was a challenge to his whole policy, his whole world outlook, the foundation on which he had built his own career and staked his future.

"I don't deny your assessment," he said with a gesture of his hand. "But I must emphasize that while leaders may come and go, Rome itself stands firm like a rock. Unfortunately, it's true that a clash seems to be shaping up, and who will be victorious is anyone's guess. But it is to Rome itself that Judea must look for its future, regardless of who may be at its head at the moment."

Herod paused significantly and folded his arms on his chest. His eyes narrowed, and his voice took on an urgent, ominous ring. "And while we're discussing what seems to be an inevitable clash, I want to remind you that there is someone else who has long had his eyes on the throne of Judea. Cassius's departure from Syria will present him with his long-awaited opportunity."

This possibility had not occurred to Hyrcanus. He knew only too well that Antigonus held him, and especially Herod, in contempt, regarding them as minions of Rome and pursuing a policy that was bound to prove detrimental to Judea. What is more, he knew that Antigonus held him partly responsible for the death of his father and brother. If he should succeed in seizing power – the very thought made Hyrcanus shudder.

"You may not know it," continued Herod, "but Cassius has ordered me to keep an eye on the country while he's away. Should Antigonus decide that the time is ripe to seize control of Judea, it would be my responsibility to repulse him."

An alarmed look swept across Hyrcanus's countenance. The thought of Antigonus trying to usurp the royal and priestly crowns made his blood turn cold. "It's not at all certain that Antigonus is planning such a move," he said hopefully, like a drowning man clutching at a straw.

"I can assure you that that is exactly what he is doing," replied Herod emphatically. "As governor of Coele-Syria, it is my business to uncover and keep an eye on seditious elements. I have excellent sources of information. You can rely on what I tell you."

Hyrcanus was familiar with Herod's suspicious nature and his penchant for establishing an efficient spy system. There was little reason to doubt his warning.

As though reading Hyrcanus's thoughts, Herod continued: "If we are allied, you can rest assured that in me you will have a strong and faithful protector."

"Until now Antigonus has not dared to move. Why would he be likely to do so now?"

"The situation is different now. First of all, Rome has been going through a turbulent stage since Caesar's death. So far Antigonus has not felt strong enough – nor was he – to carry out his designs. But he probably believes the picture has changed so much that his chances of success are good. He is undoubtedly counting on many of his countrymen joining his banner, and you know as well as I that many would do so. Hence my proposal is very much to your advantage."

Hyrcanus reflected on this for a long moment. "What you are proposing is not a military alliance, but an alliance of families. That is an entirely different matter. There are many complicated aspects," he added, pondering how to politely reject Herod's suggestion.

"I'm aware of that," replied Herod calmly. "But there are no hurdles that can't be overcome."

Hyrcanus shifted his gaze to the scene outside the window. "There is, first of all, the elementary fact that you are a married man. It would be unseemly for a Hasmonean princess to marry someone who already has a wife and a son."

Herod showed no embarrassment at this remark. "It is no secret that relations between my wife and me are not what they should be. I don't want to go into details, but I'll merely say that, while my late father had the best of intentions when he arranged the marriage, we are not compatible. It would be better for both of us to part ways amicably. So there would be no problem on that score."

Hyrcanus did not feel like mentioning the other reasons for opposing the match. The thought of a possible attack by Antigonus had thrown him into confusion, and he was anxious to put an end to the matter. "You realize, of course, that your proposal is not one that can be answered immediately."

"I fully realize that. My purpose today was to let you know of the dangers lurking and to point out some of the advantages you would enjoy from linking our two families. When you have given the matter due thought, I'm sure you will appreciate the many benefits of such a union."

Until Herod's visit Hyrcanus was thoroughly enjoying his vacation. He felt relaxed, free of the tension that had plagued him the past few months. He had banished from his mind all problems and worries and was sleeping well. That night, however, he had difficulty falling asleep, and when eventually he did, it was a fitful sleep, disturbed by bad dreams. In one his dead brother Aristobulus pointed an accusing finger at him and demanded to know how he could deign to even consider the proposal of that Idumean upstart, to besmirch the name of the Hasmoneans. "You will bring shame and doom to our people and our house," he warned.

When Hyrcanus awoke he was bathed in a cold sweat. "O Lord," he beseeched in a quiet but fervent voice, "let Your mercy shine on Your faithful servant and help me to do what is best for my people."

When he joined the family at breakfast, he was subdued, his face drawn.

"Are you feeling well, Abba?" asked Alexandra solicitously. "You look tired."

"I didn't sleep well last night. I'm a little off-color, that's all; there's nothing to worry about."

Hyrcanus dreaded the thought of broaching to Alexandra the subject of Herod's visit, and day after day he put it off. It was she who pried it out of him. She could not help noticing the change that had come over him since the visit and concluded that there was a connection between the two. When she first inquired about it, he fobbed her off with some lame remark about its having to do with affairs of state and refused to elaborate. But when she saw him growing increasingly morose and withdrawn, she determined to get to the bottom of the matter.

"What exactly was it you discussed with Herod?" she asked point-blank while sitting on the terrace one afternoon.

Hyrcanus stared at his daughter abstractedly. "I believe I told you," he said in a flat, toneless voice.

"You said something about affairs of state. I'm curious to know what affairs of state. It's obviously weighing on you."

Hyrcanus sucked his underlip thoughtfully. He saw no point in putting the matter off further, painful as it may be. He kept his gaze focused on the distant horizon, where a golden-purple mantle was enveloping the Mountains of Moab.

"Herod claims that Antigonus is planning to seize control of Judea once Cassius leaves Syria," he said, trying to keep his voice as casual as possible.

Alexandra paled noticeably. She knew her brother-in-law's views only too well, and after her visit to him in Chalcis she sensed that he might be contemplating such a move when the opportunity was ripe.

"How reliable is Herod's information?" she asked with palpable concern. Like her father, she knew that Herod's highly suspicious nature impelled him to build up a network of spies to ferret out potential sources of danger and elements hostile to him. She therefore had little reason to doubt that he might have discovered Antigonus's plans. But she also knew that he was not adverse to twisting the facts when it suited his purpose. She did not credit him with being as cunning as his late father, but he was much more ruthless and, she suspected, even more ambitious.

"I've no way of telling how reliable his information is," replied Hyrcanus. "If Malichus were alive, I could probably answer your question. But unfortunately he is no longer at my side," he added with a sigh.

These words made Alexandra wonder. Could it be that her father had been thinking of Malichus since Herod's visit, and this was another reason for his change of mood?

"Did Herod say what he intends to do in such a case?"

"He said it would be his responsibility to oppose any such move on Antigonus's part."

"I can hardly imagine that he would be asking for your assistance, seeing how relations have been between our two families of late."

Hyrcanus's brow furrowed and his eyes took on a veiled, troubled look. "As it so happens, he does want my assistance – or rather, our assistance, to be more exact."

"*Our* assistance?" exclaimed Alexandra with a surprised look. "In what way?"

Hyrcanus was slow in replying. "He didn't say so outright, but I think he might be interested in some sort of cooperation."

Alexandra strongly suspected that her father was evading the question. "Cooperation in what?" she demanded to know.

"He suggested that an – er, alliance between our two houses would be to our mutual benefit."

Alexandra stared at her father with a baffled expression. "What sort of alliance?"

"He proposed marriage with Mariamne," replied Hyrcanus in a low, dispirited tone.

A look of utter incredulity passed over Alexandra's face. "Did you say marriage with Mariamne, our Mariamne?" she stammered.

"Yes. I know you're just as surprised as I was."

"Surprised isn't the word for it! I can't believe it!" Alexandra rose to her feet, agitated and breathing hard. "It's absurd! I've never heard of anything more preposterous in my life. How dare he even mention such a thing?" she exclaimed, the words tumbling out furiously.

Hyrcanus had not expected his daughter to react placidly to this information, but he did not think she would be so upset – more upset than he had ever seen her before. Her eyes were blazing, her chest heaving.

"He claims it would be to our mutual benefit – even to the benefit of the nation," Hyrcanus added in the hope of calming her a bit.

"How considerate of him!" she spat out scornfully. "And since when has he ever been concerned for the good of the Hasmoneans or the Jewish people? Herod has always been and always will be concerned with one thing only – his own good." Alexandra thrust a finger at her father. "He, an Idumean, a pagan at heart – he married to my daughter, to a Hasmonean! I've never heard anything more shocking in my life. I hope you made it quite plain to him that the answer is an unequivocal no."

Hyrcanus lowered his eyes. He gazed at his folded hands with an expression that betrayed his uneasiness. He moistened his lips "I didn't give him an unequivocal yes or no. He left with the impression that I would give the matter some consideration."

"What is there to consider?" asked Alexandra, her voice rising in pitch. "On no account will I ever agree to such a monstrous proposal. It was our family that liberated the country from the pagan yoke. We have served the nation as high priests and kings. We restored its sovereignty, renewed its spirit; we are the pride and hope of our people. Yes, we, the Hasmonean house. And you are willing to taint our name, to debase yourself and me – and the Jewish people too – by considering a marriage with that Idumean? How could you? It's madness, sheer madness, to even think of such a thing! On no account will I agree! The very thought of it fills me with loathing."

Hyrcanus bore this searing reproach quietly, letting Alexandra unburden herself. When she finally paused, he said in a soft, fatherly voice: "I didn't expect you to like the idea any more than I did when I first heard it. I was tempted to say to Herod some of the things you have just now said, and even more. There are other reasons for opposing such a union, not just personal or family reasons. Do you think I ever dreamt of Mariamne marrying someone like Herod?"

"Then why are you ready to consider it now?" asked Alexandra fiercely.

"Because it may be the lesser of two evils."

Alexandra gaped at her father. "*Two* evils? I'm afraid I don't understand. I can see only one evil – a terrible evil."

Hyrcanus shook his head slowly. "In your agitation you have forgotten what I mentioned at the beginning of our talk. You speak of the Hasmonean house. But don't forget that you, your children, and myself, we are not the only Hasmoneans. There's your cousin and brother-in-law. Antigonus is dying to be king of Judea. He'd give and do anything to become king."

Hyrcanus paused briefly and then continued: "The matter is not as simple as you think. I'd be only too happy if it were. I've had time to reflect on it, which you haven't been able to do yet. Suppose Antigonus gains control of Judea. Do you realize what the consequences would be? Rome would oppose the usurpation of the throne with the utmost ruthlessness. There would be a heavy price to pay."

"That's a moot point," retorted Alexandra. "Antigonus, his father, and his brother engaged the Romans more than once."

"And they didn't pay a dear price? Also, don't forget that the uprisings were not successful; they were stamped out at an early stage. Let Antigonus seize the throne, and you'll see what the Romans are capable of doing. Then you'll find out how..."

At this point Hyrcanus was interrupted by the appearance of Mariamne, Aristobulus, and two of their friends.

"Imma [mother], we were looking all over for you," declared Mariamne in mock reproach. "We're starving, all of us; aren't we, Aristobulus?"

"That's right, Imma. My stomach is growling like mad."

Alexandra shook her head with an amused look. "I doubt that you're starving, any of you. You had lunch not so long ago."

Mariamne ran over to Hyrcanus and threw her arms around his neck. "Grandpa, you tell her," she pleaded in her most winning voice; "we really are famished."

Hyrcanus assumed a severe look. "Now, children, you don't give the impression that you're perishing of hunger. I think you just like to stuff your bellies, that's all. What do you think, Alexandra, should we try to appease their ravenous appetites?"

Alexandra grinned. "All right, go to the kitchen, dears, and tell the cook I said to give you something light."

"Thank you, Imma," exclaimed Mariamne gleefully. "And you too, Grandpa," she added, planting a moist kiss on Hyrcanus's cheek.

The foursome dashed off in the direction of the kitchen, their joyful laughter ringing all the way.

"Ah," sighed Hyrcanus, shaking his head, "their greatest concern is their growling stomachs. May they have no bigger problems in life."

"Amen!" agreed Alexandra. "Youth is wonderful; everything is bright and cheerful then. It's amazing how quickly youngsters get over the tragedies of life."

"We could do with some of their resilience," said Hyrcanus, picking a fig from the bowl on the small marble table beside his chair. He felt a lump rising in his throat. "Mariamne, my little Mariamne – so sweet and innocent. If she knew what we were discussing, she'd be at a loss to understand us. 'Marriage? Not for me,' she'd say. 'I'm much too young, and besides, I haven't time for such nonsense; there are more interesting and pleasant things to do.' And she would be right – there are more pleasant things than bothering her young head with talk of marriage."

"Especially to one like – like him."

"I know," commiserated Hyrcanus. After the diversion with the youngsters he was reluctant to return to the subject they had been discussing. But reluctant or not, he could not leave the matter hanging in the air. "Herod, Antigonus, the Romans," he muttered more to himself. "Sometimes I feel I'd like to trade places with any ordinary citizen. Not to have to wrestle with momentous questions of state, not to ponder whether one's young granddaughter should be given in marriage to someone who is obviously unsuited..."

"Then why do it? Tell him no and be done with it."

"If only it were that simple. It's not only the problem of the Romans, there's also Antigonus to reckon with."

"It's not at all certain that he'll try to seize power. You only have Herod's word for it, and I have no faith in the word of a vindictive schemer."

In Alexandra's voice there was a note of uncertainty, for the visit to her brother-in-law the previous autumn had left her with an uneasy feeling regarding his future intentions.

"I hope you're right," said Hyrcanus with a serious mien. "But suppose you're not, do you realize what Antigonus might do?"

"I don't imagine anything drastic would happen to us."

"Can you be sure of that? Don't forget, Antigonus has lost his father and his brother. That has been eating him like a canker. He holds me at least partly responsible for their deaths. Isn't it conceivable that he would want to avenge their deaths? But it's not only myself I have to worry about."

Alexandra gave her father a startled look. "What do you mean?" she asked in a low, quavering voice.

"Antigonus wants the throne and high priesthood. I have no doubt about that. But your children – my grandchildren – are my heirs apparent; they represent an obstacle in his way. Need I remind you what has happened in similar circumstances in other countries?"

Alexandra tried to keep a calm appearance, but her father's words upset her more than she cared to admit. "You're referring to gentile kings and princes. Antigonus is a Jew, a Hasmonean. To even think he'd do something so barbarous is unrealistic."

Hyrcanus drew a deep breath. "I sincerely hope you're right. But don't forget, you and your children are all the family your mother and I have. How can I expose you to such a risk?"

Alexandra had to concede the validity of her father's concern, but she could not accept his proposed solution. "Even if what you say should, heaven forbid, come to pass, how can we pay such a price? How can we sacrifice Mariamne's happiness, not to mention everything the Hasmonean house has stood for? How can you expect me to accept Herod as a son-in-law? The very thought turns my stomach. And you know only too well how the people feel about him. Even if he should be married to a Hasmonean, that wouldn't change their feelings toward him. If anything, it would make them more bitter, because if, heaven forbid, anything should happen to Aristobulus, Herod might conceivably become king. Think of it – Herod, a pagan Idumean, he king of the Jews! It's too dreadful to contemplate!"

Alexandra was so wrought up that her whole body shook. Hyrcanus had never before seen her so distraught. His heart ached for her, but what could he say to comfort her? "Let us hope that the Almighty will spare Aristobulus until he's 120 and enable him to serve our people with love and devotion," he declared fervently. "But even if things work out differently and Herod becomes king, the queen would be a Hasmonean; the princes and princesses they would beget would have Hasmonean blood. The Hasmonean house would not die out; it would continue to be the pride of the nation."

At the thought of a possible unhappy fate befalling Aristobulus, a terrible pallor spread across Alexandra's face. She found it hard to regain her composure, and harder still to follow her father's reasoning. "That is very little comfort to me or our people," she said gloomily. "They'd want a Hasmonean on the throne without the Idumean."

"They undoubtedly would. But what are the chances of that happening? One possibility, of course, is that Antigonus succeeds in usurping the throne. Apart from the danger this would pose to us personally, it would convulse the nation. Maybe it wouldn't lead to civil strife, as happened in my younger days – I certainly hope not. But the Romans wouldn't sit back with folded arms and let it happen. Under their imperial policy they would never let Judea slip out of their grasp. One way or another they'd drive Antigonus off the throne, and in his place they'd appoint a king loyal to their cause – someone with or without a Hasmonean wife. Don't think I relish the idea of giving Mariamne to Herod. In pondering the matter the past few days I've had no peace of mind. I have had to ask myself, in view of all the circumstances, what should I do? Perhaps you can tell me."

Alexandra was silent for a long moment. She felt small and wretched; as though contending with forces beyond her control. Her mind was in a turmoil. "I don't know what to tell you," she said at last with a helpless look. "If things turn out as you describe and our only hope is to let Mariamne marry Herod, then I'm afraid our fate is sealed. I cannot help feeling that we would be bringing disaster on ourselves, our house, our people. As long as Antigonus does not make any move against you, I cannot consent to giving my daughter to that miserable Idumean. I hope and pray that my brother-in-law will know how to restrain himself."

Antigonus Tries to Reach Jerusalem

News of Cassius's departure from Syria to join Brutus in giving battle to Antony and Octavian spread like wildfire through Rome's eastern provinces. The atmosphere was charged with expectation and tension, for another dramatic showdown was shaping up such as had repeatedly rocked the Roman Empire during the past century, and on whose outcome hung the fate of the various states in this region.

No one was more pleased to see the Roman governor leave Syria than Antigonus. From his residence in Chalcis he had been able to follow developments in Cassius's province, and as they marched toward their denouement, he hastened to complete the preparations that had long been afoot. Ever since coming to this picturesque town, his home had served as a headquarters from which he maintained contact with his lieutenants and agents, and now it was a veritable beehive of activity. With the help and encouragement of the prince of Chalcis, who had given him asylum, he had recruited a modest force of mercenaries, but it was not on them that he was pinning his hopes. Once he crossed the border, he was counting on the Galileans to flock to his banner. They had always been the most implacable opponents of the Romans and the principal reservoir of manpower in the struggle against them.

"We'll harass the Roman garrisons in Galilee," he explained to his chief lieutenant, Joab, a strapping, taciturn native of one of the northern Galilean villages, who seemed somewhat ill at ease in Antigonus's handsomely furnished study. "We'll cause them as much mischief as we can, but our main objective is to rally the Galileans to our standard and then head for Jerusalem as quickly as possible, swelling our ranks as we advance."

"And Phasael?" asked Joab, raising his bushy black eyebrows. "He has a large number of foreign troops at his disposal, including some Romans."

"We'll have a larger force of Jews," replied Antigonus with a confident grin. "And they'll be only too eager to drive those pagans out of the Holy City."

"What about Hyrcanus?"

Antigonus shrugged his shoulders. "He's so accustomed to the company of Romans that he'll undoubtedly prefer to join them. I assure you that I'll put no obstacles in his way."

"It sounds too smooth and easy," said Joab, tugging at his shaggy beard with gnarled fingers. "There's one problem we haven't given proper thought to – the most crucial problem of all."

"Herod?"

"Yes, Herod. He's not going to be twiddling his thumbs in Coele-Syria while all this excitement is going on."

"I don't expect him to. That's why we have to move fast. We must get to Judea before him. Once we're there, our fellow Judeans will join our ranks, and then Herod won't stand a chance."

Joab gave no indication that he shared Antigonus's optimistic assessment. He was a tough, seasoned fighter, but experience had taught him that plans that appear foolproof often miscarry, especially when they have to do with the Romans. He was not disposed to speculate about the future, but like Antigonus, he was eager to seize what looked like a golden opportunity to rid the country of the Romans and their Idumean lackeys. At the same time, he had no desire to shed the blood of his countrymen in vain. He wanted to know what would happen if, God forbid, Brutus and Cassius should defeat Antony and Octavian.

"It wouldn't be good either for our people or for us personally," acknowledged Antigonus with a grimace. "But I'd say the odds are against Cassius; and I'm not basing that on the entrails of any animal or any other augury, but on plain common sense, from knowledge of what's going on in Rome."

Antigonus clapped Joab by the shoulder, and added in a gently chiding tone: "You're a follower of the Pharisees; where is your faith in divine providence? Pray that our good friend Cassius does not gain the upper hand, that he'll lose his scurvy head, and not just figuratively."

"Will Antony and Octavian be any better? They're also dyed-in-the-wool imperialists. I don't trust any of them."

"I wouldn't put my trust in any Roman. But for all that, some of them are not as bad as others. Don't forget that Antony and Octavian are Caesar's men, that Octavian was even his nephew and adopted son. Most of our people think that Caesar wasn't too bad as far as the Jews were concerned."

"Maybe not, but I didn't see that he appointed you king – or ethnarch – of Judea. He preferred your uncle and Antipater."

Antigonus was stung by this unpleasant reminder. "Your memory is pretty sharp, isn't it?" he said in a tone laced with sarcasm and injured pride. "For your enlightenment, if Caesar preferred my uncle, it was because he was a pragmatist. When he saw that Hyrcanus and his Idumean puppeteer were too firmly entrenched, he took the easiest course. Sentiment was not one of Caesar's abiding qualities, and Antony and Octavian will follow his example. Except that this time it will be clear to our erstwhile Roman friends that it is Antigonus who commands the loyalty of the Jewish people and should therefore replace his superannuated uncle."

If Joab was impressed by this explanation, he betrayed no sign of it. "And you're willing to be a client-king of the Romans?"

133

Antigonus gave his lieutenant a long, hard stare. Was Joab needling him, or was he serious? "That's a prickly question you ask," he said somewhat tartly. "So you think I want to step into Hyrcanus's shoes, do you?"

"Not at all," protested Joab, realizing he had touched on a very sore point. "I meant no offense. Forget the question."

"No, that's quite all right," retorted Antigonus, recovering his aplomb. "You've asked a legitimate question and you're entitled to a legitimate answer. First of all, do I regard all Romans as our enemies? No, I wouldn't say that accurately describes my feelings. I regard Rome, the empire that spreads its tentacles everywhere and crushes its victims, as the enemy of Judea. And those who rule it – vultures like Cassius, for example – they are our enemies, they are the ones I loath," added Antigonus, flinging out his arm to emphasize the point.

"And you think Antony and Octavian will be different?" asked Joab, still unconvinced.

"At least I hope so; but of course one can't be sure. If my assessment is correct, we'll manage fine; if not – well, let's wait and see what the future will bring. But one thing I want to stress – and don't let there be any doubt about it – I have no intention whatsoever of being what you call a client-king. I will be a sovereign king, acting for the good of our people. As long as that coincides with Rome's policy, we'll get along. But if Antony or Octavian treats us like a conquered province, to be milked and enslaved, then there will be trouble ahead."

* * *

It was soon evident that Antigonus had not miscalculated the response of the Galileans. As soon as he crossed the border, they began to flock to his banner, and within a few days they outnumbered the mercenaries. Antigonus knew that ideally he should spend several weeks whipping his force into shape, but since it was essential to reach Judea and Jerusalem before Herod could intercept it, he had to reluctantly forgo this. The Galileans were a rugged lot, making up in courage and ardor what they lacked in the art of warfare. As guerrilla fighters they were unsurpassed, but in a pitched battle would they prove a match for a trained, disciplined force? Antigonus and Joab decided that their best chance of success lay in speed and surprise.

But they reckoned without Herod. He was in Damascus when he learned about Antigonus's arrival in Galilee. Nothing could have pleased him more. He saw to it that Hyrcanus was apprised of Antigonus's intentions, and his heart warmed when his courier described Hyrcanus's consternation. Herod almost felt a fond affection for Antigonus, for he was playing right into his hands.

Not one to let the grass grow under his feet, he set out to give battle. His aim was to intercept Antigonus before he reached Judea, where the ferment of revolt was giving Phasael considerable cause for concern. Herod was buoyed at the prospect of coming to grips with his foe, to inflict a crushing defeat on him and hopefully to eliminate him completely. Even more, he was galvanized to the point of exultation by the thought of the prize that awaited him – the affiancing of the young, beautiful Hasmonean princess, which meant a long step toward the throne of Judea. He did not doubt that Hyrcanus's fear of his nephew would outweigh any misgiving he might have at accepting the proposal Herod had broached during his visit to Jericho.

The elimination of Antigonus would mean one less Hasmonean claimant to the throne. Herod was confident of the outcome, but he was not going to take any chances. His army was superior in training, discipline, and generalship, but it would not be fighting for a cause that inspired it. Antigonus's men, on the other hand, were fired with a fierce determination and zeal that would largely compensate for their shortcomings. Herod therefore decided to field a force outnumbering anything Antigonus could possibly muster, and put his ablest officers in command.

On the second day of the march Herod's scouts reported the location and size of the foe. Herod convened his officers to decide on the most strategic place to engage the enemy and the tactics to employ. All signs indicated that Antigonus was taking the mountain road leading to Jerusalem, which afforded him a commanding view of the surrounding area and the best position for warding off an attack. Various ways were considered how to lure him into a comparatively flat, open space where Herod's force could exploit its advantage to the full, but it was conceded that Antigonus would hardly be likely to fall into such an obvious trap. In this case there would be no choice but to overwhelm him with their far larger numbers.

The battle took place on rugged terrain not far from the Judean border. Seeing how greatly outnumbered they were, Antigonus and Joab skillfully deployed their men to take advantage of every natural defensive feature. The odds were against them, but Antigonus was determined to put up a stout resistance in the hope of somehow affecting a breakthrough and putting Herod's men to rout. By late afternoon many of Herod's soldiers had fallen, yet his ranks remained intact. Joab reported that their own troops were weary and stood little chance of gaining the victory. He advised withdrawal under cover of darkness, and Antigonus regretfully agreed. Assembling his men in a stony field after nightfall had halted the fighting, he addressed them in a voice that betrayed no despair:

"You put up a good fight, and I'm proud of you. You fought like true Galileans, and gave an excellent account of yourselves, just as you did in years past. We did not win the battle, neither did we lose it. The enemy far outnumbered us but did not outfight us. I don't want to shed any of your blood needlessly, so we are going to break off contact with the foe. We are by no means abandoning the struggle. Our aim remains unchanged – to clear our country of the oppressive conqueror from without and the traitorous elements from within. We will abide our time until a more favorable opportunity arises. Events are moving fast in this part of the world, and the day is not far off when we will again be able to take the field, but with the odds more in our favor, and finish the job."

Avner Sold into Slavery with Other Emmaus Men

The day Avner was seized by the Romans and marched away to be sold into slavery was the blackest day in his life. But as he turned his head to catch one last glimpse of Emmaus before it disappeared from sight, he swore that he would let nothing break his spirit or humble his self-respect. His mother wept bitterly as he was bundled off with all the other able-bodied men the Romans could lay their hands on. Zechariah put a comforting hand on her shoulder and told her not to worry, for the Lord would look after their son and everything would turn out for the best. But she refused to be consoled and continued to weep.

That day was even worse than the one when he was put on the block in the slave market of Tyre along with some of his fellow townsmen. He was forced to stand stark naked for examination by prospective buyers, among them smartly dressed women. He felt like a plucked chicken dangling in the marketplace. But he bore the ordeal stoically, resolved that no matter what happened, no one was going to deprive him of his spiritual independence, to force a slave mentality on him.

He was sold to a wealthy Greek who possessed a large estate outside Tyre. He came to the slave market together with his steward, and Avner watched sullenly as they examined several males of diverse races and physiques. When the dealer ordered him to mount the platform and strip, Avner did so with a feeling of utter revulsion. The Greek seemed to be impressed with him, for he turned to his steward and conferred with him. Although Avner had picked up a smattering of Greek from his contact with pagans and could manage a simple conversation, he was unable to follow their rapid exchange. But he guessed from their gestures and the few words he grasped that he appeared to be a suitable candidate for their stable of slaves. He was then subjected to a thorough examination by the steward to see if he was as healthy and strong as the dealer claimed. Avner could not help thinking that it was the kind of examination one would make if he were contemplating the purchase of a horse or cow or some other animal for the farm. "If they think I'm just an animal or treat me like one, they'll soon find out differently," he said to himself between clenched teeth.

The Greek listened attentively to the steward's evaluation, and then there followed another exchange of comments – a rather lengthy one it seemed to Avner. He was wondering what defects they had discovered, when the Greek nodded and, turning to Avner, asked him in an easy Koine what his name was. Avner, who knew enough of this Greek dialect spoken in the eastern Mediterranean lands to understand the question, told his name in a defiant tone. The Greek was not the least perturbed by this.

"Ah, good!" he exclaimed in a somewhat nasal voice. "So you understand Greek. Can you speak it too?"

"A little," replied Avner dryly.

"To obey orders it's enough to understand some Koine. And if you can speak it, so much the better." He turned to the steward. "I think he'll do."

The steward had been scrutinizing Avner very closely and had observed the defiant look on his face, the smoldering fire in his eyes. He took his master aside and spoke to him in a low, inaudible voice.

"And did you expect him to enjoy being sold as a slave?" remarked the Greek with a grin. "As long as he does what he's told, I'll be satisfied. It's up to you to see that he obeys orders."

The Greek began to haggle with the dealer over the price. Avner took advantage of this to size him up. He was a middle-aged man with a short, squat frame, a round, clean-shaven face with shrewd black eyes peering from under bushy brows, a straight nose over thick lips, and deep lines creasing the corners of a sensual mouth. He was wearing a blue cloak of expensive stuff, and his stubby fingers sported costly rings set with rubies and other gems. He gave the impression of being a man of substance who freely indulged his taste for the pleasures of life. He did not appear to be cruel or sadistic, for which Avner was thankful.

The steward seemed to be made of sterner stuff. He had a brawny physique and a hard countenance with cold gray eyes. He would present a problem, Avner thought as the Greek concluded the negotiations and told the steward to pay the dealer.

Avner's impression of the steward proved to be correct. He tolerated no nonsense, and the slightest breach of discipline or sign of disobedience earned the guilty person severe punishment. Avner, aware that the steward was keeping a close eye on him, managed to avoid incurring his anger, but he winced every time he witnessed one of the slaves being flogged. There were more than fifty male slaves, the majority of whom worked in the fields or orchards. Avner preferred such tasks to the others, for he enjoyed working outdoors: It kept him in good physical condition, and he was able to smuggle some fruit and vegetables to his quarters, thereby supplementing his meager fare and avoiding forbidden foods.

There were, of course, female slaves too – most of them young and robust, with well-developed bodies, but also some who were older and fading in strength and appearance, who had been purchased many years ago and were now assigned to lighter tasks. The female slaves were a motley lot: Some had a fair complexion and flaxen hair, others an olive complexion and dark hair, while a few were dark-skinned. They were housed in separate quarters from the male slaves, but it was virtually impossible to keep the sexes apart; in fact, Avner did not see that any great effort was made to do so, nor did this seem to cause much concern. At first he was shocked at the sexual license allowed. When he spoke about this to a fellow slave, the man regarded Avner with an incredulous expression. "Are you serious, man? We may be slaves but we're not eunuchs. And do you think the females spend their time only in household chores? One of their duties – in fact, I'd say probably the main one – is to satisfy the desire of the master and his guests. And do you know what? They enjoy it and can't wait to do the master's bidding. Don't be crazy, man; if you get a chance with one of them, don't pass it up."

That evening Avner discussed the matter with his fellow townsman who had been sold together with him. Reuven, who was the older of the two and more worldly-wise, explained that this was not Emmaus, and other than themselves, the slaves were not Jews. This was their way of life, and they saw nothing wrong with it. Moreover, it was their only source of pleasure and relief from the drudgery of their existence.

"But the way they go about it," remarked Avner with a grimace, "it reminds me of the animals on our farm."

"That's about what most slaves are reduced to in the pagan world – animals."

As the days stretched into weeks and the weeks into months, Avner became increasingly restless. At night, as he lay on his pallet, he gloomily contemplated the bleak, endless road ahead of him. Momentous events were happening in Judea, and perhaps even more portentous ones were looming ahead, and here he was, a slave on the estate of a pagan Syrian-Greek. He must escape this intolerable bondage. But how? As he considered the various possibilities, he realized it would not be a simple matter. Even if he succeeded in fleeing the estate, how would he find his way through this strange land? Where could he take shelter at night from the cold and the rains that were likely to pelt him at this time of the year? The possibility that he might not succeed and would be punished did not trouble him very much; it was a risk worth taking.

Avner kept his thoughts to himself, but was wondering whether to confide in Reuven. He would prefer to have a companion in his attempt, but if his townsman refused to join him, what then? Once Avner's absence was detected, Reuven would certainly be interrogated and probably tortured. Dare he expose his friend to this danger? The question was settled by Reuven himself.

One night, as they were reminiscing about their families, Reuven said wistfully, "And to think, I have relatives living not very far from here – in Antioch. I visited them last year. What I wouldn't give to be with them now."

At this revelation Avner's eyes lit up. "Why didn't you ever mention that you have relatives in Antioch?"

Reuven shrugged his shoulders. "What difference would it make? Do you suggest we pay them a social visit?"

"Not a social visit," said Avner, ignoring his friend's irony, "but we could drop in on them."

Reuven threw Avner a puzzled look. "A great idea!" he said, trying to keep his voice down. "And I think we ought to invite Greekie too. I know my relatives would be highly honored to play host to such an illustrious citizen of Tyre. And I'm sure he'd also be delighted. Perhaps he would even let us accompany him in his gilded carriage."

Avner could understand his friend's mystification. "I want to get away from here," he confided with a serious expression. "I want to get out of this prison. If we could reach your relatives, we could get a change of clothing and some food to take with us. We could also –"

"And if Greekie should find out," Reuven interjected, "do you realize what danger we'd be exposing my relatives to? It's enough that I have to suffer; I can't compromise my relatives as well. When our absence is discovered, Greekie is bound to search for us in the Jewish quarter of the city."

Avner reflected for a moment; he had to acknowledge that Reuven's apprehension was justified. "Would you be willing to try and escape without involving your relatives?"

Reuven stared at Avner for a minute or two and then lowered his gaze. He sucked his lips as he weighed the pros and cons He was pining to see his wife and children and the rest of the family; there was not a single night when he did not feel acutely homesick. But he knew what fate awaited slaves who were caught trying to escape. "I don't know," he replied at last. "I don't see how we can pull it off. I don't want to stay here any more than you do, but if we're caught, we'll pay dearly."

"And if we're not caught, we're free men again. It's worth taking the chance."

Reuven remained skeptical, and Avner saw that he would not be able to budge him. Reluctantly, he decided he would have to risk going alone – a prospect he did not relish but which he preferred to his present lot.

In the following days, Avner planned his escape He studied the grounds carefully to determine where he had the best chance of climbing the high stone wall undetected. He decided that the most promising spot was the grove of cypress bordering the wall at a point furthest from the villa and other structures, and which was not guarded very closely. As regards the timing, he debated whether it was preferable immediately after the evening meal, when his absence would probably not be noticed for several hours, or before dawn, when he was fresh. The second alternative was riskier, as he would not be able to proceed very far before his escape was discovered, and daylight would make it much easier to pursue him. On the other hand, he would be sufficiently rested for the ordeal that lay ahead, and not exhausted from the day's toil. It would be advisable to wear different garments so as not to attract attention, and to take some food with him. Once he put some distance between himself and his pursuers, he would have to scrounge for food in the fields, but that should present no problem.

He waited until the last night to tell Reuven of his plan. "And if you oversleep?" asked Reuven.

"Don't worry; if I have to get up early I'll do it."

At the thought of Avner's departure, Reuven's spirits fell. He would pray, of course, for his successful escape, but knew that he would be very lonely without him. Avner, reading his thoughts, put an arm around his shoulder, and for a while they sat quietly, not saying a word.

"If, with the Lord's help, I manage to escape and get back to Emmaus," said Avner at last, "is there anything you want me to tell your family?"

Reuven shook his head slowly, and replied in a low, faltering voice: "Just tell them that they're always in my thoughts, and I hope and pray to be with them again in the near future. Apart from that, I am, thank God, in good health."

"I'll tell them that," Avner solemnly promised. "And now we had better get some sleep. There's no point in disturbing you in the morning, so perhaps we had better say *shalom* (farewell) now."

"No," protested Reuven. "You must wake me before you leave. Promise me that."

"All right."

It took Avner a long time to fall asleep. He tried to relax, but a thousand thoughts raced through his mind. He was resigned to a sleepless night, but eventually succumbed to the exhaustion of the day's work. His sleep was fitful, punctuated by bad dreams – something that seldom happened to him. In one dream he was fleeing from an enraged mob armed with scythes and pitchforks. When he was about to fall into their clutches he awoke, his body drenched with sweat. He heaved a sigh and turned over to glance through the window at the far end of the room. It was still dark outside. He had no idea how long he had slept, but he dared not let himself doze off again. There was nothing to do but wait for the first sign of dawn, when he would be able to see his way. His thoughts drifted to Emmaus – to his parents and siblings, his friends, and the familiar surroundings. He uttered a silent prayer that he soon return to the bosom of his family.

After what seemed an interminable interval, the dark mantle of night began to lift. Avner silently rose from his pallet and, after pouring some water over his fingers, he donned a warm undergarment under his tunic. He glanced at Reuven, and from his light, even snoring he knew he was sound asleep. He thought it a pity to awaken him, but he had promised to do so. He tiptoed to his pallet and tapped him on the shoulder. Reuven awoke with a start. Avner signaled to him not utter a sound lest they be heard by others in the room. Reuven threw off his coarse woolen blanket and sat upright.

"Is there anything I can do to help you?" he whispered.

"No, thanks. I got everything ready last night. I'll put my sandals on outside."

Reuven got out of bed and embraced Avner. "Good luck and God be with you," he said with a pensive expression.

"With the Lord's help we'll both be free soon," replied Avner. "Don't lose hope."

In the pre-dawn grayness Avner could hardly see the path leading to the grove of cypress, but he was sufficiently familiar with the grounds to find his way. He walked as quickly and quietly as he could and soon reached the trees. They were not unusually tall, but in the murky light they seemed to tower aloft like a phalanx of giant sentinels. He made his way to the place where the wall dipped slightly and seemed to offer a better footing.

In trying to figure out how to get over the wall, he had hit on the idea of using a grappling hook and managed to improvise one. He flung it to the top of the wall, and on the third attempt it held fast. He began to climb the wall, taking pains not to disturb any of the stones. His heart missed a beat when one of them began to give way, but he was able to keep it from slipping loose. When he reached the top of the wall, he breathed a sigh of relief, for the worst was over, but he still had to be very careful in making the descent. He saw a spot where the ground was covered with a thick layer of leaves and other foliage, which would cushion his drop. Avner crawled along the top of the wall until he reached a point directly over this spot He affixed the hook to the upper stone and started to lower his body. Because the stone was covered with lichen, he did not notice that it was not firmly fixed in place. It gave way under his weight, hurtling him to the ground below. He had enough presence of mind to try to land on both feet, but as he was off balance, he came crashing down on his right foot, turning his ankle with a sharp stab of pain.

"Damn it!" he swore softly, realizing he had sprained his ankle.

The noise of the fall aroused the dogs. Within a few seconds he could hear their barking getting closer. He pulled himself up to his feet, but could hardly hobble along. Any thought of escape was now out of the question. His one hope was to get back to his quarters before the guards found him. He knew the odds were against him, for the terrain around the wall was fairly rough, and his progress was distressingly slow. He saw two guards advancing upon him; he sighed in frustration.

"Trying to run away, are you, you bastard!" one of the guards shouted gruffly, bearing down on Avner. He and his burly partner pinned Avner's arms. "You'll soon get your come-uppance," he added with a fierce scowl.

Avner resigned himself to an unpleasant aftermath. It took him some time to cover the relatively short distance to the villa. From time to time the guards ordered him to snap it up and gave him a push. The excruciating pain made him wince, much to the amusement of his captors, who assured him that his present suffering was nothing compared to what awaited him. When they reached the villa, one of the guards went inside, and after a minute or two emerged with the steward.

"So!" roared the steward, towering over Avner menacingly, "you tried to escape did you? When a slave does that he's stealing our property. You'll pay dearly for that!"

The steward, who from the start had questioned the wisdom of purchasing Avner, felt a strong urge to vent his wrath on him physically. He ordered the guards to lock him up without food or water. Toward evening, after the work in the fields was finished, Avner was fettered and led to an open area behind the villa. There he found all the slaves standing in a wide circle in order to witness his punishment. When the steward ordered him to the center of the circle Avner felt like a dog that had been chastened by its owner. After a few minutes the master emerged from the villa and approached Avner. He folded his arms on his chest and contemplated the bound slave with a scornful grin.

"Did you find our hospitality so lacking that you decided to desert us?" he asked in a mocking voice. "You cost me quite a few drachmas, and I hate to see my money wasted. You can thank your lucky stars that you've been a good worker, but you'll have to learn that you're only part of my investment – a very small part at that; and I have to protect the rest of it. I trust that you, and the other slaves too will realize that it doesn't pay to trifle with my generosity and good nature." He turned to the steward. "All right, Demetrius, you know what to do."

"How many stripes, sir?" asked the steward.

"I'll tell you when to stop."

The steward nodded to the guards, one of whom was gripping a long snake-like whip. The other guard unbound Avner's arms and removed his tunic, leaving his body uncovered except for a loin cloth. He then retied his arms.

Avner gritted his teeth and awaited the blows. He knew the flogging would be painful, but was determined not to utter a sound; he would show them the stuff he was made of. Looking up, he caught sight of the master's wife watching the scene from a vantage point near the villa. She seemed to be taking great interest in the spectacle, as though she enjoyed the sight of corporal punishment.

"Have a good look at my body, lady, if it pleases you, for it will soon be less attractive," he muttered.

The steward nodded to the guard wielding the whip. He swung it back and then snapped it forward with a sharp cracking sound. Avner's skin quivered under the blow, and he winced with intense pain. This was worse than he had imagined. At first he counted the blows, but then he began to grow faint. His back was oozing blood and each blow lacerated it a little more. He had never before experienced such excruciating pain; his head was reeling and he knew he would soon lose consciousness. His legs sagged and the scene before him became darker and increasingly blurred. The next thing he knew he was lying on his pallet. His body was one mass of ugly, painful welts, but clean of blood and glistening with an unguent. He groaned and slowly opened his eyes. He saw Reuven sitting at his side, regarding him with anxious eyes.

"So much for your escape," he commiserated.

"Yes," agreed Avner weakly. "At least for the time being."

"Forget the 'time being' nonsense. Your punishment was bad enough – and believe me, it hurt me too – but it could have been worse. And it will be if you try again. You have a mother and father to think about. They want to see you again, safe and sound, and with the Almighty's help they will. So just curb your impatience."

It was more than a week before Avner was able to move around without pain. He was reassigned to work in the fields, as though nothing had happened. But he was aware that the guards were keeping a close eye on him. Several days later he was ordered to report to the steward. While making his way to the office, Avner wondered if he was in for some more trouble. The steward's expression was hard and cold, and he wasted neither time nor words in explaining why Avner had been summoned.

"Starting tomorrow you will work in the villa," he said curtly. "Report to my assistant, who will see that you are given new garments. You are to dress neatly at all times. That's all; you may go."

Avner stared at the steward with a puzzled look. He knew that the work indoors was physically much easier and carried with it certain privileges. If he were assigned to more strenuous work, he could attribute it to his attempted escape. But to work indoors! Frankly, he preferred to continue in the fields.

"Well, what are you waiting for?" growled the steward.

"Excuse me," said Avner, ignoring the steward's brusqueness, "I don't know if I can express any preference in the matter, but I would like to stay where I am."

It was the steward's turn to stare with an astonished look. "You seem to forget you're a slave," he barked scornfully. "You will start in the villa tomorrow. Now go!"

When Avner returned to his quarters wearing an uncustomary frown, Reuven asked why the steward had summoned him. When he heard the explanation, he too was surprised, and in reply to Avner's question about the possible reason for the transfer, he could hazard no guess. He thought maybe some of the veteran slaves might know and promised to make inquiries.

The following evening he asked Avner how he found his new duties.

"It's work for a woman, not a man," he replied sourly. "When there are guests, I have to see that they are made comfortable, their feet washed, the food brought in, and a dozen other stupid things. And when there are no guests, I'm supposed to help prepare for those who will be coming. For the life of me, I still can't understand why I was transferred. Did you find out anything?"

Reuven shook his head. "I asked around but couldn't learn anything definite."

"Did you learn anything at all?"

"The one they call Horseface, the Spaniard, you know, he gave me a knowing grin and called you a lucky dog. He said you can probably thank the master's wife."

"The master's wife! What has she to do with us slaves?"

"I don't know, and I couldn't pry any more information out of him. He said you'll probably find out soon enough."

Avner sucked his underlip. He had once heard some idle talk about her, that she was born in Rome and was very much a "new Roman woman." He had no idea what that meant, nor did he particularly care.

The Spaniard was right: Avner did not have to wait long to discover the answer to the riddle. Several days later, while he was going about his chores in the atrium, the master's wife approached silently; she stopped in the doorway and stood there watching him. When he became aware of her presence, he gave a start.

"Did I startle you?" she asked in a low, throaty voice. "I was admiring how efficiently you work."

Avner felt awkward, and not only because of what he was doing. This was not the first time he had been alone with the master's wife, but she had always worn a businesslike air. Now there was something different about her, something he could not put his finger on. She was not endowed with outstanding natural gifts: She was short and plumpish, her features undistinguished, with a low brow over green eyes, a short, straight nose the tip of which flared a little too widely, a small compressed mouth, and a receding chin. Her dark brown hair was combed straight back and gathered together in a chignon. She was wearing a bright green tunic clasped at the waist by a jewel-encrusted girdle. A gold pendant hung from her neck. There was an assortment of rings on her fingers and a gold armlet on each arm.

"I trust that you find the work here more pleasant than in the fields," she said with a seductive smile.

"I'm an outdoor type," replied Avner. "I'm used to working in the fields, and frankly I prefer it. That's what I call a man's work."

"We have enough men for that. For the house we need someone who not only can speak a passable Greek but is intelligent and presentable."

Avner acknowledged the compliment with a slight nod. "I'm glad you think I have those qualities."

"Very much so," she said, dropping her voice and moving closer to Avner. He caught the scent of her perfume, a heady jasmine scent.

"It was I who had you transferred to the house. I saw that here you could be, let us say, very useful to me."

As she said this her features seemed to undergo a transformation. Avner stared in fascination as her countenance softened and her eyes assumed a veiled, imploring look. She did not seem nearly so plain as before.

"There are certain things a young man like you can do much more satisfactorily than a female," she said in a sensuous voice. She took hold of Avner's hands and drew him to her. She caressed his arm, sending a shiver of excitement through his whole body. He had not reckoned on anything like this. He tried to free himself from her embrace, but she held him tight.

"Lady – you see, I don't even know your name – I'm only a slave," he remonstrated, making another effort to free himself.

"I know you're a slave," she purred, "and so you must do my bidding. Come," she commanded, nodding in the direction of her bed chamber.

"There are other people in the house," Avner blurted out, not knowing what else to say.

"No, there aren't – just you and me. We don't have to worry about being disturbed. We can enjoy ourselves to our hearts' content."

"If the master finds out," Avner went on, desperately seeking a way out of this predicament, "he'll punish me severely – and you too."

Lady Aurelia laughed softly. "My husband is too busy with his own pleasures to give me much thought. Besides, he's too much in my debt to deny me a little pleasure. When he married me, he not only got a plump wife but a very plump dowry. You don't have to worry about him. You only have to please me."

She took Avner by the hand and led him toward her bed chamber. As though in a trance, he followed her, her hand tightly gripping his. His head was in a whirl, as reason struggled with emotion.

Upon entering the room, she slipped the bolt quietly. Avner's heart hammered against his ribs, and there was a fierce throbbing in his temples. At the same time an inner voice warned him against yielding to her passion. It reminded him that he had so far kept himself chaste, and that when he took a wife he wanted to come to her pure in body and mind.

"I'm sorry," he said, trying to squirm out of her arms, "it, it's not right."

"If I say it's what I want, then it's right," she replied in a voice thick with desire. "Now, don't think or talk any more."

Avner did not move. He stared at her with a vague, hesitant expression. If he did not put an end to this immediately, it would be too late, for his resistance was weakening. Where was his will power? Where was his resolve not to let anyone force a slave mentality on him? True, he had not reckoned on something like this when he made that resolution, and her ardor was overwhelming. Yet he knew he must not yield to it if he wanted to remain free in spirit. But he did not want to offend the master's wife and incur her wrath, for wittingly or unwittingly he had given her the impression that he was putty in her hands, and had let her work herself into a state of intense passion.

"You must not ask me to do that," he uttered in a low voice. "It's not right for me to be here alone with you."

Avner's protesting inflamed her desire still more. "I told you there is nothing to worry about. The master will not know, nor will anyone else. Now, not one word more."

"But you don't understand. It's you I'm concerned about."

Lady Aurelia stared at Avner with a baffled expression. "What do you mean?"

"I don't know quite how to put it. It's embarrassing really. But I respect you too much to expose you to any possible..."

"Any possible what?" she demanded to know.

"Well, I – I'm afraid I have an issue." He spoke these words with a troubled conscience, for he did not like to lie, but he thought it justified in the circumstances.

Lady Aurelia fixed him with an incredulous look. "I don't believe you!" she flung at him, her voice rising in pitch. "When my husband buys a male slave, that's one of the first things he examines."

"When the master bought me I didn't have an issue. It came later."

Lady Aurelia's face turned livid with rage. She began to hurl obscenities at Avner, accusing him of leading her on and then lying to her. She worked herself into such a fury that she began to beat him with her clenched fists. He was amazed at how coarse she could be. Yet he bore her savage attack patiently, even contritely, for he could not deny that he was partly to blame. She ordered him out of the room and out of her sight.

When he left the room he knew he would not be working in the villa any more, and perhaps his life would be made miserable in various ways. But he experienced a profound sense of relief. He started to thank the Almighty, but checked himself, for he felt too sullied for that. Whatever his fate would be, he would accept it humbly.

He was not surprised, therefore, when a few days later he was ordered to report to the master. But he was very surprised to learn that Reuven too had been summoned. It was with some trepidation mingled with curiosity that he entered the master's office together with his friend. The pleasant expression on the master's face allayed his apprehension somewhat. He was even more relieved when they were asked to be seated.

"Well, my friends," said the master with a broad, slightly ironic smile, "I would like to know how you found working on my estate."

Avner and Reuven stared at each other incredulously. They could not comprehend the purpose of such a question, let alone the master's friendly manner.

"I have no complaints, sir," said Reuven warily.

"I'm glad to hear that, even if I don't believe you," replied the master amiably. "Your young friend obviously thinks otherwise. It's a pity we had to remind him, in what was perhaps a rather unpleasant manner, that one does not make his departure from here by climbing over walls. But, to use a poor metaphor, that is water under the bridge. You're undoubtedly wondering why I have summoned you. I will not keep you in suspense. I will simply say that you have not proved to be a good investment for me."

At this remark their faces fell. This provoked a chuckle from the master. "No, you have not been a good investment at all. I paid a good many drachmas for you two, and now I stand to lose my money."

Avner and Reuven were more mystified than ever. "I'm afraid we don't understand," said Avner.

"No, you probably don't. Then let me bring you up to date on what has been happening in the outside world. It will probably distress you greatly to know that your beloved Cassius has joined his ancestors. Mark Antony is the new master of his part of the empire, and he has arrived to assume control. One of the first things he's done is to decree that all Jews who were sold into slavery by Cassius are to be liberated."

The master watched with an amused look as the two men exchanged glances, unable to believe their ears. Avner felt a weight lift from his heart, and he experienced a surge of exhilaration. He and Reuven sprang to their feet and fell into a joyous embrace.

"Blessed be the merciful Lord," Reuven uttered solemnly, his eyes misted with tears. Avner added a hearty Amen. He could not believe it – he was free! Free to return to Emmaus and to rejoin his family and fellow townsmen.

The two men, suddenly recalling in whose presence they were, grinned sheepishly at the master. "We thank you for this information, sir," said Avner. "I can't say we'll be sorry to leave you, but the experience has been interesting in a way – and even quite exciting at times," he added, leaving it to the master to fathom his meaning.

"I'm glad to hear that. I shall arrange for your transportation, of course. And, oh yes," he continued, grinning at Avner, "I suggest that this time you leave through the front gate rather than over the rear wall. You'll find it much easier – and a little more pleasant."

Antigonus Meets the Parthian "King of Kings"

Antigonus had more than once been repulsed by the Romans, mostly alongside his late father and brother. This, however, had the effect of steeling his resolve, so that he continued to maintain a sanguine outlook. But his defeat by Herod, which had thwarted his advance into Judea after Cassius's departure from Syria, had left him dispirited and temporarily at wit's end – an uncharacteristic mood for him. The reason lay not so much in the setback itself, which he was confident could be rectified – as in Antony's subsequent appearance in the region. This threatened to deal a severe if not fatal blow to his long-cherished hope of gaining the throne of Judea. Antigonus knew at first hand the triumvir's prowess on the battlefield, having been bested by him some fifteen years earlier. Antony had gone on to win fame as staff officer and Master of Horse under Julius Caesar, winning a reputation as a commander who knew how to inspire his men with enthusiasm and to wrest victory in the face of overwhelming odds.

Antigonus tried to keep his feelings to himself in order not to demoralize Joab and his other officers, but they sensed that something was troubling him. Antigonus's wife was, of course, fully aware of his mood, but at his request she refrained from discussing the matter with others. In the course of their married life she had endured many agonizing spells, and while a brave woman, she suffered as all brave women do when their spouses don their armor and go off to do battle. She tried to keep up his spirits as best she could, for which he was grateful. Her loyalty and devotion were a great help during this difficult period.

Autumn passed and the air turned sharp, bringing with it the smell of rain. Soon winter would arrive, and in Chalcis this meant driving winds, bitter cold, pelting rains, and even blizzards. Normally Antigonus did not mind such weather, but this year the thought of it deepened his gloom. He would have loved to relax in a warm, sunny climate, and had a longing to visit Jericho. This, of course, was out of the question, and as a prince of the Hasmonean house, he could not simply pack up and journey to some foreign place like an ordinary citizen. It was therefore with considerable curiosity and a quickening of the pulse that he received a letter one early winter day from the royal Parthian court.

Written in Aramaic and bearing the signature of the chief minister Karenas, it informed Antigonus that the King of Kings, Orodes the Second, was pleased to invite Antigonus to an audience at his palace in Ecbatana. Since the matter he wished to discuss was of the greatest import, it would be desirable to hold the audience as soon as possible. To ensure its success, strict secrecy was essential, both in the preparations for the journey and during the trip itself. Antigonus was requested to send his reply with the courier who delivered the invitation.

The very receipt of a communication from the monarch of Parthia, one of the two greatest powers of the day, was enough to dispel Anigonus's gloom. The fact that he was to discuss a "matter of the greatest import" both intrigued and exhilarated him; his handsome, finely molded countenance recovered its decisive, confident expression. He was puzzled, however, by the venue of the audience, for he knew it was the practice of the royal court to move before the onset of harsh weather from Ecbatana, the Median capital situated in a mountainous region that turned cold relatively early, to the winter palace at Ctesiphon, a short distance from the ancient city of Babylon.

"Is His Majesty still in Ecbatana?" he asked the courier after reading the letter once more.

"Yes, sire."

"Hasn't it turned cold there yet?"

"It has, sire," was the laconic reply.

Antigonus realized it would be pointless to inquire why the court had not yet moved to Ctesiphon, which enjoyed mild weather in the winter. He told the courier that he would receive his reply on the morrow.

Antigonus had not had much contact with the Parthians. He had visited some of the Jewish communities in Babylonia, but had seldom met with royal officials. Nevertheless, he knew a good deal about the Parthians. He had heard that some of the coarseness of their forebears still clung to them – even to the courtiers and nobles, who lacked the refined manners and elegance of the Persian aristocracy. Theirs was a huge, sprawling kingdom, embracing numerous peoples. Their lack of polish notwithstanding, the Parthians possessed a faculty for governing, which enabled them to hold together the heterogeneous mass of subject peoples in the hundred years or so since their kingdom came into existence. They treated prisoners of war decently, admitted foreigners to high office, and gave asylum to refugees. They were tolerant of different religions, and the Jews were quite happy under their rule, just as they had been during most of the period under Persian rule.

Parthia had become Rome's arch rival in the east, but in their military clashes the Romans were the aggressors, while Parthia's actions were basically defensive in nature. So far they had proved to be very adept at this, as Roman generals seeking conquest and fame, such as Crassus, had discovered much to their sorrow. Parthian tactics were sound, and their mounted archers had proved to be more than a match for the highly trained, disciplined Roman foot soldiers.

On the first part of the journey from Chalcis to Ecbatana, Antigonus and his retinue of high officers and advisers traversed a long stretch of bleak, undulating plain. The traffic on the road to Palmyra and Doura-Europas was fairly light, consisting mainly of camel caravans transporting a variety of wares and some passengers. After crossing the Tigris, Antigonus's suite found their progress slowed down by the rugged terrain. The Zagras region was a country of alternate mountain and valley, with here and there a fairly extensive, and for the most, part picturesque plain. The mountains were covered with forests, mostly walnut and oak; they did not reach to the summits of the loftiest peaks, but almost completely clothed the smaller ranges. The valleys abounded with orchards and gardens, which at this time of the year were largely bare, but in the spring would burst into bloom and produce a wide variety of fruits and vegetables.

Ecbatana came into sight around noon of a cool, sunny day. Antigonus was engaged in desultory conversation with his companions when the road made a sharp turn, revealing in the distance the ancient capital of the Medes, situated at the foot of a long, lofty mountain. The sight of the city stirred Antigonus, for it was here, in the very same palace they would be visiting, that Cyrus had issued his edict allowing the Jews to return to Zion and to rebuild the Temple after their expulsion seventy years earlier.

Although it no longer possessed the grandeur it had in Cyrus's time, Ecbatana was still impressive. From the mountain on which it sat copious streams descended to a plain dotted with scattered patches of luxuriant verdure which had not yet succumbed to the winter frost. Protecting the city was a citadel of obviously great strength. Beneath it, and dominating the city, was the magnificent royal palace, nearly a mile in circumference. Imposing public buildings, temples, and other large edifices abounded, as befitted the capital of a once powerful and still flourishing province.

As the party drew near the outlying houses, they encountered numerous large, powerfully built horses. This did not surprise them, for Media was famous for the excellence of the horses bred there. The Parthians were known to spend much of their lives on horseback, conversing, transacting business, and even eating while mounted on their steeds. Moreover, their mounted archers were the terror of opposing armies, even Roman.

After reaching the palace square, Antigonus instructed his retinue to wait until they were notified to enter the palace. He adjusted the girdle of his fur-edged scarlet cloak and strode toward the majestic staircase. He identified himself to the captain of the guard, who had been expecting him. The officer conducted him into a comfortably heated anteroom, and after a few minutes he returned with a short, thick-set man whose appearance and bearing stamped him as a person of authority. His black hair, beard, and mustache were curled in the Parthian fashion, and his deep-set black eyes under thick brows were full of restrained fire. He had a large aquiline nose, and his lips were thick and curved in a warm smile. A loose green and red robe interwoven with threads of gold reached down to his feet, and was held in at the waist by a bejeweled girdle in which was thrust a long dagger in an encrusted sheath.

He strode over to Antigonus, and with a bow introduced himself as Karenas. "It was very kind of you to accept our invitation," he said in a deep, resonant voice. "Especially as the weather can be quite nasty at this time of the year, very nasty indeed."

"I am extremely grateful for the opportunity to have an audience with the King of Kings," replied Antigonus. "It is an honor that I shall cherish, regardless of such a trivial matter as the weather, which today happens to be very much to my liking."

"Let us hope that your visit will be as pleasant as the weather you have brought with you. I regard it as an auspicious sign."

Upon learning that Antigonus's retinue were waiting in the square, Karenas ordered one of his aides to admit them and show them to their apartment. He informed Antigonus that in the evening they would dine with the leading nobles of the land and that the audience with King Orodes was scheduled for the following afternoon. Anticipating a query about the food, Karenas assured Antigonus that through their friends in the Jewish community of Babylonia, they were familiar with the problem of forbidden foods and had arranged for a Jewish chef to prepare their meals.

The royal residence occupied a large area, but as they walked through the broad corridor, Antigonus saw that at least half the space seemed to be taken up by open courts, paved mostly with marble. His curiosity was aroused by the pillars and surrounding colonnades, and upon inquiring about them, learned that most of the pillars in the palace were made of either cypress or cedar wood and plated with silver or some other precious metal. Despite the sunny weather and his heavy garments, Antigonus was chilled by the dank air in the corridor, but when he entered the apartment assigned to him and his retinue, he found it pleasantly warmed by glowing braziers. The floor was covered with soft rugs that had deep piles and richly colored designs and motifs, and this too lent a feeling of warmth and luxury.

That evening Antigonus and his men were feted in the banqueting hall, where more than a hundred nobles had gathered. They constituted the higher Parthian aristocracy, and enjoyed more power and dignity than that usually possessed by the subjects of an Oriental king. Each stood at the head of a body of retainers accustomed to bear arms and to serve in the wars of the empire; they constituted, in fact, the backbone of the army.

When Orodes entered the hall, all the guests leaped to their feet and bowed deeply. Accompanied by guards and attendants, he made his way to a couch placed at a higher elevation than those of his guests. Antigonus, seated fairly close to the king, observed that his gait and bearing were those of a physically vigorous man of moderate build. He had a slightly aquiline nose, large eyes, and reddish frizzed hair, beard, and mustache. His hair was confined by a simple diadem, which was actually a band of ribbon that encircled the head and terminated in two long ends that hung behind his head. His purple robe flowed loosely to the tops of high yellow shoes.

After the king was seated the musicians struck up a lively tune with their flutes, pipes, drums, and sambucas. This was a signal for the guests to begin partaking of the food, which was served in generous portions. The banquet went on until almost midnight. Karenas spoke briefly in honor of the guests from Chalcis, and numerous toasts were proposed between the acrobatic acts performed by lithe young males and dancing by a troupe of slave girls.

Next morning Antigonus and his men were taken on a tour of the city by one of the nobles. This was followed by a military exercise on the royal parade ground, in which archers mounted on Nicean steeds displayed their famed skill.

For his audience with the king, Antigonus wore a thick scarlet robe and his favorite armlets. As Karenas escorted him to the audience, they chatted amiably until they reached the bronze-covered portals of the throne room. Here two guards stiffened to attention and then opened the doors to admit the two men. When they stepped inside, Antigonus saw that the walls were decorated with a combination of bas-reliefs and panels of glazed brick, with the predominant motif being hunting scenes. The floor was paved with blue, white, and red stones arranged in various patterns and covered in places with magnificent carpets. At the upper end of the hall was an elevated golden throne, upon which sat the Parthian monarch surrounded by guards, a scribe, and three attendants, two of whom Antigonus recognized as the king's son Pacorus and the satrap Barzaphanes; the third, he was surprised to learn a little later, was a Roman general.

Antigonus approached the throne and made a deep obeisance. He then presented the king with an exquisitely wrought pair of golden armlets inlaid with onyx, carnelian, and other gem stones. Orodes welcomed him in Aramaic and expressed his appreciation of the gift, which, he said, would go well with the golden chain he wore around his neck.

"I trust that my minister Karenas is making your stay enjoyable," he said in a friendly, somewhat thin voice. "Fortunately the weather today is fine, which we could not promise when we invited you to Ecbatana."

"Your Majesty's minister has been most considerate and helpful," replied Antigonus respectfully. "I am deeply mindful of the great privilege and honor you have conferred on me, regardless of such an insignificant matter as the weather."

"Nevertheless, there was a special reason for deciding to hold the audience here instead of our winter palace in Ctesiphon. Karenas will explain to you." The king leaned back on his throne and nodded to his minister to proceed.

Karenas cleared his throat. "As His Majesty has indicated, the royal winter palace is at Ctesiphon, where the weather is mild this time of the year – a real pleasure indeed. But, as you well know, there is a large Jewish community there, and the same is true of other nearby cities. Your presence there would attract considerable attention, and we were anxious to avoid that, for reasons that will soon become clear to you."

Antigonus gathered from the tenor of these remarks that the purpose of the audience was to discuss some major enterprise in which he was designated to play a role. He waited expectantly for Karenas to continue, but the minister seemed to digress onto something quite insignificant.

"One of the advantages of a huge kingdom like Parthia – and take it from one who intimately knows how huge it is – is that it enables the royal court to move from one palace to another with a change of season."

Antigonus failed to see the relevance of this observation. He was burning with impatience, but knew he must betray no sign of it. "Permit me to point out, Excellency, that my country is very small. Compared with Parthia, Judea is like a fly next to a lion. Yet in this tiny land one can also find a big difference in climate. In the winter one can escape within a few hours from cold, rainy Jerusalem to the balmy Jordan Valley."

"Indeed? Your country is fortunate in that respect. And you are spared the problem of having to deal with many diverse peoples. Our king must treat his various subjects indiscriminately, either with a firm hand or by keeping them satisfied. We prefer to keep our Parthians, Greeks, Persians, Medes, and yes, our Jews too, as contented as possible. That is why we have been spared internal strife."

"My fellow Jews in Babylonia are fortunate to live under such benign rule," said Antigonus with a slight bow to Orodes.

Orodes leaned forward on his throne "We find your fellow Jews a very positive and worthy element," he said with an affable smile. "I have had many enlightening conversations with your sages – both those in Babylonia and even some from your own country. Through them I know something of your customs and beliefs, which I find most interesting. I am also familiar with the different currents of thought in your country and the attitude of your people in my realm toward events there."

This remark piqued Antigonus's curiosity. "If His Majesty will forgive my boldness, may I ask what you believe is the prevailing mood of the Jews in your realm?"

Instead of replying to this question, Orodes nodded to his minister to explain.

"It is, how should I put it? – a somewhat ambivalent attitude," said Karenas, tugging at his beard. "It is exemplified in the person of your eminent uncle. On the one hand, the Jews here hold Hyrcanus, the high priest, in great esteem. But they are less happy about Hyrcanus the king – or ethnarch, as the Romans have officially designated him. Do I make myself clear, or am I being too vague?"

"I think I know what you are implying. Am I correct in assuming that you feel they are not too pleased about the situation regarding the Romans?"

"Precisely. They are worried about the growing influence of Rome and those who closely cooperate with it. They fear the possible consequences of this tendency, which they believe is not in Judea's best interests."

Antigonus now realized that Karenas's seemingly innocent remarks about the weather and the heterogeneity of the Parthian Empire were not idle talk but had a definite purpose. What was he leading up to? And what was this Roman officer doing here? Antigonus cast a sidewise glance at him, but his countenance was an inscrutable mask. Antigonus waited for Karenas to continue.

"It is not only your fellow Jews in our kingdom who are concerned about Rome's intentions," Karenas went on. "We have more than enough territory and peoples to deal with. Indeed, more than enough. We have no designs on others, and we try to keep our subjects happy and contented. But there is a danger that our leniency and benevolence might be misinterpreted as a sign of weakness. In recent years we have had to contend with the spreading power of the Roman Empire, which seems determined to swallow up more and more lands. They are like wolves, whose appetite is never satisfied. What is that saying? Their appetite grows with the eating. We made no effort to interfere with Rome as long as it did not attempt to encroach upon our kingdom. But ever since Pompey broke his treaty with us, we have been increasingly at odds with Rome. During the reign of His Majesty's father, one of the Roman aristocrats could find no better way to employ his talents and wealth than to invade Parthia. Unfortunately for Crassus, his enterprise turned out differently from what he had expected, and instead of fame, he lost not only his legions' eagles but his head as well."

"Judea also had reason to hate Crassus," said Antigonus, folding his arms across his chest. "He robbed our holy Temple to help finance his campaign against your kingdom. But his death did not bring relief to my people. In his place came Cassius, who was just as greedy and extortionate. Nor do I think Mark Antony will prove any better. True, he ordered the release of the Jews whom Cassius had sold into slavery, thereby winning the favor of my people. But from my knowledge of Antony, I do not believe that he will retain their goodwill for long."

"On that point we are in complete agreement," replied Karenas. "But perhaps our noble friend Labienus is better equipped than I am to enlighten you on that."

"Before he does so," interjected Orodes, "perhaps our guest would like to help himself to some dates. They're from Babylonia, which is famous for its date palms."

"Thank you, Your Majesty. I shall be happy to do so."

After Antigonus had taken advantage of this offer, Orodes nodded to Karenas to continue.

"Regarding Mark Antony," the minister resumed, "Labienus has valuable information to impart – very valuable and interesting indeed. But first, let me acquaint you with this noble Roman. Quintus Labienus bears an illustrious name. His father was one of Caesar's generals, who earned a reputation as a brave and able officer. Quintus himself has an enviable record to his credit. You probably wonder about his presence here – I noticed you eyeing him with a puzzled look. He came here over a year ago seeking our assistance on behalf of Brutus and Cassius in their contest against Antony and Octavian. While we were considering his petition, news arrived of the outcome of the battle of Philippi. Labienus found himself stranded here, and because of the proscriptions, he realized his life would be forfeit if he returned to Rome. Here he may not be among his own people, but he is among friends who hold him in high regard and value his expert knowledge and judgment. And now that you know something about our dear friend, I will let him explain what has been happening in the Eastern provinces that have come under Antony's authority.

Even when seated, Labienus held his carriage ramrod straight. He had a sturdy build and a typically Roman face, with a straight nose, hazel eyes, somewhat thin lips, and a dimpled chin. Antigonus put his age at abut thirty-five. He was wearing a Roman military tunic, with a dagger his only weapon. While Karenas was describing how Labienus came to be at the Parthian court, Antigonus noticed that his lips were compressed and the look in his eyes somewhat veiled and even remote. But when he spoke, it was in a strong voice, and his face assumed a resolute expression. Although naturally less fluent in Aramaic than in Latin or Greek, he chose to speak in the native tongue of his hosts.

"Karenas has told you how I came to be here in the Parthian court. As you can gather from his remarks, I am not in Mark Antony's camp; in fact, I confess that I intensely dislike the man. But that is neither here nor there. You said that Antony is liable to prove just as grasping and extortionate as his predecessors. That is exactly what is happening. The inhabitants of the various kingdoms in this region thought that with his coming their burden would be lightened. But they have discovered that it is just as bad, if not worse. At least with Cassius they knew their money was going on the Roman army. With Antony they are also having to pay for his riotous living, and they resent it bitterly. Some of the client-kings and vassals have petitioned His Majesty to help them throw off Roman rule."

That the inhabitants of the neighboring kingdoms were fed up with the Romans, Antigonus already knew. What puzzled him was Labienus. Why was he siding with the Parthians against his own countrymen? Was it solely because of his hatred of Antony? Was he hoping that Parthian intervention would help bring down the triumvirate? And what about the Parthians? Knowing their policy, he wondered what had induced Orodes to fall in with Labienus's designs – assuming that this was the case. His puzzlement, plainly written on his face, prompted Karenas to interrupt his speculation.

"His Majesty sympathized with the plight of these unfortunate peoples, but he was reluctant to intervene. As I have already mentioned, he has enough territory and peoples to cope with – more than enough; and he had no desire to extend his protection to other lands, especially if it meant a clash with the Romans."

"And what caused His Majesty to change his mind?" asked Antigonus, concluding that the Parthians were contemplating some military action.

Karenas folded his arms across his chest. He regarded Antigonus steadily with a faint smile. "His Majesty has not forgotten that the Romans more than once tried to snatch parts of the Parthian empire. As I have already emphasized, they're like a wolf in the farmyard. Yes, that's how you can put it. And he knows what sort of a man Antony is. But even so, His Majesty was not disposed to take any action likely to provoke the Romans. We Parthians do not underestimate their fighting ability, even though we have not done badly so far – indeed, not badly at all. But a new factor has arisen to change the picture: The knowledge that Rome, or, to be more exact, Antony, is contemplating an expedition against Parthia."

At this statement, spoken in a quiet, matter-of-act tone, a look of astonishment crossed Antigonus's face. "This is a most unexpected piece of news," he exclaimed. "I assume that it is based on sound evidence?"

"Very sound," replied Karenas. "Labienus will explain."

Labienus related how not long before his death, Caesar had drawn up a plan for a campaign against the Parthians. It was highly secret, and only a handful of his most trusted officers were privy to it. One of them, who had clashed with Antony on several occasions, was stunned to find himself proscribed after Caesar's death. However, he managed to escape, and upon meeting Labienus revealed to him Caesar's contemplated expedition. From a reliable source Labienus learned that Antony, after being assigned the Eastern provinces, had studied the plan and intended to implement it when the time was ripe.

This disclosure made it clear to Antigonus why Orodes and Karenas had decided to change their policy. It was also obvious that they would not have revealed this highly confidential information to him unless they were counting on his aid and cooperation.

"Am I correct in assuming that it is in this connection that I have been granted an audience with His Majesty?" he asked in a polite, guarded tone.

"You assume correctly," replied Karenas. "You understand, of course, that we would not have revealed this information to you unless we desired you to play a role in thwarting Rome's designs."

"I can appreciate that. But I don't see what role I can play. After all, I am – to be perfectly frank – living in exile in Chalcis."

A shrewd grin appeared on Karenas's round face. "If our enterprise succeeds – and we have every intention for it to succeed – you will no longer be living in exile in Chalcis."

Orodes, who was accustomed to let his chief minister steer the talk when it bore on matters of high policy, pulled himself erect and gave Antigonus a knowing look. "If I am not mistaken," he said in a soft voice, "you once tried to convince Caesar that the throne of Judea should be entrusted to you rather than your uncle. Is that not so?"

This statement took Antigonus by surprise. He wondered how Orodes knew about that meeting. "Yes, that is true, Your Majesty," he said a little hesitantly.

"You failed to convince Caesar," Orodes went on, "for reasons probably known only to himself. But they obviously had to do with what he regarded was in the best interests of Rome. In our considered opinion you are the man who should be sitting on the throne of Judea."

These words, spoken in almost casual accents, caused Antigonus's face to light up; they sent the blood racing through his veins, hammering at his heart and brain. The Judean throne! The goal he had long dreamed about and aspired to!

"We have been closely following events in your country," said Karenas after a respectable pause to let the impact of this declaration sink in. "We know what efforts your late father made to gain the throne – the valiant battles he fought in the face of overwhelming odds. We know about your attempt to fight your way to Jerusalem, also against great odds. But now the odds are in our favor – indeed they are. Like your father and brother, you have been able to rally your countrymen to your banner. We know the sentiment of your people in our kingdom. We have good reason to believe they would welcome a Hasmonean on the throne who would adopt a more independent stand toward Rome, who would be less servile to its wishes and policy."

These words were music to Antigonus's ears. He could already visualize his triumph, the triumph he had long waited for and which he had despaired of achieving. The Judean throne! What could be sweeter to contemplate? But a jarring note suddenly intruded on his thoughts. His first impulse was to brush it aside, for he did not want anything to dim the dazzling prospect dangling before him. But, he was painfully aware, the doubt would not vanish by itself. His hesitation did not escape the Parthians' notice.

"You have reservations about our proposal?" asked Karenas, arching his thick eyebrows. "If you do, please don't hesitate to express them."

Antigonus was silent for a long moment, weighing whether to voice his qualms. How could he tell them that if he cast his lot with the Parthians he would lose whatever chance he might have with the Romans? On the other hand, his prospects of securing the throne from the Romans were anyway practically nil. No, it was not advisable to mention this. But he could tell them about his other misgivings.

"Your proposal is most enticing, and I am highly honored to be deemed worthy of your confidence," he said, framing his reply carefully. "As a prince of the Hasmonean house, how can I even think twice before giving an affirmative reply. Yet two considerations give me pause."

"And what are they?" asked Karenas, surprised that Antigonus did not immediately agree.

Antigonus knitted his brow; his visage assumed a serious, meditative expression. "As you yourself have so rightly pointed out, my people have been less than happy with Hyrcanus because of his pliant, even servile attitude toward the Romans. They feel that he has let himself become too much an instrument of Rome, whether because of a lack of backbone or because he fell under the evil influence of Antipater and his two sons. Whatever the reason, he has demeaned himself in the eyes of many of our people, bringing disrepute not only on himself, but even more important, upon the Judean throne and the Hasmonean house. If I were to put myself in a similar position in relation to Parthia, it is highly conceivable that the people would point an accusing finger at me and say, 'Hyrcanus let himself become a puppet of Rome; you, Antigonus, have let yourself become a puppet of Parthia.'"

Karenas grinned upon hearing this reservation. "If that is what is troubling you, you can put your mind at rest. I won't deny that our favoring you is in Parthia's interests. It is especially important in view of Rome's designs against us. But that by no means implies we want a puppet on the throne of Judea. Indeed not, that would only work against us in the long run. We want an ally, a friend. There are strong bonds between our kingdom and Judea. Your brethren are among our most loyal and industrious subjects, and His Majesty and I enjoy cordial relations with the leaders of the Jewish community. They are wonderful men. As I have already said, we know that your people here respect Hyrcanus as high priest, but are greatly disturbed by his pro-Roman policy. They have witnessed Judea's loss of independence under his rule, its growing subjection to Rome. They are perturbed to see Judea milked by Roman governors, and what power that has been left it being actually wielded first by Antipater and now by Herod and his brother, who are regarded as outsiders, more Idumean than Jewish, more concerned for Rome's interests than Judea's. For this situation they largely blame Hyrcanus. They would welcome a strong Hasmonean on the throne. That we know. And we also know how you have succeeded in drawing thousands to your banner and putting up a stout fight against Herod. The people are for you; they would side with you in a contest against Herod."

This reminder of his battle against Herod caused Antigonus to frown. It was a memory he did not cherish, and he would have been happier had Karenas not seen fit to mention it.

"Permit me to point out," said Antigonus, keeping his voice even, "that while the people might side with me against Herod, the struggle would not be against Herod alone, but against Herod and Antony. In my younger days I met Antony in battle, and since then he has fought for Caesar and more recently was mainly responsible for defeating Brutus and Cassius. I do not underrate his ability."

"It would be foolhardy to do so," concurred Karenas. "But the picture is brighter than you seem to realize – much brighter indeed. Our good friend Labienus has something to say on this."

Labienus proceeded to describe the politico-military situation in the Roman Empire in general and in the Eastern provinces in particular. He emphasized that the position of the triumvirate was far from secure. Although the Caesarians had emerged victorious at Philippi, they were not yet firmly in the saddle. They had not succeeded in quelling all opposition. Even now Octavian had his hands full dealing with Sextus Pompey, and the outcome of the struggle was far from certain. Because of the hostilities in Italy, Asia Minor had been denuded of troops, and in Syria there were only two legions, which had originally fought with Cassius and hence their loyalty to Antony was doubtful. In fact, Labienus went on, he had it from a reliable source that they were virtually in a state of mutiny. This had not escaped the attention of Rome's client-kings in the region, who were overwhelmingly pro-Parthia.

Another thing that had not gone unnoticed, Labienus stressed, was Antony's growing infatuation with Cleopatra, who had enticed him to Alexandria. Instead of proceeding with the administration of the Eastern provinces, Antony was indulging in a life of ease and luxury, neglecting his duties and letting his subordinates manage affairs. His officers and men were dismayed at this turn of events. Their morale had suffered, since they felt they were virtually leaderless.

"From Labienus's report," said Karenas with a sly grin, "it seems that Antony is finding life in Egypt extremely interesting and is loathe to leave it or its queen, who is acknowledged by all to be a very talented and charming ruler. As long as he continues to bask in the warmth of the Egyptian winter and the embraces of its queen, we can assume that he will not display any great vigor in pursuing his plan to conquer Parthia. But we can also assume that the attraction of Egypt and the queen will eventually pall on a man with Antony's restless, ambitious nature, that his passion for the country and Cleopatra will burn itself out, or at least simmer down. This means that at present we are enjoying only a respite from his designs. We must also remember that the situation in Rome is far from stable, and no one can predict if and when events there will take a sharp turn and stir Antony into action. Because of this, and considering all the factors mentioned by Labienus, it would be advisable to take immediate action. To quote the maxim Labienus is fond of repeating: 'You should hammer your iron when it is glowing hot.' I'm sure you will agree with that."

Rumors that Cassius Battles with Antony

Zechariah loved all the appointed seasons of the Lord, but being a man of the soil, he was especially fond of the three pilgrim festivals, which in one way or another are connected with the agricultural cycle. At Passover the fields, orchards, and vineyards stir with life after the winter rains: The barley is already ripening, the wheat sprouting, the air is redolent of the blossoms of almond, apple and other fruit trees, and myriads of poppies and other wildflowers blanket the hillsides and uncultivated patches of flatland in a blaze of color. Seven weeks later comes Shavuot, when the villagers assemble in the large town of their district and go up together with their first fruits to the Temple, where they are welcomed with song by the Levites.

But no festival delighted Zechariah more than Sukkot. When the produce of his fields and vineyard was gathered in and the granary was full, he could behold the fruits of his labor and give thanks to the Lord for His bounty. The sky would no longer be a clear blue day after day, but more often than not clouds would float lazily toward the east or scurry in thick banks, driven by winds which hinted of rain. The countryside had by now donned its checkered mantle of russet, crimson, olive and forest green, and other bright hues, and the air was fresh and bracing. Booths roofed with leafy branches or straw dotted the courtyards, a temporary home for the week-long festival, a reminder of the flimsy dwellings in which the Israelites had lived during their forty-year trek through the wilderness.

Jerusalem would be thronged with pilgrims from all part of the country and the Diaspora. The hostelries would be filled to capacity and tents pitched in nearby fields to accommodate all who had come to rejoice in the Lord's House, with its colorful ceremony of the *hoshanot* prayers recited as the worshippers circled the altar carrying the Four Species – the palm branch, citron, myrtle, and willow twigs – and in the evening the water-libation rite, during which bonfires kindled in the Temple courtyard shed their light over the city, and even sages and other pious men joined in the dancing, carrying flaming torches and singing songs and praises in addition to Psalms.

But this year, with the thanksgiving festival approaching, Zechariah was not light-hearted. When he contemplated his still largely unharvested crops he sighed wistfully. His three elder sons had their own farms to attend to, and while they dutifully gave their father what help they could, they had precious little time to spare. How he missed Avner – not only his strong back and arms, which would have brought the crops in by now, but even more, his cheerful presence, his breezy good humor.

It was now more than half a year since the Roman soldiers had descended on Emmaus to round up all the able-bodied males and sell them into slavery on Cassius's order. Zechariah was grateful that his other sons were not in Emmaus at the time and were thus spared the fate that befell Avner and almost all his friends and many of the other menfolk. When Avner had been led away fettered, his mother had burst into tearful sobs, and all Zechariah's comforting words had failed to console her.

"Avner will manage, don't worry," he had told her. "He's resourceful, and with the Almighty's help we'll be seeing him again soon."

But the weeks stretched into months, and although Zechariah did not doubt that the Almighty would hearken to his prayer and watch over his son, he began to fret more and more.

His neighbor Saul was burning with indignation at the Romans and frequently vented his opinion of their brand of justice. "A pack of bloodsucking jackals, that's what they are!" he snorted while chatting with Zechariah one fine autumn day. "The Bible says that man was created in the divine image. But when I think of what that vile blackguard Cassius has done, all I can say is that he's not a man but a beast in human form."

"No, he's a human being all right," replied Zechariah, shaking his head. "But man can choose to do good or evil, and Cassius has chosen to do evil, like the men of Sodom and Gomorrah."

"Well, I can't figure it out," growled Saul, shrugging his broad shoulders. "Have you heard anything about Avner lately?" he asked solicitously after a slight pause.

Zechariah's eyes lit up. "I got a letter from him yesterday."

"A letter! From him?" said Saul, astonished at this information. "How did he manage to get a letter to you?"

"Leave it to Avner," replied Zechariah with a proud grin.

"He's a smart one, all right. And what does he write? Is he still enslaved to that rich Greek in Antioch?"

"In a suburb of Tyre," Zechariah corrected his neighbor. "He says he's not being treated too badly, everything considered; it could be worse. He's doing his best not to eat forbidden foods, and he recites the *Shema* and some other prayers every day. He also tries to recite something from the Psalms before going to sleep – as much as he can remember by heart. But he says he sometimes gets mixed up, especially when he's very tired."

"He's a real credit to you," said Saul, nodding his head; "and to all of us in Emmaus. You and Hannah must miss him terribly."

"We certainly do," admitted Zechariah with a sigh. "Just like all the others whose menfolk have been sold into slavery."

Saul, who was leaning against a stone wall, shifted his position. "Well, I have a hunch it might not be too long before we see them back again," he drawled, giving Zechariah a knowing wink.

Zechariah stared at him with a puzzled expression. He knew that Saul was invariably the first to learn of any important news. "What do you mean?" he asked in a tone of intense curiosity mingled with soaring hope.

Saul pulled himself erect and squinted at Zechariah. "Well, I'm not sure – just a rumor, you know – but I wouldn't be surprised if Cassius will soon be rotting in Gehenna, if he's not there already."

Zechariah's heart leaped up. "The Lord be praised!" he uttered with humble gratefulness.

"Now don't get too excited. As I said, it's only a rumor. One can't..."

"What exactly have you heard?"

"The story I got was that a big battle was fought somewhere in Greece or Macedonia – I'm not sure which. And it seems that Antony and Octavian got the better of Brutus and Cassius. In fact, the rumor is they're both dead."

Zechariah's face broke into a broad smile; he felt a surge of renewed hope and joy. "The Lord be praised! If only it's true. I've told you many a time that every man gets his just deserts – if not in this world then in the next one."

"Well, all I can say is that if Cassius tries to pull any of his foul tricks in Gehenna, he'll get his bones rapped good and proper."

"Are you sure there are bones to rap in Gehenna?" Zechariah joshed his neighbor.

"Just a manner of speaking," retorted Saul with a grin. "And while we're on the subject, there are a few more people I'd like to see keeping him company there. Herod for one."

"He's betrothed to Hyrcanus's granddaughter."

162

"I'm aware of that," said Saul, making a wry face. "For the life of me I can't figure out what made Hyrcanus do such a daft thing. Here he was trying to get those Idumeans off his back, and all power to him. Couldn't have done anything better than to set Antipater down a notch or two and to put Malichus in his place – may his soul rest in peace. Now he's gone and turned the wheel back again, and then some."

Saul wagged a thick finger at Zechariah. "You mark my words, no good will come of that match – for no one: not for Hyrcanus, not for our people – no one except that arrogant, swaggering son of Antipater. Imagine that! She betrothed to someone like him. She's a pretty one, I've heard. And being a Hasmonean, she could have her pick of the best families in the land, and not a rotten villain like Herod. He's evil, I tell you, evil to the core. And too close to those damned Romans."

"What did you expect?" said Zechariah with a shrug of his shoulders. "He's a pagan at heart. But is it any wonder? It was wrong to force the Idumeans to convert. Who needed them in our fold anyway?" Zechariah paused a moment. "So you say Cassius is dead, did you?" he asked again, still finding the news too good to be true.

"That's the rumor. I can't vouch for it, but..."

"That means that either Antony or Octavian will be master of Rome, or maybe both of them. They're more like Caesar. If what you say is true, then there's hope that Avner will be back with us again soon. May the Almighty be praised!"

Chapter Four

All Roads Lead to Jerusalem

Hyrcanus Retains His Office – with Herod and Phasael

Publius Quintus sometimes wondered if he was subconsciously trying to stay the wintertime of his life. But since he was still in his forties, he could hardly be regarded as washed up, especially as only half a year ago he had proved at Philippi that he was still a nimble and able commander. Nevertheless, he asked himself what made him agree to join Antony's staff on the tour of the Eastern provinces that had been assigned the triumvir under the agreement with his co-rulers Octavian and Lepidus. Why could he not be content to remain on his family estate, as he had once warned Cassius he would do if the latter persisted in his cavalier treatment of him? At the time it had seemed a capital idea, especially as he was in low spirits after the retreat from Parthia. And only a few months ago the army he had helped command had suffered defeat again – this time at the hands of his fellow Romans led by Antony and Octavian.

Two defeats like that were enough to make any self-respecting officer his age call it quits. And he did – for a while. He could thank the gods that he was still alive. In Parthia he had seen Crassus perish – quite ignominiously in fact; but a man who had devoted his whole life to money grubbing had no business seeking glory on the battlefield. At Philippi, Cassius, who had few equals as a commander, had ignored Publius's advice and paid the price. Not that the outcome would probably have been any different had Cassius not rejected his counsel, but to proceed on the assumption that Antony's lifestyle had affected his generalship was sheer folly.

Finding himself still alive after that battle, thanks largely to Antony's clemency, he had sacrificed an ox to Jupiter Capitolinus and retired to his estate.

For a few months he had enjoyed the experience of being a gentleman farmer. The peaceful countryside was a welcome relief from the life of the camp and the bloody battlefield, and he even found pleasure in the companionship of his wife. But when Antony had proposed that he join his staff so that his knowledge of the Eastern provinces could be put to good use, he had found the offer too tempting to resist.

Antony's reputation both as a soldier and as a rake was common knowledge, and Publius knew what to expect. Yet he could not help marveling at the glaring contrast between him and Gaius Longinus Cassius. The latter had been a dour, harsh, strict disciplinarian, intolerant of mediocrity and overindulgent living and inclined to be tight-fisted. Antony was, paradoxically, a more complex character, alike cruel and generous, overfond of women, an extravagant spender and heavy drinker, yet withal a brave and resourceful soldier, who earned the love and respect of his troops by sharing their hardships, occasionally eating with them in their mess, and even by his ribald talk and carousing in public. In the proscriptions that had terrorized upper-class Rome after Caesar's death, Antony had proved to be the most merciless of the triumvirs, and the way he had treated Cicero disgusted many Romans. Antony had placed him high on the list of those to be slain, and had ordered both his head and his right hand, which had penned the vituperative speeches against Antony's public policy and private life, to be hung up in the Forum. Yet when Antony had come upon Brutus's body at Philippi, he ordered it to be wrapped in the most costly of his own robes and sent his ashes home to Brutus's mother.

For better or worse, Publius had agreed to put his first-hand knowledge of the Near East at Antony's disposal. Not that Antony was a stranger to these parts. Some fifteen years earlier he had distinguished himself as commander of the Roman cavalry that fought against Aristobulus's son Alexander, but since then he had largely been out of touch with events and personalities in this region.

Antony was in excellent spirits after crossing the Hellespont into the Asian Minor province of Bithyania. The Greeks had treated him royally: At Athens he and his staff had attended games and religious ceremonies, and he even enjoyed holding discussions with scholars, who hailed him as a lover of Greece (his troops remarked that they should have added, 'and especially Grecian women').

Antony, patently flattered by all these honors, had showered gifts upon the city. Publius wondered whether things would go as smoothly in Asia Minor, where there were numerous kingdoms and factions and shifting allegiances were the rule. Several delegations had already arrived to pay their respects to Antony; some of them presented not only their compliments but also their complaints. One of the delegations scheduled to meet Antony was from Judea, and Herod had also announced his intention of coming. Knowing this young man and his relations with the Jews, it did not take much imagination for Publius to guess that the deputation would have some unkind things to say about Herod, especially his zeal in helping to raise the heavy tribute Cassius had laid on the country. Antony would no doubt want his assessment of the situation and of the personages involved. If it were Cassius and not Antony, the deputation would undoubtedly get short shrift, but Antony would probably hear them out and treat them respectfully, especially because of the high regard the Jews had for Caesar.

"Well, Publius, my faithful adviser," Antony greeted him the following morning at their daily conference, "I hope you managed to sleep off the effects of last night's celebration."

"My head is as clear as I can reasonably expect," replied Publius soberly. Truth to tell, he had early on realized that he was no match for Antony when it came to imbibing wine or engaging in other pleasures. He therefore made it a practice to take his wine heavily diluted and the other pleasures in moderation. He marveled at the ease with which Antony shook off the effects of his exuberant living. It failed to erase the noble dignity of his appearance: his curly head and beard, broad forehead, and aquiline nose gave him a bold, masculine look which the opposite sex found irresistible.

"And what delegations may we expect today with their rich gifts and even richer flattery?" asked Antony, toying with a gold figurine.

He was seated behind a lemonwood table in one of the small, handsomely furnished rooms in a palatial residence that had been put at his disposal. He was wearing a military tunic, which he preferred to the more formal and cumbersome toga he donned when receiving the deputations.

Publius, glancing at his waxed tablet, read off the list of delegations, mentioning the one from Judea last.

"From Judea, you say? And what do you think our good friends from Jerusalem will want? Would you say they intend to hold games in my honor, or to arrange a springtime saturnalia or some other amusing diversions for me?" This question was accompanied by a hearty chuckle; it was obvious that Antony was in good humor.

"My guess is that they will pay their respects to the man who is now master of this part of the world and who was a close friend of the late Caesar," replied Publius. "They will probably express their hope that you will follow in Caesar's footsteps and not those of Cassius, who, I need not tell you, did not exactly win the admiration of the Jewish nation. At the same time, I wouldn't be surprised if they also voice their sentiments about Herod and his brother Phasael, who are also not liked by the Jews."

"Ah, that again! Seems like old times." Antony pushed his chair back and crossed his legs. "Do you know, Publius, it was in their country that I won my spurs. I was in charge of Gabinius's cavalry force that routed one of those Hasmoneans – I can't remember whether it was Aristobulus or one of his sons. Anyway, whoever it was had holed up in Alexandrium – a pretty tough fortress – and put up a stout defense. Gave us no end of trouble, he did. But we also put on a good show, and who do you think won the prize for bravery? None other than yours truly."

Antony grinned as he recalled this glorious episode from his younger days. And then, mindful of the business at hand, he uncrossed his legs and assumed an attentive expression. "You mentioned Herod and his relations with the Jews. You'd better brief me on that."

Publius began by giving a short factual report on the situation. He emphasized the people's warm respect for Caesar and their hatred of Cassius. He mentioned Hyrcanus's turning his back on Antipater, which caused Antony to frown. He went on to describe the heavy tribute Cassius had laid on the land and Malichus's inability, or refusal, to collect his quota, which had provoked Cassius's wrath and led to the order to sell the male inhabitants of four towns into slavery. He then told about Antipater's sudden death, which Herod was convinced was due to poisoning, and the subsequent murder of Malichus at Tyre.

Antony, who had been an active participant in many momentous events in Rome, was intrigued by Publius's account.

"I see things have been pretty lively in Judea since my young days. A strange but interesting country. The people actually worship a god that can't be seen, and yet they're willing to sacrifice their lives if anyone should try to interfere with that right. By Hercules! I'd like to see the Roman who would do that. And Hyrcanus, where does he stand now? He always struck me as a rather tame sort, but at least he had the good sense to work together with Antipater. Hard to imagine him breaking out of harness. How are relations now between him and Antipater's son?"

Publius shifted in his seat and folded his hands. "Truth to tell, after Cassius left Syria I lost touch with events in Judea. But when I accepted your offer I made it my business to update my information. To my astonishment, I discovered that Herod is now betrothed to Hyrcanus's granddaughter."

"What!" exclaimed Antony incredulously. "Did you say betrothed to Hyrcanus's granddaughter?"

"Yes, strange as it may seem."

"I would never believe it. I know of many marriages that have been made for all sorts of reasons. But this one beats them all. How do you explain it?"

"I don't know all the details. But as far as Herod is concerned, the reason is simple enough: He's got his eyes set on the throne."

"That's quite obvious. But it's Hyrcanus that baffles me."

"In his case it seems that the decisive factor was fear of his nephew Antigonus. Antigonus, you may or may not know, tried to advance into Judea after Cassius left Syria. That must have put the fear of death in Hyrcanus."

"Hmm, I see. So Antigonus is still up to his old tricks, is he? Aristobulus and his sons were always a troublesome lot." Antony leaned back in his chair. "It really does seem like old times again. You know, Publius, I see that I'm going to feel right at home here."

"You probably will. And what will you tell the Jewish deputation if they complain about Herod and Phasael?"

Antony scratched his chin, ruffling his curly beard a bit. "I'll have to hear them out, of course, and I'll understand and sympathize with their concern. But," he added with a wink, "if Herod is affianced to Hyrcanus's granddaughter, how can I interfere with what is essentially an internal matter?"

"I doubt if they will be taken in by that line. Everyone knows that when Rome's interests are at stake, it does interfere. Besides, permit me to remind you that Herod sided with Cassius."

"And you didn't?" Antony shot back with a teasing grin. "I knew Herod's father very well. And Herod is a chip off the old block. He'll side with Rome, no matter who is in the driver's seat. That's why we have to prefer him."

Antony rose to his feet, signaling that the meeting was over. "And Publius," he said, placing an arm around the other man's shoulder, "let's make sure we stay in the driver's seat."

* * *

Herod learned about the impending visit of the deputation of Jewish notables to Antony while in Jerusalem, where he had gone to confer with Phasael after Cassius's death. It was some months since he had last set foot in the family residence, and every object evoked poignant memories of his father. How many times had he sat in the cozy study and listened to his father describe with great relish how he had pulled off some diplomatic feat, or expatiate on how some delicate problem should be dealt with, or even to administer a gentle rebuke over what seemed to him a mistaken decision or course of action.

It was a mild spring day and the sunlight streamed in through the window, casting a cheerful glow over the room. Normally Herod would have felt buoyant and optimistic in these pleasant surroundings, but today he was troubled in mind. He had never conceived a great liking for Cassius – even his father could muster little enthusiasm for that austere, sour-tempered man – but they had both served him dutifully. Moreover, it was Cassius who had appointed, or more precisely reappointed, Herod governor of Coele-Syria and given him command of a formidable armed force. Now Cassius had disappeared from the scene, and his vanquishers held in their hands not only the reins of power but Herod's and Phasael's fate as well.

"There is no reason to worry," said Phasael, who was perched on the edge of the table and regarded Herod with a concerned look. "Rome needs us as much as we need Rome."

Herod cast a dubious glance at Phasael. "You know that and I know it, but the question is, does Antony know it? Don't forget what kind of man we're dealing with. He and Octavian proscribed hundreds, if not thousands, of senators and other notables. He even allowed one of his own relatives to be put on the list, and you know what happened to Cicero. A man who could do that is not to be trifled with."

"They were avenging Caesar's murder," Phasael reminded his brother. "Those who had a hand in that conspiracy, even if only indirectly or tacitly supported it, undoubtedly deserved such punishment. No, my dear brother, don't vex yourself so much. True, Antony can claim that we cooperated with Cassius, but we had no choice in the matter. And even more important, we had no part whatsoever in Cassius's death. Antony will realize that, even if the deputation tries to show us in as bad a light as possible. So..."

"What deputation?" asked Herod with a startled look.

Phasael, realizing that this information was bound to disconcert his brother, kept his voice as calm and even as possible. "A deputation of Jewish notables is due to set out within a few days to pay their respects to Antony in Bithyania."

"Why didn't you tell me this before?" exclaimed Herod, rising to his feet in agitation. "I've been here since yesterday, and only now you tell me about this deputation!"

"There's no need to be upset. It was to be expected that, along with all the official delegations from the various client-kingdoms, certain circles in this country would want to meet Antony. As far as I can gather, the decision to send the deputation was taken only two or three days ago. I was going to tell you about it this morning; in fact, I was leading up to it now. And what if they do present their respects, or even their complaints, to Antony? Do you think he'll be influenced by what they might say?"

Herod was so wrought up that his cheeks began to twitch. "They'll do their best to blacken our names," he said, his voice rising in pitch. "Who are they? Who are the members of this deputation?"

"I don't know the entire list. It's fairly long. But I can give you a few names."

As Phasael mentioned those he was certain of, Herod's face grew increasingly dark. "Every one of them was in Malichus's camp or is one of Antigonus's men," he muttered.

"Antigonus?" It was Phasael's turn to be surprised.

"Yes, Antigonus," confirmed Herod, banging his fist on the table. "Every single one of them is hostile to us!"

"And what if they are hostile? Haven't we always had to contend with unfriendly elements? There's nothing new in that."

"They're dogs!" snapped Herod with a fierce, black expression, "the whole pack of them. They'll go whining to Antony about how we're usurping the place of their beloved Hasmoneans."

Phasael shrugged his shoulders. "Yes, they probably will do that. So what?"

Herod glared at his brother, who was drawing up a chair and calmly seating himself. He failed to understand how Phasael could be so imperturbable. Herod's face twisted into a forbidding grimace as one sensation chased another: loathing, worry, fear, frustration. His cheeks began to twitch again as he struggled to master his feelings and reflect on what his brother had said. He glanced at his father's polished high-backed chair, which was left unused out of respect for his memory; in his mind's eye he could see Antipater admonishing him to think coolly and rationally and not impetuously, and he felt a sense of shame. Phasael was right: What difference would it make if a deputation went to Antony? Are they more than a match for himself? Can they convince Antony that they are friends of Rome, a reliable ally? No, all they can do is to vilify him and Phasael, who have faithfully served the Roman cause. And yet...

"They're bound to harp on our aid to Cassius in raising the tribute," he growled. "That would be the logical thing for them to do. Cassius was the ringleader in the plot against Caesar, and Antony's sworn enemy."

"They probably will do what you say. But weren't we serving Rome's interests in raising the tribute? We were ordered to do so by the Roman authorities – in this case Cassius. If Antony or Octavian, or anyone else for that matter, had ordered us to do the same thing, would you have refused?"

Herod thought a moment before replying. "No, I wouldn't have refused. But as I said before, we're dealing with a man who proscribed hundreds if not thousands of persons of high rank for siding with the conspirators, who were led by this same Cassius. Such a person may not look at things in a cool, dispassionate light, as you evidently think he will."

Phasael crossed his legs and started to play with the reed pen with which their father had written innumerable documents and epistles. "There is that danger, I won't deny it," he remarked with a shrug. "But it's a very slight one. Since then have you not repulsed Antigonus's advance into Judea and prevented him from seizing power? Don't forget that Antony has had several encounters with that branch of the Hasmonean family. He's hardly likely to think badly of one who opposes the ambitions of a man who has clearly demonstrated his anti-Roman sentiments. Play on that point if Antony throws the business of Cassius in your face. That ought to win him over. And there's something else you seem to be overlooking: Haven't you become affianced in the meantime to Hyrcanus's daughter? Don't forget, he was appointed high priest and ethnarch by Caesar, whom Antony esteemed and superbly eulogized. That's another very important point in your favor."

Herod silently digested Phasael's arguments. And as he did so, he felt a weight lifting from his heart. He even managed a feeble smile. "Thank you, dear brother. You are wiser than I am."

"Not wiser, but I think I keep my cool a little better than you. And – oh yes, one more thing: I suggest you let the deputation reach Antony first. You'll have no trouble demolishing their arguments."

* * *

The journey to Bithynia was a long, tiring one and gave Herod ample time to decide how best to approach Antony. So far he had managed to hit it off tolerably well with the various Roman officials with whom he had dealings, from the easy-going, loquacious Sextus to the sullen, vicious Cassius. But Antony was to him a largely unknown factor. Even though some fifteen years had passed since he and the governor Gabinius were guests in their home, Herod still remembered being impressed, and a little awed, by Antony's ruggedly handsome features and dashing manner. He also recalled, with a grin, how his father had frowned at some of Antony's remarks and jokes and nodded in the direction of his sons, intimating that their ears were too young for such off-color talk. Gossip had it that Antony was addicted to the good life – wine, women, and various other pleasures; he was also given to good-natured raillery and ribald jokes, even enjoying those made by his troops at his own expense. Herod was conscious of his own rather staid, humorless nature, and while he had learned the art of ingratiating himself with those whom it paid to do so, he had little gift for small talk or light-hearted banter. It was therefore with some apprehension that he was ushered into Antony's presence in a fashionable country home built in the Greek style.

Two sentries guarded the entrance to the residence and several were stationed inside. Herod had no idea whom the villa belonged to, but as he made his way through the peristyle escorted by a young officer, it was obvious that the owner did not lack for means. The officer led Herod to the wing on the far side of the inner court and halted before a stout oaken door. It was guarded by a stern-faced legionnaire, who saluted the officer, and upon being informed the name of the visitor, knocked on the door. At a command from within, he opened it and nodded to Herod to enter.

Herod found himself in a rather small room, whose walls were surprisingly almost totally bare and whose furnishings consisted of only a moderate-sized dark table, several chairs, and a low, handsomely carved chest. Two men wearing military tunics were seated at the table. Herod could not perceive any particular change in Publius Quintus's appearance since their last encounter, but Mark

Antony had put on weight and his curly hair had grown thinner, his eyes were wrinkled at the corners and the lids a little heavy, giving him a somewhat jaded look – an impression that was soon dispelled.

"Greetings!" said Herod, bowing stiffly.

"Greetings," the two men responded.

Antony pushed back his chair and made his way to the other side of the table. He clapped Herod by the shoulder and looked him up and down; a broad smile played on his lips, and he nodded his head in approval.

"So this is the gangling youngster I once met in Antipater's home," he said in a clear, sharp voice, flashing a quick glance at Publius. "I remember the occasion as though it were only yesterday. The room was swarming with high officials, army officers, and other dignitaries, and your father was busy putting everyone at his ease in his suave manner. In you came, a young man looking very serious and self-assured, accompanied by a friend – or maybe it was your brother. Your father introduced you two around, and when it came my turn, you bowed and said in a very proper tone of voice, 'I admire your superb horse-manship and bravery. It is my sincere wish to emulate you.' I smiled, but said to myself that here is a youngster who is destined to go far in life."

"Destined to be of service to Rome, sire," said Herod with deliberate modesty, both relieved and highly pleased at Antony's cordial welcome.

"Yes, I can honestly say that you, and your father before you, have emblazoned that on your banner."

Antony seated himself on one of the chairs standing along the wall opposite the table and nodded to Herod to do the same. Publius remained seated at the table. "Your father, whose untimely death was a grievous blow to all of us," Antony went on, "was highly spoken of by Caesar. And his cousin Sextus lauded your capable administration of one of his important provinces."

Herod was inwardly glowing at these warm words of praise, but was apprehensive lest Antony go on to mention his subsequent service to Cassius. He deemed it prudent to anticipate this possibility.

"I have always endeavored to be loyal to Rome," he declared in even accents. "Rome has brought peace and order to many peoples and lands. I say this even though not all its public servants seem to be sufficiently aware of its manifest destiny or are as estimable as the great Caesar and his protégés."

Antony realized that this oblique reference to his foe was intended to take any possible wind out of his sails. He had to admire the adroit way in which Herod sidestepped what might prove to be an embarrassing turn in this highly favorable conversation. He turned to Publius and with a wink observed, "If all the rulers and their subjects in this region are as appreciative of the role Rome can and must play as our friend here is, our task will be a very happy and successful one. Don't you agree?"

"Quite so," replied Publius perfunctorily. He cleared his throat. "I want to remind you that the delegation from Pontus arrived this morning."

"See that they are given comfortable quarters and attended to. Tell them that tomorrow morning I shall be honored to receive them officially. Tonight they will be my guests along with the other delegations."

Publius rose to his feet and started to take his leave. Before he got to the door Antony called out: "One more thing, Publius: How are the arrangements for tonight's entertainment?"

Publius had half-expected this question. "Everything has been taken care of," he replied dryly. "I can assure you that they will find the entertainment quite satisfactory in every respect."

After Publius's departure Antony turned to Herod. "Now we can continue our chat. But not here. I feel the need for fresh air."

Antony led Herod to the garden, pausing to instruct an orderly to have refreshments served them. The garden was not very large, but it was laid out in good taste, with leafy bowers, fountains, and statues endowing it with an air of serene beauty. Antony found it a welcome relaxation from his official duties, although being a man of action, he discovered that if his relaxation was not shared with someone it soon palled on him.

Herod, who had a strong sense of aesthetics, was duly impressed. "A beautiful garden," he exclaimed, "and what splendid sculptures!"

"They are splendid," agreed Antony, who greatly admired the human figures – the males youthful, brawny, and vigorous-looking; the females comely and seductive. "Take this discuss thrower," he said, pointing to a white marble statue, "who but the Greeks can carve an athlete like this, capturing flowing motion in stone? In the art of warfare and governing they may be inferior to Rome, but in sculpturing they have no peers. We Romans have done them a great honor in appropriating some of their finest specimens to decorate the capital of the world," he added with a grin. "Right, Aspasia?" he said jovially, slapping the thighs of a voluptuous nude female figure mounted on a round pedestal a few feet away. "She's a bit hard to handle," he commented with a glint in his eyes, "but what an inspiring body! And best of all, she never finds any fault with me."

At this point two Nubian slaves appeared, one carrying a platter piled high with delicacies, and the other a decanter of wine, some other beverage, a mixing bowl, and two silver goblets. They laid these out on a small marble table and placed two stools around the table, after which they withdrew. Antony took Herod by the arm and led him toward the table.

"There's nothing here you can't eat," he said, seating himself and waving Herod to the second stool. "I don't know how strict you are about these so-called forbidden foods, but as you can see, I am not unfamiliar with Jewish customs. The wine, of course is a different matter. If you prefer, there is something else to drink."

"It's very considerate of you, but ever since I have served Rome in various official capacities, it has been my practice to eat and drink what the Romans do, at least when I'm their guests. Besides, there are some who call me a 'half-Jew,' so if I am sinning against the Jewish religion, I suppose it can be regarded as only half a sin," he added with a wan smile.

"As you wish," said Antony. "The deputation from Jerusalem wouldn't touch anything except fruit and vegetables, even though I assured them that special dishes had been prepared for them. Nor did they seem to appreciate our superb entertainment," he added with a grin. "I suppose in Jerusalem they're not used to that sort of thing. They gave me the impression of being straightlaced men who are boringly faithful to their wives."

At this reference to the deputation, Herod shifted his weight on the stool. This was Antony's first mention of it, and while there was nothing in his remarks or attitude to cause any disquiet, Herod was curious to learn more details, especially the outcome of the audience.

"The members of the deputation are men of repute and high standing," he remarked warily.

"So you know who they are?" said Antony, a little surprised at the mild reaction.

"I know most of them by name. They are not men with whom I or the other members of my family have been on particularly cordial terms."

Antony was amused at this statement. He regarded Herod with an arch expression. "From the tenor of their remarks I got the impression that you are sworn enemies. I don't mind telling you that they painted you and your brother in dark colors. They had so many complaints that I had to cut them short."

This information made Herod flush with fury against the members of the delegation. He paled noticeably, and a cold, suspicious look clouded his eyes. "I trust that you were able to properly judge their allegations," he said, trying to keep his voice as calm as possible.

"I more or less knew what to expect even before they set foot in here," replied Antony, who did not fail to notice Herod's altered expression. He scrutinized the refreshments on the table and picked a sweetmeat, which he proceeded to munch.

"Delicious!" exclaimed Antony, smacking his lips. "I must compliment my cook. He's new but came to me highly recommended. Makes the tastiest dishes, and for that he deserves a proper reward. What will you drink – wine or the other concoction?"

"Whatever you take," said Herod, impatient to hear more about the audience.

Antony rose and filled two goblets of wine from the mixing bowl. After handing one to Herod, he raised his goblet and proposed the traditional Jewish toast *l'chaim,* which he recalled from his younger days. Herod returned the toast, adding: "May your rule be marked by peace and prosperity, for Rome and the provinces alike."

On that note they drank. Antony downed most of his goblet at one go, and then fixed Herod with a piercing look. "The fulfillment of your good wishes largely depends on the kind of cooperation I get from the inhabitants of the provinces," he said in a voice pregnant with meaning.

"And that in turn will depend to no small degree on the caliber of the men who will direct the affairs of the provinces," retorted Herod.

"In the case of Judea I don't expect any problems on that score."

"From what you've told me about the deputation, there may very well be a problem. As you have said, they don't take kindly to me and my brother, who, together with our late father, have always made it a guiding principle to cooperate with Rome for the common good of our two countries."

Antony was amused at the adroit manner in which Herod steered the conversation back to the subject that was clearly gnawing at him. "It's true that the deputation expressed sentiments that were not exactly complimentary," he admitted, downing the rest of his drink and gazing at the empty goblet as though surprised that it was empty. "But they represent only one element in the population."

"But not an insignificant element," Herod hastily pointed out in a tone of concern mingled with suppressed wrath.

"Perhaps not, but I managed to foil their plans."

At this statement Herod felt a sense of relief. "How did you do that, if I may ask?"

Antony rose and stretched himself. He helped himself to another delicacy and contemplated another goblet of wine. "I simply asked them that if you are so bad and wicked as they claim, how is that Hyrcanus, high priest and ethnarch of the Jewish nation, nevertheless saw fit to betroth his granddaughter to you. Ho! that really made them hem and haw. You would have enjoyed the scene. I got such vague and incoherent answers that I didn't know whether to pity or to laugh at them. And speaking of the betrothal, I congratulate you."

"Thank you."

"That calls for a special toast." Antony picked up Herod's goblet and went over to the table to mix two more drinks. He handed one to Herod and raised his aloft.

"To you, whom the goddess Juno – and Venus too – have bestowed their gracious favor. May your union with the Hasmonean house prove advantageous to all concerned, and," he added almost as an afterthought, "bring you marital happiness."

Herod, who knew something of the attitude toward marriage in high Roman circles and Antony's notorious philandering, acknowledged the toast with a thin smile.

175

"When I congratulate Hyrcanus," Antony went on after quaffing a long drought, "I shall have to remember not to evoke our dear gods – or rather, goddesses. Where is it we're due to meet?" he asked, more to himself.

"In Daphna, I believe. He intends to send a small delegation to meet you in Ephesus, but he himself will probably meet you later in Daphna."

"Oh yes, that's it. I must say, I'm looking forward to meeting him. We have a lot to reminisce about. Who would have dreamed that one day you and his granddaughter – well, the ways of the gods are often inscrutable and most surprising."

"Indeed they are," acknowledged Herod perfunctorily.

"But I doubt if Hyrcanus will produce a list of complaints and dark accusations against you," said Anony, grinning roguishly.

"From what I understand, Hyrcanus has two main petitions to submit to you," said Herod, and he immediately regretted this statement, which had slipped out inadvertently.

"And what are they?"

Reproaching himself for his imprudence, Herod paused to frame his reply. Antony regarded him curiously, wondering what caused his sudden nervousness.

"Hyrcanus would like to ask for the restoration of the territory taken from Judea by the Tyrians," replied Herod in a low, flat voice.

"When did the Tyrians do that?"

"Shortly before Cassius left Syria."

"Cassius? That villain!" exclaimed Antony. He knew that Cassius was the culprit, but he sensed that Herod wanted to conceal something from him. He decided to make him squirm a bit. "Besides restoring the territory, what else is troubling our good friend Hyrcanus?"

Herod swallowed hard. He stared past Antony, but could feel his eyes boring into him. For a second he thought of fobbing him off with some innocuous reply, but realized that after his audience with Hyrcanus, Antony would know the truth. "Hyrcanus's second petition will be to free the Jews who were sold into slavery by Cassius," said Herod in a hollow voice.

"Oh yes, I once heard some vague reports about that business. You must tell me about it. I'm very curious."

Herod compressed his lips as he considered what exactly to relate to this man, who had the power to make or break him. He described as sketchily as possible how Cassius had laid a heavy tribute of 700 talents on Judea, and how one of the officials responsible for its collection had failed to raise his quota, in consequence of which the inhabitants of four of the principal towns in the area he was responsible for had been sold into slavery. Herod discreetly omitted any mention of his part in raising the tribute.

Antony, who had resumed his seat while listening to this account, burst out indignantly: "Just like Cassius! He was a blackguard through and through. When I meet Hyrcanus, I'll inform him that the Jews who were sold into slavery will be set free and the territory taken by the Tyrians will be restored."

At these words Herod breathed more easily. "Hyrcanus will be most appreciative, and so will all the Jewish inhabitants of Judea. They will hail your benevolence and wisdom."

"It's only what they should expect of Rome." Antony took another sip of wine and then fixed Herod with a searching glance. "You say that Cassius had demanded 700 talents. How much did he actually get before he enslaved the four towns?"

Beads of sweat appeared on Herod's forehead. With a conscious effort not to betray any nervousness, he replied that the figure was 600 talents.

Antony's eyebrows rose sharply. "That's a very big sum for Judea. I'm surprised he got that much. He must have had some very efficient collectors – or perhaps I should say, a very efficient method. Who raised the money for him?"

A silence ensued. Antony smiled enigmatically as he waited for an answer. In a dry, matter-of-fact voice Herod related that his father had been ordered to raise the tribute. Since the order had come from the Roman governor, he had no choice but to obey, and so he assigned the task to three men, including Phasael and himself.

At this revelation Antony stared long and hard at Herod. He noticed a pallor creeping over his long nose and a troubled look clouding his eyes. Antony smiled to himself; it would be amusing to let Herod squirm a little more.

"I trust, sire, that you will understand it was not out of any particular sympathy with Cassius that we performed this duty," explained Herod somewhat stiffly.

"Sympathy? Of course not!" Antony spat out. "One never sympathized with Cassius. But when it is obvious that an order is against Rome's true interests, I fail to see the need to display excessive zeal in carrying it out, especially when the order was issued by the man most responsible for the foul murder of the greatest Roman of all times."

Herod, taken aback at this harsh rebuke, was momentarily at a loss for words. Even though it was he who had regrettably mentioned the subject of the tribute, he had not expected Antony to become so indignant, especially when the talk had been going extremely well. Antony was clearly a man of changeable moods and could be quite touchy. He would have to bear this in mind in the future.

"Permit me to point out, sire," he said guardedly, "it was precisely because we knew what sort of man Cassius was, and out of concern for the welfare of the inhabitants of Judea, who had been most loyal to and loved the noble Caesar, that we felt ourselves bound to carry out Cassius's bidding. We knew that many cities in this region had been forced to pay him ten years' taxes in advance. When Rhodes resisted his demands, he ordered his troops to kill many of the leading citizens. In Tarsus they had to auction off municipal lands, melt down temple vessels and ornaments, and even sell free persons into slavery. That was the kind of man we had to deal with. We had no choice but to bow to his extortionate demands, even though our sympathy naturally lay with the supporters of the great and admirable Caesar, who had proved to be a beneficent ruler in the best Roman tradition and who, incidentally, had seen fit to elevate our late lamented father and his sons to high office."

Antony listened attentively as Herod presented his defense in an increasingly confident voice, and he was duly impressed. He had to admit that he and Octavian had not resorted to the gentlest of methods to raise funds. The proscriptions had been a grisly affair, even if very profitable – and not only in monetary terms. He recalled with a roguish grin how Caponius's wife had offered herself to him in order to save her husband's skin. It had been worth it, he thought, savoring the memory. True, the proscriptions had been necessary in order to punish Caesar's murderers and, incidentally, to confiscate their wealth, but it far overshadowed anything that Cassius had done; compared with it, the latter's exactions were a paltry matter. Well, Herod had perspired and squirmed, and Antony had found this an amusing diversion. Now he would let him off the hook. Actually he was pleased at the way the man acquitted himself, particularly that little bit at the end about how Caesar had appointed Antipater and his sons to high positions. Very clever that. Yes, Herod would prove very useful. Antony resumed a stern mien.

"If you're trying to prove that Cassius was a rapacious villain, you can save your breath. I know only too well what he was like. But one must know how to deal with such scoundrels, and cringing before them is not the way. Well, he's met his deserved end, and I trust that if you are put to a similar test in the future, you will know how to handle it."

Antony paused and assumed a softer, meditative look; his voice took on a different timbre. "So you and your brother raised 600 talents, did you? That took some doing. I think I should consider appointing you chief tax collector for my Eastern provinces."

This statement was accompanied by a toss of Antony's head, and together with the note of raillery in his voice, it told Herod that the danger had passed – almost as abruptly as it had blown up. He wiped his brow with the back of his hand.

"I hope you'll forgive me, but I do not regard that as a very desirable post," he declared in a more lighthearted tone. "I have yet to find anyone who willingly pays taxes, and if you're including the Egyptians, they certainly would not relish paying them to one hailing from Judea."

"No, they wouldn't," conceded Antony, folding his arms on his chest. "That vixen of a queen of theirs would have a fit. I've summoned her to appear before me at Tarsus."

"On the same charge?"

"Something much worse. She not only raised money for Cassius, she also raised a force for him. She must render an accounting for that."

"She's very clever. She knew how to twist the great Caesar around her little finger."

"She possessed magnificent gifts to beguile him with," said Antony with a sly wink. "But you needn't worry about Antony falling victim to her snares."

Antony's countenance creased into a broad grin, and his voice took on a confidential ring. "I'll let you in on a little secret. When she was young and I was stationed in these parts, I had a crush on her. But a good many years have passed since then – I'd say fifteen or so. She must be at least thirty by now – an old mare ready to be turned out to pasture. No, you needn't have any fear about Antony being trapped by her."

"I have been told that age has not faded her bloom or dimmed her other charms."

"No? Well, I shall soon be able to see for myself," replied Antony with a bold look. After briefly contemplating this delightful prospect, he recalled the business at hand. "I had better get back to the house and see what excitement is going on there."

Antony put his goblet down on the marble table and started to stroll back to the house with Herod at his side. "Speaking of feminine charms, when is your marriage to Hyrcanus's granddaughter going to take place?"

"No date has been set yet. But it will probably not be very soon; she's very young."

"All the more reason not to delay. When they're young they're fresh and beautiful, like a newly opened rose. Why wait till she starts to wilt?"

"There are other reasons," replied Herod a little stiffly.

"May I ask what they are, if I'm not too indiscreet?"

"For one thing, Hyrcanus is worried about Antigonus. He insists on waiting until the tension dies down, until this threat is eliminated."

Antony stopped dead in his tracks and fixed Herod with a serious expression. "That is of direct concern to me too. Stability in Judea is exactly what I want and need. You can count on my full cooperation and support on that point."

"Thank you, sire. It's good to know that I have the confidence of the Roman triumvir in this matter."

Antony tapped Herod on the breast with his forefinger. "You have more than my confidence. I'm counting on you to keep Judea pacified and firmly in the Roman orbit." He paused for a moment and lowered his voice. "You don't know this and not many Romans know it either, but shortly before his assassination Caesar was contemplating a campaign against Parthia. He realized that the Empire would not be secure on its eastern flank as long as Parthia remained strong and able to challenge Rome. Crassus's ill-fated expedition made this amply clear. Caesar had even gone so far as to draw up plans for such an expedition. He had no fixed date in mind, but was definitely set on it. I was one of the few who knew about the plans.

"What I'm going to say now is strictly confidential. Before embarking on my present tour I studied the plans again. The question of Parthia is high on my list of priorities. Once I have established order in my provinces and have the reins firmly in hand, I intend to deal with the question. It's essential – absolutely essential – that there be peace and quiet in Judea."

Antony paused to let the import of this revelation sink in. Herod's brow furrowed as he reflected on it and the implications for him. It was plain that he had been made privy to a secret enterprise of the utmost importance. And it was equally plain that he would not have been so privileged unless Antony was certain he could trust him and had marked him out for a significant role.

"You can be assured," said Herod with a conscious effort to keep his voice calm and even, "that your aims and mine regarding Judea are identical. You can also be assured that you can place your trust in me – in whatever capacity you deem me worthy to fill."

Antony beamed at Herod and clapped him by the shoulder. "Good! I knew I could count on you. In Rome we have a triumvirate – three men at the helm. In Judea we shall have something similar: Hyrcanus will continue to be ethnarch, and you and Phasael will be at his right hand – or, perhaps I should say, you at his right hand and Phasael at his left hand. And as for your titles – tetrarch would seem to be appropriate. How does that sound to you?"

Herod, his heart beating rapidly and his spirits soaring, replied with a look of exultation: "It sounds very impressive, and very responsible. You can rely on us to fulfill this office to the best of our ability and devotion."

Shemaiah Joins Emmaus Celebration of Avner's Return

The sun was sinking low on the horizon and a breeze started to blow up, rippling the strands of golden wheat and rustling the tree-tops. Zechariah, trudging home with his ox Kalba, was grateful for the breeze, for it had been hotter than usual for an early-summer day.

As he eyed the weed-infested fields with their skimpy crops, he sighed – not so much because it meant a smaller income with all its attendant hardships, but because it was a poignant reminder of the absence of so many of Emmaus's menfolk. Since Saul had told him about the rumors of Cassius's defeat, Zechariah had been buoyed by the hope of seeing Avner again soon. He vowed that if the rumors turned out to be true and Avner returned home, he would journey to Jerusalem to make a thanksgiving offering. Zechariah was a patient man, and he was sure that everything would turn out well, but in God's own time. Still, he could not gaze upon the stricken fields without thinking about his son. How many imaginary conversations had he held with him, how many heated political discussions. In his mind's eye he could see Avner gesturing excitedly and rebutting his arguments with all the passion and confidence of youth.

"Well, Kalba," Zechariah addressed his ox, "what do you say? Is it right to moan about our lot, hard though it may be at the moment? Should we not be grateful to the Almighty for what we have, instead of complaining about we lack? Our men are safe and sound and will probably be freed soon. What more can we ask for than that? What does it matter if our crops are meager and we will have to struggle harder this year? The good Lord will help us; He won't forsake His people – and not even you, my faithful ox," he added, patting the animal fondly. Kalba turned his big eyes on Zechariah and swished his tail, as though he understood perfectly.

Zechariah reached the courtyard to his home and was about to open the gate when his neighbor Saul hailed him: "Shalom, Zechariah!"

"Shalom, Saul," Zechariah returned the greeting, eyeing his neighbor curiously. "I see you're having guests today. Relatives or friends?"

"What makes you think I'm having guests?"

"When a man who is hale and hearty does only half a day's work, he is either getting lazy or is preparing to rejoice. Since your beard is washed and combed and you have changed into your brown striped tunic and put on a clean head-covering, I give you the benefit of the doubt."

Saul chuckled. "You're pretty shrewd, aren't you? Yes, we're expecting a guest – from Jerusalem."

"From the Holy City, no less? That's quite an honor."

"A special honor. It's my brother's son Joel, who, as you know, is a disciple of the famous sage Shemaiah."

"That *is* something special. That means we'll probably enjoy a fine sermon this Sabbath."

"Even better than you think. It won't be my nephew who will give the sermon, but someone far more exalted – Shemaiah himself!"

As Saul expected, this disclosure made a profound impression on his friend. Zechariah's face lit up, and there was a note of awe in his voice. "Shemaiah! We are fortunate to be so highly honored." Zechariah stroked his beard thoughtfully. "And to what do we owe this unexpected rare privilege?"

Saul shrugged his shoulders. "Your guess is as good as mine. You know that the sages make it a practice to visit various communities and deliver sermons. Why Shemaiah chose Emmaus for this particular Sabbath, and without letting the elders know well in advance, I can't say. When I see my nephew, I'll probably find out."

"And who will be his host?"

Saul gave a short laugh. "There was keen competition for the honor. When I told Meir the news, he insisted that as president of the synagogue he was entitled to be the host, but Eliezer claimed that since he was chief archon of the town, the honor belonged to him. They finally agreed that Meir would be Shamaiah's host, and next time a sage visits us he will stay with Eliezer."

"That sounds fair enough. I too am privileged this Sabbath. It's my turn to translate the Scripture reading."

"Is that so?" Saul shifted his weight and made a wry face. "I'm still not convinced we have to translate the Scripture reading. Who here doesn't speak Hebrew? And if there are a few who prefer Aramaic, they understand Hebrew. Why must we ape the Galileans? If they insist on speaking Aramaic and can't take the trouble to learn Hebrew properly, that's their hard luck."

Zechariah saw that Kalba was getting restless, and so he opened the gate to let him into the courtyard. "All right, Kalba, in you go. I know this conversation doesn't interest you," he added with a grin. "A fine ox he is," he commented as the animal lumbered toward the cattle-shed. He then turned to Saul to reply to his remark.

"What harm is there in translating the Scripture reading? It's not only the Galileans who don't know Hebrew, or don't know it well enough to really understand the reading. We have to face reality. Aramaic is the main language in this part of the world, much more so than Greek. It's unfortunate, perhaps, but nearly all our people in Babylonia speak only Aramaic. When they come on pilgrimage, shouldn't they be able to communicate with their brethren in the Holy City? And don't we in Emmaus have visitors from Babylonia? Sometimes on a Sabbath there may be almost a dozen outsiders in the synagogue, and that includes your cousin from Galilee. Shouldn't he understand what is being read from the holy Scripture?"

"Of course he should. And so he should make it his business to know Hebrew – in addition to Aramaic, if he wants – just as we in Emmaus know both languages and just as my nephew from Jerusalem does. And speaking of my nephew, I better go; he'll probably be arriving soon."

Saul bid Zechariah *shalom* and headed for home. But after a few steps he stopped. "By the way, Zechariah," he called out, "why don't you tell the president of the synagogue to have some extra benches put in."

"Why do we need more benches? So many of our men are unfortunately absent."

"Just the same, it's advisable to have a few extra benches. One can never tell."

Zechariah regarded Saul inquisitively. *Did he really think something would happen before the Sabbath to make extra benches necessary? It was very unlikely. Still…* "All right, I suppose it won't hurt to have a few more benches."

Zechariah watched Saul making his way down the dirt road in the direction of his home. His house was as big as Zechariah's, but it did not seem so, for three of his children were still living there. Zechariah's home, which was set between two others sharing the courtyard, seemed spacious in comparison – too spacious, he thought nostalgically, now that all his children except Avner had set up their own homes.

Like his children, he had been born in this house, but it was smaller then. Before he married, his father had added a second story for him and Hannah, and although it was not as large as the lower story, it had proved adequate for several years. After his parents' death Zechariah had moved the family downstairs and kept the second story for the day when his first-born, Yair, should marry. When the second of his four sons was about to take a wife, Zechariah had planned to add a third story or at least an attic, but Yair decided to build his own home close to the field his father had purchased for him. Over the years Yair's brothers had followed suit, and whereas the house had once resounded with the laughter and shouting of Zechariah and Hannah's eight children, now only Avner lived at home. Not that it was by any means empty and forlorn: The married children were frequent visitors, and their offspring saw to it that the grandparents did not suffer from excessive quiet.

Zechariah entered the courtyard and opened the door to the cattle-shed to admit Kalba. He removed the harness and washed the ox down with a large rag, after which he released him to the feeding trough. His ox seen to, Zechariah proceeded to the house, first looking into the woodshed and storehouse to see that everything was in order. As he neared the oven in front of the house, the smell of bread in the baking tickled his nostrils, along with the delicious smell emanating from a large pot on the clay stove next to the oven. Zechariah opened the front door and stepped inside after kissing the *mezuzah* attached to the upper part of the doorpost.

"Hannah!" he called out, "I'm here."

His wife's answering voice could be heard from the other end of the house. Zechariah walked through the dining room to the kitchen, where he preferred to eat when no guests or members of the family were present. Until a few years ago, when there were hardly ever less than half a dozen persons present, he almost invariably had his meals in the dining room; but now that Avner too was absent, he could not bring himself to eat there, even though the kitchen was quite cramped.

"How did the work go today?" asked Hannah, carrying on with the peeling of cucumbers.

Like her husband, she was short and lean. Her graying hair, which was combed straight back and gathered into a bun, contrasted with her bronzed face and neck. She had a pleasant, serene expression, with lively brown eyes, a thin nose, and smooth lips. Her voice was soft and rarely raised in anger. She was wearing her workday tunic made of coarse stuff.

"Thank God, I can't complain," replied Zechariah. He drew up a stool and seated himself. "I managed to plow as much of the barley field as I had hoped to. Actually the barley crop wasn't too bad this year. But the wheat is a different matter. That's going to be a skimpy yield. How soon will supper be ready? I'm hungry."

"And tired too, from the looks of you. Why don't you change your clothes while I get supper on the table? Maybe you'd like to eat in the dining room for a change?"

"In that big empty room? No, thanks."

Zechariah rose and filled a basin with water drawn from a clay jar. He carried it to the bedroom, where he washed and changed into a clean tunic. Glancing out the window, he saw that the sun had gone down. He thereupon proceeded to the dining room to say the evening *Shema*. He took down a small lamp from a recess in the wall and, after lighting it, placed it on a stand in the center of the room. It diffused a dim light, but it sufficed for the moment; later he would put more lamps on the stand to provide enough illumination for reading.

Bidden by the Bible to say the *Shema* twice daily, in the morning and after sundown, he was sometimes inclined to recite the declaration of God's unity rather mechanically. But not tonight; he enunciated each word slowly and with fervor, and then added a short prayer for the safety and early return of his son.

Returning to the kitchen, he saw five loaves of bread in a large willow basket lying on top of the small chest used for storing spices and pickled foods.

"Why did you bake today instead of tomorrow?" he asked his wife. "The bread won't be very fresh for the Sabbath."

"I promised to help our neighbor Miriam tomorrow. She's not feeling well enough to prepare for the Sabbath."

"A pity her husband isn't here to help," commiserated Zechariah. "It's been pretty hard for her."

He glanced at the bread and shook his head. "Five loaves – it wasn't so long ago that that would have lasted no more than half a week," he observed nostalgically. "Which of our children will be with us this Sabbath?"

"Leah."

"What about Ezra? I thought he was supposed to come too."

"The children aren't feeling well. They'll come next week."

"What's the matter with them?"

"Nothing to worry about – just upset stomachs and headache."

"I see. Well, I don't think we'll suffer from too much quiet – not with Leah's three lively youngsters in the house."

Hannah always looked forward to the Sabbath, but never more so than during the past few months. Surrounded by her children and grandchildren and with the house ringing with laughter, she was able to keep from worrying excessively about Avner. During the week it was different, but on the seventh day the home radiated with a special warmth, an entirely different atmosphere that made all problems and anxieties seem less acute. Even though Avner's fate was uppermost in everyone's mind, it was tacitly understood that on this day no mention was to be made of it in order not to spoil the Sabbath joy.

"You had better start eating," she urged her husband. "The soup will get cold."

Zechariah made the blessing over the bread, and broke off a piece for himself and another for his wife. The lentil soup was still hot, but he consumed it in no time at all; when Hannah asked if he wanted a second helping, he did not refuse. He did not speak much during the meal, but after he had eaten he was in a more talkative mood. He recounted his detachable table-tops and tripods and a pile of folding chairs. In the middle of the room, Zacharia told his wife about the conversation with Saul, and like her husband, Hannah was excited to learn that the famous sage Shemaiah would be visiting Emmaus this Sabbath. Zechariah also reminded her that it was his good fortune to be the translator of the Scripture reading this week.

After saying grace, he got up to start preparing the translation. He went to the dining room, which was the center of activity in the home. Along one wall were stacked a number of fairly large four-legged oblong tables with wooden-backed chairs at either end. Zechariah moved the lampstead next to a table and lit two more lamps. On top of one of the chests was a Torah scroll, which he had brought home in the morning from the synagogue after the reading held especially for the benefit of neighboring villagers who brought their produce to the Emmaus market on Mondays and Thursdays. He carried the scroll to the table and opened it to the correct place. As translator, he would stand beside each of the seven persons called up to read a section from the weekly portion and would render each verse into Aramaic. But this task was not limited to a mere literal translation; in fact, one who did this did not fulfill his function properly, for the translation was actually a sort of commentary that ensured that the Written Law was transmitted in accordance with oral tradition. And since the translation was regarded as Oral Law, it had to be given from memory. Zechariah also had to prepare the translation of the selected passages from the Prophets, but here his task would be easier in one respect, as the translation could be rather rough and rendered after every three verses.

Zechariah knew much of the Torah by heart, but still he had to refresh his memory, especially the oral traditions associated with the translation. And since the leading sage of the day would be present this week, it was doubly important not to make any mistakes.

Not many of the adult males of Emmaus were qualified to serve as translator, and Zechariah deemed it an honor to be among the chosen few. As a youngster he had studied in the local school, and afterward his father had sent him to Jerusalem for another year of study in one of the *yeshivot* (Talmudic colleges). Most of his fellow townsmen did not have this privilege, and he was forever grateful to his father for it, particularly as it had not been easy for him to forgo Zechariah's help on the farm.

While noting down on a waxed tablet some of the points he intended to incorporate, he was startled by a loud knock on the door. Occasionally a neighbor or some other townsman would call after dark on personal or communal business, but this was infrequent, for after nightfall few inhabitants ventured out. He put the tablet down and went to the door.

"Who's there?" he called out.

"It's not the tax collector or an uncircumcised heathen. It's someone who is footsore and hungry and far behind in his rent," came the blithe reply.

Zechariah could not believe his ears. With trembling fingers and pounding heart, he slipped the bolt and opened the door. There, clad in a frayed, soiled tunic, a makeshift rucksack slung over one shoulder, and a big grin spread across his grimy face, stood Avner.

"Avner! It's you!"

"I'm glad you recognize me. Yes, it's me – in the flesh, as they say."

With that eloquent confirmation, Avner warmly embraced his father, who was beside himself with joy. "Blessed be the merciful Lord!" Zechariah uttered repeatedly, too overcome to say anything else.

Hannah, who had also heard the knock on the door and the exchange of greetings, came running in. She fell on her son with cries of joy and embraced him so hard and long that Avner thought she would never let go.

"Come in, come in my son," she said at last, wiping the tears from her eyes.

As Avner stepped into the vestibule, he kissed the *mezuzah*. How many times had he pictured this scene in his mind's eye while enslaved; how eagerly had he awaited this moment! He uttered a silent prayer of thanks. Zechariah bolted the door, and together they went into the dining room. Hannah immediately set abut kindling additional lamps; there was radiant light not only in the room but in her heart as well. The parents took a good look at their son. He was ragged and much thinner, his cheeks were gaunt; but his eyes gleamed with their customary sparkle, and his spirits were clearly as high as ever.

"You've gone thinner," said Hannah, shaking her head. "Didn't they feed you well?"

Avner removed the rucksack from his shoulder and seated himself on one of the chairs. He was so weary he thought he would not be able to get up.

"They treated us royally," he said in reply to his mother's question. "We were served a sumptuous repast every evening while reclining on damask couches and with musicians and dancers performing for us. Nothing but the best to eat – stuffed geese and pigeons, exotic desserts..."

"Apart from fruit and vegetables, was there anything else you ate?" asked Zechariah, proud that his son had refrained as far as possible from touching forbidden foods.

"Bread – as much as I could lay my hands on. Reuven said it was all right to eat bread. There were a few other things too. I didn't exactly get fat on my fare, as you notice, but neither did I starve."

"When did you last eat?" Hannah wanted to know.

"Around noon. Some kind farmer provided Reuven and me with an ample supply of beets and cucumbers. Some day I'll have to repay him."

"I'll get you something right away, Oh, how good it is to have you back!" Hannah wiped a tear from her eye and hurried into the kitchen

"Well, Abba," said Avner to his father, fingering his soiled tunic, "what do you think of my new outfit? It's the latest fashion, straight from Rome."

"It's about what one would expect from Rome," replied Zechariah with a chuckle. It warmed his heart to hear his son jesting again. "Why don't you wash and put on something clean?"

"But it wouldn't be nearly as chic," protested Avner with a straight face. "If I'm to dine with my father and mother, I must wear my most fashionable garb."

"Then let it be in your most fashionable garb," relented Zechariah with a broad grin.

Avner, however, changed his mind, and summoning all his energy, he rose and made his weary way to the bedroom to wash and change his clothes.

Meanwhile Zechariah rolled up the Torah scroll and put it back on top of the chest. He had not managed all the reading, but the little that was left could easily be finished the next day. His heart was light and a feeling of gratitude to the Almighty welled up in him. He put two more chairs around the table, for although he and Hannah had already eaten, they would join their son in some fruit at least.

Hannah entered and set a place for Avner, putting down a copper dish instead of the earthenware generally used during the week. She returned to the kitchen to get a bowl of vegetable soup, a fresh carp, which she had intended to serve on the Sabbath, a bowl of dried figs, and a loaf of bread.

Avner emerged from his room refreshed after washing and changing into a clean tunic. His eyes lit up at the sight of the food, and he had an overwhelming urge to pounce on it.

"Imma, this is a meal fit for a king!" he exclaimed.

"You are a king today," she replied. "Now go and wash your hands and sit down to eat."

After blessing the bread, Avner broke off a big chunk, which disappeared in a trice. He then tackled the soup, followed by the fish, devouring it ravenously.

"Not so fast," cautioned Hannah, who had taken the chair on Avner's left. "You're gulping the food down like a dog. It doesn't become one who has been used to eating sumptuous meals while seated on a damask couch." They all laughed.

When everything set before Avner had disappeared, Zechariah handed around cups of wine, and they drank in honor of the occasion.

"In our rejoicing to have you back with us," said Zechariah, wiping a drop of wine from his chin with the back of his hand, "we must not forget our fellow townsmen who were taken away together with you. Have any others besides you been released?"

"I can only speak about Reuven, who was together with me. We were released at the same time and made our way back to Emmaus together. Our Greek master told us that it was at Antony's order that he was setting us free, so I imagine the others should be returning soon."

Zechariah recalled Saul's suggestion to have extra benches in the synagogue this Sabbath, and marveled at his prescience. He must have some sixth sense; he couldn't possibly have known about Antony's order, he thought to himself, shaking his head in wonder. He was very curious to know what had befallen Avner during his months of slavery, but thought it advisable to wait until he had recovered from the fatigue of his long tramp home. However, Avner was feeling better after the food, and he began to recount some of his experiences. His parents listened with rapt attention, and were more than a little perturbed by the story of his attempted escape and its aftermath. Avner did not omit the incident of the master's wife, but limited himself to a brief description, glossing over the more intimate details.

"Next week you and I will go to the Temple and make a thanksgiving offering," declared Zechaniah when Avner had finished. "This Sabbath you'll be called up to the Torah, so you better prepare for it. And prepare well, because the sage Shemaiah will be present and I'll be translating.

"We'll have the whole family over for Sabbath dinner," said Hannah. "This is a very special occasion."

Ordinarily on a Friday, Zechariah worked in the fields or, in inclement weather, on other jobs until the horn was sounded to signal the cessation of work. But this time he was in too festive a mood and decided that the fields could wait till Sunday. Avner, however, jocularly objected, saying that he had been having life too easy of late. Actually he knew that his father must have been hard put to keep the farm going during his absence, and he felt duty-bound to lend him a hand even on this short but very special day. So, despite his parents' protest, he donned his work tunic and collected the necessary tools. He himself harnessed Kalba, who showed his pleasure over the reunion by vigorously swishing his tail. They proceeded through the gate, but that was as far as they got. Saul came into view, and catching sight of Avner, greeted him effusively. He did not leave until he had heard a good part of Avner's adventures.

Thanks to Saul, news of Avner's return spread through the town like wildfire, and other neighbors came to welcome him back. It was obvious that no work would be done that day, so Kalba was returned to the barn and Avner and Zechariah changed into other clothes.

In the early afternoon the members of the family appeared with their brood of children. The little ones fell on Avner with whoops of joy and would not let him go until he had repeated his story and answered their torrent of questions. By now he was beginning to weary of recounting his experiences, so he started to embellish his tale with even more exciting adventures, which left his young audience wide-eyed and oohing audibly. In the meantime the women began to bake more bread, for it was obvious that the number of loaves made the day before would not suffice, and they lent a hand with the cooking. When this was finished, they took their leave, including Leah, who would return together with her family before the kindling of the Sabbath lights. Hannah spent the rest of the afternoon tidying up the house and making final preparations, which came to a halt with the blowing of the horn indicating that it was time for the Sabbath lights.

Over a dozen lamps and candles were lit in the dining room alone, and they gave a cheerful glow throughout the room. Two three-legged tables had been set up for the children, and the large table laid for the adults was covered with a white cloth. At the head of the table, two large loaves of bread were hidden under an embroidered cloth. Hannah took out her best dishes for the adults, together with a silver wine goblet for Zechariah and copper cups for Avner and Leah's husband.

In the meantime the men recited the evening *Shema,* after which they took their places around the tables. Zechariah rose and pronounced the benediction over the wine, thereby sanctifying the Sabbath. The meal was interspersed with the singing of Sabbath melodies, and all joined in lustily, especially the children, some of whose piping voices did not exactly harmonize with the others, much to Avner's amusement. Seated next to his father, he felt a warm glow inside him. He had always enjoyed the Sabbath with its special atmosphere, but had been inclined to take it somewhat for granted. Now, after he had been deprived of it for months and forced to labor on this day, the full significance and beauty of the seventh day of rest struck him anew.

Eventually the oil in the smaller lamps began to run out, and Zechariah noticed that some of the youngsters were having a hard time keeping their eyes open. At such family gatherings on the Sabbath he was accustomed to say a few words on the weekly Scripture reading and had prepared to do so tonight. But he decided to forgo this, and instead he incorporated in the grace after meals some of the sentiments he had intended to express.

On the morrow the synagogue was packed, for an unusually large number of women attended the service. If Avner and Reuven were back, then their own husbands and sons were likely to return soon. For the first time since their men had been taken away, there was a cheerful, expectant atmosphere in the town, and no one wanted to miss today's service, especially as the renowned sage Shemaiah would be present.

For this occasion the president of the synagogue chose their outstanding precentor. He combined a pleasant voice with a gift for composing prayers, for in this period the text of the prayers was fluid and to some extent could be improvised. The congregants occupied all the available benches, while the elders sat on chairs with their backs to the wall facing the Holy City. Shemaiah, who occupied the "chair of Moses," which was reserved for the sage who delivered the sermon, kept his eyes lowered most of the time as he concentrated on the prayers, but he knew that he was the center of attention. For all his modesty, he was conscious of the fact that the inhabitants of Emmaus considered themselves highly honored by his presence. He was accustomed to visit different towns and villages on the Sabbath and festivals to disseminate knowledge of the Torah, both the Written and Oral Law, including the recent *halachic* discussions and decisions of the Sanhedrin. But if the citizens of Emmaus considered themselves privileged to have him as their guest, he for his part considered it an honor to perform this sacred duty. He knew how much Emmaus had suffered at the hands of Cassius, and had chosen this week to visit it in order to help lift the inhabitants' morale. He had no inkling that his visit would coincide with the return of the first of the released prisoners. He regarded this as a good omen.

The precentor had prepared well, incorporating in the prayers various verses from the Psalms that expressed the prevailing mood of hope and gratitude. When he finished, Shemaiah complimented him, pleasing not only the precentor but the entire congregation. It was now time for the Scripture reading. The president of the synagogue and Zechariah mounted the dais, while the adjutant and one of the elders made their way with measured steps to the small adjoining room housing the ark of the scrolls. When they reappeared, the congregation rose and remained standing until the ark was set down in the middle of the wall facing Jerusalem and a Torah scroll was taken out and carried onto the dais.

The first of the seven persons designated to read from the weekly portion mounted the dais, and after pronouncing the opening blessing, began to read. Zechariah, standing beside him, translated into Aramaic after each verse. Moved by the solemnity of the occasion, he rendered the translation flawlessly. His voice was firm and steady, and the members of his family – the men occupying a bench in the first row and Hannah and two of her daughters seated with the other women toward the rear of the hall – looked on with manifest pride. The third person called up was Shemaiah, and Zechariah deemed it a rare privilege, if not the greatest ever vouchsafed him, to translate the reading by the most distinguished sage of the time. He was no less thrilled to do the same for his own son.

After the seventh reader pronounced the closing blessing, the scroll was rolled up, wrapped in its embroidered cloths, and returned to the ark. A smaller scroll was produced for the reading from the Prophets. The selection was from Isaiah, and to translate the most eloquent of the Prophets was a task Zechariah did not envy anyone. Fortunately, the translation of the Prophets could be less exact than that of the Torah; it could be done three verses at a time, and if necessary even a little freely.

When Zechariah returned to his seat, the congregants sitting nearby came over to congratulate him and to welcome Avner back. The president of the synagogue waited a few minutes and then called for order. When quiet was restored, he welcomed Avner home in the name of the entire community and expressed his earnest hope that all the other men would soon be back in their midst. He then introduced Shemaiah, stressing the signal honor conferred on Emmaus by the august presence of the renowned sage.

Shemaiah rose from his chair and acknowledged the president's words of praise, which he said were more than he merited. If he had been blessed with any special knowledge, it was only thanks to the Almighty, and hence it was an honor and mitzvah for him to impart it to the good people of Emmaus.

He cut a dignified figure. The noble cast of his features endowed him with an air of unassuming authority that impressed everyone. He had dark eyes under bushy brows, a high forehead, thick black hair turning gray around the temples, and a beard trimmed in the Assyrian fashion. His voice was resonant, and when delivering a sermon he spoke slowly and eloquently with seemingly little effort.

After his opening remarks Shemaiah began to expound on various points in the Scripture reading, giving homiletic interpretations, citing *halachic* decisions, and spicing his discourse with apposite parables. He invited the congregation to ask questions as he proceeded, and they eagerly responded, so that the sermon was more in the nature of a lively colloquy, which went on for over an hour.

When he finished his discourse on the Scripture reading, Shemaiah paused to drink some water and then cleared his throat. "In another two weeks," he resumed in measured tones, "it will be the first day of Sivan. In view of the momentous event that occurred in this month, it is only fitting that we devote some thought to this subject."

Shemaiah realized that some of the congregants were probably getting impatient, and he said he would not take it amiss if anyone wanted to leave. Only a few did so – women anxious to get back to their young children or to attend to dinner. Zechariah, who had found the sermon highly edifying, was eager to hear more, while Avner, who during his enslavement had been deprived of intellectual and spiritual nourishment, was also keen to listen to what else Shemaiah had to say, but at the same time he was looking forward to exchanging greetings with his fellow townsmen. Since it was obvious that he would not find any of them outside the synagogue, he waved to some of his friends and then turned to give his attention to the speaker.

Shemaiah was pointing out that only a few weeks earlier all had celebrated the exodus from Egypt – an event that had indelibly stamped itself on the consciousness of the nation. Time and again the Torah exhorts the people of Israel to remember that they had once been slaves in the land of Egypt – a fact that had colored their lives and helped mold their character, their attitude toward themselves, the stranger in their midst, and even the nations of the world.

But other nations had also suffered enslavement and succeeded in breaking the yoke of bondage. "Wherein has our destiny differed from that of these other peoples?" he asked. "What is it that has made Israel unique among the nations of the world?" He explained that paradoxically it was an event that also involved submission, but submission to the Creator and Master of the universe. Revelation at Mount Sinai, the granting of the Torah to the people of Israel, marked the beginning of the nation's spiritual history; it was the covenant whereby Israel became a holy people. But while revelation was given to Israel alone, it was not intended solely for Israel. He quoted Isaiah's prophecy that the day would come when all the nations would flow to the mountain of the Lord's house to be taught His ways and to walk in His path. "The day of revelation was as momentous as the day of creation itself," he stressed, "for without Torah, without the divine moral law, the creation of the universe would have been incomplete – nay, meaningless."

Shemaiah went on to discuss a paradox: Israel, the nation that had broken the shackles of Egyptian bondage and accepted the covenant to be a kingdom of priests, a light unto the nations, was in a sense not even master of its own house, for it could not be denied that a foreign power had in no small degree gained dominion over the land. This obvious reference to the Romans riveted the audience's attention, especially when the speaker declared that the citizens of Emmaus in particular were aware of this apparent contradiction, for many of their dear ones were presently languishing in slavery. "How can this seemingly anomalous situation be reconciled with the Lord's divine plan, His covenant with Israel?"

Probably no question had vexed the nation and its spiritual leaders more than this one since the destruction of the First Temple and the exile of the people from their land. When peace and tranquility reigned and the people did not lack for sustenance, they did not dwell overmuch on this question, but when internal strife, foreign oppression, or other tribulations reared their ugly head, it invariably surfaced anew.

Shemaiah proceeded to define the covenant, explaining that it represented a mutual obligation or commitment between the Almighty and Israel. In return for God's promise to Abraham to give the land to his seed, they were required to "keep the way of the Lord, to do righteousness and justice, to hearken to His voice and keep His commandments, statutes, and laws. And at Sinai, before He gave Israel the Ten Commandments, He bade Moses tell the children of Israel that if they keep the covenant, they shall be His own treasure, a kingdom of priests and a holy nation. The Israelites accepted this condition, but alas, they did not always abide by the covenant. They began to do that which was evil in the sight of the Lord and the land was filled with iniquity. They did not do justice and righteousness, they did not keep the Lord's commandments; they even began to worship strange gods. Retribution was not long in coming: The Temple was destroyed and the people exiled to an alien land.

"In Babylonia they reflected on their fate and repented of their misdeeds. They wept when they remembered Zion and yearned to dwell again in the Holy Land. When God's instrument Cyrus presented them the opportunity, they returned – unfortunately not in large numbers, it must be admitted.

"Just as the Second Temple falls short of the First in majesty and grandeur, so too the Second Commonwealth for long fell short of the First in one very fundamental aspect. With the return from captivity we no longer enjoyed independent sovereignty in our own land, but lived under the rule of others – subjects of the Persians and then the Ptolemaic kings of Egypt, the Seleucids in Syria. Nevertheless, we were able to live in accordance with the covenant. We made great strides forward. The Bible was canonized, an extensive external literature created, and the Oral Law continued to develop. Spiritually there was a remarkable flourishing, and economically too there was considerable progress."

Shemaiah explained that it was only when the Syrian-Greek tyrant Antiochus tried to force the people to abandon their covenant with the Lord and to embrace paganism that they rose up and fought for and eventually gained political independence – for the first time in over 300 years. "Antiochus showed what can happen when a foreign power interferes with our divinely ordained way of life." He paused and let his glance roam over the audience. His voice became grave. "And now a new world power has come upon the scene, probably the mightiest one of all time. For us it presents a dilemma: How are we to relate to it?"

Shemaiah was now addressing a question that was very real and immediate to his audience. Not a sound could be heard in the synagogue as all waited for him to continue. "If we could maintain our sovereign independence, this was undoubtedly to be preferred," he declared in a firm voice. "Our unique way of life has not evolved on an abstract, ethereal plane, divorced from the realities of life. The Torah deals with and governs every aspect of life, with relations not only between man and his Maker, but also between man and man. The Lord has sanctified us with His commandments, and in a similar vein the Prophet Isaiah proclaimed that the holy God is sanctified by justice. The pursuit of justice in its every aspect, enshrining the principle that man is created in the divine image, the hallowing of life – this is the quintessence of our way of life. This applies to and must govern each and every one of us, the community, the nation as a whole. It applies even more to those who guide the fortunes of the nation – the Sanhedrin, the high priest, and even the king, who is bidden to keep a copy of the Torah with him and to read therein all the days of his life, that he may keep all the words of this law and the statutes.

"If those who govern the nation are commanded to act in accordance with God's laws and statutes, then how can we reconcile ourselves to a situation where the ability to observe our special way of life depends, in some degree or other, on the whims of a foreign power? This is not the ideal situation envisaged in connection with our holy covenant. But reality stares us in the face, whether we like it or not, whether we understand it or not. How can tiny Judea withstand mighty Rome? The odds are overwhelming," he declared, shaking his head. "But just as a tree can withstand a raging storm if it bends a little, so we may have no choice but to bend a little until this storm too passes away. But there is a limit to how far we can bend," he added emphatically. "If, heaven forbid, another Antiochus should rise up and try to force us to abandon our divinely ordained way of life, we must draw a line and say, 'this far and no more.'"

"When the Israelites were about to enter the Holy Land, our teacher Moses declared, 'What great nation is there? They that have God unto them, they that have statutes and ordinances so righteous, this law which I set before you today.' If we observe these statutes and ordinances, if we remain faithful to the covenant, we will always be great – not in the sense that Rome is great, but in a different and far more enduring sense. Babylonia, the mistress of kingdoms, has disappeared from the stage of history, and the Persia of Cyrus's day was brought low. The Roman tide too will one day begin to recede. For it is inevitable that a nation whose might is based primarily on the sword will eventually succumb to a new rising power. But Israel, the smallest of nations, will continue to live and flourish, for its greatness lies in the realm of the spirit, against which the sword cannot prevail. As long as Israel remains faithful to the covenant it will continue to illumine the path of mankind, until the day will come when all will acknowledge that the Lord our God the Lord is one."

Shemaiah returned to his seat amid complete silence, for the congregants had been held spellbound by his words. Then they broke into a chorus of whispered approbation. The president of the synagogue waited awhile and then called for order. When silence was restored, he expressed the congregation's appreciation of the sage's edifying lesson and inspiring message, which they would long remember and take to heart. The congregants then rose and waited deferentially until Shemaiah and the president made their exit into the courtyard. Here the sage was besieged by a large number of persons who wanted to let him know how much his sermon had moved them. As Zechariah added his appreciation, Hannah and Avner stood respectfully aside. Much to everyone's surprise, Shemaiah approached Avner and clasped his hand.

"I have been told how you refrained from eating forbidden food during your enslavement," he said in his resonant voice. "When I heard that, I thanked the Almighty that He has given His people such a steadfast heart." He turned to Zechariah and Hannah. "You can be proud of your son. Of him it can truly be said that in the most trying circumstances he fulfilled what is stated in Proverbs: 'My son, keep the commandments of thy father and forsake not the teaching of thy mother.'" Turning again to Avner, he added: "We are told in the same proverb that the commandments are a lamp and the teaching is light. May your life always be bright with such light."

A beaming Avner thanked Shemaiah for his blessing, as did his elated parents. When the sage moved away, Avner found himself surrounded by a large crowd who welcomed him back and inquired about those who had not yet returned. Avner told them what little he knew and expressed his conviction that they would all be released soon, a statement that cheered them immensely. Together with his parents and other members of the family, he began to make his way home. The walk was punctuated by greetings from those few neighbors who for some reason or other had been unable to attend the service.

Zechariah, who had frequently complained of late about how quiet the house was, was pleased to observe that the dining room could barely contain all his children and grandchildren. The entire stack of small tables had to be put to use, filling every corner of the spacious room. As on the previous evening, Avner was seated to the right of his father, the place usually reserved for the guest of honor. He enjoyed being the center of attention, and even did not mind describing once again his ordeal to those members of the family who had not heard it before.

After dinner neighbors began to drop in to congratulate Zechariah and Hannah on Avner's return. To make room for the callers and, no less important, to enable them to hear one another, the youngsters were sent out to play. The main subject of conversation was, of course, Avner's experiences and the morning service in the synagogue, especially Shemaiah's sermon. All agreed that this was one of the most memorable Sabbaths they could remember, one they would never forget.

That night Avner had trouble falling asleep. Over and over he reviewed the happenings of that crowded Sabbath, which had brought him more pleasure than he had ever experienced before. Like all the others, he had been greatly impressed by Shemaiah. His dignified bearing, his modesty and sincerity, his erudition, his love of Torah and unbounded devotion to its dissemination, his deep concern for the welfare of his people, all these had profoundly moved him. He had found Shemaiah's discourse on the covenant extremely interesting and thoughtful. But one point troubled him and left him uneasy – the possible need to "bend with the wind." Avner could not deny the validity of the sage's logic, but the idea ran against his grain. He had always nursed an intense resentment of the foreign intruder, and his recent taste of Roman "benevolence" had not made them any more endearing to him. Maybe he was not being completely rational, but in his heart he felt that foreign dominion or even influence over the country, in whatever shape or form, was bound to spell trouble and possible disaster. It was something to be stoutly resisted.

Mariamne's Betrothal to Herod

Alexandra always looked forward to the annual winter stay in Jericho. The balmy air and luxuriant vegetation of this lovely spot never failed to lift her spirits and make the most vexing problems and cares seem lighter and more remote. She also enjoyed the easy, informal atmosphere and the round of social activities of the aristocratic priestly and other influential families who made Jericho their second home.

This year in particular she welcomed the winter vacation, for ever since her daughter's betrothal she had fallen into a depression which she could not shake off. As much as she loved her father and appreciated the pressures and anxieties that oppressed him, she could not accept the necessity or wisdom of the betrothal. Her mortification and sense of futility had grown more acute, and this had not escaped Hyrcanus's notice. It was therefore with no little expectation that she prepared for the journey to Jericho. But this year, for the first time, she was to be disappointed. Even the little things that always gave her pleasure failed to strike a responsive cord, and she was unable to dispel the dark thoughts that weighed on her.

It distressed her when one day Mariamne complained about the changed attitude of her friends toward her.

"What do you mean?" asked Alexandra, observing the pouting expression on her daughter's oval face. "In what way has it changed?"

"I don't know how to explain it. It's not that they're less friendly; they just seem a little… I don't quite know how to put it."

"A little reserved, more remote?"

"Yes, that's it, more reserved and remote. Take Naomi, for instance. She always used to tell me everything. We'd share our secrets and talk about what we wanted to be like when we grew up. But not any more."

Alexandra's brow furrowed. "Did you sometimes talk about what kind of husbands you wanted when you grow up?"

"Well, hardly that! After all, we're only young girls. But yes, maybe we did talk about it a few times. Naomi would say I was so pretty I'd be sure to get a very handsome husband."

"Well, that's probably the answer. You see, you're already betrothed and Naomi isn't. That makes you different in a way."

"And that's the reason?"

"I'm pretty sure it is."

"Then I wish I wasn't betrothed!" Mariamne burst out, her eyes filling with tears. "I liked it better the other way. Why do I have to be betrothed?"

Alexandra put an arm around her daughter's shoulder. "Now, dear, don't fret. You have to realize you're no longer a child. You're a Hasmonean princess, the granddaughter of the high priest and king, a descendant of the liberators of our country. That means you not only enjoy certain privileges, you also have responsibilities and obligations to your family and your people."

"If I have to be betrothed, why can't it be to someone young and hand-some? Why must it be to someone like, like him?"

It hurt Alexandra to see how her daughter could not even bring herself to call Herod by his name. What hurt her equally as much was the knowledge that aversion to the betrothal was not confined to Mariamne's friends but was shared by almost the entire populace. This Alexandra knew from one of her close friends, who had confided that in aristocratic circles in particular the match was regarded as utterly unsuitable for a member of the Hasmonean house, and it elevated Herod to a status where eventually he might constitute a threat not only to their privileged positions but to the nation as a whole.

"And now that Mariamne is betrothed, what about you, Alexandra?" the friend had asked with genuine concern. "You've been a widow too long. You should think of remarrying."

This was not the first time the suggestion had been made to her. Her father too had urged this on her more than once, and every time she would reply that as long as the children were small she could not bring herself to take another husband. When pressed to explain herself, she would become evasive or lapse into silence. Truth to tell, she herself was not sure what deterred her from this step. Many a night, as she waited for sleep to come, she would ponder the question. Her marriage to Alexander had been arranged to help heal the breach between their fathers, which had rocked the nation and hastened the loss of independence. She herself had misgivings right from the start, for Alexander, like his father, was strong-willed and vain of his Hasmonean lineage. He chided Hyrcanus for lacking in backbone, regarding him as a weakling who let himself be led by the nose by Antipater, and groveled before the Romans.

The early years of their marriage had been full of tension, and Alexandra regretted that her happiness had been sacrificed for reasons of high policy. She had been torn emotionally. She too was proud of her Hasmonean blood and did not approve of her father's policy with respect to Antipater and the Romans. But love for her father had impelled her, if not to defend him, at least to try and explain his motives, and this had resulted in considerable friction with her husband. Withal, she came to realize that Alexander had been profoundly concerned for the welfare of their people and had attracted many to his banner. His execution upon Pompey's orders to prevent him, as well as his father, from aiding Caesar, had been a great shock to her and the entire nation. The trauma of his beheading had seared her soul, and whenever her father or her friends suggested remarriage, she shrank from the idea.

As long as the children were small, they had filled part of the void in her life. But only part. The years were slipping by, and she feared that her life would be getting emptier. Mariamne was now betrothed, and it would not be very long before her brother Aristobulus would go his own way. Her friends assured her that, in addition to her lineage and station, she was still very attractive and desirable; there were many who would welcome the opportunity of having her hand. Alexandra's mirror told her that her friends were not politely exaggerating. Her features were clear and well molded, her dark brown eyes bright and intelligent; there was still a sheen and silken texture to her black hair; her body was still lithe and youthful. There was, she had to admit, a hint of pride in her features, but this only added to their aristocratic cast. Should she take her father's and friends' advice and remarry? During her stay in Jericho she gave much thought to this question, but could not arrive at a decision.

After returning to Jerusalem her attention was again focused fully on her children, for both of them became ill and had to take to bed. The weather was very raw for early spring, with driving winds and heavy downpours. It was impossible to adequately heat the private apartments in the palace, and first

Aristobulus and then Mariamne developed a rasping cough and high fever. The royal physician assured Alexandra that there was nothing to worry about, that in no time at all they would be up and about. Normally they would not have minded being confined to bed for a few days, for they liked being doted upon and receiving all sorts of gifts and attention, especially from Grandma Elisheva, who would come and tell them nice stories. But it was getting close to Purim, and they did not want to miss the excitement of this joyous holiday.

The physician had forbade visitors until the fever subsided. One of the first to call was Herod. The announcement of his presence did not cheer Mariamne up.

"I don't want to see him!" she cried, pulling a long face. "Tell him to go away!"

"Now, darling, that's no way to act toward the man you're betrothed to," Alexandra gently admonished her daughter.

"I don't want to be betrothed to him. I don't like him. I, I hate him!"

"Come now," said Alexandra a little sharply. "You're exaggerating. You're not used to the idea of being betrothed – to him or to anyone else. You still think of yourself as a child. You have to remember that you're a princess, and a princess must act graciously – at all times."

* * *

On the way to the palace Herod thought about what he would say to Mariamne, but found it hard to hit on the right note. First of all, there was the age difference: she was thirteen, he thirty-two. He was a man of the world who already had a checkered career behind him, who had held important positions of leadership and command, a man experienced with women. How was he to address this young Hasmonean? True, she was very beautiful, but also very young, a flower not yet fully blossomed. He would have to handle the matter delicately, adopting a sympathetic manner. He was perfectly aware that the betrothal had not made her happy; she had gone through the ceremony apathetically, like a puppet with no volition of her own, her countenance a frozen mask. He was realistic enough not to have expected differently, but had hoped that she would gradually grow accustomed to the idea of being his wife. He must be patient; in another two or three years she would be a striking beauty and most desirable.

Herod was polite and attentive during the visit but studiously avoided any words of endearment. Mariamne was clearly ill at ease, and Alexandra even had to prod her to thank him for the gold broach he gave her. After chatting with them for a while, Herod took his leave, wishing the ailing brother and sister a speedy recovery. As he made his way through the palace he experienced a surge of anger and even mortification. The fact that this young slip of a girl could make him, of all people, feel awkward bruised his pride. He wondered if he had done the right thing with regard to Mariamne. But he quickly dismissed the thought; so far he had no reason to regret any of his major decisions, and he doubted that he would have cause to regret this one.

When Herod emerged from the palace his litter-bearers leaped to their feet and stood stiffly at attention as he descended the staircase and crossed the court-yard. It was only a short distance to the family mansion, where he was to spend the night before returning to Galilee. For an instant he considered dismissing the litter-bearers and making his way on foot, as he felt the need to take stock of the situation. However, he thought better of this, realizing that it might be unbecoming to a man of his station.

It was not only the frustrating visit to the royal palace that perturbed Herod; his mother's state of mind was also giving him cause for concern. Cypros never seemed to have recovered from the trauma of her husband's death. Herod and Phasael had done their best to cheer her up, but with no great success. She would sit for hours on end, sunk in reverie, apathetic to what went on about her. Formerly she had always taken a keen interest in her sons' accomplishments and liked to hear about their political and diplomatic triumphs, which filled her with motherly pride. But now she was indifferent even to this. What was worse, her headaches recurred with increasing frequency and intensity.

At the betrothal ceremony she had spoken very little, and acknowledged congratulations perfunctorily, almost as though she hardly knew why they were being offered. Herod was not even sure how she felt about the alliance with the Hasmonean house. But if she kept her thoughts bottled up inside her, Salome did not leave him in any doubt about her feelings.

"And how is our darling bride-to-be?" she asked Herod in an elaborate tone of concern.

"She's feeling better," was his curt reply.

"I'm happy to hear that," said Salome with a frigid little smile. "But you don't look very cheerful. What's the matter, wasn't she delighted to see you?"

Herod glared at his sister, wondering how she had instantly fathomed the cause of his pique.

"Well, one good thing about her being sick," Salome went on, "it at least gives you a good excuse to visit the royal palace. That's more than I can say about the rest of our family. Do you realize that since the betrothal we have not once been invited to the palace?"

"I wasn't aware of that," replied Herod brusquely.

"Oh, come now," continued Salome with a scornful frown, "something like that wouldn't escape your notice. I know my brother too well."

Herod had no wish to pursue the conversation further, but realized it would be fruitless to try to brush Salome off. "They have had many things on their minds lately," he replied lamely. "And now the sickness of both children."

"A mere case of sniffles. I'm sure that didn't cause the cancellation of a single social engagement of theirs."

"I don't keep check on their social life," Herod growled, irritated at both the truth of Salome's grievance and her hammering the point home.

"Of course not. But I can't help feeling that your future in-laws think we're not high enough on the social scale for them. It's true we don't have royal blood in our veins – at least not royal Jewish blood; but we are aristocrats. You know – in Idumea we're part of the nobility."

"Idumea is not Jerusalem," snapped Herod, anxious to be done with the subject.

"I'm aware of that," Salome went on, tilting her head at a haughty angle. "But do let me point out, dear brother, that were it not for the insignificant aristocrat of Idumea, our father of blessed memory, and his two eldest sons, your Hyrcanus would not be occupying the royal palace today. No, I don't think we have any reason to feel the least bit inferior. In fact, I would be so bold as to say that Hyrcanus and his beloved daughter can consider it a great privilege to ally themselves with the family who has preserved the throne for them, and they can deem it an honor to invite us to the royal palace. In fact, I would go so far as to say that they have an obligation to do so. Don't you agree?"

Herod scowled at his sister and his mouth jerked angrily. He had to admit that she had a point. He knew that his family had not been invited to the palace, but he was not surprised. And what about Cypros? In her present condition she would not make a favorable impression. Was it worthwhile pressing the matter just now? He was of two minds about it.

"Very well, I'll have a word with Hyrcanus."

"When?"

"As soon as I think it opportune."

"You're returning to Galilee tomorrow. It will probably be some time before you're back in Jerusalem."

"It may be," concurred Herod frostily. ""I don't think the matter is that urgent."

"For you perhaps not. You have entry to the palace. But we're not as privileged as you. At least put the matter to Hyrcanus before you leave. You owe that much to your family."

"All right!" barked Herod, the color mounting in his cheeks. "I'll talk to him tomorrow morning before I leave. I hope that will make you happy."

* * *

Hyrcanus realized that it would not be easy to persuade Alexandra to hold a reception for Herod's family. Ever since the betrothal she had avoided discussing it with him, but he knew that she remained adamantly opposed to the alliance of the two families. When he broached the subject of a reception, she remained unexpectedly silent, concealing her feelings behind an impenetrable mask. She found the idea repugnant, but could not bring herself to hurt her father's feelings so insensitively. On second thought, though, perhaps it was better that he should know how the betrothal was viewed by his people. When she told him what she had heard in Jericho about the reaction in aristocratic circles, his face fell.

"And it's not only your aristocratic friends who don't like the match," Alexandra pointed out. "I doubt if there's anyone who approves of it. I know what drove you to it, but nobody else can understand it."

"Is it as bad as that?" asked Hyrcanus in a barely audible voice.

It distressed Alexandra to see his pained expression. How she wished she could spare him this, but for once and for all he had to know, if only for his own good. She told him about the denunciation of the "unholy alliance" and the call for a "true Hasmonean ruler" daubed on the walls of the marketplace. To soften the blow, she added that this was undoubtedly the work of Antigonus's partisans, but she knew that it reflected the sentiments of a substantial part of the population.

"But the deed is done," she said in a resigned tone. "Nothing will make it popular – or even understood."

"And the reception? How can we in all decency refuse to invite Herod's family?" asked Hyrcanus tonelessly.

"Let me think about it. Maybe I can find a solution that will be at least half-way palatable."

But before she devoted any thought to the matter, it had become irrelevant. Two days later came the startling news of the Parthian invasion of Syria.

Herod Assesses the Situation

In some respects it seemed to Herod that the wheel had turned full circle and he was back where he stood seven years ago, when as a somewhat brash 25-year-old he had been appointed governor of Galilee by his late father. The northern province was as difficult and turbulent as ever, seething with unrest, its Jewish inhabitants querulous and thoroughly hating the Greeks in their midst, who for their part regarded the Jews with scorn and harassed them in every possible way. Yet there were significant differences. Herod was no longer a raw, inexperienced governor, for in the meantime he had served a number of high Roman officials in important positions and had earned a reputation as an efficient, fearless administrator. Now he bore the impressive title of tetrarch, conferred on him by no less a person than Mark Antony, one of the three co-rulers of the Roman Empire and whom he regarded not only as his patron but a good friend. Moreover, the fact that Herod was now allied to the Hasmonean house was sure to elevate him in the eyes of the Jews and command the grudging respect of even the most disgruntled Galileans. Even more important, this represented a big step forward to his ultimate goal – the throne of Judea, the very contemplation of which quickened his pulse.

Herod's enhanced status could have affected him in diverse ways: It might have made him more arrogant and domineering; it might also have had the opposite effect, mellowing him in the exercise of his office. In a sense his reaction was mixed: He was determined to brook no signs of rebelliousness on the part of the Galileans, and he dealt harshly with all malcontents and agitators; at the same time he decided that now that he had gained a legitimation previously denied him, he would refrain from unduly antagonizing the Jewish inhabitants under his authority.

An example of this was the way he dealt with a delegation of Jewish merchants who complained that Herod's soldiers had roughed them up while transporting their wares to Gamla. In the past Herod had been plagued with bands of brigands preying on Greek and other non-Jewish caravans, and had detailed several companies of mercenaries to patrol the trade routes and provide protection to merchants, Jewish and gentile alike. The officer in charge of this particular patrol had vented his dislike of Jews by manhandling the merchants and confiscating part of their wares.

After hearing out the indignant merchants, Herod ordered the offending officer to report to him as soon as possible. He appeared on the following morning, and when he was confronted with his victims, a pallor spread over his visage, contorted with undisguised hatred.

"These merchants complain that you treated them uncivilly," declared Herod, fixing the dark, surly Cilician with a stern look. "What do you have to say to that?"

"I asked them what they were carrying," replied the officer in a snarling tone, "and they refused to give me a straightforward answer."

"How do you explain that?"

"They were obviously carrying contraband," replied the officer without hesitation.

"Did you try to find out if they had paid the required taxes?"

"Do you think I could expect to get a truthful answer from this bunch of, of..."

"From these Jews?" Herod completed the sentence for him.

"Yes, from these Jews."

"These Jewish merchants happen to be respectable members of their community," said Herod in a sharp, authoritative voice. "Your orders were to protect caravans – all caravans, Jewish, Greek, and others – against brigands. You have failed to carry out my explicit instructions. You were derelict in your duty; you overstepped your authority and were actually insubordinate. I will not tolerate insubordination by any of my soldiers. You are hereby relieved of your command and will be incarcerated until I decide what punishment to give you."

Herod ordered the guards to arrest the officer. He then offered his apologies to the merchants and promised to return the goods that had been confiscated. The merchants bowed deeply and thanked Herod profusely for redressing the wrong done them. When they departed Herod chuckled softly to himself. He knew that news of the incident would spread to every corner of this stubborn, contentious province, enhancing his reputation as a tough, fair, and efficient governor who would tolerate no nonsense from anyone.

He was correct in assuming that all Galilee would quickly learn about his adroit handling of a potentially explosive situation. What he did not foresee was that it would be overshadowed by a more momentous event. Three weeks later his scouts brought alarming intelligence: The Parthians had crossed the Euphrates River with a large body of foot-soldiers and dreaded horsemen! Their initial objective, it seemed, was the Roman garrison at Apamea, commanded by Decidious Saxa. This report stunned Herod. He knew that the garrison was heavily outnumbered and stood no chance of repulsing the attack. He was both puzzled and dismayed to learn that the Romans had been taken by surprise. To mount an expedition of the size indicated by his scouts required a great deal of preparation, yet the Romans had not detected any sign of an impending invasion. And while this was going on – obviously for many weeks if not months – where was Antony? In Alexandria dallying with that Egyptian whore of his. Damnation! What stupid folly! For once Herod was angry at his patron, and very worried.

He was well acquainted with the situation in Rome's Eastern provinces: The populace resented the ruinous taxes imposed on them and would undoubtedly welcome the Parthians with open arms. Moreover, many of the Roman troops had fought for Cassius and did not feel any strong allegiance to Antony. Altogether the picture was bleak. The reports that reached Herod in the following days were increasingly desperate. At Apamea the garrison offered only token resistance, and Saxa fled to Cilicia, where he was killed. The Parthian army then separated into two forces, one under Labienus advancing in a westerly direction, and the other under Pacorus marching southward. The client-kings abandoned their Roman overlords without a fight. The rulers of Cappodicia and Commagene were openly pro-Parthia, and Castor of Galatia made no attempt to check Labienus. The situation in Syria was hardly any better. Pacorus swept southward, encountering only light resistance. Only Tyre held out against him;

the rest of the country either made a half-hearted stand or went over to the Parthians.

Herod realized that his position was precarious. The forces at his disposal were too small to stem the Parthian advance even on a narrow front. Full of foreboding and in a dark mood, he convened his officers to plan his strategy. Then came the news he had been dreading: Antigonus had crossed the northern border and was proceeding in the direction of Mount Carmel, where large numbers of Jews were streaming to his banner. His objective was clear: to close in on Judea and capture Jerusalem – and with it the Judean throne. Herod had no choice but to abandon Galilee to its fate and march his troops at a forced pace in order to join up with Phasael as quickly as possible and prevent Jerusalem from falling to his rival.

Thousands Join Antigonus's March to Jerusalem

When news of the Parthian victory over the Romans and Antigonus's rapid advance through Judea reached Emmaus, Avner could not contain his excitement. This was the hour he had been waiting for; at long last Judea was going to throw off the yoke of the hated Romans and regain its independence! He was burning to join the liberating force and help end the humiliating servility to the foreign conqueror, who milked the land dry and sold him and his fellow townsmen into slavery.

But one consideration gave him pause: his parents. He had only recently returned from slavery; how could he just pick himself up and march off without giving them time to get used to the idea? Avner was a dutiful son: He loved his parents, and the commandment to honor one's father and mother was strongly ingrained in him. He was torn with indecision, and his restlessness did not escape his parents' notice. Zechariah sensed what was troubling him, but refrained from touching on the subject.

One day he saw Avner leaning against a tree, shading his eyes as he stared into the distance. "Avner!" Zechariah called out softly as he approached his son.

There was no reply.

"Avner!" he repeated a little more loudly.

Avner, startled out of his reverie, turned to face his father.

"What is it you see in the distance, son?" asked Zechariah.

"Nothing. I was just thinking."

"Emmaus is on the route to the Holy City. They'll be marching down our road, so you needn't be afraid of missing them."

Avner lowered his gaze. He knew how much his parents had missed him when he was enslaved and how hard it had been for his father to manage the farm on his own. He had an overwhelming desire to join the approaching force, but at the same time he was reluctant to cause his parents any more anguish.

"Abba," he said in a low voice.

"Yes, son," replied Zechariah, waiting patiently for Avner to unburden his heart.

"Will you be glad to see them marching past Emmaus?"

Zechariah did not answer immediately. He stroked his beard as he turned the matter over in his mind. "I am older than you, son, much older," he said calmly. "And older people usually see things in a little different light. They view them through eyes that have witnessed a great deal in their lifetime, and this colors their judgment of events and people. Perhaps if in my younger days I had not seen so much Jewish blood shed by the two Hasmonean brothers, I too would be glad to see Antigonus march against the Romans and their mercenaries and restore Judea's independence. But the idea of Antigonus fighting against Hyrcanus, his own uncle, saddens me, and also frightens me, much as I prize our independence."

"But it's not Antigonus against his uncle. It's Antigonus against the Romans and the Idumean brothers, the enemies of our people. The people are all for Antigonus. They want an end to foreign domination."

"If only Antigonus could achieve this!" said Zechariah with a sigh. "I cannot help doubting his prospects."

"But why? The Parthians are siding with us. They're a powerful nation, just as powerful as the Romans. They've defeated the Romans before and now they're defeating them again. They want Antigonus on the throne. This is our God-given opportunity, can't you see that? It would be an unforgivable mistake to pass it up. We owe it to ourselves, to our children and our children's children. How could I look my son in the eye and admit that at this historic hour I was found wanting? We must join together, all of us, and rid ourselves of this pestilence."

Zechariah gazed at his son's ardent face. He was filled with mixed emotions: He was proud of Avner's love of his country and people, but as a father he could not help being anxious about the uncertainty and dangers lying ahead. Nor was he confident of the final outcome. As Avner admitted, the Romans were a powerful nation – in Zechariah's opinion more powerful than the Parthians. And while they have suffered setbacks, it was inconceivable that they would let them go unavenged. They possessed a huge reservoir of manpower, highly trained and skilled in the art of warfare. Antigonus might gain the throne – his prospects in fact seemed quite good – but for how long? And what would be in the end? What price would the nation have to pay? And what would be with Avner, his youngest son? If only the Lord would help him to advise his son the right thing to do.

On the day Antigonus and his men marched past Emmaus the whole town turned out to greet them with cheers and refreshments. There was an air of intense excitement, and the hearts of the inhabitants beat with fierce pride. Antigonus cut a dashing figure on his white mount, his armor glistening in the sun. His men were a motley lot, sporting all sorts of weapons and some wearing helmets, but more wearing plain headcloths. They burst into song and waved to the crowd lining the road, beckoning to the menfolk to join their ranks. The patriotic fervor was contagious, and many of the younger males answered the call, including Avner.

Zechariah and Hannah embraced their son warmly. Hannah's eyes were moist and she wiped away the tears, just as she had done when he was led off to slavery. Zechariah's eyes were dry, but there was no joy in his heart.

"May the Almighty look after you and protect you, my son," he solemnly prayed as he took his leave of Avner. "When you go into battle, fight like a man, but also act like a man. Remember that you will be fighting God's creatures; so you must not only be brave, but wherever possible you must show mercy to the enemy, especially, especially..."

"Especially to my fellow Jews?" Avner said, seeing that his father could not bring himself to utter the words. Zechariah nodded his head.

"Don't worry, Abba," Avner assured him. "All the Jews will be fighting on Antigonus's side. So you can put your mind at rest on that point."

Antigonus and Herod in Battle for Jerusalem

Like his brother, Phasael was a brave soldier, and he was determined to give a good accounting of himself. But to his practiced eye the situation looked desperate, if not hopeless. No sooner had the shattering news of the Parthian invasion reached him than Antigonus appeared before the gates of Jerusalem to be welcomed by the populace as a liberating hero. Phasael's mercenaries were disciplined, seasoned warriors who could hold their own against a larger foe, but they stood little chance against Antigonus's rapidly swelling army.

Hastily convening a council of war, Phasael outlined the situation as he saw it. All agreed that there was little possibility of quelling the uprising, let alone checking the enemy at every point, especially in the narrow lanes of the Lower City, where virtually every house was a hostile fortress. The best strategy was to keep their force in a tight formation, thereby enabling them to hold their ground in the Upper City with minimal losses until Herod arrived with sufficient reinforcements to take the offensive.

In the first few days skirmishes took place along the wall separating the Upper and Lower City. Phasael's soldiers repulsed attack after attack, but Antigonus's men pressed on relentlessly, and eventually their superior numbers began to tell. The defenders were forced to yield ground, and they gradually withdrew beyond the marketplace, perilously close to the royal palace. It was at this point that Herod arrived with his troops. He did not need Phasael's report to size up the situation: It was clearly precarious.

"Withdraw your men to the palace grounds for a couple days of rest and to attend to their wounds," he instructed Phasael. "We'll relieve them in the meantime and hold off the enemy until we're ready to go on the offensive. With our combined force we'll show that Hasmonean dog a few tricks. He'll wish he stayed in his precious Chalcis."

"Do you think our chances are that good?" asked Phasael with a skeptical look.

"Don't be dismayed by their numbers. We're pitted against a mob, an untrained rabble," replied Herod scornfully. "They'll have little stomach for fighting once we start cutting them down and their blood flows through the streets. We beat Antigonus before, when he had trained men under his command. We'll chase him and his scummy rabble out of Jerusalem like a pack of frightened jackals."

"There were no Parthians in the country then," Phasael reminded his brother, with a worried frown.

Herod was acutely aware of this difference. But he had faced overwhelming odds before and emerged victorious. He had unbounded faith in his guiding spirit, and was confident that it would not let him down now.

"We didn't get this far only to see our hopes and aspirations dashed. The Parthians are keeping away from Jerusalem. Once we drive Antigonus out of Judea they'll have second thoughts about backing him. Now take yourself and your men to the palace grounds and rest up. You can promise them some good fun afterward."

Herod disliked defensive fighting; to attack the foe and crush him was to his mind the only way to win battles. But, like Phasael, he realized that this time circumstances dictated different tactics. He did not dare let the enemy break through to the palace, especially as his family was sheltered there.

When Phasael's rested troops rejoined him, Herod wasted no time in taking the offensive. His immediate objective was to push Antigonus back through the marketplace and retake those parts of the Upper City that had fallen to him, apart from the Temple, which military and other reasons made it inadvisable to attempt to wrest by arms, at least at this juncture.

The initial assault overwhelmed Antigonus's force harassing Herod's outer defenses, and drove it back to the marketplace. Here hard fighting raged all day. Herod's mercenaries inflicted heavy losses on the enemy, but reinforcements streamed in to replace the fallen, and when darkness put an end to the day's fighting, the issue was far from settled. The outcome was the same the following day and the next one. It was clear to Herod that he had underrated Antigonus's irregulars, who more than made up for their lack of training by their fierce determination and valor.

Herod had no choice but to change his tactics again – to switch back to defensive action with sporadic jabs at the enemy to keep them off balance. This, he painfully realized, would not enable him to vanquish the foe; the most he could hope for was to drain them of their strength and fighting spirit and force a stalemate on them until they decided to come to terms. This was not the kind of warfare he liked, but he saw no other possible course. There was another reason for his decision to lash out at the enemy with sporadic attacks: the festival of Shavuot was approaching, and normally thousands of pilgrims came to Jerusalem. The presence of such a huge concourse would pose a much greater threat to Herod. He did not delude himself: He knew that the overwhelming majority of the pilgrims would favor Antigonus's cause, and many could easily be inflamed and persuaded to join his ranks. By exerting pressure on the enemy and keeping Jerusalem a battleground, he hoped to deter many from making the pilgrimage.

* * *

Antigonus had witnessed only one boxing match in his life, and that was over twenty years ago in Rome, where he had been brought as a captive along with his father and sisters. He did not like the match, just as he did not like any of the less gentle Roman sports, such as gladiatorial contests and the various other kinds of carnage devised to amuse the blood-lusting spectators in the amphitheater. The two brawny pugilists had pummeled each other with their hide gloves reinforced at the knuckles with an iron band. The one who looked younger and less disfigured was more nimble and was getting better of his opponent. He drove him all over the arena until he was groggy, but could not knock him out.

Antigonus was reminded of the match when he discussed the military situation with Joab and his other staff officers. His men had clearly gained the upper hand in Jerusalem: They far outnumbered the Idumean mercenaries, especially after Shavuot when large numbers of able-bodied pilgrims joined their ranks, and they had forced the enemy to give up more and more ground until they were pushed back almost to the perimeter of the palace precincts. But although battered and bloodied, the mercenaries fought tenaciously and refused to concede defeat. They were proving a very tough nut to crack. Antigonus reluctantly concluded that he could not bring Herod to his knees unless he was ready to pay a high price in Jewish life – a prospect he shrank from. Nor did he wish to assault the palace itself, for several reasons. First of all, he did not possess the necessary siege engines, and his men were not trained nor had a taste for such warfare. But even more important, the last thing he wanted was to batter down the royal palace – the seat of power of the Hasmoneans, the symbol of the glorious role played by his family in the recent history of the nation – and to endanger the lives of his cousin, her children, and even her father.

Antigonus was in a dilemma. As he gazed upon the palace, his ambition was fired to white heat. His long-cherished dream was nearing fruition: The throne of Judea was about to fall into his hands like a ripe plum. The very thought of it filled him with elation, but at the same time with great frustration. How to finish off the business? He convened his staff officers and announced that the matter had to be brought to a successful conclusion – and soon. They deliberated and weighed all the possibilities. Various suggestions were made; several of them possessed some merit but not enough to elicit much enthusiasm. It was Barzilai, who had joined Antigonus's staff as an adviser at the beginning of the siege, who finally hit upon a stratagem that brought smiles to everyone's face.

Avner Rescued by Rachel

The smell of rain was in the air; dark clouds scurried toward the east, driven by a stiff wind. The fields were still wet from the previous week's unseasonable shower, so Zechariah decided this would be a good time to repair the stone wall that had been damaged by the heavy runoff. Fortunately the storm had not harmed any of the crops; and if it should rain again, it would be an additional boon. There would be plenty of work at harvest time, and he might even have to get extra help. A lot would depend on Avner's leg. If it troubled him, he would hire someone to do the heavy work, even though Avner would probably protest.

Zechariah was glad to have his son at his side again. He had missed him terribly during those long, interminable months after he joined Antigonus's army, and he had worried greatly about his safety. He had tried to hide his feelings from his wife, but Hannah was not fooled. A big weight lifted from their hearts the day Avner returned home – not completely sound, for he had a pronounced limp. Now, several weeks later, he no longer limped noticeably, but his leg still hurt when he tried to do strenuous work.

His parents noticed that, apart from his physical condition, a subtle change had come over Avner. He was as good-humored and optimistic as ever, but not as exuberant. He seemed to have matured perceptibly, and more often than was his wont, he would be wrapped in thought, even a bit withdrawn.

"Avner is no longer a youngster," remarked Hannah. "He's a man now – a young man. Something is weighing on his mind; he seems restless."

"That's understandable," replied Zechariah. "The fighting didn't last very long, thank God, but for all that it's not easy to get back to the old routine; it takes time."

"Avner's been home nearly two months now. That's time enough to get back to the old routine. What he needs is to get married and settle down."

"At his age? He's only eighteen. With the Lord's help he'll get married and settle down. What do you want from him?"

"When you were eighteen years old you were already about to be a father."

"Times have changed. The younger generation isn't marrying as early as we did. He's got time to catch up."

"He doesn't show any great desire to. He's a good lad, our son, even if I say so. Many a man here would be happy to have him for a son-in-law. Menahem for one. He's approached you more than once. His Sarah is a fine, virtuous girl. She'd make him a good wife."

"I agree with you," said Zechariah with a shrug of his shoulders. "But whenever I mention the subject to Avner, he doesn't show any interest. We can't force him to get married."

* * *

Avner was coming up the Emmaus road in a mule cart when it started to rain – not heavily but driven by the stiff wind. Holding the reins in one hand, he reached down with the other to extract a poncho from a basket and slipped it over his head. He urged the mule on with a flick of the whip, but by the time he entered the courtyard to his home he was wet and chilled. His bad leg began to hurt – a dull aching throb. He unhitched the mule and stabled it. Emerging from the barn, he caught sight of his father working on the stone wall. "Hadn't you better go inside, Abba?" he called out as he approached his father. "It's a pretty cold rain."

"I know, son," replied Zechariah without looking up. "I just want to get this big stone in place first."

"I'll give you a hand."

Within a few minutes the stone was in place, and Zechariah and Avner headed for the house. "I see you're limping again," observed Zechariah. "How's your leg feeling?"

"It's bothering me a little, as usual in this kind of weather – which I must say is quite freakish for this time of the year."

"When we get inside you'd better warm yourself by the brazier."

"I intend to."

"That's a nasty souvenir you brought back from Jerusalem," said Zechariah, shaking his head with a concerned look.

"It could have been worse."

"Yes, it could have. We must be grateful to the Almighty for that."

Zechariah was curious about how his son had been wounded, but most of what Avner knew was what he had heard from others. All he remembered was that he was advancing beyond the marketplace in the direction of the royal palace when he felt a searing pain in his left thigh. A sharp object had pierced his flesh, and blood spurted out. He groaned in agony, then everything went black. The next thing he knew he was lying on a pallet in a small, sparsely furnished room. He felt feverish and dazed; his tongue was dry and fuzzy. He had no idea how long he was unconscious, but he noticed that he was wearing a clean tunic and his left leg was thickly bandaged. He tried to move it, but a wave of intense pain shot through his whole body. He uttered a loud groan and sank back on the pallet, his eyes closed.

"Don't move your leg!" a female voice commanded.

The voice was familiar. Avner tried to place it, but he could not focus his thoughts. For a moment he thought it might be... He opened his eyes and regarded the person seated on a stool next to the window. "Rachel!" he murmured with a surprised look. "What are you doing here?"

"Why don't you ask what *you* are doing here?" she replied airily. "You're in our home."

"Your home!" exclaimed Avner, looking around him "This doesn't look like the mansion of a – er, wealthy notable."

"If you don't like it here, you're free to look for other accommodations," she said perkily.

Avner smiled in spite of his pain. "I'll think about it," he promised, and then added: "I'm glad to see you again, even if I'm flat on my back."

He again tried to raise himself, but with the same result. "I feel awful," he muttered. "I suppose I look awful too."

"I've seen you looking better," admitted Rachel, rising to pour some water from a pitcher onto a folded cloth "Now lie still and let me sponge your forehead; you're still feverish."

Avner liked the touch of her hand on his forehead. She's prettier than ever, he thought. He wondered if he looked any different to her. "I don't know what's happened to my leg," he said, shaking his head, "but at least there is one compensation: It's brought us close together again."

Rachel gave him an arch look. "When you talk like that, I know you're recovering."

"I hope it will be quick," he said. And then he added, almost as an afterthought: "But not too quick. The accommodations here aren't so bad, after all."

Rachel smiled. "That makes me feel better. And now you're going to get some food. You haven't eaten a thing since you've been here. You're very thin."

"How thin?" asked Avner with a twinkle in his eyes.

"I don't know. Our servant can tell you, if you really want to know."

"Right now I'm more interested in knowing to what I owe your unexpected hospitality."

"To the simple act that you were wounded in front of our home."

"Do you mean to tell me you were caught up in the fighting!" exclaimed Avner with an astonished look. "You saw what was going on in the streets?"

"Not exactly. We were all herded together in the servants' quarter – here in the rear of the house, where it was safest. We couldn't see what was happening in the street, but we could hear it. It was horrible! Thank God, the walls of our house and courtyard are very strong. Fortunately it wasn't long before the fighting moved on and we could venture out – although it seemed like ages to me."

"Where exactly did you find me?"

"Not far from our gate. An arrow hit you in the thigh. It was bleeding badly. For how long I don't know. I thought I was going to faint, but I managed to run back to the house and get a servant – or rather, two servants – to carry you inside, to this room. You looked more dead than alive. In fact, I wasn't sure if you would..." Rachel's voice trailed off, and she dabbed her eyes with a handkerchief. Avner waited patiently for her to continue.

"What happened then?" he asked in a subdued voice.

"I ordered one of the servants to summon a physician as fast as he could – a Greek slave who belongs to our neighbor."

"*You* ordered him to call a physician? Where was your father all this time?"

"He's serving as an adviser to Antigonus. He was with him at the time. In fact, that's probably where he is now."

"I see. So that's how I got here, is it? And how long have I been your honored guest?"

"You were unconscious three days."

"As long as that? All because of this little wound?"

"Your wound is not so little. The physician said you lost a lot of blood. He also said you were lucky the arrow didn't hit any of your vital organs."

"And I suppose he also said I was lucky that you called him when you did?"

"Yes, he did say that."

Avner tried to shift his position, but the pain was excruciating.

"You see," said Rachel, "it's not a little wound you have, not by any means."

Avner sighed deeply. "Does the physician think I'll heal completely, or am I liable to be crippled for the rest of my life?"

"He says you'll probably recover completely. But your leg may bother you for a long time, especially in cold weather. And now I'm going to bring you some food."

Avner lay back on his pillow and closed his eyes. It was obvious that he would be bedridden for quite a while. But he could be thankful that things had turned out the way they did, that by the grace of God Rachel had been there to help – nay, probably to save his life. Rachel – the girl he had grown up with in Emmaus. She brought back many fond memories. It had always been fun to be with her. She had been a bit of a tomboy, and until she reached an age where her father forbade her to play with boys, she was one of his favorite playmates. When her family moved to Jerusalem, he had felt a nagging emptiness.

Rachel returned with a tray of food: a slice of bread, some honey, a cup of goat's milk, and a boiled egg. "This isn't very much," she said, putting the tray down on a small table. "But the physician said you should eat only a little at a time for the first few days."

"If my stomach has to be half-starved, at least my eyes can feast on you," remarked Avner with a bold expression.

"I don't think the physician would object to that," replied Rachel, flushing a little. "But I doubt if it will help you to get better."

At Avner's request, Rachel brought him a basin of water for washing his hands. After reciting the blessing over the bread, he dipped it in the honey and began to eat it with the egg. With each bite he became hungrier.

"Don't eat so fast!" Rachel cautioned him. "You won't be getting any more food until evening."

"I didn't realize how hungry I was." Avner heeded Rachel's advice and began to chew his food more slowly. He did not speak another word until he consumed everything on the tray. He longed for more. "It's a long time since we've last seen each other," he said as Rachel rose to remove the tray. "You've changed a little since then."

"Did you expect me not to?" she replied, smiling demurely.

"Not really. But whenever I thought about you, I pictured you as you were then – a gangling youngster with long curly hair. Now you're in the full bloom of maidenhood. And no doubt affianced," he added, with a questioning look.

"Yes, I am."

Although he knew it was naive to expect otherwise, Avner's face fell upon hearing this. For a long moment he was silent, as though finding it hard to digest the information. "I had no way of knowing, of course. But I should have expected it. I suppose you're affianced to someone worthy of your present station – or someone whom your father thinks is worthy of you," he added with tinge of sarcasm.

"He's what you call of good stock – from an old aristocratic family."

"Do you love him?"

This question disconcerted Rachel. She gave Avner an annoyed look. "That's a very personal question," she admonished him.

"Yes, it is," admitted Avner, regretting his indiscretion. "Forget it."

"But I suppose it would be natural for you to ask that," she said in a softer tone. "After all, we've known each other a long time."

Her brow knitted as she considered the question. "Do I love him? To be perfectly honest, at this stage, I really can't say. We've been betrothed only a short time. But since when has that been the main consideration? People marry for various reasons – family, financial, sometimes even political. Love usually comes later, after marriage."

An incredulous expression appeared on Avner's face. "Is that your opinion or your father's?"

Rachel hesitated before answering thoughtfully: "That's how my father explained it, and my mother too. They say the most important thing is to marry well."

"Your father would say something like that," retorted Avner sarcastically.

"And your father wouldn't?"

"I really don't know," replied Avner with a thoughtful look. "We've never discussed the matter. I suppose my father, and my mother, too, assume that one day I'll marry – maybe not well, but with someone of my own class."

"I'm sure they assume that you'll marry happily," said Rachel, ignoring Avner's last cutting remark.

A thought suddenly struck Avner. "If you're betrothed, are you allowed to be alone with me?"

"We're not really alone. This is part of the servants' quarter; there are servants next door right now. Besides," Rachel went on with a big grin, "Avner, you make me laugh; until today you weren't even conscious."

* * *

Avner was bedridden for almost a whole month. The physician visited him daily to check his progress and change his bandages. During this time, Avner saw Rachel's father only once. According to her, he was extremely busy helping Antigonus set up his administrative machinery. Apart from the Sabbaths, he had very little free time to spend with his family. Avner had been surprised to learn that he was one of Antigonus's advisers, but Rachel explained that he had served as an officer under Antigonus's father. On the sole occasion he spoke to Avner, he was coldly formal. He made it clear that it was at Rachel's earnest request that he had agreed to let him stay in his home until he was strong enough to return to Emmaus.

It was a happy day for Avner when the physician informed him that he could go outdoors for a while and take a short walk. He was weak from the long confinement, and his leg pained him when he tried to walk. But he made rapid progress, and before long the physician pronounced him well enough to return home. He had become homesick during his confinement and was longing to see his parents and the rest of his family, but when he bade Rachel farewell, it was in a tone of genuine regret.

When Avner entered the courtyard to his home, it seemed ages since he had left it. He stopped to survey the surroundings. But not for long, for his parents came running out of the house. They had received several letters from him and knew approximately when he was expected to arrive. Hannah had been on tenterhooks ever since the last communication, and at the sound of every approaching vehicle she hurried to the door and looked out. When at last she saw Avner opening the gate, she called to Zechariah in great excitement, and rushed out as fast as her legs could carry her. She fell on Avner's neck, her eyes filled with tears of joy. A minute later Zechariah too was embracing his son, and in a choked voice he thanked the Lord for having vouchsafed Avner a safe return. As they started to walk to the house, several neighborhood children dashed into the courtyard and surrounded Avner. They formed a ring around him and broke into a lively dance, while singing at the top of their voices. When Zechariah finally pleaded with them to let Avner enter the house, they agreed on condition that he promise to tell them about the battle in Jerusalem.

The next few days were, like his return from slavery, very joyous ones for Avner and his family. All his siblings and their offspring and a good many of the townsmen came to welcome him back. Avner enjoyed the fuss made over him, but after a week he decided that the time had come to give his father a hand with the work. Zechariah restricted him to the lighter jobs, hiring outside help for the heavy tasks. Avner was glad to relieve his father of part of the work load, but he did not find it easy to get back to the old routine. Something was missing – something vague, indefinable. He was restless – a mood he put down at first to the difficulty of adjusting to a quiet, peaceful life after having helped to drive Herod out of Jerusalem. But upon reflection he was not sure that this was the main cause. He had spent more than two months in Rachel's home, and that in itself was a fairly long transitional period. And a most extraordinary one at that. His thoughts were constantly returning to that memorable interlude. Despite the pain that had troubled him the first two to three weeks, he had enjoyed the experience – Rachel's devoted ministration, the bantering, the reminiscing about their youthful adventures in Emmaus. Rachel was affianced to another, and he knew it was pointless to dwell so much on her. But what his mind told him his heart refused to accept.

Avner's parents were aware that something was troubling him, and Zechariah suspected that it had to do with Rachel. Avner had, of course, told them how she took care of him, and Zechariah recalled their youthful companionship. "It's no good his thinking about her," he said to Hannah. "She is betrothed, and that's that, not to mention all the other reasons why he should put her out of his mind." And the sooner the better, he decided the day he was fixing the stone wall.

"I see the mule cart is all spattered with mud," remarked Zechariah to Avner as they started to return to the house to escape the rain. "Did you get stuck in the road?"

"The road was soft in places. The calf wasn't all that heavy, but it was enough to bog the cart down near cousin Joab's house."

"It's no wonder you're limping like that. With your leg in the condition it's in, you shouldn't be putting too much strain on it."

"Joab gave me a hand. I couldn't budge the cart by myself, even after removing the calf."

"Well, that's done with. Let's hope Joab gets good use out of the calf. I could have sold it to Menahem, you know. He offered me a good price."

"Why didn't you sell it to him?"

"I had already promised it to Joab. He's family, so I couldn't even ask him the full price. Menahem won't have any trouble getting another calf. Well, here we are. We'd better get the mud off our shoes before going in."

"You might like to know," said Zechariah as they entered the house, "Menahem spoke very highly of you. He thinks you're a fine lad. I'm inclined to agree with him," he added with grin.

"Thanks, Abba," replied Avner warily.

"Oh, yes," Zecharah went on in a casual tone, "there was something else he spoke about in connection with you, but that can wait till after supper."

Avner gave his father a curious look. He thought he knew what Menahem had on his mind.

After supper Zechariah suggested that they go to the small room he usually used for studying. It was chilly and dark, but after he lit a brazier and two lamps, it became comfortably warm and pleasant. "It's cozy here," he said, rubbing his hands over the brazier, "especially after being out in the rain."

Avner too was in better spirits after a wash, change of garments, and a hot meal. He glanced at the scroll lying on the small table and saw from the name-tag that it was the Book of Proverbs. His father did not own many books; he could not afford to buy more because of their high price, but those he possessed he cherished and used well.

"One good thing about this kind of weather is that it gives me some time to study," remarked Zechariah, returning the scroll to its place in the cabinet. "When the weather is good, it's almost impossible except on the Sabbath. And it's important to study, no matter how hard one has to work. One of the proverbs tells us to receive knowledge rather than choice gold. That's pretty good advice in my opinion. Of course, if one can have both, so much the better."

"I agree with you," said Avner guardedly.

"Some of these scrolls belonged to my father," Zechariah continued as he took a chair and nodded to Avner to also be seated. "I treasure them all the more because of that. One day some of them will belong to you."

"I too will treasure them."

"I know you will. I can rely on your word. That's one of the things Menahem said about you, how reliable you are. When I mentioned what a big help you've always been to me, he said he's not surprised. He says I can be grateful to the Almighty for giving me a son like you."

Avner felt uncomfortable at all this praise, which his instinct told him was a prelude to the subject his father wanted to discuss. "Menahem has three sons of his own he can be proud of," he remarked in a noncommittal tone.

"Yes, he does. And also a daughter – about the same age as you."

This statement confirmed Avner's suspicion. "Sarah is more than a year younger than me," he said lamely.

"If you know that – then you know what a fine, upstanding girl she is." Zechariah regarded Avner with a serious look; he lowered his voice to a confidential level. "She'd make a good wife, son."

Since Avner's return Zechariah had spoken to him once before about the desirability of marrying, but in general terms. This was the first time he made a specific suggestion. Even though he was expecting something like this, Avner found it hard to frame a reply. "I'm sure she'd make a good wife," he said hesitantly. "But why tell me?" he asked, immediately realizing the inanity of this question.

It was obvious to Zechariah that Avner was disconcerted. He replied in a patient tone: "Son, when with the Lord's help you become a father and have a daughter of marriageable age, you'll know the answer to your question. A father – and a mother too, of course – want to see their daughter married to someone who will be a good husband to her, someone who is God-fearing, who has a good character, who, together with her, will make a happy home, like the one the Almighty has blessed your mother and me with. Sarah is the apple of Menahem's eye, and he wants to see her married to the right sort of person. And to him you're the right sort."

Avner stared at his father for a moment and then lowered his eyes. "It's flattering to know what Menahem thinks of me," he replied in slow, measured accents. "It's a compliment – a big compliment I admit – to be considered worthy of his daughter's hand. But this has taken me by surprise. It's not something I can give an answer to on the spot."

"I don't expect you to. It's a very serious matter – without a doubt the most serious decision a young man has to make. Menahem too understands that. I just ask you to give it your earnest consideration. But let me say this: You have reached the age where you should seriously think of taking a wife and making a home of your own."

Avner's brow furrowed and a thoughtful expression appeared on his face. "But Abba, what about –" he broke off, leaving the question unfinished.

"Yes, son, what is it you find hard to say? What about your father? Is that what's troubling you?"

"Yes," replied Avner, surprised at how accurately his father had read his mind. "How will you manage by yourself? There's too much work for you."

Zechariah was deeply touched by his son's solicitude. "And how did I manage while you were away fighting? I admit it was hard. But you see, somehow I did manage. And when those cursed Romans took you away to be sold into slavery, it wasn't hard? Of course it was, even if I was a little younger then. But don't let that worry you. Our holy Bible has put it well: 'It is not good that man should be alone; I will make him a helpmate for him... Therefore a man shall leave his father and his mother and shall cleave unto his wife, and they shall be one flesh.' That's the way of the world, the way the Almighty has commanded us."

Avner reflected on this. He too, of course, knew this passage well, but this was the first time it took on an intimate meaning for him. "To cleave unto his wife, to be one flesh," he repeated slowly. "To do that one has to love his wife as himself."

"That's right, he does. It's only when a man and a woman love each other that they are truly one flesh. But let me ask you something: When you say 'love,' what exactly does that mean to you?"

Avner was surprised that his father should ask such a simple question. But when he tried to reply, he found it harder than expected. "Well, I can't say that I've given it much thought," he said at last, "especially in connection with the matter we're discussing. But if it has to do with a young man, I'd say that it – well, if he's always thinking about a certain girl, if he's always seeing her in his mind's eye and longs to be with her, I'd say that's a sign that he loves her."

"That's a pretty good definition – or rather, description – of one kind of love. I'd call it romantic love," replied Zechariah with an understanding look. "I'd be the last person to belittle it. If one marries the woman he loves thus, and this love endures the trials and tribulations of married life – and there are bound to be trials and tribulations – then he is indeed fortunate. But there is also a love that grows slowly, that comes with sharing the problems and joys of married life, of bringing children into the world and rearing them. Maybe it's not the kind of love that sets the heart aflame. Such love, by the way, can also cool off after marriage; in fact, I'd say the chances are that it will, at least to some extent, while the other kind will more than likely grow warmer over the years. Take the story of Rebecca and Isaac, for example. The Bible says, 'Isaac took Rebecca, she became his wife, and he loved her.' When he took her as his wife, she was a stranger to him. But love came with marriage, when he learned to appreciate her good qualities, her companionship, her devotion. And that's the way it has been with your brothers and sisters. Thank God, they're all happily married and fulfilling the divine command to be fruitful and multiply. Their homes are happy homes, and their children are a treasure no gold can buy. There's where true happiness lies."

Avner had often discussed all sorts of matters with his father, including those of a personal nature, and he greatly valued his practical, down-to-earth wisdom. He knew that his father had his best interests at heart, and so he always gave his views and advice his earnest consideration. But in this particular matter the final decision must be his alone.

"Well, son," Zechariah went on, seeing that Avner had fallen silent, "this is the first time you and I have had a serious talk on this subject. That's a sign you have reached a new stage in your life. The decision must be yours, of course, and you don't have to decide right now. Menahem will understand that. But I hope you will give the matter serious thought."

"I will. But I can't promise that my answer to Menahem will be a positive one."

Zechariah studied his son's face closely. "You still have your heart set on Barzilai's daughter, don't you?"

Avner paused before admitting in a low voice: "Yes, I'm afraid I do."

"You told me she is betrothed. That means she belongs to another."

"I know. And I keep telling myself that. But I can't get her out of my mind."

Zechariah leaned forward and put a hand on Avner's shoulder. "Now, son, be realistic," he gently admonished him. "You have to forget about her, there's no other way. If she is betrothed, then that puts an end to the matter. And even if she weren't, do you think for one moment that her father would ever give her hand to you? You know perfectly well he wouldn't. We belong to two different worlds. We're simple farm people, and he's now a wealthy merchant and landowner. And what about her? Apart from looking after you when you were wounded, did she show any sign of feeling the same way about you as you evidently do toward her?"

Avner reflected a moment. "No, I can't honestly say she did."

"Did she encourage you in any way?"

"No, on the contrary."

"Well, there you are! Don't waste your time in pipe dreams. I know you're young, and young people tend to look at such matters in – well, what I called before, a romantic light. Maybe Sarah doesn't strike you that way now. That's probably because your thoughts have always been dwelling on Rachel. But if you marry a girl like Sarah, you'll come to realize she's a real jewel. She'll be a helpmate to you, and together you'll build a fine home. Look at it in that light, son. That's all I ask of you."

Loss of Hope in the Royal Palace

As the festival of Shavuot drew near, Hyrcanus became increasingly despondent. He had endured many tribulations in his lifetime, but never before had he sunk to such a low state. Even when he had been bested by his brother and was forced to relinquish both the priestly and royal crowns to him, he had been able to accept defeat with a fair degree of equanimity. But then he was a young man with his whole life ahead of him. Now, after having long served his people faithfully as high priest and king, he could not reconcile himself to his humiliating change of fortune.

He was virtually a prisoner in his own palace. Because of the fighting he could hardly venture outdoors in the daytime, let alone officiate in the Temple, which was held by Antigonus's men. He was cut off from his dear friends Shemaiah, Avtalion, and other sages, who might have been able to advise him or at least lift his troubled spirits with their learned discourse. From the upper floor of the palace he could see the priests going about their assigned duties, and the sounding of the trumpets before the wine libation and the sweet singing of the Levitical choir helped him to forget for a few precious minutes the oppressive din of fighting. How he yearned to be in the Temple! There he was in his element, there he fulfilled the task the Lord had destined him for. And to think that Shavuot was approaching, the festival when throngs of pilgrims would begin to bring their baskets of first fruits to the Temple, and two loaves baked from the finest wheat grown that year would be waved before the Lord. He would be forced to witness the ceremony from the palace, his magnificent prison. His heart ached at the thought; he felt empty and forlorn.

In the last few years he found that he needed no more than five or six hours of sleep to feel refreshed. But now he was unable to fall asleep until the early hours of the morning. And then his sleep was disturbed by a host of worries. Above all, he feared for the safety of his family. Hardly less tormenting was the sight of his fellow Jews fighting in the streets of the Holy City. When the wind blew his way he could sometimes hear the groans of the wounded and dying – his own people. His heart bled for them, even though he knew that their victory would spell the end of his reign. He was essentially a man of peace. Even during the first stormy years of his reign, when his brother had fought against him, the thought of his own people killing one another had sickened him. When Aristobulus had gained the upper hand and wrested both crowns from him, he had at least been glad that the bloodletting was ended – or so he had thought and hoped.

The mental anguish and physical fatigue showed on his countenance and bearing. Alexandra did her best to raise his spirits and keep his hopes alive. In his presence she maintained a cheerful, optimistic air, assuring him that the people had not turned against him but were venting their hatred of the Romans and Antipater's sons. But she knew that her father had not enhanced his esteem in their eyes by affiancing her daughter to Herod. They could not accept the fact that a Hasmonean princess was to be the wife of the arrogant, self-seeking "pagan" puppet of the conqueror. She too could not reconcile herself to what she considered to be a bad error of judgment on her father's part. And the bitter irony of it was that one of the principal factors that had motivated him was the deadly fear that Antigonus, like his father before him, would attempt to seize his two crowns, plunging the nation into internecine strife and threatening his personal safety and that of his immediate family.

The knowledge that they were presently dependent on Herod for protection galled Alexandra. Protection against whom? Against her own people? Against her brother-in-law? Her anguish was exacerbated by the close contact with Herod and his family. With Herod she was able to maintain a polite but detached relationship. Truth to tell, he was so occupied with the fighting that she saw very little of him. But she was thrown into daily contact with his family, and this made her plight all the more intolerable. Although born to a noble Nabataen family, Cypros was basically a simple, illiterate woman, who was almost totally ignorant of things Jewish. Alexandra knew there could never be any affinity between them, yet she had to admire her devotion to her family. With Salome it was an entirely different story. In the royal Hasmonean palace and in her late husband's home Alexandra had encountered many different types of people, who ran the gamut from the gentle, noble sort to overbearing, unprincipled opportunists. But never before did she have to contend with a spiteful, inveterate schemer like Salome.

Ungainly and angular in figure, possessing a shrill, grating voice and an abrasive countenance and manner, she took a perverse delight in sowing dissension wherever possible. Alexandra herself had a strong character and was little disposed to tolerate Salome's malicious behavior. But for the sake of peace in the palace and out of respect for her father's feelings, she refrained from paying Salome back in her own coin. She kept Mariamne as far away from her as possible, for Salome seemed to have marked her out as her chief victim.

One day shortly after the fighting had broken out Alexandra found her daughter in tears and sobbing loudly. At first she thought it might be the tension that was upsetting her. "Darling," she said, slipping an arm around Mariamne's shoulders, "you must be brave. None of us likes the fighting, but you have to remember that you're a Hasmonean princess and must learn to steel yourself."

"It's not the fighting," Mariamne blurted out between sobs. "It scares me, I admit, but it's not that what's bothering me. It's Salome. I hate her! I wish she were a bug, and then I'd step on her and crush her!"

"Now, is that a nice way to talk?" Alexandra gently admonished her daughter. "One mustn't speak that way about another person, not even Salome."

"I don't care! She's horrible! You say I must remember that I'm a Hasmonean princess. Then I ask you, does anyone have the right to slap a Hasmonean princess?"

Alexandra stiffened and an incredulous expression crossed her face. "She slapped you?"

"Yes, and hard too. I tried to kick her, but she jumped out of the way. She said that if I dared to do that again she'd slap me harder."

"What did you do to get her angry? I told you more than once to stay away from her."

"I try to keep away from her. Who wants to be near that horrible monster? But I couldn't help it; I didn't see her when I ran into the room. If I'd known she was standing next to the door, I wouldn't have gone anywhere near it."

"What happened when you ran into the room? Did you bump into her?"

"Yes. I didn't see her until it was too late. I stepped on her foot, and she screeched like a horrid old witch – and that's exactly what she is."

"She had no right to slap you," said Alexandra, trying to mollify her daughter, "but it was probably painful when you stepped on her foot. Did you apologize?"

"I tried to. But she didn't give me a chance. I did say I was sorry, but she screamed that I was lying, that I purposely did it to her and wasn't at all sorry."

Mariamne paused a moment, and the look of self-pity was replaced by a defiant expression. "And maybe she's right," she went on. "I didn't do it on purpose, but now that it's done, I'm not sorry about it. I only wish I'd stepped on her foot harder. Next time I will."

"You mustn't do that," said Alexandra, shaking her head in mild reproof. "That's not the way to behave, especially a member of the royal family. The Lord knows, we have enough troubles on our hands, and Salome too is undoubtedly affected by them. The best thing is just to keep a safe distance from her."

Alexandra knew that in the present circumstances everyone's nerves were on edge and outbursts were to be expected. With Salome, however, it was not a question of circumstances but a basic trait of her character. Alexandra realized that she could not ignore the matter. In order to let Salome's temper cool off, she waited two days before approaching her. She broached the subject with the utmost tact, speaking calmly and avoiding anything suggestive of reproach. She apologized for any pain Mariamne might have caused her, and assured her that it was not done intentionally. Salome snorted contemptuously and said that Mariamne must be very stupid if she can't watch where she's going. This brought a flush to Alexandra's cheeks, but she kept her composure. She pointed out that Mariamne was very young, and like all youngsters she might not always be as careful as she should. But whatever the cause, if in the future Salome has reason to be annoyed with Mariamne, it would be advisable to bring the matter to Alexandra's attention and let her deal with it rather than strike Mariamne – something one does not do to another person's child, let alone a princess.

Salome drew herself erect and her visage assumed a haughty, scornful look. "If a child deliberately steps on my feet, I won't go running to her mother," she declared in staccato accents. "And don't think that just because she's a princess that makes any difference to me. It's only thanks to my brothers and my late father that she can call herself a princess today. So if I were her – or even her mother – I wouldn't give myself airs and graces."

"I don't think my daughter is giving herself airs and graces, as you put it," Alexandra replied coldly. "And as for your other remark, I will only say that if you think we are beholden to your brothers or your late father, you would be well advised to disabuse yourself of the idea."

Salome placed her hands on her hips and glared at Alexandra. "Is that so! And pray tell me, who is defending the palace and protecting your father and yourself and your children if not my brothers? And against whom? Against the Jewish rabble – your own people, who have always been nothing but a festering sore, a pack of howling ingrates."

Alexandra stared hard at Salome. It was plain that there could never be any understanding or rapport between them. Herod's sister was a danger to them, and she would always have to be on guard against her. She turned her back on Salome, and without another word stalked out of the room.

A Parthian Delegation to Beseiged Jerusalem

Herod was in a fretful mood. The sun was climbing rapidly in the east, heralding the start of another day that would undoubtedly see hard fighting and a further dwindling of his forces. Normally at this hour there was a refreshing breeze, but today the air was still and dry and even a bit hazy with dust. This meant a khamsin, which would irritate his nose and throat and make him even more edgy. He was uncomfortable in his cuirass. He disliked wearing armor at the best of times and especially in hot weather, but it was foolhardy to go unprotected when volleys of arrows would rain on them throughout the day. Right now it was quiet, but soon the air would start humming with barbed missiles.

He took a quick look at his defenses. Some of the men were yawning widely; others were munching their rations while keeping their eyes peeled to detect any movement on the other side of the barricades "The men are in position, sir," his chief lieutenant reported. "What are your orders?"

"Tell the men to keep themselves exposed as little as possible. If the enemy attempt to advance, repulse them vigorously, but otherwise I want a minimum of casualties. Tomorrow or the next day, if the khamsin breaks, we'll stage a sortie. We have to drive them away from the palace."

"Yes, sir," the chief lieutenant said in reply, and strode away to join his fellow officers.

Watching his retreating figure, Herod wondered if he would be as lively at the end of the day. His musing was cut short by a familiar sound – the whizzing of the first volley of arrows, aimed directly at him. He disdainfully watched them fly overhead and moved to a safer position.

As the morning wore on the weather became more oppressive and enervating. It was evidently affecting the enemy too, for apart from sporadic flights of arrows, there was very little action. At midday Herod, relieved at the comparative quiet, ordered a light meal served him and his staff. The officers joined Herod and Phasael around a table set up in a protected spot in the courtyard. Despite the khamsin, the men were in good spirits, and they joshed one another as they helped themselves to goat milk and cheese, bread, honey, lentils, and fruit. After removing his helmet and breastplate, Herod felt more comfortable, and in a rare relaxed mood he pushed out of his mind for a brief spell all thought of the fighting. He listened to the adventures and anecdotes recounted around the table, some of which he recognized as embellished versions of tales related more than once in the past, especially of amorous conquests. He was glad to see his officers in a cheerful frame of mind.

Their pleasant respite was interrupted by the hasty appearance of a sentry. Several of the officers, assuming that something was amiss, uttered a curse and instinctively reached for their helmets. Herod, who was eating an apple, looked puzzled. There was no sound suggesting the resumption of fighting; on the contrary, there was an eerie silence in the direction of the foe. His perplexity turned to amazement when he learned that a path was being cleared for what looked like a mounted nobleman of some sort, who was heading toward the palace.

"What does he look like?" Herod asked the sentry.

"Well, sir, from the looks of him I'd say he's a Parthian."

"What makes you think so?"

"I've run up against Parthians before, and I can recognize them by their dress, the size of their horses, and the way they ride them without stirrups."

"Is he alone?"

"No, sir, there are three other horsemen with him."

Herod's eyes narrowed and he assumed a hard, suspicious look. "What the hell would bring a Parthian here?" he muttered, more to himself. "I'm as keen on seeing a Parthian in Jerusalem as I am of seeing the devil himself."

"He must have something very important to say if he's taken the risk of coming here," remarked Phasael.

"They're a devious lot and not to be trusted," Herod shot back. "This is probably a trick of some sort."

"If he's come to parley with us, we shouldn't refuse," Phasael said soberly. "In fact, I don't think we're in a position to refuse."

Herod scowled and cursed under his breath. He turned to his chief lieutenant and told him to order the men to let the Parthians advance unharmed. Rising from his campstool and pushing his plate of food aside, Herod signaled to his staff to accompany him to the barricade that had been thrown up to ward off attacks from the direction of the marketplace. The Cilicians and Syrians stationed there jumped to attention and saluted the party of officers, who made their way to the end of the barricade, where a narrow slit between the thick stones served as a peephole. Herod peered through the opening, and what he saw confirmed the sentry's report. They were Parthians, and judging from his armor and appearance, as well as the silver trappings of his steed, the leader was obviously a noble, probably of high rank.

The four horsemen advanced toward the barricade, and when they came within speaking distance they halted and the leader called out in Greek: "Hail Herod! I bring greetings from His Majesty, the King of Kings Orodes!"

Herod turned and stared in amazement at his officers, who were equally nonplused. He made a wry face and cursed softly. He glanced at Phasael with a quizzical expression. Phasael nodded his head, signifying that the Parthians should be admitted. Herod mounted the barricade and called back: "I am honored to receive greetings from His Majesty King Orodes. You will be admitted."

Herod ordered a passage cleared at one end of the barricade wide enough to admit the party single file. He took the precaution of instructing the officer in charge of the barricade to keep a close eye on the Parthians and to guard against any possible ruse. The Parthians waited patiently as a passage was cleared for them. Three of the steeds, powerful chargers protected by scale armor, as were their riders, squeezed through with difficulty; the other mount was a sleek courser without mail, and so it had no trouble getting through. The leader of the party smiled benignly at the bemused soldiers as he dismounted; he approached Herod and saluted in the Roman rather than the Parthian manner.

Herod saw before him a vigorous-looking middle-aged man of moderate build; when he removed his pointed helmet he revealed a ruggedly handsome countenance with a broad forehead, black eyes under trimmed brows, a large thin nose, and sensitive lips framed by a black square beard. His jet black hair was curled in the Parthian fashion of the time. Despite the heat he appeared quite dapper in his purple- and yellow-striped cloak clasped at the waist by a studded leather girdle in which was thrust a long dagger with an encrusted handle.

"I have never had the honor of meeting you before," he addressed Herod suavely, "but your fame has spread far. Allow me to introduce myself. I am Pacorus."

"The prince Pacorus?" asked Herod, his brow arching sharply.

"I have the great privilege of serving my lord, King Orodes, in all fidelity, but as his cupbearer, not his son. We bear the same love and veneration for His Majesty, as well as the same name, but we are not kinsmen. And now, please allow me to introduce my retinue."

In introducing his companions, Pacorus gave their titles from which it was evident that they were members of the Parthian aristocracy.

"You come at a very precarious time," commented Herod dryly after introducing Phasael and his chief lieutenant, "and at no little risk to yourself."

"It is precisely because the situation is precarious that I have come," declared Pacorus in measured tones. "And as for the risk involved, I do not fear any harm to my person. I respect the honor of your men."

"When men are under siege they may forget their code of honor," replied Herod darkly.

"Then it would be advisable to see if the siege cannot be lifted," retorted Pacorus with a polite smile.

Herod stared at Pacorus with an incredulous expression. Did this smooth-tongued Parthian dandy think it was in his power to end the fighting? Is that why he came – to persuade them to capitulate? The muscles of Herod's neck tightened and his right cheek began to twitch; his eyes took on a hard, cold look.

Phasael, recognizing the signs of his brother's mounting anger, stepped forward. "The king of Parthia would not send his envoy to us unless he had some constructive proposal to make," he said to Herod in a grave voice. "We owe him the courtesy of hearing him out."

Herod reflected on this for a moment. Then, turning to Pacorus, he addressed him in a friendlier tone. "With High Priest Hyrcanus's permission, you will be escorted to the palace, where we can confer in comfort. You may not find that in the present circumstances we can offer you the hospitality normally provided distinguished visitors."

"There is no need to apologize," replied Pacorus amiably. "I fully appreciate that there may be – er, some difficulties."

For the first time in weeks calm descended on the Holy City. True, it was a tense calm, and no one could guess how long it would last. But the respite from hostilities was welcomed by all, even those most eager to see an end to Roman influence. Everyone knew that an envoy from the Parthian court had come with the aim of arranging a settlement. They were pinning their hopes on him to end the stalemate, for the inability to bring the battle to a victorious conclusion had filled them with a deep sense of frustration.

In the palace too there was an air of expectancy. This, however, was not shared by Herod, who remained suspicious of the Parthians' intentions. During the meal served in the small banqueting hall he spoke little and responded laconically, if not brusquely, to Hyrcanus's and Phasael's attempt to draw him into the general conversation. Pacorus, on the other hand, seemed to be enjoying himself immensely: He was in an expansive mood and regaled his hosts with anecdotes about the Parthian court. He exuded an air of bonhomie and displayed the utmost politeness to Herod and Phasael and deference to Hyrcanus. Even though he had weighty matters on his mind, he did not let this affect his enjoyment of the food: he praised Hyrcanus's cuisine, a sentiment echoed by his retinue, and gave his hearty approval of the choice of wines, which he sampled in copious draughts.

After the leisurely meal Hyrcanus suggested that they repair to the audience chamber to hold their talk. When everyone was seated, Hyrcanus expressed his appreciation to Pacorus for coming to Jerusalem at a very difficult time on what was undoubtedly a highly delicate mission. He assumed that Pacorus had a message of the greatest import to convey, and assured him that his words were eagerly awaited and would receive careful consideration.

Pacorus began by thanking Hyrcanus for his kind hospitality, including the delicious meal, which, he added with a smile, he had greatly enjoyed. He was grateful for the opportunity to meet with the leaders of the Judean state, and confirmed that he had indeed come on an important mission, which he earnestly hoped would be crowned with success, for the benefit of all concerned. He brought greetings from King Orodes, who was greatly concerned about the fighting in the Jewish capital and desired nothing more than to see the restoration of peace and quiet to the country and Jerusalem spared the miseries of a prolonged siege. To this end he had authorized Pacorus to do whatever he could to help end the fighting.

"And why, may I ask, is King Orodes so solicitous about Jerusalem's fate?" Herod interjected in a cold, challenging voice. "Other cities have undergone a siege of late, especially Tyre. Has His Majesty dispatched some member of his court to seek an end to the fighting there?"

Pacorus, plainly aware of the hostile tone of Herod's question and in fact anticipating such a reaction, was unruffled. "His Majesty has conceived a particular attachment and concern for the Holy City of the Jewish people," he replied blandly. "In his kingdom there is a large Jewish community, and he enjoys very cordial relations with its leaders. He knows their anguish over what is happening in Jerusalem and feels he owes it to these loyal subjects to do whatever is in his power to bring peace and tranquility to this admirable land."

"And so he orders Antigonus to invade Judea and invest Jerusalem in order to seize control of this admirable land from its rulers!" Herod flung at Pacorus with undisguised scorn.

Pacorus knew that this charge was liable to be leveled at him. In a calm, patient voice he directed his reply not only to Herod but to Hyrcanus and Phasael as well. "I can appreciate your sentiments on this point. And if I were in your shoes, I'd probably feel the same as you do. Antigonus's arrival on the scene at this particular juncture would, I admit, create the impression you mention. But could it not also be that Antigonus, who, as is well known, has in the past aspired to the Judean throne, saw in the present situation his great opportunity and decided to take advantage of it without necessarily being ordered or influenced to do so by others?"

"Parthia had no need to order or influence Antigonus to invade Judea," Herod shot back. "He's doing your work for you."

This barbed remark piqued Pacorus, but being a consummate diplomat, he kept his composure. "Please pardon me if I take issue with you on that," he replied a little stiffly. "Judging from what I know about Judea, the majority of the people, in fact a big majority, seem to favor Antigonus's cause. No one is forcing them to side with him, least of all Parthia."

Herod did not respond to this comment, whose truth he could not dispute. "And precisely what proposal do you bring?" he asked with a defiant, metallic ring in his voice.

Pacorus turned a thoughtful look on each of the three conferees, replying in a restrained voice. "As I have already pointed out, I am the king's cupbearer. While this is an important position, there are others whose standing is higher than mine and who wield more influence. One of them is Barzaphranes, commander of the Parthian army in southern Syria. At the moment his headquarters are close to the Galilean border. Now, if you were to go to him you would find that with his sagacity and wide experience he could, I am sure, help work out an amicable solution to this – er, somewhat complicated problem. He could..."

"Are you suggesting that we put ourselves at Barzaphranes's mercy?" Herod broke in, half-rising from his seat, his eyes blazing with anger. "You insult our intelligence by such a preposterous suggestion!"

Pacorus was braced for a negative response by Herod but did not expect it to be so vehement. "I believe you may not have properly understood me," he said a little coolly. "Perhaps it is my fault that you have jumped to a hasty conclusion and misconstrued my words."

"I don't see what other meaning can be read into your words," snapped Herod. "Stripped of its diplomatic polish, your proposal boils down to one thing – our capitulation."

Pacorus's face darkened. "Your accusation is, if you forgive me, disconcerting, to say the least. You impute base motives to my proposal when my desire – the desire of my lord, King Orodes – is to help restore peace and quiet to Judea."

"And what better way to ensure that than to remove Judea's legitimate rulers from the scene," retorted Herod ominously.

"I regret that you persist in this line of argument," Pacorus countered with a sigh of resignation. "Permit me to ask you, do you have a better suggestion to make?"

Herod was silent for a moment. He lowered his eyes, and then looked up, glowering at the Parthian. "We did not seek your advice or assistance. We were holding off the enemy before you came, and we'll continue to hold them off after you have gone."

"I admire your courage, especially in the face of such overwhelming odds," commented Pacorus with a trace of irony. "It is obvious that we differ in assessing your prospects."

He rose to his feet, a signal for his retinue to follow suit. "I regret that I shall have to report to His Majesty the failure of my mission."

At these words Hyrcanus, who had listened with growing dismay to Herod's acrimonious exchange with the Parthian, experienced a sinking feeling in the pit of his stomach. "Please don't go," he said with a strained look. "There are a few points I would like to clarify."

Pacorus glanced at his men with a pleased look. He nodded and all resumed their seats. "I shall be very happy to answer any questions you wish to ask," he said to Hyrcanus with a deferential bow.

Hyrcanus threw a sideways glance at Herod and saw that he was fuming, but he was determined to proceed. He turned to Pacorus. "You suggest that we go to Barzaphranes. It is still not entirely clear to me what purpose this would serve. Perhaps you could elucidate. And one other thing: What about Antigonus? Would he also be there?"

Pacorus knew about Hyrcanus's dread of his nephew, and he observed the worried look that crossed his face. "Do you want Antigonus to be there?" he asked gently.

"I would prefer not. In fact, if he's going to be there, I will not even consider the matter."

"Then he will not be there. You will be dealing solely with the Parthian monarch's representative."

At this assurance Hyrcanus breathed a sigh of relief. He put several more questions to the Parthian, who did his utmost to allay Hyrcanus's apprehensions. When Pacorus and his retinue took their leave, it was with the understanding that his proposal would be given due consideration.

Herod was extremely annoyed at Hyrcanus, and it was only with great difficulty that he could speak to him civilly. That evening, as they discussed the situation, he warned Hyrcanus and Phasael not to be hoodwinked by Pacorus's cajolery. "The Parthians are a smooth, deceitful lot," he declared in a steely voice. "It's quite plain what they want."

"Why do you condemn the Parthians outright?" Phasael wanted to know. "What makes you so sure their proposal wasn't made in good faith?"

"Even a dunce could see that the suggestion to go to Barzaphranes is pointless," Herod snapped at his brother. "What will Barzaphranes do – decide whether Antigonus or Hyrcanus has a more legitimate claim to the high priesthood and to sit on the royal throne?" he snorted with angry disgust. "Can't you see how absurd the idea is? It's obvious who they want on the throne."

"Why are you so sure about that?" asked Hyrcanus with a worried frown.

"If you weren't so distraught by our present predicament, it would be clear to you," replied Herod sharply. "The fact is that we – you, Phasael, myself – represent Rome in the eyes of the Parthians. The Parthians are at war with Rome, at least in this part of the world. Commonsense would tell you that they prefer Antigonus, who would be only too happy to serve their interests as long as their arms ensure him his privileged position."

"What alternative do we have?" asked Phasael with a somber expression. "Our situation is desperate, even hopeless."

"Desperate, yes, but not hopeless. We've held our ground so far, and we can continue to hold our ground."

"For how long?" said Phasael, flinging his arms upward. "Eventually we'll run out of food and other supplies. And our force isn't unlimited; we can't replace our losses. We'll be forced to surrender. We'll be taken captive, and who knows what will happen to us then? This way we may be able to treat with the Parthians and arrange an honorable settlement."

"You're not being realistic," retorted Herod with an exasperated look. "If you weren't my brother, I'd say you're being naïve, very naïve."

"I don't think I'm being either unrealistic or naïve. On the contrary, I see our situation as it really is, and I don't see that we have much choice. I admit there is some risk involved in going to Barzaphranes, but we face a greater risk if we don't accept their proposal. The Parthians are known for their lenient treatment of their opponents. Why do you suspect they'll deceive us?"

Herod stared vacantly at his brother for a long moment before replying. When he did, it was in a low voice and with an odd expression on his face. "Because I know what I'd do if I were in their shoes."

Phasael's countenance fell. He loved his brother dearly, but knew that he possessed an inflexible will, a hard, even cruel streak that brooked no compromise with his plans, his aspirations. His dire words shook Phasael; a cold shudder passed over him. When he spoke there was a strained note in his voice.

"I hope the Parthians will prove to be a little more..." He was about to say "humane," but checked himself.

"Don't be foolish," Herod urged him. "The Parthians – and Antigonus – have the upper hand right now, but the wheel will turn. It's bound to. Rome will be back on top, and so will we."

"But until then, what will happen to us, to our loved ones – our mother, our sister, my wife, our little ones? Even if only for their sake we have to treat with the Parthians and salvage what we can in the meantime."

Hyrcanus and Phasael Depart to Meet Parthian General

From one of the upper-floor rooms in the eastern wing of the palace, Hyrcanus watched the priests going about their tasks in the Temple courts. He was too far away to recognize them, and he was not even sure which of the twenty-four divisions was officiating that week. Their vestments and purposeful air set the priests apart from the crowd milling about the courts – his fellow

Jews who had come as worshippers and remained to fight under Antigonus's banner. His heart ached at the thought, and he began to brood over the cruel turn of events. The melancholy observation of Koheleth (Ecclesiastes) came to his mind: "What profit hath a man of all his labor and of the striving of his heart wherein he laboreth under the sun? For all his days are pain, and his occupation vexation; yea, even in the night his heart taketh no rest."

Hyrcanus had always thought Koheleth too pessimistic, one whose sky was overcast, who was not attuned to the goodness of the Lord's majestic world. But now the preacher's words struck a responsive cord in him, gripping him like a haunting refrain. Yes, Hyrcanus had to admit, Koheleth penetrated more incisively than he the inner recesses of man's mind; it was he and not Hyrcanus who understood what drove men to all sorts of inexplicable acts, what made the Jews, Hyrcanus's brethren whom he loved as his own flesh and blood, take up arms and attempt to depose him.

As he moodily reflected on his change of fortune, the mists of time rolled away and in his mind's eye he beheld a strange people in the Temple precincts – Pompey's troops swarming through the courts with drawn swords, slaughtering all Jews they came upon – laymen and priests going about their sacred tasks. The memory made Hyrcanus shudder, and a cold fear crept over him. "O God!" he uttered, appalled at the enormity of it all. The Temple was the House of God, in the construction of which no sound of iron tools was heard, for God's House was a house of peace. How ironic and horrendous that precious Jewish blood had been shed here of all places.

Hyrcanus had seen too much Jewish blood shed in his lifetime, especially at the beginning of his reign, when his younger brother had sought to wrest the high-priestly and royal crowns from him. Hyrcanus had been ready to relinquish them, for he was essentially a man of peace. His father had despised him for this trait, and favored the more ambitious and militant Aristobulus. When Alexander Yannai died, after a 27-year reign marked by incessant warfare and oppression of the Pharisaic sages, which had made him odious in the eyes of his people, Hyrcanus experienced only mild grief. He had always been uncomfortable and even timorous in his father's presence, and avoided him as much as possible. "You're a softy, a milksop!" his father had once upbraided him. "You're fit to be a scribe but not a high priest, let alone to rule over the nation. Heaven help the people if you should become king!"

If Hyrcanus had found the courage to serve as high priest, it was thanks to his mother. It was she who understood and encouraged him in every way. She was wise and good and gentle – so unlike her spouse. The people loved her as much as they disliked Yannai. The nine years she had sat on the throne were the happiest years of Hyrcanus's life. As high priest he was content: He had found his niche and life seemed good and fulfilling. Peace now prevailed in the land, and prosperity too.

The rains were ample, the crops exceptional, the granaries overflowing. The talk in the palace was no longer about victorious campaigns, the need to impose new taxes in order to hire more mercenaries and build new fortifications, or about the brazen impudence of the Pharisees, who challenged the wisdom and moral validity of Yannai's policies and disputed his right and competence to serve as high priest. Now, more often than not, the talk was about the expanding network of schools for providing religious instruction, the growing eminence of the Sanhedrin under the dynamic leadership of the Pharisaic sages who had returned from their places of refuge, and the state of Jewish life in the Diaspora.

Judea had thrived under his mother's wise, benign rule, and she fully deserved the nation's veneration. Many a time when he had to make a major decision he asked himself what she would have done, what she would have advised him. He had sought to emulate her, but somehow fate seemed to conspire against him. He too yearned for peace; he sought the good of his people, for he wanted them to love and respect him as they did her. Why, then, were they now taking up arms against him? What had he done to deserve this?

In another hour or so, he and Phasael would be setting out on their journey to the north to meet with Barzaphranes – a meeting which Herod warned was a trap designed to ensnare them. To such a state had he sunk! Yet he did not see that he had any choice but to go through with the business, even though he too was not a little apprehensive about its outcome – a misgiving probably evoked, or at least exacerbated, by Herod's dire warning. As long as there was the slightest prospect of success he was duty-bound to accept the risk. His heart was heavy, and he could not shake off a premonition that this might be the last time he would behold the Temple, and perhaps even this room. In this somber mood he went to his study and from one of the cabinets extracted a well-worn scroll – the Book of Psalms, which he was accustomed to read when he was troubled in mind. He opened it to the thirty-first psalm and began to read in a low, fervent voice. One of the longer psalms, its lofty sentiments stirred him deeply. It spoke directly to his heart, and his spirits began to rise as he communed with his Maker, his rock and fortress.

He beseeched the Almighty to bring him forth out of the net hidden for him, to lead and guide him. He would yet rejoice in the Lord's loving-kindness, for He has seen his affliction and taken cognizance of his troubled soul. When he uttered the passage, "I am forgotten as a dead man out of mind," a surge of pain welled up in him: how lonely he had been these last few terrible weeks, when he was cut off from his dearest friends, from his own beloved people, and terror lay on every side. But he found solace in the knowledge that the Lord's goodness is abundant, especially for those who fear Him and take refuge in Him; He hears the voice of supplication and preserves the faithful, bidding those who wait for Him to be strong and take courage.

When he finished the psalm, Hyrcanus continued to stare at the words which had uplifted his spirits and infused him with renewed hope. After a few minutes he turned to another of his favorite psalms and read it in an equally fervent voice. He then closed his eyes and recited the twenty-third psalm, which is unsurpassed for sheer sublimity.

He remained seated, reluctant to break the mystical spell woven by the psalmist, to leave the room which now seemed suffused with a pure, radiant light. Some time passed before he slowly rose to his feet and, turning toward the Temple, added a short prayer of his own: "O Lord, I don't know what lies ahead of me, but whatever fate You have marked out for me I will humbly accept One thing, though, I implore: Do not take Your holy spirit from me. Let Your countenance shine on me till the end of my days on earth."

Now came the painful moment of leave-taking from his loved ones: his wife, his daughter, and her two children. They were silently waiting for him, and their grave expressions told him that they were finding his departure no easier than he.

"Is everything ready?" he asked Alexandra, assuming a matter-of-fact tone in the hope of dispelling some of the gloom. Alexandra could not bring herself to speak. She nodded her head, struggling to hold back the tears.

"Come, now," he said with a faint smile, "why are you all so glum? I'm only going on a short trip."

"When will you be back, Grandpa?" asked Mariamne in a plaintive voice.

"I hope fairly soon," Hyrcanus replied softly. "I'll be thinking of you every minute."

"And we'll be thinking of you, too," Aristobulus added, "so hurry back."

"I'll try to get back as soon as I can," Hyrcanus promised, patting his grandson's head. "But it's important that I come back with good results. So even if it takes a little longer than you or I would like, we must be patient."

He turned to Alexandra – his wise, stouthearted daughter who was his confidante and comfort during many a troubled period. He lowered his voice and his expression became more thoughtful. "If God forbid, anything should happen..."

"Don't say that!" Alexandra pleaded in a choked voice. "You will come back. You must!"

"With God's help," said Hyrcanus quietly. "You pray for the success of my mission, and I'll pray for your safety and that of all our loved ones. But we cannot know the ways of the Almighty. Whatever He has in store for me, we must accept. Come what may, be assured that I will be easier in mind because I know I can depend on you."

Chapter Five

Herod's Lone Journey to Rome

Phasael Advises Herod to Escape

After the departure of his brother and Hyrcanus, Herod fell into a sullen mood. Until the very last he had done his utmost to dissuade them, and his failure to do so both exasperated and worried him. The truce did not improve his spirits: With no active fighting to occupy him, he became a prey to mounting anxiety. If only he had a Roman legion or even a few cohorts at his disposal, he could finish off Antigonus and his wretched rabble. But damn it! Where were the Romans? How Antony could forsake his administration of the Eastern provinces in order to dally with that royal Egyptian whore was something he could not fathom.

Relations inside the palace did not make his life any pleasanter. Salome became more difficult than ever, driving him to distraction with her petty bickering and spiteful behavior toward Hyrcanus's family. He realized that the danger and tension they were all enduring would fray the nerves of the calmest of persons, and he would by no stretch of the imagination put her in this category.

Alexandra tried to keep herself and Mariamne out of her way as much as possible, but it was inevitable that their paths occasionally crossed in the course of the day. These encounters were frequently accompanied by acrimonious exchanges, and more than once Herod had to shout Salome down, especially when her venom was directed at Mariamne, who, he reminded his sister in no uncertain terms, was not only Alexandra's daughter but his betrothed as well.

Herod's mercenaries were also discontented. They had become restless during the truce, when they could not leave their confined area. They would have preferred to try and hack their way out, even at the risk of almost certain failure.

Aware of their declining morale, Herod ordered his officers to arrange contests and other diversions for them.

When more than a fortnight passed without any news from his brother, Herod became increasingly anxious. He tried to hide his feelings in his mother's presence, but she was not deceived. She too was very worried, and her apprehension was not allayed by Herod's perfunctory replies to her persistent questioning. Salome asked him outright what he thought could be happening to Phasael.

"If only I knew," he replied with a strained expression. "My spies usually keep me informed of what's going on, but this time it's different. I only hope my fears prove unfounded."

Two days later he finally received a communication from his brother. He was sitting at his desk toying with a stylus when his aide knocked on the door and informed him that one of the officers wanted to speak to him urgently. Herod immediately became alert, sensing that something important had happened; he put the stylus down and pulled himself erect. "Admit him," he ordered.

An astonished look crossed his face when the officer entered carrying an arrow with a piece of papyrus tied around the shaft. "This was shot into the palace grounds a few minutes ago," he said. "We have no idea who did it, but it seems there is a message tied to the arrow. Since it is presumably for you, I did not take the liberty of reading it."

Herod thanked the officer, and with quickening pulse untied the papyrus and unrolled it on the desk, flattening it with the palm of his hand. He immediately recognized Phasael's handwriting.

"Are there any instructions, sir?" asked the officer.

"No, thank you. You may go."

"Very well, sir," said the officer, starting to withdraw. But before he got to the door, he was summoned back. "One moment," Herod called. "You're right about it being a message for me. But I don't want the news spread around. I don't want to take any chances on the enemy learning about it. So tell those who know about the arrow to keep it to themselves. Is that clear?"

"Yes, sir," replied the officer, wondering how he could possibly enforce such an order.

After he left, Herod began to read his brother's communication. It was written in a cramped script, and in the dim light of the room he had trouble deciphering it. He got up and went over to the window, where it was easier to make out the words. The message was fairly long and it took Herod several minutes to get through it.

To my dear brother Herod, greeting.

I am sending this message through our good friend, Saramella, who managed to visit me secretly. I say secretly, because unfortunately it seems you were right in suspecting the Parthians' intentions. At first Barzaphranes received Hyrcanus and me with due honor, and treated us with the utmost courtesy and respect. But much to our surprise, he did not seem to be in any hurry to discuss the proposal raised by Pacorus. After several days he informed us that he was moving his headquarters to Ecdippa on the coast, and we of course accompanied him. When his headquarters was set up, we thought that now he would get down to business. But instead he disappeared for over a week after apologizing that urgent military matters called him away. We were naturally puzzled and not a little dismayed at this turn of events. What is more, it began to dawn on us that we were in effect being restricted to the headquarters area. Somehow Saramella found out about us – he hinted that he has a spy planted here (my guess is that he is a bribed Parthian officer or guard). Saramella confirmed our suspicion that we are under secret guard, but more than that his contact didn't know. Like you, Saramella doesn't trust the Parthians. He thinks that Barzaphranes is deliberately stalling, probably in the hope of getting you too in their hands, and that he has no intention of reaching an agreement with us. Saramella urges us to slip away and has promised to put a boat at our disposal. Hyrcanus and I have decided to wait another two or three days, and if there is no change in the situation, we will probably take his advice. I therefore hope, if everything goes well, to be reunited with you all in the near future. I can't tell you how happy this will make me. But in the meantime, do whatever you think is necessary in the circumstances I have described.

If there is any possibility of getting out of Jerusalem safely, I strongly urge you to do so. Above all, don't let the Parthians get you into their clutches. Do your best to keep our family's spirits up, and tell them that I am constantly thinking of you all. I look forward to the day when we will be together again.

Your brother Phasael

Herod and Family Flee to Masada with Alexandra

As the full import of Phasael's message hit him, a wave of desperation and physical weakness spread through Herod's body. "Phasael, O Phasael!" he muttered in an agonized tone, "why didn't you listen to me? I begged you not to go." With slow, heavy steps he made his way back to the desk and sank onto the chair. His brain was reeling. One thought kept hammering at him: His brother was a captive of the Parthians! True, he sounded optimistic about his chances of escaping, and Herod knew that Saramella would do everything in his power to help. But he did not share Phasael's optimism and feared the worse.

For several minutes Herod sat and brooded in this vein – an uncharacteristic mood for him. He who was always resourceful and sure of himself now felt helpless and at a loss. He stared abstractedly at the frieze on the opposite wall; the geometric shapes seemed to come alive and start dancing, holding him in a hypnotic spell. And then the incongruity of it all struck him. "What has come over me?" he muttered in a tone of self-reproach. "Am I a frightened puppy, a whimpering suckling, that I should be quaking like this? Has my blood turned to water? Perhaps I should also beat my breast and go in sackcloth and ashes. Will that help Phasael? Will that help us here?"

Herod's native courage and tenacity began to reassert themselves. He pulled himself erect and rose to his feet; he began to pace the room, pondering Phasael's plight. What could be done for him? Herod's brow furrowed deeply as he weighed one possibility after another, only to reject them as impractical or too risky. He concluded that there was only one course of action that held out some prospect of success – to escape the Parthian ring and seek Roman aid in saving his brother. Phasael himself had advised Herod to escape Jerusalem. But how? He had discussed this with his staff more than once, and always came to the doleful conclusion that their chances were virtually nil. And to attempt to get out with the womenfolk and young ones was folly. Their lives would be imperiled. How could he expose his family and even Mariamne and her family to this danger? The enemy would show no mercy to his family. They might spare the Hasmoneans; in fact, they most likely would. But either they all escape safely or no one escapes – on that he was adamant.

There was another matter to consider: Should he tell his family about Phasael's message? They would be relieved to know he was unharmed, but the other information would distress them. As for Alexandra, if she knew her father's situation she might wittingly or unwittingly reveal it. He sincerely hoped that news of the arrow had not reached her.

His rumination was interrupted by a knock on the door. Herod swore softly; with a sigh of resignation he bade the sentry enter.

"Yes?" he said impatiently as the sentry opened the door.

"The Princess Alexandra wishes to speak to you, sir."

"Alexandra?" Herod was both surprised and annoyed. What the devil did she want to see him for just now? It was as though she had divined his thoughts. He shrugged his shoulders and told the sentry to admit her. He quickly folded Phasael's message and thrust it under a waxed tablet.

When Alexandra entered the room, Herod noticed that there were deep lines under her eyes and her face was drawn. "I trust you are feeling well," he said politely, as she drew up a chair opposite him. "We haven't had the pleasure of your company the past two days."

"I have been keeping to my apartment," she replied in a quiet but firm tone. "I feel as well as one can in the circumstances."

"Which are quite trying, I admit," observed Herod, wondering what she wanted to see him for.

"It's the suspense that makes it so hard," she went on; "not knowing what is happening to my father, and your brother too, of course. I was certain that by now we would have heard from them. The fact that we haven't worries me. Do you think something might be amiss?"

The muscles of Herod's face tightened and his cheeks started to twitch. He picked up the stylus and began to tap it on the desk as he considered what to tell Alexandra. "I really can't say," he replied at last. "I'm every bit as worried as you are."

Alexandra shifted in her chair and leaned forward. "I understand that a message was shot into the palace grounds a few minutes ago. I would like to know if it contains any information about my father."

Herod could not suppress a start. He stared at Alexandra with a puzzled expression. How did she know about the arrow? Had she herself seen it fall, or did someone tell her about it? But what did it really matter? It was foolish to think that something like that could be kept secret. He reached over and picked up the papyrus. "It's from my brother," he said tonelessly, handing it to her.

Alexandra stared at the papyrus. She was impatient to know what it had to say about her father, but something in Herod's manner and words made her pause; she feared that it did not convey cheerful news. She too had difficulty reading the cramped writing in the dim light, but she remained seated. When she finished, a troubled look clouded her eyes. "So it has come to that!" she uttered in a barely audible voice. "I was afraid that might happen."

"You can't say I didn't warn them," said Herod with more than a trace of despair.

"No, I can't. But they believed there was no other course open to them. Or at least my father didn't think there was any other honorable course he could take."

Herod's eyebrows arched sharply. "What do you mean by honorable course?"

Alexandra did not reply immediately. She rose to her feet and with a slow step walked over to the window. "I had urged my father to escape before it was too late," she said with a note of desperation. "He said that as long as there was some chance of a successful outcome, no matter how slim, he would remain in the palace, for he was high priest and king, and it would be undignified and wrong of him to desert his people, to sneak away like a thief in the night."

Herod's expression changed to one of intense curiosity. "How could he have escaped the palace? We're surrounded by enemies."

"True," agreed Alexandra, turning to face Herod. "Yet there was a reasonably good chance that he could have gotten outside the city walls without being seen."

"How?" Herod demanded to know with burning impatience.

Before coming to Herod, Alexandra had debated whether to reveal to him the secret information she possessed. She would have preferred not to, but instinctively feeling that the mysterious message contained disquieting news about her father, she had to make a quick decision. She feared for the safety of her children – that was the overriding consideration. She had to get them to some haven where they would be out of danger from the Parthians and, as much as she hated to admit it, even her brother-in-law Antigonus. She was confident that she could get herself and her children away from the palace without being detected, but there were weighty factors to take into account. First of all, even if she did get away from the city undetected, presumably under cover of darkness, what then? She could not proceed on her own without some sort of transport or protection. Herod, with his resourcefulness could very likely pull it off; at least the odds would not be so great. It was this consideration that finally swayed her.

"You're probably not aware of it," she said, resuming her seat; "in fact, not many people are, but the Temple is not built entirely on solid rock. There are a number of subterranean passageways which enable one to get outside the city wall."

"I heard vague rumors to that effect from my father," Herod interrupted, his pulse beginning to beat more rapidly. "But how will that help us? We're not in the Temple; we're bottled up in the palace."

"True, but there is also an underground passageway connecting the palace with one beneath the Temple."

"Then there is a way out!" exclaimed Herod, his face lighting up.

"It will be necessary to avoid any commotion while going through the passageway," Alexandra cautioned. "And above all, not to attract any attention once we get outside the wall. The best time to do it would be a dark night, preferably around new moon."

"Yes, of course, you're quite right," Herod quickly concurred. His mind was already racing with plans. He would inform his troops only at the last moment in order to avoid any possible disclosure of this secret to the enemy. He could rely on the officers to hold their tongues, but not the others. He would take all his men with him, as they would be needed for future encounters with the foe. He would head toward Idumea and continue on to Masada, the rock stronghold overlooking the Dead Sea. Here he would leave his men and his family in the knowledge that they were safe. From there he would proceed to Alexandria and then, after procuring transportation, on to Rome, where he would get the help he desperately needed for himself and, above all, for his brother.

Cleopatra – Serpent of the Nile

Shafts of pale light filtered through the narrow windows of Cleopatra's bathing chamber, casting a soft glow over the tiled floor and pool. The sun had made its initial rapid ascent, but had not yet dispelled the chill inside the palace. Syrius, a lean jet-black Nubian eunuch, bent down on one knee and dipped his hand into the pool to test the water, a task he had been performing ever since he was brought to the royal Egyptian palace four years ago. He knew exactly what temperature the queen liked the water, and the gods help him if she should find it the least bit cool for her comfort. In the hot, humid summer he had little to fear in this respect, but with the approach of winter he had to be on his toes if he did not want to be subjected to a barrage of caustic aspersions on his birth and mental competence.

As he had expected, the water was not warm enough. He ordered the two brawny slaves standing behind him to add eight jugs of hot water. Watching them lug the large clay vessels from a nearby chamber and empty them into the pool, he was reminded that this task would soon be eliminated with the installation of Roman-type lead piping – an innovation he viewed with dismay as it would diminish his authority. When the last jug was emptied, he tested the water again and nodded his approval. A sharp clap of his hands was the signal for the three males to withdraw and for the queen to enter with her two attendants.

Cleopatra never started her day in the royal palace without first bathing. While pressing business might sometimes force her to forgo the ministrations of her masseuse, only a severe indisposition could make her pass up her bath. She chatted gaily with her two ladies-in-waiting as they helped her to disrobe and climb down the narrow steps until the water covered her body almost up to the armpits.

The warm water had a soothing effect on her. Afterward she would finish up in the cold-water pool, which would send the blood coursing through her veins and leave her invigorated and ready to face the day ahead. But she enjoyed most of all the immersion in the tepid scented water, which induced a pleasant, relaxed feeling.

She liked to vary the scent, and from time to time would have the court perfumer compound a new essence for her. This was a forgivable feminine indulgence, she assured herself, wondering if she should ask him to try his skill with the exotic flowering plants that had arrived from the Far East the week before. And it also benefited the royal treasury, as the scents she tired of would

241

subsequently be produced in large batches and marketed abroad at a handsome profit. How could one compare this with the ostentation of wealthy Roman matrons who, as rumor had it while she was living in Rome three years ago, bathed in asses' milk, no less? Such vulgar extravagance! Anything to flaunt their husbands' ill-gotten wealth.

But pshaw! What had gotten into her this morning? Why was she spoiling the pleasure of the bath by thinking about those parvenues? She turned over on her back and, bracing her feet against the side of the pool, gave herself a push that sent her floating across the fragrant water. As always, she got a sensual thrill out of this. Her outstretched body was as seductive as ever, she was happy to note except for her midriff which was, well, a little soft, she observed with a frown. *I must have the masseuse slim it a bit*, she decided. She had always taken great pains to keep her figure trim and lithe, and in particular to keep her waistline down. It had not proved too easy, although this did not seem to detract from her charms. Caesar, in fact, used to tease her for her obsessive concern, assuring her that in fact it even made her more alluring. Still, when he had insisted on having a golden statue of her made for the temple of Venus Genetrix, ancestress of Julius's family, she had agreed only on condition that it should not reveal the slightest suggestion of flabbiness.

She liked the statue. Archesilaus had flattered her somewhat, she conceded, but he had caught the grace of her carriage, the vivacious expression of her countenance, her sensitive mouth, firm chin, and large, liquid eyes; he had even made her nose a little less prominent than what her mirror revealed. Caesar had also been delighted with the statue and remarked, with a waggish grin, that he was not sure if he didn't prefer it to the Cleopatra in the flesh.

She did not delude herself. Her fascination for Caesar had not depended solely, or even predominantly, on her physical charms. There was no end of women as generously endowed in this respect. But which of them could match her skill in languages and learning? Who could converse in seven different languages and was at home in Greek history, literature, and philosophy? Caesar, who had not only been talented in the art of warfare and statecraft, but had been no mean writer in his own right, had fully appreciated these gifts of hers. This, together with the fact that she was queen of an ancient country with a flourishing economy and bulging treasury, had made her irresistible to the dictator of Rome. So much so that not long after his departure from Egypt, he had her and their son Caesarion brought to Rome and installed in a villa beyond the Tiber, where they could be together while ostensibly negotiating a treaty of alliance.

If she had ever loved a man – or could love one – it was Caesar. At first she had made a conscious effort to captivate him, because she was bent on regaining the dominions that had once belonged to the Macedonian dynasty that ruled Egypt ever since the death of Alexander the Great, and she realized that for this purpose she had to remain on good terms with Rome. If Egypt could no longer be independent of Rome, she saw no reason why she should not share equally in or even dominate their union. But if her original intention had been to use Caesar for her own purposes – just as he had undoubtedly intended to use her for his own purposes – she had found herself more and more drawn to him despite the big difference in age.

What a pity he was assassinated, she thought ruefully, stirring the water with her cupped hands. He was a man in every sense of the word: a consummate lover, a peerless general, a superb administrator. He had done great things for his people and was brimming with plans for further improving their lot and for raising Rome to ever greater heights. She had been privy to his hopes and aspirations, and as long as they did not clash with her own objectives, she would have given anything, even of the wealth of Egypt – well, perhaps some small part of it – to actively share in them. Together they could have done wonders.

Cleopatra realized that she was lingering longer than usual in her bath. The dioiketes would be impatient if she was late for their morning conference. "But let him be," she said aloud with a defiant toss of her head. She would be furious if her chief minister dared to show up late, but he could jolly well cool his heels awhile – the privilege of a queen.

"Will Your Majesty be much longer?" one of the attendants asked. "Shall I inform the hairdresser that you'll be late?"

"No. Tell Iris that I'll be with her shortly."

But she was feeling a little languid today, and was in no hurry to leave the bath. *Now, if Antony were here I wouldn't need the masseuse to keep my tummy in shape*, she thought with a roguish grin.

How different he is from Caesar, she mused. She had determined to captivate him for the same reason she had Caesar, and so she fell in with his moods, even though she often found his banter and pranks quite puerile.

She knew that he was being blamed for letting the Parthians invade Syria. In Rome they were taunting him for preferring to bed with the "serpent of the Nile" than to wage war against the Parthians. The "serpent of the Nile" – hah! So that's what those insolent, crass moneybags have the gall to call her! Well, let them beware of this serpent's fangs then! No doubt that prissy Octavian has a hand in this. What a triumvirate! Instead of sticking together, they spend more time sticking knives in each other's back. But this time it wasn't Antony's fault. When he learned that his wife Fulvia and his brother Lucius had plotted to overthrow Octavian's rule in Rome, he was furious, especially with that bitchy wife of his, who poked her nose too much in political affairs for her own good. Now Antony would probably have to abase himself before that sniveling juvenile in order to straighten out the mess. But the business shouldn't take too long, because the Parthians have to be dealt with, and the sooner the better. No, it probably won't be very long before Antony returns to nest once again with his serpent of the Nile.

Clad in a deep-purple robe, her hair piled high on her head and bound with a diadem, Cleopatra was ready to start another day of audiences with her officials, foreign ambassadors, and petitioners. She never wearied of the round of meetings and official functions; to her statecraft was a powerful elixir, and she served it with a passionate zeal. She even took a keen interest in minor details, especially those of a financial nature. Egypt was flourishing more than ever under her able rule, and she was determined that it should continue to do so and that as little of its wealth as possible was drained out by the Romans. If Egypt had to pay tribute, then she was going to derive the maximum compensation for it. She had her heart set on regaining the territories lost to the Seleucid kings, in particular Coele-Syria and Judea, and in moments of soaring aspiration she dreamed of even greater triumphs.

The dioiketes Theon was undoubtedly champing at the bit, but before beginning the daily conference with him, Cleopatra summoned Caesarion and his tutor Nicolaus. Nicolaus entered the queen's apartment sedately, while Caesarion burst in, his eyes gleaming with mischief.

"And how did my darling Caesarion sleep last night?" she asked her seven-year-old son, enfolding him in her arms.

"Like Acate, our goddess-cat," he replied, kissing his mother on the cheek. "If only I could jump as high as her, I'd be the happiest boy in the world. Do you think I can learn to jump that high?"

"If you jump like that you'll frighten all the birds away," replied Cleopatra in her melodious voice.

How much he resembles his father, she thought with a pang of nostalgia. The same thin face, keen dark eyes, and firm mouth with its whimsical expression. "May his life be a long, happy one and not end like Caesar's," she silently prayed to the goddess Isis.

She turned to Nicolaus. "Tell me briefly, how is Caesarion progressing in his studies?"

She was fortunate to have a tutor like Nicolaus, who possessed a gift for imparting knowledge to an energetic youngster in a way that made him, if not exactly eager, at least willing, to absorb it. Nicolaus had come to her court from Damascus upon Theon's recommendation. He was only in his mid-twenties, but already possessed a growing reputation as a scholar and a writer of tragedies and comedies. Tall, slender, slightly stoop-shouldered, and simply but neatly dressed, he was the epitome of the savant-cum-diplomat. The latter skill was no doubt inherited from his father, who filled various important civic posts and was entrusted with numerous diplomatic missions by the Seleucid ruler. Nicolaus, for his part, counted himself fortunate to be employed as tutor in the royal Egyptian court, for here he found an atmosphere of learning and culture that was extremely congenial and probably without compare, even in Athens. His patroness, the queen, was herself well-educated and often engaged him in philosophical and other learned discussions. She frequently invited him to banquets in the palace, where he had the opportunity of meeting the intellectual and literary luminaries of the day.

"Since Your Majesty is pressed for time," said Nicolaus deferentially in reply to the queen's query, "I shall sum up Caesarion's progress by quoting Isocrates: 'If you are fond of learning, you will soon be full of earning.' In this respect I am happy to state that Caesarion shows every indication of following in his mother's worthy footsteps."

"Your report is not only brief, but nobly phrased and highly encouraging," replied Cleopatra with a pleased expression. She then dismissed the two, after receiving another kiss from Caesarion.

As she approached the audience chamber, the two sentries stiffened to attention and opened the large gold-plaited door to admit her as well as Theon and a secretary, who had been waiting in the anteroom. Like the rest of the palace, the audience chamber had undergone changes during its long existence, but its marble floor and columns, its wall paintings and bas-reliefs, and its statues made as dazzling an impression as ever. It overlooked the harbor with its forest of masts, itself an impressive sight.

"I hope I haven't kept you waiting," said Cleopatra to Theon with only a trace of a smile as she mounted the throne. "I do dislike unpunctuality. It's a sign of sloth, and sloth will not keep Egypt strong and flourishing."

"Your Majesty is absolutely right," concurred Theon dryly with a polite bow. He was conscious of an exquisite scent. *Another new perfume*, he thought to himself. He was about to express his approbation, but decided that this might be taken amiss, even though the queen seemed to be in good spirits this morning.

Theon, who as dioiketes, not only managed the country's economy but headed the government, had loyally served the queen ever since she ascended the throne seven years ago. In his younger days he had been an outstanding athlete, and he still possessed a strong, well-proportioned physique. He was not handsome: His nose was misshapen due to a blow received in a boxing match, his mouth was a little too wide and the corners turned down, his lips were too thin, and a long jagged scar marred his right cheek. His hair, or what was left of it, was once a dark brown, but now mostly gray. His blue eyes, which looked out from under tufty brows, were shrewd and intelligent, and despite his rough-chiseled features, he exuded an air of quiet dignity and authority. He was a keen-sighted man of affairs and an accomplished finance minister, who had succeeded in appreciably increasing the annual income from the various sources of revenue, especially the salt, banking, and other royal monopolies. He had the satisfaction of knowing that the queen was highly pleased with his performance, even though she sometimes seemed to take a perverse delight in making him squirm, something he found disconcerting but generally managed to take in his stride.

"Well, now, Theon," said Cleopatra after seating herself on the throne, "what business awaits me today?"

"First of all, I have a short financial report to submit," replied Theon, producing a rolled papyrus from the folds of his himation. "And then..."

"I trust the report will sustain my good mood," Cleopatra interrupted in an affected drawl, whose implication was not lost on Theon.

"I am pleased to state that, all told, Your Majesty has cause to be satisfied," Theon blandly assured her.

"And if you leave out the 'all told,' will I still be satisfied?" asked Cleopatra, eyeing her minister closely. "I would like to know what exactly is the state of our revenues, in particular that from the oil trade. Please enlighten me."

Theon's brow furrowed deeply. The queen had been displeased to learn from his last report that this source of revenue had been falling off of late. He had intended to gloss over this item, but knowing her retentive memory for details of this sort, he had not been very sanguine.

"As I pointed out previously," he said in a matter-of- fact tone, "for some reason that is still not entirely clear, our income from the oil monopoly has – ah, decreased a little the last couple of months. But you can rest assured..."

"Theon!" Cleopatra cut him short, "when revenues fall off the reason is invariably clear. Are our Egyptian palms yielding less oil of late, or are we greasing more Roman palms?"

Theon was nettled by this question but did not let it show. The queen knew very well that the bulk of Egypt's oil was produced from saffron and castor and not from palms. Even allowing for her penchant for turning a clever phrase, this one was a little too barbed for his liking. "Since you have touched on this particular subject," he said, keeping his voice level, "I need not remind you that it is in Egypt's interests to maintain good relations with the Romans. And, of course, that means..."

"I know perfectly well what that means," remarked Cleopatra with an impatient gesture. "But I can't help wondering if some of our officials are not being a little too enthusiastic in promoting these good relations. I have a sneaking suspicion that our oil revenue pipeline has sprung a serious leak. I trust you will give the matter your urgent attention."

"Your Majesty's wish is my command," replied Theon, relieved to be finished with this particular subject.

"Good! Now let me hear the rest of your report, and then we'll get on with the audiences. How many are scheduled for today?"

"Six. Three with foreign envoys, and then there is Herod, and..."

"Herod?" Cleopatra's eyebrows arched sharply. "Herod of Judea?"

"That's right."

Cleopatra's eyes narrowed, and there was a sudden change of expression on her face. Her voice took on a cold, almost harsh, tone. "What, may I ask, prompts Herod to seek an audience with the queen of Egypt? You know very well that I have little fondness for persons of his ilk. If he is not yet aware of that fact, it's time we make it clear to him."

"Permit me to remind Your Majesty," Theon went on calmly, "that Herod's father was on excellent terms with the great Caesar, and Herod himself enjoys the confidence of the noble Antony, who has found him an efficient and loyal administrator."

"And also humorless and extremely ambitious, if my memory of Antony's description doesn't betray me."

"These traits are not unique to Herod, nor are they necessarily negative in themselves."

"Humorless men are terribly dull – and dangerous. And as for ambition, it may be commendable in one who lives far enough away to be relatively harmless to Egypt's interests, but it is not so commendable in one who is our next-door neighbor and thirsts for power in a land that was once part of the Ptolemaic dominions."

"Herod's fortunes are not at very high tide at the moment. I don't think that in the present circumstances you need be troubled by his ambition."

"One must always beware of a man who is both ambitious and humorless, my dear dioiketes. The dullness of his humor makes his ambition all the keener. If his fortunes are at low ebb now, he will abide his time until the tide turns. Don't underestimate such a man, my good Theon; it is most inadvisable."

Herod Heartbroken at His Brother Phasael's Death

Herod could not help wondering if his guardian spirit had deserted him. He was seized with doubt – a black, silent, bitter doubt. He had suffered setbacks before, but there had always been some influential patron to help him get back on his feet and to turn the tables on his adversary. But now misfortune beset him on every side: One tribulation followed another, and he felt like a stricken vessel floundering in a turbulent sea. True, he had escaped the Parthian net, but literally like a rat scurrying through an underground hole. He had been filled with mixed emotions as Alexandra led them through the secret passageway under the Temple precincts. He was relieved that his family would be out of immediate danger, but it galled him that he and his hardened soldiers had to flee in such an ignominious way, and to be beholden, of all things, to a woman for their safety, even if she was the mother of his betrothed. Never again, he vowed, would he let himself be trapped in a situation like this.

Once outside the walls of Jerusalem, he made his way to Masada, where he left his family and about a thousand of his picked troops while he set about salvaging what he could. All the while the fate of his brother weighed heavily on him, and he pondered how to secure his release. His original intention had been to seek Roman military aid, but upon calmer reflection he realized that this was out of the question. After Saxa's defeat at Apamea, Rome was in no position or mind to confront the Parthians, least of all for the sake of one man. In these circumstances there seemed to be only one way to rescue his brother – to ransom him. For this he needed money, and lots of it. In the early days of the fighting he had managed to remove most of his valuables from Jerusalem to Idumea, but the amount over and above his immediate needs would not suffice to tempt the Parthians. He therefore decided to go to Petra and collect the loan his father had given the Nabataean king Malichus. After learning why the money was needed, surely Malichus would not fail to repay the long-outstanding debt, especially as he had received many other benefactions from Antipater, and Cypros herself was from a noble Nabataean family. But much to Herod's dismay, Malichus did not even grant him the courtesy of receiving him. Instead, he sent a messenger to inform him, in flowery language, that he had been warned by the Parthians not to receive him.

Herod did not believe a single word of the Nabataean ruler. It was obvious that he saw in Herod's plight a convenient opportunity to renege on his debt. Herod was livid with rage, and he berated the messenger savagely. He swore that one day he would make Malichus rue his disgraceful behavior. But what was he to do now? Where could he lay his hands on enough money to ransom his brother? There was only one possible recourse left: to follow his original intention and seek help from his friends in Rome, especially Antony. He therefore decided to proceed to Alexandria and take passage to Italy. But first he returned to Masada to bid farewell to his family and his betrothed and take what he needed for the journey. In Idumea he picked up an escort to accompany him to the Egyptian border, and then he set out along the trade route traversing the Sinai desert in the direction of the coast. Early on the third day he reached the frontier post of Rhinocolura.

The morning air was pleasantly cool, and Herod's spirits rose a little. When he and his escort were halted by two border guards, he answered their routine questions in an easygoing tone. Upon learning his identity, the guards exchanged a quick glance. "Herod son of Antipater?" one of them asked.

"Yes," replied Herod, wondering how they knew his name.

"Please wait a minute. Our officer would like to speak to you."

Herod could not understand what interest the guards or their officer might have in him. He was impatient to be on his way and begrudged even the slightest delay. The guard that had addressed him disappeared into a small stone building a short distance away, but reemerged shortly with a young Greek officer and a stocky, black-bearded middle-aged civilian of uncertain origin. They approached Herod, and the officer saluted him. The deference shown him by the officer and the serious aspect of the civilian made Herod even more puzzled and uneasy.

"You are no doubt surprised that we have been expecting you," said the officer, speaking Greek with a broad Macedonian accent.

"I confess that I am," replied Herod a little testily. "I'm in a great hurry to reach Alexandria and your queen. But I don't understand how anyone in Egypt knows that. I have informed no one apart from my family and escort."

"You can be assured that no one has been spying on you, if that's what you suspect," responded the officer. "The fact is, we weren't certain you would show up here. But you have a friend – a rich and powerful one it seems – who thought there was a good chance you might appear. He dispatched one of his men with a message for you. I understand that it's a very important message – so important that the courier was instructed to wait here several days if necessary until you arrived."

Herod was struck by the urgency of this information and especially the incongruity of a civilian being allowed to tarry at a frontier post. "And if I had not come, what then?"

The officer nodded to the courier to answer. The latter, who had heavy jowls and a grave expression, spoke in a halting provincial Greek with an accent Herod did not recognize. "My master instructed me to first go to Jerusalem and deliver his message to you. If I didn't find you there…"

"How were you going to deliver a message to me in Jerusalem?" asked Herod somewhat brusquely, his eyes narrowing with suspicion. "We were under siege until the very end."

"I know," replied the courier calmly. He gave Herod a meaningful look. "Did you not receive a message before – a very important message?"

Herod stared at the courier with an odd expression. "Your master – who is he?"

"The worthy Saramalla, sir."

Herod was astonished at this revelation. Now he knew who had arranged for Phasael's message describing his treatment by the Parthians to be shot into the palace grounds. And he also understood why the officer had been so deferential to him and why he had permitted the courier to stay at the frontier post. Saramalla was not niggardly when he needed someone's assistance.

Herod was torn between two conflicting emotions. He wanted to know without one second's delay what news the courier had brought about his brother, but at the same time he had a premonition that it would not be happy news, and he dreaded to read the message. After some hesitation and trying to still his growing agitation, he asked the courier, this time in a gentler voice: "And if you did not find me in Jerusalem, why did you come to this particular place? What made you think you'd find me here?"

"I wasn't sure I'd find you here. My instructions were to try and learn your whereabouts in order to give this message to you personally. Failing that, I was to come to this border post and wait, for my master reasoned that sooner or later you were bound to escape Judea and make your way to Rome. The only way you could do that in your circumstances was to board a ship at Alexandria. And now," the courier went on, extracting a rolled papyrus from the folds of his robe, "permit me to discharge my master's orders and give this to you."

As Herod took the sealed message his heart started to beat fiercely against his ribs. With a troubled eye he glanced at the officer and then at the courier. "If there are any additional details you may wish to know," the courier said, "my master has told me what to inform you."

Herod broke the seal and began to read, at first rapidly and then more slowly. Both the courier and the officer studied him closely. They saw a pallor spread across his face. His lips quivered and his fingers began to tremble, so that he could hardly follow the writing. With great effort he forced himself to read on, his eyes filling with tears. When he finished, he stared blankly ahead of him, the papyrus hanging limply in his hand; he began to weep unabashedly.

""Phasael, O Phasael!" he cried, "why didn't you listen to me when I warned you not to go to the Parthians?"

The two men watched silently as Herod gave vent to his grief. The officer turned to the courier and asked in a low voice: "His brother is – dead?"

The courier nodded.

"Killed by the Parthians?"

"It's not certain. My master received conflicting reports. According to one, Herod's brother beat his head against a rock until he expired. But my master is inclined to believe the other report, that he was killed trying to escape his captors. That would be more like the son of Antipater, with whom my master had the honor of forming a warm friendship a good many years ago."

The courier waited patiently until Herod began to regain his composure. "My master wants you to know how grieved he is at the death of your noble brother," he said in grave tone. "He knows what a great loss you have suffered. But he says you should remember that the blackness of the night is followed by the dawn of a new day. He is certain that a bright day awaits you. He prays to the gods that it may be so."

Herod felt drained and bleak. One blow had followed another, but this was the most grievous of all. The others could be overcome somehow, but nothing could bring his brother back to life – his brother with whom he had shared his hopes and aspirations, with whom he had worked side by side in administering the Judean state, whose wisdom and prudence had often restrained his own inherent impetuosity, thereby saving him from serious missteps. Would there be an end to the darkness? Would it be followed by a bright day? Herod had no confidence that it would. Yet it was comforting to know that Saramalla had faith in him.

"Tell your master," he said in a low, trembling voice, "that I am profoundly grateful for his sympathy and kind words of consolation. I will never forget how he tried to help my dear brother in his hour of travail, nor will I forget the effort he went to in order to let me know his bitter fate. May the gods bless your master."

"I shall convey your thanks to my master. But before I take leave of you, I'd like you to explain something that has puzzled him."

"By all means. What is it?"

"As you have read in the message, the Parthians spared Hyrcanus's life, yet they did something odd before exiling him to Babylonia: They mutilated his ears. Do you know why they did that?"

"That was to disqualify him for the high priesthood. According to the divine law of the Jews, the high priest must be free of any physical blemish. By mutilating his ears the Parthians – or whoever it was – have made sure that Hyrcanus will never again serve in the Temple. Your master did not mention it, but by now Antigonus is undoubtedly serving as high priest, which office is even more exalted in the eyes of the Jews than the royal crown."

"I can't imagine a high priest being more exalted than a king," remarked the courier; "but I don't pretend to understand the Jews or their ways. And now that I have executed my master's orders, I bid you farewell. May the gods be with you and prosper all your endeavors."

Herod Meets Cleopatra in Alexandria

It was more than seven years since Herod had last visited Alexandria. He and Phasael had accompanied their father as Caesar's guests after Antipater helped the Roman to quell the armed opposition in Egypt. The impression made on him by what was unquestionably the most beautiful city in the world was still vivid in his mind. He had been amazed at its size – a metropolis more than three miles long lying between the sea and the sweetwater Lake Mareotis, and inhabited by over a million people, many of whom lived in tall, spacious houses. It boasted luxuriant parks and gardens and abounded with magnificent avenues, which in daytime resounded with an unceasing stream of vehicles conveying goods or passengers, including tourists from all ends of the world who had been attracted by glowing accounts of the city's famous sites: stately palaces and mansions; the Mausoleum, where the bones of Alexander the Great rested in a glass sarcophagus; the Museum, where literary men and scholars lived and studied, gave lectures, or wrote their books; the library, which contained nearly half a million volumes; the theater, stadium, and hippodrome; Greek and Egyptian temples with their distinctive styles; the twelve-mile long canal connecting Alexandria with the pleasure-city of Canopus, along which yachts glided day and night past the villas and gardens of wealthy citizens; and many other attractions.

Herod had never forgotten that visit, and more than once he had longed to see Alexandria again – but not in the circumstances in which he was about to see it now. During the crossing from Pelusium in a small cargo boat he was grim and withdrawn, hardly exchanging a word with the captain once they had agreed on the fare, or even with his own aide. Phasael's death had plunged him into a black despondency; he was shattered and numb inside. He could think of nothing but his brother. He relived their lives together, recollecting the major experiences they had shared since childhood, the offices and honors they had won, and, with a stab of pain, the siege they had endured together. Had he been responsible for the situation that culminated in Phasael's death? He honestly did not know, but he could not shake off a feeling of guilt. He feared it would plague him the rest of his life.

It was only when the island of Pharos with its towering white lighthouse hovered into view that Herod's spirits lifted a little, and he began to take an interest in the scene unfolding before him. He watched with ungrudging admiration as the captain skillfully guided his freighter through the narrow entrance to the Great Harbor, avoiding both the reefs against which the waves beat with unrelenting violence and the incoming and outgoing traffic. Peering about him, Herod saw that the port was throbbing with activity. This did not surprise him, for Alexandria was the greatest trading center in the world, the place where East and West met in the busy emporium. There were vessels of all sizes and shapes, ranging from small fishing smacks to long, sleek galleys; some were riding at anchor in the roadstead, others were easing their way to or from their berthing place, while still others were discharging or taking on cargo. The docks swarmed with dark-skinned stevedores who grunted and shouted and swore as they hauled aboard ship Egyptian corn, linen, glassware, paper, oils and scents, and various other local manufactures, and offloaded such wares as Chinese silks, Arabian spices and aromatics, timber from Macedonia and Crete, copper from Cyprus, purple dye from Tyre, wine and marble from Greece, honey from Rhodes, and sponges from the Black Sea.

In the confusion and rush of events that had overtaken him since escaping Jerusalem, Herod had not given any thought as to where he would stay in Alexandria. But this was a minor detail, for he had a number of friends in the city who, he was sure, would accommodate him. In this he was not disappointed, and within an hour after debarking with his aide and a slave, he was comfortably ensconced in an attractive Greek villa in the Tycheum Quarter, a relatively short distance from the Museum.

On the following morning Herod dispatched his aide to the royal palace with a written request for an audience with the queen, and was pleased to learn that it was set for two days hence. This would give him time to take stock of his situation and regain his bearings. At Rhinocolura he had been dealt a crushing blow, but now his native courage and tenacity had begun to reassert themselves; the pain in his heart had eased somewhat, the black clouds had dispersed a bit, and he could better see the road he had to take. Nothing could fill the empty spot left by Phasael's death, but the memory of his brother would spur him on until he reached his divinely destined goal. The road to this goal led through Rome; now more than ever his destiny was bound up with the mistress of the world. Rome could not suffer Parthia to retain control of Judea, a wedge in its Eastern empire; it could not suffer Antigonus on the throne of Judea. Rome needed a friend, a dependable ally, on the throne, and who was a more loyal friend and reliable ally than Herod son of Antipater?

He knew that when the throne of a client state fell vacant, it was Rome's policy to choose, wherever feasible, the new ruler from the old line, in the belief that this was the best way to ensure domestic tranquility and obedience to Rome. But in the case of Judea what male issue was left to the Hasmonean house? Hyrcanus was in exile and Antigonus had thrown in his lot with Rome's sworn enemy; as for Aristobulus, it was hardly conceivable that Rome would place on the throne a youngster whose competence was unknown and allegiance uncertain. No, Rome would have to look elsewhere for a suitable candidate for the Judean throne. And who was more suitable than Herod, especially as he was now affianced to Hyrcanus's granddaughter?

In a sense he and Rome were in the same boat: They had both suffered a temporary setback, but they had the same compelling objective, and together they would achieve it. His destiny and Rome's aims in this part of the world were inextricably intertwined. The prospect fired his imagination. Antigonus was now sitting on the Judean throne, but his days were numbered, like a candle burning down to nothing. The certainty of Antigonus's impending fate filled Herod with intense malicious pleasure. "Enjoy your taste of rule, my friend, for it will be brief. And as sweet as you find it now, so its end will be bitter. I have a score to settle with you; the blood of my brother is crying for revenge, and you will pay dearly for your foul deed."

Herod spent the next day relaxing and enjoying the sights of Alexandria with his host. His host, who had been invited to a banquet that evening, asked Herod if he would like to go along even though he was in mourning. He understood perfectly when Herod politely refused. Truth to tell, Herod had another reason for turning down the invitation, which in normal circumstances he would have gladly accepted. His audience with the queen was scheduled for an early hour, and it was important that he get a good night's sleep.

He had heard a great deal about Cleopatra and knew her to be a shrewd ruler who combined a talent for administration with a feminine charm that had captivated two of the greatest Romans of the day. Her journey to Antony in Tarsus to answer charges of having aided Cassius was the talk of the whole Eastern world. While Antony sat on a throne in the forum waiting for her to appear and explain her actions, she sailed up the river Cydnus in a barge with purple sails, gilded stern, and silver oars that beat time to the music of flutes and fifes and harps; her maids, dressed as sea nymphs, were the crew, and she herself, dressed as Venus, reclined under a canopy of gold cloth.

Whether this story was true in all its details was a moot point, but there was no doubt in Herod's mind that Antony's folly in letting himself be ensnared by this cunning siren was the main cause of his present sorry plight, of the humiliating need to beg her for such a trivial favor as accommodation aboard one of her ships. He also had reason to believe that Cleopatra was determined to recover the territory that had been lost to the Seleucids, which included Judea, and in this she was pinning her hopes on Antony, as previously she had on Caesar. He would have to tread carefully with her, seeking her help in procuring passage to Rome without her exacting too high a price or in any way jeopardizing his relations with Antony.

After a good night's sleep he felt refreshed and confident. He took considerable pains with his dress, donning a new tunic and an elegant fine-woven crimson robe. He oiled and combed his thick black hair and beard, which had been trimmed the day before, and dabbed a few drops of musk on his forehead and arms. Examining himself in the mirror, he was pleased with the effect. Since it was essential that his head be as clear as possible, he contented himself with a light breakfast consisting of a slice of bread, some pickled herring, and a few olives, washed down with a glass of barley beer. His host put a handsome carriage at Herod's disposal and wished him luck.

The weather was ideal – a clear sky and a bracing sea breeze. Within a few minutes the carriage was rolling down the Canopic Way, a hundred-foot wide avenue flanked by a marble colonnade on either side and extending the entire length of the city. They encountered a steady two-way stream of vehicles and pedestrians. A similar picture presented itself when Herod's driver turned left onto Boulevard Argeos, an equally wide avenue which was also colonnaded on both sides and ran from the Sun Gate, close to the canal at the southern end of the city, to the Moon Gate, near the Royal Harbor and palace.

The ride along Alexandria's two main thoroughfares took Herod past Greek-style temples, imposing public buildings, and verdant gardens. Since he had already seen these sights the day before, he tried to concentrate on his audience with the queen, but was unable to keep his eye from drinking in their beauty once again. He could not help marveling at the skill and ingenuity of the architects, master builders, and sculptors, who could fashion out of stone such magnificent structures and statues that filled one with wonder and demonstrated what heights of perfection could be attained by mortal man blessed with a divine sense of beauty. He had also seen the royal palace, which was set in spacious grounds on a promontory at the mouth of the Great Harbor, but from a distance. Now, as he was ushered through the official residence of the Ptolemaic rulers, he was awed by its grandeur, which surpassed anything he had ever beheld before. A little too ornate though, he thought – almost effeminate and even decadent, like the Egyptian monarchy itself. Nevertheless, he could not help feeling envious. One day, he vowed, he too would possess a palace that would arouse universal admiration.

In the anteroom to the audience chamber, Herod was greeted by the diokites Theon, who escorted him to the queen, seated on a golden throne adorned with elaborately carved ivory figures. She regarded him with a curious expression as he approached and bowed deeply. "Your Majesty is most kind to grant your humble servant an audience," said Herod in a slightly stiff Greek.

"I could do no less to one whose father had rendered the great Caesar invaluable military aid and of whom Antony has spoken so highly," replied Cleopatra in a fluent Hebrew with only a slight accent.

Herod was taken aback by her use of Hebrew. Was she showing off her skill in languages, or was she trying to take him down a notch? Despite his annoyance, he decided to stick to Hebrew. After having heard so many tales about this seductive siren, he was surprised to see that she was not the raving beauty he had imagined. True, she had a shapely figure, but her features were not remarkable. He knew many women who were just as good-looking. He wondered what she possessed that had so fascinated Caesar and Antony.

Herod presented the queen with a gift he had managed to get out of Jerusalem in the early days of the siege – an exquisitely wrought gold necklace with a Nabataean motif, from which hung a golden pendant inlaid with precious stones. It had cost a pretty obol to have his most skilled jeweler make it, but if it helped him to win something from this royal vamp, he would not begrudge the outlay.

"Your Majesty undoubtedly possesses many necklaces that are more beautiful and costly than this one," he said, bowing slightly, "but I assure you that none was given with greater esteem. I would deem it a great honor if occasionally it adorned what is without question the most beautiful neck in the world."

As Cleopatra accepted the gift, she studied its giver more closely. This was no uncouth foul-breath desert chieftain who stood before her, but a man of sturdy bearing, virile features, and a suave manner, who, even if he was lacking in humor, could probably rival her in the art of flattery. This was a man who bore close watching.

"Your words delight me no less than your gift," she acknowledged with a smile. "As the wise Xenophon has so aptly noted, 'No sound is sweeter than the sound of praise.' To which I may add, especially when it is sincerely uttered." She turned to Theon. "What do you say, my good diokites? Does not such an eloquent expression of esteem please the ear as well as the eye?"

"I heartily agree, Your Majesty," he replied dutifully. "The gift does honor to both its recipient and its giver."

Cleopatra was so delighted with the necklace that she could not wait to try it on. She replaced the one she was wearing with the new one. "What do you say now?" she said to Theon after allowing the two men enough time to judge its effect.

"It is very original and – er, eye-catching," he replied primly, thinking that only a woman like Cleopatra could flout what he considered proper royal decorum, but then he was used to her ways.

"As you can see," she remarked to Herod with a twinkle in her eyes, "my chief minister is as stinting in his praise as he is generous with the royal purse."

Theon, who was still smarting from the queen's insinuations about the declining oil revenue, made a wry face. "There are many needs to provide for," he said stiffly, "including some of a special nature."

"Ah, yes," agreed Cleopatra, who could not resist the temptation to chaff her minister. "It does take a lot of money to keep my subjects contented. And then, Alexandria is also a drain on the treasury. You know," she went on, turning to Herod, "we Ptolemies pride ourselves on having made Alexandria the most beautiful city in the world. And like a beautiful woman, she must be constantly groomed if she is to remain that way."

"Women who are very beautiful attract many hungry eyes," commented Theon dryly, seeing that the queen had ignored or deliberately misconstrued his last remark.

"You are being very subtle, my dear Theon," retorted Cleopatra with a toss of her head. "One would hardly know that you are referring to Rome. Yes, Rome is also a drain on our treasury, but considering that her founders were suckled by a she-wolf, is it any wonder that her rulers and high officials are so wolfish?"

She flashed Herod a coy smile. "I dare say, you too have undoubtedly had first-hand experience with their voracious appetite. But Judea being more bone than flesh, you have probably been spared more than we."

"I am in no position to make a comparison, Your Majesty," replied Herod, puzzled by the seemingly aimless exchange between the queen and her chief minister. "Crassus stripped the Temple in Jerusalem of its gold, which was quite a fortune. And Cassius laid a heavy tribute on the land."

"In whose successful collection I understand he was more than a little indebted to you," remarked Cleopatra with a sly grin.

Herod's face flushed. "I assure you that it was purely from lack of choice. We could not defy the governor of Syria, even if we knew or suspected that the tribute was intended to help finance the struggle against Octavian and Antony, who has always been a true friend of Judea. We knew what happened to Rhodes when the citizens refused to pay the tribute Cassius had laid on them. There was good reason to fear that he would order his legions to batter Jerusalem too and rob it of its wealth. How would Judea have then been able to aid Antony? Besides, we knew that the gods would help those whose cause was the more just."

Cleopatra gave Herod a shrewd, calculating look. How cleverly he wriggled out of that, she thought. "How fortunate for Judea that the gods were so perceptive with regard to Cassius," she said with an arch smile. "It's a pity they have been less perceptive with regard to Parthia."

"From long experience I have found that the gods are disposed to help those who help themselves," interjected Theon in a voice laced with a hint of censure.

Cleopatra glared at her minister. This was a sore point between them, for he had frequently warned her that Antony's prolonged stay in Alexandria would have undesirable repercussions for himself and Rome, as well as for Egypt. "The gods sometimes work in devious ways, whose consequences are not always immediately apparent," she rejoined with a petulant gesture.

"I'm sure Herod will agree with you," said Theon, realizing that they had not yet given him an opportunity to explain why he desired an audience with the queen. "He is without question the one who has suffered most from the change in fortunes in our part of the world."

Herod had followed with great interest the spirited exchange, with all its subtle innuendoes, between the queen and her minister. He had had audiences with many high officials, but never had one proceeded in such an unconventional manner. He did not know whether to put it down to the fact that this audience was with a female sovereign, but whatever the reason, it was clear that he was dealing with a very shrewd woman, and he would have to be on his guard not to fall victim to her wiles.

"Your Excellency is unfortunately correct in your assessment," remarked Herod to Theon with a grave expression and tempted to add that he could largely

257

thank Cleopatra for his vicissitudes. "I have been forced to flee my country, at whose helm noble Antony saw fit to appoint me and my late brother alongside the most worthy Hyrcanus." At these words, uttered with a catch in Herod's voice, a look of shocked surprise crossed Cleopatra's and Theon's faces. "But I know that this is only a passing episode," Herod went on after regaining his composure, "and before long Rome will push the Parthians back to their own borders."

"I'm very sorry to hear that your dear brother is no longer in this world," commiserated Cleopatra. "You have indeed suffered most grievously. May you find consolation in the knowledge that, as has been so sublimely observed, 'the gods take those whom they love most.' As for the Parthians, I share your conviction that their presence here will be short-lived. We don't want them on our doorstep any more than you want them in Judea."

Cleopatra scrutinized Herod reflectively. What was it he wanted from her? Asylum in Egypt? Perhaps, but if she read his character correctly, he had something else on his mind. "Until the happy day of the Parthians' departure," she went on, leaning forward, "we would be honored if you made Egypt your home. I'm sure you have not been unimpressed with Alexandria and the many delights it has to offer. We would be pleased to put a villa at your disposal."

"Your Majesty is most kind," said Herod with a deferential nod. "Your gracious offer has lifted some of the weight from my heart. Alexandria is indeed a most wonderful city, and when one has beholden its beauty, it is extremely hard not to accept such a tempting offer. But it is my earnest desire to reach Rome as quickly as possible. I would therefore be most grateful if you permitted me to make the voyage in one of your fast galleys."

Cleopatra's eyes narrowed and she compressed her lips. She had suspected that it was Herod's intention to proceed to Rome, and she did not like the idea at all. She too was certain that it was only a question of time until Rome regained control of the provinces lost to Parthia. In view of Antony's high regard for Herod, he would clearly be a strong contender for the throne of Judea or whatever other high office might be created. But whether he bore the title of king or some other designation, he would be an obstacle to her own designs on Judea. It was essential to deter him from proceeding to Rome.

"When a beehive has been stirred up, do you think it advisable to thrust your hand in?" she asked with an enigmatic smile.

Herod stared at the queen with a quizzical expression. "I'm afraid I don't know what you're referring to."

"No, you probably don't. For while you were under siege, you had no way of knowing what was happening in Rome. In brief, relations between Octavian and Antony have again taken a turn for the worse; in fact, they are at daggers drawn, and an armed clash seems imminent. It would not be advisable to go to Rome now."

Cleopatra paused to let the import of this disclosure sink in. "This news is highly distressing, I admit – for both of us. But we don't have to sit idly by in the meantime. For whatever the outcome of the triumvirs' quarrel, Parthia will remain the foremost problem for all of us – for Rome, for you, and for Egypt too. The sooner we act, the better. We must begin preparations now for the eviction of the Parthians. It is my firm intention to do so. And here is where you can play an important role, and most effectively help the Romans."

Herod listened with amazement to Cleopatra's fervent declaration. How in the name of all the gods did she intend to drive the Parthians back? Was this another of her cunning wiles? He was intrigued in spite of himself. "And what is that role, if I may ask?"

Cleopatra turned to her minister. "Theon, please explain the plan Antony broached before he left Egypt."

Theon was surprised at this request. He wondered why she stressed the trouble between Octavian and Antony, and it was only when she continued to dwell on it that he realized she probably wanted to keep Herod from going to Rome. He still did not know how she expected to accomplish this, but in obedience to her command he described the conference that had taken place in the palace shortly after the Parthian invasion, in which were discussed its repercussions and ways of driving the enemy back. One possibility Antony had thought held reasonably good prospects of success was a two-pronged attack, with the Romans advancing from the north and Egyptian forces from the south.

"And here is where you can render a very valuable service to our common cause," declared Cleopatra with an emphatic gesture. "Either as a commander of our forces, or if you prefer, in an organizational capacity."

Herod stared at the queen incredulously. At first blush Antony's plan seemed to possess some merit, although he was unable to judge it on such short notice. But he, a Judean – or an Idumean, as some insisted – in command of Egyptian troops! It didn't make sense; in fact, it was preposterous. "I am highly honored by your offer," he said, wondering what Cleopatra's real intentions were, "but surely Egypt doesn't lack for competent officers of her own."

"Egypt has grown soft, like a pampered woman," replied Cleopatra. "Our soldiers are brave enough, but without efficient organization and leadership they are like a flock of sheep; they don't stand a ghost of a chance against the Parthians. Antony has told me about your organizational talent, and that is something we badly need."

"I am flattered by your praise," said Herod, searching for a way to politely turn down the queen's proposal. "But since Judea has enjoyed close ties with Rome and I personally owe my office as tetrarch to Antony, I feel obligated to go to Rome as quickly as possible and put my services at his disposal. I'm sure that if you were in Antony's shoes you would expect no less of me. I would therefore be greatly indebted to Your Majesty for accommodation on one of your swift galleys."

Seeing that her offer had proved fruitless, Cleopatra decided on a different tack. "From your request, one would know that you are from Judea, which has no major port or international shipping to speak of," she said in a deceptively mild voice that did not betray her annoyance at his rejection. "Winter has already set in and the sea is extremely treacherous. Except for an odd ship now and then and in the most compelling circumstances, you won't find any navigation on the Mediterranean until spring. Many a captain, rash enough to attempt the crossing at this time of the year, has gone down with his ship. Our war galleys remain in port, or if they do venture out, they hug the coast and that only for a short distance. So I'm afraid there is no possibility of providing you accommodation aboard a galley. And if by chance there should be a cargo ship risking the crossing, for your own sake I'd advise you to wait until winter has passed and the seas are more favorable."

For all his distrust of Cleopatra's motives, Herod knew she was speaking the truth. He had heard tales of ships floundering in stormy waters and did not have to be reminded that the Mediterranean was dangerous in winter. To attempt a crossing now was indeed a risky matter. But to tarry would be fatal to his plans. The quarrel between Antony and Octavian was distressing, but they had quarreled before and managed to patch up their differences. By the time he arrives in Rome, he hoped they will have composed their dispute. But even if they fail to do so, this would not deter him; he must let nothing stand in his way – absolutely nothing! Looking up, he saw the queen was patiently awaiting his answer.

"I appreciate your solicitude for my safety," he said with a polite nod, "but I have always made it a rule to strike when the iron is hot. If I linger here, I will surely enjoy the many delights Alexandria has to offer, but I fear that I may later have cause to regret it. I therefore prefer to commit my fate to providence and board the first vessel that sets sail for Italy. And when, with the help of the gods, I reach Rome I will inform Antony of your sympathy and kindness to me in my hour of tribulation."

Risky Journey by Sea

More than two weeks passed before Herod could find a ship with available accommodations. When he, together with his aide and a slave, boarded a merchantman bound for Rhodes, he was greeted by the captain, a burly middle-aged Greek with a leathery, weather-beaten face, piercing black eyes under beetle brows, and a somewhat brusque manner. Over the years he had carried a number of prominent persons, but never in winter nor one whose passage had been arranged by a royal court. He did not relish the responsibility thrust on him.

"You should know, sir," he said to Herod in a gravelly voice as he escorted him to his cabin, "we ain't likely to have smooth sailing. In fact, you can count on a pretty rough voyage. At this time of the year, you're damn lucky to find a ship making the crossing."

"I'm quite aware of that," replied Herod laconically, glad to be on his way at last, even though he had enjoyed some pleasurable diversions during his stay in Alexandria.

"Mind you, I don't want to throw a scare in you," the captain went on, "but I know of more than one ship that's gone down in the winter months. And stout ships they were too. If I was in your shoes I'd wait till spring."

"You're in your own shoes, yet you're making the crossing. And you don't look any the worse for it, if I may say so."

"Well, let me tell you, sir, normally at this time of the year, you'd find me back home in Piraeus chewing the fat around the hearth with my old Melissa or spinning yarns to my grandkids. It's only because there was a cargo of corn that had to be hauled to Rhodes to keep the people's stomachs from growling – this was a bad year for grain around these parts, you know – that I'm risking my neck like this. Me and my crew were promised a fat bonus, but even so I had a devil of a time rounding up enough men to sail this ship."

The captain halted before a heavy oaken door and pushed it open, nodding to Herod to enter. "It's not very fancy, I'm afraid. But it's the best we can offer."

"It's fine," said Herod, hastily surveying the cabin. He was pleased to note that it was clean, and the few pieces of furniture were solid and well-made.

"Now, if you waited till spring you could get much nicer accommodations. Then there are lots of galleys and other ships for you to choose from."

"It's important for me to get to Rhodes as quickly as possible," Herod patiently explained.

"You're a brave person is all I can say," commented the captain with a shrug. "I'll have one of my crew give your man a hand with the luggage."

The first week out of port was pleasant enough, with moderate winds and a clear sky. An active man who hated to sit around idle, Herod regarded the prospect of a two- to three-week voyage with singular lack of enthusiasm; but recalling the captain's and Cleopatra's warning about a winter crossing, he knew he should be thankful if it proved to be uneventful or even boring. The daylight hours he whiled away walking the deck to keep in trim and chatting with the crew. After dark he played dice or draughts with his aide or, more often, with the captain in the latter's cabin. The hours spent with him were the most enjoyable, for then the captain was more relaxed, and he was a good raconteur, possessing an inexhaustible stock of sea tales and an ample supply of Cyprian wine and Egyptian barley-beer to go along with them.

Despite the wine, Herod generally had trouble falling asleep, mainly because of his relative physical inactivity. As he lay on his bunk, a kaleidoscope of reminiscences crowded in on him: scenes from his childhood, memories of his father, his humiliating experience with the Parthians, and the suffering subsequently undergone by his family as well as Alexandra's. Since the betrothal he had not given much thought to Mariamne. Truth to tell, subsequent events had so occupied him that he was able to devote little attention to purely personal affairs, apart from the safety of his family and Phasael's cruel fate. But, he had to admit, the plain fact was that to him Mariamne was primarily the means whereby he hoped to gain acceptance by the Jews and thereby enhance his prospects of winning the throne. That he would also win a strikingly beautiful wife was of added but not paramount importance. Not that he was insensitive to feminine beauty; on the contrary, he was quite susceptible to it, and over the years he had enjoyed his share of comely women, most of them Greek-Syrians. But he never attached much significance to these affairs; for the most part they were merely a pleasant diversion. It gratified his masculine ego that women were willing to bestow their favors on him, but he would never let any of them deflect him from the course he had charted for himself.

So it had been even with Doris, his wife whom he had to put away as one of the conditions for his betrothal to Mariamne. But, he smiled wryly to himself, this had not really been much of a sacrifice: He could never abide her sharp tongue and shrewish ways, her constant moaning. Their life together had been one long succession of quarrels, which almost invariably ended with her shrill accusation about his cruel treatment of her. No, it had not been any sacrifice to put her away in favor of a Hasmonean princess – a princess of the royal house of Judea. He liked the sound of that title; it symbolized the apex of his dreams, the lofty heights to which he aspired.

But let no one think that this was a one-sided affair, not by any means. The Hasmoneans – or at least this branch of the family – could count themselves fortunate too. He might not be a prince of the blood, but hadn't his father been the power behind the throne? And wasn't he, Herod son of Antipater, the one who really wielded power in Judea after him? The Hasmoneans had passed the zenith of their glory; their sun was setting. A new day was dawning, and it promised to be a glorious bright day for him.

His betrothal to Mariamne had not yet gained him the legitimation that he hoped for; on the contrary, so far it had the opposite effect. Alexandra treated him with undisguised reserve; it was obvious that she had not reconciled herself to the union of their two houses. Nor had the Judeans. "A half-Jew" – that was one of the taunts hurled at him; a "Roman lackey" was another. And that rankled.

He despised them for the superior airs they gave themselves. So they did not consider him a suitable match for the Hasmonean princess, did they? Well, just let them wait and see who will be grateful for the match. Like the Hasmoneans, they were living in the past, basking in the glory that was once theirs but now was rapidly fading. If his hopes materialized – and he was confident that his guiding spirit would vouchsafe him this – his journey to Rome would prove the supreme turning point in his life. He had fled Judea in ignominy – a despised "Idumean commoner"; hopefully he would return to Judea with a royal crown, a friend of the mightiest empire of all times. It would be the Hasmoneans and their subjects who would then welcome the alliance between the two houses.

On the eighth day out of port the weather changed abruptly. Almost without warning the wind sharpened, sending dark-gray clouds racing across the sky. The sea turned heavy, causing the freighter to pitch and roll with a vengeance. Feeling queasy, Herod staggered out to the leeward side of the deck to get some fresh air. The captain, who was barking urgent orders to the crew, caught sight of him. After issuing the necessary instructions he made his way to Herod. He had to shout to make himself heard above the roar of the wind and the pounding of the waves: "I wouldn't stay out on deck if I was you! It's too dangerous. A bad storm has blown up and we're in for a rough time. It's going to be tough for us old salts too." Herod saw the wisdom of this advice and returned to his cabin.

The wind grew stronger during the day, and since it was a northerly, the ship could make little progress. The next two days were even worse, and the captain's efforts to tack the vessel did not avail much. However, no one seemed unduly worried, for such a fierce storm was bound to blow over soon. But instead of doing so, to everyone's dismay it reached gale proportions, and sheets of driving rain swept the deck, drenching the crew and chilling them to the bone. The ship tossed wildly, riding high with an onrushing wave, so that its paddle-shaped rudder was exposed, and then came crashing down with a thunderous shudder.

Sleep was impossible, and Herod gave up trying to hold any food down. His guts ached from constant retching; his face turned a greenish hue and he was glassy-eyed. The air in his cabin was fetid and biting cold, and even though he padded himself with several layers of thick woolen garments, he still shivered. He had never felt so wretched in his life. He took to his bunk and remained prone, staggering out only to perform his most urgent needs. Time passed with infernal slowness; it seemed as if the day would never come to an end, and who knew how many days it would be before he set foot on dry land again – or even if he would ever see land again? He cursed himself for not heeding the advice to wait until spring. True, he was in a hurry to get to Rome, but he wanted to get there safe and sound. The creaking of the mast added to his anxiety; if it snapped they were all doomed.

The captain looked in on Herod on the second day of the gale. "I told you we could expect a rough voyage," he said, observing Herod's disheveled appearance and dismal countenance. "But I didn't think it would be as bad as this. This is more than even I bargained for. One of the worst storms I've ever run into in all my thirty-odd years of sailing."

Herod was glad that the captain called on him, but this revelation did nothing to raise his spirits. "Is there any danger of..."

"Of capsizing? Well, let me put it this way," the captain went on, seating himself on a low three-legged stool, "I said this was one of the worst storms I've ever seen; I didn't say it was the worst. The fact is I'm still sailing boats across the Mediterranean and, by Hercules, I intend to keep on doing so for another ten years at least before I become a permanent pest to my old Melissa. Still, when I get back to Piraeus, I'm going to make a votive offering."

"Is it as bad as that?" asked Herod, not sure whether to be encouraged or not.

"We've changed our course a bit, in case you don't know it," said the captain, ignoring Herod's question.

"No, I didn't realize it," replied Herod dully, seeing no difference in the heaving mass of water.

"Yep," said the captain, rubbing his stubby beard. "We've tacked to the east, and are heading toward Pamphylia. We'll hug the coastline until the storm blows itself out. It's bound to pretty soon. Even the loudest shrew eventually runs out of breath. In the meantime I've given orders to dump part of the cargo so we can ride out the storm better."

"You're dumping the corn?" asked Herod with a surprised look.

"No, not the corn; some other goods first. But even that's a pity, because it's pretty precious stuff. But if the ship goes down – which it won't, of course – there won't be any cargo reaching Rhodes anyway. And if it's a choice between the ship and the cargo, I don't have to tell you what comes first. No, we'll make it all right, don't you worry. But to be on the safe side, I suggest we both do a little praying. I'll pray to Neptune – or Poseidon, if that's what he prefers to be called – and you pray to your god. Between the two of them we should make port safely."

Two days later the storm began to subside, and the captain jubilantly told Herod that the gods had heard their prayer. They had even been able to save all the corn and much of the other stuff. The news greatly cheered Herod, and brought a glimmer of hope to his dull, rheumy eyes. The ship was still pitching and rolling, but not nearly as bad as before. Even more important, it began to pick up speed. Herod still had trouble holding down food, but it no longer mattered. After his excruciating and seemingly interminable ordeal, he could now look forward to its happy end. When the city of Rhodes hovered into view, he was never more relieved. He was even exultant, because he knew that his gamble to reach Rome was going to pay off.

Before debarking Herod bade the captain farewell. He slipped off one of his gold rings and presented it to him – "a gift for bringing the ship through safely with superb skill." The captain thanked Herod, assuring him that he would cherish this memento of an eventful voyage, which would enlarge his fund of sea yarns. With a big grin, he added that any time Herod wanted to make a crossing again, he and his ship were at his service – even in winter.

No carriages were to be seen in the Rhodes port area at this time of the year. Eventually Herod's aide procured transportation, and they started to make their way through the lower part of the town. It still showed signs of Cassius's harsh treatment, especially in the vicinity of the port. But everything looked peaceful as they ascended the bluff where the fashionable homes were situated. After a short drive along quiet streets, the vehicle drew up before a large limestone villa, which the driver announced as Sappinus's residence. Herod instructed his aide and slave to remain in the carriage while he ascertained if Sappinus was in.

Herod's knock was answered by an elderly servant. "Yes, sir?" he said in a thin, high-pitched voice, regarding with considerable suspicion the gaunt, haggard man whose expensive-looking cloak hung loosely on him.

"I'm Herod of Judea – an old friend of your master. Is he in?"

The servant looked Herod up and down, trying to decide whether he should be admitted. "Yes, sir," he replied at last.

"Please inform him of my presence," Herod requested in a cool, imperative tone which reflected his annoyance at the scrutiny he was subjected to.

The servant showed Herod into the anteroom and then disappeared. After several minutes he reemerged with his master, whose face lit up when he beheld his visitor. "Herod!" exclaimed Sappinus with a big smile and hearty embrace. "You, of all people! Who'd expect to see you in Rhodes, and in the winter, of all times? I thought my servant must have gotten the name wrong. Greetings, my friend, greetings!"

Sappinus, who had been a good friend of Herod's father, was one of the leading citizens of Rhodes. He had started his business career as a merchant but over the years had branched out into other lucrative fields. In his late fifties, he was still vigorous-looking and debonair. Tall, clear-eyed, possessing strong features, with a high brow, straight nose, a firm, mirthful mouth, and sensitive lips, he conveyed an impression of a man who knew how to live and to get things done. He stepped back and took a good look at Herod.

"Now I understand why my servant hesitated to admit you," he said with a chuckle. "It's obvious from your green, emaciated face what kind of a voyage you had. It takes an extremely good reason and strong will power to brave the seas this time of the year. There must be an exciting story behind this, and in this dull season I'm just in the mood for one. Oh, by the way, I assume you're not staying with anyone else here?"

"No. To be perfectly frank, I arrived in Rhodes only an hour or so ago."

"Then you'll be my guest. I dare say, you'll present a challenge to my cook. I wonder how long it will take to put some flesh back on those bones of yours and a little color in your cheeks. I must make a wager with Ptolemy on that. Your luggage?"

"It's in the carriage with my aide and slave."

"Tell them to come in. I suppose they're in the same shape as you. I'll show you to your rooms, and afterward you'll have something light to eat. It's advisable to let your stomach get used to food again only gradually."

"That's very considerate of you," said Herod, touched by Sappinus's warm concern and hospitality.

"By the way, Ptolemy is coming over for dinner tomorrow night. I'm sure you remember him. He'll also be delighted to hear about your adventures."

Herod was weaker than he thought, and at Sappinus's suggestion he spent the rest of that day and most of the next one in bed or relaxing in a comfortable chair. After being confined for over a month in a cramped, foul-smelling cabin, it was a pleasure to sleep in a large bed in a spacious, airy room, under clean sheets on a mattress stuffed with swan's down. Above all, Herod appreciated the fact that the room was stationary and not bouncing in all directions. The rest did him good, and by the time Ptolemy arrived he was more like his old self, free of the aching, exhausted feeling that had gripped him since the onset of the storm.

Sappinus and Ptolemy would frequently meet at each other's home to discuss business and other matters of common interest. The dinners were small, intimate affairs, with occasionally another guest or two present. Herod had met Ptolemy only once before, and that was several years ago in Syria, but he recognized him immediately. He was about the same age as Sappinus, but looked a little older. He was a stocky man, with a ruddy, amiable face; his voice was deep and his speech rather blunt. Like Sappinus, he was one of the leading citizens of Rhodes.

"I told Ptolemy yesterday how you looked," said Sappinus, turning to Herod with a grin after the two guests had exchanged greetings. "But you're already beginning to lose that scarecrow appearance. I'm not so sure I'll make that wager with him."

"I must say, Herod, you've got a lot of guts," remarked Ptolemy, eyeing a tray of tidbits being carried into the room. "You'd never get me to cross the Mediterranean in winter."

"Come to think of it," chaffed Sappinus with a twinkle in his eyes, "it might not be a bad idea for you to try it sometimes. You say your wife complains about your expanding paunch; I can think of no better way to get rid of it."

"I'm grateful for your advice, Doctor Sappinus, and will give it all the consideration it deserves," replied Ptolemy in mocking solemnity. "But right now I'm more interested in hearing about Cleopatra. Ever since her visit to Antony at Tarsus, I've been greatly intrigued by her. That really must have been quite a spectacle she put on – far better than anything we poor Rhodians have been privileged to behold. Herod, what's it like in her court? I haven't been there since her father's day and am out of touch. And tell me, how did you manage to escape her seductive charms? Or did you?"

"Your profound interest in Cleopatra is quite understandable," Sappinus interrupted with an amused look, "and I too would be delighted to hear about her from a first-hand source. But my servant informs me that dinner is ready. So if you gentlemen will please repair to the triclinium, we'll begin our repast, and Herod can enlighten us about that bewitching queen."

For all its spaciousness, the triclinium was a cozy room, with rich tapestries and vividly colored scenes adorning the walls; a skillfully wrought statue stood in one corner and large vases in the others. Bronze candelabra gave a soft light, and glowing braziers diffused a pleasant warmth.

The three men took their places on a couch drawn up before a square table covered with a linen cloth. Herod never felt comfortable eating in a reclining position, his left elbow propped up on a cushion. But since it was the custom in upper-class Greek and Roman circles, he shrugged his shoulders and decided that he might just as well get used to the idea. A slave poured perfumed water over the diners' hands from an ewer, and wiped them with a towel carried on his arm. Two other slaves brought in trays of food; one contained a variety of cheeses, oysters, and pickled mullet garnished with asparagus, mint, and black olives; the other tray was loaded with assorted meats. There was also a bowl of apples and citrons.

Herod's appetite had begun to return to normal, and he was ready to do justice to the dishes set before him. But his companions seemed to be hungrier for news about his recent experience than for food. They plied him with so many questions about the Parthians and especially the Egyptian queen that the candles had to be replaced and the oil lamps refilled by the time Sappinus ordered the dessert to be served.

"It still baffles me how she was able to cast her spell over two of the most powerful men in the world," said Sappinus. "Caesar was always an easy prey for a pretty woman, but for one to hold his interest for any length of time was unusual. And the same goes even more for Antony. He has an insatiable appetite and isn't the least discriminating; he likes all kinds, high-born or low, and he's not fussy about looks either. For someone who likes variety that much to stick to one woman is really amazing."

"If you ask me," commented Ptolemy, wiping his fingers on his napkin, "with Caesar I think it was simply that he was getting on in years and had begun to burn out. He was probably getting fed up with campaigning and woman-izing, and craved a more enduring relationship with a beautiful, intellectually stimulating companion."

"From what I understand it was more serious than that," replied Sappinus. "Rumor had it that he was seriously considering making Cleopatra his wife and co-ruler of a Roman-Egyptian empire. But as for Antony, I'm less able to under-stand why he frittered away so much precious time in Alexandria. If he hadn't done that, the Parthians wouldn't have dared invade Syria. What do you think, Herod? Can you shed any light on the question?"

Herod looked thoughtful for a moment and then answered in measured tones. "I don't believe the matter is as puzzling as you think. Whether Cleopatra is beautiful is open to question. I personally have my reservations on that point. That she is physically attractive I'll grant you. And as for her reputation for wit and intelligence, I have no reason to doubt that it is well deserved. But to my mind her greatest asset is Egypt's wealth. That is a prize that would tempt any Roman, and especially one with imperial ambitions, like Caesar or Antony. I agree with you that Antony would have been well advised to pay more atten-tion to the administration of his Eastern provinces. I for one would have been spared considerable anguish if he had. But in view of Rome's grand design and the power struggle going on there, he needed money – lots of it. In Egypt, he found a treasure."

"In the form of hard gold and the soft fleshy sort – an irresistible combina-tion," remarked Sappinus with a smile playing about the corners of his mouth. "Yes, you have a point there, a very valid one I admit. But I'm still not convinced that it's the full explanation. Man is a complex creature – very complex."

"And he can do very strange things – like sailing the Mediterranean in win-ter," interjected Ptolemy with a roguish grin. "Herod, I still don't know why you did it. Now that you've filled your belly with Sappinus's savory victuals, perhaps you'll be kind enough to explain."

"He's already explained to me," said Sappinus. "He wants to go to Rome because of the situation in Judea. It's a perfectly natural thing for him to do in the circumstances."

"But why just now, the worst time of the year for sailing? Surely it could have waited another couple of months. It was too great a risk, and he might have paid for it very dearly."

"Fortunately the gods were kind to him. Maybe they let him get shaken up a bit, but they saw to it that he arrived in Rhodes safe and sound."

"They would have been even more cooperative if he'd made his voyage after the worst of winter was over," replied Ptolemy a little testily. He turned to Herod. "You're anyway going to have to wait in Rhodes for some time, I'm afraid. The situation in Rome is pretty cloudy right now. I don't know if you're aware of it, but Antony's wife and his brother Lucius have been giving Octavian quite a time. Fulvia is no Penelope. Not for her to sit by the hearth and work her loom; she loves to dabble in politics – it's in her blood. They've caused Octavian no end of trouble, and it's finally come to open warfare. Antony has had no hand in all this; it's in his interest to keep the triumvirate intact. I understand that he threw a fit when he learned what Fulvia and Lucius had done while he was in Egypt. But Octavian isn't convinced that Antony is innocent; he suspects that he's behind the whole business. Right now it's touch and go between them, and nobody can tell how it's going to turn out. Until the dust settles, I'd keep away from Rome if I were you. What do you think, Sappinus? Do you agree with me?"

"Yes, definitely. It would be very unwise to go there now. I'm confident that the two triumvirs will iron out their differences; it would be disastrous for all concerned if they don't. But in the meantime, Herod, I think you'd better stay put."

"I suppose I'll have to," conceded Herod in a subdued voice. "It so happens that I do know something about the trouble between Antony and Octavian. Cleopatra mentioned it to me."

"And still you risked a voyage to Rhodes?" remarked Ptolemy incredulously.

Herod realized that Ptolemy had good reason to ask this pointed question, which made him seem impetuous if not downright foolish. He thought it best to be candid with him. "You asked me before how I managed to escape Cleopatra's seductive charms. Well, that's how, by putting a lot of water between us, and at the same time bringing myself closer to my destination."

"That's probably the best way to avoid getting entangled in that spider's web," commented Sappinus blandly. "And how do you intend to get to your destination – the same way you got here?" he asked with a trace of gentle mockery.

"I hope I can do it in a little more style this time," replied Herod a little stiffly.

"You must, if you want to make any impression in Rome," exclaimed Ptolemy, wagging his finger to emphasize the point. "Go there as befits a man of your station – not in an old rickety fishing smack, but in a sleek ship – say, a trireme."

An astonished expression appeared on Sappinus's and Herod's faces. "And why a trireme?" asked Sappinus, not sure whether Ptolemy was serious or jesting. "Why not a quadrireme, or better yet, a quinquereme? Five banks of oars – that would really make a splash!"

"Sappinus, you're making fun of me," retorted Ptolemy with a mock-injured air. "I mean it when I say a trireme."

"I'd be quite happy to travel in any kind of ship that's half-way decent," protested Herod. "Just as long as I get there."

"No, no!" cried Ptolemy. "You won't go in any kind of ship. You'll go in your own ship."

Herod gaped at Ptolemy. "My own ship?" he uttered, wondering at this seemingly unrealistic demand. "I don't see why it's so important to go in my own ship. Besides, how and where am I supposed to get a ship of my own? In my present circumstances it's out of the question. Even to charter a ship is beyond my means."

Ptolemy folded his arms across his chest and fixed Herod with an authoritative look. "Did I say anything about chartering a ship? I said your own ship."

The last words were spat out almost contemptuously, as though Ptolemy were barking orders to an underling. And then, in a gentler tone, he added: "Well, to be more precise, let's say, your own ship for the time being."

Sappinus cocked an inquisitive eye at Ptolemy. "You're being very mysterious, my dear Ptolemy, and very dramatic too. Don't keep us in suspense."

"All right," said Ptolemy with an inscrutable grin. "As you know, I have my fingers in a lot of pies. I'm not only a banker, but among other ways of keeping myself from getting bored and to earn a few extra drachmas I dabble in the grain trade, build homes, and now – ships too."

"Ships!" exclaimed Sappinus. "Since when?"

"Since last month. Leonides, the Corinthian shipbuilder, defaulted on a big loan I gave him. I didn't have the heart to have him declared bankrupt and let him sink. So I made a deal with him – a partnership in return for wiping out the debt."

"Why, you old rascal!" declared Sappinus, shaking his head waggishly. "What do you mean by keeping secrets from your good friend? Now I'm beginning to see the light. You mean..."

"I mean that the trireme Leonides was building should be finished in a few weeks. That may not be the ideal time to launch a ship – the sea will still be a bit rough – but it's an excellent way to test its seaworthiness and to find out how good a shipbuilder my partner is. Besides, as a banker I can smell a good investment, and my nose tells me that Herod will be a pretty sound investment."

Facing the Triumvirs in Rome

As Herod's carriage neared Rome, the fatigue of the long journey fell away and he was filled with a sense of eager expectation and wonder. Here was the most powerful city-state ever known, the capital of the greatest empire of all time, the hub of the world to which all eyes were directed. Here was enacted the great drama that determined the lives and fate of nations near and far. From here marched the legions that brought country after country under Roman sway, that brought back in their train a horde of captives of all colors and races and spoils so vast that they greatly enriched the national treasury, high officials, conquering generals, and patricians – wealth that financed the construction of imposing temples, forums, stadiums, and theaters, as well as stately mansions and villas lavishly furnished and adorned with statues, paintings, and other works of art looted from the vanquished cities of the Greek world.

From Rome also came orderly government. Herod knew that this was not generally appreciated by the subject peoples, who associated it almost solely with the payment of tribute and heavy taxes. But there were those farsighted enough to perceive the benefits flowing from a strong central government ruled by able men and imposing peace within the borders of the far-flung empire and throughout its sphere of influence. Like his father before him, Herod prided himself on being one of those who fully understood and valued the role played by Rome. In linking his destiny to that of Rome he was not only staking his own future, but, he was convinced, he was promoting the welfare of Judea as well. His fortunes were now at their lowest ebb, but as the outlying houses on the Appian Way came into view, he was aware that he had reached the most decisive turning point in his life, and in pinning his hopes on the triumvirs, especially Antony, he was confident that he would not leave Rome a disappointed man.

He was no stranger to the city, for many years earlier he had accompanied his father here on a diplomatic mission. He had never forgotten the profound impression it made on him, although time had dimmed his memory of individual edifices and other features, so that it was as though he were seeing the metropolis with fresh eyes. And in a sense he was, for it had expanded greatly in the meantime, especially under Caesar's impetus.

As Herod's carriage approached the Capena Gate, he heard what sounded like the roll of thunder. He looked up in surprise: A stiff late-afternoon breeze whipped the treetops and made him huddle into his heavy wool cloak for warmth, but the sky was clear except for a few fleecy clouds scurrying high overhead. He leaned out the window and, shouting to make himself heard, asked the driver for an explanation, and was informed that this was the day of the races in the Circus Maximus, which was located only a mile or so away. The rumbling grew louder as they proceeded, bringing back memories of the chariot races he had attended during his previous visit. He described to his aide the excitement evoked by the contests, how as the day of the races approached, all Rome seemed to talk about nothing else than their favorite jockeys and charioteers, who wore the distinctive colors of their stables – white, green, red, or blue; the feverish gambling, often of very large sums, that went on during the day; how some fans would even get down on the ground and smell the dung to make sure that the horses of their favorite drivers had been properly fed.

As the hippodrome came into view, Herod saw that it was more immense than the last time he beheld it. He learned from his driver that Caesar had enlarged the eastern and western sides of the arena and carved out the hillsides so as to seat over 150,000 persons. The roaring of the crowd grew louder until it reached a deafening crescendo. Herod told his aide that the contestants had probably reached the seventh and last lap. He could picture the spectators rising to their feet and frantically waving their arms and handkerchiefs, shouting themselves hoarse as the panting stallions dashed to the final post, with the winner being greeted with a storm of applause and overwhelmed by the crowd's frenzied enthusiasm.

Herod's carriage came to a halt outside the Capena Gate. He was about to ask the driver why he did not go on, when he caught sight of the ranks of parked carriages and remembered that all wheeled vehicles were forbidden in the city during the daytime. Antony had once explained to him that with only a few exceptions the streets of Rome were mere alleyways, wide enough for the passage of only one vehicle at a time. It was the heavy congestion and tortuous lay of the streets that had prompted Caesar to ban all traffic during the daylight hours except for pedestrians, horsemen, litters, and carrying-chairs.

The driver arranged for a porter to help Herod's slave remove the chests and other luggage from the carriage, and after receiving the agreed fee plus a generous tip, bade his passenger a pleasant stay in Rome. Herod ordered his aide to have the luggage moved to a nearby inn until evening, when it was to be transported by cart to the specified address.

Thanks to the races a large number of litters and carrying-chairs were available, and Herod was soon moving in the direction of the Esquiline hill. The sky was becoming overcast, hinting of rain or possibly even snow, and the stiff breeze would have chilled him if he had not put on an extra wool tunic beneath his cloak. As his litter-bearers proceeded through the maze of narrow, winding streets, Herod better understood the reason for Caesar's decree. They had to pick their way through a ceaseless, noisy flow of pedestrians, who jostled and swore at one another and more than once almost toppled Herod's litter. Their progress was frequently blocked by a surging mass in front and a dense mass pressing from behind.

On either side of the foul-smelling streets were blocks of tenements six or seven stories high; many of them had shops, taverns, or workshops on the ground floor and balconies on the second, and a few were connected at the top with a tenement across the street by an arched passage containing additional rooms. Here and there, squeezed between the blocks of tenements, were mansions belonging to the wealthy, which were shut off from public view by a high wall and with their doors and windows opening on interior courts. The juxtaposition of the two classes of dwellings amazed Herod, who could not help comparing it with Alexandria's residential quarters, where stately homes surrounded by spacious gardens were set off straight, wide, clean streets and boulevards.

Herod's head began to ache from the din that rose on every side, but he was fascinated by the passing scene. The ground-floor tenement shops were crowded, and in many cases the display of their wares spread into the street, aggravating the congestion. Loquacious barbers shaved their customers in the open air, untroubled by the chilly breeze, and peddlers hawked a wide variety of goods from all parts of the world, while the owners of cookshops hoarsely sang the praise of their piping hot sausages. Money changers rang their coins on dirty tables, and a beater of gold dust pounded with his mallet on a well-worn stone. Everywhere tinkers' hammers resounded, and beggars loudly recited their piteous tales of woe.

It was well over an hour from the time he set out before Herod arrived at the home of Lucius Marcellus, with whom he had become friendly when Lucius was serving on the staff of Sextus Caesar, the late governor of Syria. Herod had written him from Rhodes inquiring whether he could stay with him while in Rome, and had received a cordial invitation.

"It's a great pleasure to meet you again after all these years," said Lucius after welcoming Herod. "And I want you to know that I consider it a special privilege to meet someone who has crossed the Mediterranean in the heart of winter. It's more than I would do, Antony or no Antony. For me it's *terra firma* [dry land] in the winter."

"After my experience, I can only echo your sentiments," replied Herod, resigning himself to the fact that his voyage would be a recurring theme during his stay in Rome.

He noted that, except for a thinner crop of hair, his friend had changed very little during the past five years. Lucius was nearly fifteen years older than Herod, but regular exercise and moderation in food and drink had kept him in good physical condition, so that he looked younger than his age. He was of medium height, had a somewhat elongated countenance with keen brown eyes under thick brows, a short straight nose, thin lips, and a saber scar on his left cheek.

They were seated in the atrium, around which were ranged the main rooms of the home. Like the other mansions Herod had passed on the way, Lucius's had an unprepossessing brick-and-stucco exterior. The atrium was tastefully but not pretentiously furnished, with several small bronze and marble statues, frescoes adorning the walls, and bronze lamps to provide illumination; the furniture was of excellent design and workmanship. Thick carpets covered the floor, and their exquisite coloring and pattern evoked Herod's admiration.

"Babylonian carpets," Lucius pointed out with a touch of pride. "In the spring most of them are stored away, but in the winter they add warmth."

"It's pleasantly warm here," remarked Herod, looking about him, "but I don't see any braziers."

"You will in your bedchamber. In this part of the house there is central heating – conveyed through tile pipes in the walls."

Herod had heard that many of the fashionable Roman dwellings were equipped with central heating. He queried his host about the technical details, which interested him greatly. He saw no reason why he should not enjoy a pleasant, even heat in Jerusalem, where the winters were hardly less severe than here, and resolved that one day he would have it installed in his residence.

"From your letter I gather that your path hasn't exactly been strewn with roses of late," said Lucius, passing a dish of sweetmeats to Herod. "But in coming to Rome, I dare say you are now on the right path. And speaking of paths, I trust you had a pleasant journey on the Appian Way."

"A little tiring but quite pleasant on the whole," replied Herod, helping himself to a cake. "What I found very interesting was the journey from the Capena Gate to your home."

"Yes, it is very interesting but quite tortuous. I sometimes think our narrow, twisting streets strongly influence our politicians, and help to explain their deviousness," he added with wry grin. He rose to his feet. "Now let me show you to your room so you can wash and rest up from your journey before dinner. Where is your luggage?"

"My aide will bring it after dark."

"Oh yes, of course, Caesar's decree – one of the many excellent things he did for Rome. If only he had devised some way to deal with the noisy carts at night, we'd be forever indebted to him. What a racket they make, and what juicy curses one hears! If you intend to improve your Latin while in Rome, I suggest you don't try to do it from what you hear in the streets. Now, please come with me."

Herod rose and followed his host to the sleeping quarters. Lucius opened the door to one of the rooms and nodded to Herod to enter. "You'll probably want to rest up a bit until your luggage arrives. We'll have dinner after that, but in the meantime I'll send you some refreshments in case you're famished."

By the time Herod sat down to dinner, a warm bath, rest, and change of clothing left him in excellent spirits and with a hearty appetite. Apart from himself and his aide, only Lucius and his wife Olivia, a tallish, slender woman of average appearance, occupied places around a large table in the triclinium. The food was ample and wholesome but by no means sumptuous, for Lucius did not favor heavy, multicourse meals or exotic dishes except on very special occasions. After some small talk he began to question Herod about developments in Judea and Syria, in which he retained a keen interest; but, like Sappinus and Ptolemy, he was intrigued most of all by the audience with Cleopatra.

"A very clever woman," declared Lucius with frank admiration after hearing Herod's account. "It's no wonder she's twisted people like Caesar and Antony around her little finger."

"That takes nothing more than a shapely figure, a passable face, and a willingness to grant one's favors," Lucius' wife commented tartly. "That's enough to ensnare any man."

"I hope you will allow some exceptions to your perceptive judgment, my dear," said Lucius. "But you must admit that when she was in Rome she was faithful to Caesar."

"And how would you know, my dear husband?" asked Olivia, tilting her head at a cocky angle. "And why shouldn't she have been faithful? She was scheming to marry Caesar and make herself queen of an Egyptian-Roman empire."

"Nonsense!" Lucius flung out with a deprecatory gesture. "Utter nonsense! That's the story you women cooked up and spread. You see, Herod, what a stir Cleopatra made in Rome. And that even though she was smart enough to keep out of the public eye as much as possible. She knew her Romans, she did. And speaking of Caesar, in your audience with her did she mention him at all?"

"Not as far as I can recall. She seemed more concerned about Antony at the time."

"And so were we Romans," exclaimed Lucius, making a wry face. "When he returned from Egypt things were in a pretty sorry mess here. The business with Fulvia and my namesake Lucius left Octavian in a sour mood, and he and Antony almost came to blows. Fortunately their armies had more sense and refused to fight each other. Right now the two have patched up their quarrel, but who knows for how long?"

"If it depends on Octavia, it will stay patched," declared Olivia. She urged the two guests to have another helping of lobster. When they politely refused, she ordered one of the slaves to remove the dishes and bring in an ewer of perfumed water to pour over the diners' hands before the next course was served. While waiting for this, Lucius ordered the second slave to refill their goblets. After taking a sip of wine he turned to Herod. "In case you're wondering who Octavia is, my wife is referring to Octavian's sister and Antony's new wife."

"Yes, I know," replied Herod, putting down his goblet. "I heard about the marriage shortly before leaving Rhodes. She's what – his third or fourth wife?"

"Fourth. Antony, like so many of our upper-class males, seems to prefer variety also in his lawful spouses. Anyway, after Fulvia died – some say of frustrated ambition, others because of Antony's neglect of her; your guess is as good as mine – he married Octavia as a pledge of good behavior."

"She's much too good for him," Olivia opined. "She's a gentle, virtuous sort, not at all like those actresses and tarts he amuses himself with."

"My dear, they're no more to be condemned than many of our high-born Roman women," Lucius chided his wife. "At least you can't say he's married any of those actresses or tarts. But it's true that Octavia is a good woman," he confirmed to Herod with a nod of his head. "If Antony should mistreat her, or fly off to Cleopatra again, who knows what will happen? There's been enough bad blood between him and Octavian, and I'm not sure that we've seen the last of their feuds. But you at least will find them on reasonably friendly terms and doing their best not to tread on each other's toes. That will be to your advantage."

Herod's audience with the two triumvirs was scheduled for mid-morning of his third day in Rome. The night before he had trouble falling asleep. He tried to keep from thinking about the meeting and to relax, but without success. After tossing on his bed until long after midnight, he resorted to copious draughts of wine to induce at least a drugged sleep. "What rotten luck!" he muttered. "Of all times for this to happen." With a sigh of desperation he sank back on his bed; within a few minutes he was snoring softly. He was surprised to learn, when a loud knocking on his door awoke him that it was well past sunrise. He threw off the covers and jumped out of bed. He would have to hurry, but that did not matter: His head was clear and he even felt refreshed. A good omen, he thought. He opened the shutters to admit the daylight.

This would undoubtedly be the most crucial day in his life, and it was important that he make the right impression on the triumvirs. He decided to wear the same garb he did for his audience with Cleopatra. He was pleased with the way he had acquitted himself then, and thought it inadvisable to risk his luck by wearing something different. So over thick undergarments he put on the same tunic and scarlet cloak; he also put on the same brown leather shoes. He oiled and combed his hair and beard and dabbed on a few drops of musk. He decided to have a light breakfast in order to avoid any possible indigestion and to have a clear head for the audience.

"If you eat like a bird, your stomach will start growling, and that will be just as bad as indigestion," Lucius cautioned him. "It will take more than an hour to get to Antony's house, and in this brisk air you're bound to get good and hungry. So if I were you, I'd have a fairly substantial breakfast."

Herod accepted this suggestion, and as it turned out he was glad he did. The fresh air sharpened his appetite so much that by the time he reached his destination, he regretted that he had not eaten more.

For the first half of the journey the litter-bearers followed the same route Herod had taken upon his arrival, but then they turned off to the right and before long were making their way up the Palatine hill. The streets here were also narrow and twisting, but there were more temples and mansions than on the Esquiline, the stream of pedestrians seemed a little thinner, the hawking of wares and begging less noticeable, the din less deafening. Yet it was hard to believe that this was the fashionable residential district of Rome, the one most favored by patricians and business magnates.

Like the other mansions Herod passed on the way, Antony's was hidden from public view by a high wall. Before approaching the sentry stationed at the entrance gate, Herod stopped to straighten the folds of his cloak. Much to his surprise, his heart began to beat a little faster and his hands turned clammy. This both disconcerted and puzzled him, for he prided himself on his iron will and unshakable self-confidence. Moreover, he had gotten along well with Antony. Could it be that it was the prospect of confronting Octavian – about whom he had heard so much but had never set eyes on, the man who, together with Antony, had not shrunk from proscribing hundreds of senators and over 2,000 other leading citizens of Rome after Caesar's murder and had subsequently bested Antony in battle – that brought on this sudden nervousness? Or was it the knowledge that now his hour of destiny had arrived?

He squared his shoulders and advanced toward the sentry, who upon learning Herod's identity admitted him through the gate. At the entrance door he was met by a servant, who ushered him down a long corridor into a medium-sized room, and bade him be seated while he informed his master of his arrival.

The room gave the impression of being Antony's office. The major item of furniture was a large desk with carved legs. In one corner of the room was a black basalt bust of Caesar, and in another a statue of a discuss-thrower. An ebony cabinet contained trophies and souvenirs of Antony's military campaigns and travels, and behind the desk was a small cabinet with pigeon-holes filled with rolled scrolls. On the wall behind the desk was a display of foreign swords, and on the opposite wall, directly facing the chair behind the table, was a large painting of a sylvan scene featuring a fleshy nude maiden frolicking in a glen. Herod was gazing at the picture when Antony entered the room. Seeing what had caught his visitor's eye, he chuckled. "There's no more inspiring way to start a day's work!" he exclaimed. "A good look at that and you're raring to go."

Antony, dressed in a military tunic and looking very fit, embraced Herod. "Greetings, friend! And welcome to Antony's humble abode."

"Greetings, sire," responded Herod, his tension melting in the warmth of this welcome. "It's good to see you again and looking so well and in such good spirits after, er..."

"After our woeful misadventures, eh?" said Antony without a trace of embarrassment. "Don't be afraid to say it. Even the most stouthearted has to know that the wheel of fortune sometimes turns in the wrong direction."

"But when he is favored by the gods, he can rest assured that it will right itself, especially when he is descended from no less a divinity than Hercules," said Herod, pandering to Antony's inordinate pride in his professed divine ancestry. This rejoinder pleased Antony. Grinning broadly, he perched himself on the edge of the desk.

"Speaking of shifting fortunes," Herod went on, pursuing the opening Antony had given him, "I was very sorry to learn about the death of your wife Fulvia, but rejoice to know that you have since married the noble Octavia. My heartiest congratulations."

"I humbly accept both your condolences and your congratulations. Some scandal- mongers – how dull life would be without them – claim that I ought to have waited longer before remarrying and that Octavia, who also has been but recently widowed, should have waited at least the customary ten months. But when the lady is the sister of a fellow triumvir and reasons of state are involved, one makes an exception to the rule. Even the Senate agreed on that. Besides," Antony continued with a sly wink, "I rather imagine that Fulvia is now romping in the Elysian Fields and vigorously meddling in whatever politics goes on there. So I don't think she should begrudge me a partner to console me in my profound grief."

"I understand that your wife – your new wife, that is – is not only beautiful but a gentle and virtuous woman."

"So I have been reminded by every confounded Roman matron! They all seem to think it odd for Antony to marry such a woman. And they're probably right," he added with a chuckle. "Even in this room you can see how I have had to bow to Octavia's benign influence."

Herod looked perplexed. There was nothing in the room remotely suggesting a woman's touch. "I'm not referring to the furniture – what little there is of it – nor to my statues and trophies," explained Antony, grinning at Herod's reaction. "I'm referring to that enchanting picture on the wall – the one you were studying so intently when I came in."

"Do you mean to tell me that Lady Octavia approves of that picture?" remarked Herod with a dubious look.

"Good heavens, no! That wouldn't be at all like her – completely out of character. I wanted that picture in the atrium, where all our visitors could feast their eyes on that delectable damsel prancing about in all her ravishing undraped beauty. But Octavia wouldn't hear of it. So here it is, relegated to this secluded workroom of mine. All my efforts to point out the merits of this masterpiece failed to impress her – neither the perfect draftsmanship, the marvelous coloring, the subject itself. I even told her that some experts think the young lady is probably none other than Venus. She said that if the goddess were decently clothed, she wouldn't object to her. Ha! Who would look twice at a Venus draped in a stola? I didn't think it advisable to tell her that the model who posed for that picture was a high-class courtesan. Oh well, I suppose one can't expect everybody to appreciate good art."

Antony rose and strolled over to the window. "I wonder what's holding up that brother of hers?" he said, peering at the passing scene. "I know he's a late riser, but he should have been here by now. Well, until he comes let's warm our innards a bit."

Antony summoned a slave and ordered him to bring a flagon of Falerian wine and one of Raetian wine. Turning to Herod, he explained: "Octavian – for the life of me, I can't get used to calling him my brother-in-law – probably won't drink at this time of the day, but if he does he prefers Raetian wine. What I really should offer him is bread soaked in cold water, together with a sliced cucumber or some green figs; that I know he'll eat. What a diet! If I ate like him I'd be as thin as a broomstick. It's no wonder he suffers from so many ailments. The list reads like an encyclopedia of medicine. And wait till you see him. I'll bet you 10,000 sesterces he'll be wearing at least three or four tunics and a heavy toga over a woolen chest protector and undershirt. And more than likely he'll have his thighs and shins wrapped too. With all due respect, he's about the puniest man I've ever laid eyes on."

"Yet he carries a heavy load as triumvir. And from what I understand, he's a very able ruler," ventured Herod, careful not to tread on either of the triumvirs' toes.

"Oh, ho! That was almost my undoing," snorted Antony. "I discovered that inside that puny frame of his is an iron will and a cold, calculating brain. And what a glutton for work! That's probably why he's late now. I'll bet you another 10,000 sesterces that he was up half the night reading and writing documents."

At this point the slave returned with a large tray laden with two flagons of wine, a mixing bowl, and three goblets. He set these down on a small table. "Ah, here's our Falerian wine," said Antony, rubbing his hands. "Nectar for the gods and mortals alike."

The slave mixed the contents of one of the flagons with water and filled two goblets, which he handed to Antony and Herod. This was the first time Herod tasted Falerian wine, and he found it excellent. "I'll have to take your word for it that this is nectar for the gods," he commented with an approving nod, "but I can truly say that it's the best wine I've ever tasted."

"I knew you'd like it," said Antony after downing a big quaff. "Compared with this, that Raetian swill Octavian favors is undiluted vinegar, fit only for pickling those cucumbers he relishes so much. Here, lad, fill it up again."

The slave took the empty goblet and began to refill it when Antony's aide appeared in the doorway. "The triumvir Gaius Octavian has arrived, sir," he announced.

279

"Ah, so dear Thurinus is here at last!" said Antony with a wry grin.

"Who, sir?" asked the officer with a puzzled frown.

"Gaius Octavian! That's what you said, isn't it?" Antony snapped with a mock-severe expression. "Admit him."

As the officer disappeared through the door, Antony chuckled. "Thurinus is Octavian's cognomen," he explained to Herod. "He doesn't like it, though, and never uses it. He takes umbrage whenever I call him that."

Despite Antony's description of Octavian, Herod expected to find him an imposing figure. But he was surprised to see how young and ordinary he looked. He could not have been much more than twenty years old. He had a slight build and was much shorter than Antony. His features were so delicately molded as to be almost effeminate. He had high cheek bones and a thin, tapering face; his teeth were small and widely spaced, his hair sandy and slightly curled. His nose was high-bridged, his eyes a luminous gray. He wore a calm, mild expression that seemed incapable of commanding much respect, let alone fear. It was the expression more of a bookworm than of one worthy to step into the shoes of the great Caesar.

It was now clear to Herod why there had been so much friction between the two triumvirs. They differed greatly not only in age and physical build, but more important, in their personalities. It was hard to imagine this young man being partly guilty of the proscription of over 2,000 of the most prominent Romans; it was harder yet to picture him standing up to Antony in the struggle to inherit Caesar's mantle and even besting him on the battlefield. Anyone who could do that must truly have, as Antony asserted, an iron will and a cold, calculating brain, external appearances notwithstanding. Such a person would have to be treated with the utmost deference.

When Octavian entered the room, Herod noticed that he limped slightly, as though suffering from a weakness in his left leg. For a person who ate as sparingly as Antony claimed, he did not seem to be unduly thin, but when he removed his cloak Herod saw that he was indeed wearing a number of tunics, which padded him out.

"I trust that I haven't kept you gentlemen waiting very long," said Octavian, spreading his hands over the glowing brazier. "If I did, I apologize."

"No harm done," Antony assured him. "It gave me an opportunity to expatiate on the masterpiece gracing this room."

"Ah yes," remarked Octavian dryly as he cast a disdainful glance at the painting on the wall. "I understand from my sister that there is difference of opinion about the merits of that picture, especially its subject. But I admit that in such matters no one is more expert than you."

The corners of Antony's mouth turned down. He wondered if he had been given a backhanded compliment. "Will you join us in a drink?" he asked, recovering his convivial mood.

"No, thank you. I got up only a short while ago. I spent a good part of the night working on documents."

"That's one way to spend the nights," said Antony with a shrug of his shoulders. "Every man to his own tastes." He nodded in the direction of the small table. "That's Raetian wine you see there, a superb vintage. Are you sure you won't have some? It'll warm you better than all your tunics."

"Well, maybe later – after my breakfast has settled a bit."

"Good! We'll all have a snack then. The wine will go down well with – what do you say to sliced cucumbers and a piece of coarse bread?"

"That'll be fine," agreed Octavian, seating himself on one of the straight-backed chairs. He turned to Herod. "I understand from Antony that you didn't have a very pleasant voyage from Alexandria."

"No, sire, I didn't."

"Please don't call me sire," protested Octavian with an impatient wave of his hand. "I dislike being addressed that way."

"Yes, sir," said Herod, surprised at Octavian's objection to a title customarily used when addressing a Roman of high rank – a title he himself felt awkward using when addressing someone several years his junior.

A roguish smile crossed Antony's face. "I can just picture that ship of Herod's bouncing up and down and him retching his guts out," he said, knowing what effect his words would have on Octavian, who was such a poor sailor that he preferred to travel by land even over the greatest of distances wherever possible.

"At least he didn't have to worry about pirates, as Caesar did," retorted Octavian tartly, annoyed at Antony for making him feel queasy, which he suspected had been done intentionally. "When winter comes even pirates prefer to stay close to their hearths."

"Or their mistresses' hearths."

"It seems it's not only pirates who prefer to spend the winter warming themselves with their mistresses," Octavian observed dryly.

At this veiled accusation Antony's face darkened. This did not escape Octavian's notice, and he quickly changed the subject. "I think all this is beside the point," he said in a more amiable tone. He turned to Herod. "What we would like to hear is your assessment of what has been happening in Judea. We were most distressed to learn about Saxas's futile stand against the Parthians and his death. We have had little first-hand intelligence about developments in Judea itself, and here you can enlighten us."

Herod proceeded to give a brief account of the Parthian crossing of the Galilean border, Antigonus's advance on Jerusalem, and the skirmishes inside the city, which culminated in Pacorus's crafty stratagem to lure Phasael and Herod outside the walls where they could be seized. He stressed his suspicion of

Pacorus's offer, which unfortunately proved to be well-founded. He went on to describe his escape from the city and, with moist eyes, the fate of Phasael and Hyrcanus. He was about to describe his audience with Cleopatra when Octavian cut him short.

"One thing is not clear to me. We know that the Parthians crossed into Judea with only a relatively small force, yet Antigonus was able to advance swiftly to the gates of Jerusalem and even to sweep through most of the city. How do you explain that?"

Herod had anticipated this question, which could prove highly embarrassing. "The garrison in Jerusalem was comparatively small," he said in measured tones. "As long as the rest of the country was fairly quiet, it was adequate to deal with local disorders. But when the Parthians overwhelmed the Roman legions in Syria, your allies in Asia Minor lost heart, and the situation took a drastic turn for the worse."

"And the people in Judea – how did they react?"

"When they learned about the rout of Saxas's troops," replied Herod, playing up the Roman defeat and glossing over Antigonus's enthusiastic reception by the Jewish population, "it was clear that Parthia was now the dominant power, at least for the time being, and so the people had no choice but to cooperate with it."

"How did they take to Antigonus's crowning?"

"I was no longer in the country."

"Of course not, I forgot. You were making your way to Egypt then, I take it."

"That's correct: to the royal court in Alexandria, to be precise. I must say, Cleopatra was very civil to me, and she even offered me the command of an expedition she was contemplating."

"An expedition!" exclaimed Octavian with an astonished look. He shifted his gaze to Antony, awaiting an explanation.

This revelation came as a surprise to Antony too. "This is news to me," he said with an uncustomary frown. "I had no inkling of it. Of course, communication with Egypt in winter is very slow, almost nonexistent, as you can gather from Herod's account of his voyage."

"But if she mentioned an expedition to Herod, she must have been contemplating it long before winter. Surely you must have some notion of what she had in mind," Octavian persisted in a voice that had suddenly hardened. "After all, Egypt is one of your provinces, by far the most important of all our Eastern provinces, in fact. And you, er, enjoyed very close relations with the queen."

Antony's brow wrinkled as he pondered the matter. "Yes, come to think of it, I believe I do have some idea of what she was referring to," he said after a while. "Because of the confusion of events at the time it slipped my mind. When I was about to leave Egypt I wasn't sure how the situation stood in Syria."

"Or in Rome either it seems," Octavian interjected with more than a trace of reproach.

Antony's gorge rose at this oblique reference to the conspiracy by his wife Fulvia and his brother Lucius, and he had to struggle to keep his cool. "Nor in Rome either," he conceded, glowering at Octavian. "Anyway, it was clear to me that the Parthians would have to be flushed out of the territories they had overrun. This was also clear to Cleopatra, who had no desire to see them on her doorstep. One of the options we discussed was a two-pronged attack, with the Romans advancing from the north and the Egyptians from the south. It was all quite vague. We didn't go into details, and the matter was left up in the air. I suppose it was this she had in mind."

"And you turned down her offer?" Octavian asked Herod somewhat incredulously.

"Yes, sir, I did," replied Herod in a firm voice. "I had one overriding desire – to reach Rome as quickly as possible."

"It was a very tempting offer," Octavian went on. "And you could have helped Rome out of a tight spot."

"I'm aware of that. It is my earnest desire to render whatever assistance I can to Rome. That, you undoubtedly know, has always been my policy. But I want it to be effective assistance."

"And you didn't think her proposal gave you an opportunity to render effective assistance?"

"I would prefer to put it differently. The way I saw it, it would be some time before Rome was in a position to take the field against the Parthians. In Egypt I would, in a sense, be more or less languishing in the meantime, not in the center of things."

"And the center, of course, is Rome?" Antony interposed.

"Rome above all, and Judea too – at least as regards the role I can most effectively play."

At this remark Antony and Octavian exchanged a meaningful look. "And in what role do you think you can most effectively serve our mutual interests?" asked Octavian.

This was the question Herod had been yearning to hear ever since he decided on his course of action after Phasael's death. He glanced first at Antony and then Octavian. His voice was calm and steady.

"As you know, for the past seven years I have faithfully served Rome in various capacities – first as governor of Galilee with the confirmation of the late noble Caesar, then as governor of Coele-Syria for his kinsman Sextus. I continued in this post under Cassius, not because I favored his cause, but because I favored the cause of Rome. And more recently Antony saw fit to appoint me, together with my late lamented brother, tetrarch, second only to Hyrcanus, the ethnarch and high priest. It was Caesar who first appointed Hyrcanus to these two offices, but the assumption of both the royal and priestly crowns by the same person was a relatively recent innovation. There are many in the country – and they constitute an influential and growing party – who strongly oppose this. The main reason is that in governing a country, a king – or an ethnarch, if you will – has to perform certain functions and take actions that are not considered compatible with the office of high priest."

"Caesar served as pontifex maximus, and so did many of our leading political figures," Antony pointed out. "What's wrong with that?"

"I'm not an authority on the Jewish religion. The sages could explain it to you much better than me. But I can say that the Jewish concept of the high priesthood differs from the Roman concept of the office of pontifex maximus. The Law of Moses puts great stress on holiness, or what can perhaps be described as spiritual perfection. For this reason the high priest, to take one example, may not come in contact with a dead body of any kind, for it is considered impure and so defiles him. He is even forbidden to set foot in a burial ground. On the other hand, as king he might have to wage war, and it would not be unusual for him to lead the army into battle. So it was with Hyrcanus's father Alexander Yannai, who was both king and high priest, and in his early days as high priest Hyrcanus himself had to fight against his own brother."

Herod saw that Antony and Octavian were impressed with his explanation. He did not, of course, tell them that there were other reasons for the people's discontent with the recent Hasmonean rulers, especially Yannai: the heavy taxes levied to finance his unceasing warfare, his recruiting of pagan mercenaries, the growing Hellenization of his court, and above all, his cavalier treatment of the Pharisees, which eventually led to the banishing or flight of many of the sages. Nor did Herod mention that Hyrcanus had respected and dealt generously with the Pharisees, thereby winning the favor of this party, which commanded the loyalty of the majority of the Jewish population, and apart from the armed struggle with his brother Aristobulus over twenty years ago, which was of the latter's making, he had basically sought to steer a peaceful course and would have been liked by most sections of the population except for one thing – his acquiescence in the Antipter's pro-Roman policy.

"In what office do you think Hyrcanus's subjects would have preferred him?" asked Octavian, regarding Herod closely.

Herod looked thoughtful for a moment, before replying. "The people respected him as high priest. In fact, I'd even go so far as to say that they probably revered him in that office. That's why Antigonus had his ears mutilated – to disqualify him from serving in the Temple."

"Antigonus doesn't have any qualms about being both king and high priest," remarked Octavian stiffly. "And according to our intelligence there isn't a great deal of opposition to him, if any at all. In fact, it seems that the Jews welcomed him with open arms."

This observation, with its implied censure, would have disconcerted Herod had he not anticipated it. Nevertheless, he hesitated for a moment before framing his reply. "A new man on the throne is very often welcomed by his subjects, even if his predecessor was well liked," he said guardedly. "Unless there is good reason to think otherwise, they assume that the new ruler will also be benevolent, and so they place high hopes in him. It's only when he begins to wield power, which must inevitably benefit some and disadvantage others, that they can really judge him. It's too early for the people to judge Antigonus's rule, and so naturally there is little or no opposition to him. But what will the situation be like half a year or a year from now? No one can know for sure, but I would like to emphasize one point that is of vital importance to Rome and was the cause of some controversy during Hyrcanus's reign. With all due modesty, let me remind you that Hyrcanus had the benefit of sagacious advice, first from my father and then from my brother and myself. It was no mere coincidence that on the whole relations with Rome were good and the land calm and peaceful during most of his reign. Now take Antigonus. He's totally different from the mild and peace-loving Hyrcanus. He's like his grandfather Yannai, whose greatest ambition was to conquer more and more territory and bring more and more people under his sway. This brought him into conflict with his own people, whose hatred of him grew increasingly intense. Antigonus also takes after his own father, of course, and I don't have to tell you what trouble he and his two sons caused Rome."

"I can personally vouch for that," said Antony with a grin as he rose and sauntered over to the wine bowl to refill his goblet. "I gained most of my early military experience fighting them. A troublesome lot they were."

Octavian moved restively on his chair. "This is all very interesting and important," he declared abruptly, "but we seem to be straying a bit. I originally asked Herod in what role he thinks he can best serve our mutual interests."

"Well, Herod, what do you say to that?" asked Antony, cocking his eye.

Herod took a deep breath. This was a fateful moment, and it was essential to strike the right note, sounding neither too covetous nor too modest. "As I have already pointed out," he replied in a calm, even voice, "I have been privileged to serve Rome in several important posts. The fact that I was chosen to do so by the foremost leaders of the empire is clear proof that they could rely on my unswerving devotion and ability. As tetrarch, I was second only to the ethnarch, and this gave me an opportunity to learn at first hand the problems facing the ruler of Judea and how to deal with them. Now that Hyrcanus has been exiled to Babylonia and is getting on in years, I am confident, in all due modesty, that it is in this role that I can be of greatest service to Rome. Rome could be assured that in my hands Judea would be a loyal and staunch ally."

At this declaration Antony smiled broadly; Octavian's brow furrowed deeply. Antony decided to let his fellow triumvir speak first. "To be perfectly frank," said Octavian, fixing Herod with his cool gray eyes, "we are not surprised by your statement. After receiving your letter we actually expected it, and have given some thought to the matter."

At this revelation Herod tensed with expectation. He waited impatiently for Octavian to continue. "We are fully aware of the devoted service you and your late father and brother have rendered Rome," he said, "and we know we can rely on your allegiance. But there are other considerations that have to be taken into account."

"May I ask what they are?" asked Herod, trying to avoid any indication of his sudden anxiety.

Octavian rose to his feet and walked over to the brazier to warm his hands. "When Rome has to appoint a king in one of the countries over which it has – ah, extended its protection," he explained in a casual tone, "its policy has been to choose a member of the old line wherever possible. This helps to avoid a struggle between rival claimants to the throne and generally ensures a greater degree of tranquility among the inhabitants, something we are most desirous to promote. This is a consideration we cannot ignore even in the case of Judea."

"Then you would prefer Antigonus?" Antony challenged Octavian with a toss of his curly head.

"Of course not!" retorted Octavian sharply. "I've already made that clear to you. But surely Antigonus is not the only male issue left of the Hasmonean line. There must be someone from Hyrcanus's side."

"He has no sons," Herod pointed out. "There's only one daughter."

"And she?"

"She has a daughter and a son. The son is thirteen, or maybe fourteen years old."

Octavian screwed up his face. "Fourteen years old? Hmm, too young for these precarious times."

"And too uncertain as regards his feelings toward Rome," added Antony emphatically. "We have no idea what his attitude is, or more important, what it will be when he grows up. Don't forget, his mother is not only Hyrcanus's daughter, she was married to Antigonus's brother. As I have already stressed, there's only one logical choice."

"Perhaps," said Octavian, returning to his seat. "But we must be prudent and consider all the possibilities and implications."

"I know!" snapped Antony, flinging his arm out in an exasperated gesture; "more haste, less speed."

"Exactly!" exclaimed Octavian with an annoyed look. He did not like having one of his favorite sayings flung in his face by Antony.

From the tenor of their remarks it was clear to Herod that Antony was backing him but Octavian was hesitant. "Permit me to say, sires," he broke in, forgetting Octavian's request regarding this title, "I can appreciate your caution. It is always advisable to consider all the possibilities and implications. And Rome's policy of choosing a new ruler from the reigning line wherever possible is a wise one – provided that other things are equal. But the question is, are they equal? As you yourself have so rightly pointed out, these are precarious times. The situation in Judea is fraught with grave danger as far as Rome is concerned, and it requires a firm, loyal hand at the helm there. I'm sure that you too will agree that this is the paramount consideration. As for choosing a ruler from the old line, permit me to remind you that I am espoused to Hyrcanus's granddaughter. This means that I will soon be a member of the royal family. So I think you can set your mind at rest on that score."

Antony's face lit up. "That solves it! A royal filly and a royal crown! Well, dear brother-in-law, what do you say to that?"

Octavian paused to reflect on Herod's statement. He could not deny that it would seem to meet his reservation. Still, the knowledge that Herod was Antony's man rankled. In case of future conflict with Antony, a possibility Octavian was realistic enough not to rule out, who would Herod side with? The matter was not as simple as Antony thinks. But something has to be done about Judea. It has to be regained from Parthian control, along with the other lands lost through Antony's blundering. And it has to be governed by someone Rome can rely on. There did not seem to be much choice. He turned to Herod and looked him straight in the eye. "Herod, king of Judea," he pronounced slowly and in a grave, well-modulated voice, his lips twisting into a thin smile. "How does that sound to you?"

Herod is Crowned "King of Judea" by the Senate

When Herod entered Antony's residence, it was with a feeling of hope and expectation mingled with anxiety; when he left, he was glowing with exultation. "Herod, King of Judea" – how impressive it sounded, and uttered by no less a personage than a triumvir of the mighty Roman Empire! This was the pinnacle of his long-nursed aspirations. Within a few days, Antony had informed him, the Senate would be convened to name him King of Judea, friend and ally of the Roman people. How grateful he was for the existence of this great empire, whose friend and ally he would soon be, not only in fact but in name.

His senses were fully alive, and everything took on a brilliant hue. As his litter bore him toward the Esquiline hill, he did not see the grime of the streets nor smell the stench; he saw throngs of people, and he wanted to proclaim to them that he, Herod, would soon be king. Three days, four days hence, you people will not be so nonchalant when I pass. Then you will stare with deference and awe and exclaim: "There goes Herod, King of Judea!"

His host, Lucius Marcellus, knew the moment Herod stepped into the house that the audience had gone well. He did not have to wait long to get a detailed description of the meeting, including the business of the picture Octavia had objected to, which he found very amusing. When Herod told him about the triumvirs' decision to name him King of Judea, he was duly impressed.

For the second night running Herod had trouble falling asleep. But this time the cause was feverish excitement after, rather than before, the audience. He tried to divert his thoughts to the entertaining comedy Lucius had taken him to the previous day, but his mind kept drifting back to Antony's office, reliving the scene word for word. He would no doubt be exhausted on the morrow, but he had time to recover before his appearance in the Senate.

As he lay on his bed, his whole life passed before him in his mind's eye. On the whole it formed a richly patterned mosaic bound up with the leading figures of the day, men who had shaped historic events. He reflected on the milestones in his own rise to power. It was not a straight, even road he had traversed, but one that had its twists and turns, its ups and downs. For the most part he had made gratifying progress, but there were also some pitfalls that had proved very vexatious. He grimaced when he recalled the humiliating summons by the Sanhedrin to answer charges of illegally executing the brigand Hezekiah in his capacity as governor of Galilee. His blood boiled when he recollected how they had sought to condemn him. But they'll pay dearly for their brazen insolence – of that they can be sure.

And then there was the abortive march on Jerusalem when he was governor of Coele-Syria. This had the approval, albeit somewhat less than enthusiastic, of Sextus Caesar; but how his father had upbraided him and made him feel thoroughly naive! He could clearly picture him, his arms akimbo, as he told him in no uncertain terms how rashly he was acting. His dearly beloved father – how wise and farsighted he was! What would he say now that his son was soon to be King of Judea? He would be very proud of course, but he would also offer words of advice in his calm, urbane manner. "Govern wisely, my son," he would no doubt urge. "Don't forget that your subjects don't have any great love for us; in fact, most of them heartily resent us. They don't regard us as fellow Jews; we're outsiders to them. They have never forgiven us our positions of influence or our pro-Roman leanings. They must be made to see that this is to their advantage. This will require patience and wise rule. You are by nature inclined to be impetuous and suspicious; you can be harsh – yes, admit it, even to the point of cruelty. You have learned over the years to temper your impetuosity, but you have yet to bridle your harshness. Be severe with those who deserve chastisement or seek to undermine you, but don't oppress the others. Heed my counsel and your reign will be a successful and memorable one; you will bring honor and distinction to yourself and to our house."

Antipater's imagined words were ringing in Herod's ears two days later when he and Lucius were riding to the Senate-house in his host's canopied litter. The weather smiled on Herod, for the previous day's cold rainstorm had passed, leaving the streets reasonably clean and free of foul odors. The red roofs of the houses, stretching in undulating waves across the hills of Rome, stood out vividly against a clear azure sky. The air was fresh and invigorating, the kind of weather that makes one glad to be alive and capable of doing great deeds. The streets were thronged more thickly than usual, for the previous day's inclement weather had forced most of the inhabitants to stay indoors, unable to attend to their purchases or other business. Lucius had taken this into account and allowed extra time for the journey, starting out well before mid-morning.

Like all his colleagues, Lucius did not attend every session of the Senate – it would have been impossible even to seat all of them in the Senate-house or the various temples where it convened – but he would not miss today's session for anything in the world. "It's not every day that I have an opportunity to see a new king confirmed by the Senate, let alone one who is my honored guest," he confided to Herod.

Lucius was in an expansive mood, entertaining Herod with choice items of political gossip when he was not pointing out important buildings and other sites of historical or general interest. When they reached the Sacred Way, Herod did not have to be told that he was approaching the heart of Rome. This was one of the most imposing streets in the metropolis. It was flanked by a serried mass of columns, statues, and porticoes. The numerous shops were more fashionable than any he had seen elsewhere in Rome, especially those displaying jewelry and metalwork.

"If you're impressed by what you've seen so far, wait till we come to the Forum and Capitol," commented Lucius in response to Herod's unstinting admiration. "This whole area is one we Romans are very proud of. It's the hub of Rome – the center of the commercial, government, and religious life of the empire. The Forum is where elections are conducted and the most important political events take place. This is the route of the triumphal processions of our victorious generals. They enter the city through the western Triumphal Gate, circle the Palatine hill, and then move down the Sacred Way to the Forum, ending up at the Temple of Jupiter on the Capitol.

"The triumphal processions are extraordinary. There's nothing like them for color: the flourish of trumpets, the soldiers in their smart military dress, the steeds in their burnished trappings and bright plumes, the spoils and trophies of the campaign, the tableaux, the general in his purple toga and rounded chariot, the cheering crowds. All this stirs your blood and makes you proud to be a Roman. I attended all five of Caesar's triumphal processions. The crowds cheered wildly – an incessant deafening roar. We're now going over part of the same route that Caesar and the others took. And this is your triumphal procession," Lucius added, clasping Herod by the shoulder. "Not in a chariot perhaps, no cheering crowds, but still your triumphal procession – your great day."

As they entered the Forum, Herod felt that he was truly on hallowed ground. It possessed a magnetic fascination for him. As Lucius had pointed out, nearly all the great political events had taken place here. In his own day, Antony had eulogized Caesar from the rostra at the upper end of the Forum, and Caesar's funeral pyre had been lit close by. It was from the same rostra that Cicero had delivered some of his famous orations. Others had been delivered in the Senate-house nearby, the venue of many a momentous debate that had shaped the course of Roman history as well as the fate of numerous other nations. The area was steeped in history – a vibrant, pulsating history. Right now it was thronged with people wending their way along the flagstone pavement or through the colonnades to attend to their business in the marketplace on the fringe of the Forum, or the law courts and offices of bankers in the basilicas, or moneychangers' booths, or the temples. It was a magnificent scene that greeted Herod's eye, with a multitude of statues surmounting splendid lofty temples and huge commemorative columns, and towering over all, the temples of Jupiter and Juno Moneta on the Capitoline hill.

Lucius was glad he had allowed extra time for the journey, for the Forum was rapidly filling up with handsome litters carrying their distinguished passengers to the Senate-house. "It looks like we're going to have a good turnout," he declared. "There's old Marcus Gellius," he said, waving to the passenger in the litter drawing abreast of his. "It's months since I've last seen him at a session. He suffers from a bad case of gout. If he's coming today, you can take that as a big compliment."

Lucius's litter came to a halt before the Senate-house, a yellowish-brick building whose austere lines contrasted strikingly with the magnificent, ornate exteriors of the temples and basilicas in the Forum. The two men alighted from the vehicle and joined the throng of Senators and visitors inching their way through the bronze portal into the vestibule. Here the Senators would await the signal to take their places in the chamber, while all others would remain in the vestibule.

The Senators were distinguished from the visitors by their dress: those of the highest rank – the magistrates and former magistrates – had a broad purple stripe on their white togas, while the ordinary Senators had a stripe of the same color on their tunics; all wore high red leather shoes. While awaiting the opening of the chamber, the Senators gathered in knots to exchange the latest news and gossip. When Lucius and Herod entered the vestibule, they came over to greet Lucius and to be introduced to Herod. Before long the vestibule was overflowing, and as still more people tried to squeeze their way in, an attendant opened the doors to the chamber. The Senators respectfully let Lucius and Herod enter first so they could occupy seats of their choice, and then they filed in to take their places on benches standing on three tiers ranged along the two sides of the oblong chamber.

"This is the best attendance I've seen in months," Lucius commented to Herod as they took seats close to the dais. "There's nothing the Romans like more than a spectacle, and the appointment of a king is always a fine show – and more humane than some others that are presented in the city."

Herod, attired in his most elegant garb, was buoyed by the drama unfolding before his eyes, in which he was the central figure. He surveyed the interior of the chamber. The walls were paneled in wood, the floor composed of mosaic in elaborate patterns. Along the walls stood statues in oval niches, and beneath each statue was a small altar on which incense was burning. The benches were all occupied, but the large marble chair in the middle of the dais and the ivory-inlaid curule seats on either side were still vacant.

At this point a rustling reverberated through the chamber as the Senators rose to their feet and turned toward the entrance. In strode Octavian and Antony, accompanied by a Senator of magisterial rank.

"That's the praetor Valerius Messala," Lucius enlightened Herod in an undertone. "He's the one who convened today's session and will preside."

Messala took his seat in the middle of the podium, flanked by the two triumvirs. Octavian sat down with slow dignity and stared before him with an aloof expression. Antony moved his seat a little to the right with his foot and sat down with a bold, pleased look. This was the first time Herod had seen him wearing a toga, and he found the effect a little startling.

Messala, a middle-aged man of moderate build and refined features, cleared his throat and began to speak in a low, well-modulated voice. He apologized to the honorable Senators for having convened them on such short notice, and thanked them for responding to his call; he was heartened to see how many were present today. He went on to relate how in days gone by the noble Cato would end his speeches in the Senate with the pronouncement that Carthage must be destroyed. Not that he, Messala, had any pretensions of emulating the great Cato or of producing the same dramatic effect. "But," he continued, raising his voice, "which of our distinguished colleagues did not feel the deepest chagrin and humiliation at Parthia's invasion of Rome's Eastern provinces, which sullied the honor of all good patriotic Romans? Resorting to deception and aided and abetted by the betrayal of the perfidious Labienus, they succeeded in gaining the upper hand over the valiant and heavily outnumbered Roman legions under the command of Saxa, who, true to the Roman code of honor, fought bravely to the death.

"The outcome was Parthian mastery over the Eastern provinces and Judea too. Judea is a small country but indispensable to Rome, as it is the bridge between Asia Minor and the most important kingdom in that part of the world – Egypt. It is absolutely essential that Judea be freed of its Parthian shackles."

Here Messala paused and glanced at Antony who nodded and rose to his feet, indicating his desire to speak. Messala gave him the floor. Antony gazed at the Senators, smiling at some and nodding to others. He was clearly in fine fettle. He complimented Messala on his lucid description of the situation confronting Rome and reiterated the need to bring Judea back into the Roman fold. To achieve this, Rome had to ensure that the man sitting on the throne be a friend and ally, whose loyalty could be relied upon. "The man who by a quirk of fate occupies the throne today is a mere puppet of the Parthians, a man of fractious, rebellious nature, who has always nursed a virulent hatred of Rome and, like his father and brother, has repeatedly taken up arms against it."

Antony went on in this vein, painting Antigonus in the darkest colors possible. He then pointed out that in glaring contrast to Antigonus has been the exemplary friendship and loyalty displayed by Herod. "He too joined his father and brother in playing an active role in the affairs of Judea," Antony stressed, "but his has been a praiseworthy role, distinguished by an appreciation of the mutual advantages of maintaining good relations with Rome." Antony then gave some notable examples of such cooperation. He was no mean orator, and Herod flushed with pleasure at the flattering description of his virtues, and especially when Antony declared that no one was more suited to govern Judea, that no one more fully understood that only in working hand in glove with Rome could he promote the welfare of his country and his subjects.

"It is essential," Antony stressed, "that the Parthians be expelled from the territories they have seized. We must make them disgorge their ill-gotten gains, and in this Herod can play an important role, giving assistance on the flank. And once the enemy is expelled from the land, peace and tranquility must be ensured. There is only one man who can be relied upon to perform this task competently and faithfully. The Senate is therefore requested to advise that Herod be named King of Judea." The vote was unanimous.

When Messala declared the session closed, Lucius embraced Herod and the Senators began to troop over to offer their congratulations. Herod felt supremely honored, for these were the richest and most powerful men in Rome. His heart beat a little faster when he saw Antony and Octavian approaching and the Senators making way for them. Octavian gave a thin smile and, a little stiffly, expressed his hope that Herod would fulfill the trust Rome placed in him. Antony, who always enjoyed making a spirited speech in the Senate and was especially pleased with the effect of his present effort, was more exuberant. "Well, Herod," he said with a big grin, "the crown of Judea is yours to wear now. It may not feel very heavy on your head, but it symbolizes a heavy responsibility – to your subjects and to Rome. So wear it well, for both our sake and Rome's."

When the triumvirs withdrew, Lucius informed Herod that the day's proceedings would be capped by a procession to the Capitol for the ceremonial sacrifice to Jupiter and the depositing of the Senate's decree. After the Senators filed out of the chamber, the ushers formed them into ranks. Heading the procession were the two consuls, Gnaeus Domitius Calvinus and Gaius Asinius Pollio; behind them came Herod, flanked by Antony and Octavian, and then Messala and the other Senators and distinguished visitors. A flourish of trumpets was the signal for the procession to start. In solemn step, as befitted a body of men conscious of their high station, it proceeded to the western end of the Forum and skirted the Temple of Saturn, ascended the steep, narrow street leading to the Capitol, a comparatively small area crowded with a number of temples as well as several shrines and altars and a host of statues of deities and famous Romans, including the early kings. The procession came to a halt before the Temple of Jupiter, the largest and most imposing temple of all. Dedicated to the chief god and his companion deities Juno and Minerva, it was the symbol of the sovereignty and power of Rome and its immortality. It had over the years become a repository of works of art of many sorts, the gifts of Roman generals and foreigners, as well as dedicatory offerings and trophies of victory.

The pediment and roof were decorated with terra cotta figures, and in front of the steps was a large altar where sacrifices were offered at the beginning of the year, at the celebration of triumphs, and various other major occasions like the present one. Herod gazed in fascination at the statue of Jupiter, which stood in the middle of three cellae. Tall and magnificently carved, the god held a thunderbolt in his right hand and was draped in a tunic adorned with palm branches and a purple toga embroidered with gold.

The procession came to a halt before the altar, on which a fire had been lit. Priests in white togas emerged from one of the cellae, and the victim, an ox with gilded horns, was led to the altar. The priests washed their hands with holy water from a special stoup and dried them on linen cloths. Then they covered their heads with the folds of their togas and took up a square wooden platter heaped with the sacred flour mixed with salt. This they sprinkled between the horns of the animal, held by attendants, and on the sacrificial knife. The sacrificing priest, standing on the right of the animal, asked Herod: "Do I strike?" Upon receiving an affirmative reply, he struck a well-aimed blow with a hammer at the animal's head, which stunned it and caused it to sink on its knees to the ground. Then a knifeman, holding its head upward, slit its throat. As Herod watched the victim expire, there flashed in his mind the second of the Ten Commandments, which forbids Jews to worship foreign gods. But he shrugged this off with a crooked grin. Didn't the Judeans insist that he was only a half-Jew? Besides, he was not really worshipping a strange god: He was merely conforming to Roman convention. No, there was no need for his conscience to trouble him.

The ceremony came to a close with the depositing of the Senate's decree. This was engraved on a bronze tablet, which had been prepared the day before. In slow, measured steps Messala proceeded with the tablet to the middle cella, and going around the statue of Jupiter, attached it to the wall, adding one more tablet to the many already there. Herod gazed at the tablet, his whole aspect suffused with pride and joy, his spirit exalted. His name was now emblazoned for all Rome to behold. Now he was officially King of Judea.

Chapter Six

Bringing Glory to the House of Antipater

Recruiting Mercenaries

Shortly after dawn on a cold mid-winter day a Roman war galley slipped past the two towers guarding the mouth of the Phoenician port of Ptolemais and berthed alongside one of the quays at the far end of the mist-shrouded harbor. No stevedores or porters were to be seen, nor was anyone on hand to greet the vessel apart from the harbor master and his assistant. The harbor master had been asleep in his quarters when an urgent message arrived from the towers informing him that a Roman trireme was approaching the port. He muttered a curse at being aroused from a sound sleep, but when his head had cleared enough for him to realize that the vessel was a Roman war galley, he was galvanized into action.

This was the worst time of the year for sailing. For weeks traffic in the port had been at a virtual standstill; the few vessels that made their way between the watchtowers were fishing smacks that cast their nets not far from shore or small coastal freighters that did not venture out of sight of land. That a Roman trireme braved the rough seas to reach Ptolemais would have struck him as incredible if the archon had not given him advance notice of its arrival. And this not only because of the weather, but even more because communication with Rome had been severed ever since Ptolemais opened its gates to the Parthian invader the year before. While no Parthian officials or troops were in the city or the immediate area, admitting a Roman ship – and a war galley at that – was a risky business.

The harbor master had tried to pump the archon for information, but that was like trying to pump blood out of a stone. All he could learn was that the vessel would be paying a brief visit, mainly to replenish its supplies of victuals and water. The archon had cautioned him not to talk about the ship to outsiders, for reasons he was not at liberty to divulge. This had exasperated the harbor master. He pointed out sarcastically that the arrival of a large ship at this time of the year was bound to excite the curiosity of every man, woman, and child in Ptolemais, and once they discovered it was a Roman trireme, they would flock to the port to get a close look. Perhaps the archon wanted him to wrap the ship in goatskins in order to hide it from public view? The archon's reply had been brusque and frosty: Shut the gates to the port and keep the people out.

* * *

Herod heaved a sigh of relief as he prepared to disembark. The voyage had taken the better part of a month and was by no means a pleasure cruise. It had been almost as rough as during the latter part of his crossing from Alexandria to Rhodes, but the trireme rode out the heavy seas better than the Greek freighter. Apart from the voyage itself, whose ill effects would pass off in a day or so, Herod was even more relieved at the absence of any attempt to prevent the ship from entering the harbor. Saramella had done his job well, he acknowledged with a satisfied grin.

When the euphoria he felt after being named king of Judea had worn off, Herod was seized with apprehension over his likely reception by the authorities of Ptolemais. The city had surrendered without a fight to the Parthians, and reportedly was anxious not to antagonize them in any way. It could hardly be expected to welcome anything that jeopardized this relationship. Yet Herod had to somehow get permission to land there and establish a base of operations. Ptolemais was geographically close to Judea and, even more important, free of enemy troops; it was about the only place where he could hope to raise and train an army in relative safety.

When Herod had pondered his situation before embarking, its incongruity struck him full force. Here he was, a newly crowned king without a throne, money, or army. All he possessed was a mandate from Rome to press ahead with preparations to wrest the Judean throne from Antigonus. As for Roman military and financial assistance, Antony and Octavian had made it clear that at this juncture they could not spare it, because they were preparing for their imminent campaign against the Parthians in northern Syria and Asia Minor. But if Herod did not possess material or financial resources, he had supreme confidence in his ability and destiny; he also had an influential friend whose help he knew he could count on. So several days before leaving Rome, he had written to Saramella, thanking him once again for his efforts to save his brother Phasael from a dire fate at the hands of the Parthians, and then explaining his present predicament. His request to Saramella had been twofold: first, to persuade the elders of Ptolemais to allow him to land there and set up a base of operations; and second, to give Herod a loan to finance the raising of a mercenary force.

To help win over the city elders, Herod had suggested that Saramella should stress Rome's preparations for an early campaign against the Parthians, which was sure to end in their defeat. "You know what else it will probably take to induce the elders to give their consent," Herod had added. "Be as generous as you think necessary, for I assure you that you will be fully reimbursed for every drachma you expend on my behalf."

Since it was essential that this letter reach Saramella as quickly as possible, Antony had arranged to send it by overland courier service, which, he had assured Herod, should deliver it within a week to ten days, depending on the weather. The logical thing would have been for Herod to await Saramella's reply before proceeding further; but Antony had explained that in view of the plans he and Octavian had drawn up for preparing and dispatching a Roman force to Asia Minor, it was to their advantage that Herod proceed without delay to Ptolemais. To Herod's protest that he had no way of knowing how successful Saramella would be, especially with respect to the reception he could expect at Ptolemais, Antony had bade him set his mind at rest: He would send his own message to the city elders, which would convince them of the seriousness with which Rome viewed this request.

Herod was in an excellent mood as he walked down the gangplank, followed by his aide and two slaves carrying his luggage. Everything seemed to be going smoothly so far, much more so than he had expected. The harbor master had sought him out in his cabin and informed him that accommodations had been arranged for them, and as soon as their luggage was off the ship, they would be driven to their destination. This turned out to be the villa of Lysias, a middle-aged well-to-do merchant who, when Herod was governor of Coele-Syria, once had occasion to petition him for a favor.

"It's an honor for me to be able to repay your kindness," he said to Herod that evening as they were comfortably seated in a warm, richly furnished room leading off the atrium. "And Saramella's too. We're very good friends, you know. In fact, it was to me that he came after getting your letter."

"Judging by my reception so far, it's obvious that you possess considerable influence with the elders of the city," commented Herod, putting his half-drained wine goblet down on a small marble table.

"It so happens that I'm one of the elders," acknowledged Lysias with a smile. "But of course matters of such great import must be carefully studied and deliberated by all the elders, and here you can thank your friend Saramella. He was most persuasive in presenting your petition."

"I'm very grateful for his invaluable assistance, and yours too. I realize that my petition was unusual and quite delicate."

"Indeed it was. At first we were rather skeptical; in fact, I would even say we were taken aback by your request. It seemed to pose grave dangers to the safety of our city, and most of the elders were inclined to reject it outright. But Saramella convinced us that it was to our advantage to admit you, which sentiments were strengthened by Antony's letter. What finally allayed our doubts was Saramella's assurance that you would take every possible precaution to minimize the potential dangers inherent in this situation."

The last sentence was uttered in a tone of voice and accompanied by a look that clearly indicated that Herod's confirmation was desired on the point in question. He uncrossed his legs and leaned forward. "I can appreciate your concern," he replied with a serious expression. "I have been fully aware of the problem from the very start and have given much thought to it. If any danger comes to Ptolemais, it will also endanger my enterprise. It is essential that my activities attract as little attention as possible. It would therefore be most advantageous if I could secure the use of premises outside the city walls – preferably located, say, in a secluded wooded area which would offer a reasonable degree of concealment from cautious eyes."

Lysias mulled this over for a moment. "Yes, that would be a sensible thing to do – very sensible for both you and us. Of course, there is no guarantee that you will be able to keep your activities completely hidden from view, especially when the number of men involved increases. But I think it's a risk we can live with, at least for the time being. And I think I have just the place for you – one that will suit your needs and ours."

The place Lysias had in mind turned out to be a rambling country house a few miles from the city. Set amid thick groves of pine and cedar, as well as orchards of various kinds, which were now bare but would provide an additional mantle of green in another month or so, and surrounded by a high wall that hid the grounds from the gaze of outsiders, it was an ideal site for Herod's purposes.

Now that this problem was solved, Herod had to wait for Saramella to put funds at his disposal. This took about a week, after which he set to work getting the premises into shape and recruiting a force of mercenaries. He decided to choose his officers from among those who had previously served under him and proved their mettle. Although the number of men involved was not large, it was time-consuming to approach each of them separately, for they lived in different Greek cities in the coastal area and the interior of the country. He would have preferred to form the nucleus of his force with Cilicians and Phisidians, who had proved to be tough, disciplined soldiers, but to recruit men in territory under the nose of the Parthians was out of the question. He therefore decided to turn to the nearby Greek cities. This was not an ideal solution, for relations between Greeks and Jews had been marked by considerable friction. To Jews the very presence of pagan Greek cities in the Holy Land was a painful reminder of the low state to which the nation had fallen after the destruction of the Temple and dispersion to Babylonia. No less disturbing was the Greek cities' role in disseminating Hellenism, which the Jews regarded as a grave threat to their divinely ordained way of life.

Herod himself was an ardent admirer of Hellenism, and he intended to make the Greek cities an important prop in his realm, not least in order to counteract the Jews' antipathy to him. He realized that Hellenism and Judaism were inherently incompatible and could not exist side by side without generating friction. But the Jews would constitute the majority of his subjects, and while he would not brook any opposition from them and was determined to mercilessly stamp out the slightest manifestation of it, it was not advisable to deliberately provoke them. So, while he had no choice at this stage but to raise the bulk of his force from among the Greek cities, he intended later on to rely to a significant extent on his Idumean compatriots, whom he could trust and who were at least nominally Jewish to boot.

The next few months were a period of intense activity: recruiting mercenaries and whipping them into an efficient fighting machine. The latter task Herod assigned to Nikias, his trusted lieutenant during the Jerusalem siege. Herod watched with patent satisfaction as the force grew in numbers and preparedness, and he eagerly awaited the day when it would be ready to take the field, to launch the campaign that would culminate in the vanquishing of Antigonus and possession of the coveted throne of Judea. Not for one moment did he doubt his success: he was fully confident that his guardian spirit, which on the whole had prospered his endeavors, even turning what at times had first seemed a setback into a shining triumph, would continue to guide him along the path that led to glory and greatness. The very contemplation of this prospect filled him with elation.

There was another reason why he was impatient to give his men the order to march. Ever since he left his family at Masada, their welfare had caused him considerable concern. He was not worried about their physical safety, but about the anguish they must be suffering because of the oppressive siege conditions, and even worse, uncertainty about his own fate. He had several times tried to get a message to them; but even though the couriers had taken the utmost precaution, they had failed to get through the enemy lines.

It was now more than half a year since he had left them, and he was yearning to see them again, especially his mother. He was, somewhat to his own surprise, more than a little curious about Mariamne. At her age she had undoubtedly matured perceptibly in the meantime. He had to admit, with a tinge of conscience, that apart from the voyage to Rhodes, when time had hung heavily on his hands, she had hardly been in his thoughts. The intervening period had been so packed with dramatic events that she seemed far away in more than one sense. Had she thought about him at all during his absence? She must have, for while the most momentous event in his life so far had been the impressive session of the Roman Senate followed by the majestic ceremony on the Capitoline hill, the most important event in Mariamne's life was unquestionably the betrothal. Not that he had any illusions on this score. It was quite clear that she was not ecstatic about the betrothal; it was something that had been arranged for reasons of high policy, and which she, as an obedient daughter – or more precisely, granddaughter – was duty-bound to accept. Yet he had to make allowance for the fact that she was young and inexperienced in the ways of the world – a rose just beginning to bloom. He, on the other hand, was in the prime of life, a man of no little consequence, who was on friendly terms with some of the greatest personages of the day, a man experienced with women. But Mariamne would mature fast enough; in another two or three years she would be an extraordinary beauty – a proud and, he suspected, a somewhat arrogant one. For she was a Hasmonean, and the Hasmoneans were a proud family with an inflated opinion of themselves, who were unaware that the radiance once associated with their name was dimming rapidly. But, he had to admit, they still stirred the hearts of the Jews – that he could personally attest to. They occupied a prominent place in the annals of the Jewish nation, and he envied them for that. But the house of Herod would occupy an even more prominent place. And its greatness would not be confined to tiny Judea; Herod's name would resound throughout the Greco-Roman world.

By the beginning of summer, Herod's mercenaries numbered some 2,000, and in another month or so he expected to have another 1,000 or more under his banner. A force this size could not, of course, be kept from the enemy's eyes, and it had to fend off increasingly frequent attacks by bands emanating from Galilee. This, however, did not perturb Herod. On the contrary, he and Nikias welcomed it, because the skirmishes hardened their men and provided a good test of their performance. Their success in beating off the foe with only light losses boosted their morale immensely and made them all the keener to do battle.

Herod had from the start decided that his initial major objective was to raise the siege of Masada and set his family free. He and Nikias spent many hours studying a rough-drawn map to determine the best line of march to take. From information his scouts had gathered on the disposition of Antigonus's troops and considering the lay of the land, the best prospect seemed to be to move down the coastal plain to Ascalon and then advance eastward through Idumea to Masada. In his native Idumea, Herod was counting on filling out his ranks with his compatriots, who, he knew, would be eager for the opportunity to win rich booty and, for some, high office in his administration. But before reaching Idumea it would be necessary to reduce Joppa, the major stronghold blocking his way.

By late summer Herod and Nikias considered their army sufficiently large and trained to move. The inhabitants of Ptolemais turned out en masse to watch its departure, for they loved a spectacle. The elders of the city, however, breathed a sigh of relief as the foot soldiers, archers, javelin-throwers, and slingers marched through the city gate and disappeared down the coastal road. The skirmishes with the Galilean bands had made the elders increasingly nervous, and they feared a possible punitive action by the Parthians for having harbored their enemies. Their fears were allayed only when reports reached them that Rome had dispatched an army under the command of Publius Ventidius to Asia Minor, which would undoubtedly engage the Parthians' complete attention. This turn of events was welcomed by Herod, for he could now feel more secure against any possible Parthian intervention against his force, especially as it advanced on Joppa.

Misery in Masada

Perched atop a craggy rock that soared precipitately to a height of almost 1,300 feet and commanding a clear view of vast stretches of surrounding territory – the Dead Sea, the mountains of Moab, and the tawny, crinkled desert marching into the distance as far as the eye can see – Masada kept a lonely watch over Judea's southern border. From time immemorial this strategic height had provided a haven to those fleeing persecution or seeking the solace of isolation. But it was only during the reign of Alexander Yannai about half a century earlier that its large flat summit was converted into a virtually impregnable fortress.

In leaving both his family and Alexandra's with a garrison of 800 picked troops under the command of his younger brother Joseph, Herod was confident when he set out on his fateful journey to Rome that they would be safe from any enemy force that might try to storm Masada or lay siege to it. But if Masada gave them a sense of security, it was inevitable that after being confined here for a protracted period they would succumb to ennui.

As the weeks and months passed and no word was received from or about Herod nor any sign of relief appeared, Alexandra found it increasingly difficult to keep up the spirits of her two children, not to mention her own. She kept them indoors as much as possible during the daytime in order to protect them from enemy arrows and missiles. This made them all the more restless: healthy, energetic youngsters, they chafed at this forced confinement, which followed on the heels of the harrowing siege of the royal palace in Jerusalem. They missed their friends, the companionship of children their own age. They felt like prisoners, except that prisoners were not exposed to such dangers as they had to face the past year. True, the siege of Masada was not nearly as oppressive as the one in Jerusalem. The garrison easily warded off the sporadic assaults by Antigonus's men, and the stock of victuals would suffice for many months. Water, however, presented a worrisome problem. The capacity of the cisterns was not unlimited, and there was no way to replenish them until the winter rains. Joseph had early on instituted a strict rationing of this most vital necessity.

As in Jerusalem, Alexandra tried to keep a distance between her family and Herod's, especially Salome, who was becoming increasingly irascible. She screamed at Mariamne and Aristobulus whenever she chanced upon them, and frequently even vented her spleen on the members of her own family. Alexandra often heard her voice raised against her brother and sometimes even her mother. As a rule Joseph, who possessed a more equable temper than the rest of the family, would let Salome shout herself hoarse and then calmly put her in her place. Alexandra had several encounters with her, which invariably ended in vicious accusations against Alexandra's "cursed kinsman, who was the cause of all their suffering." Alexandra knew it was pointless to try and reason with her; in fact, she found it repugnant to speak with her at all and would generally turn away with a contemptuous toss of her head. But when Salome's ranting was directed at her children, she did not hesitate to give her a piece of her mind.

At night, when the children had gone to bed, she would tell them legends and other tales about their people and especially their own forbears, who had performed heroic deeds for the nation, delivering it from the cruel yoke of the pagan Syrian-Greeks, who had persecuted the Jews for practicing their religion. "It's the story of a few against many," she related with manifest pride. "The enemy sometimes numbered tens of thousands, and they were armed with all the weapons of warfare, even elephants. Our Hasmonean forbears – Mattathias, his eldest son Judah, who was called the Maccabee, and Judah's four brothers – usually had less than two or three thousand men under their command. But they possessed something the enemy did not have: an unshakable faith in the Almighty and a fierce determination to break the yoke of the pagan, to cleanse the land of the abominations that had been forced on it. And in the end they prevailed. That is why their name, their brave deeds, have ever since struck such a resounding chord in the hearts of our people. We have a glorious tradition to uphold, you and I. You can be proud to be a Hasmonean, my children. Never forget that. Let that always be your guiding light when, with the Lord's help, you grow up and assume the responsibility of leadership."

Aristobulus, in particular, never tired of hearing about these heroic exploits, and he would often ask his mother to relate them again. But one night, instead of dropping off to sleep with a serene expression, he sat up and looked at her with a puzzled frown: "If our forbears did so much for our people," he said a little hesitantly, "why are we hiding from Antigonus? He's my uncle; doesn't he like us any more? Why did he make us run away from Jerusalem, where all my friends are? And why did he make Grandpa leave us and go to Babylonia? I miss him very much, even if he likes to tweak my ears."

This question, asked with all the innocence and seriousness of a thirteen-year-old, made Alexandra's heart skip a beat. She felt the same whenever Mari-amne asked her – heaven knows how many times – why she, a Hasmonean prin-cess, was betrothed to someone like Herod. In both cases Alexandra fobbed her children off with a vague, indefinite reply. How could she explain to them the reasons for their predicament? These questions always upset her, and she would not sleep well afterward. She herself was perplexed at the way fate had buffeted her: widowed at a comparatively young age these nine years under cruel circum-stances, her father rendered physically disqualified for the high priesthood and languishing in exile, her daughter betrothed to a man beneath her station and hated by her people. And why? Because her father was deadly afraid of his own nephew and for the safety of his grandchildren. To such a pass had things come!

A woman of lesser fortitude would have succumbed to despair. The clouds started to gather on her horizon when she was only a few years older than Mari-amne today. Life in the royal palace had been pleasant, and she cherished fond memories of that period. Sitting on the throne of Judea was her grandmother Salome Alexandra, and while no longer young (she was in her sixties), she was vigorous and clear-headed till the very end. Apart from the Sadducees, she was loved by her people, who found her a sagacious and benevolent ruler, who worked indefatigably for the good of the realm. Peace had returned to the land after the turbulent years of warfare waged by her husband Alexander Yannai; the Pharisees provided wise spiritual and religious leadership after winning control of the Sanhedrin, the supreme judicial-religious institution, from the Saddu-cees; the harvests had never been more bountiful. A cheerful, optimistic atmo-sphere prevailed in the land and court. Dignitaries and other important visitors from Babylonia, Egypt, Rome, and the rest of the Diaspora sought audiences with the queen and her first-born son Hyrcanus, whom she had appointed high priest, an office for which he was admirably suited by temperament and training and which he delighted in performing.

Alexandra had been a very beautiful maiden – so she had often been told by her grandmother and parents. Wherever she went in Judea or elsewhere her physical charm and engaging personality had won ungrudging admiration, in-cluding that of her cousin Alexander. Tall, handsome, and well built, he cut a dashing figure; he also possessed a strong character, being energetic, bold, fiercely patriotic. But little did she dream that their marriage would take place in the circumstances in which it did: to effect a reconciliation between their respec-tive fathers after a bitter struggle for the throne of Judea, which had degenerated into internecine strife. Hyrcanus, who as the first-born had been designated as the queen's successor, was forced to surrender royal power to his brother after being defeated in battle shortly after their mother's death. He once confided to Alexandra that he would have been content to let his younger brother wear the royal crown if he could continue to serve as high priest, but Aristobulus coveted both crowns.

The aristocratic Sadducee party had found in Aristobulus a kindred spirit and backed him to the hilt, but in the eyes of the rest of the populace he too closely resembled his father, Alexander Yannai, who had waged an incessant campaign of territorial expansion against the neighboring peoples, in the process alienating his heavily taxed subjects and in particular the Pharisees, who had come to regard the king's wars as fought more for self-aggrandizement than the legitimate restoration of Judea's historical borders, and unbecoming to one who also served as high priest.

Alexander Yannai's reign came to an end after twenty-seven years, but the stage was now dominated by a family whose machinations eventually brought disaster to the state of Judea and the Hasmonean house alike. In the conflict between the two Hasmonean contestants for the throne, Antipater saw a golden opportunity. Crafty, calculating, an adroit negotiator, he was content to wield power behind the scenes, which was the most he could hope for in the circumstances. Upon the death of Salome Alexandra, whom he had served as governor of Idumea, he shrewdly sized up the situation. He had reason to distrust and fear Aristobulus, who was spirited, ambitious, militaristic, and hardly likely to appreciate Antipater's service to his mother. In stark contrast to his brother, Hyrcanus was conciliatory and pliant.

Antipater repeatedly reminded Hyrcanus that as the first-born he was the rightful heir to both the high priesthood and the throne, and the people much preferred him to his brother. To Antipater's dismay, however, his exhortations fell on deaf ears; Hyrcanus was too dispirited to respond to them. When he saw that he could not budge him, Antipater resorted to a different stratagem, confiding that he had secret information that Aristobulus was plotting to eliminate him, and advising him to take measures to save himself. At first Hyrcanus refused to believe that his brother was capable of such a vile deed, but Antipater gave him no respite, constantly urging him to flee to neighboring Nabatea. Hyrcanus finally yielded and sought asylum there. Antipater then persuaded the ruler of that kingdom – by offering him the return of twelve cities that had been seized from Nabatea by Alexander Yannai – to march with a large army against Aristobulus and depose him. Aristobulus was defeated, but the issue was not finally resolved until Pompey arrived on the scene and decided in favor of Hyrcanus, who, largely because of Antipater's influence, was more tractable to Rome.

Aristobulus stoutly resisted Pompey, but by the time the fighting came to an end, Jerusalem had fallen to the Romans, Aristobulus and his younger son Antigonus were taken prisoners to Rome (his elder son Alexander had escaped), and the high priesthood was restored to Hyrcanus, who was simultaneously appointed ethnarch, or political head, of the state of Judea. But Judea was no longer independent, being reduced in area and autonomy and made dependent on the Roman governor of Syria, to whom he had to pay tribute.

The conflict between the two branches of the Hasmonean house had greatly distressed the entire nation, but no one more so than Alexandra. For her it had been a personal tragedy: She was loyal to her husband and she dearly loved her father. To him she was more than a daughter: She was both daughter and son – the son the good Lord had denied him. Her greatest desire was to repay him in some measure for everything he had done for her, to bring him whatever happiness she could. She was aware that while he was generally well liked by the people as high priest, many felt that he had been too pliant in his relations with Rome, too subservient to its interests, and therefore as much to blame as Aristobulus for the loss of independence.

She herself was of two minds about Rome. It was as plain to her as it was to her father that Rome was the greatest power in the world, and it would be foolhardy to openly oppose or antagonize it. But, and on this point she had taken issue with her father, this did not mean that Judea had to meekly submit to Rome's every dictate. This, she feared, would only lower Judea in Rome's eyes and invite humiliating submission to every pernicious whim of Rome's rulers, who were hardly likely to properly appreciate the national-religious sensitivities of the Jewish people. It was therefore imperative to seek a middle path in Judea's relations with Rome. She had sought to persuade her husband, no less than her father, of the wisdom of such a course. But Alexander had belittled Rome's power, arguing that Parthia was more than a match for it, as clearly attested by the crushing defeat Crassus had suffered at their hands. Alexandra had cautioned him against underestimating the Romans, but to no avail. Even before her marriage she was filled with dread every time Aristobulus or his sons took the field against them; but this was nothing compared with how she had felt the day Alexander was seized by the Romans.

It had come like a bolt out of the blue. Alexandra had no way of knowing that when Caesar had become master of Rome after Pompey fled the country, he released Alexander's father from captivity with the intention of sending him back to Syria with two Roman legions at his disposal in order to win support for Caesar's cause in that country. But partisans of Pompey had gotten wind of this and poisoned Aristobulus, while Pompey ordered the governor of Syria to seize Alexander and execute him.

His death had shattered Alexandra. If it were not for the children – the need to look after them, the hopes she reposed in them – she doubted if she could have carried on. Her father had consoled her, assuring her that time would help to ease the pain. But now, nearly ten years later, the wound was still raw. Her sleep was often disturbed by nightmares; she would wake with a start, her heart palpitating, her brow and the palms of her hands clammy. She was careful not to let the children know her anguish. She always put on a brave face in their presence, but with the passing of the years she felt more and more like a withering flower, her beauty fading and wasted. Her father had often urged her to remarry, insisting that she was too young to remain a widow, that sterile widowhood was not good for her or her children. He even suggested a number of suitable matches. But she could not bring herself to seriously consider the matter. For what reason, she herself was not certain. Was it because she felt that she would be betraying Alexander's memory if she married another? Or could it be that family pride had conditioned her against marrying someone who did not have Hasmonean or at least aristocratic blood in his veins? It might also be that she did not want to do anything that could prejudice her son's succession to the high priesthood, and – who could tell? – perhaps even the throne. Whatever the reason, she had to acknowledge that her father was right: Sterile widowhood was not good for her or her children. She was still physically attractive and longed to share her life with a man of her own class, who could also help fill the void in her children's lives, especially now that their grandfather was no longer around to do so.

As autumn drew to a close and there was still no word from Herod, life at Masada took on a more somber aspect. The prolongation of the siege was exacerbating its ill effects on the civilians confined there and even the soldiers. Aristobulus, for one, was having bad dreams, and this troubled Alexandra. Even more worrisome to all concerned was the water supply. Despite strict rationing, the situation was becoming desperate, and it was clear to Joseph that until the start of the winter rains he would have to reduce the already small daily ration. He issued orders that henceforth every man, woman, and child would be limited to one pitcher a day for all needs. The soldiers, who were inured to a strict water regimen, took this in their stride, but for the others it imposed a real hardship. For Alexandra it became especially serious when Aristobulus developed a high fever. His daily ration barely sufficed to quench his thirst, let alone provide for other needs. The first few days Alexandra gave him part of her ration, but as this did not leave enough for cooking and her personal needs, she decided to approach Joseph on the matter. "Until now I haven't asked for any favors," she explained to him. "I didn't want any special privileges, either for myself or for my children. But now it's a question of Aristobulus's health."

"How long has he been ill?" asked Joseph solicitously.

"Four days, or to be more exact, nearly five. I must admit I'm worried. Instead of getting better, his fever seems to be worse. He's had fever many times before, of course, but not as bad as now."

"We're fortunate to have a physician here," said Joseph with genuine concern. "I'll tell him to examine your son."

"That's very kind of you, but he's already examined Aristobulus. I asked him to do so yesterday."

"And?"

"He said the fever may get worse in the next two or three days, but then it would probably break. He's given Aristobulus some medicine, which he said should help. In the meantime he said Aristobulus should drink a lot. That's why I've come to you."

"I see. So you want more water, do you? That's no problem. Tell your daughter to bring an extra pitcher with her until your boy is better. And if you need some water right now, tell her to go to the soldier in charge of the distribution. I'll see to it that he's notified."

Alexandra, who had early on discovered that Joseph was a kind person, was visibly relieved. "I'm very grateful to you. You're most considerate."

"Not at all," replied Joseph with a deprecatory gesture. "I'm glad to be of service to you. I wish your son better."

Upon returning to her apartment Alexandra gave Mariamne an empty pitcher and told her to take it to the soldier in charge of the water supply.

"Does he know he has to fill it up?" she asked hesitantly.

"Yes, darling. Now run along."

Mariamne hurried out with the pitcher. When she returned, she was trembling, her face was white, her eyes red from tears.

"Darling, what happened?" asked Alexandra, alarmed.

"That, that wicked Salome," Mariamne blurted out between sobs.

"What did she do? And where's the pitcher of water?"

"It's broken!"

"Broken? How did that happen?"

"She – that horrible old witch – she broke it. She pulled it out of my hands and threw it on the ground. It smashed to pieces."

Alexandra clasped Mariamne to her bosom and let her cry. When she calmed down a bit, Alexandra asked her to explain what happened.

"After the soldier filled the pitcher, I started to go back the same way I came. All of a sudden there was that horrible witch in front of me. I didn't see her coming. If I had, I would have kept out of her sight until she was gone."

"And then?"

"And then she asked me in that screechy voice of hers what I was doing with a pitcher of water. I tried to ignore her and get past her. But she wouldn't let me; she grabbed hold of me and yelled, 'I asked you a question and I demand an answer!'"

This information filled Alexandra with cold anger, but she kept her composure. "What did you tell her?"

"I told her the truth – that it was for Aristobulus, who is ill."

"Then what happened?"

"She began to scream that just because I'm a Hasmonean I think I'm better than everyone else and can get whatever I like. She said there are no privileged people here. She grabbed the pitcher out of my hands and smashed it on the floor. She's horrible, she is! I don't ever want to see her again. I hate her! I hate her!"

Alexandra waited until Mariamne's fury cooled somewhat, and then asked in a quiet tone: "Why didn't you explain that it was at Joseph's order that you got the water?"

"I did tell her that. I forgot to mention it to you."

"And what did she say to that?"

"She said I was a big liar."

"I see," said Alexandra, a steely look crossing her face. "She'll soon find out whether you were lying or not. Go back to Aristobulus and keep him company. I'll be back soon."

Alexandra returned to Joseph's headquarters and related what had happened.

"I'm sorry about this," he said apologetically. "The situation must be affecting Salome's nerves; that's the only way I can explain it. I'll have a talk with her. In the meantime tell your daughter to bring another pitcher, and I'll have one of my men accompany her back to your son."

When Alexandra withdrew it was with some doubt that Joseph would rebuke his sister; but she hoped that he would at least make it clear that she was not to give free rein to her tongue and that she must act with at least a modicum of decency toward Mariamne.

It was not until the following afternoon that Joseph summoned Salome. She stalked into his room with head held high and breathing defiance. "Yes, my young brother," she said challengingly in her strident, high-pitched voice, "you wished to see me?"

Joseph knew that this was not going to be a pleasant scene. He looked his sister straight in the eye; she returned his gaze unflinchingly, her lips twisted in a tight, scornful grin. He was painfully familiar with that look. "Please sit down," he said a little stiffly.

"No, thanks," Salome snapped. "I prefer to stand."

"Very well, suit yourself."

Joseph tapped the table abstractedly. How formidable she looks, he thought to himself. She was clearly prepared to cross verbal swords with him; in fact, he knew she was itching to do so. "Salome," he said in an even, matter-of-fact voice, "you called me your young brother; you even stressed that word. It's true I'm younger than you, but I happen to be in charge of this garrison. And I was put in charge by your older brother. I'm responsible for the safety and welfare of the soldiers and all civilians entrusted to my care, including you, our mother, Alexandra, and her two children. And so..."

"And who is stopping you from fulfilling your responsibility?" Salome interjected. "I don't see why you had to send one of your minions to call me. If there is something important you want to discuss with me, you could have come yourself. Or you could have waited until we were all together tonight."

"Yes, I could have done that. I also could have summoned you yesterday and not today. But I purposely waited in order to let you have second thoughts, to cool off a bit and think rationally."

"To think rationally about what?" Salome spat out. "I've no idea what you're getting at. And I resent being spoken to in this manner, my young brother. Come to the point or I'll leave!"

Joseph's countenance changed abruptly. "You'll stay put until I dismiss you!" he barked.

Salome gaped at Joseph incredulously. He had never before spoken to her in such a sharp tone. Her face was contorted with wrath. "I never thought I'd see the day when my brother – my *young brother* – would dare to speak to me like that," she retorted through clenched teeth. "I've had enough of your impertinence!"

She turned on her heels and headed for the door. Joseph sprang to his feet and blocked her way. "Oh no, you're not walking out on me! You'll leave when I say you can. Now sit down!"

To make sure he was obeyed, Joseph took his sister by the shoulders and forced her into the chair. "Let's get this straight," he went on, standing over Salome menacingly, "I'm speaking to you now not as your brother, but as commander of this garrison. I want to know why you snatched the pitcher of water out of the girl's hands yesterday and spilled it on the floor."

"So that's what is eating you, is it?" she said in a voice more rasping and contemptuous than before.

"Yes, that's what is eating me," replied Joseph, setting his mouth firmly. "And you knew it when you walked into this room. So do me the kindness and explain yourself."

"Very well, my dear commander. But with your kind permission I'll first straighten my tunic. I'm not accustomed to being seated so rudely."

Salome proceeded to leisurely smooth her tunic, after which she fixed her brother with a dark look. "For your information, I not only spilled the water on the floor, I smashed the pitcher in the bargain. And I'll do it again if I catch that little brat pulling the same trick."

"Pulling what trick?" exclaimed Joseph, his eyes narrowing.

"Taking more than her fair share of the water. If our precious water has to be rationed, then let it be rationed for everyone. There are no privileged characters here. I won't tolerate any special treatment."

Joseph gaped at his sister incredulously. "*You* won't tolerate!" he sputtered. "It doesn't matter the slightest whether *you* tolerate it or not. This is a matter for me to decide and nobody else. I want that to be absolutely clear! Do you understand?"

There was a biting scorn in Salome's glance. "No, I don't understand. When we've been confined here for months on end, like a flock of chickens in a coop, all because of Alexandra's brother-in-law, I don't think that she – or her precious daughter – is entitled to any special privileges."

Joseph folded his arms across his chest. "Now let's get this straight, dear sister. Alexandra's son has a high fever, and she asked permission for some extra water for his burning thirst. And that was the physician's orders too. I gave her permission. I'd do the same for anyone else in the same circumstances – including you. Is that clear?"

Salome hesitated briefly before grudgingly conceding: "It hasn't escaped my notice, dear brother, that you've been showing considerable leniency to Alexandra and her brood – more than is called for."

This remark brought an angry flush to Joseph's countenance. "To be civil to Alexandra is what you call considerable leniency? How would you have me treat her – like an outcast, a leper? Don't forget, she's a member of the royal family. And her daughter happens to be betrothed to our brother – our big brother. She will be your sister-in-law. Have you forgotten that?"

"Not at all. I have never ceased regretting that fact. Both she and her mother are insufferable snobs, even if they have royal blood in their veins. Or maybe it's because they have royal blood that they think they're in a class far above us and give themselves such airs and graces. It makes me sick, it does!"

Joseph compressed his lips and leaned forward before sounding a note of caution. "If I were you, I wouldn't let our brother know how you feel about the young woman who is going to be his wife. And our queen, the queen of Judea."

Salome stared at Joseph with a puzzled look. "What do you mean, queen of Judea?"

"Just what you heard." Joseph's voice took on a different timbre. "You know very well that Herod has had his heart set on winning the Judean throne. Well..."

"I'm perfectly aware of that," Salome cut him short, burning with curiosity. "But what has that to do with – Joseph, are you keeping any information from me?"

"Not really, that is, not more than a few hours," replied Joseph in a softer tone. "Last night I had an unexpected visitor. Under cover of darkness a courier made his way through the enemy lines and up the Snake Path. He demanded to be taken to me, saying that he had an important message to deliver. The guards were naturally suspicious; they thought he might be a spy or an impostor bent on foul play. They made him hand over his weapons and then frisked him to make sure he didn't have anything concealed under his tunic. Two of the guards escorted him to this room."

"And the message – who was it from?" asked Salome impatiently.

"It was from Herod."

"Herod!" exclaimed Salome, unable to suppress a start.

"Yes, from our brother. When the courier handed me the letter I could see that it was quite long. I tore open the seal and began to read. I couldn't believe my eyes. Herod has been in the country for several months. He tried more than once to communicate with us, but the courier couldn't get through. He's raised an army and is marching south to raise the siege."

At this information Salome's face lit up. "That means our suffering will soon be over. What wonderful news! The gods be praised!" She paused abruptly and her eyes narrowed. "What else was in that message? What's all this nonsense about Mariamne going to be queen?"

"Oh yes, of course," said Joseph in a deliberately casual voice. "I almost forgot about that little piece of information. Rather careless of me, I admit," he added with a grin. "You can stop eating yourself up about Alexandra's and Mariamne's royal blood. Our brother is now King Herod – by virtue of a decree of the Roman Senate."

Victory in Joppa – On to Masada!

When Joppa came into view, Herod felt a quickening of his senses. The anticipation of pitting his skill and courage against an adversary, especially one against whom he nursed an intense hatred mingled with envy, exhilarated him. He and his chief lieutenant halted their mounts on a rise and took a long look at the city that served as Judea's outlet to the sea. The houses were for the most part set close together, but there were a few separated from these; they were larger and more stately and were surrounded by gardens and tall trees – the homes of wealthy merchants and shipowners. The city walls were high and broad.

"Well, Nikias," said Herod, glancing at his lieutenant, "how long do you think it will take?"

"It won't be easy," replied Nikias, shading his eyes from the strong sunlight. "Those walls look pretty stout from here, and judging from all those ships in the harbor, it will be hard to starve the inhabitants out, if not impossible. They can bring in all the supplies they need by sea. They should be able to withstand a long siege."

"A long siege is out of the question," declared Herod in a crisp, resolute tone. "We must reach Masada as quickly as is reasonably possible."

"We don't have much in the way of siege equipment. If we try to batter our way into the city, we may lose a lot of men."

"That's also out of the question. We have to put our heads together and figure out a better way."

"Well, there's an old trick that has sometimes worked in situations like this. And that is to lure the enemy out from behind those walls and fight them in the open, where we can gain a fairly quick decision."

"That's it! That's the strategy we'll use."

Nikias was pleased at Herod's reaction, but thought it advisable to sound a note of caution. "Let's hope the enemy falls for it. If they're smart, they'll know better than to let themselves fall into a trap like that."

"That may not be as hard as you think. According to our spies, their soldiers are poorly trained, and I doubt if their officers are much better. After we set up camp we'll hold a staff meeting and make our plans."

Fortunately for Herod – perhaps not for his ego – the defenders' hatred of him was so great that it proved easier than expected to draw them out from behind the walls in the hope of slaying or at least capturing him. After three weeks of siege the defenders began to venture out from behind the walls, and time after time charged through the gate, only to be beaten back by Herod's well-trained mercenaries. On the last day of the fighting, the defenders' losses mounted steadily with each furious charge.

By sundown Joppa was in Herod's hands. His mercenaries had suffered comparatively light losses and were drunk with victory. They looked forward to reaping the fruits of victory. Great was their disappointment when Herod issued strict orders against pillage and rape. They openly voiced their resentment, and were appeased only when Herod promised to reward them handsomely after the campaign was over. To his officers he explained that the inhabitants of Joppa would in the near future be his subjects, and he didn't want to turn them into implacable foes.

"What about the prisoners?" asked Nikias. "What should we do with them?"

"The soldiers who surrendered willingly are to be released. Those who resisted are to be executed."

"And the officers?"

"They are to be executed."

"All of them?" asked Nikias with a quizzical look.

"All of them – without mercy," declared Herod in a tone of cold finality. "With their officers eliminated, the people of Joppa won't have any stomach to cause us trouble as we advance on Masada. And to make sure they don't, we'll assign two or three companies to garrison the city."

Herod allowed his men the better part of a week to recover from their wounds and to rest up for the next objective. In the meantime his scouts reported that there were only a few scattered, lightly manned garrisons along the planned route of march. Even more important, no formidable body of enemy troops was sighted in the area, and Antigonus's force besieging Masada did not seem to be very large – only several hundred men all told.

"It's too good to be true," was Herod's guarded reaction to this report. "That slimy Antigonus must have something up his sleeve. That he didn't come to the aid of Joppa surprised me, but it could probably be excused. But now that Joppa has fallen into our hands, where is his resistance? That I can't understand."

"We haven't reached Masada yet," replied Nikias. "My guess is that we'll meet plenty of resistance – maybe not by a large body of troops, but ambushes to hold us up and wear down our strength."

Herod's eyebrows arched sharply. "Ambushes are mere pin pricks," he said with a disdainful expression. "They can annoy us, but not hold us up for any length of time. And as for wearing down our strength, in Idumea I'll pick up plenty of reinforcements, more than enough to make up for any possible losses. Antigonus must surely be aware of that."

"It would be reasonable to assume as much," agreed Nikias. "Let's look at the possibilities. First, how large a force does Antigonus have? And what sort of soldiers does he have – volunteers or mercenaries?"

"Mostly volunteers I'd say, if not entirely so."

"Well, since this is harvest time, some of his men may have gone back to their farms to help bring in the crops in the meantime. That would deplete his available forces."

Herod shot his lieutenant an incredulous look. "When we're advancing into Judea? Nonsense!"

"Nevertheless it's a possibility. Let's consider another one. Antigonus has been besieging Masada for quite some time without success. It must be obvious to him that he has no chance of succeeding now. So why should he dissipate his strength at this stage for no good purpose? My guess is that he intends to husband his strength for Jerusalem, where it will be a completely different story. He's probably counting on us dissipating our strength there."

"By the time we reach Jerusalem we'll hopefully be getting some help from the Roman legions."

"And Antigonus may be counting on help from the Parthians."

"The Parthians were beaten by Ventidius only a short while ago."

"One defeat doesn't mean the end of the war. The Parthians have shown that they're a match for the Romans. Don't underestimate them."

"Good advice," Herod conceded. "Let's get back to Masada. With the 800 troops I left there, we'll box the enemy in from the front and rear. We'll crush them; we'll scatter them like chaff in the wind."

It was imperative for Herod to get a message through to Masada in order to inform his brother of his impending arrival and to coordinate their plan of action; no less important was his desire to reestablish communication with his family. Since his return from Rome he had several times tried to get a message to them, but without success. This time there must be no failure. He picked two of his best scouts and gave them detailed instructions about the route they were to take and how to avoid detection, a matter he had given considerable thought to.

Herod marched his army down the coastline and then turned left in the direction of Marisa. He cherished fond memories of this town, for in his youth he had spent many happy days on his father's nearby estate and explored the surrounding territory on both foot and horseback. It was like homecoming, he confided to Nikias. But as he approached the town his heart turned cold. The scene before him was one of widespread destruction. Hardly a single house or courtyard was left untouched; charred ruins were everywhere. He caught sight of an elderly man standing in the gateway to one of the courtyards and suspiciously eyeing the advancing column of troops. Herod halted his mount and called out: "Tell me, old man, whose work was this?"

There was no reply, only stony silence.

"Don't be afraid to speak," Herod assured him. "Don't you recognize Herod, son of Antipater?"

The old man peered at Herod. "The gods be praised!" he uttered. "So it is. And never more welcome. Whose work was this, you want to know? I'll tell you whose work it was, may Satan take their cursed souls! It was those cursed Parthians."

"Not Antigonus?"

"No, just the Parthians."

"How long ago was this?"

"Not long after Jerusalem fell into their hands. That would be about – let me think a minute; how many months is that?"

"Never mind," said Herod, waving the question aside. "It's a good few months for sure. These houses should have been repaired by now, or at least a start made."

"With Antigonus's men not far away and the Parthians ready to come back at any time? It would be wasted effort."

"Not any more. The Parthians have been beaten by the Romans and Antigonus will soon be on the run. My fellow Idumeans are going to help me see to that."

Herod ordered his men to pitch camp outside Marisa while he went about recruiting reinforcements. Within a few days several hundred Idumeans joined his banner. They did not make much of an impression on Nikias, who would have preferred to forgo this untrained and, he suspected, undisciplined addition to their army. Nor was he convinced by Herod's assurance that what they lacked in training they would more than compensate for by their loyalty and motivation, fanned by an intense desire for revenge.

The march from Maris to Masada was more difficult than expected. In spite of the scouts' earlier optimistic reports, Herod's force encountered frequent ambushes, which slowed its advance and took a growing toll. By the time it reached Masada it was only a little larger than when it started the campaign, the Idumean reinforcements notwithstanding. Herod had not reckoned on this, and his ire grew fiercer with each ambush. He gave orders to show no mercy to anyone who fell into their hands, but to dispatch him on the spot.

Herod's ugly mood lifted only when the lofty silhouette of Masada emerged from the morning mist on the third day out from Marisa. He halted his mount and stared at the rock fortress in wonder. So many momentous events had happened since he left his family here that he found it nothing short of incredulous. He had come here at the nadir of his fortunes – after the departure of his late brother Phasael to treat with the Parthians and the humiliating withdrawal from Jerusalem. He was returning as king of Judea, crowned by the Roman Senate no less. His path had taken him to two of the world's greatest capitals – to the incomparably beautiful Alexandria and an audience with Cleopatra; and then, after a journey to Rhodes that had almost ended in disaster and still gave him nightmares, to all-powerful, glorious Rome, capped by the majestic ceremony on the Capitoline. Fate was marching with him hand in hand and nothing could stop him now. He would make a quick end to the siege and liberate his family.

And so it came about. Realizing that they stood no chance against a foe who now virtually surrounded them with far superior numbers, Antigonus's men offered only token resistance before retreating in the direction of Jerusalem.

Stirring Up Strife at Dinner

Unlike the others lining Masada's outer defense wall, Alexandra and Mariamne watched impassively as Herod's troops made their laborious way up the narrow, twisting Snake Path. Aristobulus, however, could not contain his excitement, especially when the men reached the top and began to form ranks outside the gate.

"Look, Mariamne," he exclaimed, "isn't that something?"

Mariamne continued to stare blankly at the soldiers.

"Aren't you even a little bit excited?" asked Aristobulus with a puzzled frown. "Doesn't it do something to you to watch soldiers lining up for a parade?"

"I'm glad the awful siege is over," replied Mariamne in a low, flat voice.

"So am I glad it's over. But to watch soldiers getting ready to parade – that's something special."

"Now, son," Alexandra gently chided Aristobulus, "you must realize that marching soldiers don't excite girls as much as they do little boys."

"I'm not little," protested Aristobulus.

"You're right, you're not little," replied Alexandra with a grin.

"And besides, look at all those people. They're excited too – all of them, even grown men and women. Listen to their cheering."

"They're cheering mainly because most of them are Idumeans who fled to Masada for protection. And now they can safely return to their homes."

What a difference between her two children's reaction, Alexandra thought. She could understand Aristobulus's excitement. He's a young boy, and it doesn't take much to enthuse him. With Mariamne it's a different story. She is now a young woman, and instead of being properly groomed for her role as a Hasmonean princess, she has been caught up in a maelstrom that would overwhelm a much older and experienced person. The poor dear is obviously bewildered, and Herod's arrival has only made matters worse. According to Joseph, the Romans have crowned him king of Judea. Any other woman would rejoice at the prospect of becoming queen of Judea, but how can Mariamne rejoice? This is the ultimate humiliation of the Hasmonean house. Herod, King of Judea – how preposterous, how degrading! What would her father say to that? She wondered if he would say that if Herod sits on the throne of Judea, Mariamne should sit at his side. Maybe it was this possibility more than anything else that made her father agree to this awful match.

* * *

Herod had decided even before the start of the campaign that he would enter Masada as befitted a triumphant general who was now king of Judea. In his message to Joseph he had informed him accordingly and instructed him how to proceed.

When the last of the long sinuous column of soldiers reached the top of the Snake Path, the officers formed the men into rows of four; once inside the gate, they would fan out six abreast. The standard-bearers took their place at the head of the formation, followed by the trumpeters, then Herod and Nikias, the staff officers, and the various companies of troops.

Meanwhile, at the far end of the fortress square the garrison force lined up six abreast. Their burnished shields and helmets glinted in the bright sunlight, adding an additional touch of color. A slight breeze had blown up, keeping the temperature at a comfortable level. At a signal from Joseph, the blast of trumpets rent the air. The formation started to march, while simultaneously the standard-bearers of the other formation emerged through the gate, to the cheers of the spectators lining two sides of the square. When Herod came into view, the spectators' excitement reached its peak.

The two formations met in the middle of the square, forming one large compact body, with Herod in front. As his eye roamed over the soldiers lined up in perfect order, he experienced a feeling of intense pride and satisfaction. A hush descended over the scene as he prepared to speak, and everyone strained to catch his words. He praised the men for their bravery and exemplary fighting qualities, and spoke of the significance of this great victory, the first of many more to come until the foe is completely vanquished. When he finished, a loud sustained roar echoed across the neighboring heights. The troops then paraded around the square twice before being dismissed.

Herod assembled his officers and gave them instructions, after which he strode over to greet his family. He warmly embraced each member, starting with Cypros, who made no attempt to stem her tears of joy. She was oblivious to all the eyes riveted on her. To see her son again after such a long absence was happiness enough for her; to see him return as king of Judea was beyond her wildest dreams. How her beloved Antipater would have rejoiced!

Herod turned to Joseph and thanked him for faithfully fulfilling his duties as commander of the fortress, and said that later on he wanted a full report from him. He sympathized with Salome for all the discomfort she had suffered during the siege and assured her that never again would she or any other member of the family have to endure such an ordeal.

Herod looked around him, wondering where Alexandra and her children were. He did not expect to find them together with his family; nevertheless it rankled him that they kept themselves aloof. He caught sight of them a short distance away. The impassive expression on Alexandra's and Mariamne's faces disconcerted him. When he left Masada relations with Alexandra had been, if not cordial, at least correct. Why this sullen mood? Wasn't she happy to see the end of the siege, to see him return victorious and as – of course, that was it. How could she, a Hasmonean princess, be glad to see him return as king of Judea? Well, so be it; let her bemoan the decline of the Hasmonean house.

The crowd parted to let him approach Alexandra. She summoned up a faint smile, but there was no joy in her eyes. Herod greeted her pleasantly enough, making a conscious effort to keep any stiffness or formality out of his voice. He turned to face Mariamne. To his consternation, he experienced an awkward moment, but he immediately recovered his aplomb. His eyes lingered on her for several seconds. He was struck by how much she had matured since he had last seen her. Her features were more delicate and beautiful than ever, and her figure had rounded perceptibly. He framed his greeting so graciously that the expression on her countenance thawed noticeably, much to his delight.

After conferring with Joseph and Nikias about accommodations for the troops, Herod closeted himself with his brother in order to learn what had happened during his absence. "The siege must have been hard on the civilians," he said, shaking his head. "How did they hold up? How did our family take it? And what about food? Was there enough for everybody?"

"No one got fat, but neither did anyone go hungry. Water was the big problem. With 800 soldiers and all these civilians, I knew it wouldn't be long before the cisterns were empty. I ordered a strict rationing, but watching the level of the water dropping day after day turned my hair gray. It got so low that I feared the worst. Some of the officers thought we would have to abandon Masada or even capitulate. Fortunately we finally got some rain – not a heavy one, but enough to replenish part of the cisterns with the help of flash floods in the two nearby wadis. And to save me from an unpleasant family squabble."

Herod's eyebrows arched sharply. "Such as?"

Joseph related how Salome had clashed with Mariamne over the pitcher of water and how he had to reprove her. Herod did not seem unduly perturbed. "In the circumstances you described something like that was bound to happen. It's understandable."

Joseph gave his brother a puzzled look. He had expected a stronger reaction. "Of course you were right to take her to task," Herod added, noticing Joseph's disappointment. "Apart from the business with Salome, how was Alexandra during my absence? Did she give you any trouble?"

"Trouble?" remarked Joseph with a baffled expression. "Why do you ask that? In the incident with Salome she acted quite properly, even more than could be expected. No, you can put your mind at rest on that score."

Herod's eyes narrowed and his tone hardened noticeably. "All the same, I want you to keep an eye on her."

Joseph regarded his brother with an astonished expression. "The mother of your *fiancée*?" he exclaimed.

"Yes, the mother of my fianc**é**e," confirmed Herod, the corners of his lips tight and unsmiling. "You know very well that she's disapproved of our betrothal from the very start. She's a Hasmonean, with all the pride of the Hasmoneans. Now that I've returned as king of Judea, you can hardly expect her to take kindly to that."

"In other words, you suspect her, and you want me to do the same, is that it?"

"Exactly!"

This remark made Joseph uneasy. "I can swear that she hasn't shown the least sign of opposition. On the contrary, I've come to have considerable admiration for her. Our relations have been excellent."

"That's to your credit," retorted Herod a little tartly. "But you are not me. You're not king of Judea. Now that I'm back, we can expect her to show her true colors. I want you to inform me immediately of any sign of opposition or even discontent on her part. And that goes for all our dear Judean friends. We have to be doubly vigilant now. Any threat to my throne will be dealt with severely and without mercy. Is that clear?"

"Yes, that's clear," replied Joseph drearily.

"Good! Now let's get down to other business. I want you to arrange a victory celebration for the soldiers. Make sure the tables are laden with food and drinks. That means plenty of meat, wine, and all the other good things. And don't forget entertainment. That's just as important as food and drinks."

Joseph gaped at his brother. "After all these months of siege, where am I supposed to get meat for so many people?"

"Are there no flocks in the area?" asked Herod with an impatient gesture. "Surely you can convince the nearby villagers that a lamb or a kid is a small enough gift to offer for the liberation of their land by their new king. You'll have to learn to exercise our royal prerogatives," he added imperiously.

"The matter will be attended to," said Joseph, swallowing his brother's stricture. "About entertainment, what do you have in mind?"

"Obviously not what the men want most. This is not the time or place for that. But music, singers, dancers..."

"And where do you suggest I look for them – in the same place as the lambs and kids?" asked Joseph with a tinge of sarcasm.

"Of course not! Our officers are nearly all Greek, and so are many of the soldiers. Not that it really matters. So I suggest you see what you can round up in Ascalon."

That evening Herod dined with his family in the apartment that had been readied for him. He was in a relaxed mood and even light-hearted. Everyone was eager to hear his story, and they listened with rapt attention as he recounted his experiences from the day he left Masada. Salome was particularly intrigued by the Egyptian queen. "Is she as beautiful and clever as they say?" she wanted to know.

"I wouldn't say she's very beautiful. I've seen more beautiful women – plenty of them. But clever, yes – very clever and seductive. After all, to snare Caesar and Antony is no mean achievement."

"And what about Herod?" asked Salome with a sly wink. "Did he also fall victim to her charms?"

This question evoked laughter from all present, even Cypros.

"I'm not quite in the same class as Caesar and Antony," Herod admitted with an unruffled demeanor. "Especially when I had my audience with her. Then I was a mere commoner and not exactly in the most prosperous of circumstances."

"Then she didn't try to exercise her charms on you?" Salome persisted.

"She offered me a command in her army. I would like to think it was because of whatever talents I may have in that direction. But I suspect the real reason was to keep me from reaching Rome. Oh yes, she's clever all right. But your brother is no slouch either."

"Maybe she values your administrative ability," commented Joseph. "After all, you made quite a name for yourself as governor of Coele-Syria."

"I'm proud of my record, I admit," said Herod with a pleased look. "But I'm still convinced that her offer was a ruse to keep me away from Rome."

"Why should she want to do that?" asked Joseph.

"It's quite simple. Cleopatra is an ambitious queen, who dreams of restoring the Ptolemaic empire to its ancient boundaries. And that includes Judea."

"But Judea is to all intents and purposes under Roman influence, or, if not Roman, then Parthian," Joseph countered.

"And who is Rome? In this part of the world Rome is – or was – Caesar, and now Antony. Do you think she's passionately in love with Antony? Her passion is power and all that goes with it – territory, money, and all the rest. That's what she loves. And she'll do anything for that."

"Even prostitute herself?" interjected Salome with a snide look.

"Yes, even prostitute herself, if you want to put it that bluntly. But I doubt if she regards it in that light."

"You'll have to tread carefully, my dear brother," Salome went on with a sudden undertone of scorn. "To contend with one female adversary is trouble enough; to contend with two is more than double trouble."

Herod looked at his sister sharply. "More than double trouble? What do you mean?"

"What could be more natural than for the power-hungry queen of Egypt to join hands with the arrogant Hasmonean princess? The two of them together would make a very formidable adversary."

"You're very perceptive," Herod conceded. "You're sounding a warning that I'm quite aware of."

"You yourself admit that Alexandra has never reconciled herself to your betrothal," Salome went on, her voice becoming more strident and contemptuous. "It was her father's doing, not hers."

"I'm perfectly aware of her attitude toward our betrothal," said Herod, searching for a way to divert the conversation.

"She despises you," Salome spat out, her eyes hard and vindictive. "She despises all of us. She'll always despise us!"

Cypros, who had spoken very little during the meal, felt constrained to intervene. "Now, Salome," she said in a tone of mild rebuke, "you're getting over-excited. It has been very pleasant until now. Let's keep it that way and not spoil it with harsh talk."

"Mother is right," Joseph added. "You can never speak about Alexandra without getting worked up. She's not nearly as bad as you make out. She may not love us, but that doesn't mean she despises us."

Salome glared at her brother. "Oh, no?" she retorted heatedly. "The desert sun must have affected your senses, my dear brother. Can't you see that she puts herself on a pedestal far above us miserable Idumeans? She looks down on us. We're dirt in her eyes – dirt! And her daughter is the same. For your own good, Herod, put her away; break the betrothal!"

Herod grimaced and stirred uneasily on his seat. Salome's burning hatred of Alexandra was an old story. "Have you witnessed anything suspicious about her – anything that could be regarded as harmful to my interests – to our interests?"

Before Salome could reply, Joseph pushed away his bowl of fruit and drew himself erect; his mouth was firmly set. "As commander of this fortress, I believe I'm in a better position to judge that. As I've already told you, I haven't found any fault with her behavior."

"No, of course not!" Salome hurled the words with mounting fury. "You may know how to command a fortress, but you don't understand a woman's heart or mind." She pointed an accusing finger at Joseph. "Tell me, why does she keep aloof from us? Why is it she doesn't even deign to speak to us? Because she hates us, that's why!"

Joseph was taken aback by the vehemence of his sister's outburst. His face clouded. "You haven't exactly been a paragon of decency toward Alexandra and her children, if I may say so. If she keeps a distance from you, she has good reason. I've talked with her quite a few times, and I can honestly say she has never tried to make me feel the least bit inferior."

"You're not affianced to her daughter," replied Salome with a scornful toss of her head. "You're no threat to the Hasmoneans." She turned to face Herod. "Now that you're king, you don't need Alexandra's daughter. Put her away!"

Herod gave his sister a long, hard look. "I appreciate your concern for my welfare," he said irritably. "But in spite of your misgivings, I have no intention of terminating the betrothal."

"You don't need her now!" Salome repeated fiercely.

"I must be the judge of that," replied Herod.

"And what valid reason have you?" she flung at him defiantly. "Reasons of state, perhaps?"

"Yes, reasons of state. You may not like Mariamne, you may not like her mother or any of the other Hasmoneans. But the people of Judea do. And since they will be my subjects, I must take that into consideration. And besides, did it ever occur to you that I may have another reason for desiring this match – a personal reason?"

Antigonus – King on a Threatened Throne

Antigonus, wearing a purple woolen robe that did justice to his well-proportioned figure and handsome features, hummed softly as he studied one of the numerous reports piled on his desk in the royal Hasmonean palace. A glowing brazier kept the small room comfortably warm despite the cold drafts that penetrated the window and beneath the door opening onto the unheated corridor. Using a reed pen, he underlined or made marginal notes of points he intended to discuss with his advisers. When he finished the report, he rolled it up and took another from the pile. After an hour or so he began to grow weary, so he pushed the remaining documents aside. Studying reports was an essential part of his daily routine, but sometimes he felt they tended to get the better of him.

Setting up an administrative machinery had proved to be more difficult and time-consuming than expected. He had to admit that his efforts had not been crowned with conspicuous success – at least until the last few weeks. Some of his advisers and confidants had begun to grumble, especially after Herod's arrival in the country. But, as Antigonus had explained to them, it was precisely the return of that despicable scoundrel that had frustrated his efforts. When Herod fled Jerusalem, Antigonus was sure he had seen the last of him, at least for a long time to come. But less than half a year later he showed up at Ptolemais with a Roman crown no less! Now Joppa was in his hands and the siege of Masada lifted. What a wretched business this was turning out to be! Who could have foreseen that after leading the Parthians to a glorious victory over the Romans the year before, Labienus would be defeated in a return engagement, with the result that the Romans now posed a threat to Antigonus's throne? In these circumstances it had been very difficult to organize his administration and to get it functioning properly. However, things were looking up now that Barzilai was one of his chief advisers. He was proving to be an able administrator, and was relieving Antigonus of much of the tedious day-to-day detail. If only his reports were a little shorter, he said to himself with a grin.

Antigonus stared idly at the desk. It was a beautiful piece of work, made of a thick-veined knotted wood he could not identify and with exquisitely carved legs. Whatever he thought of his uncle, he had to admit that he had good taste.

And the desk had been placed in an ideal spot: It faced a large window that overlooked the stately homes of the Upper City, the bustling marketplace, the city wall with its gleaming battlements and towers, and in the distance the pine-covered hills. It was an inspiring view, and Hyrcanus had undoubtedly found it conducive to studying the numerous books in the polished cabinets lining the cedar-paneled walls. He was essentially a bookish man, Antigonus mused with a wry expression, and it would have been much better for himself and the nation if he had devoted himself to such pursuits instead of fighting his own brother over the right to wear the royal and priestly crowns. He was unfit to govern: That had been clear to their father, Alexander Yannai, who had bequeathed the throne to his widow instead of his first-born son. What had Hyrcanus accomplished? The weakling – there was no other way to describe him – had let those accursed Idumeans lead him by the nose, causing Judea to become a vassal of the arrogant Romans and bringing about the death of his own brother and his elder son, Antigonus's brother.

The people could be grateful to Antigonus for having Hyrcanus banished to Babylonia with his ears mutilated to render him unfit to serve as high priest. They wanted, and needed, a real Hasmonean at their head, not one who let himself become a pliant tool of those Idumean scoundrels. Even the distinguished Pharisaic sage, Shemaiah, had wished Antigonus well upon his coronation. True, he was not happy at the way Hyrcanus had been disqualified for the high-priesthood, and he had certain other reservations, which he had not hesitated to express. He ardently hoped that there would be no repetition of the civil strife that had marred the long reign of his grandfather Yannai and the short reign of his father, and that both parties – Pharisees and Sadducees – would work together for the common good.

A knock on the door interrupted Antigonus's musing. He knew that would be Barzilai for his daily meeting. He called out to him to enter; he came in with an armful of documents. He was a thick-set, middle-aged man of medium height, with a strong masculine countenance that bespoke a shrewd, forceful man of affairs; his square black beard was sprinkled with a few gray hairs. He was wearing an elegant red robe clasped at the waist by a bejeweled girdle.

"Well, Barzilai," said Antigonus with mock severity, signaling to his adviser to draw up one of the high-backed chairs, "I see you're determined to ruin my eyesight."

A puzzled expression crossed Barzilai's face. "Heaven forbid!" he said in a deep voice. "I don't know what you're referring to."

Antigonus chuckled. "Come now, my good man, don't be alarmed. I'm referring to all those reports you've submitted for my edification."

"Oh that! I have to admit there were quite a few yesterday – more than usual."

"And today too, from the looks of it. Well, that's a sign you're not letting the grass grow under your feet."

"There are many matters that have to be dealt with," replied Barzilai with a serious expression. "And urgently, too."

"But not so urgently that we can't have refreshments first. After poring over your reports I can do with some nourishment."

Antigonus ordered a servant to bring sweetmeats and wine. As he disappeared through the door, a draft of cold air from the corridor caused the window to rattle. The howling of the wind grew stronger. "A gentle reminder that winter has arrived," remarked Antigonus with a wry smile. "Sitting in this room, you hardly realize it."

"It's a very cozy room," commented Barzilai, crossing his legs. "And done in good taste."

"The credit belongs to my uncle. You know, I lived in this palace for over three years, and for the life of me I don't remember this room. I've no idea what it was used for in my day. Do you happen to know?"

"I'm afraid not. Even though I was an officer in your father's army, I didn't have many opportunities to visit the palace. Besides, that was more than twenty years ago."

"A whole generation," said Antigonus, shaking his head wistfully. "A lot of water has flown under the bridge since then. Yet I must confess that when I set foot in this place last summer I felt that I was returning home – my real home. Even when things looked darkest – and there were many dark periods during the past twenty years – I knew that one day I would be back in the royal palace."

"Your rightful home, and may you reside here for many more years, to the glory of our nation," intoned Barzilai, anxious to get down to business.

The most pressing matter was the military situation, but Antigonus preferred to defer its discussion until Joab, commander of the army, joined them. The first item they took up in the meantime was the state of the royal finances. Barzilai reported that collection of the new taxes was proceeding smoothly, with no noticeable resistance. The need for additional revenue was recognized by all, and there did not seem to be any attempt to speak of to evade the extra burden.

This information pleased Antigonus. "That should make some of my disgruntled friends begin to sing a different tune," he declared.

Barzilai knew that when he had agreed to be Antigonus's adviser there was growing dissatisfaction at the slow progress made in organizing the administration. Some of the key officials had not been up to the mark. The most sensitive area of all, the military, had also given cause for concern, but this did not lie in Barzilai's competence. His appointment had not pleased all circles. He was telling the truth when he said there was no attempt to speak of to evade the extra tax burden, but this was because the people were aware of the dangers facing the country rather than a reflection of their respect for him. He knew that the inhabitants of Emmaus, for example, had never forgiven him for foreclosing mortgage loans he had given them in years of severe drought. They grumbled when his agent came to Emmaus, but they paid their taxes.

Nor was Barzilai greatly liked in aristocratic circles, in particular the leading families of priestly lineage. A man of humble origin, he had to use all his ingenuity in attempting to gain entry into these circles, who looked down upon him as a parvenu. This rankled him, and so he found it all the sweeter to show them who was fit to hold one of the most prominent positions in the court. He had obtained Antigonus's approval to replace the inept officials. Antigonus had, however, made one stipulation: That he appoint not only Sadducees but also some Pharisees. Barzilai had objected to this, insisting that running the administration was a task for men of affairs, and the Sadducees were better suited for this. But Antigonus was adamant, explaining that he did not want to repeat his father's mistake in exacerbating relations between the two parties, regardless of his personal inclinations. "The enemy," he emphasized, "is Rome and its stooges and they alone."

After discussing the financial situation, they proceeded to the next item of business. "The recruiting of men for the army, how is it going?" Antigonus wanted to know.

Barzilai raised his eyebrows. "Shouldn't this be discussed in Joab's presence?"

"Not necessarily. We'll inform him later."

"Excuse me for bringing up a subject which I think it is advisable to discuss before he arrives. It's something I've mentioned before."

"About appointing a military adviser?"

"Yes. It may strike you as a novel idea, even a bit odd; but I think recent developments have made it desirable to seriously consider the suggestion. I'm not a military man myself, even though I was an officer in your father's army. I may know something about tactics, but not much more than that. Your reputation is unquestioned, and Joab is an excellent commander. But in view of the – er, complexities of the military situation, I think it would be advantageous to also have the advice of someone who is not directly involved in the actual fighting."

Antigonus frowned. Behind the dexterous phrases was an implicit criticism of the way things had been going of late. Some of Antigonus's advisers were outspoken on the subject. "You think the loss of Joppa could have been avoided?" he asked bluntly.

Barzilai knew this was a sore point with Antigonus. The presence in the country of the Roman general Ventidius after defeating Labienus had upset the strategy devised by Antigonus and Joab and made them pursue a more cautious course than originally planned. "As I've just mentioned," Barzilai explained, "I'm not a military expert. I can only repeat what others are saying in private."

"And that is?"

"That we abandoned Joppa to its fate. We made no attempt to come to its rescue."

This accusation was no secret to Antigonus. It had vexed him greatly when he first heard it; it annoyed him to have his chief adviser repeat it to his face. His voice took on a sharp edge. "They know very well that we had reinforced the garrison and dispatched a number of officers to help train the local recruits."

"With all due respect, the defenders' stand can hardly be described as glorious or even valiant. It was not a happy reflection on the officers."

"No, it wasn't," conceded Antigonus. "Joppa should have been able to withstand a long siege and sap the enemy's strength. That was the intention. Why the officers failed to restrain the men and let them abandon the protection of the walls is a mystery to us. Unfortunately, none of the officers are alive to enlighten us."

A knock on the door signaled Joab's arrival. He looked tired and somewhat disheveled. He apologized for his appearance, explaining that he had just returned from an urgent visit to the Beit Horon region.

"We were discussing the loss of Joppa," said Antigonus with a grim expression after Joab seated himself. "Barzilai tells me that my advisers are very unhappy about it; they're still grumbling."

Joab grimaced but made no attempt to minimize the gravity of the setback. "They have every reason to be unhappy," he said stiffly. "It was an unpleasant shock to me too."

And an unpleasant reflection on you, thought Antigonus. But he knew that this applied equally to himself. Maybe Barzilai's suggestion has some merit. He would have to give it serious consideration. "There's no use crying over spilt milk," he said in a firm tone. "We must learn from our mistakes and make certain they don't happen again."

Barzilai cleared his throat. "May I suggest that one way we can ensure that is to try and anticipate more accurately the enemy's likely moves."

"That goes without saying," remarked Joab dryly; "it's elementary."

"Well then, gentlemen," said Antigonus briskly, "let's put our heads together and try to figure out what that Idumean's next move is likely to be. What do you think, Joab?"

Joab reflected a moment and then replied in a deliberate tone with frequent pauses. "To me his next move is quite obvious. One doesn't have to be a military man to guess what it will be. Let's examine the situation. Herod is at Masada now. So what objectives can he have? To march up to the northern part of the country? What for? That's where he started from. Besides, he knows from first-hand experience that the Galileans are tough; they've given him more than one bloody nose. No, you can forget about any move in that direction. Then what?"

Joab paused and gazed thoughtfully first at Antigonus and then Barzilai, allowing them to draw their own conclusions. Antigonus's eyes narrowed; an intense, half-incredulous look crossed his face. "Are you suggesting – do you honestly think the bastard would dare to attack Jerusalem?"

Joab nodded his head slowly. Like Antigonus, Barzilai was skeptical; he leaned forward. "With his relatively small force of mercenaries it would be extremely risky for him, if not hopeless."

"Jerusalem is not Joppa!" exclaimed Antigonus, banging his fist on the desk and half-rising from his chair. "It would be suicide for him, yes suicide!"

Joab's composure was not ruffled by this sudden outburst. "With his mercenaries alone it would be suicide," he agreed. "But together with a Roman force..."

This possibility made Antigonus wince. He had clashed with the Romans before and had a healthy respect for their prowess. True, shortly after defeating Labienus, Ventidius had withdrawn the greater part of his force to restore order in some of the Syrian towns, but he had left the rest of his troops in the charge of Silo. Together with these hardened soldiers, Herod would pose a threat that could not be lightly dismissed. "How many men does Silo have?" asked Antigonus.

"To the best of my knowledge, five or six cohorts plus auxiliaries," replied Joab.

Antigonus's brow furrowed. "Hmm, together with Herod's men they may be strong enough to lay siege to Jerusalem."

"Not a very pleasant prospect," remarked Barzilai. "Jerusalem has seen enough fighting lately."

"Unfortunately it has," agreed Antigonus. "But if it comes to a siege, the city will stand firm. We may have to resort to defensive action for a while, until the Parthians return. Then we'll give that Idumean a drubbing he won't forget."

"Can we count on the Parthians returning?" asked Barzilai. "Even after Labienus's defeat?"

"They have informed me of their determination to drive the Romans out of this region," replied Antigonus.

Barzilai's mind was not put at ease by this information. The prospect of a siege dismayed him more than he cared to admit. Jerusalem was strongly fortified; its walls were stout, its inhabitants determined to protect the city and the Temple. True, twenty-three years earlier Jerusalem had fallen to Pompey, but then the country had been rent by civil war, and one of the factions had even opened the city gates to the enemy. Today the picture was different. The people were united behind Antigonus and in their hatred of Herod. Yet a siege, even a comparatively short one, would bring suffering to the inhabitants; and, heaven forbid, one could not rule out the possibility of widespread destruction, including his own home, before Parthian assistance arrived. He shuddered at the thought. The threat had to be nipped in the bud. It was not Herod's force he feared, but the Romans. They were trained, hardened warriors, with excellent officers. Excellent – but still human, with human frailties. A crafty smile appeared on his lips. Neutralize their commanding officer and you've neutralized the Roman threat. There were rumors about Silo. They had aroused Barzilai's curiosity, and he prided himself on his thoroughness. How wise of him to have had the rumors investigated. Which of Antigonus's aristocratic friends would have been clever enough to do that?

"Your information about the Parthians is heartening," he said to Antigonus. "But until they return – and may it be soon – we must do whatever we can do discourage the Romans. And I think I know how we can pull it off."

Antigonus and Joab gave Barzilai an intensely curious, almost astonished, look. They waited for him to continue. "Herod will not dare to attack Jerusalem by himself," he went on, pleased at the effect of his words. "Even Joab agrees with that. But with Roman help he may be foolhardy enough to try it, even though, considering the size of the Roman force now in the country, his chances of success would be pretty slim. Now, if he should not be sure of the Romans, if for some reason he begins to doubt their ardor for a cause that doesn't directly concern them, he would quite likely lose heart, giving us a breathing spell until the Parthians could mount a new offensive."

Antigonus was intrigued by Barzilai's analysis of the situation but was dubious about his conclusion. Before asking for details, he wanted to hear Joab's opinion. Joab turned his shaggy-browed eyes on Barzilai. "To put it bluntly, there's a basic flaw in your reasoning, or what we've heard of it so far. Since when do Roman soldiers fight because of their ardor for a cause? They fight for the simple reason that they are ordered to."

"Exactly!" exclaimed Barzilai, stabbing the air with his finger. "I agree with you completely. They fight because they are ordered to." He paused briefly and then continued with an enigmatic smile. "But if the order is not given or if it is given half-heartedly, if the general lacks enthusiasm for one reason or another, then you have a different situation."

Antigonus unfolded his arms and leaned forward, fixing his adviser with a questioning look. "The man who gives orders in this case is Silo. He himself receives orders from Ventidius, and Ventidius from Antony. Do you mean to tell me that Silo would dare disobey Antony?"

"Antony is far away from the scene, in Athens. From there it is hard to know what exactly is going on here."

"I'm not so sure about that," said Antigonus with a frown. "But even assuming that you're right, why would a general like Silo lose enthusiasm, as you put it?"

Barzilai's voice took on a confidential ring. "I think you know me well enough to realize that I don't do things half-way. I've made it my business to find out whatever I could about Silo. As I suspected, he has his weaknesses."

"He likes women?" Joab ventured.

Barzilai gave a short laugh. "What Roman doesn't like women? There's more to it than that. He also likes to live in style when he's not in uniform, but that too is no sin – provided one can afford it. But it seems that Silo is a better general than businessman. He's made some bad investments and is heavily in debt."

Antigonus immediately caught the drift of Barzilai's remarks. "Is your information reliable?" he asked with heightened interest.

"It came from what I believe to be a reliable source."

"So you think our friend may not be averse to a little – ah, financial assistance, do you?"

"I have little reason to think he would object strenuously."

"But his orders!" Joab broke in.

"Orders can be obeyed full-heartedly or less than full-heartedly," replied Barzilai with a patronizing smile. "It's not always easy to tell the difference. Besides, from what I know about Silo and Herod, I'm willing to wager that they're not going to hit it off together."

Antigonus rose from his chair and ambled over to the window. He gazed abstractedly at the scene before him as he weighed Barzilai's words. And then he turned around. "You're sure this is going to work, are you?"

"I can't guarantee it," replied Barzilai with a satisfied grin. "But I'm reasonably sure." He paused briefly before adding: "What have we to lose?"

"Nothing. All right, it's worth trying. You go ahead with this. We only have to decide how much we are ready to offer."

Herod Deserted by Roman Commanders and Soldiers

Herod did not tell his family about his intention to visit the ancestral estate at Marisa. He knew they would want to join him, in fact would insist on it, in particular his mother. But he wanted to spare her the sight of the ruined homestead; he also wanted to be alone with his thoughts and memories.

Leaving his mount with the armed escort in the courtyard, he entered the sprawling structure, or what remained of it. Having witnessed a fortnight earlier the extensive damage done to the town by the Parthians, he did not expect to find any leniency shown the ancestral home. Fortunately, it had not been razed to the ground. His heart ached at the sight of the charred ruins, but enough of the building was standing for him to recapture scenes and events that had taken place here in the bosom of his family. A host of recollections crowded in on him, most of them happy, some less so. Most poignant of all were those of his father and his elder brother Phasael, which filled him with acute nostalgia.

From the back room he stepped out onto a graveled path and made his way to a mound a little beyond the walled enclosure. He was relieved to see that two large boulders were still where he had placed them when escaping the Parthians. This meant that the ancestral tombs had not been disturbed. He summoned two of his escorts to roll away the boulders, revealing the mouth of a burial cave. Taking a lighted lamp from one of the men, he descended the few steps to the entrance hall, which led to three burial chambers. The air in the main chamber was damp and chilly, and he wished he had brought a heavier cloak. The lamp shed a fitful light. When his eyes adjusted to it, he could discern the gabled niches in the walls of the chamber and two sarcophagi resting on a shelf hewn along the length of the walls. An awesome stillness pervaded the chamber, and the spirits of the dead seemed palpably near. As he walked over to Phasael's sarcophagus, his eyes filled with tears. "Dear Phasael," he uttered in a low, choked voice, "how I miss you. You were my right hand, and I loved you more than myself. The enemy dealt treacherously with you, but be patient, my brother, you will be avenged."

Next to this sarcophagus was an even more ornate one, the work of a noted Greek sculptor. This had been Herod's idea, to which Phasael had readily agreed. Herod could feel his heart beating as he lingered before his father's remains. As if he had conjured it up, Antipater's image appeared before him. Herod stretched out his hand as though to touch it. "You were always wise and noble, my father," he solemnly declared. "Your counsel stood me in good stead, and saved me from many a misstep. Even when you were no longer in this world, when I was deprived of your physical presence, I could consult you. For your spirit has always been near to me, and you often appeared to me in a dream. My dearest wish, my greatest desire, is to bring fame and glory to our house. Help me to be strong, to resolutely pursue this supreme goal, to overcome and crush all who would oppose me, to go forward, always forward. I am now about to take a momentous step – to march on Jerusalem and capture the throne that is now rightfully mine. Once before, I wanted to march on Jerusalem, but you dissuaded me, and rightly so, for the time was not ripe then. But now the time is ripe. Then I was young and inexperienced; now I am king of Judea – King Herod, friend and ally of the Roman people. Yes, I have come this far, and nothing can stop me now, nothing! Our name will ring throughout the land, throughout the whole of the Hellenistic world, and even Rome will know who is Herod, son of Antipater. That I solemnly swear to you."

Herod lingered awhile before his father's sarcophagus, then leaned forward and kissed the cold stone. He was reluctant to depart. He stepped back and let his eyes roam over the chamber. He never ceased to be impressed by the rich ornamentation, but what moved him even more were the niches containing the remains of his ancestors; these filled him with a mystical awe. After a few minutes he turned and slowly retraced his steps. Before emerging into the daylight, he heard a faint sound as of a drop of water dripping on stone. A pebble had fallen from the ceiling of the entrance hall and almost hit him. For a second he was startled: could this be an omen of some sort – an ill omen perhaps? No, that it could not be. He smiled and stopped to pick up the pebble. It was an ordinary one, small and unprepossessing. He would have it set in filigree and wear it around his neck. It would be his good luck charm.

* * *

Nikias was not keen on the idea; Joseph opposed it. "With our small force and winter already set in, we don't stand a chance," said Joseph. "Remember, it's Jerusalem, not Joppa or Masada."

"It's precisely because it is Jerusalem that I intend to press ahead," Herod countered. "Fortune is smiling on me. We've been victorious everywhere so far. Besides, let me remind you that whenever I've taken the field against Antigonus, I have had the upper hand."

"That may be," said Nikias thoughtfully, "but it's risky to count on it. There's a first time for everything, you know."

The three men were seated in their Masada headquarters. Sunlight streamed through a small window, giving the room a warm, cheerful aspect. It was hard to realize that only a relatively short distance to the north Jerusalem was in the grips of winter.

Herod turned his gaze on his younger brother. "You're worried about the size of our force. With what we have at present you're right to be worried. But you're forgetting two things. First, Costabarus is recruiting more Idumeans. And second, we won't be fighting alone: Silo's army will be joining us."

Nikias frowned. He was not impressed with the first argument, for he did not have a high opinion of the fighting qualities of the Idumeans. But knowing Herod's origins, he refrained from saying so outright. "The recruits will not be trained or battle-hardened," he said flatly. "I doubt they will be of much help."

"We're not going to storm into Jerusalem," replied Herod. "We'll have to lay siege to the city, so by the time it comes to the final assault they'll be hardened enough."

"And what about Silo?" asked Joseph. "Can we rely on him? From what you've told us of your meeting with him I got the impression that he's not enthusiastic about attacking Jerusalem now."

Herod grimaced, for his brother had touched a raw spot. The meeting with the Roman general had gone badly and left a sour taste in his mouth. He had entered the general's headquarters with a proud, confident bearing, as befitted a friend and ally of the Roman people. But Silo had treated him like a bungling subaltern. After recovering from the shock, Herod had resorted to the cajolery that worked so well with other, more highly placed, Romans. But Silo was made of different clay. His manner had been brusque and arrogant. He said tersely that it was inadvisable to launch an attack at this time of the year, and especially considering the relatively small size of their army. When Herod had tried to convince him otherwise, he fastened his hard, cold eyes on him and barked in a fierce, snarling voice: "You may be king of this stinking province, but I'm commander of the Roman army here. And if I say it's not advisable to attack Jerusalem now, that puts an end to the matter!"

Herod was stunned. Never before had he been so humiliated. His fury mounted, and he had a powerful urge to grasp the arrogant Roman by the throat and throttle him. But he quickly mastered this mad impulse, which would have been the end of him. He took a deep breath to calm himself and then, drawing himself up, declared in firm, clipped accents: "Permit me to remind you, general, that I have been proclaimed king of Judea by the Roman Senate, on the recommendation of Mark Antony and Gaius Octavian. I have also been proclaimed friend and ally of the Roman people and given a mandate to drive Antigonus out of the country. If I am prevented from fulfilling my mandate, I shall have no choice but to inform Antony."

Silo stared at Herod with sullen fury and half-rose from his chair. Herod returned his gaze unflinchingly. After a second or two the general's features slackened, and he sank back onto his chair. Herod knew he had won: Silo would join him, but there would never be any real understanding or cooperation between them.

* * *

Most of the faces in the company Avner was assigned to were unfamiliar to him. He recognized less than half a dozen men from the previous year's campaign, but within a few days he was on friendly terms with nearly all of them. A spirit of camaraderie prevailed among the men, who shared the same burning desire: to keep Jerusalem from falling into Herod's hands.

When Avner had reported to the recruiting officer in Jerusalem, he was asked if he had any physical disabilities, to which he had replied in the negative. The officer looked at him with a curious expression and asked how his leg was. Avner said that it was almost as good as new; it would cause no trouble. He asked the officer how he knew about the injury. "You were in front of me when it happened," he explained. "I didn't expect to see you bearing arms again."

Nor did Avner's parents. Zechariah had tried to convince him that he had done his share, and had suffered a severe injury that still caused him to limp a bit. Now it was the turn of other able-bodied men. Avner had replied that the need for volunteers was especially great, because this time the enemy was not only Herod but also the Romans. Departing from his parents had been harder than ever. He could not help feeling sorry for them, because he knew the anguish they had already endured and how much more they would suffer this time.

He found an air of tension in Jerusalem. Knots of people gathered in the marketplace, at the city gates, in the Temple precincts, to discuss the situation. After having undergone a siege only a little over a year earlier, the inhabitants dreaded the thought of another one, especially as rumor had it that Romans would be fighting alongside Herod's troops. Antigonus ordered supplies of victuals, wood and charcoal for heating, and other necessities to be brought to the city for immediate distribution to the populace and for storage in guarded warehouses.

Soldiers were to be seen everywhere. Their numbers had swollen as volunteers streamed in from all over Judea and even Galilee. Children and grown-ups alike watched in fascination as they drilled in all available open spaces. The sight stirred the children and boosted the morale of the adults.

Despite the tension, life in the city went on pretty much as usual. In the Lower City could be heard the pounding of anvils, the braying of asses, the cries of vendors hawking their wares; priests and Levites went about their assigned tasks in the Temple; the Sanhedrin sat in judgment and deliberated new religious legislation.

Avner loved Jerusalem from the moment he had first set foot in it many years ago, when as a youngster he accompanied his family on a Passover pilgrimage. The city had teemed with people from all parts of the country and from all lands of the Diaspora. He loved the surrounding hills, the Kidron and Tyropoen valleys, the Temple Mount; the Upper City dazzled him with its stately homes, magnificent public buildings, majestic royal palace, and wide streets. It was in this quarter that he had been wounded, and he longed to revisit the scene. On his first free day he did so together with a fellow soldier. They threaded their way through the crowded marketplace and then proceeded toward the Hasmonean palace. As they walked down the lovely avenue, Avner described the fighting that had taken place here. "In the street, in front of all these homes?" asked his companion with an astonished look.

"That's right. You can imagine how the residents felt. And here is the spot where I was hit by an arrow. I remember it as clearly as if it happened yesterday. I don't remember very much after that because I was unconscious."

At the mention of his injury, Avner smiled. He recalled how he had regained consciousness in a small room and found Rachel at his side. He wondered where she was now. Her father had undoubtedly sent her to a safe place far from the impending siege. Avner had heard that he now held a very important position in the court – one of the king's advisers, if he remembered correctly. He confided this to his friend as they approached Barzilai's mansion. While they were gazing at the building, the front gate open and out stepped an elegantly dressed man followed by an attendant. When they drew closer, Avner recognized Barzilai and greeted him pleasantly. Barzilai, who was speaking to his attendant, returned the greeting perfunctorily without looking up. It was only after he had taken a few more steps that he realized who had addressed him. He halted and called in a dry tone: "Is that you, Avner?"

"To the best of my knowledge, sir," said Avner, piqued at Barzilai's lack of cordiality.

Barzilai ignored the somewhat brash reply. "What brings you to Jerusalem at a time like this?"

"One can never see too much of Jerusalem. And like the last time, I've come to help defend the city against the enemy."

"After that bad wound you got? It was the leg, wasn't it?"

"That's right. It's almost like new now. Your physician did a good job."

He wanted to add that his nurse also did a good job, but thought better of it. Yet if he did not inquire about Rachel, it might seem boorish of him. "I trust Rachel is well," he said, trying to keep his voice casual.

"She is, thank you," replied Barzilai, a little curtly. "Well, it was good to see you again, and this time don't try to stop any arrows."

* * *

Avner did not have many more free days. The company's training was stepped up and it was posted to the western part of the city, which was expected to see the heaviest fighting. Herod's army came into view on a cold, misty morning, advancing along the Bethlehem road. The city gates were immediately closed and trumpets blared a warning to the inhabitants. Avner's company took up positions on the western ramparts, ready to check Herod's men; the Roman force, smaller than Herod's but equipped with siege engines, was approaching from the north.

Herod's army encamped a short distance from the western wall, as expected. That night hundreds of watch fires dotted the area, making it glow like a bright jewel. The defenders braced themselves for an attack on the morrow. Very few soldiers or civilians slept that night.

The next day dawned cold and cloudy, but there was no rain. The defenders took up their positions and waited. To their astonishment a lone soldier approached the wall and halted on a rise just out of bowshot. A hush descended on the ramparts, for it was obvious that this was a herald with some message to deliver. His voice was strong and carried a great distance.

"Citizens of Jerusalem," he called out, "Herod proclaims that he has come as your friend. He has your welfare at heart and has no desire to see the holy city of Jerusalem destroyed. He is concerned for your safety and the safety of the Temple. He bears no grudge against those who have openly opposed him, and is ready to forgive them. Do not cause needless bloodshed. You cannot prevail against the combined forces of Herod and the Romans. Lay down your arms and open the gates. It is for your own good. You will be forever grateful for doing so."

In the ensuing silence the herald stood motionless as he awaited a reply. It was not long in coming. A Jewish soldier mounted the parapet opposite the herald. In a voice equally as powerful he called out: "To Herod, His Majesty Antigonus declares as follows: 'Your words do not deceive us; they are empty words, devoid of sincerity. The citizens of Jerusalem know only too well how concerned you are for their safety and welfare. To one who has sacrificed to an idol in Rome our Temple is not holy, our city is not holy, our land is not holy. Your gods are not our God, your cause is not our cause. You come as a foreign conqueror. Your army is an army of pagan mercenaries; you are supported by a pagan Roman army. To you we have but one reply: We will defend our holy city and our holy land with all our might until, with the Lord's help, we rid ourselves of this vile pestilence!'"

* * *

Herod was in a filthy mood. The cold, damp air crept into his bones, and he swore at his subordinates apart from Nikias. There was no building or structure of any kind that could serve as his headquarters, for Antigonus had ordered the area outside the city wall on the western side to be laid waste. Herod had no choice but to use his tent for headquarters. It at least protected him from the heavy rain that fell much of the time, but when he stepped outside he generally got drenched in spite of his poncho. He developed a racking cough and his chest ached. The physician warned him that he was liable to get worse in the present conditions. He did not dare say more than that, for he had already been subjected to a barrage of scathing comments on his professional competence and that of physicians in general.

Joseph tried to keep out of his brother's way as much as possible. When he reminded him about his opposition to a winter campaign against Jerusalem, Herod silenced him with a stream of invectives. Never before had Joseph seen him so frustrated, so livid with anger. Two weeks had passed since they began the siege. The initial sorties had failed miserably, but it was not this that upset Herod so much, for he had reckoned that a direct assault would not budge the defenders. What enraged him was the behavior of the Romans. There was no coordination between the two armies. Silo was surly and imperative, and he made it clear that the Roman army would fight as he, and no one else, ordered it. To Herod's angry rejoinder that he would be happy to see the Romans fight in any way whatsoever, Silo had leaped up from his camp stool and dressed Herod down as if he were a schoolboy caught in some mischievous prank. He capped this by warning that if his troops were not supplied with proper food, he would withdraw them to winter quarters. Herod knew this was no idle threat, for his men too were complaining about the small rations. He detailed a whole company to scour the countryside for food and forage. Their efforts were not very successful, while the besieged, ironically, did not lack for food.

In the following week it rained incessantly for three days, turning the ground into a sea of mud. The rain changed to sleet and then snow. A bitter wind whipped the snow flurries, reducing visibility to almost zero. Herod's men did not have sufficiently warm clothing, and many took sick. On the fourth day the snow stopped and the sun peeped out. Herod's spirits lifted a bit, but not for long: The Roman army had vanished from sight.

The Romans Spare Emmaus

Emmaus never looked more peaceful and flourishing. Its fields groaned under bumper crops of wheat and vegetables, the vines were beginning to swell with grape, the chirping of sparrows harmonized with the cooing of doves, bees sucked their fill of pollen and nectar, and went buzzing to their hives, cows grazed placidly in the pasture or lowed contentedly in their barns. It was a scene calculated to gladden the hearts of the inhabitants. But their hearts were heavy, for Jerusalem was again under siege. Only half a year ago, it had been threatened by a combined force of Romans and Herod's mercenaries. Now a much larger Roman army had joined Herod in a second attempt to capture the Holy City. The people of Emmaus had watched in trepidation as two legions and a sizable body of cavalry marched toward Jerusalem.

"O Lord," Hannah had implored as she gripped Zechariah's arm, "protect Jerusalem and its defenders. Watch over our dear Avner; let him return to us safe and sound."

"We must trust in the Lord's mercy," Zechariah had consoled her, putting an arm around her shoulders.

The townsmen grasped at every scrap of information they could get from wayfarers and neighboring villagers. Their spirits rose a little when they learned that the enemy was not having an easy time: Jerusalem was holding fast! And then, much sooner than they had expected or dared hope, came the sensational news: The enemy had broken off the attack and the Romans were retreating along the same route they had taken only a few weeks earlier.

The city elders decided to hold a special thanksgiving service on the following Sabbath. But fate decreed otherwise: Their joy was short-lived. The day after the meeting Zechariah was startled to see a wagon dashing pell-mell up the road leading to Emmaus, raising a thick cloud of dust. Both the horse and driver seemed possessed. When he neared the entrance to the city, the driver shouted out: "Take shelter everyone! The Romans are coming! Take shelter!" He continued to shout the warning until he reached the city square.

"What's got into you, Eli?" asked Zechariah's neighbor Saul when the wagon came to a halt. "Why the panic? You're as pale as whitewash."

The driver, a young man in his late twenties, jumped down from the wagon. From the panicky look on his face it was clear that something drastic had happened. "The Romans are coming!" he repeated to the gathering crowd in a hoarse voice.

"The Romans are going, you mean," Saul corrected him. "We've heard they've been defeated and are retreating."

"They're retreating all right," retorted Eli, "and killing every person they meet on the way. I was lucky to escape them. For God's sake, shut the city gate and let everyone bolt the gate to his courtyard. Stay in your houses and keep out of sight. With luck maybe they'll pass by without harming us."

The people stared at one another, fear written on their faces. They hastened to lock the city gate, fully aware that the Romans could easily break their way in. They rushed their cattle and other animals into the barns and then retreated into their homes.

Toward sundown the Romans came into view. They marched in their usual ranks of six, but made no attempt to keep in step. There was a fairly large number of wounded among them, the more serious cases being transported in wagons bringing up the rear. The Romans had clearly sustained heavy losses. Ordinarily the inhabitants of Emmaus would have been pleased at this, but they were more concerned with their likely fate if the enemy decided to wreak vengeance on them. When the Romans reached the Emmaus approach road, the commanding officer reined in his mount and signaled the column to halt. The inhabitants' hearts turned cold, and they silently prayed for the Romans to continue their retreat. Their prayers were not in vain, for after a few minutes the commander shook his head and pointed straight ahead.

The people of Emmaus heaved a sigh of relief when the column resumed its march. But in several homes there was profound anxiety, for not all the inhabitants had succeeded in taking shelter with their families: Some had gone to neighboring villages for one reason or another. Had they escaped the Romans? Their fate was revealed in the following days. In more than half a dozen homes there was bereavement; in all Emmaus there was mourning and anger – a fierce, consuming anger.

"O Lord, You created man in Your image," Zechariah cried out as he returned with Saul from consoling the families of two of his fellow townsmen. "How can Your creatures be so cruel? How can they cut down good, pious Jews going about their peaceful pursuits, even young innocent children?"

Saul, less given to such speculation, burst out: "May those damned Romans roast in hell, every last one of them! If these are Your creatures, Lord, wipe them off the face of the earth!"

Zechariah thought Saul's words were a little blasphemous, but he could not blame his friend. There was not a single person in Emmaus who did not feel as Saul did, even if they did not express their sentiments as vociferously. When news had reached Emmaus of the enemy's defeat, there was great rejoicing. Machaeras's army of two legions and a thousand cavalry, while not very big by Roman standards, was nevertheless a formidable force, unlike Silo's few cohorts. But while Silo had been content to withdraw his men to winter quarters after a half-hearted attempt to breach Jerusalem's defenses, Machaeras had vented his angry frustration by slaughtering all Jews encountered on his retreat. He spared no one, not even women, children, or the aged. Their pierced, hacked bodies made a gruesome sight. Zechariah, who had helped prepare the corpses of the Emmaus male victims for burial, was haunted by it.

"At least the dead are beyond suffering," he said to Saul, more in order to console himself. "They have returned their souls to their Maker and will abide in everlasting peace."

"May those damned Romans return their rotten souls and go straight to hell!" Saul spat out as he viciously kicked a pile of leaves lying along the path. "They can all go to hell, every last one of them! Anything to get rid of this pestilence. Who wants them here? Who asked them to stick their noses in our affairs? That damned Herod, it's his fault they're here. Crowned king of Judea by those wicked bastards! How low can the man get? I hope to God that Antigonus finishes him off."

Zechariah knew that Saul was not being very logical, but he saw no point in trying to refute him. The Romans were in the country not because of Herod, but because it was part of their policy, and it suited their purpose to make Herod king of Judea. Yet he could not deny that in Herod they had a willing collaborator. The people hated him as much as they did the Romans. After this latest display of Roman cruelty, their hatred of both was boundless. It was no wonder that Avner felt so strongly about them. Zechariah had been inclined to put it down to youthful impetuosity; now he realized that it was more than that. The Roman presence boded ill for Judea. Only the Almighty knew what the final outcome would be.

* * *

Joseph did not look forward to the meeting with Herod, which he instinctively knew was not going to be a pleasant one. He was only too familiar with his brother's mood; when he was angry or frustrated, it was advisable to give him a wide berth. And Herod was exceedingly angry and frustrated. Even if he had wanted to keep his distance, Joseph knew it was out of the question. He had been ordered to leave Idumea and come to Samaria without delay. He had tried to pry information out of the courier, but without success. However, it did not require much imagination to realize that the summons had been prompted by the retreat from Jerusalem. Like all strong, ambitious men, Herod hated being thwarted, and woe to him who happened to be in his presence when the black mood was upon him. The wisest course would be to let him shout himself hoarse and then try to give him the benefit of calm, sagacious advice. More than likely the advice would be rejected as utter nonsense, but after sober reflection it would produce the desired results.

Joseph had arrived the previous afternoon after a long, tiring journey. He had taken an escort of only three stalwarts in order not to attract undue attention as they traveled a circuitous route to avoid territory infested with hostile bands. When he neared Samaria he had been able to relax; the air here was lighter and cooler, and his fatigue had begun to lift a bit. By the time he reached the villa that had been requisitioned for the family, he was in reasonably good spirits. He had not expected his family to be in a similar state, so he was not greatly disconcerted to find his mother suffering from a bad headache and repeatedly wringing her hands and moaning about the trouble they had to endure because of that horrible Antigonus. Salome was her usual acerbic self, roundly vilifying the Hasmoneans in general and even finding fault with Joseph. When he asked how Herod was feeling, she replied that he was in a terrible mood but otherwise all right. Joseph was also curious about Alexandra and her children, but was prudent enough not to ask in Salome's presence.

Joseph saw his brother only later in the day, when the family sat down for the evening meal. Herod greeted him curtly, merely thanking him for coming. He wore a grim expression and, most uncharacteristically, spoke very little during the meal. Joseph was anxious to hear about the battle for Jerusalem, but realized that this was not the time to ask. Herod's appearance worried him. His face was strained and drawn, his jaws set tight, his eyes hard and heavily lined, his complexion sallow. He needs to relax more, Joseph thought; he's driving himself too hard. And he needs the soft touch of an understanding woman. He would deny it, of course. His thoughts, his ambitions ran to "higher" things: the kingship, affairs of state, power – these were the stuff that gave his life meaning and direction. Women played a relatively small part in his scheme of things. It was more than four years since he had sent his wife Doris away. Relations between the two had never been harmonious, and Herod had not been faithful to her. Nor had he been living the life of a celibate since then, but these were casual affairs; none of the women could even be regarded as his mistress, who in times of stress or adversity could soothe his bruised ego, in whom he could or wished to confide.

Conversation at dinner was desultory. Herod asked Joseph about the situation in Idumea, and apart from throwing in a question from time to time, he kept silent. Joseph was glad when the meal was over, for he had eaten heartily, and this, together with the fatigue of the journey, made him drowsy and eager for sleep. Herod bade him goodnight, and told him when to be at his headquarters in the morning.

Joseph ran into Nikias at the entrance to the room serving as headquarters. They exchanged greetings and shrugged their shoulders, as though to say they knew they were in for an unpleasant session. When the sentry admitted them into Herod's presence, they found him studying a papyrus roll.

"Good morning, gentlemen," Herod said in a crisp voice. "Be seated. I just want to finish reading this and then I'll be with you."

After drawing up a chair, Joseph studied his brother's face. His appearance and manner had changed markedly since the previous evening: He seemed rested and less tense; his features had regained their strong, confident aspect. Joseph marveled at the change and wondered what had produced it. When Herod finished reading the papyrus, he rolled it up and put it down on the desk.

"Well, Joseph," he said, folding his arms on the desk, "I suppose you'd like to know what happened at Jerusalem. To put it in a nutshell, we didn't succeed. We weren't exactly defeated, but neither were we victorious. But that's not news to you."

"No, it's not. The news got around pretty fast. What I don't know is why the attack failed, and so quickly."

Herod's countenance underwent an abrupt transformation: His eyes narrowed, his jaw was thrust forward; his voice took on a snarling tone. "It failed because of all the generals in the Roman army, they had to send me their most stupid jackass. Any more such help and I am undone."

"Who was the general this time? His name escapes me."

"Machaeras. Right now he's here in Samaria, but the less I see of him, the better. He's caused me a very serious problem, and I'm not referring to the military setback."

"And what is this serious problem?"

"Before explaining, let me tell you one thing: This Machaeras is as bad as Silo – a puffed-up toad. After defeating the Parthians, Ventidius sent him to me with two legions and a thousand cavalry. That's not a small force by any means. With the right strategy we stood a good chance. But not a quick breakthrough."

"Was that what he tried to do?" remarked Joseph, his eyebrows rising sharply.

"That's right! Against Jerusalem's strong walls and fanatical defenders, mind you. He thought that after they had beaten the Parthians, Jerusalem would be easy prey. Did you ever hear such nonsense?"

"Couldn't you talk him out of it?"

"Did you ever try to talk to a stone wall? He's every bit as arrogant and rude as Silo. He thinks that only the Romans know how to wage war. He treated me like dirt – me, the king of Judea!"

"And what were the consequences? What was the big problem he caused you?"

Herod sat back with a grave look on his face. "As you know, we had to retreat from Jerusalem. My force – or rather, our force," he corrected himself with a fleeting grin at Nikias, "withdrew to Samaria in good order. But Machaeras, in retreating beyond Emmaus, killed every Jew he came across, even including some of our supporters."

"What a terrible thing to do! And completely idiotic."

"That's right! The Jews, I don't have to tell you, have never taken kindly to me – to any of our family. And now they're burning with hatred, far worse than anything in the past. And they're going to be my subjects. Do you know what that means?"

"Is the hatred widespread, or is it more or less confined to the route of retreat?"

"My spies tell me that it's widespread. How could you expect otherwise? And for this I have to thank that asinine Roman."

Joseph reflected a moment. "You once told me that Antony and Octavian never promised you military aid, that you would have to go it alone."

"Until they defeated the Parthians," Herod explained. "The campaign isn't over yet, even though the Parthians have lost a major battle. That's why Ventidius was able to spare two legions and a thousand horse. If only he had spared a general who knew his business, not one who's only fit to be a mule driver."

"Well, what's done can't be undone. Or can it?" Joseph added, knitting his brow.

Herod cocked an inquisitive eye. "What do you mean? Have you any ideas?"

"Perhaps."

"Let's hear it."

Joseph drew a deep breath before replying. "You say the hatred is intense and widespread. You have to counteract it."

"How?" asked Herod impatiently.

"You've been betrothed to the Hasmonean princess for a long time now – four or five years, I believe."

"Almost five. So?"

"She's very popular; the people adore her. If I'm not mistaken, that was one of the reasons you wanted the betrothal in the first place. I know things haven't been normal the past couple of years, that you've had plenty of other concerns on your mind. But now is the time to finish the business. Don't put off the nuptials any longer."

Joseph did not utter a sound as he watched his brother turn the matter over in his mind. Herod's eyes lit up, and his countenance underwent a subtle change. He leaned forward and turned to his chief lieutenant, who had been silent all this time. "Nikias, you're Greek, so I don't expect you to understand the Jewish mentality or the intricacies of the situation. Still, you may have something worthwhile to say on the subject. What do you think?"

Nikias replied without hesitation. "As you say, I don't understand the intricacies of the situation. I can only speak as a military man. And as a military man I say, finish the military business first. Secure the throne and then marry the Hasmonean princess."

Herod's brow furrowed. He picked up a stylus and began to tap the desk abstractedly as he pondered Nikias's advice. "I see you two differ on the timing of the marriage. I'll have to give it careful thought. Joseph, thank you; you have eased my mind considerably. Now let's get down to military business. Nikias, what's the situation with our troops? How many men have we lost? How is morale?"

"We've lost less than a third of our men. That's tolerable, I'd say, but our force has never been very big."

"True," Herod agreed with a frown. "And morale?"

"So-so. Some of the men are disgruntled after the unsuccessful siege. And they haven't been paid for some time."

"I'll see that they get paid," said Herod in decisive tone. "Let the men start taking leave – staggered of course. We'll have to recruit replacements, and that's not going to be easy. It's clear to me that by ourselves we'll never finish this business. We need Roman help, it's no use denying it, but proper help, with an adequate force, siege equipment, and above all, a competent general."

"I agree with you," said Nikias. "What are the prospects for such aid?"

"That's what I intend to find out. What I was reading when you came in was a letter from Antony. It was delivered to me late last night. He's back in Syria and has taken over command of the Roman army from Ventidius. Right now he's besieging Samosata."

"Samosata? Is that in Parthia?" asked Joseph.

"It's close to Parthia, but it actually belongs to Parthia's ally, Antiochus of Commagene. It's the capital city. I'm going there to explain our situation to Antony. From the tone of his letter I'm quite hopeful. In my absence, you, Joseph, will be in charge here. Don't get into any arguments with Machaeras. He's not going to be happy when he discovers that I've gone to Antony. And don't let him talk you into any reckless adventures. Stay put, I'm warning you."

Chapter Seven

Hyrcanus in Babylonian Exile

A Letter from Alexandra

The view from his home in the Jewish quarter of Babylon reminded Hyrcanus of the royal palace at Jericho. Toward the west a treeless desert stretched as far as the eye could see, reminiscent of much of the scenery between Jerusalem and Jericho, while date palms abounded along the banks of the Euphrates, rivaling those in the vicinity of the Hasmonean winter palace.

Sitting at his ease on the roof of his villa in the late afternoon, when the air had cooled a bit, Hyrcanus watched the riverboats making their way downstream. With their high prow and aft and propelled by poles, they were a picturesque sight. Their cargo consisted mostly of agricultural products and woven stuffs, some of which Hyrcanus was quite certain belonged to his fellow Jews. While most Babylonian Jews engaged in agriculture, there was a considerable number of merchants among them, some of whom traded surplus nonperishable farm products for silks and spices from the Far East.

"Now you can get some idea why relatively few of our people returned to the homeland after Cyrus's decree," Hyrcanus remarked to his wife Elisheva, who was sitting beside him knitting a scarf for their granddaughter. "Once the trauma of captivity wore off, they soon got used to life here. Where do you find such fertile soil as that between the Euphrates and Tigris rivers? Apart from perhaps the Nile basin, I doubt if there is richer, better-watered soil anywhere. It's no wonder that Babylon and nearby Seleucia are the hub of numerous trade routes and that so many of our people live in this region. And not only here; there's hardly a city or even a village in this country without a sizable Jewish population. Whenever I bring up the subject of returning to the homeland, the people give me a vague look and stammer an evasive reply.

"Can you blame them?" said Elisheva. "We've been here only two years, while most of our Babylonian brethren probably have roots here that go back even to Nebuchanezzar's days. That's more than 500 years ago, a very long time. The Temple means a lot to them and the homeland is still the homeland. But apart from an occasional pilgrimage, what compelling urge do they feel to pick themselves up and return for good? Here life is – well, more peaceful for one thing."

Hyrcanus gave his wife a sidelong glance. Only three years younger than he, she still had an alert, vibrant look. Her features were finely molded, her skin bronzed by the summer sun; she had large brown eyes, a lofty brow, and a well-poised neck. She had always been a pillar of strength to him, sharing his joys and his many tribulations with fortitude and solicitude. If not for her, he doubted whether he could have borne the humiliation of being led captive to Parthia.

"The peaceful life here depends on the character of the ruler," he replied meditatively. "If he happens to be benevolent, life is good and peaceful for our people. But if there should arise a new king who knew not Joseph – I don't have to tell you about the Egyptian bondage. And the same goes for our people in other countries, even Rome. I wouldn't be surprised if more of our people aren't living in the diaspora than in the homeland. It's not a healthy situation by any means."

"I agree with you, but the way things are at present it's unrealistic to expect any change – at least in the foreseeable future. Antigonus and Herod have been fighting each other nearly two years, and who knows how much longer it will go on or how it will end? People who want to go on pilgrimage from here are afraid to do so. You think it doesn't distress them? They may not want to go back to live there, but they do want to visit the Temple."

Hyrcanus sighed. He wished his wife had not mentioned the Temple again. She knew how much it pained him to be reminded, even indirectly, of what Antigonus had done to disqualify him from serving as high priest. His mood darkened. "The ways of the Lord are sometimes mysterious," he said with a note of pathos. "When I was high priest, I was very curious about the Jewish communities in Babylonia and yearned to visit them but never managed it. Now I yearn to see the Holy Land again and can't do so."

"You'll see it again," Elisheva reassured him.

"I wish I could be as confident of that as you are. But even if the Almighty grants me the privilege, I will return as Johanan Hyrcanus, no longer high priest, no longer ethnarch or king – just plain Johanan Hyrcanus."

Elisheva put down her knitting. "You will never be just plain Johanan Hyrcanus," she said resolutely. "You are royalty, a Hasmonean. Nothing can take that away from you. Even here in Babylonia the people haven't forgotten who you are. When you appear in public, don't they greet you as their high priest and king?"

Hyrcanus's lips twisted into a wry smile. What his wife said was true, and this both pleased and puzzled him. The Jews of Babylonia were strongly pro-Parthian in the conflict with Rome, and so they favored Antigonus. Yet they called Hyrcanus their high priest and king and showed him every respect. He had to admit that, everything considered and whatever he thought of his nephew Antigonus, he had been treated deferentially. He had never felt so devastated as when he was led fettered before the Parthian monarch, who had received him cordially and released him from his bonds. He had also allowed him to live wherever he wanted in Babylonia, the province in the Parthian empire with the densest Jewish population. After discussing the matter with some Jewish notables, Hyrcanus had decided on Babylon, where he was provided with a spacious villa and an income sufficient for maintaining a household if not on a royal than at least a decent scale. He enjoyed complete freedom of movement, and was highly gratified at the honor bestowed on him by the Jewish community. It was at his first public appearance that he had been greeted as "our high priest and king." This had brought tears to his eyes, and helped to ease somewhat the acute distress he had felt after the cropping of his ears. The memory of that dastardly deed still made him shudder. To think, his own nephew had dared to render him unfit to serve in the Temple! No longer a high priest, but – as his wife so rightly said – neither was he just plain Johanan Hyrcanus.

Dear Elisheva! What a wonderful helpmate she has been to him. He knew how bad she felt at her failure to give him a son, or even another daughter or two. Her miscarriages had caused her great anguish. He assured her that he was grateful to the Almighty for giving him a daughter like Alexandra, who in many ways was like a son to him. He missed her greatly, and his grandchildren too. He longed to see them again, to delight in their youthful spirits, to tell them stories about their family. With all the turmoil in the country, were they safe? He prayed to the Almighty to watch over them.

Communication with Alexandra was an uncertain matter. Occasionally she managed to get a letter to him; and this, together with the reports brought back by those pilgrims who braved the journey to the Holy Land, kept him abreast of developments there. He remembered every word of the letter she had written while still at Masada, when Herod had set out to attack Jerusalem. She grieved for her fellow Jerusalemites and prayed for their safety. She had taken a great risk is writing this, for interception of the letter could have had unpleasant consequences for her. But she was not alone in her sentiments. News of the siege of Jerusalem had filled Babyonian Jewry with trepidation. Special prayers had been recited for the safety of the city and the Temple. Hyrcanus had joined in the prayers, but he could not escape a feeling of some unease, for while no one remarked in his presence about his close association with Herod, he felt as though an accusing finger had been pointed at him. When news of the withdrawal of the besieging force reached Babylonia, it was greeted with immense relief. And so too was Herod's subsequent discomfiture. For it was clear that while he had achieved some successes in Galilee, they were not of a decisive or lasting nature: In many instances the inhabitants rose up and regained much of what had been lost.

Hyrcanus managed to get letters to Alexandra even after the move from Masada to Samaria, a safer and more comfortable place. She looked forward to these letters and begged him to keep on writing, as this bolstered her spirits. "I wonder how Alexandra and the grandchildren are," Hyrcanus remarked wistfully to Elisheva when she returned from the kitchen with a bowl of dates. "It's some time since we've heard from her."

"I know," replied Elisheva with a frown. "I can't help worrying about them, what with the unsettled life – the fighting, Herod's family..."

The mention of Herod's family made Hyrcanus grimace. This was a very sore point with him. Not a single member of his family was happy about Mariamne's betrothal – not even Elisheva. Like Alexandra, she had tried to dissuade him from this step, but after hearing his reasons, she refrained from criticizing him on this score. Occasionally, however, she would forget herself, and her true feelings would emerge, as they did just now.

"When they were at Masada, Joseph was quite friendly and helpful," said Hyrcanus a little lamely.

"Joseph, yes; but the trouble is not with him – you know that. It's Salome. She goes out of her way to make life miserable for Alexandra and her children. Besides, Joseph is only occasionally at Samaria, where he can keep Salome in her place."

Hyrcanus sighed. When he had agreed to Herod's proposal of the match – how long ago it seemed – he had not reckoned on Salome. He had heard rumors about her but did not think this was a relevant consideration. He now had to admit that he had underestimated her spiteful, malevolent nature. "Alexandra is a strong person," he remarked confidently. "She's more than a match for Salome. I wouldn't worry too much about her."

"I hope you're right," said Elisheva, her brow furrowing deeply.

"Now let's forget about them for a while and relax."

For a few minutes they sat in silence, enjoying the tranquility of the scene. They nibbled at dates while watching the boats heading south. It was quiet and peaceful at this hour, when the sun was sinking and the oppressive heat of the day had let up. Overhead birds circled, their chirping adding a cheerful note. "Is everything ready for your journey tomorrow?" asked Elisheva, breaking the silence.

"Yes. I understand that I'll be traveling in a comfortable carriage and accompanied by an escort."

"Provided by the exilarch?"

"Of course. We're both looking forward to this meeting. It's almost half a year since we last saw each other."

"Wouldn't it have been proper for him to call on you, and not the other way around?"

Hyrcanus regarded his wife with an amused look. "The exilarch, dear, is head of the Jewish community in Babylonia and a high official in the Parthian court," he explained patiently. "I am a – well, you might say, a guest here. Besides, he came to see me the first time, and it was largely thanks to him that I have been treated so well and provided with this fine villa. Also, I'm curious to see what sort of a court he maintains, and to meet our people there. So…"

Hyrcanus broke off as a servant appeared in the entrance to the roof. "Excuse me, sire, a courier has arrived with a letter for you."

"A courier?" Hyrcanus's face lit up as he rose to his feet. "I'll come right down."

The courier, a moderately tall, slim man in his late twenties, was wearing a dun-colored tunic covered with dust; lines of fatigue showed on his face. From his girdle he extracted a papyrus roll and handed it to Hyrcanus. "I was ordered by the princess Alexandra to deliver this to you, sire."

"How long ago was that?"

"About a week."

"You made very good time. Did you encounter any danger on the way?"

"A little. Even in Samaria."

"Your services will not go unrewarded."

Hyrcanus turned to the servant. "Show the courier to the room next to yours, and give him a basin of water so he can wash himself." To the courier he asked, "Would you like to rest first or eat?"

"If it's all the same to you, I prefer to eat something light now and then rest a bit before having a proper meal."

"It shall be as you wish."

After the courier left, Hyrcanus opened the papyrus roll. "It looks like a long letter," he remarked.

"Read it aloud," Elisheva requested. "I'm impatient to know what she has written." Hyrcanus sat down and began to read the letter aloud:

My dear parents,

May the Lord bless you and keep you in good health and spirits. I am sending this letter with a trusted courier, and pray that he succeeds in delivering it to you. In these difficult times one has to be grateful for even things like this.

I am happy to learn from your last letter, which took almost a fortnight to reach me, that you are comfortably settled in the spacious home put at your disposal, and that our brethren in Babylonia are according you the respect you deserve. I hope that this compensates you in some measure for the unhappy change in your fortunes. As for me, it has made our separation more tolerable.

In one respect I envy you. You are living among our people and in a land that is enjoying peace and relative calm. We, on the other hand, are now living in Samaria, which, as you know, was once the capital of the ancient Israelite kingdom but now is completely Greek in character. If I find this a cause for dismay, for Mariamne and Aristobulus it is even more so, but I am doing my best to protect them from pagan influences.

"The poor dears must be having a hard time," commiserated Elisheva.

"At least they're safe from physical danger – as safe as one can be in these times," said Hyrcanus with an encouraging nod. "I see that Alexandra goes on to mention this. Listen:

I am thankful to the Almighty that for the time being at least we are enjoying a degree of safety: no siege, no shortage of water or food. We must be grateful for that.

Your grandchildren, thank God, are growing fast. Aristobulus is no longer a young child but will soon be a gangling youngster. And Mariamne is a very beautiful young maiden. She has always been beautiful – and this is not a mother's biased opinion – but now she is strikingly so. Evidently this has not been lost on Herod, for whenever he comes here – and this seems to be increasingly frequent of late – he never fails to bring her a costly gift. He is showing her a lot more attention. While my feelings about the betrothal have not changed, one good thing has happened: Salome does not dare to openly create trouble, as she did at Masada. Herod has made it quite plain that he will not tolerate any of her nonsense.

The fighting, unfortunately, is still going on. From time to time, Herod summons Joseph and his staff officers to a meeting here in Samaria, and from the tone of his voice and his angry looks I gather that matters are not going too well. He evidently thought that within a relatively short time after being crowned king of Judea he would be sitting on the throne. But even though his army wins battles, it cannot hold on to its gains for long. This makes him furious, and everyone around him is clearly aware of it. You should have seen him when he learned about the death of Ptolemy, the general he put in charge of the region around Arbela after flushing out some Galileans from the caves there. The Galileans, as you well know, are a tough lot, and they hate Herod like poison. They will never forgive him for executing Hezekiah.

"I should say not," remarked Elisheva. "And what a time Herod gave you when he was brought to trial before the Sanhedrin for what he had done!"

"You still remember that?" said Hyrcanus, raising his eyebrows. "That was almost ten years ago."

"How can one forget something like that? I remember it as though it happened yesterday. And that nasty letter the governor of Syria sent you – whatever his name was."

"Sextus, Sextus Caesar. Now where was I? Oh yes, the Galileans. Let me continue:"

The Romans assigned a general called Silo to help Herod, but he proved to be more of a hindrance than help, and on his departure Herod remarked that it was good riddance. Another general – I think his name is Machaeras – was then sent to help Herod, but he turned out to be not only just as incompetent, but extremely cruel, and he caused a very serious problem. What the final outcome will be, only the Lord knows. I pray that it will be good for our people, our country, and our family.

You are always in our thoughts, and we miss you very much. The children keep asking when you will be coming back to them. Let us hope and pray that, with the Lord's help, it will not be long before we are reunited. Until that happy day may the Almighty keep you and grant you good health and good spirits.

Your loving daughter, Alexandra

"Poor Alexandra," said Elisheva with a deep sigh.

Hyrcanus gave his wife a curious look. "Why poor Alexandra? Apart from having to live among pagans, I'd say she sounds quite cheerful on the whole – more so than in her other letters."

"That may be. But still she – and the grandchildren, too, of course – are really prisoners in a war-torn land. How can they live a normal life in such circumstances? Look how peaceful and quiet it is here. You can't compare the situation here with what they have to endure."

"Do you think it has always been peaceful and quiet here? Do you know how many wars have been fought here, how many times possession of this land has changed hands? We're fortunate that the Parthians now rule the land. They've been tolerant and good to our people. But how can we be sure that something won't happy to change all that?"

Elisheva reflected on this for a moment. "Yes, I suppose you're right, if you look at it in that light. But I can't help worrying about the situation in Judea, and especially about Alexandra and the grandchildren. It's not good that she's been a widow all these years. She should have remarried."

Hyrcanus, who had heard this plaint innumerable times, gave his usual reply: "I agree with you completely. But we can't tell Alexandra what to do. It's for her to decide."

The Former High Priest Meets the Exilarch

Hyrcanus enjoyed the ride to Nehardea, which was made in one of the exilarch's handsome carriages. He took great interest in the passing scenery, especially the irrigated fields and the system of canals, sluices, and dams that drained the marshy soil between the Tigris and Euphrates rivers. The region was noted for its bountiful crops, and after observing the plentiful water supply and rich alluvial soil, he could clearly see why.

Hyrcanus arrived at his destination in the early afternoon. The exilarch's residence was not nearly as large or majestic as the royal Hasmonean palace in Jerusalem, but it was nevertheless a fairly sizable, imposing edifice. Built of stucco-covered brick, it was enclosed by a tall wall, much of which was covered with flowering climbers.

"My dear High Priest," the exilarch greeted Hyrcanus cordially, "it's an honor and a pleasure to welcome you to my residence. And I'm pleased to see you looking so well – much better than at our previous meeting. May I take it that the accommodations you were provided with is one reason for this happy change?"

"They are most satisfactory," replied Hyrcanus, warmed by the exilarch's hearty welcome. "I'm very grateful for your intervention with the Parthian monarch. I'm perfectly aware that he had ample reason to be less magnanimous with me."

"His Majesty is a very tolerant and generous man," said the exilarch with an engaging grin. "After I explained your situation, he was most understanding and even expressed a desire to invite you to an audience." The exilarch took

Hyrcanus by the arm. "Come, let me take you to your room so you can put your luggage away, and then I'll show you around my modest home."

Hyrcanus was impressed by the exilarch's residence. It was even more state-ly than what its exterior suggested, consisting of a large hall, two smaller ones, and a number of apartments ranged around the central courtyard and a smaller one. The rugs, tapestries, and furniture were rich and costly; exquisite green-glazed vases and other ceramic objects graced many of the rooms. It was obvious that the exilarch did not lack for means.

After showing his guest through his home, the exilarch ushered him into the audience chamber, where they were joined by another man, who was in-troduced as Avraham. It was pleasantly cool here, and after partaking of some refreshments, including spiced date wine, Hyrcanus began to recover from the tiredness of the journey. While engaging in small talk, he studied the two men. The exilarch was a dynamic-looking man in his early fifties; he had a medium build, full face, slightly beaked nose, shrewd, penetrating eyes, and a well-trimmed mustache and square-cut beard. He wore a long purple silk robe fastened at the waist by a wide girdle made of beaten gold. The other man was also clad in silk, but of a light blue color, and his girdle was made of studded leather. Hyrcanus, however, was struck more by the man's physiognomy than his dress: He was in his mid-thirties, had a graceful figure, noble brow, and a handsome countenance that did not look the least Semitic.

"If I read your thoughts correctly," said the ethnarch with a wry smile, "you are curious about my worthy official's origins."

Hyrcanus gave an embarrassed grin. "I didn't realize it was so obvious. It wasn't polite of me to stare."

"But perfectly understandable. Avraham is a convert of Greek origin. You see, we have converts in Babylonia too, although maybe not as many as in Judea. Avraham – I still find it hard to call such a fine specimen of Greek manhood by that name – not only has a perfect command of Greek, he knows four other languages; and this, together with an excellent knowledge of the Greco-Roman world, has made him an invaluable aide. He is my adviser on matters relating to Rome and the Hellenistic world in general."

"You are fortunate to have the services of such a talented adviser," said Hy-rcanus, flashing a smile at Avraham. He wondered why the exilarch wanted his adviser on Hellenistic affairs to be present at the audience.

"I am aware of and grateful for my good fortune," acknowledged the exi-larch. "A faithful convert, a faithful adviser – a rare combination indeed. Such a convert is to be highly prized and welcomed with open arms." The exilarch kept his voice casual as he added with an enigmatic smile: "That is more than one can say about those who have been converted against their will, without any real conviction whatsoever."

At the last remark Hyrcanus stiffened visibly. He regarded the exilarch with a puzzled expression. The latter continued to smile benignly, but the import of his observation was not lost on Hyrcanus. They had been conversing pleasantly; what impelled him to introduce such a jarring note? Hyrcanus felt challenged to reply, but for a long moment he groped for words. Finally he said in a firm voice: "The Idumeans, Exilarch, and I assume that's whom you are referring to, were given the choice of either converting or leaving their land. Incidentally, let me remind you that the land they now occupy was not originally theirs, but was part of the territory that had belonged to the tribe of Judah. They lived further south and moved north when our people were exiled to Babylonia. My grandfather could have dealt with them in another way: He could have put them to the sword. That is not an unheard-of thing in this part of the world. Or he could have exiled them or sold them into slavery – the way many kings have dealt with a conquered foe. But my grandfather chose a different way – a more humane way."

"Humane it may have been," agreed the exilarch, regretting that he had not framed his remark a little more carefully. "But was it wise?"

Hyrcanus gave the exilarch a long, thoughtful look. "Put yourself in my grandfather's shoes and tell me what you would have done. What was the situation then? Judea was relatively weak, and there were enemies on every side who threatened to snuff out the nation's newly won independence. I'm referring not only to the Syrians, who more than once tried to reconquer Judea. Idumea, our southern neighbor, was also hostile. They sided with the Syrians, and it's no coincidence that in their campaigns against Judea the Syrians more than once attacked from the south, through Idumea. And there's something else you must remember: The Idumeans were pagans. That too was a danger to our way of life. Hebron, the city of our patriarch, in pagan hands – you don't think that was intolerable?"

Avraham, who so far had listened intently but said nothing, now addressed Hyrcanus: "By converting the Idumeans did your grandfather think he had purged them of their paganism?" he asked in perfect Aramaic with a Greek lilt. "Did he think he could turn them into loyal citizens or loyal subjects?"

Hyrcanus shifted his position on the chair. "No, of course not. He didn't delude himself. He knew that this would take time. After all, the Israelites wandered around in the desert forty years before the Lord considered them ready to enter the Promised Land. And this after they had witnessed His many miracles – in Egypt, at the Red Sea, Mount Sinai, and elsewhere."

"A pity your grandfather didn't foresee that his policy would also produce a Herod. He's undoing the very thing your grandfather held most dear."

"Most dear? What exactly are you referring to?"

"The sovereignty and yes, the very safety of Judea, no less! Ach, my friend, look what has happened: Herod crowned king of Judea – by whom? By the

Romans – the pagan Romans! And your grandfather was worried about the pagan neighbors to the south – a small, insignificant people, How ironical! Your grandfather must surely have turned over in his grave."

Hyrcanus's face clouded. There was no denying the validity of this statement. He remained silent and waited for the exilarch to continue. "We in Babylonia – in all Parthia for that matter –" he went on, "are dismayed at the turn of events, especially the fighting that is now raging in the land. We are distressed at the plight of our brethren in the Holy Land, in the Holy City. Our people hesitate – nay, are afraid – to make pilgrimage, to visit the holy Temple, to bring their offerings. You as high priest can appreciate what that means. And not only that. Our young men who want to continue their studies in the Holy Land, to sit at the feet of the sages, how can they do so?"

The exilarch raised his voice a bit, his expression was grave. "All this gives us cause for the utmost concern. It also places us in an awkward position vis-a-vis the Parthian government. Many of us – the overwhelming majority in fact – belong to families who have been living here for over 500 years, ever since the Babylonian Captivity. Nevertheless, our hearts are with our brethren in the homeland. What happens to them affects us as well. At the same time our sympathies lie with the Parthians. They have treated us very favorably. As you see, I am the head of an autonomous community. And as such, I am also part of the Parthian hierarchy. We owe the Parthian monarch our allegiance, but otherwise we enjoy complete freedom in our religious and cultural life. We also..."

"Our people in Rome also enjoy such freedom," Hyrcanus interposed. "Nor have the Romans interfered with our religious life in Judea. On the contrary, it was Caesar who appointed me high priest and ethnarch."

"Ach, my dear friend," the exilarch snorted, flinging his arms out, "and that is not interference of a sort? Why should Caesar – a Roman, a pagan – have appointed you high priest? Ethnarch, that I can understand: it's not much different from appointing you king. But high priest, head of the Temple, responsible for the religious and spiritual life of the nation – what has that to do with a pagan Roman?" The exilarch paused briefly, then continued: "This is not the only example of Roman interference; there are others. My worthy adviser can cite them to you. Avraham, please refresh our dear friend's memory."

Avraham straightened the folds of his robe and cleared his throat. His voice was resonant and well modulated. "Roman intervention in Judea began with Pompey, about twenty-five years ago," he began, noticing a pained look crossing Hyrcanus's face. "When Pompey captured Jerusalem, his soldiers entered the Temple and killed all the people they found there, including the priests going about their sacred functions. Then..."

"Not only that," the exilarch interjected, "Pompey himself entered the sanctuary – the Holy of Holies – an unheard-of sacrilege. Only the high priest is permitted to enter the Holy of Holies, and that only on the Day of Atonement. Proceed."

"After Pompey, there was Crassus. He plundered the Temple of all the money he could lay his hands on."

"And that was an enormous sum," the exilarch emphasized. "All the half-shekels sent each year by our people in the homeland and every country in the diaspora, as well as the money deposited in the Temple for safekeeping." The exilarch nodded to his adviser to continue.

"And not only that. Crassus stripped the sanctuary of all its golden vessels – worth a fortune. After that there wasn't much left for Cassius to take. So he imposed a heavy tribute. When this was not met in full, he enslaved the men of four towns – sold them to gentiles – pagans."

"So you see, my friend," said the exilarch, leaning forward in his chair, "it is not correct to say there has been no interference by Rome. Maybe it has not been as flagrant or direct as in the days of wicked Antiochus Epiphanes – may his name be blotted out – but still not exactly commendable acts of benevolence."

"No, they were not benevolent acts," conceded Hyrcanus with a shrug of his shoulders. "But in a way they can be regarded as exceptions."

"Exceptions!" exclaimed the exilarch, raising his eyebrows. "Pompey, Crassus, Cassius – that's a lot of exceptions in such a relatively short time."

Hyrcanus stirred uneasily in his chair. He had not expected the audience to be confined to an exchange of pleasantries, but neither had he expected to squirm like this. He felt his good name was being impugned. "They may seem like quite a few exceptions," he reluctantly admitted. "But if we're discussing Roman intervention in Judea's affairs, let me ask you something: Do you think Parthian intervention has been all to the good? You mentioned Herod before – the fact that he was crowned king of Judea by the Romans. Don't forget that until the Parthians came to Judea I was high priest and king – or ethnarch, if you want to use the Roman designation. So if Herod is now king, the Parthians are largely to blame. They set in motion the train of events that led to his crowning."

The exilarch mused on this for a moment. "You have a point there, I agree. But I wonder whether a vassal, or a client king – and that's what Herod will be if, heaven forbid, he is victorious, and what you, if I may say so, would have been had you continued to sit on the throne of Judea – is that for the good of our people in the homeland?"

The exilarch glanced at the ceiling for a second, and then continued with a grave expression. "Since we're speaking about Herod, there's something I'm extremely curious about. It's a very delicate matter, and you don't have to explain if you don't want to." The exilarch paused briefly and then spoke slowly, as he weighed his words. "I can think of no greater contrast than that between Herod and the Hasmonean house. This is not only my opinion; I can safely say it is shared by all our people wherever they live. When we learned about the betrothal of your granddaughter to Herod, we were astounded. We couldn't believe our ears. I have discussed this with a number of people, and have heard all sorts of possible reasons. But it is all speculation, and frankly I'm still puzzled. Was it for personal reasons, or perhaps national? Either way, it's hard for me to understand. I don't want to press you or cause you any embarrassment. As I have said, you needn't explain if you don't want to."

The exilarch folded his arms and waited for Hyrcanus's response. Hyrcanus cupped his chin in his hand and lowered his gaze; a pallor crept over his face as he pondered his reply. When he raised his eyes, they were at first troubled and then thoughtful. He moistened his lips and spoke in a low voice: "Time will tell whether I was wise in espousing my granddaughter to Herod. Apart from my family and a few close friends, I have not confided my considerations to anyone, even though I'm aware of the general negative reaction. But since you ask, and considering your exalted office, I feel you have a right to know. Was it for personal or national reasons, you ask. It was both. I have to admit that my initial and probably overriding consideration was to protect my daughter and grandchildren, who, apart from Antigonus, are the last of the Hasmonean line."

"Protect them from what?" asked the exilarch with a baffled look.

"Antigonus."

"Antigonus – your own nephew!" exclaimed the exilarch incredulously.

"Yes, my own nephew. And events have shown that I have had good reason to fear him. For one thing, it was he who mutilated my ears."

"A dastardly deed, I admit. I can't condone it by any means; but presumably that was to ensure that he would be high priest and hence king."

"And who can guarantee that he won't go further than that?"

Utter disbelief was written on the exilarch's face. "You mean..."

"Yes, that's exactly what I mean."

"Preposterous! His own family, his own kin!"

"Aren't there enough examples in the world around us? You have never heard of pretenders, or successors, to the throne doing away with the members of their own family in order to eliminate any possible rivals?"

The exilarch and his adviser exchanged a meaningful glance. "Phraates," murmured Avraham, nodding soberly.

"Yes, Phraates, the Parthian king of kings," declared Hyrcanus with a note of emphatic self-vindication. "Phraates, who only a short time ago murdered his father Orodes and all his younger brothers – all thirty of them. This is only one example; there are others."

"But they all have to do with people who did not receive the Torah, which prescribes capital punishment for murder," countered the exilarch without much conviction.

"Is it inconceivable for Antigonus to so manipulate it that the Parthians would perpetrate the actual deed? As you see, they would have no compunctions on this score."

The exilarch was visibly shaken by this possibility. For a long moment he was silent as he digested the import of what he had just heard. Fixing Hyrcanus with a grim look, he said, "I pray to the Almighty that it will never come to this. It's too terrible to contemplate. I find it hard to believe that Antigonus could be guilty of such a heinous crime. But now I can at least understand your apprehension. Yet I still fail to see how uniting your house – the Hasmonean house – with Herod's offers a solution. Besides hating Herod for his servile pro-Roman policy, our people don't regard him as Jewish, certainly not in spirit, if not *halachically*. We could never accept him as a Jewish king."

"But our people could accept my granddaughter as a Jewish queen. Their offspring would be Jewish in the full sense of the word. You may disagree with me, but I'm convinced that Rome will be in this part of the world for a long time to come. It may not be a pleasant fact, but we in Judea will have to live with it, within reasonable limits of course. And it's also a fact that Rome has proclaimed Herod king of Judea. This too is not an ideal situation as far as we are concerned. But through my granddaughter we can at least ensure that those who follow Herod on the throne will have Hasmonean blood in their veins. This was my second major consideration – what you could call the national consideration."

The exilarch shook his head dubiously. "I wish I could agree with you, but it strikes me as a prescription for disaster. I'm afraid our people would prefer Antigonus, without the other business you alluded to, of course."

"The Parthians would have to drive the Romans out of Judea for that to happen. I have grave doubts they can do it."

The Sanhedrin Debates Involuntary Conversion

Shemaiah had never forgotten the words uttered many years ago by his revered teacher Shimon ben Shetah during a discussion of Israel's role in the divine scheme of things. "The Jewish people," ben Shetah had told his disciples, "have three crowns: the priestly crown, the royal crown, and the crown of Torah. The Babylonian Exile showed that, if necessary, Israel could survive without the Temple; for 500 years it had survived without a king; but without Torah, the teaching and observance of God's word, Israel is just a tiny, insignificant nation doomed to drift aimlessly like chaff in the wind until it vanishes, like all such nations."

This statement had made an indelible impression on Shemaiah, and he could still vividly recall his master's noble appearance as he enlarged on this theme. Shemaiah was humbly grateful that he had been privileged to sit at the feet of the greatest sage of the day, to imbibe his knowledge and wisdom, and to follow in his footsteps and help carry on the sacred task of disseminating God's word through teaching, preaching, and dedicated service in the Sanhedrin, the supreme ecclesiastical and judicial body of the Jewish people.

The Sanhedrin had experienced more than one change of fortune during Shemaiah's lifetime. As a youngster he had witnessed its humiliation by Alexander Yannai, who brooked no interference with or criticism of his military adventures or his secular, Hellenistic ways, and in the end persecuted the sages belonging to the popular Pharisaic party. The Sanhedrin regained its exalted status during the reign of Yannai's widow, the beloved Queen Alexandra Salome, and it continued to enjoy harmonious relations with Hyrcanus. But with his banishment to Babylonia, it again faced a period of uncertainty. Not that Antigonus displayed any hostility toward it; on the contrary, he was careful to avoid any semblance of discord. Besides, apart from the first few months, he was too occupied with Herod to devote much attention to the Sanhedrin. But the turmoil caused by Herod's latest attempts to wrest the throne from Antigonus had made it difficult for the institution to function properly, especially when a full quorum was required. With the withdrawal of Machaeras's Roman legions from Jerusalem, the sages who had been stranded in their home towns and villages were able to resume their places in the Sanhedrin.

As Shemaiah made his way up the Temple Mount on a warm summer day, he was greeted deferentially by worshippers proceeding to the daily morning sacrifice. It was gratifying to know that he and Avtalion, president and vice-president respectively of the Sanhedrin, were held in high esteem by the people, who looked to them for spiritual leadership in these troubled times. Shemaiah had reservations about Antigonus, who in some respects reminded him of his grandfather Alexander Yannai. He deplored Antigonus's attempt to usurp the royal and priestly crowns from his uncle Hyrcanus and the way he had disqualified him from the high priesthood by mutilating his ears. But there was no denying his immense popularity with the people, who had welcomed him with open arms and flocked to his banner. They hated Herod and Rome's growing domination over the country – a feeling exacerbated by the brutal behavior of generals like Machaeras and several years before him by Cassius's enslavement of the males of Emmaus and three other towns. Shemaiah knew that many of his colleagues in the Sanhedrin shared the widespread enthusiasm for Antigonus.

Shemaiah was essentially a man of peace, and the turmoil and agony convulsing Judea distressed him greatly. He could understand the rejoicing with which the people had greeted Parthia's victory over Crassus's Roman legions some fifteen years earlier and its occupation of Syria only two years ago, but he was less sanguine than most even then. To his mind its feudal structure put the sprawling polyglot Parthian empire at a considerable disadvantage in its struggle with Rome for hegemony over this part of the world – a judgment reinforced by the subsequent Parthian setbacks. This, however, gave him no cause for satisfaction: Like all his colleagues, he was dismayed at the prospect of Herod's occupying the throne of Judea, even if he shared it with Hyrcanus's granddaughter.

How was he to relate to Herod? One thing was indisputable: Herod could not be regarded as a Jewish king, for Scripture states, "One from among thy brethren shalt thou set king over thee; thou mayest not put a foreigner over thee, who is not thy brother." Despite the widespread hatred of the man and the prevailing opinion that he could not be regarded as "one of thy brethren," especially as regards the kingship, the question of his Jewishness was not as clear-cut as was generally thought. But there was no denying that if, heaven forbid, he should occupy the throne of Judea, it would not be because the Jewish people had set him king over them. He was appointed king by Rome, and while arguably he might be nominally Jewish – or half-Jewish, as many claimed – in his outlook and way of life he was thoroughly Hellenistic. Many even regarded him as an outright pagan, for how else could they view his sacrificing to Jupiter in Rome? Even more disturbing to Shemaiah was the fear that if he gained the throne, Herod would suppress the Sanhedrin or at least strip it of most its powers.

When Shemaiah entered the Chamber of Hewn Stone, the members of the Sanhedrin stopped chatting and rose to their feet as he made his way to his chair in the middle of three rows of benches ranged in a semicircle. He nodded to Avtalion and the two scribes seated on either side of his chair, and signaled to the elders to be seated. The benches were totally occupied, which meant there was probably a full quorum, a fact confirmed by the scribes. Unlike Shemaiah, whose stride was still vigorous and his thick hair and beard black with only a sprinkling of gray, most of the members were elders in years as well as in title. All were garbed in long robes, with fringes dangling from each hem; they each wore a phylactery on their forehead and one on their left arm, with its black leather thong of the latter entwined around the fingers of the hand.

Shemaiah opened the proceedings by calling on one of the elders to invoke God's blessing on the deliberations, after which he addressed the assembly. "Our deliberations have been beset with many difficulties of late," he began in a low voice. "For too long we were unable to deal with matters requiring a full quorum. Litigants who turned to us as a court of appeal had to wait an unduly long time for their suits to be adjudicated, with all the inconvenience and worry involved. Even worse, a number of capital cases could not be heard, leaving the defendants in great anguish. In addition, many inquiries concerning our beliefs and practices – inquiries submitted by our brethren in this country and in the various lands of the diaspora – have gone without reply.

"I am happy to state that during the past fortnight we have made good progress with respect to civil and capital cases. I have therefore decided to devote today's session to dealing with some of the inquiries and perhaps also with the enactment, or discussion, of such decrees as may be deemed necessary or desirable.

"First, the inquiries. As you can see for yourselves, there is a large pile of letters on the table before each of the scribes. Where we all agree with my suggested response, the scribes will draft a reply. Where we do not agree, I shall decide whether to defer the discussion to a future session or refer the inquiry to a committee of elders for further study."

The inquiries covered a wide range of subjects. Some had to do with the service in the synagogue: which prayers were mandatory and which optional, who may lead the service, and so forth; some wanted to know if certain activities fell into the thirty-nine categories of work forbidden on the Sabbath; a few were questions of a theological nature. In many cases Shemaiah was able to bring his considerable erudition and interpretive skill to bear, and his suggested responses elicited the admiration and concurrence of the elders. Some inquiries resulted in an animated discussion and were referred to a committee for study.

Shortly after noon Shemaiah called a brief recess. When the elders reassembled, he announced that since they had dealt with many of the inquiries, the rest of the session would be devoted to discussing whatever matters the members might wish to raise. One of the elders, Ezra ben Yair, immediately rose to his feet and received permission to speak. A moderately tall, lean man in his early fifties, he was known to be a staunch supporter of Antigonus and a bitter foe of Herod. Despite his rather frail physique, he had a powerful voice, which in the heat of debate resounded throughout the chamber. He had strong views on many subjects, but none more so than Judea's relations with the surrounding peoples.

"I would like to raise a matter that has long been troubling me and, I suspect, a good many members of this Sanhedrin," he began in a soft tone which gradually rose in volume. "It has assumed growing importance of late, but to the best of my knowledge it has never been formally discussed by the Sanhedrin, either during the time I have been a member or before. It has to do with the very essence of our Jewish identity. I refer to involuntary conversion to our faith."

This statement riveted the attention of every single elder. They exchanged looks of surprise mingled with intense curiosity. What the speaker said was true: This *was* a question that had long troubled them, and they had frequently discussed it in private but never in the Sanhedrin itself. It was a delicate issue with extremely important implications, especially in the present circumstances. The chamber buzzed with whispered exclamations.

"Silence, please!" Shemaiah called out. "Allow the speaker to continue."

"It is obvious that you all know who I'm referring to," ben Yair went on when quiet was restored. "So be it. When some ninety years ago John Hyrcanus gave the

Idumeans the choice of converting to the Jewish faith or being expelled from their land, he acted, I contend, without *halachic* sanction. Perhaps he felt he was not transgressing any commandment or injunction, perhaps he thought he was not violating any halacha, for the simple reason that at the time there was no halacha regarding forcible conversion, either of individuals or – and this is of the utmost importance – especially of an entire people. I can only assume that he took this step on his own volition, without consulting the sages of his day. His motives may have been valid, his reasons compelling, but they were purely political reasons."

"Is that against halacha?" one of the elders interjected. "Halacha deals with all sorts of problems, with all aspects of life."

"I don't dispute that point," the speaker retorted. "But halacha, as you all know, must reflect God's will as revealed in the Written Law given to our teacher Moses and, even though my Sadducee friends may disagree, also in the Oral Law, which was also given to Moses, and in a wider sense can be said to include all inter-pretations and conclusions which the prophets and sages deduced from the Written Law, as well as the regulations they instituted, and which is just as binding as the Written Law. And nowhere I say," the speaker went on, raising his voice and bran-dishing his arms, "can we find sanction or any textual support for admitting to our faith a non-Jew against his will, not even a slave and certainly not an entire people."

"The Idumeans agreed to convert," an elder objected.

"Only when given the choice of converting or leaving their land," the speaker shot back. "How different from the example of our father Abraham! He brought heathens to believe in God through persuasion, through kind deeds, not by coercion. And how different from Ruth the Moabitess, the ancestress of King David, who clung to her mother-in-law Naomi, proclaiming, 'Your people shall be my people and your God, my God.' Righteous proselytes like her are to be welcomed with open arms. They are a precious addition to our people, to our faith, for they have come to recognize that the God of Israel is lord of the whole universe, and withal Israel is a people apart, a people bidden to be a holy nation, a kingdom of priests. They willingly accept what this entails – the yoke of the Law, to obey God's commandments. But to *force* an entire people to accept our way of life on pain of expulsion from their homes! Can we expect such converts to be a welcome addition to our fold? No! I say – a thousand times no! They will inevitably bear a resentment against us. Maybe outwardly they will pretend to conform to our way of life, but in their hearts they are pagans and will remain pagans. How can it be otherwise?"

The speaker paused to clear his throat, and then resumed in a quieter tone. "Have we not had enough bitter experience with paganism? In days of yore, be-fore the first Temple was built and even when it was standing, the surrounding nations seduced many of our people to go astray, to go awhoring after strange gods. For this we were exiled from our land. And in more recent times – yes, even today – do we not witness another form of paganism in the more alluring guise of Hellenism?

"Now we stand at another turning point in the annals of our people. We are witnessing a bitter struggle between two forces for dominance over Judea: One led by Antigonus, descendant of the Hasmonean liberators of our land and our holy Temple from the wicked Antiochus, may his name be blotted out; the other led by Herod, the evil Idumean pagan. The man who all his life has bowed and scraped before the Roman idolaters, the man who committed the abomination of offering a sacrifice to Jupiter in gratitude for being crowned king of Judea – by the Romans no less! The man who with the help of these same Romans has twice tried to conquer Jerusalem. Such is the man who would sit on the throne of Judea, who would rule over the Holy Land, over God's holy people.

"When John Hyrcanus made the Idumeans convert, little did he dream that matters would come to such a pass. If he were alive today, he would surely rue his impulsive act, just as we rue it and, God forbid, I fear we may have even more reason to rue it in the not-too-distant future. We cannot undo what has already been done, but if we are to preserve the unique character of our people, to keep the Lord's covenant inviolate, we must prevent the recurrence of such rash, ill-conceived acts. I call on the Sanhedrin to determine that only those gentiles who through conviction seek to shelter under the wings of the Divine Presence, to cast their lot with the people of Israel and wholeheartedly accept our way of life, will be admitted to our faith."

Ben Yair resumed his seat amid a profound silence. His passionate words had gripped the assembly, and for a long moment they quietly digested his speech. The silence was so palpable that the chirping of birds penetrated the thick walls of the chamber. And then, after the elders reflected on what they had heard, there arose a babble of voices.

"Silence, please! Silence!" Shemaiah shouted above the din. "Let us conduct ourselves as befits members of the Great Sanhedrin." He waited until order was restored, and then proceeded to address the elders. "Our distinguished colleague has raised a matter of the utmost importance, one fraught with serious implications and demands earnest thought and calm deliberation. In the short time remaining at our disposal today, we cannot possibly do justice to it. For this we need a full day's session, if not more. But we can make a start. At this point I would like to know if anyone wishes to express any reservations about the proposal put before us or to take issue with the speaker."

Several elders immediately rose to their feet. Shemaiah recognized Meir ben Eliezer, one of the senior members of the Sanhedrin. Possessing a composed, thoughtful visage, he had a reputation for dispassionately and incisively analyzing controversial issues. He contended that there were two sides to every question, and in arguing what he believed to be even the minority view, he helped to sharpen the issue under discussion. He spoke in a calm, level voice, unruffled by the most pointed interjections.

"Our learned and eloquent colleague has indeed raised a matter of great importance, one which, as our distinguished president has so aptly put it, is fraught with serious implications. It has long weighed on our minds, and the wonder is that it has never been discussed by the Sanhedrin until now. Perhaps it was because neither we nor our predecessors felt any compelling need to do so, or maybe because the circumstances did not seem appropriate. But the circumstances have changed: We face the prospect of a man ascending the throne of Judea whose Jewishness is questioned by many. It therefore behooves us who are charged with preserving and strengthening our precious heritage, our divinely ordained way of life, to give serious thought to the problem of forcible conversion.

"Let us first clarify what exactly we understand by the concept of conversion. The term designating a convert today, *ger zedek*, a righteous proselyte, or simply *ger*, differs in some important respects from the *ger* appearing in Scripture. In Scripture it is not always clear if the reference is to a resident alien or a full-fledged convert. The resident alien, you will recall, was one who chose to dwell in the land of Israel for various reasons – economic, family, political, or anything else that induced him to leave his country and to seek a haven here, to become a resident of the country and enjoy its protection. This he did without any intention or particular desire to become a Jew in the religious sense. But he had to keep some of the fundamental commandments of the Torah. He had to observe the seven Noachide Laws, for example, including the renunciation of idolatry. In return, he was permitted to live in the country and enjoy many of the privileges enjoyed by all Jews. We are bidden to be solicitous of his welfare and to befriend him – to 'love the stranger in our midst,' as Scripture puts it.

"In many cases – in fact, I dare say in most cases – the resident alien was gradually weaned to our faith. He began to accept more and more of our customs and ways, to celebrate our festivals, to perform many other commandments, until in effect he became one of us. The final step, of course, was circumcision; with this he became a full convert. Now Scripture, as I have already mentioned, does not clearly distinguish between the resident alien and the full convert, the righteous proselyte, and this can cause some confusion.

"With the exile of our people to Babylonia, the status of resident alien became virtually meaningless. We were no longer an independent, sovereign state; we were subject to a foreign power even after our return to the tiny province of Judea. In these circumstances obviously few if any gentiles would come here seeking civil privileges or a haven. Only those who knew something about our religion, our belief in the one and only God, who sought to shelter under the wings of the Divine Presence, were attracted to join our fold. The proselyte enjoys all the privileges of born Jews with a few minor exceptions. He cannot be appointed king for one thing, and while he can act as a judge in monetary cases, he cannot be a judge in criminal cases involving the death penalty. There are other examples, but these will suffice.

"All this you know, and I crave your indulgence if I am wearying you by describing the obvious. Now what about the Idumeans? In which category do they belong? Can we say that in spite of what I have explained about the present status of alien residents, we can nevertheless regard the Idumeans as such? Hardly likely. Even though, with the Lord's help, we were once again an independent state in John Hyrcanus's time, the only converts today, ignoring emancipated slaves, are righteous proselytes, those who want to become one of us, to fully accept our faith through conviction. The Idumeans did not come to dwell in our midst, to seek our protection, yet they are expected to keep more than the seven Noachide Laws.

"Are the Idumeans, then, to be regarded as true proselytes? When they were forced to convert, they were pagans who worshipped the god Kos. They had no desire to become Jews. So how did John Hyrcanus justify their involuntary conversion? Did he consider them non-Jewish slaves, captives of war, who had to undergo circumcision and keep some of the commandments, and who upon being liberated were regarded as converts? This is a far-fetched supposition: We have no evidence that the Idumeans ever acted or were treated as slaves.

"Can we find any *halachic* support whatever for their compulsory conversion? I think we can. I think it is possible to regard it as an emergency measure of a sort – a one-time act like that of Ezra. Just as Ezra had persuaded those who took foreign wives after the return from Babylonia to put them away in order to preserve the small and weak Jewish community, to prevent its unique character from being diluted to the point where it was in danger of extinction, so too John Hyrcanus had resorted to an emergency measure. He..."

"He did the exact opposite of Ezra," one of the elders protested. "Ezra made the men put aside their non-Jewish wives; John Hyrcanus made a whole people become Jews."

"You're absolutely right," concurred the speaker. "But the circumstances were completely different. How many of our people returned from Babylonia? Only some 40,000 – a tiny island in a sea of paganism. By taking the daughters of the surrounding peoples for wives, they endangered the survival of the small remnant. Did not our teacher Moses warn against making marriages with the daughters of the heathen peoples living in the Promised Land? 'They will turn away your sons from following Me, that they may serve other gods.' In John Hyrcanus's day Judea was no longer a tiny state. It had grown in area and numbers, and was not in danger of physical extinction. Nevertheless, the Idumeans were a threat to our unique way of life; we were, and still are, surrounded by heathen peoples.

"Don't forget, John Hyrcanus's father and his four brothers – the glorious Maccabees – had liberated the land from the pagan yoke, the Syrian-Greeks and their king Antiochus, who had persecuted our people, forbidding them on pain of death to keep the holy commandments and defiling our holy Temple with their abominations. With the Lord's help the enemy was defeated in one campaign after another until the land was liberated and the Temple cleansed. What could be more natural than John Hyrcanus's desire, after he had conquered the Idumeans, to cleanse of paganism the territory that had been the inheritance of the tribe of Judah, especially Hebron, where the Patriarchs are buried, which David had made his first royal city – to restore Torah to this territory that is an integral part of the Holy Land?"

"And has Torah been restored to Idumea?" one of the elders challenged the speaker. "Do you want us to believe that the Idumeans have shed their pagan ways?"

Ben Eliezer was not perturbed by this provocative question. "No, I don't claim that the Idumeans have become faithful, Torah-observant Jews," he replied calmly. "It would be unrealistic to expect them to. This will take time; it will be a slow, gradual process, like that of the resident aliens I mentioned earlier. At first the resident aliens kept only the seven Noachide Laws; little by little they conformed to our way of life until eventually many, if not most, of them became full proselytes.

"So it will be with other pagans too. Did the prophet not foretell the day when all the peoples of the earth will recognize the one and only God? As the Lord said to Isaiah, 'Unto me every knee shall bow, every tongue shall swear.' How will this come about? 'I will give thee for a light unto the nations, that My salvation may be unto the end of the earth.' At present the world is steeped in paganism. But the day is not far off when the inhabitants of the earth will begin to lose faith in their gods – gods who fornicate with goddesses and mortal women, who fight among themselves, who bring to this world not order but disorder, who do not offer solace or hope to the oppressed, consolation to the bereaved, or salvation to mankind. Even now there are Greek philosophers who have misgivings about their pantheon and speak of the one God. The doubts will grow, and the inhabitants of the earth will begin to perceive the light of Torah and be receptive to its message.

"So you see, my distinguished and very patient colleagues, John Hyrcanus did not act irresponsibly when he gave the Idumeans the choice of leaving their land or converting. He acted humanely and with perhaps greater foresight than even he himself realized. Let us bear this in mind in debating the issue before us."

Like the previous speaker, ben Eliezer took his seat amid total silence. This, together with the rapt attention with which his argument had been followed and the paucity of interjections, was a clear indication that his words too had made a strong impression. More than a minute passed before one of the elders rose and requested permission to speak; several others followed suit. Shemaiah pointed out that the session would have to be adjourned soon, and so he would allow only one or possibly two more members to briefly express their views.

Judah ben Yoezer, one of the younger members of the Sanhedrin, began by complimenting the previous speaker. "It is always a pleasure and highly instructive to listen to our learned colleague expound his views. He has marshaled facts that many of us may have forgotten and analyzed the issue in such a comprehensive and lucid manner as to hold us spellbound. It is only when we pause and reflect on his words that we realize we have been presented a masterly description of an idealized situation, the end of days no less, when, in the words of the prophet, 'All the nations shall flow to the mountain of the Lord to be taught His ways and to walk in His paths.' Who can gainsay such an exalted state? But alas, we are living in a world that has made very little progress in this respect. We do not behold nations beating their swords into ploughshares and their spears into pruninghooks. On the contrary," the speaker went on, his voice abruptly assuming a sharp tone, "we still have vivid memories of Pompey's legions smashing their way into the Holy City and in cold blood slaughtering innocent men, women, and children; and more recently Machaeras's murderous retreat through the countryside after failing to conquer Jerusalem. Who aided the Romans, who implored their help in order to usurp the throne of Judea? The Idumean, no less! The leading son of that people whom John Hyrcanus had seen fit to bring into our fold, to swell the ranks of God's chosen people.

"It is heartening, I admit, to contemplate the day when the wolf will lie with the lamb, but can any of you envision the Romans putting away their arms and devoting themselves solely to peaceful pursuits in the foreseeable future? Do any of you think the Idumeans really share our belief in the Almighty and have truly joined us in walking in His ways? We must face reality. Not for nothing did the prophet Malachi proclaim, 'Was not Esau Jacob's brother? saith the Lord; yet I loved Jacob and hated Esau.' Esau – father of the Edomites, or the Idumeans as they are now called; and Jacob – two brothers, yet how different in their ways! John Hyrcanus may have had good intentions, but he failed to realize that the differences between the two brothers, between the two peoples, are irreconcilable. We owe it to ourselves and to posterity to ensure that never again will this folly be repeated."

The next speaker spoke in a similar vein. Shemaiah was about to adjourn the session when Meir ben Eliezer requested permission to make a final statement. Shemaiah said it was almost time for the afternoon sacrifice, when the Sanhedrin had to adjourn, and suggested that he make his statement on the morrow. Ben Eliezer, however, insisted that it was extremely important for him to sound a note of caution before the members dispersed and weighed the arguments for and against the proposed decree. He promised to be brief. Shemaiah gave his grudging consent.

"As I had more or less expected," ben Eliezer began, speaking more rapidly than was his wont, "the sentiment of the Sanhedrin seems to be in favor of interdicting forcible conversion to our faith. I can appreciate the apprehension of those who advocate such a decree, but I feel compelled to utter a note of caution – nay, a warning. It is my earnest conviction that it would be advisable to leave the resolution of this issue to some future time. Our distinguished colleague ben Yoezer has urged us to face reality. I too urge you to face reality. During the past year, Herod has twice tried to conquer Jerusalem – fortunately, without success. But mark my words, he will make a third attempt, and this time we can assume that he will have all the Roman help he needs. If, heaven forbid, he should seize the throne of Judea, he would take a dim view of our prohibiting forcible conversion. Not because he favors such conversion – the opposite is true; but because he would regard our action as a personal affront, a deliberate attempt to stigmatize him. He would not want to be regarded as a foreign king foisted on his subjects with the help of Roman arms. Not for that did he betroth the Hasmonean princess. Knowing him as we do, I shudder to think what might happen. The Sanhedrin must not shrink from performing its sacred duties, from dealing with all problems submitted to it. But this particular issue can lead to dire consequences. We have lived with it until now. Prudence dictates that we continue to live with it until a more propitious time."

Shemaiah was glad that he had allowed ben Eliezer to make a final statement. From the expression on the members' faces it was clear that the appeal for caution had a sobering effect. Some of the elders would no doubt regard the appeal as a sign of timidity and vote in favor of interdicting forcible conversion. But others, perhaps a majority, would have second thoughts and see the wisdom of deferring a decision. How ironical, he thought, that after personally condemning the conversion of the Idumeans, he should now favor the rejection or deferment of the proposed decree. His learning and interpretive skill told him that little or no *halachic* sanction could be deduced for compelling the Idumeans to accept the Jewish faith, and today's debate only reinforced this opinion. Moreover, while it might have been unrealistic to expect John Hyrcanus to foresee all the implications of his act, the danger now confronting Judea could in no small measure be laid at his door. It was not only the sovereignty of Judea that was threatened, but the independence and perhaps the very existence of the Sanhedrin, the guardian of Israel's spiritual heritage.

The vote tomorrow would be one of the most fateful in the Sanhedrin's history. He knew that even if the proposed ban should be voted down, Herod would react strongly to the Sanhedrin's even deliberating the question. The prospect filled him with foreboding. He felt a heavy burden of responsibility resting on him. Like all the other members of the Sanhedrin, he would spend a good part of the night pondering the day's debate. But he would not be weighing so much the arguments for and against the proposal; he would be pondering the fate of the Sanhedrin itself.

Chapter Eight

Seclusion in Samaria, Satisfaction in Samosata

Mariamne Resents Her Betrothal to Herod

Mariamne hated Samaria. From the moment she set foot in the city, to which Herod had moved his and Alexandra's families from Masada, she was repelled by it and everything it stood for. She was almost eighteen years old, in the bloom of youth, but instead of enjoying what should have been the happiest period of her life, she felt as if she were confined in a gilded prison, one that stifled any possible joy.

Her mirror confirmed what her mother often told her, that she was blessed with extraordinary features and figure. But apart from her mother and brother, who cared whether she was beautiful or not? She was cut off from her friends – the young daughters of aristocratic families, most of whom were already married. For what seemed an interminable period she had lived under the shadow of armed conflict, of death and suffering. The siege of the royal palace in Jerusalem still gave her nightmares. She could not banish the memory of those terrible weeks, when she did not know what the morrow might bring. The land was still convulsed with warfare; in fact, it seemed to her that apart from a few brief respites it had never ceased.

In Samaria she was far from the scene of fighting, and so was spared the sight and smell of the wounded and dead. For this she should have been thankful, but like her mother, her heart was with her people in Jerusalem, who had already undergone more than one siege and feared they had not seen the end of their suffering.

For five years now she was betrothed to Herod. She did not know of anyone in her circle who was betrothed for such a long time, except in the case of minors. She was neither a free maid nor a married woman, but perhaps it was better this way than being the wife of a man she felt no affinity to. In the first years of their betrothal he had showed little interest in her, but of late he was displaying a courtly manner toward her. He gave her expensive gifts, but she took little pleasure in them. He spoke to her gently, but she frequently overheard him shouting to others in a way that used to frighten but now repelled her.

How different was his younger brother Joseph. He had been a good-hearted person and had a soft spot for her. More than once he had rescued her from Salome's vicious temper. She liked him, and his recent death in battle saddened her greatly. She felt that she had lost a good friend. She had never seen Herod so grief-stricken, and she was touched by this.

Of late he had been coming to Samaria more frequently, usually accompanied by Roman officers, whose stern visages both fascinated and unnerved her. She had several times encountered them in the corridor, and was flustered whenever their eyes lingered on her. Their attention annoyed Herod, who, she discovered, had a very jealous nature and did not take kindly to others revealing too much interest in her, not even his uncle, also named Joseph, who had recently married Salome. He showed a respectable attitude toward Alexandra and her children, and intervened whenever Salome vented her ill-humor on Mariamne. Salome was quick to report this to Herod, who did not hesitate to rebuke his uncle. This, of course, exacerbated relations between Joseph and Salome, whose frequent quarrels were clearly audible to others.

Alexandra had thought that marriage would help curb Salome's temper somewhat, but she soon discovered how naïve this was. She wondered what had induced Joseph to marry her, knowing as he did what kind of a person she was. Mariamne said he probably did it because he knew that no one else in his right mind would want to live with such a shrew. Alexandra had given Mariamne a chiding look, followed by a grin.

The thought of having Salome for a sister-in-law galled Mariamne no less than that of being married to Herod. For five years now she had suffered the ignominy of being in effect part of this family. She loved her grandfather dearly, but how could he have done this to her? She asked herself time without number. In the meantime the circumstances that had prompted this wretched decision had changed drastically: Hyrcanus was now living in exile in Babylonia, permanently disqualified from wearing the priestly crown and with virtually no chance of wearing the royal crown. She pleaded with her mother to inquire whether the betrothal could be annulled or otherwise terminated. Alexandra communicated with Shemaiah, who replied that he had considered the betrothal ill-advised right from the start, but his advice had been rejected for reasons he did not find very convincing. The matter was also *halachically* complicated, not the least because Herod's Jewishness was the subject of considerable controversy. He suggested that Alexandra should first determine whether her father had second thoughts about the betrothal in view of the changed circumstances. Alexandra immediately wrote him, but it was some time before she found someone whom she could trust to deliver the letter. Hyrcanus's reply reached her a month later. Mariamne studied her mother's face as she read the letter.

"What does Grandpa write?" she asked with an anxious frown.

Alexandra did not respond immediately. From the expression on her face Mariamne knew the letter would not please her. "His answer is no, isn't it?" she uttered in a low, faltering voice.

"Your grandfather has not changed his mind," Alexandra solemnly confirmed. "In fact, he's more concerned than ever about our safety."

"But that's absurd! Antigonus wouldn't harm us. I still remember how nice he was to us in Chalcis. He wouldn't hurt a hair on our heads."

"I agree with you. But your grandfather feels differently. He's even more worried now."

"But why? What's happened to make him feel that way?"

"He's had a terrible shock. Orodes, the Parthian king, was murdered by his oldest son, who also killed all his own brothers."

Mariamne gasped. "How awful! I thought the Parthians were more civilized than that."

"They're no more or less civilized than most other peoples. This is not the first time a prince has murdered his brothers – or even his father – to gain the throne. It's happened more often than you realize, and not only in this part of the world. That's why your grandfather is afraid."

"But it's absurd to think Antigonus would do something as terrible as that. He's a Hasmonean, a Jewish prince, not a pagan."

"That's right. But you have to understand that your grandfather has seen a lot of bloodshed in his lifetime, especially in his younger days. He's still haunted by the memory of the war against his own brother and nephew – my husband Alexander and Antigonus."

"But they didn't do Grandpa any harm, not even when his brother was king for – how many years was it?"

"Three years.

"Three years, and he didn't touch Grandpa."

"That's true. But your grandfather was young then, and his whole life – or practically his whole life – lay ahead of him. Now the better part of his life is behind him. We're all the family he and Grandma have. That's why he worries so much about us, why he's so anxious about our safety."

"Is my safety more important than my happiness? What kind of a life can I look forward to married to a man like Herod and with a sister-in-law like Salome?"

"You can at least console yourself with the prospect that one day you may be a queen – a Hasmonean queen on the throne of Judea. Your grandfather probably also had that in mind."

"To sit on the throne beside that man! It's a horrible prospect!"

"I'm not happy about it either. But it would at least ensure the continuation of the Hasmonean line. Our people would welcome that."

"But I wouldn't!"

Mariamne's voice broke and she burst into tears. Alexandra drew her to her bosom and let her cry her eyes out. She could not help feeling sorry for her daughter. Life was not always kind, she mused, thinking of her own fate. For too long they had been cut off from their own people, and this was having a bad effect on her and her children. Circumstances had conspired to throw them together with Herod and his family, who she was convinced were pagans at heart. And when she stepped outside the villa Herod had taken to accommodate their two families, she was in a completely pagan environment.

She was worried about her children. Aristobulus was now fifteen years old, the formative period of his life, and for the past three years he had virtually no contact with Jewish children and only what Jewish environment Alexandra was able to provide under the most difficult circumstances. She did her best to teach him and Mariamne something about the history of their people after the Babylonian Exile, with special emphasis, of course, on the Hasmonean period. She would have also liked to impart to them some of her knowledge of Ben Sira and other post-biblical literature, but was handicapped by the lack of books. Aristobulus already knew much of the Bible, but his other studies had been interrupted by their tribulations. She decided to hire a teacher for him, and after considerable effort she obtained the services of one of Shemaiah's former students. Gadiel, a young married man in his mid-twenties, was at first reluctant to live, even if only temporarily, in a pagan city, but was finally persuaded that it would be especially meritorious to teach Hyrcanus's grandson precisely in such a place.

Aristobulus was an eager student, and Gadiel was pleased with his progress. He saw that the youngster was hungry not only for learning but also for companionship. He tried to satisfy this need as best he could, devoting part of the day to story-telling and various games. He discovered that Aristobulus had a sensitive nature, as revealed by the incident of the lame pigeon. Aristobulus had found the bird in the garden of the villa, unable to fly and barely able to drag itself along the ground.

"Gadi, come here!" he called out. "There's something wrong with this pigeon."

"Its wing is broken," said Gadiel after a quick look.

"Will it get better?" asked Aristobulus with a worried frown.

"If we take care of it, it probably will. If you hadn't found it, it wouldn't have much of a chance."

Together they made a bed of twigs and provided seeds, rice, and leaves for nourishment. Whenever he had a free moment Aristobulus would come to see how his feathered friend was progressing. He was happy to see its wing healing and its cooing assuming a more cheerful ring. The day came when it tried out its wings, and was able to fly for a few seconds. "It's only a question of time until it can fly almost normally and rejoin its friends," Gadiel said. When that day came Aristobulus was sad. "It's natural for you to feel that way," Gadiel consoled him "But you can be proud that you helped the pigeon to get better."

Unlike the situation in Masada, where they were confined to a small area, in Samaria Alexandra and her children were able to roam the countryside. They avoided the residential area and center of the city because of the pagan environment and especially the hostility of the inhabitants. Alexandra had not expected them to be friendly, for her great-grandfather had conquered the city and destroyed much of it. She did not realize how virulent was their hatred until one day shortly after their arrival she and her children strolled through the city and came upon the ruins of a temple. A gang of youngsters passed by and began to revile them. Aristobulus started to answer back, but Alexandra restrained him. When they saw that their scurrilous taunts were not having the desired effect, they started throwing mud, bespattering their victims' garments. Summoning her most authoritative bearing, Alexandra advanced upon them and ordered them to leave.

"We don't take orders from dirty Hasmonean Jews!" one of the boys shouted. "This is our city, and this is where one of our temples stood until your scurvy ancestor burned it down. We don't want you here, so get out, you Hasmonean pigs!"

The gang took up the refrain, "Get out, you Hasmonean pigs!" accompanied by indecent gestures. When one of them pushed Mariamne, Alexandra gave him an unregal kick in his rump. At this point, when the situation was threatening to get out of hand, Herod's uncle Joseph happened to be walking nearby, and attracted by the noise, he hurried over to investigate. When he saw who the victims were, he ordered the rowdies to disperse. Knowing that Joseph was a member of Herod's family, they took to their heels.

Alexandra, relieved to see them beat a hasty retreat, thanked Joseph for coming to their aid. "It was an elementary duty and an honor," he said with a polite bow. "Those young ruffians are a vile lot. With your permission, I'll accompany you until you're safely out of their reach."

This incident, Alexandra later learned, had an unexpected sequel. News of the encounter spread fast and reached Salome's ears. "So, my big hero," she snapped at her husband, "you have become the protector of the Hasmonean women. How noble of you!"

"Elementary courtesy, my dear. I couldn't have done less."

"You most certainly could have! You could have let them get their just deserts."

"Permit me to remind you, dear wife, that they happen to be in effect part of our family now. I'm the uncle of Mariamne's husband-to-be, you know."

"And you're my husband! In the future you be a little less gallant to them, my fine cavalier."

Herod Assured of Massive Roman Help

Herod set out for Antioch accompanied by twenty horsemen. This was a large escort, but both Nikias and Joseph agreed that it was necessary since hostile bands were known to be operating in the territory Herod had to traverse. The first part of the journey was through a region familiar to Herod from the days when he was governor of Coele-Syria. *How much water had flown under the bridge since then*, he thought with a tinge of nostalgia. Then he was young, burning with ambition, his sights set on great things. But he did not dream that his path would also be beset by grievous personal blows – the deaths of his father and elder brothers and frustrating military setbacks. And now here he was on his way to Antony in the expectation of finally bringing to fruition his long-cherished goal – the throne of Judea.

The scenic coastal road passed through several moderately large towns, where Herod replenished his supplies and lodged his men for the night. He knew they were hoping he would stop long enough for them to sample the pleasures the towns had to offer, but it was not until they reached Antioch that he informed them that they would halt for an entire day before entering what was reportedly dangerous territory.

While seeking accommodations for his men, Herod's curiosity was aroused by the large number of soldiers milling about the marketplace and basilica. He approached a squat, powerfully built man who gave the impression of being in command. "Excuse me," he said in an even tone, "may I ask if you and your men are on your way to join Antony?"

The officer eyed Herod suspiciously. "What business is it of yours?" he replied in a surly voice.

"My men and I are headed for Samosata," said Herod, ignoring the man's churlish response. "If you have any information about the safety of the route, it would be very useful to me."

The man looked Herod up and down with a contemptuous expression. He glanced at the men surrounding Herod, and his practiced eye told him they were hardened soldiers. "We hope to get to Samosata to join Antony," he said a little less scornfully.

"Hope to? Why hope?"

"Ambushes. Of the last group that left for Samosata only half got back here alive."

"Why did they come back? Why didn't they press ahead to Antony?"

Three of the soldiers, overhearing the exchange between their commander and the inquisitive stranger, gathered around them. It was clear that they did not like what they heard. "It's none of your damned business," one of them growled. "We've come to help Antony, and dead men ain't much help."

"If you're going to sit on your butts in Antioch, you'll be even less help," Herod shot back.

This remark infuriated the officer. "Save your sass for your own men," he barked. "Who do you think you are talking to us like that, the king of Parthia?"

Herod fixed him with a scathing look. "No, the king of Judea."

"Judea? What's your name?"

"Herod."

"I've heard that name before. Can't remember where, but you're not the king of Judea. It's someone called An, Antigonus, or something like that."

Herod looked the officer straight in the eye; his voice was authoritative, steely. "I'm king of Judea by virtue of a decree of the Roman Senate. If you don't believe it, when we get to Antony, and I assume you do intend to get there, I suggest you ask him."

From the altered expression of the officer's face Herod knew that his words had made an impression. "How many men you got?" the officer asked, a little less brusquely.

"Twenty."

"Twenty! That's all? And you spouting off like that! If you run into an ambush you don't stand a chance."

"Maybe not. But together with your men we can outwit and outfight any ambush. How many men do you have?"

"Nearly a hundred. Plus pack animals."

Herod's brow furrowed. "Pack animals? Hmm, that could be a problem. On the other hand, they would make good bait – yes, very good bait."

"Bait? What are you talking about?"

Herod chose to ignore the question. "Am I correct in assuming that the ambushes have been taking place in wooded areas?"

"That's right. In the woods right before you get to the plain."

"How many roads run through the woods?"

"Around these parts there is only one real road and one or two narrow ones, actually paths, where the going is pretty rough."

"We'll take the good road."

The officer's eyebrows arched sharply. "That's where all the ambushes have taken place."

"I know. And that's where we're going to give them a little surprise."

"What do you have in mind?"

"This isn't the place to explain. We'll discuss it in private, after I arrange accommodations for my men."

True to his word, Herod let his men have a whole day to themselves. When they started out for Samosata, they were in high spirits, regaling one another with embellished accounts of their amorous pleasures. The other men were also in good spirits, their morale having risen after hearing Herod's bold plan. Herod reckoned that if all went well it would take about three days to reach their destination. On the second day they approached a densely wooded area. Herod, who had been leading the column together with the officer, signaled the men to halt. "If there's going to be an ambush, this is the place," he said to the officer.

"I still think it would have been better to take our chances on one of the other roads. I'm afraid I stand to lose many of my animals, not to mention men."

"Whatever losses we have, they're going to have a lot more."

In accordance with Herod's plan, the force was divided into three roughly equal units. One, led by the officer, was to go ahead of the baggage train, while a second one was to trail well behind, taking care to avoid being sighted by any ambush party and ready to rush to the aid of the first unit. The remaining men, including Herod and his escort, were to make their way single file to a point beyond the clearing ahead, which was reckoned to be the most likely spot for an ambush.

"Now remember," Herod said to the officer, "if there is an attack, be sure to sound the trumpets. That will be our signal to converge on the road."

The skirmish developed pretty much as envisaged. When the lead unit reached the clearing, it was on the alert for an attack. The ambush party was larger than expected, surpassing the total number of defenders. Espying the baggage train, it swept down on what looked like easy prey. The officer and his unit fought valiantly, warding off the foe long enough for the second unit to rush to its aid. The attackers were taken by surprise, but emboldened by their superior numbers, they continued to press ahead. When Herod's unit bore down on them from the rear, they were thrown into confusion and took to their heels, leaving behind many casualties.

When Herod reached Samosata he came upon a familiar scene – a city under siege. Only this time the city was not Jerusalem, and it was not Herod who was frustrated but Antony. From the latter's reply to his letter, Herod knew that the siege had been dragging on much longer than expected with no sign of a decision, and Antony, impetuous by nature, was growing increasingly impatient. He had even requested Herod to bring as many reinforcements as possible. Herod gave a short, dry laugh. Antony knew very well that it was he, Herod, who needed reinforcements. Could it be that Antony wanted to reprove him for the friction that had marred his relations with both Roman generals sent to his aid? Possibly, but it would be easy to prove that the blame lay with Silo and Machaeras.

If Antony was frustrated, it was not apparent from his appearance. He looked fit and was in an excellent mood when Herod was admitted into the headquarters tent. "Hail the conquering hero!" Antony greeted Herod, rising from his campstool and embracing him. He stepped back to take good look at Herod. "Excellent condition – lean and hard, as a warrior king should be."

Antony turned to the two officers in the tent. "Gentlemen, you have the honor to meet Herod, recently crowned king of Judea and hero of a skirmish with the band of marauders that had been inflicting heavy losses on reinforcements trying to get through to us."

"You've already heard about our victory?" said Herod, extremely pleased with his warm reception. "How did the news reach you so fast?"

"Ah, that's our secret," replied Antony with a sly wink. "Let's say the birds brought us the news. They told us that you used bold tactics to rout a far superior force. Later on you must give me a full description."

Antony peered through the half-opened flap of the tent. "Those men over there are yours, I take it?"

"The mounted soldiers on the far right are my bodyguards. The others are reinforcements who have come to join you."

"We'll make good use of them. We've been having a tough time here, much tougher than expected," said Antony with a grimace. "When I relieved Ventidius, I didn't realize what a hard nut we had undertaken to crack. Ventidius is a good man. He deserves to celebrate a triumph for his brilliant victory over the Parthians. He helped redeem the Roman honor lost by old Crassus. But we still haven't recovered the standards lost to the enemy. Before we finish, though, those standards are going to be back in our hands, or my name isn't Mark Antony."

"All Rome awaits that glorious day. And so do I," said Herod with an ingratiating smile.

"By Hercules, that day isn't going to be far off either. And now, let's get you and all these men fixed up. Afterward I'll show you around the area."

An aide led Herod to his tent. He unpacked his gear and then stretched out on the camp bed to rest a little before joining Antony and his staff officers for lunch. The meal was a simple affair, not much different from that of the troops. Herod, who had not eaten a warm meal since the skirmish, was ravenous and ate heartily. When he finished, Antony rose and told his officers about Herod's victory, following which he asked him to describe the tactics used. After having his self-esteem deflated by Silo and Machaeras, Herod welcomed the opportunity to show the high-ranking Roman officers what he was capable of, and was gratified to see that they were impressed.

After lunch Antony and Herod toured the area on horseback. The scene was familiar to Herod: The besieging force drawn up around the walls, the defenders taunting them from the battlements, the air humming with arrows. But what differentiated the situation here from that in Jerusalem was the large number of siege engines, which Silo had lacked and Machaeras had not deigned to employ. At the moment, fighting was fairly light, being confined mostly to the archers on both sides and the sporadic hurling of missiles into the city by the catapults.

"It's pretty quiet today," said Antony, sitting erect on his white charger.

"The walls look stout enough," remarked Herod. "Maybe not as stout as Jerusalem's, but still capable of taking a lot of pounding. But you have something we lacked in Jerusalem: adequate siege engines. With all these catapults and battering rams, it shouldn't take long to breach the walls."

"You'd be surprised how much punishment those walls have taken already. We can't seem to make any headway. It looks like it's going to take some time to finish this business, but we'll finish it one way or another."

"At least you're confident of victory. That's more than I could say about Machaeras. He didn't even think it was necessary to bother with siege equipment."

"You're pretty bitter about him, aren't you?"

"I think I have good reason to be."

"I can understand your feelings. He's Ventidius's favorite, not mine. He did a good job against Pacorus, though."

"That was a pitched battle, not a siege. He's probably better at that kind of fighting."

Antony grinned. "You can say the same about me. This siege is getting on my nerves. I prefer a pitched battle any time: one day, two days, and it's over. If only I had another Roman legion or two, this business would be over by now. There aren't better soldiers anywhere. You can't compare these foreign auxiliaries with them."

Antony's mount suddenly reared up. "Careful!" he shouted as an arrow fell in front of them. "They must have spotted us. We'd better move back."

"Another legion or two shouldn't be a problem," said Herod after they were out of bowshot.

"It shouldn't be, but it is, thanks to my fellow triumvir."

"Octavian?"

"Yes, my dear brother-in-law."

From Antony's scathing tone it was clear that relations between the two triumvirs were still far from harmonious. Herod realized he would have to tread carefully; he waited for Antony to explain.

"Under our agreement we have equal rights to recruit troops in Italy. But he's taking advantage of my absence from Rome to put every possible obstacle in my way. I'm losing patience with my dear brother-in-law."

"I'm sorry to hear that. Rome can only be the loser. And it must make your wife unhappy too."

"There's nothing she desires more than peace between us. She's very attached to her brother, and she seems to be fond of me too. You may not believe it, but during the past two years I lived a peaceful and virtuous life in Athens, well, let's say a virtuous life by my standards. Octavia and I attended more lectures than I had in all my life until then. I was even appointed head of the Athenians' gymnasia. Imagine that, me a minister of education!" he added with chuckle.

Herod found it hard to believe that a man as vigorous and active as Antony, and a confirmed philanderer to boot, could be content to live what he described as a peaceful and virtuous life. As though he read Herod's thoughts, Antony added: "But too much of that kind of living can be stifling. I'm a man of action, and it's action I crave. But not sitting in front of Samosata's walls. How they mock me, those walls! I must finish this business without further delay. It's holding up my campaign against Parthia. And it's important that you too finish your business. I can't risk having an enemy in our rear. I want to see you sitting on the Judean throne."

"There's nothing I desire more ardently," said Herod, trying to conceal his exaltation.

"You'll have all the assistance you need. As soon as we finish this siege, I'll put two legions at your disposal."

The smile on Herod's face vanished as quickly as it had appeared. "Permit me to remind you that Machaeras had two legions under his command. Yet we had to withdraw from Jerusalem."

"I see I haven't made myself clear," replied Antony with a cryptic smile. "The legions will be under your command."

Herod stared at Antony incredulously. He had never heard of a foreigner commanding Roman legions. This would be signal honor for him and an eloquent expression of Antony's faith in his generalship. But what could he accomplish with two legions? It would be a repetition of the previous fruitless sieges.

"You honor me greatly with this offer," he said with some reserve. "I regard it as an expression of your faith in my leadership and loyalty. But if you are having trouble taking Samosata with all your legions, I will undoubtedly have even greater difficulty with just two legions."

Antony grinned. "I didn't say this is all the help you'll get. The two legions should enable you to drive Antigonus back to Jerusalem. After we finish this blasted siege, Sossius will join you with enough legions to take Jerusalem and your throne."

Elaborate Wedding for Herod and Mariamne

Herod returned from Samosata in a jubilant mood. The assistance rendered Antony, while limited in scope, strengthened the bond between the two men. It was a brilliant move that paid off handsomely – far more than he had dared hope. The two legions Antony put at his disposal in themselves were nothing to get excited about, but the assurance that a large army under Sossius would soon be joining him put an entirely different complexion on the matter. The outcome of the struggle against Antigonus was now a foregone conclusion, and it was only a question of time until he entered Jerusalem and occupied the throne.

With the aid of the two Roman legions he put down uprisings in Galilee and inflicted a crushing defeat on Antigonus at Jericho, thus opening the road to Jerusalem. Antigonus withdrew his army to positions behind the city walls, confident that he could withstand a siege by the enemy's relatively small force, little suspecting that it would soon be swollen to eleven Roman divisions of foot soldiers and 6,000 mounted troops, plus auxiliaries. His previous abortive assaults against the city had taught him not to underestimate the strength of its defenses or the courage of its defenders. He therefore contented himself at this stage with encamping close to the northern wall at a point where it could most easily be breached. Here he made three lines of earthworks and erected towers.

While awaiting Sossius's arrival, Herod was free to turn his mind to other matters. First and foremost was the finalization of his relationship with Mariamne. When he was not occupied with military matters, he found himself increasingly thinking about her. On his frequent visits to Samaria he was more conscious than ever of her extraordinary beauty. He always brought her a gift, which she invariably acknowledged with a cool politeness. This both baffled and disconcerted him. She was, after all, his betrothed, his wife-to-be; the least she could do was to show a warmer, more appreciative response.

He found her whole attitude toward him extremely puzzling. Here he was, the man crowned king of Judea by the Roman Senate and who would soon be sitting on the throne, whose word would be law, who would have the power to bend everyone to his will, even this Hasmonean princess. Yet she possessed some indefinable, almost mystic, quality that eluded him – the magic spell the Hasmoneans cast over the Jews. All its vicissitudes and setbacks failed to dim the luster of the Hasmonean house. He told himself that this was a trivial matter. What mattered was the throne: the power and glory that went with it. He did not require legitimation by the Hasmonean house; that of the Roman Senate was what counted. He was actually conferring a benefit on the Hasmoneans by making Mariamne his consort. And yet..

He vividly recalled the day he broached the subject of a marriage alliance to Hyrcanus. Then Mariamne was only thirteen years old, but it was already obvious that she was going to be a very beautiful and desirable woman. He admired beauty in all its forms, but he had to admit that his primary motive in proposing the alliance was more pragmatic – to soften the opposition of the Jews to him and to win their approval, for even then he had his sights set on the throne of Judea. With Mariamne at his side, he would win the respect of his subjects, and the union with the Hasmonean house would bring enhanced glory to the kingdom of Judea.

It was five years since he had put Doris aside as a condition for affiancing Hyrcanus's granddaughter. He felt the need for a wife – not so much in the physical sense, for he had not lacked for women, but as a consort worthy of his exalted station. This was a role Doris could never play. He had never loved her, despite his father's hopes that the match he had arranged would develop into a satisfying relationship. He supported her and their son in style, and would continue to do so, but her stodgy, small-minded ways were as irritating as her temper. Their son, whom he had named after his father, had Doris's traits more than his own, and he was unable to feel any real paternal love for him. He strongly desired sons, to follow in his footsteps and to carry on his name. This was another reason why he wanted to finalize his relationship with Mariamne.

There were some practical problems involved. First of all was the style of the marriage ceremony – strictly Jewish or more like the Roman. Some features of the latter appealed to him, but if he was to gain the approbation of his subjects, he would have to forgo this. Nevertheless, he would introduce some changes. There was the question of who would officiate. This presented considerable difficulty, for it was only fitting that the officiant be the recognized leader of the Sanhedrin. This meant Shemaiah, or possibly Avtalion, but they were cooped up in Jerusalem, which he himself had put under siege. Besides, he doubted if they would agree to officiate even if it were physically possible, for the sages did not take kindly to him. This left him with only one alternative – to seek a less prominent sage who was not shut up in Jerusalem. But even this did not prove to be simple. The first few men his agent approached turned down the request on the plea of ill health or some other flimsy excuse. This infuriated Herod, and he instructed his agent to threaten the next candidate with dire punishment if he refused. He also told the agent to make sure there was at least a quorum of ten Jewish adult males, as required for the nuptial benedictions.

The next few days were spent in feverish preparations for the wedding, including the inviting of guests. Herod decided to consult Alexandra with respect to the marriage rites and customs, but in view of her opposition to the betrothal, he was not sure how she would react. He was pleasantly surprised at her cooperation: If she did not display any marked enthusiasm, neither did she betray any overt animus.

He wanted no scenes to spoil the ceremony on the part of the members of his own family, and he told them so bluntly. He was glad to see how excited they were at the coming event, with the exception of Salome, who could not desist from giving vent to her spiteful opinion of the bride-to-be and her family.

On the wedding day a large crowd gathered in the courtyard of the villa. Samaria had never before witnessed such a distinguished assemblage: Roman and Greek officials whom Herod knew from his days as governor of Coele-Syria, the rulers and high officials of neighboring states, the commanders and staff officers of Herod's two Roman legions, and other dignitaries from Syria as well as from Samaria and nearby cities. In addition to these, kinsmen and friends had arrived from Idumea, and standing apart from the others and conversing among themselves in low, subdued voices, a knot of Jews, who were ill at ease.

At dusk the doors of the banquet hall were opened to admit the guests. The spacious room was aglow with the light of bronze oil lamps suspended from the cedarwood ceiling, the walls were adorned with wreaths, and festoons of fruit and flowers stretched between the pillars. The tables were covered with white cloths and grouped on either side of a passage to the canopy of gold and scarlet cloth, the symbolic representation of the nuptial chamber, where Herod would take Mariamne for his wife.

While waiting for the bride and bridegroom, the guests were entertained by singers accompanied by pipes and lyres, and between songs by a jester who poked good-natured fun at the institution of marriage. Even though many of his bon mots were familiar to the crowd, they relished them anew. He had just finished one of his quips when a fanfare of horns brought an abrupt halt to all laughter and conversation. All eyes were fixed on the door leading to an inner apartment, from which Herod emerged, flanked on either side by his groomsmen.

Herod cut a royal figure: a golden crown sat on his jet black hair and a silken purple robe flowed down to his ankles. He held himself erect, his dark eyes glowing with pride and authority. With slow, dignified step he and his groomsmen marched to the canopy. The groomsmen took up positions on either side of the opening to the canopy, while Herod seated himself on one of the two throne-like chairs to await the arrival of his bride.

When Mariamne appeared, attended by Alexandra and Herod's mother Cypros, the Jewish guests began to chant "A sweet and lovely bride" and clapped their hands to speed her on her way to the canopy. The singing and clapping were restrained and barely audible at the opposite side of the hall. Alexandra sighed softly, for she knew that the few Jewish guests were motivated by a sense of duty more than real joy. She couldn't help thinking ruefully that if her daughter were being married in Jerusalem, all present would join lustily in the singing, even the sages, for it was a mitzvah to gladden the bride and bridegroom.

Like Herod, Mariamne wore a golden crown. Her bridal robe was of fine white flax bordered with gold stripes, and she was adorned with some of her mother's best jewelry. Her face and hair were veiled, so the guests were unable to see how beautiful she was. But neither could they see her misty eyes. Herod saw them when Alexandra lifted the veil under the canopy. As the blessings were about to be pronounced, he took her hand and whispered to her not to be nervous.

Upon the conclusion of the wedding ceremony, Herod and Mariamne took their places at the head of the table reserved for members of their families. This was the signal for the guests to begin feasting. The tables groaned with platters of meat and other viands, and the wine flowed freely. The conversation and singing grew louder, the laughter at the jester's bold quips more raucous. Mariamne stared at the sea of faces before her. There were Roman, Greek, and Syrian faces; in only one corner did she see faces of her own people, hardly more than a quorum. Her heart ached and her eyes again filled with tears.

The tears were still there when later that evening she lay beside Herod in the bridal chamber. "This is no time for tears," Herod murmured. "This is the start of a long, happy life together – I as king of Judea, and you as its beautiful queen. You will share my throne, and all Judea will sing your praises. We'll produce beautiful princes and princesses. So, no more tears, my lovely bride."

"Yes, sir," Mariamne responded stiffly, stifling a sob.

"Not *sir*. I'm now your husband."

"Then what shall I call you?"

"Just Herod, or even dear husband."

"Yes, sir."

The consummation of the marriage was not particularly gratifying for Herod, but he had not expected it to be otherwise. He was thirty-seven years old, double Mariamne's age. He was a man with considerable experience, having been married and known other women. Mariamne came to him a frightened virgin in the nuptial bed. She was cold and trembling when he took her in his arms; she remained stiff and impassive despite his ardor and soft words. But he was not disheartened; he would have to be patient with her, for he was certain that she would come to love him as much as he loved her, his beautiful Hasmonean bride.

Mariamne Asserts Her Identity

Mariamne did not possess a large wardrobe, certainly nothing befitting a princess. This was not because she was indifferent to clothes; on the contrary, she liked beautiful things, but circumstances during the past three years had made it virtually impossible to satisfy this desire. The large mahogany chest in her room in the royal palace in Jerusalem was filled with garments of the finest material, but they would be too small for her now, she realized nostalgically.

In a small ivory casket Mariamne had kept her jewelry, most of which had been given to her over the years by her grandparents and her mother. She had loved to deck herself with this finery, to the admiration of her girlfriends. It seemed ages since she had last seen them; she missed them terribly and envied them. They were all married by now, and as far as she knew, happily so. When they moved into their husbands' homes it was with joyous anticipation. How different from what she herself felt as she moved her belongings into Herod's apartment. While the number of garments was pitifully small, she did not lack for jewelry, for Herod had given her many gifts since their betrothal, but they did not have the same sentimental value to her. She had no desire to take them with her; in fact, it was with a heavy heart that she moved any of her things.

"That's no way to act," Alexandra admonished her. "For better or for worse, you're married to Herod, and you have to accept that. You're a grown woman now and a Hasmonean. The people love you and look up to you. You must show yourself worthy of their love and respect."

"Does that mean we won't be seeing Mariamne very much now?" Aristobulus asked with a worried look.

"Of course not, darling. As long as we're here in Samaria, your sister will be living only a short distance away, at the other end of the corridor."

"And after we leave Samaria?"

"Maybe you won't see her as much as now, but you'll see her often enough."

* * *

Mariamne's brooding did not, of course, escape Herod's notice. "Is this the way to start our life together?" he remonstrated. "You look as if you're going to your execution."

Seeing that Mariamne was struggling to hold back tears, he softened his tone. "I know how attached you are to your mother and brother. And I know it's not easy for you to get used to the idea of being married. It will take a little time. But you'll see, you're going to be happy, because I want you to be happy."

These words touched Mariamne, and a wan smile appeared on her pallid face.

"Now, that's better!" exclaimed Herod. "Here, let me give you a hand with your things."

"Thanks, but I can manage. There isn't very much to take with me."

"One day, and not too long at that, you'll have so many garments you won't be able to say that. And we won't be living in a cramped apartment. We'll be living in a magnificent palace, one of the biggest and most beautiful in the world – a palace fit for the most beautiful queen in the world. It will be even more beautiful than Cleopatra's palace in Alexandria. It will be the envy of the entire world."

Mariamne did not know whether or not to be pleased at this prospect. It wasn't like Herod to wax so enthusiastic in her presence, or to praise her so effusively. Nevertheless, her spirits rose a little.

In keeping with Jewish tradition, Herod spent the first week of marriage together with Mariamne. Every day there was a celebration in the hall where the wedding took place. The guests were Romans, Greeks, and other gentiles. Herod invited a number of Jews, but knew that few if any would accept. Mariamne experienced the same detached, remote feeling she did at her wedding, but heeding her mother's admonition, she put on a brave face and forced herself to smile and be gracious to the guests. This pleased Herod, and he let her know it. But he was not pleased when they received an invitation from a highly placed Roman official. Mariamne refused to go.

"What do you mean, not go?" Herod demanded incredulously. "Perhaps you will be good enough to explain why."

"I cannot eat his food or drink his wine," replied Mariamne in measured tones.

Herod was familiar with the Jews' avoidance of certain foods and wine used for idolatrous purposes, but he had never let this interfere with his enjoyment of a meal or his dealings with gentiles. "That's a mere triviality," he said irritably; "not of any real importance."

"Maybe it's not important to you," Mariamne countered in a low, firm voice, "but the Bible forbids Jews to eat certain animals and fowls and other things too."

"Once the food has been eaten, what difference does it make?" Herod retorted with growing exasperation. "The stomach can't tell the difference."

"A Jew who knows the Bible will know the difference."

This oblique reference to his Idumean origin angered Herod. He stared coldly at Mariamne. This was not the frightened, timid bride who had indifferently shared his marriage bed. Whence her sudden boldness? "Don't tell me you have always been able to keep this prohibition," he said with a scowl. "When you were under siege at Masada, and even here in Samaria, you couldn't possibly have done so."

"We did, and we still do, to the best of our ability, whether you believe it or not. My mother instructs the cook how to prepare the food, and she keeps an eye on her."

Herod realized that Mariamne was not to be easily swayed in this matter. This was something that would have to be settled, as it had very important implications. "When we sit on the throne of Judea, we'll have many contacts with non-Jews. You can't let yourself be restricted by these taboos. They may be all right for commoners but not for royalty."

This remark made Mariamne gasp. Observance of the dietary laws was deeply ingrained in her, and any thought of violating them was repugnant, while to Herod they were meaningless taboos. What would her grandfather say to that? Had he taken that into account when he agreed to affiance her to Herod? "The people may not expect *you* to keep these so-called taboos," she said defiantly, "but they will expect it of me."

Herod regarded Mariamne with a baffled look. The truth of her statement struck him. He wanted the best of both worlds: to find favor with his Roman overlords and at the same time to win the respect of his Jewish subjects. Was this possible? "All right," he said after some reflection, "we'll find a solution. I'll explain the situation to our host, and I'm sure he'll arrange it so you can attend with a clear conscience."

* * *

After the prescribed week of celebration, Roman officers began to appear in the villa. Although Mariamne was not allowed in their presence, from the lengthy conferences and the snatches of talk she overheard, she suspected that what they were discussing boded ill for the inhabitants of Jerusalem and for all Jews for that matter. When Herod told her that he would be gone for several days, she did not know whether to be glad or not. "May I ask where you are going, or is it a secret?"

Herod hesitated briefly before replying somewhat brusquely: "I'm going to see how my soldiers are getting along."

"And to prepare them to destroy Jerusalem?" said Mariamne with undisguised scorn.

Herod looked angry at this bold accusation. "To prepare them to finish the business with Antigonus," he retorted ominously.

"And to murder my people in the process?" Mariamne flung at Herod.

Herod's mouth twitched in anger as he struggled with his temper. "I have no intention of murdering the inhabitants of Jerusalem. After three years of fighting the business has to come to an end, so that you – yes, you – can take your rightful place beside me on the throne of Judea."

Mariamne stared at Herod icily. "A throne won by shedding the blood of my people is abhorrent in the eyes of the Lord," she declared in a tone of disgust.

Herod's face turned livid with fury. "Did the Hasmoneans win the throne of Judea by peaceful means? They had to fight for it."

"They fought against a foreign conqueror, who sought to make pagans of us all."

"When I sit on the throne, the people will have reason to be grateful to me," Herod retorted before storming out of the room.

Jews Fight Valiantly as Jerusalem under Siege

As Antigonus gazed at the Temple from his headquarters room in the royal Hasmonean palace, his mood was subdued. The last of the Passover pilgrims had returned home, and an anticlimactic air hung over the Holy City. This was typical of the conclusion of every major festival, but this year it was more pronounced than ever.

The number of pilgrims had been smaller than usual, for the enemy force encamped near the northern wall of the city had deterred many from making the pilgrimage, especially from Babylonia and other Diaspora communities. Antigonus's defeat at Jericho and subsequent withdrawal to Jerusalem also had a dampening effect.

Antigonus's chief lieutenant, Joab, and Barzilai would soon be arriving for the daily morning meeting, and it would not do to let them find him in a somber mood. Antigonus had a resilient nature, and after helping himself to some wine, his spirits began to rise. *Am I a stranger to adversity?* he asked himself. *Haven't I experienced setbacks before and overcome them? More than once that Idumean lackey of Rome had tried to get the better of me in Jerusalem, and we sent him whimpering like a whipped dog. The same thing will happen to him again.*

Joab and Barzilai arrived together. They had expected to find Antigonus in low spirits, but were pleasantly surprised to see they were wrong. "Good morning, gentlemen," he greeted them amiably. "I trust you had a good night's sleep."

"Not bad," said Barzilai laconically as he drew up a chair. The rings under his eyes did not escape Antigonus's notice.

"How's your arm, Joab? Is it feeling any better?"

"I can't complain. It's healing slowly but surely, and in another couple of days I'll probably be able to get rid of this sling. Considering what happened at Jericho, it could have been much worse."

"Hmm, yes," muttered Antigonus, frowning. "Things didn't go well for us at all."

"We lost a lot of men," said Joab grimly. He had opposed Antigonus's decision to dispatch part of his army to Samaria under the command of Pappus, with the object of cutting Herod's line of communication. As Joab had warned, Herod concentrated the bulk of his force, which consisted largely of the two Roman legions Antony had put at his disposal, against Pappus, inflicting heavy losses before Antigonus could come to the aid of his general, who fell in battle.

Greatly weakened, Antigonus was unable to check the enemy at Jericho and had to withdraw to Jerusalem.

"The men we lost at Jericho weren't trained soldiers," Joab added, "but we could certainly do with them now."

"There's no point in dwelling on the past," replied Antigonus brusquely. "We've got to put our heads together and plan our strategy carefully. What's the mood in the city, Barzilai? That's important to know."

Barzilai's brow creased as he weighed his words. "It's not easy to judge. The people are disappointed at what happened at Jericho, of course, and are dismayed to be under siege again. At the same time, they remember how Silo and Machaeras had tried their luck and with what success, and this makes them more hopeful."

"A good thing Silo likes money more than glory," remarked Antigonus with a wry grin. "A pity we can't try that tactic again."

"No chance whatever," Barzilai agreed. "Herod is aiming at much bigger things."

"And using my niece to help him gain his ends."

"The people don't like it one bit," said Barzilai. "It's an odd situation, really. The people are with us wholeheartedly, yet they greatly admire, I'd say even love, Mariamne. They could never understand why Hyrcanus affianced her to Herod – a pagan Idumean who kowtows to Rome's every whim."

"And cruel too. It was a terrible mistake – typical of the old fool's perverted judgment. Sacrificing his granddaughter, and for what? I pity the girl; she deserves better."

"And yet..."

"And yet what?"

Barzilai's eyes clouded; he sucked his underlip.

"And yet she may be queen of Judea – is that what you were going to say?"

Barzilai nodded soberly. "If Jerusalem should fall..."

"Jerusalem will not fall! You can be sure of that. And it's up to us to see that our people are sure of that."

* * *

When his company had marched off to repulse Herod at Jericho, Avner was ordered, because of his ailing leg, to remain behind and help man Jerusalem's walls. His request to be allowed to join his comrades was turned down. The suspense of waiting to learn the outcome of the battle was nerve-racking, and he grasped at every rumor that floated his way. When he saw the army retreating to Jerusalem, he realized that it had been defeated. He got some idea of the magnitude of the defeat when he rejoined his company and saw, with a sinking feeling, how much its ranks had shrunk. He knew many of the missing men by name and even something of their personal history. Were they dead or wounded, or perhaps captives? It was a gloomy thought, and he was especially upset by the absence of his buddy, Nahum. No one knew what happened to him. Next day he turned up, a wounded straggler.

"Thank God!" exclaimed Avner as he embraced his friend. "How glad I am to see you."

"The Lord forgive me for saying this," replied Nahum with a weary look, "but I'm glad to be here behind these walls."

"Was it as bad as that?"

"I'm afraid so."

"Herod's army isn't that strong, and he's no great shakes as a general."

"Maybe not, but he had two Roman legions under his command. Even so, for the life of me I can't understand why Antigonus divided our army and sent part of it under Pappus in the direction of Samaria. That was a fatal mistake."

"Why did he do that?"

"I haven't the faintest idea. Whatever the reason, Herod dispatched most of his army against Pappus and inflicted heavy losses. That's what undid us."

As he stood guard duty, especially in the deep of night, Avner's thoughts would turn to his family, who he knew were worrying about him. And he could not help worrying about Rachel, even though she was betrothed and perhaps even married by now. He had several times walked past Barzilai's home in the hope of catching a glimpse of her, but to no avail. He assumed that she had been evacuated from the city, or perhaps was even living in her husband's home.

* * *

Herod ordered his troops to strengthen the earthworks that had been thrown up at the beginning of the siege, but made no attempt to breach the city walls. The inhabitants of the city were more annoyed than dismayed at this situation. But on the morning of an early summer day it changed drastically. A huge Roman army began to arrive on the scene, like a swarm of locusts. It was equipped with numerous siege-engines, and the pounding of hammers in the next few days told the besieged that more catapults and battering rams were being constructed. The hearts of the Jerusalemites turned cold with apprehension. Heightening their trepidation was the knowledge that the commander of this army was no Silo or Machaeras, but Sossius, one of Rome's most successful generals.

* * *

Seated on a dappled stallion, Herod gazed at the crenellated walls of Jerusalem. A crafty smile creased his face as he recalled his previous futile attempts to assault these walls, first as the twenty-five-year-old governor of Coele-Syria, and more recently together with the bungling and undoubtedly bribed Silo and Machaeras. But this time success was assured. And once he took his place on the throne, he would settle accounts with all who had opposed him over the years, especially those stuffy graybeards who had the audacity to make him stand trial in the Sanhedrin. Revenge would be swift and sweet. The siege-engines had already started to hurl their projectiles and to batter the walls. It was only a question of time until the northern wall would be breached, and then the second wall. After that – well, he pitied Antigonus and his supporters.

* * *

"We're in for a tough fight," said Joab bleakly, observing the enemy from a vantage point on the northern wall. "We're badly outnumbered."

"As long as our soldiers and inhabitants don't lose heart, we'll hold them off," said Antigonus with more bravado than conviction.

Barzilai was less optimistic. If the enemy broke into the city, everything he had striven to achieve would be lost – his position, his wealth, and very likely even his life. Thank goodness, he had at least gotten his wife and Rachel out of the city in time. After considering all the possibilities, he had evacuated them to Emmaus, which the Romans had largely ignored so far. He knew he was not well liked by the people of Emmaus because of his foreclosure of unpaid loans in the past, but this was a minor considerations compared with the safety of his family.

* * *

The ordeal endured by the Jerusalemites weighed heavily on Shemaiah. Fewer people than usual had made the Passover pilgrimage this year, yet it was heartening to see how many had braved the danger and uncertainties to fulfill this mitzvah, which normally was a very joyous occasion. Their faith that the Lord would not forsake His people or His temple was inspiring. Nevertheless, he could not forget that the city and the Temple had fallen to Roman legions under Pompey. That was almost quarter of a century ago, when he had only recently been ordained. The memory of the fighting still haunted him. Was that catastrophe about to repeat itself? The possibility was depressing but very real. Even now Roman siege-engines were taking innocent lives, and the toll was growing with each passing day.

Much as he hated bloodshed, he had to do whatever he could to help sustain his people in this fateful hour. Antigonus was a charismatic leader who could inspire his fellow Jews to flock to his banner in defense of the nation against its enemies, even mighty Rome. But the prospects did not look promising to Shemaiah. When the struggle took a turn for the worse, the people would look to him, as the spiritual leader of the nation, for guidance. The responsibility was a heavy one. He prayed to the Almighty to give him the wisdom and fortitude to discharge this responsibility in the best interests of his people.

* * *

"What do you say, gentlemen, how long will it take?" Sossius asked his staff officers and Herod as they surveyed the city from a vantage point out of bowshot.

"The walls are very stout," Herod cautioned. "My father reinforced them, so I know."

"I've come up against plenty of stout walls in my time," Sossius retorted crisply. "I know what our siege-engines can do, and I can assure you that I wouldn't like to be shut up in that city. I give them two weeks, three at the most. That's…"

"Look! Over there!" an officer shouted. "Something is burning."

The officers looked in the direction indicated. Near one of the earthworks smoke was curling upward. Roman soldiers were engaged in hand-to-hand combat, and their shouts were clearly audible.

"What in hell is going on there?" barked Sossius.

"Looks like the enemy's set fire to some of our siege-engines," one officer said.

"How did they get out of the wall undetected?" Sossius demanded harshly. "Where were our sentries? Were they asleep?"

"I don't know, sir."

"Find out and see to it that the guilty ones are duly punished."

"Yes, sir."

* * *

The defenders proved to be more resourceful and courageous than Sossius had reckoned. Time after time they slipped out from the walls and set fire to siege-engines and even to engage the enemy in close combat, usually after nightfall, when it was hard to detect their approach. Sossius, growing increasingly exasperated, gave orders to step up the bombardment of the city. But this did not daunt the defenders; they fought valiantly and devised various ways of frustrating the enemy. Sossius thereupon decided on a bold tactic – to scale the wall at a point which his scouts reported was lightly manned at night. This was to be carried out after midnight, when most of the Jewish troops would be sleeping.

A platoon of hardened legionnaires would make the initial assault and secure a foothold, while reinforcements swarmed over the wall. Sossius had resorted to this stratagem before and, while not without its risks, it had succeeded often enough to make the attempt worthwhile.

He chose a night shortly after new moon, when there was just enough light to enable the legionnaires to negotiate the terrain. He and his staff stationed themselves a short distance away and watched with tense expectation as the assault party stealthily made its way toward the wall. He breathed a little easier when three ladders were raised against the wall seemingly without attracting attention, and the men began to climb upward. They had almost reached the top when suddenly the battlements became alive with shouting defenders, some brandishing their weapons and others, much to the Romans' surprise, carrying large jugs. The latter contained oil, which was poured onto the ladders, making them too slippery to grip. The legionnaires fell to the stony ground, where they were easy targets for the defenders' arrows. Realizing that he had fallen into a trap, Sossius cursed loudly.

* * *

After the enemy's abortive attempt to scale the northern wall in the fifth week of the siege, the night watch was doubled along the entire perimeter and the defenders placed on high alert, ready to rush to any threatened spot. Avner sorely missed his occasional brief leaves, when he could roam the city and rub shoulders with those inhabitants who dared to venture outdoors in defiance of the missiles. In the early days of the siege he particularly enjoyed visiting the marketplace with its display of colorful vegetables and other commodities, but as the siege wore on the supply of food and other products became scarcer until they all but disappeared from the stalls. This was reflected in the faces of the shoppers, which became increasingly haggard, the eyes duller. He noticed that whereas formerly they had been accustomed to haggle over prices, they now purchased their needs with a minimum of bargaining, so that they could quickly return to the relative safety of their homes. Some of them were not lucky enough to escape the projectiles, and their cries of pain sent a shudder through Avner's body. He would rush over to the victim, and together with others administer whatever first aid he could. As a soldier he had had his share of brushes with death, but he could not get used to the suffering of innocent civilians, especially children. On such occasions he would have trouble falling asleep no matter how exhausted he might be.

It was not only the physical wounds that upset him; the gnawing hunger of the inhabitants also gave him no peace of mind. The troops were no longer getting full rations – in fact, these were getting progressively smaller – but neither were they going hungry. Whenever he had a precious leave, he would take some food in his rucksack to give to a needy person. He got a lot of satisfaction from this, and in this way he was also able to strike up a conversation. One day, while walking through the Lower City, he came upon a little girl, no more than four or five years old, who had a racking cough. "What's the matter with you, little one?" he asked solicitously.

"I, I," she started to reply, but was unable to continue because of a bout of coughing. "I'm not feeling well," she finally blurted out.

"I can see that. Why aren't you indoors?"

"Imma said I can go out for a little while and get some fresh air, but not to go far because it's too dangerous to be outdoors."

"What your mother says is right. It is too dangerous."

"Here she comes now. That means I'll have to go back in."

"Before you do, why don't you tell me your name."

"My name is Rachel."

"That's a beautiful name," said Avner, recalling another Rachel. After introducing himself to the mother, Avner added, "Your daughter seems to have a bad cough,"

"She's caught a nasty cold in spite of the summer weather. I hope she doesn't give it to the other children."

"Wouldn't hot drinks and honey help her coughing?"

The woman threw up her hands in a gesture of despair. "It would, but where can I find honey? We've used up the little bit we had."

Avner opened his rucksack and extracted a small jar of honey, which he had intended to spread on his bread. "This isn't much, but you're welcome to it."

The woman's face lit up. "It's very kind of you to offer me this. But I can't take it. You need it more than we do."

"If I can help my little friend, it will make me very happy. So please take it with my best wishes."

"May the Almighty bless you," said the mother, taking the precious jar of honey. "Rachel, tell the soldier how thankful you are."

"Thank you – ah, what is your name?"

"Avner."

"Thank you very much, Avner."

"May I offer you a glass of wine and some cake?" the mother said. "We're not short of wine, and we have cake left over from the Sabbath."

"Thanks, but I must be getting back."

"Some other time then. Whenever you're free, you're always welcome. We live over there," she said, pointing to a courtyard with a green gate. "May the Lord bless you and keep you and all our soldiers. And may we quickly see an end to this awful siege."

Avner had a sudden hankering to visit the spot where he had been wounded nearly three years ago when driving back Herod's mercenaries to the royal palace. As he headed toward the Upper City he could not get the encounter with the little girl and her mother out of his mind. They reminded him of his sister and her young daughter. But what a difference! In Emmaus the inhabitants enjoyed peace and quiet. They could send their children outdoors to play without worrying about falling missiles, nor were they going hungry. If a child needed some honey for a cough, it was no problem to obtain it. Above all, there was no fear of what the morrow might bring – the breaching of the walls and enemy soldiers rushing through the streets with drawn swords and battle axes.

Rachel – what a beautiful name. He would always associate it with the comely child to whom he had given a little honey. But it was also the name of the girl with whom he had grown up in Emmaus and who had helped nurse him back to health after being wounded in front of her home. She was now a young lady, probably already married. And, unless she had been evacuated, presumably she now lived in the Upper City, the quarter of the wealthy, aristocratic families. She had grown quite distant from her Emmaus days. Yet, when she had helped him recover from his wound, it was almost like old times. Avner grinned as he recalled her father's reaction: He had not tried to hide his lack of enthusiasm at having Avner as a "guest" in his home, for more than one reason. Avner's father had never forgiven Barzilai for squeezing the financially strapped farmers of Emmaus, foreclosing the mortgages of those unable to repay the loans he had given them in years of poor harvest. How many times Zechariah had advised his son to forget about Rachel. "You're wasting your time if you think anything serious can come of this," he had often admonished him. "Barzilai will never consent to anything so demeaning in his eyes."

Avner was so absorbed in his thoughts that, almost without realizing it, he was approaching Barzilai's mansion. Here too the streets were deserted, for missiles were falling with frightening regularity, and he had to take shelter several times. When he neared Barzilai's residence, he wondered if by some chance Rachel was inside and how she was taking the bombardment. It couldn't be pleasant for her, and maybe she was even longing for the days when she had lived in the pleasant quiet of Emmaus, far from the siege. A sentry was posted at the gate to Barzilai's residence, which had a forlorn, deserted air. He was tempted to approach the sentry and ask if Rachel was in, but realized how ridiculous this would seem.

* * *

The brave resistance of the greatly outnumbered defenders and their daring countermeasures heartened the inhabitants of Jerusalem, but did not curtail the bombardment of the city. In fact, Sossius, his temper growing shorter the longer the siege exceeded his original estimate of two to three weeks, ordered the construction of more catapults and battering rams and stepped up the assault, taking an increasing toll of Jewish lives. Added to the people's woes was a growing shortage of food. Realizing that the end was drawing near, Shemaiah and Avtalion decided to address the Sanhedrin.

The atmosphere in the chamber was somber; the elders were bleary-eyed and weary owing to anxiety and lack of sleep. They had been carrying on the business of the Sanhedrin as best they could in the face of the most trying circumstances, ignoring the dangers that lurked on every side. The crashing of stone projectiles onto mansions and humble dwellings alike was clearly audible. Mercifully the cries of the victims did not penetrate the thick walls of the chamber, but it did not take much imagination to realize what was happening outside. When Shemaiah rose to speak, the elders leaned forward and some cupped their ears, for they knew he had a fateful message to deliver.

"The facts stare us in the face," declared Shemaiah in a grave voice. "The situation has become desperate. Our men are fighting valiantly and have given the enemy more than they bargained for. But how long can we hold out against such a huge, formidable army? It is only a question of time until it breaches the northern wall and overruns the city, with results too horrible to contemplate. Even now we're paying a heavy price: Every day more and more of our people are being killed or wounded. The dead cannot be removed from the city for burial. The stench of their rotting bodies assails our nostrils, and disease is rampant. Moreover, the specter of famine stalks our streets. We can prolong the fighting, but what will it avail us? The choice before us is not an easy or pleasant one. It has caused me many a sleepless night. If the suffering of our people would culminate in victory, then I would say that it's the price we have to pay, grievous as it may be. But in the present circumstances, when victory is remote – nay, beyond our grasp – my conscience impels me to advocate an accommodation with the Romans. I therefore propose that we send a delegation to Antigonus and inform him that this is the consensus of the Sanhedrin."

Shemaiah's proposal cast a pall of gloom over the chamber. Several elders spoke in favor of the proposal, albeit somberly. The few that opposed it were particularly worried about the likely fate of Antigonus, and no less distressing, their own fate. It was clear to all that the country had reached a crucial turning-point that did not bode well.

The next day Shemaiah and Avtalion were ushered into Antigonus's headquarters in the Birah, the fortress at the northwestern corner of the Temple Mount, where they found Antigonus, Joab, Barzilai, and another adviser seated around a long table. "We know you have very urgent matters to attend to," said Shemaiah after returning Antigonus's greetings. "We are therefore very grateful that you agreed to receive us."

"When the distinguished heads of the Sanhedrin request an audience, I assume it is of great importance," replied Antigonus.

Not having seen Antigonus for more than a fortnight, Shemaiah was struck by his appearance. Normally a handsome, self-confident man who radiated an air of command, he was showing the strain of conducting the defense of Jerusalem against a powerful, vastly more numerous foe. His face was drawn and there were dark rings under his eyes; when he sat down he slumped instead of holding himself erect.

"I hope the Sanhedrin has been able to carry on its business in the face of the, er, annoying interruptions," Antigonus said with a trace of a smile.

"Fortunately, we have been able to manage tolerably well so far. But how long we can continue to do so is doubtful."

"And that, I take it, is why you have requested an audience?"

"Among other things," replied Shemaiah gravely. He glanced at Antigonus's advisers. "With all due respect, we would prefer to speak to you privately."

A puzzled look crossed Antigonus's face. "That is a rather unusual request. My advisers are generally privy to my audiences. They must be if they are to advise me properly."

"We understand that," said Avtalion, "but the matter we wish to discuss is very delicate and personal. When you have heard us out, we're sure you will understand."

Antigonus knitted his brow as he considered the request. "Very well," he said, frowning. He dismissed his advisers but told them to stay within calling distance. After their departure Antigonus leaned back in his chair and folded his arms. "If it's the military situation that is troubling you, I fail to see why you wanted me to dismiss my military advisers. That's precisely what they're here for."

"What we have to say concerns you personally, and we don't want to cause you any embarrassment in the presence of your advisers," said Shemaiah.

"Embarrassment?" said Antigonus with an even more perplexed expression. "Please explain yourself."

Shemaiah cleared his throat and spoke calmly. "Let me begin by saying that we admit we are not experts in military matters. Far from it. We fight the Lord's battles in a different way – by disseminating knowledge of our holy Torah and applying it to our daily lives. We are concerned with everything that affects our people, and right now our people are suffering terribly. At this very moment we can hear the crash of missiles hurled by enemy catapults, and if we were outdoors we would hear the cry of the victims. This has been going on for several weeks. Besides the constant bombardment, the food supply is dwindling. The people are getting hungrier and weaker with each passing day. If they don't fall victim to the catapults, they'll soon fall victim to famine and disease. If we felt there was hope for a successful conclusion of the siege, we could say that this is the price that has to be paid, distressful as it may be. But considering who we are up against, we don't see any hope for a successful conclusion."

Antigonus, visibly upset by the last remark, flashed a swift, questioning glance. "And so what do you suggest?"

Shemaiah looked thoughtful for a moment and then answered with care: "It is the consensus of the Sanhedrin that an accommodation should be sought with the Romans."

Antigonus's eyes narrowed, and his jaws set firm. "Surrender to the pagans!" he exclaimed in disbelief. "Does the Sanhedrin think this will bring salvation to our people?"

"Perhaps not salvation," replied Avtalion. "But we hope it will at least bring an end to the people's suffering."

"For how long? Surrendering to the Romans means that the throne of Judea will fall into the hands of that despicable Idumean. This is a man whose brand of justice we know only too well. Have you forgotten what he did to the brave partisan leader Hezekiah? And what about the Sanhedrin? Have you forgotten how he marched on Jerusalem with the intention of taking revenge for being summoned to stand trial for that crime? Is that the kind of man you want on the throne of Judea?"

"No, it isn't," said Shemaiah with a grim expression, "but what is the alternative? To let the siege go on, with more and more of our people being killed or wounded until the enemy breaks into the city and slaughters everyone in sight? If we agree to stop fighting, the Romans may treat us leniently, including you."

Antigonus snorted. "I'm afraid you don't know the Romans as well as I do. They are not the least squeamish about how they treat their prisoners. There is nothing a victorious general desires more than to be voted a triumph, when he and his soldiers parade through the streets of Rome with huge crowds cheering them on together with the spoils of war and captured prisoners, who are subsequently executed."

"You have twice been a prisoner of the Romans, yet they didn't harm you," Shemaiah pointed out.

"That was because I escaped the first time, and the second time I was released under an agreement with Gabinius. But what happened to my father and brother? My father was poisoned and my brother beheaded."

"That was due to the civil war between Pompey and Caesar," replied Avtalion.

"True. But I could just as easily have suffered the same fate."

Antigonus leaned back in his chair and fixed the sages with a piercing look. "Don't think I'm afraid to die," he said in a quiet, intense tone. "A man who has rallied the people to his banner and led them into battle against the Romans and Herod's mercenaries knows he is risking his life. But have you considered that I am actually the last of the Hasmoneans, a descendant of those who led the nation against the Syrian-Greeks and saved it from pagan Hellenism? Our people have not forgotten that glorious chapter in our history. If I depart the scene, it will be the end of the Hasmonean house, and who knows what fate awaits our people."

"Hyrcanus is still alive," said Avtalion.

Antigonus gave a short, hard laugh. "Alive, but completely powerless, disqualified from wearing the priestly crown."

"There is his grandson, your nephew Aristobulus."

"Do you think Herod will let him be a rival for the throne? I pity the boy. No, I'm really the last of the Hasmoneans, and our people know that. I'm no less sensitive to the people's suffering than you are, but I know the stuff they're made of. They'll fight like lions, and I'll lead them, a Hasmonean to the end. That is my answer to the Sanhedrin."

* * *

The two to three weeks that Sossius had originally estimated it would take to subdue the city stretched to almost six weeks before his battering rams breached the northern wall. Two weeks later the second wall was also in Roman hands. Enemy troops overran the Lower City and the outer precincts of the Temple. The defenders put up a stout resistance, but were overwhelmed by the sheer weight of the enemy's numbers. The Romans showed no mercy to the Jews, slaughtering everyone they came across, soldiers and civilians alike, young and old. Herod was at first jubilant at the rapid advance of Sossius's forces, but once they spread through the city, he began to fret at the wanton massacre which they perpetrated. "These people will be my subjects," he protested to Sossius. "There won't be many left if your troops keep on like this."

"Your subjects haven't shown any great love for us Romans," Sossius replied coolly, "but that was to be expected. Neither do they seem to show any great love for their new king."

Herod's visage darkened. "They will in time," he said stiffly. "But if you don't order your men to stop murdering and plundering, I'll be ruling over a wilderness."

"My men have risked their lives so you can sit on the throne. They deserve some reward for that."

"Order them to stop, and as soon as we finish with Antigonus, I'll see to it that they get their reward, each and every one of them."

* * *

Antigonus convened his advisers in his headquarters in the Birah. The gravity of the situation was written on everyone's face; all knew the end was drawing near. The din of battle was ominously loud, for the enemy now occupied practically all of the city and even part of the Temple Mount.

"How much longer do you think we can hold out?" Antigonus asked Joab.

"A week at the most, I'd say."

"We have nothing to be ashamed of," remarked Antigonus with a somber expression. "We gave the Romans a good fight – more than they bargained for, I'm sure. They had to send one of their best generals with an army big enough to fight the Parthians. That says something about our soldiers and our people."

"What galls me," said Barzilai, "is that their sniveling puppet will now sit on the throne. Who knows what he'll do to our country. Nothing good, that's for sure."

"Obviously not," agreed Antigonus. "My ancestors liberated the country from the pagan yoke. That was a glorious chapter in the history of our people – one that will forever be enshrined in the hearts of our nation. And to think that my uncle was partly responsible for bringing us to this wretched state. The question is, what now?"

"Fight to the end!" declared Joab.

"You mean to the last man," retorted Antigonus. "The end is a foregone conclusion. We have to face the bitter reality. Our people are being slaughtered mercilessly. When our troops fall in battle I grieve, but I have to accept it, because that's the risk all soldiers take, myself included. But old folks, helpless women, young children – that's a different matter. I have to stop the slaughter."

"How?" everyone asked.

"By giving myself up to the Romans."

All present gasped. "They'll execute you," said Joab glumly.

"They probably will," agreed Antigonus with a resigned look. "But I'm ready to pay the price. The Romans will learn that a true Hasmonean knows not only how to fight for his people, but if necessary how to die for his people."

Chapter Nine

Herod Controls Jerusalem with an Iron Fist

The Wounded Avner Meets Rachel in Emmaus

Zechariah was proud to be one of the elders of the Emmaus synagogue, and he took his responsibilities seriously. Too seriously, his wife complained. "If the roof needs fixing," she said one late autumn day, "who says you have to see to it? Is that the responsibility of an elder? Asher is the president; let him worry about it. Or the *hazzan* [beadle]. He's paid to see to the running of the synagogue."

"The hazzan has a lot of duties to perform," Zechariah patiently explained. "Sometimes he needs help. Right now the schoolmaster is sick, so on top of everything else the hazzan is taking charge of the school."

"So how long will the schoolmaster be sick? With God's help, at most a couple of days."

"We've already waited longer than we should with the roof. We can't risk having the rain leak through and get the people wet. Rain is good for the fields but not for people trying to concentrate on the service."

"There's still plenty of time before the rainy season starts."

"Who says we have to wait for the rains to start? You have to harvest your crops when the weather is good. The same goes for fixing a roof."

"I don't like you on the roof of that building. It's dangerous."

"I won't be doing the actual work. I'm only going to show Eli where the leaks are and see that he mends them. Besides, haven't I fixed the roof of our house dozens of times?"

"You're not as young as you used to be."

"None of us are. I just have to be a little more careful, that's all. Don't worry, with God's help, nothing will happen to me."

As Zechariah made his way to the synagogue he reflected on his wife's anxiety. "She's worrying more than ever," he sighed aloud. "It must be the situation; it's making a lot of people nervous." He related this to his neighbor Saul, whom he met two hours later when returning home.

"My helpmate is the same," replied Saul, leaning against the gate to his courtyard. "The minute I get home, off she goes. It's Herod this and Herod that. Now it's the business about the high priesthood. It's causing a lot of hard feeling."

"I've said it before, but if Hyrcanus hadn't given his daughter to Herod, maybe things wouldn't have turned out so bad."

"Who knows? Unfortunately, it's not only Herod; it's also those damned Romans. Look at how many of our people they killed in Jerusalem and how many homes they destroyed. When I was there a couple of weeks ago, I was shocked at the amount of damage."

"I've heard that Herod's got the people working hard to repair the damage."

"I certainly hope so. And speaking of repairs, what's happening with the synagogue roof? Where you elders sit it's nice and dry; where I sit it's like being in a *mikvah* [ritual bath]."

"Aren't you exaggerating a little?" said Zechariah with a grin. "It was never that bad."

"Then maybe you'll trade places with me?"

"It won't be necessary. The roof has just been fixed. That's where I'm coming from now."

"You mean to tell me that *you* fixed the roof?"

"Eli did it. I just supervised."

"Well, that's a big relief. I must say, you're getting pretty high up in the world," Saul chuckled.

"My wife wouldn't think that's funny. She doesn't like me being on rooftops, not even if someone else does the work. Next time I'll let you have the honor."

"No, thanks. With all due respect, I'm too small a man for such a big honor. To change the subject, how's Avner feeling?"

"His wound is healing nicely, and he's in better spirits."

"Every time I think about how he got out of Jerusalem it makes me shudder. That was a pretty close call."

"We thank the Almighty morning and night for that. And we also pray that he give up his crazy ideas and settle down."

"What crazy ideas?"

"About joining some resistance group. We've made it clear that he's no longer a youngster; he's done more than his share of fighting, and it's time to settle down."

"Does he still have his heart set on Rachel?"

"I really can't say. Avner says she keeps pretty much to herself since the disappearance and death of so many of her family members. She's lucky her father had the foresight to get most of the family out of Jerusalem before the siege began. At least they're safe."

"I never had much love for Barzilai, as you know. He wasn't exactly charitable to our people here who were hard up and had to borrow money from him and couldn't repay their loans, and are now without any land of their own. Still, I can't help being sorry for what happened to him, and more so for his family."

"I wonder how they feel being back in Emmaus. Avner has told us about their big mansion in Jerusalem – in the Upper City, where the wealthy aristocrats live. To come back where they started from is a big comedown, however you look at it."

* * *

When Avner, limping noticeably from a wound to his left leg, opened the gate to the family courtyard after making his laborious way from Jerusalem, he braced himself for the reception that awaited him. His parents fell on his neck, and with tears of joy thanked the Almighty so many times. Avner wondered that the Lord Above did not lose patience. But he could not blame them. For weeks – how many he wasn't sure – he had been unable to get a message to them, and obviously they were extremely worried, especially when news of the fierce fighting in Jerusalem and its tragic outcome reached them. Their intense relief at his safe return was tampered with concern about his injury – "a superficial wound," Avner assured them.

"Superficial or not, it has to be looked after," his mother declared. "This is the second time you've been wounded in that leg. I'll heat some water up."

"Avner must be very hungry," his father said. "I think he ought to have something to eat first. How bad does it hurt, son?"

"So, so. If I've gotten this far with it, it can wait a little longer. I *am* starving. I haven't eaten a thing all day. I'll go wash up a bit."

Avner fell on the food voraciously. His parents were eager to hear about his experiences, but thoughtfully did not question him. When his hunger was appeased, he was ready to relate what had happened in Jerusalem, but his mother said that could wait; first, his injury had to be treated. "I'll ask Bracha to come and look at it."

"Bracha! The midwife?"

"That's right."

"I'm not about to give birth."

"Such miracles I don't expect. If your wound is superficial, she can dress it for the time being. Tomorrow we'll call the physician. Right now he's seeing a patient in the neighboring village."

Bracha's diagnosis, which was confirmed the following day by the physician, was that the wound was not serious, but Avner would have to stay in bed for several days at least.

After she left, he described, briefly and unemotionally, his escape from Jerusalem. "Fortunately, it turned out to be rather easy, now that I look back on it. When I saw that the battle was lost and the enemy had overrun the city, I managed under cover of darkness to climb down the wall with the help of a stout rope, at a point where I knew I was least likely to be detected. I stripped the armor off a dead legionnaire and made my way safely through the enemy lines."

"And that's it?" exclaimed Zechariah with a look of amazement. "The Lord was surely watching over you."

When his parents asked him about the siege, a pained expression came over Avner's face. "The inhabitants suffered terribly," he said in a subdued voice; "first from the catapults and hunger, and horribly when the enemy broke into the city." More than that Avner would not relate, and his parents did not press him.

That night his sleep was disturbed by a nightmare. His fellow soldiers were being cut down and the inhabitants were falling victim to the catapults and then to the enemy troops pouring through the narrow streets, slaying everyone they came across. Once he groaned so loudly that his parents woke up and hurried to his bedside. "You must be having a bad dream," his father said solicitously.

"I'm afraid so." Avner apologized for the disturbance. "I'll stay with you a little while," Zechariah said

"Thanks, Abba, but it's not necessary. I'll be all right. Go back to sleep. Please."

For several days Avner suffered not only from nightmares but also from depression over the fall of Jerusalem and the entire country to the enemy. He tried to keep his feelings from his parents, but they were not deceived. Even though they too were distressed at the turn of events, they did their best to cheer him up. "We cannot fathom the ways of the Lord," declared Zechariah, "but we must have faith that He will not forsake His people."

Avner hated being confined to bed and treated like an invalid, he moaned to his parents. But in getting out of bed several times a day to relieve himself he found that he was weaker than he thought. Gradually, however, his strength returned, and this, together with the visits of his family and fellow townsmen, boosted his spirits. But none more so than the visit of one whom he least expected. Awakening from a nap one cloudy afternoon, he was surprised to see sitting in his room none other than Rachel.

"Am I dreaming or is it really you?" he asked with an incredulous look.

"Pinch yourself and you'll find out," she replied with a wan smile.

"How did you know I was here? You surely didn't come to Emmaus just to see me."

"We've been living here for several weeks."

Avner's eyebrows arched sharply. "Living here! My parents never told me."

"I asked them not to."

"Why not?"

"I had my reasons."

"I wish I knew you were here. I've been very worried about you. There were rumors that you had been evacuated from Jerusalem, but I didn't know how true they were." Avner shook his head dolefully. "I'm very sorry about your father. May the Lord console you and all your family."

"Thank you," said Rachel in a low, choking voice, dabbing at a sudden tear. "I'm sorry," she apologized. "I've come to help cheer you up. Your father told me how depressed you were."

"Thank goodness, I've more or less gotten over that. But that's nothing compared with what you have all suffered. I take it your mother is here?"

"Yes, and so is my younger sister."

"And your brother?"

"We don't know what's happened to him."

"I see," Avner murmured with a grim expression. "Let's hope for the best. And your *fiancé*?"

Rachel shook her head with a helpless air; tears welled up in her eyes.

"How terrible!" Avner commiserated. "May the Lord give you and the rest of your family the strength to bear your grievous losses."

"Thank you," I'm afraid my visit isn't going to make you feel more cheerful."

"That's all right, don't let it bother you. Life isn't always a long cheerful road." After a pause he continued, "I'm curious about something: What made your father decide to bring you back to Emmaus? He owned property in other places."

"He thought Emmaus was safer than the other places, the one least likely to be troubled by the Romans in case things didn't go right."

"I see. Do you have any idea how long you'll be living here? Oh, that's a silly question. I don't suppose you know."

"We have no definite plans at the moment. Frankly, we're very confused. We don't even know what's happened to the rest of our family on either my father's or mother's side."

Avner fell silent as he considered the painful news. Rachel's sorrow plainly showed on her face. Gone was her radiant smile, her sanguine, cheerful manner; there was an anguished look in her eyes. He was deeply touched.

"My mother sends you her best wishes for a speedy recovery," Rachel said quietly, breaking the awkward silence.

"I'm very grateful. In a way it's odd when you come to think about it. The last time we were together, I was also wounded – and in the same leg. But thanks to the expert ministration of your physician and especially the devoted care of my nurse, I was soon back on my feet."

A trace of a smile appeared on Rachel's pallid face. "We had an obedient if somewhat impatient casualty on our hands. And besides, I'd like to remind you that it took some time before you were back on your feet."

"I know your father, may he rest in peace, came to see me briefly," Avner responded, wondering if it was wise to evoke what were likely to be painful memories.

"Did you ever see my father again after that?"

Avner nodded. "I saw him once when I had some time off from guard duty. I took one of my buddies to see the Upper City, and we ran into your father as he was leaving home."

"He never mentioned that to me."

"You were probably evacuated to Emmaus at the time. Besides, I don't suppose he attached any importance to it," remarked Avner with a conscious effort to keep any rancor out of his voice.

"He had many things on his mind," said Rachel defensively. "The fate of Jerusalem worried him greatly."

"It worried all of us. I can't help thinking about the little girl and her mother I befriended in the Lower City. I wonder if they survived the siege."

"You must tell me about it.'

Rachel listened with rapt attention as Avner recounted how he had come upon a little girl with a racking cough and how he had given her mother his small jar of honey to help her recover. "That's a very touching story," Rachel commented when Avner finished. "You had a big mitzvah. The mother must have been very grateful."

"She was. And the little girl has a beautiful name."

"What is it?"

"Rachel. One day, when I get back on my feet," Avner continued, intrigued by the surge of color suffusing Rachel's cheeks, "I intend to go to Jerusalem and see if I can find out what happened to them."

"When you do, you must let me know."

"With God's help I'll do that; it's a promise."

Resentment as Hannanel, a Babylonian, Appointed High Priest

When Alexandra herded her two children into the coach that was to take them back to Jerusalem, she was filled with mixed emotions: immense relief at leaving Samaria and trepidation over what awaited them at the end of the journey. The closer she came to the city, the more uneasy she felt, and when it came into view, her heart sank at the sight. A gaping hole in the northern wall testified to the spot where the Romans had penetrated the city's defenses, and shattered rooftops and crumbling walls were grim evidence of the ordeal suffered by the inhabitants. When the coach passed through the main city gate she saw that many of the streets were littered with the rubble of devastated homes, and a putrid smell assailed her nostrils. Worst of all, the sight of grieving mourners accompanying through the gate the bodies of those who had succumbed that day to wounds incurred before the end of the fighting nearly a fortnight ago sent shivers down her spine. *How many of my fellow Jews had perished in the siege?* she wondered. Judging from the evidence that met her eye, the number must have been painfully large.

When the coach came to a halt before the royal Hasmonean palace, it seemed ages since she had last been here. Could it possibly be only three years? So many momentous events had taken place in the meantime that her world seemed to have become completely disordered. She was wistfully gazing at the building that had been her home for most of her life when an officer approached and saluted.

"Greetings, Your Highness," he said with a strong foreign accent. "His Majesty has ordered me to escort you to your apartments."

His Majesty? For a second she wondered whom he was referring to. She studied the officer's face. She could not tell whether he was a Syrian-Greek or some other nationality, but he was definitely not Jewish.

"That's kind of you," she replied a little stiffly, "but quite unnecessary. I have lived here more years than you possess. But I would be grateful if someone brought our luggage in."

As she and her two children walked down the corridor toward the private apartments, the mist of time rolled away, and a host of memories crowded in on her. Some harked back to her youth, when she was younger than Mariamne today. She could hear the voices of her parents – occasionally admonishing but more often encouraging: her dear father and mother, who were now living in exile. She could see the knots of visitors from Babylonia, Rome, and other lands, not to mention from every corner of the Land of Israel, who had come to pay homage to their high priest and king. Where were these people now and how were they faring? Who would have ever dreamed that matters would come to such a pass? Herod and his family living in the palace of the Hasmoneans! "His Majesty" – the words stuck in her throat. She gave a short, bitter laugh.

She passed the study where her father had sat reading Psalms before going to meet the Parthian general Barzapharnes – the last time she saw him. He had been confident that the meeting would have a favorable outcome, but she had been less sanguine. Had the study been used during the past three years? Had Antigonus sat here over the numerous books that filled the handsomely carved cabinets? Probably very seldom, if at all. Dear Antigonus! How his fortunes have come to grief – a prisoner of the Romans in Antioch, his life at the mercy of Mark Antony, whose hands are stained with the blood of hundreds of Roman aristocrats. The memories chased one another, some pleasant, others less so. And now what? The Hasmonean house had been cast low, its glory dimmed almost beyond recognition. But as long as there was even a single Hasmonean alive, she would do her utmost to ensure that the ember be not extinguished, that it should again glow brightly.

Alexandra paused at the door of her apartment. For three years it had presumably been occupied by another. When she entered she immediately knew it was Antigonus's wife Roxane, for under the divan she saw one of her rings, undoubtedly overlooked in the haste of vacating the palace. Where was she now, with Antigonus or elsewhere? And where were their children? With all her heart she hoped they were not prisoners of the Romans.

A knock on the door interrupted Alexandra's reflections. Two servants had arrived with the luggage.

"We've brought your baggage," one of them said. "Where do you want us to put it?"

"Now let me see. These four chests are mine. You can leave them here. And these two go into Aristobulus's room. That's the third door down the corridor. And as for Mariamne – hmm, that's a problem."

"That's no problem," Mariamne protested; "they go into my old room."

"My dear, you're forgetting that you're a queen now. I don't know myself where your apartment will be. That's for Herod to decide."

Mariamne shook her head despondently.

"What's the matter, dear?"

"Nothing," Mariamne replied dully.

"You'll have to get used to the fact that you're Herod's wife, Queen of Judea," Alexandra gently admonished her daughter. "Whatever our people think about Herod, they love you. You're a Hasmonean, and that means a lot to them. You must not let them down, especially in these difficult times."

"And what am I supposed to call Herod?" asked Aristobulus with a contemptuous look. "It's certainly not going to be Your Majesty."

"I don't think he'll expect you to, son."

Alexandra sighed. She realized that many complications lay ahead, and it would not be easy to cope with them. In Samaria she had gained a better insight into Herod's character. That he was crafty and had a fierce temper when crossed she already knew; she also knew that he could be ruthless when thwarted in his designs. What puzzled her was his attitude toward Mariamne. Whatever his reasons for marrying her – she assumed the principal one was dynastic – Mariamne had a strong fascination for him, so much so that he was extremely jealous of anyone who showed too personal an interest in her. This worried Alexandra, for Mariamne did not reciprocate his feelings – a situation that did not bode well for the future.

The servants recalled Alexandra to the business at hand. "These other chests," one of them said, pointing to Mariamne's, "what have you decided, Your Highness?"

"Take them to Mariamne's old apartment for the time being. She'll show you where it is."

"Thanks, Imma," Mariamne said with visible relief.

"You must realize, of course, that this is a temporary arrangement. Now go and show them where to take your things."

Before Mariamne reached her apartment, she saw Salome approaching. For a moment she was flustered, and her first impulse was to hastily retreat into the nearest room. But she immediately realized how foolish this would be; it would only make her more contemptible in Salome's eyes. She must show her that she was no longer a young child who could be intimidated by her. She decided to simply ignore her sister-in-law. But Salome would have none of this.

"Welcome to the royal palace, Your Majesty," she said with a spiteful smirk, stressing in her high-pitched, grating voice the royal title. "I trust you find it suitable to your eminent station. But, of course, I'm forgetting: Unlike our humble family, you're not a newcomer here."

"No, I'm not," replied Mariamne brusquely. "Now if you'll excuse me, I'll get on with my work."

Disregarding this abrupt dismissal, Salome added: "The apartments here are very plain – too plain for a queen, or even for the other members of the royal family for that matter. I doubt if His Majesty will approve of them."

"His Majesty can decide that for himself. Now if you'll excuse me, I'll get on with my unpacking."

Turning to the two servants, Mariamne ordered them to bring the chests into the apartment. Salome, following behind, peered through the door. "As I thought, very plain. But what can one expect from a Jewish – er, a Hasmonean king? Knowing my brother, he won't be content with this poky palace. He'll want, and deserves to have, a magnificent palace, one befitting the glorious reign he's initiating."

Three days later Alexandra received a request from the sage Shemaiah for an audience with her. She was eager to meet the president of the Sanhedrin, for the news she had heard since returning to Jerusalem was most distressing. When he was admitted to her presence, she was taken aback to see that while his bearing was as dignified as ever, his face was drawn and his eyes red-rimmed.

"Welcome back to Jerusalem, Your Highness," he greeted her with a deferential bow.

"Please don't be so formal," Alexandra said with a wan smile, waving the sage to a seat. "We've known each other too long for that. I'm still Alexandra to you."

"Of course, Your... Excuse me, Alexandra. It's a long time since I've had the honor of speaking to you. But please tell me, how are you and your dear children?"

"As regards our physical health, thank God, I can't complain. But I can't say as much for our spirits, especially since returning to Jerusalem."

"I can understand that. Much has happened in the meantime, too much – to you and your family, to all our people. And little Mariamne – now Queen of Judea! It's hard for me to believe.

"I don't know whether to congratulate you or not, especially as I know your feelings on the subject. If it weren't for the fact that her husband, the king, is Herod, there would be no question about it. But – well, time will tell. The ways of the Lord are mysterious. Our history is one of ups and downs, and what seems disastrous now may turn out happily in the end. Nay, it must. We must be strong and not lose faith."

"May it be as you say. But what kind of hostess am I? Let me offer you some refreshments. Do you have any preference? Fruit, cake, whatever you fancy."

"Thank you, I'm not fussy; anything will do."

Alexandra summoned a manservant and told him what to bring. She then turned to Shemaiah with a grave expression. "Am I correct in assuming you don't bring happy tidings?"

"Unfortunately, I don't."

"Since my return, I've heard stories of terrible things happening in Jerusalem, and especially to many of my dear friends."

"Alas, the stories are only too true. I don't have to tell you that the inhabitants of Jerusalem suffered greatly during the siege. The well-to-do may not have gone as hungry as the poor, but death rained down on the city indiscriminately, irrespective of class or wealth. And when the Romans broke into the city, it was terrible to behold. Their brutality knew no bounds."

"It was not only the Romans," Alexandra said in a low, solemn voice, "it was also my dear son-in-law. I've discovered that many of my friends are no longer in this world; they were murdered in cold blood – after the fighting stopped."

"No mercy was shown to those known or suspected of being supporters of Antigonus," Shemaiah confirmed with a somber expression. "Nearly fifty of the leading citizens have perished. Their wealth has been confiscated, their widows and children left forlorn and destitute. Many of those executed were members of the Sanhedrin, my worthy colleagues. Nearly all of them sat in the Sanhedrin ten years ago, when I warned them that they might suffer a dire fate. Perhaps your father told you about that."

"Are you referring to Herod's trial?"

"Yes. It was an incredible affair, a harbinger of things to come. I can see it as clearly as if it happened only yesterday. Herod was governor of Galilee at the time, appointed by his father. The Sanhedrin had summoned him to stand trial for executing the partisan leader Hezekiah without benefit of a trial, when he knew, or should have known, that only the Sanhedrin has the right to try capital cases. He entered the chamber wearing a purple robe instead of a black garment, as is customary in such cases, and was accompanied by an armed bodyguard, even though he knew it was strictly forbidden to bring weapons into the chamber, or anywhere on the Temple Mount for that matter. This so overawed the elders that no one dared to speak up against him, not even those who had previously denounced him. I warned them that if they didn't try Herod he would one day punish them. To my great sorrow, this prediction has come true."

"Couldn't they escape the city?"

"Some of them tried, but Herod had stationed guards at the city gates to seize all wealthy citizens and nobles who had sided with Antigonus, and to confiscate any valuables they might be trying to smuggle out. I was with many of them in their final hour. It's something that will haunt me to the end of my days."

"My dear friends, my dear friends!" Alexandra murmured as she wiped a tear from her eyes. Her head fell on her chest. After a long moment she looked up; her voice was barely audible. "I can't tell you how relieved I am that Herod spared you at least. In view of your warning ten years ago, how do you explain that?"

"Herod knew I was on excellent terms with your father, who was deprived of the high priesthood and the throne by Herod's arch-enemy, Antigonus. Moreover, your father enjoyed good relations with Herod and Antipater, and his granddaughter, your beloved Mariamne, is now Herod's wife. But probably the main reason is that Herod has a certain soft spot for me."

"Soft spot!" remarked Alexandra incredulously. "I can't imagine him having a soft spot for anyone whom he even vaguely suspects of standing in his way."

Before Shemaiah could explain himself, the servant entered with a tray of refreshments, including cakes, a pitcher of fruit juice, and two glasses.

"Thank you, Yosef," said Alexandra as he set the contents of the tray on a low table and filled two glasses of juice. "Please help yourself," she bade Shemaiah. "Are you sure you don't prefer wine?"

"No, thanks, this is fine," he replied, helping himself to a cake, over which he made the required blessing.

For a few minutes they made polite conversation as they enjoyed the refreshments. When they finished, Shemaiah gazed abstractedly out the window for a moment before continuing.

"You're curious, and rightfully so, to know why Herod has a certain soft spot for me. Allow me to explain myself. When I saw that the situation in Jerusalem was hopeless, that it was impossible to withstand much longer the huge Roman army, and more and more of our people were being killed or wounded every day, I advised the Sanhedrin to try and persuade Antigonus to surrender, in the hope that this would end the terrible ordeal of the inhabitants and prevent their slaughter once the enemy entered the city. Also, I thought, perhaps naively, that if Antigonus did this, the Romans might be persuaded to spare his life. Word of my counsel must have reached Herod's ear. Antigonus, however, rejected my advice, and when he finally did surrender, the enemy showed no pity. They slaughtered our people like sheep."

"How horrible! May the Almighty have mercy on their souls. And Antigonus, is there any hope for him?"

"He was taken to Antioch and handed over to Antony, who I assume will keep him for his triumph over the Parthians."

"Poor Antigonus! He gave my father a lot of trouble, but I can't help feeling sorry for him. Can't anything be done to save him? Ah, that's a foolish question. The Romans will show him no mercy."

"And not only the Romans. Herod too. I'm afraid he'll do his best to have him eliminated. As long as Antigonus is alive, Herod will never feel really secure."

Alexandra shook her head gloomily. "I never thought I'd see the day when Judea was brought so low. It almost brings us back to the time of Antiochus."

"Heaven forbid! The situation is serious, very serious indeed, but not comparable. The queen is Jewish – and a Hasmonean. Herod will not dare to tamper with our religious practices, I'm quite sure of that. And as for the Sanhedrin, we still have some powers left."

"What do you mean, *some* powers?" Alexandra asked with a puzzled expression.

"Herod asked me to appoint new members in place of those who had been executed. But he made it quite plain that he's the ruler of Judea – the sole ruler. The Sanhedrin will henceforth be able to deal only with matters of a strictly religious nature; it will have no say in the governing of the country, no political powers whatsoever. This means that if Herod does anything contrary to halacha, so be it; his will is law."

"That's awful!"

"I agree. He's already begun to set up his administration, and the men he's appointed so far are all Gentiles – good Hellenists all."

"And you say he's not going to be another Antiochus! Apart from the fact that the queen is my daughter, what Jewish character will the court have?"

Shemaiah rolled his eyes upward, as though he were communicating with the Almighty. "There's no doubt that we're headed for a difficult time," he declared gravely. "The court will be more Hellenistic than Jewish, if not entirely so. But that doesn't mean Herod will try to prevent us from living according to our holy Torah, our divinely ordained way of life, as Antiochus did. Many of our people call Herod a half-Jew; that's better than being a complete pagan. The Sanhedrin, for one thing, will continue to function."

"You said its powers will be curtailed."

"Curtailed, but not eliminated. Even if the Sanhedrin will no longer share in the governing of the country, it will continue to guide and inspire our people to go in the way of the Lord. Our sages will continue to teach the written Torah and the Oral Law and strengthen their observance, to adapt ancient *halachot* to new circumstances, to solve new problems in accordance with Torah."

"And what about the Temple?" Alexandra asked with a worried frown. "Antiochus desecrated the Temple, turned it into a place of idolatry. Herod is quite capable of doing the same."

"You can put your mind to rest on that score. Herod has no intention of doing that," Shemaiah replied firmly.

An odd look crossed Alexandra's face. She stared intently at Shemaiah, before speaking in an urgent tone. "It will soon be Yom Kippur, the holiest day of the year, when the high priest alone performs the entire service. Now that Antigonus is a prisoner of Rome, there is no high priest."

Shemaiah's brow furrowed deeply; he sat back with a solemn expression. After a moment, he said in a low, even voice. "There is a high priest. Herod has appointed Hananel of Babylonia."

For a second Alexandra thought she had not heard correctly. Hananel of Babylonia! It couldn't be; surely Shemaiah was mistaken. Hananel – she was stunned; her face turned livid with rage. "What gall! That's the height of impudence!" she exploded. "The high priesthood belongs to a native of Judea, to a Hasmonean, and not some unknown priest from the Diaspora. That was decided long ago by the Great Assembly, when it conferred the high priesthood on my ancestor, Simon, and his descendants forever. Can you deny that?"

Shemaiah paused before replying quietly. "No, I don't deny it. What you say is true. But let me ask you, what Hasmonean is left who can serve as high priest?"

"Aristobulus, of course."

Shemaiah had expected this answer. "Yes, there is Aristobulus, but how old is he? Only sixteen, if I'm not mistaken. That's a young age for a high priest, very young."

"No age limit has been specified for the high priesthood that I know of," Alexandra countered. "Am I correct?"

"That's essentially correct, although there is an opinion that the high priest must be at least twenty years old. But apart from the question of age, I wonder if your suggestion is advisable," he added cryptically.

Alexandra stared at the sage with a bewildered look. "What do you mean?"

"Knowing Herod as I do, I doubt that he'll welcome a Hasmonean high priest."

At this statement the blood rushed to Alexandra's head; her eyes blazed with anger. "There's a limit to his impudence!" she snapped. "It's not for him to decide! It's unthinkable that a man who is a pagan at heart if not in fact should be the one to decide who will be the high priest. It's for the Sanhedrin, the sages, the people to decide that. And I don't have to tell you who the people prefer.

Oh, I know that my father's policy regarding Antipater and Herod, especially as it had to do with the Romans, was not popular, but the people respected him as high priest. And in the eyes of our people the high priest is more highly regarded than the king. Let Herod be king, if that must be our fate, but the high priest must be a Hasmonean. There can be no question about that!"

"I see you're very determined," Shemaiah said with a shrug. "But Herod obviously thinks differently. How do you intend to convince him?"

Alexandra cupped her chin as she pondered the question. After a long moment she regarded the sage steadily, with a thin smile on her lips. "Herod owes his kingship to the Romans, especially Mark Antony," she said firmly. "He dare not lose favor with him, and Antony will not risk losing favor with Cleopatra, who, rumor has it, he intends to marry."

"And so?"

"I'll write to Cleopatra, who is no great admirer of Herod, and appeal to her sense of justice."

This statement took Shemaiah by surprise. He looked thoughtful for a moment and then spoke with care. "I'm afraid I have less faith in her sense of justice than you do. I'm reminded of the admonition, 'Put not your trust in princes.' But don't misunderstand me, I don't doubt her dislike of Herod, and it's quite conceivable that she'll welcome the opportunity to take him down a peg. But I confess that I feel uneasy about the idea."

"Even if it succeeds?"

"Precisely because very likely it will succeed. Herod will not take kindly to Cleopatra's intervention, and even less to yours. When he's crossed or feels threatened, he can be very dangerous."

"The Hasmoneans have never shrunk from danger," Alexandra declared firmly. "That is what won the hearts of our people from the very start. They love Mariamne – that is quite clear – and I know they'll love Aristobulus too, young as he is. Any other choice will antagonize them. With all my reservations about Herod, I don't think he'll want to rule over hostile subjects. That would not please his overlords or satisfy his craving for glory."

"I hope you're right," said Shemaiah, shaking his head skeptically. "But I'm afraid that if Herod is confronted with a choice between his craving for glory, even in the eyes of his subjects, and power, assuming there is no contradiction between the two, he'll choose power."

Effort to Introduce the Queen to Hellenistic Culture

A month after the siege ended Jerusalem was still a stricken city. Whenever Herod contemplated the scene from the small audience chamber he used for meetings with his ministers, he groaned at the sight. The damage to the houses and other buildings stood out like festering sores on the carcass of a rotting beast.

"Dreadful!" he remarked sourly to his chief minister. "One would think the fighting was still going on."

"It's only been over a couple of weeks," Ptolemy replied calmly.

"One month is not a couple of weeks," Herod said irritably. "From the minister in charge of finance I can expect a more precise calculation."

Ptolemy shrugged off this stricture. He was used to Herod's temperamental outbursts, and being familiar with life in the courts of Hellenistic kings and princes, he regarded such barbs as an occupational disease of royal ministers. In fact, he found they added zest to the daily routine. He had not sought the office of Herod's chief minister. He had been recommended by a friend who knew of his service to the ruler of one of the neighboring principalities.

A short, rotund, middle-aged man, Ptolemy did not cut an impressive figure. In his youth he had been proud of his strong, sinewy physique and moderately good looks, but with the passing of the years his fondness for good living took its toll. This, however, did not trouble him greatly, and if he could roll back the years, he would not have chosen differently.

He had been reluctant to accept the offer of the highest office in Herod's court. What little he knew of the Jewish state and the life of its inhabitants had not appealed to him. But when he learned of Herod's connections with the rulers of the Roman Empire and his plans for his kingdom, he was won over.

Herod turned away from the window and, hands on hips, faced his minister. "I'm not going to have my capital a city of ugly ruins," he declared. "I want all the damage repaired and the city cleaned up. Give that top priority."

"A very commendable desire," Ptolemy replied placidly, "but who will be responsible for doing the repairs?"

"As regards the houses, the tenants, of course. And the sooner, the better. The rains will soon set in."

"And if they don't have the means for it? I understand that the Romans did a thorough job of looting."

"That may be. But we're talking about houses – modest houses – not mansions."

"And where the tenants have fled or are no longer alive? There are quite a few such houses. Who will repair them? And who will cover the cost?"

"That's your problem. I was told that you're an expert at things like that."

"Bees can't make honey if there are no flowers," replied Ptolemy blandly.

"If you prod the people hard enough, you'll find enough flowers in their secret hiding places. And if it comes to the worst, give them loans to be repaid over the coming year or so. And while we're on the subject of money, we're going to need a lot of it. So get your tax collectors busy in all the districts."

"What about Costobarus?"

"He's confiscated all the wealth he could lay his hands on."

"No more wealthy Hasmonean supporters left?"

"None that we know of, except for the Sons of Baba."

"Who are they?"

"Influential relatives of Antigonus. They've disappeared from sight. With all my spies, we haven't been able to lay hands on them. We've combed the city, but with no luck so far. But mark my words, we'll nab them eventually, or my name isn't Herod."

"Costobarus has no clue as to their whereabouts?"

"So he claims. But forget about Costobarus and start worrying about taxes."

"Collecting taxes won't be a simple matter. The people have a special reason to evade them."

"People always have a reason to evade taxes. Twist their arms and you'll find them more amenable."

"It would be easier if it weren't for the business of the high priesthood. I understand that the people are fuming over your appointment."

Herod fixed his minister with a hard, cold look. "What do you know or care about the high priesthood?"

"I admit I don't know very much about it. Personally, I can't see where it matters very much one way or the other. What does the high priest do apart from overseeing the examination of the entrails of sacrificed animals or the taking of auspices in order to determine the will of God, and a few other duties?"

"Those are some of the main functions of priests in the Hellenistic-Roman world. It's not the same in this country. You wouldn't believe it, but the Jews think more highly of the high priest than they do of the king."

"Oh, so that's it! And you, of course, aren't happy about that, I take it."

"You take it correctly. But that's the way things were until now; they're not going to be that way in the future. Under the Hasmoneans the king and the high priest were one and the same. But no longer. From now on the king is supreme."

"That's the way it should be – the civilized way."

An annoyed expression appeared on Herod's face. "What's keeping Costobarus? He should have been here by now."

"Maybe he's snared another rich Hasmonean follower," said Ptolemy with a roguish grin.

Herod was not amused by this statement.

"While we're waiting for him," Ptolemy went on, "there's something I'd like to speak to you about. It's rather delicate, and I hope you'll take it in the spirit with which it is intended."

Herod regarded his minister curiously. "What is it?"

"It's about the queen."

Herod's eyes narrowed; he gave Ptolemy a dark, suspicious look. "What about the queen?" he asked coldly.

"Let me put it this way," said Ptolemy, taking note of Herod's changed expression and conscious of his touchiness about his consort. "As you know, when you proposed that I join your court, I was reluctant to accept. I couldn't see myself in a royal Jewish court. I admit that I knew next to nothing about the Jewish people and their way of life, and still don't know very much. But I do know that they differ greatly from what I have been accustomed to. When you told me of your admiration of the Hellenistic-Roman way of life and your intention to make your court as Hellenistic as possible without offending the sensitivities of your subjects, I was dubious, but eventually you managed to persuade me."

"I'm aware of that," Herod interjected impatiently. "What is it you're trying to tell me?"

"Simply this. You made it quite clear that part of my duties and responsibility is to help give your court the proper tone, to make it a shining example in the Hellenistic-Roman world."

"That's right. And so?"

"To do that, I advise you in such matters as the titles of courtiers – 'friends,' 'relations,' and so forth. And more important, court etiquette – how to receive distinguished guests, how to entertain them, proper manners, ceremonies, and things like that."

"Yes, yes, of course; that goes without saying. What is it you're driving at?"

Ptolemy realized that Herod was growing increasingly impatient, but it was necessary to tread cautiously. "The king, of course, is the one who sets the tone of his court. But the queen too plays an important role."

"The queen! What has she to do with all this?"

Ptolemy knew how sensitive Herod was on the subject of the queen, how jealous he was of anyone who showed too much interest in her, how violently he could react. He chose his words discreetly. "A queen is a symbol to her people, a gem, as it were, in the royal crown. This is especially true in the Hellenistic world, where the people worship beauty, regarding it as a divine gift. In this respect you are very fortunate, for Her Majesty has few if any peers. She is a dazzling gem, and needs but a little polishing to be a perfect one."

Herod gave his minister a perplexed, searching look. "What do you mean by a little polishing?"

"The queen is naturally a product of her environment and upbringing, which are not exactly compatible with what we find in a Hellenistic society."

"You mean she is too Jewish?"

"I wouldn't put it quite that way."

"But that's what you mean, isn't it?"

"Well, yes, you could say that," Ptolemy replied in a somewhat apologetic tone. "Mind you, in itself it is undoubtedly highly commendable in the eyes of her people. But if I understand you correctly, you aim to be a luminary in the Hellenistic world."

"You understand correctly. I'm determined that Judea shall be more than a tiny, insignificant principality in the Hellenistic-Roman world. Judea will always be physically small – nothing can change that – but its fame will spread far and wide."

"And with it the fame of its king."

"Exactly! And I'm counting on you to do everything in your power to bring this about."

Ptolemy nodded politely. "You may be assured that I will devote all my efforts to this noble objective. It is for this very reason that I have brought up the subject of the queen."

"We seemed to have digressed a bit," said Herod with a frown. "What do you have in mind?"

"First of all, the language. The queen knows only a smattering of Greek. Since most of your officials and guests, if not all of them, will presumably be Greek-speaking, it is important that she become more fluent in the language. Together with this, she should broaden her knowledge of Greek culture – its literature, its philosophy; in short, Greek civilization. This, in my humble opinion, is fundamental – a must. It will be necessary, of course, to have a tutor, and with my connections I can easily arrange it."

Herod mulled this over for a long moment. "What you advise is sensible, and in principle I fully agree with you. But the matter is not so simple as you think. The Jews – or at least the big majority – hate anything smacking of Greek or Hellenism. Their heroes are the Hasmoneans, who liberated the country from the Syrian-Greeks. The queen is a Hasmonean, and so they naturally love her."

"More than they love you, I take it?"

Herod thought this remark was in bad taste and uncalled for. "After three years of civil war and the elimination of that wretched Antigonus, the answer is obvious," he growled. "But whether they love me or not, they'll learn to respect my power – and the power of Rome. That you can be sure of."

* * *

Upon Costobarus's arrival, the discussion shifted to matters of more immediate concern. In appointing his distant relative to the second highest office in his court, subordinate only to himself and Ptolemy, Herod knew he was creating a potential source of friction, for the two men differed markedly in character and background. Whereas Ptolemy was a refined, highly educated

Helene, Costobarus was a rough-hewed Idumean noble, a desert chieftain, scornful of men of learning. He was of medium height, had a broad, muscular build, a swarthy complexion, with black hair and black eyes that peered craftily under thick brows. He and Herod had spent much of their youth together, but whereas Herod had been molded by his father, the consummate statesman who consorted with prominent Roman and other distinguished personalities, Costobarus was an outdoor man, whose favorite diversion, apart from women, was hunting. He knew the Jews frowned upon this sport, but he didn't care a fig for their opinion. He rued the day when his grandfather had been forced to forsake the religion of his ancestors, who had been priests of Koze, and embrace the Jewish religion after John Hyrcanus's conquest of Idumea.

Costobarus was well suited for the office Herod had assigned him – the governorship of Idumea and Gaza, and even more important, responsibility for internal security. In the latter task he was in charge of guarding the gates of Jerusalem after the city had fallen and preventing the escape of wealthy supporters of Antigonus. That some of the victims were only lukewarm supporters of Antigonus, or were even known to be sympathetic to Hyrcanus, had not troubled what little conscience he had; their wealth was enough to condemn them. Nor was he the least squeamish about executing his victims; in fact, he took a diabolic delight in making them plead for their lives. His instinct told him when they were lying about their wealth, and he would pretend to be susceptible to their offer of a bribe in exchange for their freedom, only to laugh in their faces before informing them that part of their wealth would anyway wind up in his hands. Now that all, or nearly all, known supporters of Antigonus had been dispatched, this lucrative source of income had dried up, but the wealth he had amassed so far would enable him to live in handsome style for the rest of his life.

"Ptolemy tells me the people are unhappy about my choice for the high priesthood," Herod said to Costobarus. "What's your opinion?"

Costobarus gave a short, dry laugh. "Unhappy is too mild a word. They're in an ugly mood."

"Any signs of rebellion?"

"No open signs to speak of, apart from some graffiti in the marketplace. But I can imagine what they're saying in the seclusion of their homes."

"Imagine!" Herod shouted hoarsely. "I don't give a damn what you imagine. I want to know the facts. Where are our spies?"

"They can't be everywhere," replied Costobarus with an effort to suppress his annoyance. "They try to eavesdrop on every gathering they come upon outdoors, but as soon as the Jews see an outsider approaching, they shut up. From the expression on their faces it's not hard to guess their mood."

"It shouldn't be hard to make them reveal their thoughts," barked Herod with a menacing look. "You're an expert at that."

Ptolemy coughed lightly. "Excuse me for interrupting, but I can't help feeling that what you suggest will not have the desired effect. It will only stir the people up more and create a highly inflammable situation, which is not advisable in the present circumstances. You have made it quite clear that you want Jerusalem cleaned up and all damaged buildings repaired or demolished if they can't be restored, so that the city will be a fitting capital. That implies a quiet, peaceful capital. And then there is the matter of collecting taxes from the citizens."

Herod regarded his chief minister with a thoughtful expression. "What do you suggest?"

"The question of your network of spies I leave to your discretion. If necessary, you can increase it. But no matter how many spies you have, it will be hard, in fact impossible, to ferret out secrets discussed in the home. But outdoors is a different matter. You can forbid gatherings of more than, say, four or five people for instance. This is not a perfect solution, but it should be of some help."

"An excellent suggestion!" exclaimed Herod. "We'll ban gatherings of more than three people – no, even two. Costobarus, see that notices are posted in the marketplace, where everyone will see them. And make sure the people know what penalty awaits them for disobeying this order. Is that clear?"

Costobarus's brow furrowed, and he shrugged his shoulders. "Not quite. What do you mean by a gathering of two people? If someone stops to ask a question – directions, for example – then what?"

"I mean exactly what I've said. That's disobeying the order."

"That's going to keep my men extremely busy. And the penalty?"

"Imprisonment. And even worse if they resist arrest. See to it that enough spies are posted to keep an eye on the people."

"We'll need a lot more spies than we already have."

"Then recruit them. Now what about the Baris? What has been done so far?"

"Excuse me," Ptolemy broke in, "what is the Baris? It's not something I know about."

"You're right," agreed Herod. "It's a matter I discussed with Costobarus, but you should also know about it. The Baris is the castle, or fortress, or whatever you want to call it, at the northwestern corner of the Temple Mount. Right now there's a Roman garrison there, but not a very big one – a single cohort – to keep order in the city. I want to make it both impregnable and more esthetic, fit for residential use in case of need. I'm not taking any chances with these subjects of mine. I don't trust them very much; in fact, I don't trust them at all."

"I understand," said Ptolemy. "In the present circumstances it's advisable to be prepared for any and all eventualities."

"Exactly! I intend to strengthen all the existing fortresses and build a few more. I also have a special project in mind not far from Jerusalem, the spot where I fought off an enemy force after the Parthian invasion. I plan to build a palace there worthy of my station and strong enough to withstand any attack. But that's still far ahead. Right now I want to deal with the fortress on the Temple Mount. That's the most urgent one."

Herod Dines with Queen Mariamne

In the late afternoon, after concluding his audiences with various envoys and meetings with his ministers, Herod enjoyed a rare moment of solitude. Sitting in a high-backed chair next to the window commanding a view of the Temple courts, he watched the priests performing the afternoon sacrifice. He strained to see if Hananel was officiating, but the altar was too far away to determine this. What a headache Hananel was causing him, Herod grimly mused. When he appointed him high priest, he knew many would be displeased, but he did not dream it would stir up such a hornet's nest. He had reckoned that he could safely ignore Aristobulus because of his age; after all, he was still a youngster. But he had clearly miscalculated public sentiment. Nevertheless, his mind was made up: The people could cry all they wanted; it would not budge him one iota. On no account would he tolerate a high priest who rivaled the throne, least of all a Hasmonean, who was certain to be a focus of opposition to his reign.

He could not, of course, reveal this to Alexandra or Mariamne. He had fobbed them off with lame excuses, which he knew were not convincing. Alexandra was furious; Mariamne was deeply hurt. Mariamne's reaction disconcerted him more than he cared to admit to himself.

When he had asked for Mariamne's hand, he realized he was courting possible trouble. It had been easy enough to persuade Hyrcanus, because the timid old man was deathly afraid of his highly popular, ambitious nephew Antigonus – now safely eliminated, Herod grinned maliciously. But Alexandra was hardly likely to approve the match, and as for Mariamne, he was confident that eventually she would get used to, and even welcome, the idea of being married to one clearly destined for greatness. In this he was disappointed so far. He was not a romantic person who could utter endearing sentiments. Instead, he showered her with expensive gifts in the hope of winning her heart and showing her how much she meant to him.

During the past three years, when he was fighting Antigonus, he had not been able to spend much time with Mariamne, but now that hostilities were over and he could turn his mind to other pursuits, he was free to devote more time to her. It would have been simple for him to find another woman who would gladly accept him for what he was. As king, he could take more wives and even concubines. Why, then, did he put up with Mariamne's aloofness, her sullenness, her passive submissiveness in the marital bed? The answer was not simple. There was, of course, her extraordinary beauty. He worshipped beauty – almost as much as power – but it was more than that. There was something ethereal about her. It was as though she inhabited a domain inaccessible to him, something beyond his comprehension, his reach. The fact that she was a Hasmonean had an unfathomable, almost mystical, effect on him. His driving ambition had always been to scale great heights, to reach the top, and this meant displacing the Hasmoneans. At the same time, she exercised a magnetic pull over him precisely because she was a Hasmonean.

He was not very conversant with the Bible; in fact, he was almost totally ignorant of it. But there was one passage that made his blood boil. When the patriarch Isaac blessed the younger of his twin sons in the mistaken belief that he was Esau, ancestor of the Idumeans, he declared: "Be lord over thy brethren and let thy mother's sons bow down to thee." This unforgivable affront had gnawed at Herod's soul like a canker. He deeply resented the deceitful Jacob, and prayed for the day when this prophecy would be nullified, when the yoke of Jacob would be shaken off Esau's neck, as Isaac himself had proclaimed. And now that day had arrived: Herod, the Idumean, was ruler over the descendants of Jacob; the Jews bowed to him, their lord and master. And the beautiful Hasmonean, the darling of the Jewish people, bent her will to his, her lord and master.

* * *

What Ptolemy had urged about Mariamne's acquiring a basic knowledge of Greek language and culture was eminently desirable, but could he persuade her to accept this? He realized that he himself could benefit from a better grounding in Greek culture, and the more he contemplated the idea, the more it appealed to him. He had never attached much importance to a formal education, but if he wanted Judea to assume its rightful place in the Hellenistic-Roman world, as Ptolemy put it, he too would have to apply himself to this end. He was not a studious sort; in fact, he had always disliked studying. His father had urged him to learn at least the rudiments of Greek literature and thought, but to no avail. Now the situation was different. Despite his many pressing duties, he would somehow have to fit it into his program. As soon as he had the most urgent business in hand, he would consult Ptolemy on this.

* * *

Mariamne was a little puzzled but not greatly surprised when Herod told her that he would dine alone with her that evening. She was accustomed to dine most of the time with her mother and brother in her mother's apartment, and frankly she preferred it, for she could not abide her sister-in-law Salome or her mother, both of whom grated on her nerves. But she could hardly refuse Herod this modest request. When she wanted to know if there was any special reason, he asked, somewhat dryly, if it was unusual for a husband to want to dine alone with his wife.

Mariamne was very tidy, and her apartment reflected her taste. She kept the furnishings to a minimum, thereby lending a more spacious feeling to the rooms. The furniture was made of the finest imported wood and superb workmanship and was kept highly polished. Bright tapestries lent a warm touch to the walls of the main room.

She dressed modestly for the occasion, choosing a blue linen robe edged with golden embroidery and fastened about her loins with a girdle of beaten silver. Apart from earrings, her jewelry consisted of only a necklace and two rings. At first she chose her favorite necklace, a birthday present from her grandparents, for which she had a great sentiment; but thinking that Herod might be hurt by this, she replaced it with one of his recent gifts.

Together with her maidservant, she laid the table and told her what courses to serve. Satisfied that everything was ready, she sat down to write a letter to her grandparents. She was still at this task when Herod arrived. Darkness had already fallen, but the apartment was aglow with the light of candles and oil lamps. Having wondered in what mood she would find her husband, she was relieved to see that his countenance was not stern.

When she rose to greet him, Herod's eyes lit up. The fragrance of the flowers and Mariamne's perfume was intoxicating to his senses, and so too was his wife. How much like an exquisite rose, he thought. Her figure was very appealing, if a little fuller than usual. Her features were flawless, unsurpassed in beauty. His heart began to beat faster, and he had an ardent desire to take her in his arms, to crush her to him, but that would have to wait. "You look wonderful," he remarked with uncharacteristic gallantry. "And your perfume is exhilarating. It's new, isn't it?"

"You're very observant," said Mariamne, pleased with Herod's manifest delight in her. "Yes, it's new – an Egyptian import."

The smile on Herod's face froze. "Egyptian!" he uttered in a tone abruptly turned cold. "Not one of Cleopatra's concoctions, I hope?"

Mariamne knew that Herod did not harbor any great love for the Egyptian queen, and she had not meant to reveal the origin of the perfume, but the words had slipped out inadvertently. "Yes, it is," she admitted, flustered by her gaffe. "I think it's odd for a queen to have such a hobby," she added hastily. "Not that she herself makes the perfumes – she has an expert do her bidding, from what I've been told. But I must say, her perfumes are superb, the best there are."

"How did you get this perfume?" Herod asked sharply, a dark, suspicious look creasing his face. "I've a good mind to ban the import of Egyptian perfumes."

"That wouldn't make them disappear from the market stalls," Mariamne flung out, both baffled and resentful at Herod's sudden change of mood, which threatened to spoil what had promised to be a pleasant occasion.

"Someone who gives perfume to the queen doesn't buy it in the market. Who gave it to you?" he demanded to know.

"A friend."

"What friend?"

"You wouldn't know her," replied Mariamne, growing increasingly indignant.

"A woman friend?"

"Of course. What did you think?"

Herod realized he was straying from the purpose of this private dinner: It was not about perfumes that he wanted to discuss. Regretting his impulsive outburst, he poured some wine into his goblet and drained it to calm him down. Regaining his composure, he said apologetically: "You must admit, it struck me as a little odd to know that you possess one of Cleopatra's perfumes, or, to be more exact, another one. But let's forget about that royal hussy and enjoy our dinner."

Relieved that the storm had passed almost as quickly as it had blown up, Mariamne summoned her maidservant and told her to serve the first course – a thick vegetable soup. Herod, who had not eaten since noon, devoured his portion and two slices of bread before Mariamne was half-way through hers. "Delicious!" he pronounced, smacking his lips. "I'm tempted to ask for another helping, but I don't want to spoil my appetite for the next course."

"You seem to have a big appetite tonight."

"I do, and not only for food," said Herod with a knowing wink.

Mariamne pretended to ignore this remark. Herod's eyes were fastened on her in a way whose meaning was abundantly clear. "I take it you had a very busy day. Is it some outdoor activity that has given you this, er, big appetite?"

"I made a tour of the Lower City in the late afternoon. But the rest of the day I conferred with my ministers."

"I see," said Mariamne somewhat dryly, wondering if some new affliction was being hatched against her people. She knew it was pointless to ask.

"By the way," Herod said as the next course was being served – a baked trout smothered with spicy sauces and garnished with olives and marrows, "Ptolemy brought up a matter that concerns you."

Mariamne's eyebrows arched sharply. "Perhaps I should be flattered that your chief minister found me a worthy subject of discussion," she replied in a slightly frosty tone. "Did all your ministers take part in the discussion?"

"No, only myself. The matter isn't particularly urgent, but it merits consideration."

"And what is it, if I may ask? I hope it won't spoil your appetite or mine. It would be a pity if it did."

Herod did not fail to notice the hardening of Mariamne's tone and her wary expression. He had no desire to spoil the atmosphere, which, after his initial outburst had been pleasant enough. It was imperative that it remain so if he wanted to win her over. In a conciliatory voice he related Ptolemy's urging the desirability of Mariamne's acquiring some knowledge of Greek language and culture and proper etiquette in a Hellenistic court. She listened silently as Herod spoke, repressing her growing consternation.

"With all due respect to your chief minister," she declared, making a wry face, "he seems to have forgotten that Judea is a Jewish state. I grant that there will inevitably be contacts with the outside world, the Greek-speaking world, but that's a far cry from – it's asking too much; in fact, it's brazen of him to expect me to devote myself to learning pagan Greek literature, philosophy, and what have you. Except for a few brief periods, in the last three years I've been deprived of the opportunity of learning more about my own heritage. That's something that concerns me much more."

"The two don't necessarily conflict; you can learn both," said Herod placidly.

"Maybe, but the result would be like a half-baked loaf of bread, neither Jewish nor Greek. Hardly better than raw dough."

"Raw dough?"

"Yes, raw dough. Look at your court. Is there a Jew among your ministers and courtiers? I feel like a stranger in their midst, not a Jewish queen. How can I expect my people to respect me?"

"The people respect you because you *are* a Jewish queen – a Hasmonean queen."

"Forgive me for saying this, but since you are now king of Judea, don't you think it would be advisable for you to learn something about the heritage of your subjects – their religion, their history, their culture?"

Herod stared at his wife in amazement. Whence this sudden boldness, this persuasive argument? Never before had she spoken to him in such a vein. He felt the blood rushing to his head. He strove to master his mounting agitation.

"I know for a fact," Mariamne continued, "that your father tried to learn something about our people. It was my grandfather himself who encouraged him and even arranged for one of the sages to instruct him. Your father made a conscientious effort to learn something about the Bible, our history, our laws and customs. Of course, he couldn't master all this – it was rather superficial on the whole – but he learned enough to appreciate our heritage. And he knew the sensitivities of our people and did his best to avoid offending them."

"And I don't?" asked Herod heatedly.

"I must leave that to your judgment."

"What specifically are you referring to? Antigonus, perhaps?"

"Not necessarily. I was thinking of something else. But now that you mention it, yes, the manner of his execution. A king beheaded! Ghastly!"

"My dear wife," said Herod in a cool, superior tone, "you evidently know very little about the Romans. Do you think they have any qualms about executing their enemies? Do you know how many Roman aristocrats lost their heads in the proscriptions? And speaking of execution, isn't beheading one of the prescribed Jewish methods of capital punishment? I may not be learned in Jewish law, but I do know something about the Sanhedrin. From personal experience, no less!"

Mariamne stared at Herod with a defiant gleam in her eyes. "The rumor is that Antony wanted to take Antigonus to Rome for his triumph, but you persuaded him not to delay his execution."

Herod fixed Mariamne with a cold, hard expression. "I don't know who started this rumor," he snapped, "but let me ask you: If the boot had been on the other foot and Antigonus were victorious, what do you think my fate would have been? No, my dear wife, I don't think you have a valid argument there."

"Well, maybe not," Mariamne conceded, "but there are other things."

"Such as? Please let me know what else is disturbing your precious sleep," he remarked scornfully.

Mariamne paused briefly before responding in a slow, deliberate tone. "The high priesthood, for one: your appointment of Hananel."

"Ah, so that's it!" exclaimed Herod. "I thought you would bring that up. Let me ask you, is Hananel not a priest? Is he an ignorant Jew? I have it on good authority that he is well qualified for the office and is performing satisfactorily. What fault can you and all the others find in his appointment?"

"You know very well whom the people want as high priest," Mariamne replied firmly. "The high priesthood has been in the Hasmonean house for over a hundred years."

"That doesn't mean the high priest must forever be a Hasmonean. Before the Hasmoneans the high priests belonged to other houses. I don't know their names, but I know that for a fact."

"The high priest before the Hasmoneans was hated by the people. He was a traitor to our people – a Hellenist, a pagan at heart."

The epithets *Hellenist* and *pagan* hit Herod close to the bone. His mouth jerked silently as he struggled to control his temper. "Can anyone accuse Hananel of being a Hellenist, a pagan at heart?"

Mariamne paused before answering quietly. "No, I can't say anyone can accuse him of that. But he's not what the people want. He's not even a Judean: You brought him over from Babylonia – something unprecedented. It's obvious you don't trust a Judean."

Herod looked angry at this accusation. How well she read him; how convincingly she argued. Was this the demure, staid young woman he had taken to wife – she who hitherto had been aloof, cold, passive? He could hardly contain his astonishment. She was alert, breathing fire, brimming with passion. He stared at her, consternation mingling with wonder. But he was visibly upset by the turn the conversation had taken. He had intended this to be a quiet, pleasant dinner; instead it had gotten out of hand. He was relieved when the maidservant appeared to remove the dishes.

"Shall I bring in the next course, Your Majesty?" she asked.

Mariamne glanced at Herod. He was hungry, but his stomach was churning. After a moment he nodded his assent.

"You may bring it in," Mariamne said. "Make sure it's still hot."

While they were waiting, Herod turned the talk to lighter matters. He related some anecdotes about Antony. Mariamne was especially amused to learn how Antony's wife Octavia had made him move the picture of the voluptuous nude in the glen from the atrium to his private office. "I don't know why he needed the inspiration of a picture," Mariamne commented with a twinkle in her eye. "He did quite well with Cleopatra in the flesh."

"Quite true!" agreed Herod, smiling a little.

At this point the main course was brought in – roast duck garnished with sliced citron and asparagus, served with hot rice flavored with cinnamon.

"Ah!" uttered Herod, smacking his lips, "my favorite dish. And to be enjoyed with my favorite woman."

Mariamne stared at her husband with an odd expression. She could not remember when he had last paid her such an affectionate compliment, and she marveled at his swift change of mood.

They engaged in small talk while relishing their food. But gnawing at Herod's mind was the uneasy feeling that the matter they had discussed before was too important to leave dangling in the air. It was imperative to reach an understanding, but in a way that would not create a bad feeling. Pushing back his chair and folding his hands, he regarded Mariamne reflectively. "I don't like to return to the subject we discussed before," he said as amicably as he could; "it upset both of us. But if we don't clear it up now, it will only crop up later to plague us."

"Must it be now?" asked Mariamne with a deep frown. "Our dinner started pleasantly enough, and right now we're both enjoying our food and conversation. It's not very often that we're so fortunate. Can't we finish it on a pleasant note?"

"Don't worry. I too appreciate this occasion, and I intend to keep it pleasant."

Mariamne sighed. "All right," she said dubiously, "what is it you want to clear up?"

Herod spoke in slow, measured tones. "You say the people want a Hasmonean high priest. What Hasmonean is left to fill this office? Antigonus is no longer alive, and as far as I know, he's left no eligible son."

"What you say is true," Mariamne replied calmly. "But there is another Hasmonean – in my own family."

"In your own family? Surely you're not referring to your brother Aristobulus?"

"I am," said Mariamne quietly but firmly.

"But he's young, too young for such an important office. He's not even sixteen years old, if I'm not mistaken. Maybe in another few years."

"I agree that he's young, in both years and experience. But he'll learn. He has the makings of a good high priest. The people like him. They want him and not an outsider."

"I'm afraid the people are letting their sentiments get the better of their common sense," Herod countered with an exasperated look. "The high priesthood is too important an office to entrust to one so young."

"He won't always be young."

"No, but..."

"It would make the people happy, and me too. And our son will be proud to know that his uncle is the high priest."

Herod stared at Mariamne in astonishment. "Did I hear correctly? Did you say 'our son'? Mariamne, are you..."

"Yes, I am. Haven't you noticed that my belly is starting to swell, and I haven't been feeling well in the mornings?"

Herod broke into a broad smile. "Why did you keep this from me? I thought you looked a little fuller than usual, but I didn't associate it with – oh, what wonderful news! A baby! A little Herod!"

"And a little Hasmonean too," responded Mariamne with a blissful expression.

Silence in the Marketplace

After traveling nearly two weeks from Babylonia in his private coach, Nehunya shook off the fatigue of the journey the moment he beheld Jerusalem's skyline. The crenellated walls, the Temple perched atop its mount, the homes sprawling over the hilly terrain, the surrounding heights – the view never failed to stir him. The disaster that befell the city dampened, but could not extinguish, the spiritual exultation that filled his heart. Perhaps it was wrong to feel this way when Jerusalem had suffered so much, but to one who had visited many large, beautiful cities during his checkered career none could excite him as much as the Holy City, the navel of the world.

It was nearly five years since I had last set foot in Jerusalem – too long a time, he mused as his coach approached the main city gate. Much had happened in the meantime – catastrophic events which were not calculated to delight the heart of one who loved his people with every fiber of his being. Of the three principal figures in this drama, one was dead, one was living in exile in Babylonia, and the third was sitting on the throne of Judea thanks to the crushing might of Roman arms. In addition, many of the leading citizens of Jerusalem had been executed, including forty-five members of the Sanhedrin, which had been shorn of much of its powers.

As he gazed at the Temple, his thoughts went back another five years, to Hyrcanus's confrontation with a group of women who were clamoring for Herod to be tried by the Sanhedrin for executing their sons together with the partisan leader Hezekiah without benefit of a trial. Hyrcanus had been badly shaken and had sought the advice of the distinguished personages forgathered in the royal palace.

That fateful trial! It had touched off a long chain of events that culminated in the city's present woeful plight. Nevertheless, Nehunya knew that despite the low state to which Jerusalem had presently fallen and other setbacks it had suffered in its long history, the city was eternal, its spirit inextinguishable, and this buoyed him.

He was not unduly perturbed when the sentries at the city gate demanded to know where he was from, the purpose of his visit, and how long he intended to stay. He maintained his sangfroid even when they searched his coach for suspicious objects. He had expected this inconvenience, but he was unprepared for and extremely annoyed at the rude treatment that subsequently awaited him. After being admitted through the gate, he had a desire to see from close up the havoc wreaked by the enemy, and instead of going directly to the Hasmonean palace, he ordered his driver to proceed through the Upper City in the direction of the marketplace.

He was pleasantly surprised to see only relatively minor damage in the Upper City residential quarter, but the closer he came to the marketplace, the more glaring were the signs of destruction: jagged walls, burnt and broken beams, and even empty lots testified to the fierceness of the fighting. At the same time, he was amazed at the extensive reconstruction going on. The pounding of stonemasons' hammers, the sawing of fresh beams, and the hammering of nails drowned out the usual sounds of the marketplace. Roman and other soldiers walking in pairs patrolled the streets, and they seemed to outnumber the shoppers and other pedestrians. What particularly struck Nehunya was the relative quietness of the marketplace, which normally rang with vendors' exuberant hawking of their wares and animated haggling over prices. This puzzled him. He ordered his driver to halt the coach, whereupon he got out and strolled over to one of the stalls to satisfy his curiosity. Approaching some customers who were examining the goods displayed, he excused himself and asked for an explanation of this extraordinary phenomenon. To his great surprise, they shrank from him with a nervous look. When he persisted in questioning them, they turned their backs and moved away. One intrepid youngster pointed to a notice prominently displayed on a public bulletin board. Nehunya sauntered over to read the notice, and he immediately understood the strange behavior he had witnessed. "Well, well, so Herod has banned all public gatherings!" he muttered with a derisive smirk. "A fine measure of his confidence in his subjects."

His mirthless laugh was cut short with the pinning of his arms behind his back in a vice-like grip. "What do you think you're doing!" he shouted at two ill-clad men with harsh faces. "Let go of me at once!"

"You will accompany us to our officer," one of the men ordered in a rough voice.

"You can go to the devil first," Nehunya shot back. "Do you realize who you're talking to?"

"Someone who has read the public notice and should know better," the second man answered gruffly.

"You'll pay dearly for your brazen impudence!" Nehunya warned in his most authoritative voice.

"And you'll come with us quietly if you don't want us to drag you along."

Fuming fiercely, Nehunya realized he would get nowhere with his two captors, who evidently were carrying out official orders. He signaled to his driver to follow him as he was hauled, much to his surprise, before a Roman subaltern in what served as headquarters of a sort in an abandoned house a short distance from where he was apprehended.

The officer, an intelligent-looking clean-shaven man in his late twenties, was perusing some papers when Nehunya was ushered into his presence. Nehunya waited until he finished and looked up. "Your roughnecks are over-zealous in performing their duty," Nehunya said to the officer with an effort to keep his voice calm and well-modulated.

"That's what they're supposed to do," replied the officer in a halting Aramaic. "What is the charge?" he asked the two men.

"Talking to others in the marketplace," one of them answered.

"Ah, yes, suspected subversion – a very grave offense."

Nehunya wasn't sure whether the officer was serious or not, as there was a half-cynical ring to his voice. "Now look here, but first tell me, what language is easiest for you? There's no need for you to break your teeth on Aramaic. May I assume it's Latin?"

"Latin or Greek," replied the officer, realizing from Nehunya's dress and bearing that he was addressing no ordinary citizen.

"Let it be Latin then. I don't want to tell you what I think of that notice posted in the marketplace. I'll keep that to myself. But whatever my opinion, I was not aware of it until your two gorillas grabbed me in what could be described as a not very gentlemanly manner."

The officer threw a question to the two men, after which he turned to Nehunya. "They say you resisted and cursed them."

"If someone crept on you from behind and yanked your arms out of their sockets, what would you do – quote Euripides or Cicero to them? When they ordered me to accompany them, I merely informed them that they could go to the devil first."

The officer grinned in spite of himself. "They have their orders, and so do I."

"And your orders, I assume, come from His Majesty, King Herod?"

"That's right."

"Then do me the kindness and take me to him."

The officer's jaw fell at this startling request. "I'm afraid that's out of the question," he said after recovering his aplomb.

"Then please inform him that the person you have apprehended is Nehunya, an emissary of the King of Kings Phraates."

The officer knitted his brow and sucked his underlip before responding: "Can you prove that?"

Nehunya thrust his hand between the folds of his elegant robe and extracted a letter bearing the Parthian monarch's seal. He handed it to the officer without a word. The latter examined the seal, then returned the letter to Nehunya. "Please convey my felicitation to the King of Kings," he said with a smile. "And whatever you may think of this particular order, I trust you won't inconvenience my men in the future."

* * *

When Nehunya related his encounter in the marketplace to Alexandra, she was both amused and indignant. "Can you imagine that! That's the kind of king Judea has. Do you know of any other country where the king is so distrustful of his subjects that he has an army of spies to arrest anyone who even dares to ask directions to a public toilet, for instance? You're lucky you were taken to a Roman officer who seemed to be a decent sort, and not to one of Costobarus's thugs."

"An officer who also knows who Euripides is," said Nehunya with a grin. "That must have made some impression on him."

"I suspect that Phraates's seal impressed him even more."

"You're undoubtedly right. And now let me give you his letter."

Nehunya took out the letter from the folds of his robe and handed it to Alexandra together with another one. "It's from my father," she exclaimed, glancing at the second letter. "I've been waiting to hear from him."

"Then go ahead and read it first. Phraates's letter, I am sure, is more a formal statement of his good wishes. Your father's letter will undoubtedly be of greater interest."

"Do you know what he has written?" asked Alexandra with an expectant look.

"Only one thing – something he discussed with me first."

Nehunya and Alexandra were seated in the small audience chamber. The sun was sinking low on the western horizon, enfolding the brooding hills in a crimson mantle. A breeze had blown up, rattling the windows. A servant entered and lit a number of oil lamps, and a second one brought in warm drinks, wine and cakes. Alexandra told Nehunya to help himself, after which she broke the seal of her father's letter. Before reading it, she asked, "How are my parents? Do they look well?"

"Thank God, they are quite well."

"And their spirits?"

"On the whole, not bad."

Alexandra gave Nehunya a questioning glance. "What do you mean, on the whole?"

"When you read the letter, you'll know what I mean."

As Alexandra read the letter, her brow furrowed deeply. She read the letter again, this time more slowly. When she finished, she gazed intently at Nehunya. "My father wants to return to Jerusalem," she said in a subdued voice.

"I know. He discussed it with me several times. He and your mother miss you and the children very much. And they miss Jerusalem."

"What did you advise him?"

Nehunya studied his fingernails for a minute or so before replying in a level, earnest tone. "I told him I could understand his yearning to see you and the children again. It was only natural and to be expected. But I advised him to consider the situation as it now stands."

"That is to say?"

"For one thing, Herod is now king of Judea, and this does not please the people one bit. In fact, they're very disgruntled. If your father should return, some may associate this unhappy situation with him and even hold him at least partly responsible for it."

"What did he say to that?"

"He said that as high priest he enjoyed the people's respect. But, I reminded him, that was in the past. He can no longer serve as high priest; Antigonus made sure of that. The man Herod has appointed high priest is not a Hasmonean, but a little-known Babylonian. What is more, the fact that the people hold your father in great esteem could paradoxically cause a serious problem."

"A serious problem? I don't understand."

"Herod as king is not Herod the aspirant to the throne. I don't have to tell you what kind of a man he is – his deep-seated suspicion of anyone who might outshine him in the eyes of the people. He would not tolerate anyone whom he even slightly suspects of plotting to supplant him on the throne or being a rival to him in any way."

"It's obvious you don't trust Herod."

"I trust him as much as I do a snake. I don't have to tell you how dangerous he can be when he's thwarted or feels the least threatened. That's unquestionably the reason why he appointed an insignificant Babylonian as high priest – one who by no stretch of the imagination can be a rival to the throne."

"Even though the people are very upset by this appointment? Even though they prefer – nay, demand – a Hasmonean?"

Nehunya gave Alexandra an earnest, piercing look. "Am I correct in assuming that you're referring to your son?"

"I am."

Alexandra was puzzled by the sudden change that came over Nehunya. His eyes looked troubled, and his face assumed a strained, sober expression. "Why does that surprise you?" she asked.

"It worries me, it worries me greatly. Let me ask you, is there any movement afoot to replace Hananel with your son?"

Alexandra stirred uneasily in her chair. Her gaze was fixed on the ceiling as she weighed her reply. "I have written to Cleopatra," she said in a low voice. "I asked her to intervene with Antony."

Nehunya shook his head slowly. "Excuse me for asking, but did you consult any of your advisers before taking this step?"

"I intimated my intention to Shemaiah."

"What did he say to that?"

"To be frank, like you he was concerned about Herod's reaction."

"Yet you ignored his advice. Don't you think that was a risky thing to do?"

"I admit there was some risk," Alexandra responded stubbornly. "But I pointed out that the Hasmoneans do not shrink from risks."

"Permit me to remind you that the Hasmonean house has paid dearly of late for taking risks," said Nehunya solemnly. "And with Herod on the throne, the risks are much greater."

Nehunya, starting to feel weary from the long journey, helped himself to some wine and cake. Alexandra took advantage of this break to reread her father's letter. Refreshed by the drink, Nehunya waited until she finished before continuing. "I can appreciate your parents' desire to be near you. But, as I stressed to your father, in Babylonia, in all Parthia for that matter, he is held in high esteem and greatly honored by the entire Jewish community. What is more, he enjoys excellent relations with the Parthian monarch. If he returned here, I confess I would feel very concerned."

"How did my father react to that?"

Nehunya looked thoughtful for a moment and then answered in a grave, deliberate voice. "He said he is no longer a young man but in the twilight period of his life. His life has, on the whole, not been a smooth, easy one, like the one his mother enjoyed, especially after ascending the throne. He has suffered many vicissitudes. At the same time, as high priest he enjoyed great satisfaction and fulfillment. He doesn't know how many more years the Almighty will spare him, but he wants to spend them in Jerusalem, the Holy City, where he was blessed with the great privilege of serving God and his people with all his heart. And when the time comes to return his soul to his Maker, he wants it to be in the bosom of his family."

At these words Alexandra's heart grew numb, and her mind was in a turmoil. She could not deny Nehunya's doubts about how her father might be received by some of the people. But much more worrisome was the potential danger that Herod posed to her father and to her whole family in fact. And as to Aristobulus, had she placed him in a precarious position by writing to Cleopatra? She was filled with doubt, a dark, tormenting doubt. Aristobulus was the last surviving male of the Hasmonean line. If, God forbid, anything should happen to him – she could not bring herself to finish the thought. "Oh, God," she silently prayed, "don't let anything happen to him." But her tenacity quickly reasserted itself, though her face remained pallid, but resolute and courageous.

Nehunya observed with wonderment the play of emotions, and could guess what was passing through Alexandra's mind. "I'm very sorry for causing you such anxiety," he said with deep regret. "I struggled with my conscience whether to remain silent or to voice my apprehension. I wish with all my heart that I could have spared you this."

"You meant well," Alexandra uttered quietly, "and for that I am grateful. So don't blame yourself." She paused and then resumed in a lighter, more cheerful tone. "When you return to Babylonia, please inform my parents that, God willing, they will have a great-grandchild in the near future."

At this announcement, Nehunya's demeanor changed dramatically. He smiled broadly and his eyes brightened. "That is excellent news! Your parents will be delighted. May the Lord grant Mariamne an easy pregnancy, and may the baby imbibe with the mother's milk her abiding faith in the Almighty and in the destiny of our people."

Chapter Ten

Enter Cleopatra – And Antony

Cleopatra Unwillingly Agrees to Meet Antony in Antioch

The rapidly rising mid-autumn sun heralded the start of a day that would be oppressively hot by noon, but at this early hour was pleasantly cool, especially inside the royal Ptolemaic palace. The palace was still quiet as Cleopatra, refreshed by her daily morning bath in the two scented pools, made her way to the children's room to have a look at her little ones. She was accustomed to rise early, regardless of how late she had gone to bed the night before, but in the afternoon, after her audiences, she would take a short nap if she felt tired, and then carry on with her crowded schedule with renewed vigor. Her chief minister, Theon, marveled at her stamina, but thought she was overtaxing herself, and occasionally ventured his opinion that she should ease up a bit.

"My dear Theon," she would invariably chide him, "do you prefer me to be a slothful queen? Egypt would be the poorer for it, don't you agree?" Theon would dutifully agree, and brace himself to submit his periodic financial report, which more often than not would turn out to be a chastening experience. He had never known a woman, or anyone for that matter, with such a profound grasp of royal finances, and he had to be prepared for her sharp questioning of even the smallest details. When his memory sometimes betrayed him and he had to pause to recollect the information requested, he knew instinctively that she would eye him like a cat about to pounce on a mouse, with arms folded across her chest, and her foot tapping impatiently until the information was forthcoming. Most perturbing of all was her querying of certain expenditures which he explained were necessary in order to obtain a result that was eminently desirable but involved the offering of a special "inducement" to the party concerned. In such cases he had to be at his most persuasive, and often her pointed questions would make him squirm. Withal, he had the satisfaction of knowing that she valued his loyalty and devotion to duty, and he was inwardly pleased whenever his suggestion that perhaps she would be better served by someone more qualified than he, would elicit a blunt order to stop talking nonsense.

When Cleopatra entered the children's room she was greeted by a chorus of piping voices, and in a trice she was smothered by two pairs of soft arms and a torrent of wet kisses.

"And how are my darling babies?" she asked the nursemaid when she managed to disentangle herself.

"We aren't babies any more," protested Alexander. "We're children now."

Cleopatra chuckled. "How right you are, my darling three-year-olds." She turned to the nursemaid. "They look as if they had a good night's sleep and an ample breakfast."

"They have, Your Majesty. Alexander ate everything I gave him, and little Cleopatra – well, her appetite isn't as big."

"She's probably concerned about her figure, like any female," said Cleopatra with a grin. "And Alexander takes after his father when it comes to food."

"When will our father come to see us?" asked Alexander, pouting a little. "Doesn't he like us?"

A wistful expression crossed Cleopatra's face. "Of course he likes you," she said somewhat abruptly.

"I don't know what he looks like," Alexander went on, "but I know his name. It's Mark, Mark Antony, isn't it?"

"That's right, my dear. He's a very famous man and a very brave one." To herself she muttered, "And also a very fickle man."

"When are you going to tell us a story?" asked little Cleopatra. "We like your stories."

"Especially about heroes," echoed Alexander.

"Maybe this afternoon," said Cleopatra. Turning to the nursemaid, she asked, "And how is Caesarion feeling? Has his fever gone down?"

"He's feeling much better today. He's already awake and wants to get out of bed."

"We'll let the physician decide that. If he feels up to it, he can have a lesson with Nicolaus. I'll go and see him, and then I must get down to business. Bye-bye, my darlings," she said, giving each of the twins a hug and a kiss. "Be good and do as Tares tells you, and I promise you an exciting story later in the day."

Proceeding to the audience chamber, she stopped before one of the tall windows in the corridor which commanded a striking view of the port. The sight of vessels of all shapes and sizes riding at anchor or making their way to and from the numerous wharves that lined the Great Harbor always thrilled her. The flourishing maritime trade was the life-blood of the country's economy, transporting its grain and a wide range of other goods to all parts of the Mediterranean and beyond, and bringing spices, dyes, copper, marble, and many other products for the Egyptian market or for transshipment. After gazing at the scene for several minutes, she continued with a light step to the audience chamber, where Theon was waiting for her.

"Good morning, Your Majesty. I trust you slept well," he greeted her.

"Thank you, Theon. I'm pleased to say that I did," she replied as she took her place on the throne. "We have a lot of audiences scheduled for this morning, so we better get down to business. And that means, of course, your financial report first of all, which I trust will keep me in my present good mood."

Theon, who knew from long experience that her earnest hope that the financial report would sustain her good mood was often the prelude to a spirited, trying session, cleared his throat. "Before we go into the financial report, I have to inform you that someone is already waiting for an audience with you – someone very important."

A look of surprise flashed across Cleopatra's face. "An audience so early in the morning! And without an appointment? He can jolly well wait his term."

"I don't think that would be advisable," said Theon calmly.

"Advisable or not, he has some nerve! Did he sleep in the palace last night? Get on with the financial report."

"It's true that his request for an audience is a bit irregular, and he apologizes profoundly," Theon replied with an unruffled demeanor. "But he's a Roman envoy with an urgent message from Mark Antony."

The mention of Mark Antony's name made Cleopatra's hackles rise. Did he think he can defy established procedures and encroach on her time as his fancy strikes him? And after all that has happened since he left Alexandria some four years ago? His envoy can cool his heels.

"Whose message did you say he wishes to convey?" she asked with a bemused, mocking solemnity.

"Mark Antony, Your Majesty."

"Mark, Mark who did you say?"

"Mark Antony," repeated Theon, acutely aware of the queen's abrupt change of mood, and realizing that he was about to witness one of her capricious scenes, and that he would have to humor her.

"Mark Antony?" muttered Cleopatra, feigning a perplexed look. "The name is vaguely familiar. Is he someone I know?"

Theon suppressed a sigh. "Yes, Your Majesty. He used to, er, visit the palace quite frequently."

"And when was that?"

"About four years ago."

"Four years ago, you say?" murmured Cleopatra as though searching her memory. "Oh, yes," she said with a sudden look of recognition, "that fellow who claims to be a descendant of Hercules. I wonder what he could possibly want to convey to me. A request for money, no doubt. Well, see that the envoy is comfortably seated in the anteroom, and we'll admit him as soon as we've gone over the financial report."

"Excuse my impertinence, Your Majesty," Theon said with the utmost tact, "but if the Roman envoy requests an audience so early in the morning, what he has to say is undoubtedly of great importance, and very likely he'll take umbrage if he is kept waiting. He is, after all, Antony's envoy, a Roman envoy."

"But my dear Theon, we must adhere to established procedures. And the Romans are sticklers for established procedures. I'm sure he can appreciate that. But – oh, well, maybe we'll make an exception in this case. Admit him."

The envoy, a slender, slightly stoop-shouldered middle-aged man, with stern, searching eyes, bowed deferentially as he approached the throne.

"I apologize to Your Majesty for requesting an audience so early in the morning," he declared with an air of self-assurance. "I know it may be some-what irregular, and I am very grateful for your kindness in receiving me."

"If my memory serves me correctly," replied Cleopatra in a cool, scoffing tone of voice, "his lordship is inclined to be rather impetuous when he wants something very badly. I can't imagine what could be so urgent as to necessitate a virtual pre-dawn audience, especially considering the absence of communica-tion between us the past four years." *And considering his cavalier treatment of me*, she thought to herself. "Please enlighten me."

The envoy, who had been forewarned about the possibility of a cool re-ception, took Cleopatra's scornful response in stride. "I can understand your surprise, and wish to explain that His Excellency, the governor of the eastern provinces of the Roman Empire, is presently in Antioch, where he is preparing to embark on an enterprise of the greatest import."

"The greatest import to whom?"

"To Rome, to all the eastern provinces, to Egypt too."

"And this project, I take it, will require a great deal of financing?"

"I am not qualified to answer that."

"Then what is it you're qualified to convey to me?" Cleopatra asked some-what acidly. "I have a personal message for you from His Excellency," said the envoy, handing a letter to Cleopatra.

Cleopatra broke the seal and quickly read the letter. "So His Excellency requests my presence in Antioch, does he?" she exclaimed contemptuously. "Well, you can inform him that if he has anything worthwhile to say to the queen of Egypt, she may condescend to grant him an audience at her palace in Alexandria."

"Permit me to explain, Your Majesty," the envoy replied without betraying any sign of annoyance: "Antony has established his headquarters in Antioch, where he arrived only a short while ago, and as much as he would prefer to behold your gracious presence in your own palace, military considerations make it imperative for him to remain in Antioch at this juncture."

"I have not noticed that military considerations prevented him from finding his way to Alexandria in the past," Cleopatra retorted with a disdainful toss of her head.

"Antony is quite aware of that, but he wishes to stress that you will have no reason to regret his request. In fact, he assures you that it will be the most momentous, the greatest milestone in your life."

"And how much will this great, momentous milestone cost the Egyptian treasury?" asked Cleopatra tartly.

"Not everything can be measured in terms of money, Your Majesty," the envoy countered in a calm, dignified voice. "There are noble objectives that transcend purely materialistic considerations."

Cleopatra cocked an inquisitive eye at the envoy. "Are we speaking about the same person?" she asked in slow, scoffing accents.

She knew very well that if the Roman triumvir, the governor of the eastern provinces, summoned her, a client-queen, to Antioch, she could not refuse, but her pride as the Egyptian monarch made her bridle at this manifestation of her subservience to Rome. Even more galling, her womanly pride was offended at the need to bow to the whims of the man who had dallied with her the whole of the winter four years ago and had sired her twin children before returning to Rome to effect a reconciliation with his fellow triumvir, and cementing it by marrying his widowed sister.

She too had a sensual nature, but she was more discreet in choosing her lovers – usually for advantageous reasons. To one man she had given her heart – Julius Caesar, to whom she had borne a son. In Caesar, the dictator of Rome, she saw the key to her great ambition – power. For she was bent not only on keeping a firm grip on the Egyptian throne, but also on restoring the foreign dominions of the Egyptian Empire in its heyday, under her renowned ancestor, Ptolemy II.

Caesar's assassination while she was installed in his villa beyond the Tiber had put an end to her dream. That is, until Antony appeared on the scene shortly after her return to Egypt. When, as governor of the eastern provinces, he had summoned her to Tarsus to answer charges of aiding Cassius, she saw her opportunity to realize her dream. Knowing his love of pleasure and overwhelming weakness for women, she had set out to captivate him. She had invited him to Alexandria, and for the whole of the winter she had joined him in riotous living, to such an extent that he had neglected all preparations for his projected invasion of Parthia.

It was the Parthian invasion of Syria that had impelled him to return to Rome – that and mounting friction with Octavian. She could not abide that "young puppy," as Antony often called him. But he enjoyed the support of the Roman Senate, and Antony had deemed it advisable to seek a reconciliation with him. She had not dreamt that it would involve his marriage to Octavian's sister, who had been widowed less than the required ten months.

What did Antony want from her now? If he had established his headquarters in Antioch, it probably meant that he was finally preparing to conquer Parthia, an assumption to which her ambassador to Rome lent credence. For such a campaign he would need money, lots of it. He knew that she had an overflowing treasury, much of it inherited from her Ptolemaic predecessors, plus what she herself had accumulated through her own business acumen. Well, if that's what he had in mind, he was going to be sadly disappointed. None of her money was going to be thrown away on military adventures intended to glorify his reputation as a worthy successor to the great Caesar.

Antony's envoy was waiting for her reply. What was she to tell him? "I don't know what his lordship has in mind by – how did he put it? – a great, momentous milestone; but I regret that important considerations prevent me from accepting his most gracious invitation to come to Antioch."

The envoy had hoped for a positive response, but had taken into account the possibility of a refusal. "His Excellency is not accustomed to have his requests rejected," he said in a tone that held a note of stern disapproval. "He will undoubtedly want to know what considerations can outweigh this magnanimous demonstration of his esteem for the queen of Egypt."

"Considerations that have to do with him intimately," declared Cleopatra, setting her mouth firmly. "I am the mother of his twin children – a boy and a girl not yet three years old. They are of a tender age and require my personal attention. I'm sure that His Excellency would not want anything to happen to them in my absence."

The envoy's lips twisted into a thin smile. "His Excellency has thought of that," he said reassuringly. "He ardently desires to see his offspring and requests that you bring them with you, along with Cesarean. You can rest assured that every provision will be made for their comfort and other needs."

Pomp and Ceremony on Cleopatra's Arrival

When the galley carrying Cleopatra, her children, and attendants, accompanied by an escort of three triremes, set sail from Alexandria, she recalled the voyage she had made some four years earlier in response to Antony's summons to answer charges of helping Cassius raise money and troops. How meticulously she had planned that voyage, she thought with a grin – a voyage that was still the talk of the whole Mediterranean world.

She had sailed up the Cyndus River in a barge with purple sails, gilded stern, and silver oars that beat time to the music of flutes and fifes and a harp. Her maids, dressed as sea nymphs and graces, were the crew, and she herself, dressed as Venus, lay under a gilded canopy. So overpowering had been the impression made not only on the spectators lining the banks of the river, but above all, on Antony himself, that he had virtually ignored the reason for summoning her. The outcome had met her fond expectations: She easily convinced him of her innocence of the charge, and had stirred his passion to such an extent that he eagerly accepted her invitation to visit her in Alexandria. She had set out to captivate him, and had succeeded so well that he neglected to deal with the Parthians. They had a riotous time together that winter, when he forgot that he had left a wife in Italy, the meddlesome Fulvia, whom he would have been glad to be rid of. And what did he do, that self-proclaimed descendant of Hercules? When Fulvia died shortly after his return to Italy, some say of a broken heart, he took to wife Octavian's sister. Such was the lasting impression made on him by his stay in Egypt's capital. But what could one expect of such a fickle man? And now what did he want from her? Money, no doubt. Well, if that was the case, he could induce his wife to appeal to her brother for funds. But she knew that relations between the two triumvirs were again strained. This time, though, Antony wasn't going to find her a convenient source of funds and a willing bed partner while he prepared for his long-mooted expedition against the Parthians.

When her ship docked at Seleucia, the port of Antioch at the mouth of the Orontes River, Cleopatra was pleasantly surprised to see that an effort had been made to receive her in royal style. The wharf where the ship moored was festooned with flowers and banners bidding her welcome, and an honor guard stood at attention. When she and her party came down the gangplank, a fanfare of trumpets and the roll of drums rent the air. Awaiting her at the head of the honor guard was Antony, dressed in the full regalia of a general. His face beaming, he greeted her with a light kiss on both cheeks.

"You used to do better than that," she remarked in an undertone and smiling archly. "You must be out of practice."

"We have too big an audience," Antony whispered in her ear. "Wait till we're alone, and then you'll see if I'm out of practice. And these delightful children," he said, raising his voice, "are they..."

"These two young one are our twins, and the taller one is Caesarion."

Antony bent down and picked up each of the twins, giving them a resounding kiss. "How beautiful and innocent they look. And what is your name?" he asked the boy after putting him down.

"Alexander," was the chirpy reply.

"And yours?" he asked the girl.

"Cleopatra," she answered shyly.

"Beautiful names and very fitting." He turned to Caesarion. "My, how you have grown!" he exclaimed, patting the youngster on the head. "We'll have to get re-acquainted, I see."

"It will be a great honor, sir," replied Caesarion stiffly.

"For both of us," Antony chuckled. "And now let us proceed to Antioch, where you will have accommodations befitting Egyptian royalty."

The party boarded several carriages: one for Cleopatra and Antony, another for the children and the nursemaid, and the others for the rest of the queen's retinue. Alone with Cleopatra, Antony's desire for her was rekindled to a glowing pitch. He yearned to tell her how much he had missed her, how much he wanted her, but feared she might dismiss this as so much humbug. Later, he decided; let her first get used to his presence.

"My envoy told me you were hesitant about accepting my invitation," he said as they left the port area. "He had to use all his powers of persuasion."

"It would be more correct to say that I was reluctant to obey your summons," she replied with bold candor.

"It grieves me to hear you say that. I assure you on my word of honor that my invitation was extended in good faith. How could you have doubted my sincerity?"

"Simply because my memory is a little better than yours. And also because I have not undergone as many personal changes in the past three years, or is it four?"

"To give birth to twins – our twins – isn't a big change?"

"It is. But it still can't compare with what you have experienced – burying one wife and taking another. And that reminds me, how thoughtless of me to forget! I congratulate you on your marriage to Octavia. I understand that she is a very beautiful and virtuous woman. I wish you every happiness."

"Thank you," acknowledged Antony dryly. He thought he detected a note of reproach in Cleopatra's voice.

"I also understand that she is quite fertile. How many children have you been blessed with?"

"Two daughters and another baby on the way."

"How fortunate they are. Their father is no stranger to them."

"But Antony is a stranger to our twins. That's what you're implying, isn't it?"

"I leave that to your imagination, which I have reason to believe is as fertile as your procreative prowess."

"Do the twins know anything about me?"

"They have asked about their father many times, especially Alexander."

"What did you tell them?"

"That you are a brave and famous man. I didn't tell them that you are also a fickle man."

Antony chuckled. "I plead guilty to the first charge. But fickle? Isn't that reading too much into our relationship? After all, you knew I had a wife when we were enjoying each other's company that winter."

"That's true, I admit. But I thought our relationship was more than a passing diversion to you. When Fulvia died..."

"For the sake of peace with Octavian, he proposed that I marry his recently widowed sister."

"Whom you love, I take it?"

"What has love to do with marriage? In Rome, as well as elsewhere, marriages are contracted for all sorts of reasons – in many cases political. For love one looks elsewhere. Marriage for love is a rarity."

"So it would seem."

"But I am one of the fortunate ones."

Cleopatra gave Antony an inquisitive look. "Does Octavia feel the same way about you?"

"Perhaps. But I'm not referring to her."

"No? Then who, may I ask, is the fortunate one?"

"You may ask. I'm talking to her."

Cleopatra gaped at Antony with an incredulous expression before bursting into laughter. "Am I supposed to be amused by your jokes?"

"Not at all. I'm serious."

"I think you're delirious."

"I'm deliriously in love. Do you know how much I've missed you? How much I've thought about you?"

"I can imagine what kind of thoughts you had. Octavia must have gotten a lot of pleasure from them."

"And now you can have the pleasure. And our twins will know who their father is."

Cleopatra reflected on this avowal for a long moment. Could it be that Antony *was* serious? The message his envoy had brought her did mention something about a momentous milestone. Was this what he was referring to? Antony – that philanderer– did he really want to bind himself to her, or perhaps she should say, bind her to himself? It was preposterous, but who knows? Stranger things have happened or could happen. After all, she was a queen, the queen of a fairly large country.

"Mark Antony," she said with a coy look, "are you by any chance proposing marriage to me?"

Antony flashed a big smile. "For one as brilliant and quick-witted as you, it's taken a long time to reach that conclusion."

"But you have a wife – a beautiful, virtuous wife, who it transpires is also quite fertile and the sister of your fellow triumvir to boot."

"And there in essence lies the answer to your question. It's true that Octavia is beautiful and virtuous and a very good woman, but I nevertheless found myself thinking about you more and more and longing for you."

"I who am no raving beauty, who can hardly claim to be a paragon of goodness, and least of all, virtuous – you have been longing for me?"

"Day and night. I missed the excitement of your company, of having you close to me. You're like heady wine to me. I want to have copious draughts of you."

And to get hold of some of my wealth, Cleopatra thought to herself. "What about Octavia? Do you intend to divorce her?"

"For practical reasons it wouldn't be advisable – at least not at this stage. She will continue to be my wife in name, but you will be my real wife."

"Oh, I see," said Cleopatra in a voice suddenly turned heavily sarcastic. "In other words, I will share you with Octavia, and you will share my wealth. So that's the great, momentous milestone you were referring to in your message! I must say, it's an extremely tempting offer; I simply can't resist it. I can't tell you how grateful I am. And for that I had to come all the way to Antioch."

"You're imputing wrong motives to me," replied Antony, anxious to soothe Cleopatra's ruffled feelings and to clear up any misunderstanding. "You know very well that in this part of the world a man can have more than one wife."

"But you're a Roman citizen," declared Cleopatra petulantly, "and I happen to know that in Roman law you can have as many mistresses as you like, but only one wife. And a Roman wife at that, not a foreigner."

"Do you care what Roman law and the Roman people might say about this?" asked Antony with a resolute expression.

"Not really."

"Then don't let it bother you. The Romans can think and say what they like, and that includes my fellow triumvir."

Cleopatra immediately grasped the significance of this defiant outburst. "I take it you've had a falling-out with dear Octavian."

"It hasn't yet reached that stage, but it's pretty close to it." Antony went on to explain that while he himself has abided by the agreement, Octavian had repeatedly reneged on it. Most galling of all has been his obstructing of Antony's efforts to recruit soldiers in Italy for the Parthian campaign despite their treaty providing equal rights on this point. Antony mentioned several other examples of Octavian's violation of their agreement, from which it was clear to Cleopatra that Antony's real enemy was not the Parthians but Octavian, and sooner or later there was bound to be a showdown between them.

Did she love Antony enough to be his wife? Or, to put it more bluntly, did she love him at all? It's true they had enjoyed themselves immensely that winter four years ago. But she did not delude herself that that was true love. In fact, she wasn't sure if she knew what true love was. What was it Antony said? – "marriage for love is a rarity." Well, then, what advantages would she and Antony derive from this union? As for Antony, the benefits were obvious: She was queen of a fairly large, prosperous country with a thriving economy and a bulging treasury. And, allowing for some personal vanity, she was no ordinary queen but one with enough gifts and other charms to have captivated the great Julius Caesar. And what could Antony offer her? First of all, the opportunity – in fact, the sole hope – of realizing her dream of recovering the foreign dominions of her famous predecessor, Ptolemy II. But there was an even more compelling motive: Cleopatra knew that Egypt's wealth attracted the cupidity of mighty Rome, and the best and probably only way to preserve the country's sovereignty and her throne was to marry the master of Rome – in this case, Antony, governor of the eastern provinces.

Antony himself had once spoken about the benefits that would accrue from a union of Egypt and Rome. But Cleopatra had not been greatly impressed by his argument, for she suspected that the glowing picture he painted masked a naked desire to procure Egyptian help in financing his military adventures. What did Rome – or rather, Antony – need Parthia for? To gain fame as a great general, to prove that he was a worthy successor to Caesar? Rome had swallowed enough of the Mediterranean world. A huge morsel like Parthia was bound to give it a bad case of indigestion. To squander lives and money on such a reckless adventure was extremely foolhardy. Antony would be well advised to husband his resources for an eventual showdown with Octavian.

Cleopatra was so engrossed in her thoughts that she didn't realize Antony was scrutinizing her with an amused look.

"I was wondering whether you're simply wool-gathering or if it's the lovely scenery that is holding you spellbound. Or may I be so bold as to assume that you've been considering my proposal?"

"Is it that obvious?" asked Cleopatra with a grin. "I'm sorry."

"There's no need to be sorry. I would be surprised and disappointed if you weren't giving the matter your earnest thought. After all, it's not every day that a woman, especially a queen, receives a proposal of marriage. But I can assure that when you have weighed the pros and cons, you will see that it's the ideal solution for all of us – you, me, and our children."

"In weighing the pros and cons, I find a few details that need to be clarified."

"Such as?"

"For one thing, a bride, even if she is a queen, is entitled to a wedding gift. Since we are presumably thinking in terms of a Roman-Egyptian union, the gift must be commensurate with the greatness of the occasion and considering who you will be getting for a wife."

"That goes without saying," replied Antony exultantly, taking Cleopatra's response as an acceptance of his proposal. "The only question is, what gift can I possibly give to one who already possesses everything?"

"Not quite everything."

"No? Ask, and if it is my power to grant your request, it shall be yours."

"I want the foreign dominions that belonged to my famous predecessor, Ptolemy II."

This request was totally unexpected. Antony stared at Cleopatra in astonishment and with a wrinkling of the brows. "Did I hear you correctly? Did you say the foreign dominions of..."

"Your hearing is perfect," confirmed Cleopatra firmly. "That's exactly what I said."

"What in the name of Zeus do you want them for? They'll only be a millstone around your gorgeous neck. You've no idea how troublesome they can be."

"They couldn't be any more troublesome than some of my Egyptian subjects. And yet I can say with all due modesty that on a whole the Egyptians like and respect me."

"You forget that the Ptolemys have been ruling Egypt for some 300 years. You would be regarded as a foreign monarch foisted on these new subjects of yours."

"With wise rule they would be grateful for the change."

"I doubt that very much."

"An Egyptian Empire would be a more worthy partner in a Roman-Egyptian union. You too would benefit from that."

"My eastern domain would shrink appreciably," replied Antony with a frown.

"Our joint domain would be larger and more powerful."

"Perhaps, but not certain. What lands do you have in mind?"

"Cyprus, Coele-Syria, Phoenicia, Judea, Idumea..."

"Judea is out of the question," retorted Antony decisively.

"Judea is the bridge between Egypt and Syria. In the past it benefited from Egyptian rule. The Jews liked the Ptolemys and trusted them. It was the Seleucid kings who misruled and caused them to rebel."

"That could be, but you're forgetting that since then Judea has been an independent, sovereign state. And even more important, it was I, or rather, Octavian and myself, who persuaded the Roman Senate to crown Herod king of Judea. Like his father before him, he has proved his loyalty to Rome. He'll make a strong ruler, and that's what I need when I embark on my Parthian expedition."

"Maybe Herod will be a strong ruler, but his Jewish subjects don't like him; in fact, they hate him. The land will seethe with unrest, and that doesn't bode well for you or Rome."

"The land was peaceful before? Do you know how much trouble Antigonus caused us? And his father and brother before him?" Maybe Herod will have to contend with some unruly elements, but at least I know I can trust him to support Rome's interests. Besides, he's married to Hyrcanus's daughter, who, I understand, is very popular with the Jews."

"It's true she's very popular. But she won't have any influence on Herod. He's already antagonized his subjects in spite of her – deliberately antagonized them."

"Deliberately antagonized them! What do you mean?"

"You don't know what a furor he's stirred up by his appointment of a high priest. The people won't forgive him that. Is that going to help the Roman cause?"

"What's so important about the high priesthood? Is that something to get excited about? I'm a pontifex maximus, which I understand is similar to the high priest. The Romans couldn't care less."

"The situation is not the same. In case you don't know it, to the Jews the high priest is more highly regarded than the king. For the past hundred years or so the high priest and king have been one and the same – a Hasmonean. Herod, of course, cannot be a high priest, so what has he done? He's appointed an obscure Babylonian priest to this supreme office, deliberately snubbing the Hasmoneans."

"How do you know all this?" asked Antony, narrowing his eyes.

"Alexandra has written to me. She is upset – extremely upset. And I know for a fact that the Jews are too – and not only in Judea. Do you want a resentful people in your client kingdom? If you're planning to invade Parthia, Herod will back you to the hilt, but not his subjects. Their sympathies will be with the Parthians. Is that going to help your cause?"

Antony's brow furrowed as he pondered Cleopatra's warning. He didn't like to interfere in Herod's domestic affairs, but he could not deny the soundness of her argument.

"So what do you advise? What Hasmonean is left who can serve as high priest?"

"Alexandra's son, Aristobulus."

"He's young, isn't he?"

"Yes, he's young, but not too young?"

"How old is he?"

"Seventeen, I believe."

"Seventeen! He's a mere youngster."

"He's what the people want."

"The question is, is he what *I* want?"

"Invite him to Antioch and see for yourself."

Antony considered this for a moment. "Hmm," he uttered with a pleased expression, "that's an idea – an excellent idea. For that you deserve a kiss."

"But *you* don't deserve one," said Cleopatra, pouting.

"Why not? Because of Herod's kingdom?"

"That's right."

Antony gave Cleopatra a compassionate look. "I hate to see you miserable. Suppose I give you Herod's balsam groves at Jericho, will that make you happy?"

"Well – I'm not sure. I'll have to think about it."

"Balsam is famous for its medicinal properties. The Jews call it the balm of Gilead. And even more important to you, it makes a superb perfume. Those groves are a very profitable source of income. You won't regret it. What do you say to that?"

"That's only a small part of what I want. For that you can have a *small* kiss."

At these words Antony broke into a broad smile. He eyed Cleopatra longingly. "I'll accept that," he exclaimed triumphantly. "For a start."

Herod Fumes on Hearing of Cleopatra's Marriage to Antony

Ptolemy had never seen Herod in such a foul mood. In the relatively short time he had been serving as the king's chief minister he discovered that he was liable to veer from a state of elation when affairs were proceeding satisfactorily to black dismay and even fierce anger when they took a turn for the worse. But never before had the change been so drastic. It was as if the gods had banded together to conspire against the king of Judea. Ptolemy, however, was confident that with patience and a skill born of long experience he could help Herod surmount the obstacles that had sprung up in his path.

One blow had fallen close upon the heels of another. First was the stunning announcement of the marriage of Antony and Cleopatra. Herod was dumbfounded when he heard the news. "How could Antony do such an asinine thing?" he snapped at his minister. "If he wanted to amuse himself with that Egyptian whore, that's his privilege. But marriage! He's already a married man, and to whom? To the sister of his fellow triumvir, no less!"

"You have good reason to be upset," agreed Ptolemy. "In my opinion he's done a very impulsive and unwise thing. It's bound to have serious repercussions.

First of all, Octavian won't take kindly to this marriage, not only because of his sister, but also for political reasons. It will deal a severe if not fatal blow to the triumvirate, with all its negative implications. What's more, Antony is defying the Roman Senate and the Roman people, who have never taken to Cleopatra. This will quite likely make them suspect Antony of planning to establish an independent Eastern empire with Cleopatra and himself as co-rulers."

Herod was livid with rage and despair at this dire prediction. "That's all I need," he groaned. "Our whole policy – my father's, Phasael's and mine – has been built on loyalty to Rome, the master of the world. Do you realize what a predicament this would put me in?"

"I realize it only too well. But it's too early to jump to conclusions. What I have said is only a conjecture."

"But a very plausible one!"

"Yes, it is. And not least because in marrying Cleopatra, Antony has violated Roman law."

"How so?" asked Herod, lifting his eyebrows.

"Under local law, that is, the law in this part of the world – a man can have more than one wife, but under Roman law a citizen can have only one legitimate wife, and she too must be a Roman citizen. Now, if he had divorced Octavia..."

"Has he?"

"Not that I know of. And I very much doubt he would do that. It would be virtually tantamount to declaring war on Octavian. The Romans have suffered enough from civil wars in recent years, and they wouldn't welcome another one, especially over such an issue."

"Then how do you explain Antony's action? Cleopatra I can understand. That slut would do anything to gain more power and territory, especially *my* territory."

Ptolemy paused briefly before replying. "About Antony, I'd say it's probably a combination of factors. First of all, all indications are that he's planning to invade Parthia. For that he needs money – lots of it. And Cleopatra doesn't lack for money."

"And the other reasons?"

"For one thing, love."

"Love!" snorted Herod. "Antony doesn't know what love is. Lust is more like it – lust for her favors and, as you say, for her money."

"As you wish," replied Ptolemy with a wry smile. "It's not always easy to distinguish between love and lust; more often than not they go together."

"With Cleopatra that's undoubtedly true," remarked Herod scornfully. "She's gotten what she most covets – a large part of the old Ptolemaic Empire, including a good chunk of Judea."

Ptolemy took a sip of wine from his goblet before responding calmly. "Pardon me for saying so, but aren't you exaggerating a bit? Antony has only given her the balsam and palm groves at Jericho."

"Maybe that's not a big area," retorted Herod, his eyes blazing indignantly, "but it's very valuable property – my property, part of my kingdom. Isn't it enough that I already have her as a neighbor in the south? There at least we're separated by a body of water and a long stretch of desert. Now she'll be breathing down my neck, wafting her obnoxious perfumes in my face."

"The perfume she can now make from balsam is renowned for its superb scent," said Ptolemy with a perverse grin.

Herod gave his minister a sharp, reproachful look. "I hope she chokes on that perfume. But it's not only that I'm worried about. Antony also gave her the bitumen deposits in the Dead Sea. That too is a valuable product."

"Those deposits belonged to the Nabatians," Ptolemy politely reminded Herod.

"That may be, but the Dead Sea is only a few miles from Jericho. That gives her a sizable foothold in my territory. I know her only too well. She won't be satisfied with that. She'll pester Antony to death for more of my kingdom. And he'll give in. She'll twist him around her little finger in return for her favors."

"Favors?" remarked Ptolemy with a quick, questioning glance. "She's married to him now, you know."

"Well, whatever you want to call it then. It's an intolerable situation I tell you – absolutely intolerable! You're my chief minister; give me some practical advice."

Ptolemy knit his brow as he turned the matter over in his mind. "Hmm," he uttered at last; "yet, maybe I can suggest something. I'm not sure it will work, but..."

"Let's hear it!"

"Cleopatra, I don't have to tell you, likes money. In fact, it would be more correct to say she loves money. She never has enough of it. The smell of drachmas is as heady to her as the smell of her perfumes. With a little persuasion, she may agree to lease you those groves – for an adequate compensation, of course."

"What! I pay that vixen for *my* groves!" came the fierce, incredulous protest.

"From what I understand, those groves are no longer yours," replied Ptolemy with an unruffled demeanor.

This reminder goaded Herod to black fury. "That hellcat! That blasted, foul hellcat! I'd like to wring her neck."

"Most inadvisable," counseled Ptolemy patiently, "especially now that she's Antony's wife. If you accept my suggestion, at least she won't have a foothold in your kingdom. Isn't that better than having her perfumes assailing your nostrils?"

"Damn it all!" exclaimed Herod, banging his fist on the table. How much do you think that bitch – I mean, Antony's wife – will want?"

"That would have to be negotiated. I understand she's pretty tough at that. Do you want me to deal with the matter?"

Herod weighed this for a moment. "All right," he growled. "As much as it galls me, go ahead. And don't be lenient with her."

"I'll do the best I can. Now, there's one more thing that has to be done."

"And what's that?" asked Herod with a cold, hard look.

"To congratulate Antony and Cleopatra on their marriage."

Ptolemy did not expect Herod to take kindly to this suggestion, but he was taken aback by the vehemence of his reaction.

"To congrat..." spluttered Herod, his face contorting with revulsion. "After that conspiring, greedy hussy has stolen my groves! Not on your life!"

"Permit me to remind you," said Ptolemy dispassionately, "Antony is the master of the Eastern provinces, and with his marriage Cleopatra now shares his power. So, much as I can understand and sympathize with your wounded pride, it would be an unforgivable breach of etiquette, let alone poor statesmanship, to get into their bad graces. Since you are obviously not in a very inspired mood, I am willing to draft a message for you, which you can accept or alter as you see fit."

When the congratulatory message was dispatched, Herod thought the matter was closed. Little did he dream what it would bring in its wake. Two weeks later a courier arrived from Antioch with a letter from Antony. As Herod read it, a baffled expression appeared on his face. The usual good wishes for his well-being were followed by Antony's gratitude for Herod's eloquent, heartfelt congratulations on his marriage to Cleopatra, which heralded a new, glorious era in this part of the world. As he continued reading, Herod's expression darkened into a grimace, for Antony had an important message to convey to his dear friend, and would be grateful if Herod received his emissary at his earliest convenience.

"What do you think he wants?" he asked Ptolemy after his chief minister also read the letter.

"I haven't the slightest idea," said Ptolemy, puckering his mouth.

"With Cleopatra at his side, or I should say, in his bed, I anticipate trouble."

Antony Insists on Aristobulus's Appointment

Antony's emissary turned out to be the same one who had conveyed Antony's request to Cleopatra to come to Antioch. Herod remarked, with a thin smile, how delighted they were to learn about the marriage of these two exalted sovereigns, which was certain to be a blessing to all the states in the region.

The emissary acknowledged these warm words with a polite bow. "I am happy to state that Cleopatra too was deeply moved by your most felicitous congratulations. She also wishes to inform you that she welcomes your proposal to lease the balsam and palm groves at Jericho, and in view of the cordial relations existing between Egypt and Judea, she is confident that an amicable and mutually satisfactory arrangement can be negotiated."

"I'm very pleased to hear that," replied Herod, managing to summon up the ghost of a smile. "My chief minister Ptolemy will conduct negotiations on my behalf, and I too am confident that we'll reach an amicable and mutually satisfactory arrangement."

"That is also Antony's ardent desire," affirmed the emissary, his lean head craning forward. "It is essential that harmony should reign among the various states in this region. This is true at all times, but especially so at present. For it may now be revealed that Antony is preparing to put an end to Parthia's brazen threat to Rome's Eastern empire."

This news did not surprise Herod, for Ptolemy had earlier intimated that Antony was probably preparing to challenge Parthia's hegemony in this part of the world. Personally he was not confident of the outcome of such a confrontation, but deemed it prudent not to voice this opinion. "I am very pleased to hear this," said Herod, "especially as I myself had the misfortune to be a victim of Parthia's belligerency. I wish Antony every success in this historic enterprise."

"Then you will appreciate that to ensure its success harmony must prevail not only among the various states in the Eastern empire, but also within each of the states."

Herod and Ptolemy exchanged puzzled glances. They wondered what lay behind this statement which, uttered casually, seemed to convey a cryptic message. They waited for the emissary to elucidate.

Observing the effect of his words, the emissary went on to explain himself. "The compelling need for domestic harmony applies to all the states, but especially so in Judea, as it is the bridge between Rome's Eastern provinces and Egypt, which has now assumed an even more strategic role in Rome's grand design."

"I fully appreciate the enhanced importance of Egypt to Rome's grand design and the part Judea can play in furthering it," said Herod with mounting wariness and even trepidation.

"Then you will also appreciate the need to keep the inhabitants of Judea pacified – at least insofar as can be expected in these rather turbulent times."

"That goes without saying," interjected Ptolemy, who was also becoming increasingly uneasy at the drift of the emissary's communication. "As long as whatever suggestions you may offer pose no threat to the stability of Judea's regime, you will find we have a willing ear. So perhaps you will be kind enough to tell us what specifically Antony has in mind."

The emissary leaned forward in his chair and regarded the two men with a grave expression. "It has been brought to Antony's notice that what is causing considerable concern among the inhabitants of Judea is the appointment of the high priest."

Herod gaped at the emissary in astonishment; he stiffened visibly.

"Antony has been informed that the people of Judea are unhappy about the choice of an outsider for this office," the emissary went on, aware of the impression his statement had made. "In fact, we understand that feelings are running so strongly that it could even lead to civil unrest – a situation exacerbated by the distress the Jerusalemites suffered during the recent siege and the death of Antigonus, the former Hasmonean high priest."

That Antony, a military man to the core, who had played a leading role in the proscription of hundreds and probably even thousands of prominent Romans, should concern himself with what was essentially an internal, relatively insignificant matter as the high priesthood shook Herod profoundly.

"Permit me to point out," he said with quiet intensity, "that the question of the high priesthood has assumed an entirely different character since the termination of hostilities. Whereas formerly the Hasmoneans wore both the priestly and royal crowns, I am now, by virtue of a unanimous decision of the Roman Senate, king of Judea, and the high priesthood has reverted to its rightful former status as the religious head of the Jewish nation. It may take some time for the inhabitants to understand and accept the altered role of the high priest, but it is in Rome's interest that they do so."

"What you say possesses logic," conceded the emissary, "and I can assure you that Antony has taken it into account. But because of the overriding need to keep Judea peaceful, especially in view of the planned termination of the Parthian threat, he deems it advisable to placate the inhabitants. But before making a final decision, he wishes to inform you of his intention to invite Hyrcanus's grandson to Antioch in order to see with his own eyes what sort of person he is and especially whether he can be relied on to maintain amicable relations with Rome."

At this information Herod could not suppress a start. He half-rose from his chair, only to fall back. His face was overcast and gloomy. "I would like to point out," he said in a grim voice, "that Hyrcanus's grandson is very young – too young for the office of high priest. That is why I appointed someone else to that office. Antony may not be aware of that consideration."

"Antony knows the young Hasmonean's age," replied the emissary dryly. "He's seventeen years old."

Herod eyed the man with an odd expression. How could Antony know Aristobulus's age? It might be common knowledge among the Jews, but Antony? Someone must have told him, someone close to him; and he had a strong suspicion who it might be.

"Aristobulus is not quite seventeen," said Herod lamely. "But apart from the question of his age, Antony should be aware of an even greater danger that the appointment of Aristobulus to the high priesthood, or even inviting him to Antioch, would create."

"And that is?"

"It would lead to the very unrest that Antony is so anxious to avoid."

"Why is that?"

"As you yourself have noted, the inhabitants of this country have a strong attachment to the Hasmonen house. Even though Aristobulus is the grandson of Hyrcanus, who during most of his office as high priest wisely pursued a pro-Roman policy, this did not find favor with many of the people – even a large majority. If Aristobulus were to be appointed high priest, it would rekindle their hopes for the restoration of a Hasmonean regime. This, I need not tell you, would have the opposite effect that Antony wants. It would be in Rome's interest to prevent such a development at all costs."

* * *

After the emissary took his leave with a promise to convey Herod's warning to Antony, Herod turned to Ptolemy with an ominous look. "I'd like to get my hands on the person who put Antony up to this," he burst out indignantly. "I'd break her neck."

"What makes you so sure it's a woman?"

"Who else could it be? Only that she-devil could make him take leave of his senses like this."

"Perhaps. But it's also possible that Antony's advisers gave him the idea. They're undoubtedly aware of the people's dissatisfaction, which very likely would make them favor the Parthians even more strongly."

"And if I appoint Aristobulus high priest, will that make the people less sympathetic to the Parthians? There's a strong bond between them and their brethren in Babylonia. They know that Hyrcanus is being treated with honor not only by the Jewish people living there, but also by the Parthian monarch. Maybe the people here didn't think too highly of Hyrcanus as ethnarch, but they greatly respected him as high priest. That's another reason why they would most likely favor the Parthians if it comes to a clash between them and the Romans."

"One way to lessen or even eliminate that danger would be to invite Hyrcanus to return here."

"What!" exclaimed Herod with an incredulous look. "The Jews would rally around him."

"He could never be high priest again. Antigonus made sure of that. The people would respect him – even hold him in high honor – but as the grandfather of your wife. And there's another important factor you should take into account. You admit you're not confident that Antony will defeat the Parthians. If the Parthians win, they will no doubt seek to bring Judea back into their sphere of influence. While Hyrcanus could no longer serve as high priest, he could serve as king – a loyal ally to the Parthians. You could forestall any such move by the Parthians and at the same time keep your eye on the high priest, assuming you agree to appoint young Aristobulus to this office."

"Suppose Hyrcanus refuses to return? The situation today is not the same as when he went into exile. There have been many changes, drastic changes."

"Even so, common sense would say that he longs to be reunited with his family. It shouldn't be hard to convince him to return."

Herod paused to consider this suggestion. "I see your point. It sounds reasonable, but I don't want to decide on the spot; I'll think it over."

* * *

"You're very quiet tonight and hardly touching your food," Mariamne said to Herod that evening at the dinner table. "Is something troubling you?"

"Yes," replied Herod with a weak grin, staring at his wife's swollen belly. "I'm wondering whether I'm about to be the father of a prince or princess."

"Would it matter which it is?"

"If all prospective fathers were honest, they'd hope for a boy. But in that case where would we get our lovely wives from?"

Mariamne knew that Herod was captivated by her and was intensely jealous of anyone who showed too much interest in her, but he was not given to uttering endearing sentiments. "You won't have to wait very long for your answer," she said, touched by his compliment.

"How soon does the physician think it will be?"

"Two weeks, more or less."

"Is everything all right?" he asked with palpable concern.

"He assures me that everything is fine. There's no reason to worry."

"Still, I'll be glad when it's over."

Mariamne's pregnancy had not been particularly difficult, and the knowledge that she was about to bring a human being into the world filled her with immense joy. Occasionally it was tempered with regret that Herod was not the man of her choice, but she was pleased to note that they were having fewer disputes whenever she brought up the subject of the high priesthood. Herod, in fact, was showing a softer, more solicitous attitude toward her, and he was becoming increasingly excited as her time drew near. How different, he thought, when his former wife Doris was carrying his first-born son. Then he was largely indifferent, much to his father's dismay. True, the circumstances were not the same. If Mariamne gave birth to a boy, he was certain it would favorably influence his subjects' attitude toward himself, and perhaps even make them forget or ignore the question of the high priesthood. Or would it? For no less important was Antony's personal interest in this question that he dared not ignore. Would Antony heed his warning about the likely consequences of inviting Aristobulus to Antioch? Even more crucial, would he reconsider the advisability of appointing Aristobulus in place of Hananel? He might if it weren't for one thing – Cleopatra. Herod knew that the chances of this happening were slim, if not nil.

And then there was also the question of Hyrcanus. Herod could not lightly dismiss his popularity with the Jewish community in Babylonia and especially the Parthian monarch. Antony was undoubtedly well advanced in his preparations for invading Parthia, and in view of Crassus's ill-fated expedition, Herod was not confident of a Roman victory. A Roman defeat would enhance Hyrcanus's standing in Parthia – another possible source of trouble for Herod. Ptolemy was right: It was advisable to have Hyrcanus close at hand, where one could keep an eye on him.

"Does your grandfather know you're about due?" Herod asked Mariamne as the next course was being served.

"Of course. In his last letter he wrote that he misses his family very much and longs to be present at the birth of his great-grandchild and watch him grow up."

"If I made it possible for him to watch his great-grandchild grow up, would that make you happy?" asked Herod with an enigmatic smile.

"Of course it would!" exclaimed Mariamne, elated at the thought. But the smile suddenly froze on her face. "But how can you do it? In spite of all the honor he's received – even from the Parthian monarch – he's still formally a prisoner of the Parthians."

"I can try to persuade the Parthian monarch to let him return."

"Oh, if only you can! Do you think you can succeed?"

"I can't say for sure. But one thing I promise – I'll do my best."

Salome Loosens Her Venomous Tongue

"When can we expect Her Majesty to present the king with an heir?" asked Salome in her high, abrasive voice that evening when Herod called on his family in their apartment.

"If everything goes well, in another fortnight or so," replied Herod, disregarding the irritating tone of his sister's inquiry.

"The main thing is that the birth should be easy and the baby healthy," said Cypros.

"And may you be just as fruitful," she wished her daughter, who so far showed no sign of following Mariamne's example.

"It takes two to produce a baby," retorted Salome frostily.

"What does that mean?" asked Cypros with a frown, suspecting that relations between Salome and her husband were not very harmonious.

"Exactly what I said," snapped Salome.

"Now, let's not get worked up over that again," remarked Herod, furrowing his brow. "There are more important things to worry about."

"Such as?" asked Salome.

"Affairs of state," replied Herod laconically in a flat voice.

"That covers a lot of ground. Be more specific."

"That's specific enough," retorted Herod gruffly.

"You wouldn't by any chance be referring to your audience with Antony's emissary, would you?"

Herod threw his sister a hard, questioning look. "How do you know about the audience?"

"I have my ways of finding out," replied Salome with a smirk. "If Antony sent his emissary to you, it must have been about something very important, wasn't it?"

"Yes, it was important," confirmed Herod dryly.

"It wouldn't be about the high priesthood, would it?"

Herod winced and then stared at his sister with an odd expression.

"Well, was it about the high priesthood?"

Herod was becoming increasingly annoyed at this interrogation. "What we discussed was a private, confidential matter and no concern of yours," he rebuked his sister harshly.

"But it is my concern. What causes my brother anguish causes me anguish as well. It was about the high priesthood, wasn't it?"

Herod's dark eyes narrowed. "What makes you think it was about the high priesthood?"

"Because that's what all the people are grumbling about, including your wife and your mother-in-law."

"How do you know what my wife and her mother are talking about?" asked Herod sharply. "Are you eavesdropping on them?"

"I wouldn't put it that crudely," protested Salome scornfully. "You have your methods of getting information, and I have mine. Maybe mine aren't as efficient as your network of spies, but they are quite adequate for my purposes."

"I wouldn't put it beyond you. And what did you find out?"

Salome's lips twisted into a tight, triumphant grin. She waited a moment before replying in her usual acerbic tone: "Alexandra, the blue-blooded princess so beloved by the Jews, is unhappy about your choice of high priest."

"That's not news to me," said Herod, shrugging his shoulders.

"But Cleopatra also doesn't like your choice. That, I take it, is news."

"How do you know about Cleopatra?" he asked suspiciously.

"Have you already forgotten that my ears hear things they're not supposed to – eavesdropping, which you so disdain," retorted Salome contemptuously.

"What are you trying to tell me?"

"Has it occurred to you to wonder how Antony knows about the people's discontent in the matter of the high priesthood?"

"There's nothing surprising about that. He has agents and advisers."

"And what about Cleopatra? How would she know?"

"The same way that Antony found out – agents and advisers."

"And Alexandra, she's taking all this in her stride?" Salome continued.

"What are you getting at?"

"Simply that Alexandra has undoubtedly played a more sinister role in this than you think. She couldn't approach Antony, but she could approach Cleopatra."

The muscles of Herod's jaws tightened, and a shadow of doubt swept across his face. "How could Alexandra approach Cleopatra?" he asked sternly.

"My dear brother," replied Salome with a crafty smile, "you disappoint me. You are so wise in many things, it shouldn't be hard to figure that out. Is it a problem for Alexandra to write to Cleopatra?"

Herod glared at his sister. "Did she?" he demanded to know.

"I'm sure she did."

"Do you have any proof of that?"

"Well..."

"Do you?" repeated Herod even more harshly.

"Maybe not definitely. But it's very plausible. I don't like to see my brother being taken advantage of. I think you should bear in mind what I have said and take appropriate action."

Knowing his sister's penchant for scheming and her antipathy to the Hasmoneans in general and Alexandra in particular, Herod was not sure how much credence he could place in her allegation. But he could not afford to take chances. Cleopatra had already caused him enough trouble, and she would have no compunction about taking further advantage of her enhanced power. If Alexandra was secretly communicating with her, the results could be very unpleasant. Whether his sister was right or wrong, prudence dictated that he keep a careful eye on Alexandra; otherwise he was liable to pay dearly.

Chapter Eleven

A Hasmonean Prince Is Born

Hyrcanus and Elisheva Overjoyed at Birth of Their Great-grandson

Two letters that were to have momentous consequences reached Hyrcanus within a few days of each other. The first was from Alexandra, which arrived about a fortnight after Nehunya's visit to him upon returning from the Holy Land. The letter contained news of both personal and national import. Some of it brought immense joy to Hyrcanus and Elisheva: the birth of a great-grandson, who was named Alexander after their daughter's late husband. They had been on tenterhooks ever since Nehunya told them that Mariamne was due to give birth any day, and they were overjoyed to learn that the birth had not been unduly difficult and both mother and son were doing well.

Another very pleasant surprise was the news that Aristobulus had been appointed high priest in place of Hananel, which had been received with great acclaim by virtually the entire nation.

"I wonder what made Herod change his mind," Hyrcanus remarked to his wife. "I didn't think he'd do it, even though he knew that our family and practically everyone else wanted it."

"Nehunya didn't seem very happy about it," replied Elisheva guardedly.

"Nehunya takes a dim view of Herod. He can't believe that he would do anything to please the people."

"Don't you think he has good reason to feel that way? Look what Herod did to the members of the Sanhedrin and other notables after the siege. And don't forget how many of our people lost their lives in the siege itself. You can't ignore that."

Elisheva knew how sensitive her husband was on the subject of Herod. She herself had grave doubts about this relationship, which had culminated in the betrothal and marriage of their granddaughter to this man. But she generally kept her thoughts to herself, leaving it to Alexandra to question the wisdom of Hyrcanus's decisions. A devoted wife, she regarded it as her duty to support her husband and uphold his spirits in the face of the many vicissitudes he had to endure over the years. She knew how much he needed her support and how grateful he was for it. But she had overheard his conversation with Nehunya, whose reservations about returning home had upset her. She missed Jerusalem and especially her family no less than did her husband and yearned to be reunited with them. At the same time, she was uneasy about what the future held in store for them if they returned. Nehunya's account of his encounter in the marketplace heightened her apprehension, and even more so did Alexandra's suspicion that her movements were being watched, especially when she ventured out of the palace.

"Why would Herod do something like that?" asked Elisheva with a troubled expression.

"You know Herod is a very suspicious man," replied Hyrcanus soberly. "He's always been like that, and it's no secret that he has spies working for him. When little Alexander starts to crawl, you can be sure that Herod will have his movements closely watched too," he added with a wry smile.

"Do you think Alexandra had any influence on Herod's decision to appoint Aristobulus high priest?"

"She may have urged this on him, but whether she could persuade him is another matter. But why break our heads trying to figure out Herod's motives?"

"If it's true that Alexandra is being spied upon, I can't help feeling that there may be some connection with Aristobulus's appointment as high priest or that Herod suspects such a connection."

Hyrcanus pursed his mouth as he reflected on this possibility. "The only way we'll know is to ask Alexandra herself."

There was another thing that troubled Elisheva, but she refrained from mentioning it to her husband. And that was his possible reaction when his grandson and not he himself officiated in the Temple. It was bound to make him nostalgic for the time when he performed this function. As though he read her mind, Hyrcanus himself commented on this. "I can't tell you how much it will mean to me to be in the Temple again. It was the center of my life, the source of my greatest satisfaction, apart from my dear family, of course. When Aristobulus performs, I'll be seeing myself performing."

"With a difference of a few years, of course. That's something that worries me."

"Why is that?" asked Hyrcanus with a puzzled look.

"Aristobulus is young – very young. He has no experience whatsoever. Who is going to teach him?"

"If I were back home, there would be no problem."

"But you're not back home. So there is a problem."

* * *

Less than a week later another letter arrived from Jerusalem. It was delivered by a royal carrier and bore the seal of Herod, King of Judea. Hyrcanus stared at the letter with mixed feelings, for this was the first time he received any communication from Herod since being taken a captive to Parthia. He contemplated the letter with a troubled eye. Did it bear bad news about Mariamne or her new-born son? What else could have induced Herod to write to him now of all times?

"Go ahead, open it," Elisheva urged him. When he continued to hesitate, she suggested that he give her the letter to read. Realizing how ridiculous this would seem, he broke the seal and started to read. Elisheva, observing him closely, saw the puzzled look change to one of intense curiosity and then palpable relief. When he finished, he handed the letter to her to read, and her reaction was the same.

"So Herod wants you to return!" she uttered with a dubious expression. "That's quite a surprise coming from him. I wonder what made him do it."

"As you can see, he wants to repay me for saving him from punishment by the Sanhedrin when it made him stand trial for executing the partisan leader Hezekiah and some of his men."

"That was a long time ago, and a lot of water has flowed under the bridge since then."

"Maybe the birth of a son has mellowed him. Or perhaps Mariamne persuaded him to invite me back."

"I doubt that he could be influenced by Mariamne or anyone else. I can't help feeling that he has some ulterior motive."

"What does he stand to gain from having me back?"

"I don't know, and that's what puzzles and worries me."

"If he urges me to return, why shouldn't I accept?"

Elisheva saw how elated Hyrcanus was at the prospect of returning to Jerusalem and being reunited with his family, and she didn't have the heart to deny him this compelling desire, yet a sixth sense made her hesitate. "Before you decide, why don't you have a talk with the exilarch? Anyway, we can't leave without saying good-bye to him and Nehunya, not to mention the Parthian monarch, whose captives we still are, formally speaking."

"You're right. I'll write to the exilarch today and request an audience with him."

The Exilarch Advises Hyrcanus Not to Return

It was several months since Hyrcanus had conferred with the exilarch, and he looked forward to the meeting with considerable expectation. He always enjoyed the exilarch's warm, stimulating hospitality and valued his sagacious advice, but doubted whether in view of the changed circumstances in Judea he would regard Hyrcanus's contemplated return with any enthusiasm. Nevertheless, elementary courtesy demanded that he inform him of his plan and hear his opinion.

The exilarch received Hyrcanus with open arms. "My dear High Priest," he greeted him effusively, "it's a great pleasure and honor to welcome you again to my modest residence. It does my heart good to see you looking so fit."

"For that I am indebted to you and my brethren in this hospitable country, who have been so kind and helpful to my wife and me."

"Nehunya tells me that there may be an additional reason. May I assume that you are now great-grandparents?"

"You may, Exilarch. According to Alexandra's letter, the little one is now more than a month old."

"And the mother?"

"The birth was uncomplicated, and she is recovering nicely."

"The Lord be praised! My heartiest congratulations. And what is the little one's name?"

"Alexander. He's named after my daughter's late husband."

"Let us hope and pray that the Almighty grant him a long and happy life and that he will be a comfort to your family and a blessing to all our people."

"Amen," responded Hyrcanus, beaming proudly.

"I understand that you have another mazel tov coming – also of great significance to our people."

"That was an even bigger surprise to me. As the Psalmist has so pithily and eloquently declared, 'My cup runneth over.'"

"You deserve it after all the tribulations you have suffered in recent years."

Thank you. Your good wishes gladden my heart more than you realize."

"I extend them on behalf of all our people in Babylonia. Our eyes and hearts will be directed to the new high priest, who we are confident will serve with the same devotion with which you dignified this holy office."

"I shall do my best to see that he does not disappoint your high expectations."

The exilarch regarded Hyrcanus with a curious expression. "Excuse me if I confess that I don't quite grasp the implication of your last statement."

"It's simple, really. Aristobulus is young, much younger than I was when I assumed this exalted office. I had to be trained for it, of course. And Aristobulus even more so. And who is better suited to train him than his grandfather?"

The exilarch's eyebrow lifted sharply. "Am I to understand that you intend to return to Judea?" he asked with an astonished look.

"It is my ardent desire."

"If I'm not mistaken, there are some complications. First of all, there is Herod to consider. Thanks to the Roman Senate, he is king of Judea."

"He wants me to return," Hyrcanus uttered in an even tone.

"What!" exclaimed the exilarch, flashing a quick, questioning glance.

"That's correct," confirmed Hyrcanus, extracting a letter from the folds of his robe and handing it to the exilarch. "Here, read this. It's from Herod himself."

The exilarch quickly read the letter. He could not believe his eyes. He read it a second time. "Unbelievable!" he said, shaking his head. "He's sending his envoy Saramella to beg King Phraates to allow you to return."

"According to the letter, Saramella should be arriving any day now."

The exilarch rose and began to pace the room, his hands clasped behind his back as he mulled over this startling information. When he swung around to face Hyrcanus he wore a grave expression. "I can appreciate your desire to return to the Holy Land and be reunited with your family. But I must confess that I can't help feeling uneasy. What I know about Herod makes me wonder what induced him to change his mind about the high priesthood and to invite you to return. Herod is not one to be influenced by sentiment or compassion. His whole career to date, all his moves, have been calculated with one end in mind – to further his ambitions."

"He claims he wants to repay me for saving him from punishment by the Sanhedrin when it ordered him to stand trial for executing Hezekiah and his men."

"Ach, my dear High Priest, what he writes is one thing, what his real intentions are is something else. But if it is honor and respect you also desire, what do you lack here in Babylonia? Here you are living among friends, highly respected by everyone. If you return, you will have to contend with Herod, and frankly that worries me."

"And what about my family?" asked Hyrcanus soberly. "Don't they face the same dangers I would have to face? Don't they have to contend with Herod?"

The exilarch strode to the other side of the room and gazed abstractedly out the window, musing on Hyrcanus's statement. He turned around and gave his guest a piercing look. "What you say is true, I can't deny it. I know how you feel. But it doesn't make me happy. I can't help fearing that in a way you would be entering a lion's den – or maybe I should say, a pit of serpents. Herod's deeds so far do not inspire me with confidence. Nor do they inspire Nehunya, whose judgment and advice I greatly value."

Hyrcanus knitted his brow before responding to the exilarch's dire reservations. "If the picture is as black as you paint, that's all the more reason for me to be with my family. Wouldn't you do the same if you were in my shoes?"

"Ach, my dear friend, you ask a difficult question. I thank the Lord that I don't have to face such an intimidating problem. But I see your mind is made up. If King Phraates allows you to return, I shall do nothing to dissuade him. I extend to you my sincere wishes for a safe journey and my heartfelt prayer to the Almighty that He watch over you and keep you and all your family, and may He prosper your endeavors, for the good of all our people, wherever they may be."

Avner Approaches Shemaiah

When Zechariah suggested to Avner that he take a load of produce to the Jerusalem market and then make a thanksgiving offering for his recovery from the wound suffered in the siege of Jerusalem, he was not enthusiastic about the idea. The cruel fate inflicted on the defenders and especially the inhabitants by Sossius's legions and Herod's mercenaries still haunted him and intensified his hatred of the man who now occupied the throne of Judea. It was only when Queen Mariamne gave birth to a son, and her brother Aristobulus was appointed high priest, giving rise to rumors that their grandfather Hyrcanus was planning to return from Babylon, that Avner agreed to his father's suggestion.

He hesitated to tell Rachel about it, lest it exacerbate her painful memories as well as her mother's. The death of both Rachel's father and fiancé had plunged them into a deep despondency, and Avner's attempts to cheer them up did not help much. Rachel's mother suffered the most, for, in addition to her personal loss, she could not reconcile herself to the deterioration of her material and social situation. Born into a prominent, fairly well-to-do Jerusalem family, she had never felt at home in Emmaus, where she lived for more than a decade after marrying Barzilai. She had made few friends among the local residents, and she was greatly relieved when they moved to Jerusalem's fashionable Upper City. Now she was adrift, not knowing which way to turn.

She could not even shed tears on her husband's grave, for she had no idea where he was buried; and even if she did, she dared not risk setting foot in Jerusalem. There was also the problem of Barzilai's property that had escaped confiscation. When he had evacuated her and their two daughters from the city, he gave her a list of his extensive properties, indicating which ones were not likely to be known to Herod's agents. What would happen to these properties? Who would inherit them and who would manage them? She did not even know the fate of most of her family: Who had survived the siege, who had escaped Herod's executions. In her desperation she thought seriously of emigrating – to Babylonia or perhaps Egypt. But if she did that and one day discovered where her husband was buried, she would not be able to prostrate herself on his grave. She did not confide these agonizing problems to Rachel, though the daughter had a good idea what was disturbing her mother's peace of mind.

Another cause of some concern to Rachel's mother was, paradoxically, Avner's attempts to lift Rachel's spirits. "He's visiting you too often," she complained, "and I don't like it."

"But Imma," Rachel protested, "if not for his visits, I don't know what I'd do. He's only trying to repay me for our kindness in taking care of him when he was wounded in front of our house."

"Your father wasn't happy about that."

"What did he expect me to do – let Avner die in front of our house? He would have if we hadn't taken care of him. It would have been a cruel thing to do, absolutely unforgivable."

"He wasn't the only wounded soldier. Someone else could have taken care of him."

"But we knew him personally, or at least I did. We were good friends for many years; we practically grew up together."

"That's why your father wasn't happy about what you did. I admit it was kind of you, but you were betrothed at the time – to someone of good family."

"Good family!"

"Exactly! From one of the leading families; someone who was – well, someone who was not..."

"Not what? A farmer's son – is that what you can't bring yourself to say?"

"Please, Rachel, I don't mean to belittle him or his family. But you must remember who your father was, to what an important station he had risen. We had high hopes for you."

"And what kind of hopes do you have now? Our world has been destroyed. So many of our good families have been wiped out by that wicked monster. We're no longer rich and influential. We're practically destitute."

"We may not be as destitute as you think."

Rachel gave her mother a puzzled look. "I don't understand. What do you mean?"

"Your father owned land in a number of places, even here in Emmaus – land that Herod's agents don't know about. They yielded a good income, and they can still provide a good income for us and your sister's family too. I know where these properties are, but there are some problems that have to be cleared up. First of all, there's the question of inheritance. I don't know what the law is on that point. If we were in Jerusalem I could easily clarify the matter."

"Even if you could clarify it, how would we get the income?"

"That too is a problem. Your father had agents to oversee the properties and collect the rents from the tenants. I'd have to give some thought to that. About the inheritance, that's a question I have to clarify with one of the sages. If we were in Jerusalem there would be no difficulty, but I don't dare set foot there."

"Avner said he's going to Jerusalem in a couple of days' time. Maybe he could be of some help."

"Avner! How could he possibly help us?"

"He told me he's going to take a load of produce to the market and then go to the Temple to offer a sacrifice for his recovery."

"That's very commendable, but what good would that do us?"

"Maybe you could write a letter to one of the sages and ask Avner to deliver it to him."

Rachel's mother turned this over in her mind. "Yes, that's a possibility," she said a little dubiously. "But how can Avner approach any of the sages? Does he know someone who can help him in this?"

"I don't think he needs help."

"Why not?"

"Well, there's Shemaiah, for instance."

"Shemaiah! What are you talking about? He's the president of the Sanhedrin."

"I know."

"How can someone like Avner approach Shemaiah? Why, Avner's only a, a..."

"A farmer's son? Not from a prominent family?" said Rachel with a faint smile.

"Well, yes, if you must put it that way. It's a crazy idea."

"It's not as crazy as you think. I've heard that Shemaiah visited Emmaus when the first of their men returned from slavery, and after the services in the synagogue he came up to Avner and shook his hand and told his parents, in everyone's hearing, how proud they could be of their son."

"I've never heard that before," said Rachel's mother, impressed in spite of herself. "But tell me the story later. Right now I'm trying to figure out how to get the information I need from one of the sages." After a pause she continued: "Shemaiah, you say? Are you sure you heard right? Did Avner tell you this?"

"I heard it from someone else, but Avner confirmed it."

"Amazing! It's hard to believe. A letter, you say? Hmm, that's an idea. When is he going?"

"He said probably in a couple of days."

"That doesn't give me very much time. Ask him the next time he comes here. Or maybe it would be better if I ask him."

"As you wish. But, Imma, don't..."

"Don't what?"

"Talk to him nicely, not like a – well, a farmer's son."

"Don't make me seem hard-hearted. Of course I'll talk to him nicely. Oh yes, one more thing, don't mention to him what I said about the properties in Emmaus and elsewhere."

"I have no reason to mention it to him."

"No, you don't. But still, I don't know what you two talk about."

Rachel laughed lightly. "Oh, Imma, I'm not a little girl. The next time he's here why don't you come in and listen to us?"

"That won't be necessary," was the curt retort.

* * *

Avner could not help feeling sorry for Rachel's mother. She had suffered a grievous blow, and so he overlooked her usual brusque manner of speaking to him. When she questioned him about his acquaintance with the sage Shemaiah, he was surprised at her curiosity and especially the courteous way she addressed him. He readily agreed to her request to deliver a letter to the eminent sage, which she intimated had to do with a problem about inheritance and also the possibility of reinterring her late husband's remains.

When Avner approached Jerusalem, he was beset by painful memories of the bitter fighting in which he had participated. He gazed as though mesmerized at the section of the wall where he had been stationed and fought to repulse the legionnaires attempting to break their way in. When the enemy finally breached the wall and poured into the city, he was sure his end had come. His one thought had been how hard his death would be on his parents. When he found himself alive, he was filled with mixed emotions: deep distress at the large toll of Jewish lives, and profound gratitude at having made his way through the enemy lines and returning safely to Emmaus.

At the main city gate he was questioned by the sentries, who eyed him suspiciously and carefully examined the contents of his wagon before letting him pass through. He had a sudden urge to detour to the Upper City in order to visit the spot where he had been wounded the first time, in the initial victorious stage of the battle for Jerusalem against Herod's mercenaries, and where his life had been saved by Rachel's devoted ministrations. But the thought of what subsequently happened to Barzilai and his mansion made him change his mind.

This was the first time Avner set foot in Jerusalem since the fall of the city, and as he neared the marketplace he hardly recognized the scene. His heart ached at the sight of the large number of homes that had been destroyed or heavily damaged, but it was heartening to see that rebuilding was proceeding apace. When he entered the marketplace, he was surprised, like Nehunya before him, at how quiet it was. When he read the notice banning public gatherings and saw foreign soldiers patrolling the area, his blood boiled, and it was only with great difficulty that he kept from venting his anger.

After disposing of his load of produce, Avner proceeded to a hostel to arrange for a night's lodging and to leave his horse and wagon. There was still enough time to offer a sacrifice and determine the possibility of meeting the sage Shemaiah. Since the Sanhedrin sat until the daily afternoon offering, Avner waited patiently until he saw Shemaiah emerging from the Chamber of Hewn Stone in the company of two colleagues.

"Excuse me, sir," he said reverently when he approached the sage, "I apologize for disturbing you, especially as I'm not sure if you remember me. I hope you'll forgive me for being so bold as to ask if you would be kind enough to help an unfortunate woman who was widowed in the recent executions of so many of our worthy leaders?"

All three sages stared at Avner with an expression of surprise mingled with intense curiosity. They were not accustomed to being approached in this manner, and they looked askance at this young man who solicited the help of the president of the Sanhedrin no less. Nevertheless, they were touched by Avner's earnest plea, and Shemaiah regarded him thoughtfully as he searched his memory. "If I'm not mistaken," he said at last, "you're the young man from Emmaus whose return from slavery I had the honor of commemorating."

"That's right, sir," affirmed Avner with visible relief. "And that is why I have the audacity to seek your help."

"I shall never forget that memorable Sabbath," remarked Shemaiah with a broad smile. "Allow me to introduce you to my colleagues." Turning to them, he declared: "We can be proud of this young man, whose name is, er..."

"Avner, son of Zechariah."

"That's right; thank you. Avner was sold to a Greek in Cassius's infamous punishment of the four towns that had failed to raise their quota of the tribute laid on them. And during the whole time he was enslaved he refrained from eating forbidden foods and every day would recite as much of the daily prayers as he could remember. We can be proud of such young men who faithfully keep the Lord's commandments even under the most trying circumstances."

Shemaiah's two colleagues shook Avner's hand and added their warm approbation. "And now, my good man, what can I do for you – or rather, for this unfortunate woman?" asked Shemaiah.

"She asked me to give you a letter she wrote. I understand that she seeks help, or rather advice, on two very important confidential matters."

"And who is this woman, may I ask?"

"The wife, or rather the widow, of the late Antigonus's adviser Barzilai."

"I see. She has indeed suffered a most distressful loss. May the Lord comfort her and all the other unfortunate women in similar circumstances. I'll gladly do what I can to help her. Now let me think a minute. I'll have to deal with the matter at my home, but I won't be there for a little while. I'll explain where I live, and you can wait for me there."

When Avner arrived at Shemaiah's home, he was welcomed by the sage's wife, who bade him make himself comfortable while she brought in refreshments. When she disappeared into the kitchen, Avner reflected on the signal honor of being invited to the home of the most famous sage of the day. When he had approached Shemaiah as he emerged from the Chamber of Hewn Stone, it was with considerable diffidence and even nervousness, but the sage's friendly manner and willingness to help had put his mind at ease. When Shemaiah arrived home and asked to see the letter, Avner thanked him profusely.

"If I can help this unfortunate widow, I have to thank you for letting me earn a big mitzvah. Now, let me see what she has written."

Avner sat quietly as the sage carefully read the letter. When he finished, he puckered his lips as he pondered the points raised. "One of her questions has to do with inheritance. Before I can answer that, I have to know about survivors. She mentions two daughters. Are there any sons?"

"To the best of my knowledge there are only daughters."

"I see. Her second question is about the reinterment of her late husband's remains when she finds out where he is buried. Do you know where she wants to have him reinterred?"

"Right now she's uncertain. I know she isn't keen on staying in Emmaus. She would, of course, prefer Jerusalem but that is out of the question in the present circumstances."

"Unfortunately, it is. But as long as it's somewhere in the country, it won't be a problem. These seem to be the two main questions troubling her. Now, help yourself to some refreshments while I write a reply."

"You are very kind, sir, as I know how busy you are," Avner protested mildly. "I don't feel I have a right to trespass on your precious time."

"You would deny me the privilege of earning a mitzvah?" replied Shemaiah with mock severity. "Now, not one word more of protest."

Shemaiah wrote rapidly, and in less time than Avner thought possible he received the sealed reply. "Here you are, my young friend. I've added my condolence to the widow, but you can also tell her personally that we all mourn the loss of her husband and that of so many of our leading citizens, many of whom were my dear colleagues in the Sanhedrin. May the Almighty grant their souls eternal repose, and to those they left behind, the fortitude to bear their grievous loss. May they be consoled among the other mourners for Zion and Jerusalem, and may the Lord bless you and keep you and all your family."

After taking his leave of Shemaiah, Avner started to return to the hostel where he had arranged to sleep overnight. There was still light in the sky, and on a sudden impulse he decided to visit the home of the woman to whom he had given his jar of honey during the siege. He was eager to find out how she and her family were faring, praying that they had escaped the fate of so many of the inhabitants. In particular, he longed to see the little girl Rachel, who had won his heart and whose rasping cough had prompted him to offer her his ration of honey.

When he eventually found the house, he saw that it had suffered some damage, but on the whole it was in fairly good condition. With considerable expectancy, he knocked on the front door, which was soon opened by the mother. "Yes, sir?" she said with a questioning look.

"Shalom," said Avner with a pleasant smile.

"Shalom," she replied guardedly. "May I help you?" And then she recognized the caller. "Why, it's you! What a pleasant surprise. Do come in."

When Avner stepped inside he was happy to hear young voices in the next room. "I know I've taken you by surprise, and it's no wonder you didn't recognize me right away. I happened to be in Jerusalem today, and I just had to come and see how you all are, especially my little Rachel. How is she?"

"Thank God, she's fine – completely recovered from her bout of coughing, thanks largely to your kindness. I'll call her."

When Rachel, followed by her siblings, appeared, she immediately recognized Avner. "It's the honey man!" she exclaimed, throwing her arms around him. "I'm awfully glad to see you. I can't remember your name, but you'll tell me, won't you?"

"Of course. Does Avner sound familiar to you?"

"That's a nice name, and you're a nice person. Isn't he, Imma?"

"Yes, he is. Let's ask our guest to come into the next room and tell us all about himself."

Rachel held Avner's hand as she led him into the main room of the house. Although rather sparsely furnished, it was very clean and tidy. Two more children followed them into the room: a boy who looked about two years older than Rachel and a girl a year or so her junior. After introducing them to Avner, the mother told them to return to their playing, but they begged to stay.

"Only for a little while and if you're quiet. They can be pretty noisy," she apologized. "Now, before we talk any more, let me offer you something to eat. You must be hungry."

"Thank you, but I've eaten only a little while ago."

"Then maybe some fruit?" She brought in a bowl of grapes and dried figs. "Please help yourself."

"Thank you. I, ah, please excuse me, but I must confess that I have a poor memory. I'm trying to recall your name. I just can't call you Rachel's mother."

"Your memory is fine. I never told you my name when you were here."

"How boorish of me not to ask."

"I'm Dinah. And now, may I ask what brings you to Jerusalem? It can't be just to visit us."

"It wasn't the only reason, but it was an important one. I've often thought about all of you. I know what a terrible time you went through, and I prayed that the Almighty spare you and all your family."

"And we prayed to God to watch over you," said Rachel with a serious look. "Didn't we, Imma?"

"Yes, we did. You don't realize how happy you made her. She often asked about the 'honey man' and wished he would come back to see us."

Avner was touched by their solicitude. "Well, here I am, safe and fully recovered."

"Recovered! Were you wounded in the fighting?" asked Dinah.

"A little. But thanks to Emmaus's good midwife, I was well taken care of."

"Midwife!" remarked Dinah with a surprised look.

Avner chuckled. "I must tell you about that."

Dinah was amused to learn how Avner's mother had summoned the midwife to tend to his wound.

"What's a midwife, Imma?" Rachel wanted to know.

"She, ah, well, she helps to bring new babies into the world."

"How?"

"I'll explain some other time. Right now I'm curious to know what else brought our friend to Jerusalem. That is, if I'm not being too personal."

Avner related how at his father's suggestion he brought a load of produce to the market and then went to the Temple to make a thanksgiving offering. "I also did a big favor for a woman who was widowed by the terrible events and is now living in Emmaus."

"Really? And who is this unfortunate woman, if I may ask?"

"The wife of one of Antigonus's advisers."

At this information, Dinah gave Avner a curious, perturbed look. "What was her husband's name?" she asked in a low, subdued voice.

"Barzilai."

Avner was astonished to see Dinah pale noticeably and her lips tremble. "Do you by any chance happen to know her?" he asked, wondering why she was so affected by this information.

"She and I are distant relatives – second cousins, in fact."

"I didn't realize that. I'm very sorry."

"Of course you didn't realize it. As you can gather, our lives have taken quite different paths. Her branch of the family are – or perhaps I should say, were – quite prominent Jerusalemites, while ours are, well, you can judge for yourself. My husband is an artisan struggling to make ends meet. We were shocked by her husband's execution. I can imagine how terrible a blow it was for her and her daughters. Who is with her in Emmaus?"

"Rachel."

"I'm Rachel," came an emphatic protest.

"I know, darling, but we're talking about a relative of ours who is also named Rachel." Turning to Avner, Dinah asked: "How are they?"

"They're in low spirits, as you can imagine. When she heard that I was coming to Jerusalem, she asked me to clarify some questions – about inheritance and reinterring her husband's remains."

"Did you get the information?"

"Fortunately, I did. I have a letter for her from the sage Shemaiah."

"Shemaiah! The president of the Sanhedrin?"

"That's correct."

"Well, I must say, I'm astonished. How did you manage to do that?"

"It's quite a story."

"I'd love to hear it. If you don't mind, that is."

"Not at all."

Dinah listened spellbound as Avner briefly described his enslavement and Shemaiah's subsequent appearance in Emmaus with its dramatic denouement.

"How exciting! You must have been thrilled to be praised so warmly by the president of the Sanhedrin. And your meeting with him today too. May I ask when you're returning to Emmaus?"

"Tomorrow morning. I see it's beginning to get dark. I had better get back to the hostel while there's still some light."

"May I ask you for a favor?"

"Of course."

"I haven't seen my second cousin for a long time. Her name, by the way, is Leah, in case you don't know it. I'd like to write her and Rachel a short letter of condolence. I don't want to make you late, but..."

"Don't worry, I'll wait. I know how much it will mean to them."

"That's very kind of you. I'll be as quick as I can."

Before leaving, Avner gave Rachel a fond hug. "Next time I come I'll bring you a large jar of honey. Your mother can make a big cake with it for all of you. How would you like that?"

"That would be wonderful! And I'll get to see you again."

After Avner's departure Rachel said to her mother, "I'm awfully glad he visited us. I like him a lot. When do you think he'll come again?"

"I can't say for sure, but something tells me that we'll be seeing more of him – maybe a lot more," she added with an enigmatic smile.

* * *

Realizing how anxious Rachel's mother Leah was to know what Shemaiah had written, Avner decided to go straight to her home upon returning to Emmaus.

"I'm very grateful for your help," she said. "But I see you're giving me two letters."

"That's right. The other one is from a relative of yours, Dinah."

"Dinah! My second cousin?"

"That's right."

"I haven't seen her in years. How do you happen to know her?"

"That's an interesting story. But if you don't mind, I've returned to Emmaus much later than expected, and I know my parents will be worried. With your kind permission, I'll be happy to come back later or even tomorrow and tell you about it."

"And without my kind permission you won't come back?" remarked Rachel's mother, trying to assume a stern look but succeeding only in breaking into a wry grin.

After Avner left, she immediately unrolled Shemaiah's letter and read it with intense concentration.

"Has he given you the information you want?" asked Rachel.

"He has. And a little more besides."

"A little more? What about?"

"About that young man who visits you so often."

"Avner? What does he have to say about him?" asked Rachel with an eager expression.

"Let's just say it seems Avner has made quite an impression on Shemaiah. And now, let me see what my second cousin has written."

Rachel observed her mother closely as she read the second letter, and the expression her face ran the gamut of emotions – sadness, pensiveness, curiosity, amazement.

"Well?" said Rachel, somewhat impatiently.

"She's written how sorry she is to learn about our tragic loss and prays that the Almighty give us the strength to bear it courageously."

"Anything else?"

"It seems our young man has made quite an impression on her too, and especially her older daughter, whose name is also Rachel. She also explains how they happen to know Avner. So is there need for him to come and tell us?"

"Oh, Imma, I don't have to tell you my answer to that."

"No, you don't. It's quite obvious," she said, unable to suppress a big smile.

Chapter Twelve

Joy In Emmaus, Tragedy In Jericho

Zechariah in Emmaus Deputation to the Temple

After hitching his ox Kalba to a wagon loaded with tools and various supplies, Zechariah was ready to begin his day's work when his neighbor Saul emerged from his home.

"What field are you doing today?" he called out.

"The vegetable field," replied Zechariah, opening the gate to his courtyard.

"You've got a fine crop there. I wish I could say the same about mine," replied Saul as he approached Zechariah.

"You could if you worked harder," Zechariah joshed his friend. "You know that proverb about the ant: 'Go to the ant, you dawdler, consider her ways and be wise.'"

"Maybe you admire the ant, but when I see how the whole clan comes swarming over whenever I drop bread crumbs, I can't feel any admiration for her."

"Anyway, it's a good thought to start the day with."

"You're entitled to your opinion," said Saul with a chuckle. "Wait till you come back from your vacation and see how your field will look then. When are you leaving?"

"The deputation is leaving tomorrow. And if you think that accompanying the priests as they offer the communal sacrifices, and that while you have to fast a good part of the week, is a vacation, then you had better think again."

"So why did you agree to go?"

"It's the turn of the Emmaus region this coming week, and since I'm one of the elders, it's my duty to go. Besides, it's an honor that doesn't come very often.

Figure it out for yourself: Apart from the festivals, during the year no less than 24 courses of priests and laymen from all parts of the country take turns serving in the Temple. And then there is the possibility that we may be lucky enough to get a look at our new high priest."

"The rumor is that he will officiate the first time on Succot – a little over a month from now."

"That's probably true. I understand that his grandfather is instructing him in his duties."

"I take it Avner will be looking after the farm in your absence. Can he manage by himself?"

"My older sons will take turns helping him."

"I'm glad to see him back at work again. Does that mean his leg is better?"

"Thank God, it is almost completely healed."

"I suppose having a devoted nurse – and a pretty one at that – to keep an eye on him did him good."

"Rachel was a big help. And frankly, it was good for her too. It helped keep her mind off their troubles."

"How about her mother?"

"It's been pretty hard for her. Left a widow with two daughters – one living with her husband and young children quite a long way from here. But you have to hand it to her, she's bearing up better than I expected."

"How is she managing financially?"

"Avner's not sure. He thinks she's not finding it easy. It seems Barzilai owned a lot of property in different places – almost all of it unknown to Herod's agents. But what good does that do her if she's hardly getting any income from it?"

"What's the problem? Some of that property is located right here in Emmaus – property that Barzilai got mostly by foreclosing loans he gave in those bad years. Those fields yield as good a crop as any. Isn't she collecting the rent from the tenants?"

"I really can't say. In many cases the tenants were originally the owners of the property, and she probably finds it unpleasant to deal with them, knowing their feelings about her husband."

"If that's the case, she's going to have a hard time making ends meet."

"It's a pity really. Well, I'm not going to get much work done at this rate. Even Kalba is eyeing me impatiently."

When Avner told Rachel that his father was a member of the deputation that would accompany the priests in the Temple during the coming week, she was duly impressed. "How wonderful!!" she said. "He's very fortunate, especially as it's getting close to the High Holidays. How I envy him! I would give anything to see our home again, or what was our home."

"I'm afraid it wouldn't make you happy. To see others, most likely Romans, living in your home would upset you."

"I suppose you are right," agreed Rachel with an audible sigh. "I can dream though, can't I?"

"You and your mother aren't very happy in Emmaus, are you?"

"I wouldn't say that. We're grateful that at least we're living in comparative safety. That's more than we can say about many of our friends."

At this point Rachel's mother entered the room and greeted Avner. "Avner tells me that his father is a member of the deputation that will serve in the Temple this coming week," said Rachel.

"That's quite an honor. Please give him my compliments."

"Thank you, I will," Avner replied. "He would like to know if there is any favor he can do for you while he's in Jerusalem."

"That's very kind of him. When is he leaving?"

"The deputation is leaving tomorrow."

"That will give me time to write to my cousin Dinah and thank her for her letter."

Rachel knew that, like herself, her mother missed her husband most keenly on Sabbaths, when the house seemed painfully empty. With no man in the house, they themselves recited the blessing over wine and grace after meals – a poignant reminder of their great loss. Avner's parents had several times invited them to a Sabbath meal, but Leah politely turned down the invitations, much to Rachel's disappointment.

"It's not right, Imma," she protested. "Except for those who have lost their property through foreclosures, the people here are quite nice and helpful."

"I would say they are pitying us. That's not quite the same thing." replied Leah a little haughtily.

"That's no reason to keep ourselves aloof."

"That young man of yours doesn't seem to think we are being aloof. I must say, he's a persistent sort."

"Do you want to stop him being persistent?"

"What I want doesn't seem to make much difference to him. He doesn't take no for an answer."

"I'm glad of that," said Rachel, coloring slightly.

Leah gave her daughter a long, thoughtful look. "So I gather. I suppose there are worse things in life. I think I had better have a talk with your young man."

"What about?"

"Don't worry. It's nothing bad. I have a proposition to offer him."

"A proposition! What kind of proposition?"

"When I see him, you'll find out."

"Talk to him nicely, Imma."

"Of course I'll talk to him nicely. But I don't think he's as thin-skinned as you seem to fear."

When Avner called on Rachel later in the day, he was pleasantly surprised at her mother's warm welcome. "Rachel tells me that you'll be managing the farm in your father's absence." she said after seeing that he was comfortably seated.

"That's right," he replied, wondering at her interest in what he considered a mundane matter.

"Am I correct in believing that you have a lot of experience in farming?"

"We have been farmers for many generations."

"Don't think me too personal, but can I assume that you're about the same age as Rachel?"

Avner was so surprised by this question that he stared at Leah with an odd expression. "I have never asked Rachel how old she is, but I think we're about the same age."

"That means you're about eighteen years old; is that right?"

"That's a good guess."

"A bit young. It would be better if you were a little older."

Both Avner and Rachel were puzzled by Leah's questions, and they wondered what lay behind them. "With God's help I hope to grow older," quipped Avner.

Rachel's mother's lips twisted into a thin smile. "I wish you long life," she said.

"But right now. I'd like to make you a proposition which I'm sure you will find both interesting and advantageous in more ways than one."

His curiosity aroused, Avner waited for Leah to explain.

"You may know that my late husband owned property in a number of places. He had an agent – or rather, several agents – to oversee these properties and to collect the rents. At present I'm getting very little income from these properties. In fact, I don't know what is happening to them. I need someone, actually more than one person, to keep an eye on them and collect the rents, I need someone I can trust and rely on. It is true you're young, but you have the necessary farming experience and, above all, there's a way about you that people like, especially – well, let's leave it at that for the time being. This in essence is the proposition I'm offering you. I don't expect you to give me an immediate answer, but I want you to think it over. There are undoubtedly a number of questions you would like to clarify, especially after talking it over with your family. But I just want to emphasize that, all things considered, you would find this an excellent opportunity."

Avner had listened with rapt attention to this offer, which filled him with great expectation but also with many questions. First of all, why did she choose him for this job? It's true he was no stranger to her, and she knew how reliable he was. But he *was* young, and he would be dealing with people older than himself. On the other hand, it's also true that he got along with people, and many knew what the sage Shemaiah thought of him, which was a big plus. At the same time, since the properties were spread over a fairly large area, he wouldn't be able to give his father as much help as at present, if at all. This was a very important consideration, especially as Abba was getting on in years. And what about those Emmaus farmers who had lost their fields when Barzilai foreclosed the loans they had to take in order to survive in those lean years and consequently were reduced to the status of tenants? They did not have kind feelings toward Barzilai. And the same was undoubtedly true of many others living elsewhere. These were the most important factors he had to consider.

When he raised them with his father, he was pleasantly surprised at his reaction. "It is a great opportunity for you, son. True there is a problem about those who have been reduced to the status of tenants. But it's not an insurmountable problem."

"I don't want my fellow townsmen to think badly about me. That is, if I agree to the offer. What can I do about this problem?"

"If you're really interested in the offer, you can make it a condition that those who can repay the foreclosed loans be allowed to do so and get their land back."

"That's an excellent idea!" exclaimed Avner.

"I'm not sure about the *halachic* aspect of such an arrangement. That would have to be clarified. But explain it to her."

"Assuming she agrees to this condition, there is an even bigger problem. How can I let you do all the work here on your own?"

"And when, with God's help, you get married, you won't have this problem? The solution is easy: I'll hire a worker or two. Since you say your responsibility will be limited to the Emmaus region, this problem is not quite a serious as you think. Besides, you can oversee my farm too while you're about it," Zechariah added with a grin.

Avner was greatly relieved at his father's reaction, but one thing still puzzled him. "I don't understand why of all people she offered me this job. It is true she knows me quite well, but I'm young. An older person would be more suitable in my opinion."

Zechariah put an arm around Avner's shoulder. "Son, let me ask you a simple question. Are you too young to get married?"

Avner stared at his father with a perplexed expression. "I don't see the connection," he murmured.

"No? Then let me ask you another question. Doesn't Leah – I see I'll have to get used to calling her that – doesn't she have a daughter who you've been in love with for a long time?"

Avner's cheeks reddened at this question. "You mean? You think?" he stammered.

"Exactly," Zechariah confirmed with a big smile. "Leah is no fool. It's plain to her as it is to me and your mother. Not only would she be getting a reliable agent, but a son-in-law who is not just a plain farmer, which she evidently finds it hard to reconcile herself to, but a son-in-law who would be doing more prestigious work and is highly thought of by no less a personage than the president of the Sanhedrin."

A Joyous Avner and Rachel are Betrothed

Avner was visibly relieved when Rachel's mother agreed to let those tenants who could and wanted to repay the foreclosed loans do so and thereby redeem their fields. This gesture was enthusiastically acclaimed in Emmaus and even won the admiration and blessing of the Sanhedrin, which realized the necessity of keeping the matter from reaching Herod's ear. It also enabled Avner to assume his new duties with the goodwill of all parties concerned.

Most important of all, what brought profound joy to Avner's whole family was his betrothal to Rachel. As more than thirty days had passed since Barzilai's death, she was *halachically* permitted to become affianced, but because of their bereavement the ceremony took place in modest circumstances, with only the immediate members of the couple's families and closest friends attending. At Avner's express request and Leah's hearty approval, an invitation had been sent to her relatives in Jerusalem, who accepted with great pleasure.

Avner's face lit up when little Rachel appeared with her parents and siblings. "It's the honey man!" she excitedly informed her family as she dashed over to Avner and gave him a big hug. When Avner managed to free himself, he introduced her to the rest of the family and to the other guests.

"She's very cute," said Avner's fiancée-to-be. "Now I see why you talk so much about her. But if she's Rachel and I'm Rachel, how will we know which of us you re referring to?"

"That's no problem," replied Avner with a grin. "You will continue to be Rachel, and my young friend will be Rachela. Is that all right with you, Rachela?"

"Of course," the child replied with a big smile. Turning to her namesake, she asked, "Are you going to be Avner's wife?"

"Yes, I am, but not today. Tomorrow I'm going to become his betrothed."

"What's a betrothed?"

"A betrothed is, er, to put it simply, it means I'm not exactly Avner's wife, but I will be later on."

"You'll take good care of him, won't you?"

"Of course I will. And you come to visit us often to make sure."

"I'd love that. He's a very nice man. Did he ever tell you about the jar of honey he gave my mother when I was sick?"

Rachel smiled. "He's told me many times. And you know what? I never tire of hearing the story."

The betrothal took place on the morrow in the presence of both families and as many guests as could be accommodated in the triclinium – most notable Saul and Zechariah's fellow elders and their spouses. Upon the conclusion of the formalities, they repaired to a neighboring courtyard, where tables had been set for the festive meal.

Because of the bereavement, no music was played, but this did not dampen the joyous mood. Between courses Zechariah called upon his fellow elders to extend their greetings to the young couple and their families and to wish them a happy and blessed life together.

Avner, drinking in their words, found it hard to believe that at long last he and Rachel were to be united in marriage. It was a dream come true. He recalled their carefree childhood days, how happy they had been playing together. Glancing at Rachel's mother, he saw her in earnest conversation with Dinah, her second cousin, and was grateful that he was largely responsible for bringing them together. As long as Herod sat on the Judean throne, Leah would not dare to set foot in Jerusalem, but Avner was determined that henceforth she and Dinah would not be separated from each other.

Thousands Converge on Jerusalem for the High Holidays

With the approach of the High Holidays Jerusalem began to take on a different air. Despite the tension still prevailing in the city, pilgrims started to arrive in increasing numbers from all parts of the country and the diaspora, ignoring both the notices banning public gatherings and the foreign mercenaries patrolling the marketplace and the main streets. When all available accommodations were occupied in the city's hostels and private homes, the swelling crowds turned to nearby villages and even tents set up in all open spaces in and around the city.

From his headquarters room in the royal Hasmonean palace, Herod surveyed the scene with a worried look. He confided to his chief minister Ptolemy that he thought the recent siege would deter Jews from making the annual pilgrimage, especially as the memory of the bloody fighting and execution of many of the most prominent citizens was still fresh in their minds. The presence of such a huge throng at a time when his popularity with his subjects was at a low ebb made Herod uncustomarily edgy.

It was a strange people he was ruling, he mused with a sullen frown. He found it hard to understand their mentality, their way of life. Their exclusiveness, their abhorrence of everything smacking of what he thought of as worldly culture, both baffled and irked him. They were a small kingdom in a vast Roman-Hellenistic world, which had given its inhabitants law and order, superb art, magnificent architecture, great literature (not that he himself was very familiar with it, but so Ptolemy assured him), and all this they shunned. He was cut out to be the ruler not of a tiny state inhabited by small-minded people, but of a large, thriving state, an important factor in the Roman-Hellenistic scheme of things. He doubted that he would ever understand let alone appreciate, the Jewish people. But for better or for worse, they were his subjects. He did not delude himself: He knew they did not like him; in fact, harbored a deep suspicion, even a profound aversion to him. They were a stubborn, rebellious people, and he would have to rule with an iron hand. He glanced out again at the jostling throng. "This is causing a serious problem," he declared in a strident voice to Ptolemy.

"What is?" asked Ptolemy with a puzzled look.

"All these people. They're ignoring the ban on public gatherings. Why aren't Costobarus's men doing their duty?"

"No one expected so many pilgrims. It's impossible to cope with a crowd like this."

"Nothing is impossible!" barked Herod. "Tell Costobarus to assign more men to enforce the ban. At least have him assign more spies to mingle among them."

"I'll tell him as soon as possible."

"As soon as possible means now – today! Right after our meeting," Herod growled. After a pause he continued: "Now that we've dealt with this problem, let's get down to other business. What audiences are scheduled for the next couple of days?"

"Today you know about. There's the envoy from Rhodes."

"And tomorrow?"

Ptolemy's eyebrows lifted sharply. "Permit me to remind you that tomorrow is the eve of the Jewish New Year. There's always the possibility that an audience might last longer than expected."

"And so?"

"Do you think it's advisable to conduct such business on what to your subjects is one of the holiest days of the year?"

"That's for me to decide," Herod snapped with a defiant expression. "If I think it's important, it shall be as I decide."

"Very well," remarked Ptolemy with a resigned look. "While we're on this particular subject, I'd like to mention that the tutors I recommended for the queen tell me they're having difficulty with her."

"What difficulty?" asked Herod, his eyes narrowing.

"It seems – and I want to emphasize I'm quoting the tutors – that Her Majesty doesn't show a great deal of interest in learning Greek culture. In fact, they believe she actually dislikes it."

This information did not surprise Herod, as it was a bone of contention between the royal couple. Screwing up his face, he explained that since the queen is again pregnant, this probably accounts for her present attitude, which will undoubtedly change once she has given birth.

"I didn't realize Her Majesty is again expecting," Ptolemy apologized. "Please convey my best wishes to her for an easy pregnancy."

"I'll be happy to do so," replied Herod, doubting that Ptolemy found his explanation very convincing. He did not reveal that in reality the situation had been the cause of bitter recrimination, especially on Mariamne's part. When he had upbraided her for not being sufficiently cordial to his guests, she had burst out indignantly, "How can you expect me to be cordial to your pagan guests? You are king of a Jewish state, and I am its queen. When do we have Jewish guests? Is there any Jewish atmosphere in the court? Is there any talk of Jewish subjects or any matters of Jewish interest?"

Herod glared at his wife. He knew there was some justification for her accusation. He had tried to explain more than once that Judea maintains relations with non-Jewish countries, that it could not remain a small, isolated state with a narrow outlook on life, but had to take its rightful place in the Roman-Hellenistic orbit. Their wrangling turned especially bitter on the eve of the New Year, when Mariamne reminded Herod not to come back late as they were to join her family and some important guests for a festive meal.

"I may be a little late," he apologized rather lamely, "but don't let me hold you up."

"Late! On such an important occasion?" Mariamne blurted out with a look of dismay. "Why must you be late? Surely this is more important than any meeting or any other business you may have scheduled, presumably without realizing the date. Whatever it is, postpone it."

"I'm afraid I can't. I'm meeting with some foreign architects whom I've specially invited."

"So let them wait till after the festival. It will do them good to see how our people observe Rosh HaShanah."

"I don't think they'll find it to their taste."

"So it won't be to their taste. I can assure you they won't be any the worse for it.

What can be more important than celebrating the holiday together?"

"If I tell you why I've invited them, you'll understand its importance. I want to get their ideas for a new palace."

Mariamne gasped at this revelation. She stared at Herod incredulously. "A new palace! I can't believe it."

"Why is it so hard to believe? I want Jerusalem to be one of the most beautiful cities in this part of the world. And that means, among other things, a palace befitting my reign – or rather, our reign."

"Perhaps you will be kind enough to tell me what is wrong with this palace?"

"It was all right for the Hasmonean kings, but times have changed."

"For better or for worse?" Mariamne shot back.

"For better," replied Herod dryly. "We'll have visitors and guests from many lands, and I want them to be duly impressed. But don't worry, I'm not going to build a new palace tomorrow. I just want to get some ideas now. If I had remembered about the holiday, I would have changed the date of the invitation."

"And will there be any Jews among the visitors and guests you want to impress?"

Mariamne asked scornfully.

"Hopefully there will be."

"But I assume they will be greatly outnumbered."

"That will depend entirely on them."

"In other words, whether or not they have Hellenistic leanings?"

Herod's face contorted at this insinuation. "I would say, whether they have narrow, parochial leanings or can accommodate themselves to the new wind blowing through this part of the world."

Mariamne gave a short, derisive laugh. "New wind!" she snorted. "Before the Hasmoneans drove them out, Judea was plagued with Hellenistic Jews, including the high priests Jason and Menelaus. Now we're plagued not only with Hellenistic Jews but also with pagans. Do you expect me to be a humble, submissive consort in a pagan court? If you do, I'm afraid you're going to be disappointed."

Aristobulus is Drowned, Herod Pleads Innocence

The day Hyrcanus and his family set out for Jericho was quite raw, with a hint of rain and possibly even snow. This was his first trip there since returning from the relatively mild winters of Babylonia, and he felt the cold more keenly than usual; but the knowledge that he would soon be basking in the balmy air of his favorite winter resort filled him with happy anticipation.

"Are you warm enough?" Elisheva asked as their party of four coaches and an armed escort passed through the main city gate and headed in the direction of the Mount of Olives.

"It's a little too chilly for my taste, but it won't be long before we'll enjoy warmer weather," replied Hyrcanus. "I wonder how Mariamne and her baby are doing."

"She's a lot younger than us, so you can be sure she isn't as sensitive to the weather as we are."

"It's a long time since our last trip to Jericho. A lot of water has flowed under the bridge since then," Hyrcanus remarked pensively.

"I agree with you, but let's not get too nostalgic."

"It's rather strange when you think about it," said Hyrcanus with a thoughtful look.

"What's strange?"

"This is the first time Mariamne, or Aristobulus too for that matter, aren't riding in the same coach with us on our trip to Jericho."

"Aren't you forgetting how long we lived in Babylonia? Once we arrive in Jericho we will all be together – Mariamne and her baby, along with Aristobulus and Alexandra of course."

"And Herod too," Hyrcanus added with a grimace.

"I still don't know why he was so adamant on coming with us." said Elisheva. "I would think he has enough matters to keep him fully occupied in Jerusalem."

"Too many matters," Hyrcanus asserted with obvious displeasure. "Our palace – the royal Hasmonean palace – is becoming too much like a Hellenistic palace. You hear more Greek spoken there than Hebrew, or even Aramaic for that matter. Every week, it seems, you see a new foreign face roaming the corridors."

"Why don't we drop the subject and just relax? We want to enjoy our stay in Jericho."

"You're right. No more talk or thought about our granddaughter's husband."

Unlike her grandparents, Mariamne was unusually quiet, giving all her attention to little Alexander.

"I'd be very grateful if you condescended to converse with me," said Herod with obvious annoyance. "After all, I am your husband, you know, not to mention the not so insignificant fact that I also happen to be king of Judea."

"I'm sorry," said Mariamne apologetically. "But Alexander is demanding all my attention. And so is this one who has not yet seen the light of day," she added, patting her swollen abdomen. "The ride is evidently making him – or her – a bit restless."

"Are you nauseous?"

"A little, but that's to be expected. I also feel jittery for some reason."

Herod gave Mariamne a piercing look. "It probably has something to do with your pregnancy. You had the same problem when you were carrying Alexander."

"I hope that's all it is." said Mariamne with a troubled expression.

"Why do you say that? There's no reason to feel worried or whatever it is that's making you jittery."

"I really don't know. Maybe it's the sight of those mercenaries of yours. They give me the creeps with their fierce-looking faces."

Herod gave a short, derisive laugh. "They are coming along for protection. I always have an escort when I travel through potentially dangerous territory."

"Dangerous territory! The Jerusalem-Jericho road you call dangerous?"

"One can never be too sure or too careful. That's a lesson I learned long ago. What's more, we have some very important people with us – your mother and the grandparents of the young high priest, to mention a few. We can't take chances. Better to be safe than sorry."

Mariamne, anxious to change the subject, patted Alexander on the back to burp him. "I wonder if he'll be jealous of the new arrival."

"Why should he be jealous? He – or she – will be a playmate for him."

"That's true, but still it happens quite often, especially at first, until they get used to each other. The first-born gets a lot of attention, and then he has to share it with someone else."

"It didn't happen with me – as far as I can remember. My siblings and I have always been on excellent terms. Take Salome, for instance, we got on well."

"So I've noticed." replied Mariamne with a scornful expression.

Herod flashed Mariamne a perturbed look. The hostile relationship between his wife and his sister caused him considerable anguish. "I wouldn't say that Salome is a paragon of virtue." he conceded grudgingly, "but she does have my interest at heart."

"I am quite aware of that," replied Mariamne, thankful that she didn't have to suffer Salome's presence on this trip.

"Incidentally," said Herod, "maybe this isn't the time or place to mention it, but your Greek instructor has again complained about your lack of enthusiasm – or even interest."

"He can complain all he wants," Mariamne shot back defiantly. "It won't make me more enthusiastic."

"That's not the proper attitude to take," said Herod with a frown. ""I thought I had impressed on you the desirability, or I should say, the need, to learn as much as you can about the Greek language and culture."

"For whose benefit?" Mariamne asked coolly. "As I pointed out, I believe it is more profitable to learn all I can about our own heritage – the Jewish heritage." She was about to add that Herod too would do well to emulate her, but checked herself, not wanting to spoil the family's vacation by injecting a discordant note.

Herod, unwilling to drop the subject, emphasized the importance of at least a basic knowledge of the language and culture: "You can see for yourself how many of my advisers and other officials are either Greek or Greek-speaking," he added.

"Far too many," said Mariamne disdainfully. "I would prefer to see some Jewish advisers in the court."

"Herod's mouth jerked noticeably as he struggled to restrain his pique. "My dear wife," he said dryly, "may I remind you once again that we are a tiny state in a vast Hellenistic world."

"I am aware of that," replied Mariamne stiffly. "But let me remind you that a growing number of non-Jews are showing an interest in our way of life. And what is more, they are even coming to visit our Temple."

"It's plain curiosity, that's all." Herod responded with a dismissive gesture. "But one day they will all come to see the Temple because of its unique beauty. I'll personally see to that; it's one of my plans for the future. And they will be reminded who was responsible for this marvel – one of the wonders of the world."

Hyrcanus had always looked forward to his winter vacation in Jericho, not only because of the pleasant weather, which enabled him to brush aside, at least temporarily, the vexing cares and tribulations of his office as high priest and to enjoy his early morning walks through the luxuriant, well-tended grounds of his own palace, as well as those of the neighboring villas. The occupants of the villas, in turn, were honored to exchange greetings with the high priest. This time, though, he feared he would not find the same cordial relationship as in previous years, not only because of the loss of his priestly office, but even more because so many of his friends had fallen victim to Herod's cruel vengeance. But much to his surprise, he found that the attitude toward him of his fellow vacationers and residents of Jericho had not changed; in fact, he was welcomed perhaps even more cordially than before.

Equally heartening was the enthusiastic welcome extended to Hyrcanus's successor to the high priesthood. All the worshipers had been thrilled by Aristobulus's initial performance in the Temple on Succot, which not only gave them renewed hope and made them forget, at least temporarily, Hyrcanus's deprivation of both the royal and priestly crowns. There was not a single aristocratic priestly family that did not regard Aristobulus as a most desirable consort for their eligible daughter, and the number of proposals received by the royal Hasmonean family was overwhelming.

Herod, whom the aristocratic Jewish families avoided as much as possible, was highly envious of the exceptional popularity of the young high priest, and he bided his time until making his long-planned move. To disarm any suspicion, he made a conscientious effort to display a friendly attitude toward Aristobulus, extolling his virtues, which, he emphasized, were a credit to the entire nation. Having been accustomed to the king's cool, distant attitude, Aristobulus was puzzled at this apparent change of heart, so much so that when on one very hot day he was invited to join Herod in a swim in one of the palace's spacious pools, he readily accepted the offer. Herod was an accomplished swimmer, and Aristobulus had to admire his skill.

"You're very competent yourself," Herod returned the compliment. "How about a race, say, the length of the pool two or three times – as many as you want?"

Aristobulus welcomed the challenge, but before they began an unexpected obstacle arose: They were joined by three brawny swimmers, who seemed to appear out of nowhere. "I suppose that puts and end to our race," said Aristobulus regretfully.

"Not at all," replied Herod. He ordered the newcomers to leave the pool, but then relented and said they could stay if they kept to the left side of the pool and did not disturb his race with Aristobulus. They agreed, saying they were eager to see who would win and even placed bets on their favorite. Herod and Arisotobulus decided on three lengths, and on the given signal they dived into the water and began to swim at a rapid pace, staying almost neck to neck. Churning the water as fast as he could, Aristobulus did not notice that the three "invaders" had crossed over to the right side of the pool and headed directly toward him. They fell upon Aristobulus's legs, while another tried to shove his head into the water. Realizing their evil intention, Aristobulus struggled with all his might and even managed to cry out for help, but his pitiful appeal was in vain. For a minute of so he succeeded in freeing the grip of the most powerful of his assailants, but then all three of them pounced on him, and after thrashing about in the water, they managed to keep his head submerged until his body went limp. The struggle was over. "All right," said Herod after making sure that Aristobulus was dead. "You've done your job well." he declared with a look of malicious satisfaction. "Leave the pool nonchalantly and go separately to the designated place. Get dressed as quickly as you can, and when you have made sure that no one has seen you, return to the rest of your men. Later on you'll get your reward. Now, just one word of warning: If any of you dare squeal or talk about this business to anyone, you can say good-bye to your heads. Remember that. Now go!"

News of Aristobulus's death spread like wildfire and plunged all Jericho and the entire Jewish nation in the homeland and abroad into a profound gloom. The royal Hasmonean family was devastated. They could not reconcile themselves to the fate of their beloved Aristobulus. "Oh, why did he have to die" sobbed Mariamne. Alexandra drew her to her bosom and did her best to comfort her, but she was inconsolable.

When Alexandra questioned Herod, he admitted that he was present when the terrible "accident" had occurred. He claimed that Aristobulus had suddenly complained of violent stomach cramps and called for help. "I rushed to his aid," declared Herod, "but it took me a couple of minutes to reach him. To my horror it was too late. I pulled Aristobulus out of the water and tried to revive him, but to no avail. My dear brother-in-law!" he moaned, wringing his hands and with tears streaming down his face. "What a grievous loss!"

Herod declared a week of official mourning and went out of his way to arrange a royal funeral for Aristobulus. But all his pious protestations of grief and his efforts to arrange a funeral befitting Aristobulus's preeminent station failed to move Alexandra. She knew it was a hypocritical, cold-blooded sham. She recalled Nehunya's warning and her own apprehension. Nehunya had foreseen what would happen, maybe not in all its horrible details, but in its inevitable outcome. How artful was Herod's deceit, she thought to herself, how cleverly he dissembled! She vowed that this abominable crime would not go unpunished. She would exact retribution from Herod, the man who had snuffed out the life of her beloved son. She wrote to Cleopatra about Herod's duplicity, his murderous deed, and appealed for help.

A Fearful Herod Ordered to Meet Antony

Antony was in a buoyant mood when he arrived at the royal Ptolemaic palace in Alexandria. Preparations for his forthcoming Parthian campaign had progressed so satisfactorily that he decided he could spend some time in Alexandria with Cleopatra and their children. It was a welcome relief to temporarily get away from the atmosphere of the camp and enjoy the pleasures of Alexandria, especially the company of his recently espoused Cleopatra and their offspring, including Caesarion.

The youngsters crowed with delight upon beholding the bulging packages he brought and waited impatiently for them to be opened.

"Don't think I have forgotten you," Antony said to Cleopatra after distributing his gifts to the children. "It's beautiful!" she exclaimed upon being presented with a diamond necklace set with precious stones.

Antony's manifest joy in being reunited with his Egyptian family made Cleopatra wonder if he knew what had happened in Jericho. It was hard to believe that he was unaware of the death of Aristobulus, but she did not want to mention the subject on the first day of his visit. Next morning he himself brought it up. "I assume that you know what happened in Jericho," he said with a serious expression.

"Unfortunately I do," replied Cleopatra. "It was a big shock to all of us here."

"A pity that such a fine specimen of youth should drown. It's hard to believe."

"It won't be hard to believe when you read the letter I received from Alexandra," she said, handing Antony an unrolled missive.

As Antony read the letter his brow furrowed deeply and a troubled look clouded his face. "Her accusation is serious, extremely so. But it's her version of what happened. From my information she has never taken to Herod or his family. I understand that she – like almost all Judeans – was opposed to the marriage."

"She had good reason to oppose it," replied Cleopatra. "I myself found it hard to accept for many reasons."

"That may be so, but what has that to do with Arisobulus's death?"

"It is quite obvious. Aristobulus was very popular, and Herod regarded him as a dangerous rival. Don't forget that Herod had appointed a little-known Babylonian as high priest, but public pressure made him replace the Babylonian in favor of Aristobulus. Knowing Herod, that would be reason enough to have Aristobulus eliminated."

"But the elaborate funeral and all the trappings Herod arranged – how do you explain that?"

"It was all a show to throw dust in the public's eye. You can't let this murder – and that's exactly what it was – go unpunished. You will lose the trust of the Jewish people; you'll have a rebellious nation to contend with."

Antony pondered on this for a long moment. Either way he foresaw trouble. If he found Herod guilty and punished him, he would lose someone he could trust to pursue a policy favorable to the Romans and especially to himself. On the other hand, if he ignored the matter or dealt with it superficially, he would anger the Jews, and not only those living in Judea. Until now, thanks to Hyrcanus's wise policy when he was king and high priest, relations with the Jews were reasonably good on the whole – as good as could be expected in the circumstances. Moreover, in view of his planned campaign against the Parthians, it was not advisable to stir up the Jewish masses, who sided with the Parthians. After giving due thought to the matter, he decided that his best strategy was to play it both ways – to summon Herod to defend himself and to pass judgment that would be most favorable to his own ends. He therefore informed Cleopatra that he would order Herod to appear before him in Laodicea to defend himself.

Herod was conferring with his chief minister Ptolemy when his adjutant informed him that a courier had arrived with a message from Antony. Herod stiffened visibly and his heart turned cold, for he had a premonition that this had something to do with Aristobulus's death.

"Admit him," he ordered the adjutant.

When the courier handed Herod a sealed letter, he stared at it with a troubled look before breaking the seal. He paled as he read the contents.

"I assume that it's not pleasant news," said Ptolemy with evident concern.

"Antony has summoned me to meet him in Laodicea in connection with Aristobulus's death," replied Herod gravely.

"Hmm, I see," said Ptolemy. "I can understand how you feel, but in my opinion the letter was to be expected, and is no particular cause for worry."

"No cause for worry!" exclaimed Herod, banging his fist on his desk. "You don't seem to realize what a bitch that new wife of his is. She has her heart set on regaining the old Egyptian Empire, which includes the Jewish state – my realm!"

"That doesn't mean Antony will give in to Cleopatra's wishes," said Ptolemy in an unruffled tone. "He needs you; he knows he can rely on you."

"He needs Cleopatra's money too."

"Yes, he probably does. He needs both her money and your reliability."

Herod paused to consider Ptolemy's statement. He had to admit that it possessed some merit. Could he convince Antony of his innocence? He wasn't sure. "Will Antony believe me if I plead innocent? Don't forget there is Alexandra's accusation."

"Whether he'll believe you or not, I can't say. But Antony is no paragon of virtue. His hands are stained red with the blood of hundreds and probably thousands of prominent Romans. Didn't he and Octavian dispatch many an innocent man in avenging Caesar's death? And that's not all. I can cite many more instances where he relieved good men of their heads."

Antony's summons had directed Herod's anger at the two women who brought him to this humiliating and extremely dangerous pass. He had a fierce desire to seize them by their throats and put an end to their diabolical scheming. When his ire had cooled a bit, he realized how impractical and impossible this would be. What was it Ptolemy had said: "This doesn't mean that Antony will give in to Cleopatra's wishes. He needs you; he knows he can rely on you." Yes, Ptolemy is right. Still, Herod knew that the Fates are fickle, and it was not advisable to take chances. Cleopatra coveted his territory – that was clear. She had already caused him plenty of trouble, and she holds Antony in her grip. No, it was not wise to take any risks with her. He must be prepared for any and all exigencies.

One that weighed particularly heavy on his mind – and heart – concerned Mariamne. If it should come to the worst and Antony takes a dim view of the situation, sentencing Herod to dire punishment: imprisonment or – may the gods preserve him – even capital punishment, he could not bear the thought that Mariamne would fall into someone else's hands. If he couldn't have her, then no one must have her. On that he was resolved.

When Salome learned that her husband Joseph had been summoned to an urgent meeting with Herod her curiosity was aroused. "What does he need you for so urgently?" she asked. "If it's a matter of state, he invariably consults Ptolemy."

"I can't answer your question," replied Joseph, who was very familiar with his wife's prying ears and eyes, especially if it concerned members of her family. "After I have seen Herod, perhaps I'll be able to answer your question."

When Joseph was admitted to Herod's presence he was puzzled to see him wearing a worried frown, but, even though he was Herod's uncle, he refrained from commenting.

"You are no doubt wondering why I have summoned you," Herod said after Joseph had taken a seat. "I am going to trust you with a very important responsibility."

"Pardon me for asking, but if it is so important wouldn't it be better to have Ptolemy deal with the matter?"

"You are right to ask this question, but when you have heard me out, you will understand why I have chosen you."

Herod began to pace the room with his hands on his hips: "You may have heard rumors that I was responsible for the death of Aristobulus. Well, they are just that – rumors. And who is manly to blame for them reaching Antony's ears? None other than that diabolical vixen Cleopatra herself. And what is more, she has persuaded Antony to summon me to appear before him in Laodicea."

Herod ceased pacing and sat down fixing his eyes on Joseph. "Now what is it I want from you? Listen carefully. When I go to Antony, I'll have no idea how he will react to this wretched matter. He is very unpredictable and I have to be prepared for anything. Ptolemy will, of course, handle any and all developments of a political nature. But there is also the domestic aspect."

"The domestic aspect," Joseph remarked, his eyebrows rising sharply. "What are you referring to?"

Herod replied with a certain ominous quietness: "I am referring to Mariamne."

"Mariamne! I don't understand. What has she to do with all this?"

"Mariamne is my wife."

"I am quite aware of that," replied Joseph, more puzzled than ever.

"Then you must know that she means all the world to me. I want you to keep an eye on her."

"It is still not clear to me. What do you think – or suspect – that she will do in your absence?"

"Anything can happen. She belongs to me, and me alone."

"That's understood. No one disputes that."

"If anything drastic happens to me, Mariamne must not – she cannot – belong to anyone else." Herod's tone was decisive.

Joseph wasn't sure he heard properly. He was unable to grasp the significance of this statement. "I'm afraid I don't understand."

"If things turn out for the worse and…?"

"What do you mean by 'the worse'?"

Herod was getting exasperated. Joseph's obtuseness was setting his teeth on edge. "I mean if he has me executed," he said bluntly.

"I don't think he'll do any such thing."

"Maybe you don't think he will," Herod flung out, "but you don't know for sure. I have no intention of risking it."

"So what do you want from me?"

"I want you to see to it that Mariamne will not belong to anyone else."

Joseph gaped at Herod with a bewildered look. "Am I to understand…"

"You are to understand that if Antony orders my execution, Mariamne must join me in death. It's as clear as that."

Joseph gasped. "I can't do anything like that. You mustn't ask it of me."

"I am not asking it of you," Herod shot back. "I am ordering you. And to make sure that you do as I say, I am instructing Ptolemy to see that you carry out my order."

Joseph couldn't believe his ears. He stared at Herod in utter bewilderment. He knew what Herod was capable of doing when he felt threatened or even thwarted. His heart went out to Mariamne. His head was bowed in sorrow when he took his leave, praying that no harm would come to Herod, for his own but equally for the sake of Mariamne.

Herod Again Triumphant

Herod made his way to Laodicea on the Syrian coast to give an accounting to Antony about what had happened. Most of the soldiers in his royal escort sensing his depressed mood, kept silent. It was unusual for him these days

491

to be undermined by a sense of defeat or to questioning the wisdom of any of his actions. A spark of hope momentarily broke through his black mood, knowing how much Antony needed his services and how little the Roman cared about the many deaths of his own people that he had caused.

On arrival, he was shown to comfortable quarters and given time to wash and rest from his journey. The warm welcome that awaited him when he was finally shown into Antony's presence went far beyond his wildest imagination. Much to the disappointment of Alexandra and Cleopatra, Antony was quite uninterested in the private scandals of Herod's court. "The internal affairs of dependent kingdoms are of no concern to me," he declared while digesting all that Cleopatra had reported. What was uppermost in Antony's mind was his own strategic planning against the Parthians. The serious setback of the previous year still rankled with him: an insult to the great Roman Empire. Antony was determined to attack the Parthians again with a very large force that he was now successfully assembling. The kingdoms on his frontiers had to be governed by those he could trust.

And he had no doubts regarding Herod's loyalty to Rome. So, instead of chastening his visitor, he entertained him lavishly.

Antony was concerned that his actions constituted a snub of Cleopatra's wishes. He therefore requested Herod to let her have another gift. It was the Gaza Strip that would round off the coastal territories previously ceded to her.

Not an easy prize to give to someone he detested so, but Herod had no alternative. Without the Gaza Strip, his kingdom would be virtually landlocked. Despite this set-back, on his return journey from Laodicea, he felt the thrill of triumph. *He was still alive and remained the King of Judea.*

Afterword

By Malka Hillel-Shulewitz

A nd the rest is history, goes a popular saying. But is it? When writing about
events that took place over two thousand years ago, surely we don't know it
all. So much has been lost over the centuries. Miraculously, the work of Flavius
Josephus was saved. Nevertheless, he was not a critical historian. To quote from
one of the three seminal volumes of *The Rise and Fall of the Judean State* by Dr.
Solomon Zeitlin: "… he [Josephus] used in his own writing a variety of sources
without recognizing that they were mutually contradictory. …It was therefore
necessary carefully to scrutinize his statements and reject one while accepting
another."

I know that the author of this work studied Josephus in detail, as well as
criticism of his work, including the one quoted. However, since he was writing
a novel and not a history book, he had to capture the atmosphere of the period
while sticking to available facts as far as possible.

I can understand why he chose the Herodian period: it is as varied and
colorful as it is tragic. Few people know this period well.

There is the problem of Herod the Great himself. ("Herod the Great" was
a title given to Herod I by Josephus after his death to distinguish Herod I from
those that followed.) A perfunctory knowledge would deem him a madman. After all, he killed every remaining member of the Hasmonean House, including
his own beloved wife, for fear of rivals to his throne. But this is a simplification
of a multi-dimensional character that has left its mark on the stage of history.

To quote again from a noted historian of that period, Michael Grant in
his very readable *Herod the Great*: "The career of Herod [I]… is an astonishing record of public adventures and successes, and of private melodramas and
disasters. Yet it is difficult to think of any other man of the same degree of
significance who is so little known outside specialist circles, and who is the

subject of so many misunderstandings and confusions. This is partly because he stands at the confluence of the Jewish and Greco-Roman civilizations, in a no-man's-land of cultural territory where it would be rash for any student to believe he can tread with confidence.... The empire, as a whole, consisted of Roman provinces under the control of Roman governors, but beyond the actual frontiers themselves there were also native kings who enjoyed the confidence of Rome and governed their territories as Roman 'clients,' enjoying internal independence in return for loyal collaboration with imperial policy... and perhaps the most remarkable of all was Herod the Great.... In his life-time and under his rule, Jewry developed apace in ways and directions that have often escaped notice.... He had to be enough of a Jew to retain control of his Jewish subjects, and yet pro-Roman enough to preserve the confidence of Rome.... Herod was a man of contrast; the conflict between Jewishness and pro-Roman Hellenism was only one of them. Another was the strong contradiction in his temperament and career between enlightened, civilized rationalism and passionate, murderous savagery."

Yet Herod did bring peace to his kingdom for the thirty-three years that he reigned. The "ordinary" people – peasants, merchants and citizenry – prospered. As well, Herod's extensive public building brought full employment and an absence of social agitation.

To again quote Michael Grant (ibid.): "Herod was truly eager to integrate Judaism and Jewry with the surrounding world. One of the reasons for this desire was psychological, and not particularly credible.

"Even if the tuition of Nicolaus [of Damascus, Herod's tutor and friend who also influenced the work of Josephus] had left him, in the words of [scholar] W.W. Tarn, only 'moderately well varnished,' he longed to cut a figure in that opulent, chic other world. For he had to be a match for both the Greco-Roman and Jewish worlds, and in neither of them did he feel really at ease. Jew by religion, Idumaean and Arab by race, Greek by cultural sympathy, Roman by political allegiance.... Yet to describe him as a man without any roots... would be an injustice to the spirit that lay behind his cosmopolitanism. For he possessed the absolute conviction that the only way his country could survive was by aligning itself... with the wider world outside: an ambition that was all the more realizable because his own territory had been enlarged to include so many non-Jewish lands."

Herod admitted that he could not understand the people he ruled. A pagan at heart, how could he? Even less so the Romans and the Greeks with their pantheon of gods and their slave-centered societies. Greek culture, though totally pagan, was vibrant and had virtually conquered the Roman world. They believed in multi-racial and multi-national societies. They hated the Jews' particularism. It was an irreconcilable hostility and has continued through the centuries with Christianity adding fuel to the flames.

On the other hand, the Jews were a Covenantal people: they had a covenant with the One Omnipotent God. Despite the Hellenized Jews and other schisms that unfortunately existed among them, they fiercely believed in the idea of ethical monotheism that they hoped to bequeath to the world. Judaism was a revolution; it gave the world a moral purpose. In societies where slaves were mere chattels, Judaism created a day of rest – the Sabbath – also "for thy maidservant and thy manservant." And this, thousands of years before the West woke up to the idea of a worker's day of rest.

Like faith in One God, freedom and the pursuit of justice were other ideas at the core of their belief. Never did they forget that they were freed from their bondage in Egypt – not even when freedom eluded them under the many conquerors of the Land of Israel, which was – and remains – on the cross-roads of all the major empires. Nor did they forget this later, in the Diaspora, under the bondage and frequent injustice of Christian and Islamic rulers.

In the ancient world, when a people were conquered, it usually accepted the gods and ways of the conquerors. Not so the Jews for whom Faith, Freedom and Justice were among the signposts that guided them on their way to accomplishing what they believed was their God-given mission – to make the world a better place for all mankind.

I hope, reader, that this historic novel has interested you and helped you better understand the complex character of Herod I, and the period – at once tumultuous and fascinating – in which he lived.

Malka Hillel-Shulewitz